T0113996

VINTAGE MOVIE CLASSICS

Vintage Movie Classics spotlights classic films that have stood the test of time, now rediscovered through the publication of the novels on which they were based.

Movie Adaptation of Walter D. Edmonds's

DRUMS ALONG THE MOHAWK

1939: Produced by Twentieth Century Fox Film Corporation. Directed by John Ford. Starring Claudette Colbert, Henry Fonda, and Edna May Oliver. Screenplay by Lamar Trotti, Sonya Levien, William Faulkner, and Bess Meredyth. Academy Award nominee for Best Actress in a Supporting Role and Best Cinematography, Color.

Walter D. Edmonds

DRUMS ALONG THE MOHAWK

Walter D. Edmonds was born in 1903 in New York State. His 1936 novel, *Drums Along the Mohawk*, was a bestseller for two years. His later works received major literary awards, including the National Book Award and the Newbery Medal. He died in 1998.

ALSO BY WALTER D. EDMONDS

DRUMS ALONG THE MOHAWK

Walter D. Edmonds

Foreword by Diana Gabaldon

Vintage Books
A Division of Penguin Random House LLC
New York

The Library of Congress Cataloging-in-Publication Data
Edmonds, Walter Dumaux, 1903–1998.
Drums along the Mohawk / Walter D. Edmonds ; foreword by
Diana Gabaldon. — First Vintage Books edition.
pages ; cm. — (Vintage movie classic)
1. Mohawk River Valley (N.Y.)—Fiction.
2. New York (State)—History—Revolution, 1775–1783—Fiction.
I. Title.
PS3509.D564D7 2015
813'.52—dc23 2014039499

Vintage Books Trade Paperback ISBN: 978-1-101-87267-3
eBook ISBN: 978-1-101-87268-0

www.vintagebooks.com

147468846

FOREWORD

by Diana Gabaldon

When I talk to school kids for Career Day about what writing and publishing are like, I usually take along a couple of my books as props. Invariably, one kid will raise a hand and ask (in tones of mingled respect and horror), "How do you write such *big* books?" To which I answer, "The same way you write a short book. You just don't stop."

My books run in the neighborhood of nine hundred pages. As my husband once asked, looking at a German paperback edition (1248 pages), "Do you win some kind of prize if it's a perfect cube?"

Now, there actually are good reasons why most books aren't nine hundred pages, and why most movies aren't four hours long. Any art form that's continuous rather than static—film, literature, music—is constrained by two major factors: the cost of production and the attention span (or possibly the bladder capacity) of the audience. This is why most books fall between seventy-five thousand and one hundred thousand words, and why most movies are between ninety and one hundred twenty minutes long: Those are the points at which cost and interest most often intersect.

Unusually long specimens generally have some special appeal that justifies their size. Historical novels, for instance, are generally longer than nonhistorical fiction, because people are deeply interested in the details of life in earlier times—and such details take up a lot of room on the page. These same details, though, take up much less room on the screen, because a picture really *is* worth a thousand words. You can communicate an enormous amount of information visually in a very brief span of time. But can you tell a good story that way? Maybe.

This is the art of film adaptation: condensing a written story (of varying size) into a form of strictly constrained length, with specific expectations and structural requirements imposed by the new medium. And believe me, it *is* an art. Having witnessed (and, in a minor way, been involved in) the adaptation of my first novel, *Outlander* (1991), into a sixteen-episode television season, I've been impressed, entertained, and not infrequently shocked at how it all works.

With regard to *Drums Along the Mohawk*, I loved the book. It's based on good research, covers an interesting period (not that I am biased toward the eighteenth century or anything), and best of all, it is very skillfully structured, with intersecting rings of story that link a wide range of engaging characters. The novel gives a striking picture of the struggles of rural life during the American Revolution and makes a powerful but subtle statement about the messy, painful—but necessary—nature of war. It's a nice, hefty, satisfying read.

No matter how long or short a book is, though, it can't be translated directly to the screen, page by page. The pacing, rhythm, and structure of a story work differently in a visual medium—and if one is faced with the necessity of turning a six-hundred-page novel into a ninety-seven-minute film, obviously

Things Will Need To Be Changed. So how does one go about this?

Well, to start with, clearly things are going to be left out. Walter D. Edmonds has at least half a dozen notable major characters (and a lot of fascinating minor ones) whose lives wind in and out of the story. Something like this *can* be done in film—*Traffic* (2000) did it brilliantly—but it's so difficult that it's rare, and nobody was trying anything that experimental in 1939, when the film version of *Drums* was made.

The first question, then, was plainly: Whose story do we tell? And the obvious choice was the young couple who begin and end the book: Gil Martin and his new bride, Magdalana, who set out to farm in the half-settled Mohawk Valley in 1775, only to be harried and discomposed by the American Revolution going on in their immediate vicinity, with the British army essentially hiring independent groups of Indians to kill and scalp settlers and burn their houses and crops. A story—as I tell the school kids—begins with an interesting character in a situation where conflict can happen. And the way you tell a story is to open the conflict and ask, "And then what happened?" So we have characters—Gil and Lana—and obviously we have a situation of conflict. What does our adapter do next?

Well, choice of subject (character) dictates the choice of scenes, and the emphasis to be placed on different parts of the story line. A novelist has a lot of space and time in which to manipulate things and thus the climaxes of the story can be controlled and happen when and as the author likes. A film, though, has a set time period, must have a dramatic arc, and a good film must end in a satisfying way.

So an adaptation—or at least one meant to be faithful to the original source material—begins with selecting the scenes that pertain to the main characters, and among those, scenes that can be engineered into (roughly) a three-act structure, in which the major climax occurs at the end. In pursuit of this goal, scenes are often partially deconstructed and/or flexed a bit, and may be moved out of their original chronology.

Having evolved a rough story line (this process is sometimes called storyboarding, as scenes are written down on separate sheets of paper or cardboard or on magnetic strips, to facilitate being moved around), the adapter then has to consider the problem of focus—the art of getting an audience to look where you want them to look and to see what you want them to see. I won't go into the techniques one uses to do this in a novel, save to say that they're often complex and delicate. It's much simpler with film: Essentially, you point the camera at what you want to focus on, and that's what your viewer is going to see. (I'm ignoring howls of outrage from DOPs here. . . . A DOP is the Director of Photography, a Very Important Person on set.)

A subtler aspect of focus is the question of viewpoint. Whose head are you, the writer, in? In text, viewpoint normally works best if you stay in one character's head for a good stretch of time, giving clear signals to the reader when and if the viewpoint changes to another character. Film (or other visual media, like graphic novels) has an advantage in this regard, in that you can easily have more than one viewpoint working simultaneously, without confusing the audience.

In the film, soon after the young bride Lana (played by Claudette Colbert) enters her new home—a depressing, dark, cold, cramped cabin—she turns from warming her hands at the fire her husband has made and screams. The camera shifts at once to what she's seen: a tall Indian, feathered and wrapped in a blanket. We're sharing her viewpoint, and continue to do so as she has hysterics up one side of the cabin and down the other, in spite of her husband's efforts to reassure her that this is a friendly Indian, an acquaintance of his called Blue Back (played by Chief John Big

Tree). He finally resorts to slapping her face (and not a minute too soon, if you ask me) and then proceeds to straighten things out; at this point, we're seeing *his* viewpoint, but without losing Lana's.

Now, this particular scene doesn't occur at all in the novel. Neither does the brief scene on the new couple's wedding night, in which a sinister gentleman in an eye patch approaches them during supper at an inn and demands to know Gil's political affiliation. But these brief "new" scenes condense a number of minor but important plot points into no more than a minute or two—and even seconds count, in film.

To the same end, a good adaptation often shares lines and blends characters from the original material, in order to reduce the number of important characters, simplify the story, and improve the focus of the film, without sacrificing too much information or dramatic content.

For example, the novel of *Drums* has a wonderful multipage sequence wherein the "timber beast" (i.e., hunter and scout) Adam Helmer escapes from a party of Mohawk Indians by outrunning them over a staggering distance and most of a day. This is plainly cinematic, very dramatic, and a cool thing to have in your movie, but as a filmmaker, you (a) don't have time to develop the burly Adam as more than comic relief and occasional Indian-fighter; (b) can't take the time to deal with an incident from the novel that has no plot point beyond saving Adam's life; and (c) can't take the focus off your main characters for more than a few moments—not nearly time enough to do justice to this heroic chase. So what do you do? You assign the heroic chase—and a better motive: racing to a distant fort to summon help—to Gil, portrayed by poor, spindle-shanked Henry Fonda, who to his credit manages a reasonable imitation of a stork doing wind sprints over short distances before the camera shifts to the rather more athletic trio of Indians chasing him.

So far, most of what I've talked about is the concern of the scriptwriter, director, or showrunner: the basic content and out-line of the story, boiled down as far as possible to make a simple, clear story that can be filmed reasonably easily. And that's where the art of adaptation begins—but it's sure not where it ends.

A novelist is God. The whole of the book is mine, to do with what I will. A film is the work of dozens—if not hundreds—of people, most with very specialized skills, and while a bad script will ruin a show, so will any number of other failures, from poor direction to bad acting—especially bad acting—to subpar pho-tography, set-building, and location scouting.

Finally, the quality of the finished show lies in the hands of an editor, who will cut the raw footage, select the particular shots needed for maximum impact and then put them together in a way that makes visual and dramatic sense. And *then* along come the post-production people, the color-correctors, the special-effects people, and—the cherry on top—the composer who will score the music to stir the audience's emotions and cue their moods, subtly backing up the actors' performances. The blended crea-tivity of all these people is an awe-inspiring thing to see—when it works. Sometimes it works spectacularly, and sometimes . . . not so much. (This may possibly be why there are fewer great films than there are great novels. On the other hand, it may just be that people have been writing novels longer than they've been making movies.)

One (last) important consideration with respect to the film version of *Drums Along the Mohawk* is that it's not merely a period piece; it's a *double* period piece. Shooting any sort of "costume drama" requires innumerable small considerations that affect more than the costumes. Ideally, a film set in a specific histori-cal time period or, for that matter, within the confines of any unique community (vide *Witness* [1985], which, while set in modern times, takes place almost entirely within a traditional Amish community) will make some effort to represent not only specific events characteristic of the period, but also the ethos of that period, as well as its appurtenances.

(I'm continually nonplussed by people who seem to think that it's "inappropriate" to show things in a book or a film that are Not Done by Civilized Enlightened Twenty-first-century People [i.e., them], but that's a different discussion.)

The film version of *Drums* handles its primary period fairly well, if simplistically. The historical events of the Revolution in the Mohawk Valley are condensed to a couple of Indian incursions, one offstage battle, and one onstage attack on a fort, but in visual storytelling terms, those are more than sufficient. Daily life is given fairly short shrift (for good reason: it's boring, unless you can mingle personal conflict with it, and that takes a good bit of room—room you don't have in a ninety-seven-minute movie), but there is a fair amount of realistic wood chopping, and the mustering of the militia is endearingly awkward. Politics are completely ignored, and the entire British army is condensed into the person of Captain Caldwell (aka Snidely Whiplash in an eye patch), played by famed character actor John Carradine.

But this is Hollywood in the 1930s—the second "period" that affects the film. Back then, "gritty" was not expected in a historical movie, *The Birth of a Nation* in 1915 notwithstanding. So audiences in the '30s presumably had no problem with the thirty-six-year-old Claudette Colbert playing an eighteen-year-old dewy bride with bright red lipstick, false eyelashes, and blue eye shadow, because that's what leading ladies were expected to look like.

In the same spirit, the eighteenth century at war is prettified; no one is dirty (save when coming off a battlefield), people die decently out of shot, and no one is starving or cold, in spite of all their crops and houses being burnt. Children are not killed, and God forbid anyone should actually be scalped. (The filmmakers chose to use flaming arrows to indicate the Indians' essential wickedness instead, these being dramatic and not horrifying.)

All the "gritty" characters and the dark aspects of their stories have been eliminated—such as Nancy, the dim-witted servant girl with the strong sex drive, and John Wolff, the storekeeper unjustly laden with forty pounds of irons and hounded into a prison sunk seventy feet belowground—or shrunk into insignificance, like Joe Boleo (Francis Ford), the scout who saves Lana and her children from the Indians, and John (Robert Lowery) and Mary (Jessie Ralph) Weaver, the fourteen-year-old lovers. And there are the musical set pieces—singing and dancing at a party and later at a harvesting—that were expected features of this sort of film, but seem quaintly old-fashioned to modern moviegoers.

In the end, though—is it a good adaptation? Does the film version work as a story? Is it recognizable as the *same* story? In truth, it does. It's a very watchable film, with a coherent arc, and it is recognizably Edmonds's story, effectively conveying his novel's underlying message: that war often makes no sense to the people engulfed by it, even as they are compelled to fight for their lives, in spite of having only the faintest idea of what's going on. That's no small achievement.

But the book—of course—is better.

Diana Gabaldon is the number one *New York Times* bestselling author of the wildly popular Outlander novels, as well as the related Lord John Grey books; two volumes of *The Outlandish Companion*; and the Outlander graphic novel, *The Exile*. She lives in Scottsdale, Arizona, with her husband.

DRUMS
ALONG THE
MOHAWK

To my son and daughter
and to the descendants
in their generation
of these men and women
of the Mohawk Valley

CONTENTS

BOOK II

THE DESTRUCTIVES

AUTHOR'S NOTE

To those readers who may have felt some curiosity about the actual occurrences in the Mohawk Valley during the Revolution, I should like to say here that I have been as faithful to the scene and time and place as study and affection could help me to be. A novelist, if he chooses, has a greater opportunity for faithful presentation of a bygone time than an historian, for the historian is compelled to a presentation of cause and effect and feels, as a rule, that he must present them through the lives and characters of "famous" or "historical" figures. My concern, however, has been with life as it was; as you or I, our mothers or our wives, our brothers and husbands and uncles, might have experienced it. To do that I have attempted to be as accurate in the minutiæ of living as in the broader historical features. Food, crops, game, and weather played an important and ever-active part in the Mohawk Valley. As far as possible I have checked them through old journals, histories, and dispatches, so that, before I was well embarked in the writing of the book, I knew when snow was falling, and how deep it was; how high the river came, and when there was a rain. Naturally, for spaces of time, no data were available, and there I had to rely on my own knowledge of our climate. In those cases, however, the action usually concerned the purely imagined characters of the book.

How few these imagined people are may be another point of interest. Let me list them. Gilbert Martin, Lana Martin, Joe Boleo, Sarah McKlennar, John Weaver, Mary Reall, Mrs. Demooth, Jurry McLonis, Nancy Schuyler, Gahota, Owigo, Sonojowauga, Mr. Collyer, and the paymaster. All other characters named played actual parts. As I learned more about them, it astonished me to see how a simple narration of their experiences carried the book along with only slight liberties with the truth. Even so, I found it necessary to alter the facts of very few of their lives. One case was that of John Wolff. He must have had Tory inclinations, but he was never arrested or tried. But the grafted episode in the novel is taken from the experience of a very similar man whose story may be encountered in the Clinton papers. Only the similar man, with far less evidence against him, was taken out and shot.

Of the other actual characters with the circumstances of whose lives I have tampered, I shall name George Weaver, Reall, Captain Demooth, Mrs. Reall, Adam Helmer, and Jacob Small. For one reason or another I altered the numbers of their families, or the characters of their relations. But in so far as they act for themselves in the pages of the novel, anyone with little pains may check their histories. Women and children, of course, are the bane of the student. Often they are listed without names given. "Dependants over 16, dependants under 16." When confronted by that wall, the novelist must see through as far as his conscience will permit.

The description of Newgate Prison at Simsbury Mines is strictly according to facts—most of them offered by the patriotic party, at that. It was, however, no worse than British prisons, and the prisoners, I suspect, had infinitely more to eat.

In the book, I have not set out to belittle the efforts of Congress and the Continental command so much as to show their almost light-hearted disregard of actual conditions. The maintenance at vast expense of Fort Stanwix is a case in point. I cannot but believe that the reactions of the valley people, who have been vilified for years, were justified by those conditions. Some of the letters which appear in the novel are proof sufficient.

All of these quoted documents may be read in the records, with one exception—Mr. Collyer's summary of his report to General Clinton of the seizure of the grain by the starving populace. But as the general used Mr. Collyer's argument in his own report on the matter, no doubt the inspector, whoever he was, used very similar words.

I owe several debts which I should like to acknowledge. First to two helpful booksellers: Mr. Lou D. MacWethy of St. Johnsville, and Mrs. James C. Howgate of Albany. To Mr. Howard Swiggett for his suggestive study, *War Out of Niagara.* To the older historians, Benton, Stone, Jones, and the inimitable Simms. And to that invaluable listing of the military roles, *New York in the Revolution,* compiled under the direction of Comptroller James A. Roberts. A complete bibliography would be out of place in a novel, perhaps, but I must add the names of Morgan and Beauchamp, whose Indian studies first roused my interest in the Iroquois. There, I suspect, I shall find the kernel of many controversies. Finally, for those who would like to understand what valley life was really like before the actual hostilities commenced, when the fear of the Indians was first maturing, I suggest an hour spent with the *Minute Book of the Committee of Safety* of Tryon County, printed in 1905 by Dodd, Mead, and Company.

To those who may feel that here is a great to-do about a bygone life, I have one last word to say. It does not seem to me a bygone life at all. The parallel is too close to our own. Those people of the valley were confronted by a reckless Congress and ebullient finance, with their inevitable repercussions of poverty and practical starvation. The steps followed with automatic regularity. The applications for relief, the failure of relief, and then the final realization that a man must stand up to live. They had won at Oriskany, without help, the first decisive battle of a dismal conflict; Burgoyne was helpless once the Mohawk Valley had been made safe from the British possession. They suffered the paralysis of abject dependence on a central government totally unfitted to comprehend a local problem. And finally, though they had lost two-thirds of their fighting strength, these people took hold of their courage and struck out for themselves. Outnumbered by trained troops, well equipped, these farmers won the final battle of the long war, preserved their homes, and laid the foundations of a great and strong community.

WALTER D. EDMONDS

BOOK I

THE MILITIA

I

GILBERT MARTIN AND WIFE,

MAGDELANA (1776)

It was the second day of their journey to their first home. Lana, in the cart, looked back to see how her husband was making out with the cow. He had bought it from the Domine for a wedding present to her. He had hesitated a long while between the cow and the clock; and she had been disappointed when he finally decided on the cow, even though it cost three dollars more; but now she admitted that it would be a fine thing to have a cow to milk. As he said, it would give her companionship when he was working in the woods.

Privately she had thought at the time that she would show him that she could manage their first house and help him with the fields also. She was a good strong girl, eighteen years old the day she married, and she thought that if they both worked hard, in a few years they would have money enough to pay thir-teen dollars for a clock if they really wanted it. There were only two cows anyway at Deerfield Settlement, and she might make money with the extra butter.

The cow had given a good deal of trouble yesterday, leaving its own village, but this morning it seemed to be anxious to keep up with the cart. Lana supposed the land looked strange to the poor beast, and that now the cart and the small brown mare were the only things it felt at home with.

Gilbert smiled when she looked back, and raised the hand in which he carried the birch switch. He had taken off his jacket, for the weather was warm, and his shirt was open at the neck. She thought, "He's handsome," and waved back cheerfully. Anyway, the Reverend Mr. Gros made two clocks a year which he tried to sell to any couple he was marrying, and no doubt a year or two from now there would be one to pick out if they ever came back so far.

The Domine had wedded Magdelana Borst to Gilbert Martin in the Palatine Church at Fox's Mills two days ago. There had been just her family in the little stone structure, Mr. and Mrs. Gros, and a couple of Indians, half drunk, who had heard of the ceremony and happened over from Indian Castle in hopes of getting invited to the breakfast. Lana's father had given them a York shilling to get rid of them and they had gone down to Jones's tavern to buy rum, saying "Amen" very gravely in English.

It was a pleasant breakfast in the Dutch-like kitchen with its red and black beams. They had had glasses of the hard cider saved over from last fall, and sausage and cornbread, and then Gilbert had gone out to get the cart and cow and Mother had slipped tearfully upstairs and come down again with the air of a surprise and given Lana the Bible for a departing present.

It was a beautiful book, bound in calfskin, with a gilded clasp. She had taken it to the Domine for him to write in, and he had put her name very elegantly on the flyleaf, Magdelana Martin, and then very solemnly he had turned to the empty pages at the back and had written there:—

> July 10, 1776—married this day *Gilbert Martin*, of Deerfield Settlement, Tryon County, the State of New York, North America, to *Magdelana Borst*, of Fox's, Tryon County, by Reverend Daniel Gros.

They had all thought it was very impressive, seeing "the State of New York," and Mother had looked tearful again for a moment or two, because, as she said, there was no telling what kind of country it was now, with its name changed, and all the troubles of the war in Canada.

But that had passed over quickly. It had been too late then to bring up the old argument about the Indian menace, by which for a week they had tried to persuade Gilbert to settle on their own farm. His place seemed so far away—it would take two days to get to—it was more than thirty miles.

But Gilbert had been unshakable. He had paid for the land in Hazenclever's Patent beyond Cosby's Manor. He said that it was good land. He had worked there all fall and got his house up and cleared some ground already, and would have a crop of Indian corn, on part of it. It was something no one in his right senses could abandon. And he was capable of looking after Lana as well as any man.

She remembered how he and her father had talked together, and that talk had impressed her father. "He has paid for his land," he said, "and he has built his house alone so that he could buy himself a yoke of oxen, with the money saved."

"But, Henry," said her mother, "Lana knows nobody up there. It is so far away."

"Gilbert has friends and neighbors," he said. "I think Lana will get along all right," and he had smiled at her. "You can't keep all your daughters to yourself, you know, Mummschen. What would the poor young men do, if all the mothers in the world did that? Where would I have been, if your mother had done that to you? I ask you." He had even laughed about it, while Gilbert, for some reason, looked embarrassed, maybe because Lana's sisters were looking at him so admiringly. It seemed a wonderful thing to them for a girl to start off to a strange place with a man like Gilbert, whom she had seen not more than half a dozen times before in her life.

That first time she had seen him seemed long ago now, though it was still less than a year. Ten months and four days, to-day, Lana said to herself, shaking the reins over the mare's back. She and her sisters had been drying flax over the pit on the hillside. They had been playing at kentecoying, and perhaps they had become careless, for they had not noticed the young man coming along the road. And when they had at last seen him just below them, looking up at Lana and smiling, Lana had stepped back inadvertently onto the poles on which the flax was spread, and the poles had come loose from the hillside, throwing her and the flax at once into the pit of coals. The flax instantly burst into flame, but with the quickness of lightning, the sisters said, the young man had flung down his pack, run up the hill, and jumped down into the pit. Lana's heavy linsey petticoat had not caught fire; but by the time he had hoisted her out, her calico short gown was burning; and with great presence of mind he had lifted her petticoat over her head, wrapping the upper half of her body in it and so smothering the flames.

If he had not saved her daughter's life, Mrs. Borst told him half an hour later, he had certainly saved her from being badly scarred. She called it a noble action and asked him to stay the night. He had accepted. At supper he had told them that he was going west. He had no family, but he had enough money to buy some land with.

Little did Mrs. Borst or Lana herself guess how it would turn out. But when he left he caught her alone outside the door and whispered that he would return some day, if she were willing he should. Lana could not answer, beyond nodding; but that had seemed enough for him; and he went away with big strides while her father said behind her, "That's a fine young man."

Lana had dreamed about him during the winter. Often she thought he would not come back. But in the end of the winter, just when the sugaring was beginning, he had arrived one afternoon. He told them about his experiences in the westward. Up there they didn't hear much of the political doings of the lower valley. They knew that Guy Johnson and the Butlers had gone west, of course, and Mr. Weaver, Gil's neighbor, attended Committee meetings from time to time, which gave them some news. But Mr. Kirkland, the missionary, had made the Oneida Indians so friendly that one did not have the same feeling about the possibility of an Indian war. And besides, when people were clearing land they were too busy all day and too tired at night to think much about other things.

Gilbert himself had started clearing his first five acres. He had boarded during the winter with the Weavers, who had been very nice to him, paying for his food by helping George Weaver one day a week. He had got his cabin walls laid up and a good chimney in. The cabin was set right at the turn the road made for the Mohawk River ford. One could look from the door south across the marsh to the river itself, a fine prospect. Behind the house there was a natural spring.

Though he told the family about these things, Lana, in her heart, knew he was telling them to her alone. She was afraid, after supper, to go out, knowing that he would follow her. But nothing she could do could keep her from offering to step down to Jones's for her father's beer. And as she knew he would, the young man offered to go with her to carry the jug.

On the way down he had told her still more about the place. It sounded like the most wonderful place she had ever seen. He was going to buy a plough and also get a yoke of oxen this summer. There was some natural pasture along the river on his place. The loam was deep. He expected it was four feet deep in places. He had built the cabin with an extra high roof, which made the sleeping loft quite airy. He had never slept better in his life than he had slept in that loft. In March he had bought two window sashes from Wolff's store in Cosby's Manor, glass sashes, so that the kitchen seemed as light as a church. He wished Lana could see it.

Though Lana wished so herself, they had by that time come to Jones's, and she had had to go in after the beer. When she came out again, the young man had been quite silent. Even when she had asked him a shy question or two, he had hardly answered. It was only as they came in sight of the lighted windows of the Borst house that he asked her suddenly whether she would come and look at it as his wife.

"Yes," said Lana. Though she had expected the question all along, and though she knew what her answer was going to be, the word put her into a panic. "You'll have to ask Father," she added.

He had done so, much more calmly than he had asked her; and after their talk together, her father had also said "Yes." And then Gilbert had arranged to come back for her when his first rush of spring work was ended, so long as he should not be called out on militia duty.

Now they were on the Kingsroad. It ran from the ford at Schenectady the length of the Mohawk Valley; passing the Johnson land, Guy Park and Fort Johnson, Caughnawaga, Spraker's, Fox's, Nellis's, Klock's, and on to the carrying place at the falls. Then past the Eldridge Settlement, which was on the north side of the river opposite German Flats, and so to the settlement at the West Canada Creek crossing. From that settlement it continued into the woods through Schuyler, to Cosby's Manor, and then to Deerfield, where it crossed the river. West of there it was a barely passable track into the Indian camp at Oriska on Oriskany Creek. It ended at Fort Stanwix, which some people were saying would be repaired this summer by the Continental government.

From her high perch on the cart, Lana had looked out over the Mohawk all day. Last evening they had climbed the steep ascent beside the falls. A little before that, Gilbert had come alongside the cart to point out to her the fine red brick house of Colonel Herkimer with its gambrel roof, higher than any roof she had ever seen. But once past the falls they had burrowed into a stretch of woods, and for a way the land seemed wild. There was only one house, a small one, glimpsed through an opening in the trees. Then, almost at dark, they had emerged on the broad intervale lands that marked the beginning of German Flats. A little tavern stood beside the road, and they put up in it.

Lana thought of their arrival with swelling pride. The land-lord, a Mr. Billy Rose, was smoking an after-supper pipe in the door. He was in his shirt, with a leather apron, and had bidden her "Good evening," quite politely.

Gil came up, harrying the cow. He walked directly to the innkeeper and asked for a night's lodging. "Two shilling for you and the missis," said the innkeeper, "and one for the mare. You can turn the cow in by the apple tree."

"We'll want a room to ourselves then," said Gil.

"You can have the top room," said Mr. Rose. "I can't guarantee not to have to stick in someone else, though."

Gil never so much as batted his eye. He held his purse open in one hand and put his fingers in. "Would two fips be worth a guarantee, Mr. Rose?"

"Seeing it's the top room," said Mr. Rose, "I'll guarantee it." He took the two fips and slipped them into a pocket under his apron; and after that he became most obliging, addressing Lana continually as "Mrs. Martin" and calling Gil "Mister," and once even "Esquire."

Lana fixed her hair in the back shed with Mrs. Rose's glass, shook the dust from her dress with a whisk of twigs, and came back to Gil. They had supper at a table for themselves in the tap, as quietly as any well-wedded couple in the world. There was only one other man there and he hardly noticed them. He was a one-eyed man, a stranger, Mr. Rose said, on his way up from Albany.

They had had some blood sausage with pig greens, sauerkraut, and smoked trout, and Gil had insisted on her taking a small glass of gin with him. "Seeing it's to-night," he managed to whisper. "Just especial." The whole affair seemed to Lana ruinously expensive, but after the drink she found herself flooded with a feeling of utter irresponsibility. She even enjoyed it when a small stout man named Captain Small, with a couple of friends, dropped down from Eldridge's and started talking in loud voices about Sir John Johnson's having broken his parole and taken off the Highlanders to Canada. One side said that that was a good thing, getting the Scotch out of the valley; and the other said that it meant there would be nothing to hold back the Tories. But Mr. Rose reminded them that it had happened two months ago, nearly to the day, and there had been no change in the war.

Lana felt herself very mature to be sitting in a taproom listening to men, and she tried to understand what they were saying about the army's being driven back out of Canada. Small said, "Georgie Helmer come back last month. He was with Montgomery's regiment. He said it all went fine till the last day of last year when they didn't take Quee-bec. Then he said everything went to pieces. Arnold got hurt and since then the smallpox has got into the army. He had it. He said he bought an inoculation off a Dr. Barker for fifteen cents cash money. And he was the first man in his company to get it. Everybody that bought inoculations off Barker got the disease. They thought it was because his hands was dirty and he didn't clean his nail, which he scratched them with. Then they found out he'd been all through the army and everybody he touched got it. Ain't that an awful way to fight, though?"

Everybody nodded. Lana watched the shadow of Mr. Rose's queue nodding up and down along the neck of a bottle. When she looked at him, he was still nodding, and the eelskin his hair was clubbed in glistened a greenish gray.

"The trouble is," he said, "there ain't anybody up there worth two cents except Arnold, and Captain Brown."

"Brown says Arnold is no better than the rest."

"John Brown's a good man."

They argued. The one-eyed man in the corner, who hadn't said anything, now raised his voice. He had a pursy mouth and spoke softly.

"The trouble with the American army is your Continental Congress," he said.

"What do you mean?" It was Gil who asked, and the truculence in his voice thrilled Lana. All the others were looking from him to the stranger.

But the stranger said calmly, "I mean what I said. It's no better than a cesspool. What good there is in it is hid by the scum that keeps getting on top."

Captain Small said, "I guess you mean Adams and that Yankee bunch."

The one-eyed man nodded, looking at Gil. The patch over his eye gave his face an oddly sinister expression.

"They're a bunch of failures and they talk loud to keep themselves in power. I wouldn't put the dependence in them I'd put in a bedbug. They all bite when you're asleep. Why, if I lived up here, I wouldn't take chances playing with them."

"Wouldn't you?" said Gil. "Why not?"

"Because they only play politics with the army. How many regulars do they send up here? None. Why not? Because you don't count to them for votes. You can't bring pressure on them. And I hear there's seven hundred British troops moving up to Oswego this fall. But that won't bother them, safe in

Philadelphia. Why, anybody could see this war would have to be won up north."

"Say, what's your business up here?"

"My business is to see what's going on," the man said equably, "and my name's Caldwell." He got up from his corner and moved towards Billy Rose. "How about my tally?" he asked.

Nobody said anything as he paid across the plank bar. But when he stopped in the door to ask how far it was to Shoemaker's, they told him it was eight miles.

"He's a queer-acting cuss," observed Small.

Rose said, "There's a lot of queer people in the valley, now. Did he mean the Indians was coming down?"

"I think," said Gil, "that there's a lot of foolish talk about this Indian business. Just because it happened in the French war, don't mean it will now."

"Listen, young man," said Captain Small. "How would you feel if you'd been drove out of your land and house? If you was a mean man naturally?"

"You mean the Butlers and Johnsons?"

"Them," said Small. "Them and all their bunch."

"But that don't mean they'll bring the Indians."

"Listen, Mr. Martin. The Mohawks went west with them. They've got to feed them, hain't they? They plain can't do that in Niagara. Ten to one they get them foraging down here."

"Well," said Gil, "I guess we can look after them all right."

"I guess we'll have to, young man."

Gil rose and, feeling his hand on her arm, Lana rose with him. As she saw the others watching her, she went suddenly pink. She felt she was blushing all over while they said good-night. Mr. Rose picked up his Betty lamp and took them to the stairs.

"Have a good sleep," he said.

"Good night," they said.

Gil went first. When Lana climbed through the trapdoor into

the small stuffy room with its cord bed in the middle, like a fortress in a little clearing, he was facing her.

"You didn't get scared with what they said?" he asked anxiously. "You hear that kind of talk all over the place."

She was still faintly tingling from the unaccustomed drink. And she looked at him, so straight and tall, with his good features and his blue eyes, and lean broad shoulders, remembering the way he had picked her out of the flax kiln. She felt proud and reckless and gay.

"Not of Indians," she said.

Then her eyes dropped and she couldn't look at him again as they undressed.

It was odd that in the morning she felt fidgety under Mr. Rose's eyes as they prepared to leave the inn. Mr. Rose brought a small book of blank paper and a pen. He said apologetically, "The way George Herkimer's rangers check up on a man he has to keep record of whoever stays in his place. Would you just sign your name, Mr. Martin?"

Gil complied. He took the pen and filled in beside the date, "Gilbert Martin and wife, Magdelana."

Watching round his arm, Lana thought it marked the beginning of a life. She wondered whether she had pleased him, and now she was thinking, whatever came, it would be her duty to please him, and she swore a small oath to herself that she would always be a good wife to him.

The mare went slowly and the cow kept up to the cart without trouble. They passed through the German Flats where the new fort was being built. It was called Dayton, after the colonel in charge. Peeled logs were being skidded down from the spruce-covered hills behind the village; and soldiers, militia, and hired farmers were working together at setting the stockade.

Gil must have seen her watching it as they went past, for shortly after they had left the settlement behind, he came up beside the cart. He had been silent all morning, and now as she looked down into his face he seemed to her to be troubled.

"How are you?" he said, fetching a grin.

She smiled back timidly, wanting to ask him what was worrying him.

"Just fine."

He said, "It isn't so far now. It's not above fifteen miles." He looked at her again. "We ought to get there before dark, Lana."

"That will be nice," she said.

She looked so pretty and young to him, high up on the cart, with her feet in their cloth shoes demurely side by side. Her face was shaded by a calico bonnet to match her short gown. Her hair curved away under the wide brim; it was almost black. When she met his look, she flushed a little, and her brown eyes grew solemn. He thought of her gay light-heartedness, and he looked ahead to where the road entered the woods towards the Schuyler settlement. But instead of saying what was on his mind, he described the place to her.

"They've got nice bottom land. And they've built big framed houses. You'll like it, Lana, I think."

She said, "The country's nice."

They lunched before they came to Schuyler, by a little stream in a patch of hemlocks, eating bread and cheese side by side on the carpet of short brown needles and tossing crumbs to the chipmunks. It was cool there, for the trees held the sunlight far above them. In front of them the mare drowsed in the shafts and the cow found a cud to chew.

Looking at the cart, Lana imagined placing her things in the cabin before dark.

"Will we set the bed up downstairs," she said, "or put it in the loft?" He looked at her. "I've heard Mother say that in the cabins when she first came to Klock's they sometimes had the bed set up in the kitchen."

If he was worrying about her, she would show him that she was prepared.

"You're not scared coming west so far with me, like this?"

She shook her head.

"It'll be different from living in a house." He poked the needles with a stick. "It seemed so fine to me, because I built it, that I didn't think it might look different to a girl who was raised in a big house like yours."

He was trying to prepare her.

"Mother started the same way," she said. "In a few years we'll have all those things. But beginning this way, Gil, we'll like them better when we get them." She glanced sidewise. "I've always thought it would be nice living in a cabin. It'll be handy to look after if it's small."

He said, "It ain't much cleared."

"We won't have to buy much now," she added. "Mother was awfully good to me."

He touched her hand.

Quite unexpectedly they came out on Schuyler. The open land, well cleared and cultivated, with men mowing hay along the river, and broad-framed houses, was like a release after the woods. Lana knew, as she looked about her, that their place was only a few miles farther on. It would not seem so far out of the world, now that she had seen these healthy farms.

Some people came to the fences to watch them by. They greeted Gil by name and looked curiously towards Lana. They asked for news, and when Gil said he hadn't heard any worth telling, they smiled and said, "You've brought along quite a piece of news of your own, though."

They were half an hour traversing Schuyler. Then once more the woods closed in on the road and river, great elms, and willows and hemlock along the brooks. Now and then through swampy pieces the cart lurched and tottered over corduroy, and the mare had to set her feet carefully.

When they reached Cosby's Manor, it seemed to Lana a queer lost place. There was a fine house by the river, and a store built of logs, and a tenant's house. But all had a forgotten aspect.

A woman came to the door of the store, shading her eyes with her hand. She did not seem like a live and healthy person. She seemed like someone in a trance. And she did not call to them, but met Lana's shy nod with a dull stare.

Gil came hurrying up beside the cart.

"Never mind her, Lana. She's queer. They're Johnson people here, and they haven't got friends."

"Who is she?"

"It's Wolff's wife. I get along with Wolff all right, but people here don't speak to them much. I guess she gets lonely."

He lifted his voice to call good-day to her.

"Hello," she said, flatly, and turned as if to reënter the store.

"You all alone, Mrs. Wolff?" Gil asked.

"John's round somewhere," she replied over her shoulder. "You want him?"

"No. I only thought the place looked lonely."

"Thompsons left last Thursday," she said.

"Left?"

"Yeah. They went for Oswego. They say the Congress is going to fix the fort at Stanwix, and that means trouble. I wanted John to go, but he said he couldn't afford to. You can't leave if you ain't got cash money to live on up there, he says." She tilted her head to the northwest, stared at them, and then went into the store.

Gil and Lana looked after her. Then he turned to the house. "They've boarded the windows," he said. That explained the blankness. "I guess they've taken their cattle, too."

In spite of herself, Lana shivered.

"Do just she and Mr. Wolff live here?"

"I guess so. He's got a daughter married to Dr. Petry. But Doc's a Committee member, and I guess he don't let her come up here any more."

"It's a terrible thing," whispered Lana.

Gil glanced quickly at her.

"It don't have to bother us," he said. "We're all the right party."

Lana did not answer. They were in the woods again now, and the road had become both narrower and rougher. Their pace was reduced to a mere crawl under the hazy slanting bars of sunlight, yet for the first time every step the mare took seemed to Lana to be drawing her an irrecoverable distance from her home. She told herself, "But we're going home." But it didn't mean the same thing any more.

The light through the leaves softened, became more golden. Off on a hill to the right a cock grouse began drumming, starting with slow beats, and gradually gathering pace.

A great mess of flies collected round the mare's head, like sparks in the sunlight, deer flies, and horseflies an inch long, that drew blood when they bit. The mare kept shaking herself. She stopped to bite at them, and kicked and snorted, and then went on with a sullen resignation. Lana could have cried. She looked back at Gil and saw that he was switching the cow with a branch of maple; and the cow had moved up close behind the wagon.

"Are they always like this, Gil?" Lana asked.

"There's always flies in the real woods," he said shortly. "It must be going to rain, though, the way they take hold."

He had a lump on his forehead, with a red trickle issuing from it. She said, "They never are so thick at home."

"You'll have to get used to it then. Here, take this and slap them off her."

He gave her the branch and stopped to cut himself another. Lana kept switching the mare, and after a moment she was glad of the occupation. There had been no driving for her to do for some time, for the mare had to have her head in getting over the rough spots. Lana became so absorbed in batting off the flies that she did not notice the small side road turning off to the left, or the clearing through a narrow fringe of trees. It was only when Gil said, in a pleasanter voice, "That was Demooth's place," that she realized she had missed something.

"Where?"

"We've passed it. But Weaver's is just ahead."

She raised her eyes to see the leaves thinning at last. The sun was just ahead, nearing the horizon, and putting fiery edges on some overtaking slate-gray clouds.

While she watched, the clouds overlapped the sun, and at the same moment a fresh east wind struck the road, dispersing the flies, and they emerged into the clearing with the rain.

Lana saw Weaver's, dimly, through the slanting spear-like fall of rain. A square cabin, with a small wing added on, in which the logs were unweathered, a roof of bark, and a chimney sending up smoke. It stood in the midst of the clearing, surrounded on three sides by Indian corn through which the stumps, blackened by their burning, still showed. In front of the house, like a show-piece, was a three-acre patch of wheat in well-worked ground. A track ran through it toward a low log barn, and just in front of the cabin door two hollyhock plants, one red, one yellow, stood together with a small border of pinks.

Nowhere was there any sign of people. But on the edge of the woods a new road ran off, making a Y, which Gil told her led to Reall's on the creek.

"We're straight ahead," he said.

The Kingsroad burrowed into the woods again, but they ended shortly, and Lana looked out over a long swamp of alder.

Half a mile to the left lay the river, sluggish and dark. Beyond, behind a fringe of old willow trees, the ground rose again. Suddenly the road turned left down to the alders, going straight through to the ford.

The mare stopped there, and Gil came alongside with the cow. His face was streaming wet, but he smiled at her.

"Well," he said, "we're here at last."

"Where?" asked Lana, dully.

"Home."

He looked at her.

"Giddap," he said roughly to the mare.

She turned off the road onto a winding pair of wheel tracks. Then Lana saw.

A small new cabin standing on the higher ground. Beyond, a muddy brook flowed widely through some scattered alders. On the far side the land widened out in swamp grass for perhaps two acres. She saw, almost without seeing these things.

Her heart was in her throat. "You mustn't cry," she said to herself, over and over, "you mustn't start crying."

It seemed to her so utterly forlorn. Behind the cabin were the marks of Gil's first struggle with the land: the stumps, half burnt, surrounded by corn of all heights, the most uneven patch she ever saw. All round the cabin the earth was bared to the rain and fast turning into mud. Beyond was a low shed to shelter the horse and cow.

Then Gil cried out, "Look, there's smoke!"

She saw it feebly beginning to rise from the chimney. Somehow it made the rain seem drearier than ever. She wanted to say, "Oh, let's go home." But then, in a saving moment, she took hold of herself. For better or worse she had married him, she was out of reach of home; it would have to be her business to change the looks of the place.

They came up to the door, the cart creaking in the rain. The door opened. A raw-boned gray-haired woman, in a faded, dirty calico dress that had been blue once upon a time, was holding a basket with two pinks in it. She looked completely taken aback.

"Why, Gil," she said. "You surely did surprise me. I was figuring to get the place ready for you. I'd only lit the fire and was going to set these pinks out by the door."

Gil held out his hands to help Lana down.

"You go inside," he said. "I'll unload. This is Mrs. Weaver, Lana."

The woman opened her arms and clasped Lana, without letting go the pinks.

"My God," she said. "I'm surely glad to see you. I've heard enough about you, Lord He knows it. But you're even prettier than Gil let on!"

II

DEERFIELD (1776)

I

The Peacock's Feather

A small haystack stood beside the shed. That was one of the great advantages of the Martins' place—the fact that part of it was already open land and covered with swamp grass. Most people, opening new land, had to let their cattle browse for what they could find in winter, having barely enough corn leaves to subsist their horses on. "We could keep two teams on the natural grass in that old beaver fly," Gil said more than once, "if we could afford to buy that many horses." They had harvested the hay together, Gil mowing and Lana raking, and both pitching it onto the cart through a week of dry breezy weather. Her father had taught her a little about thatching and she had put in two days' work on the stack. Though it looked to her a bungling kind of job compared to the work her father did, Gil swore that there was no better-looking stack between Schenectady and the Indian country.

But everything she did seemed to please him. The way she had fixed the cabin over, arranged their scanty furniture to make the place look, he said, as if they'd lived in it for years. The way she sanded the floor every morning; and the little cotton curtains she made for the two windows, stringing them on cord. It had been exciting, after that first gloomy day of their arrival, to unpack the two trunks and the boxes from the cart. Gil had had no idea of all the things in them. "You brought a complete outfit," he said. She felt a little shy, replying, "I told Mother there wasn't any sense in me bringing a lot of clothes, and such things. I told her I'd rather have the money spent in house things."

The cabin lost its dreariness when they had the dresser set up against the wall beside the fireplace, with its dishes laid out on the shelves. It was one her father had made of pine in his young married days, with scalloped mouldings, but it had been put by upstairs years before when he brought home the maple cupboard he bought in Caughnawaga. It had seemed like an old and clumsy piece. When Lana asked for it, her mother had been glad to let it go. But now, in its new place, the dresser looked impressively handsome. It gave Lana a comforting feeling to see it there, and to think that her father and mother must have admired it together in their first house.

On its shelves she placed her brown earthenware plates, the baking dish, and the six glasses from Albany. On the top shelf out of harm's way she put the Bible and the white china teapot that had been her Grandmother Lana's, and the peacock's feather that her mother had given her out of the cluster of six, so that she should have a reminder of home always in sight. War on sea or land could not affect its fantastical colors.

When Mrs. Weaver saw it first, she held up both her hands and marveled stridently.

"It's like the feather off an angel's wing. You say it comes from an actual bird?"

"Oh, yes," said Lana.

"What might such a bird be called?"

"A peacock, Mrs. Weaver."

"Think of that!" exclaimed Mrs. Weaver. "I wonder what he looks like."

"I couldn't say."

"Would they be wing feathers, do you suppose?"

"My mother had an uncle who went to sea," said Lana modestly. "He said it was off the peacock's tail. Mother inherited them. She has five at home."

"You certainly know a lot," Mrs. Weaver said admiringly.

Mrs. Weaver made Lana feel very proud. She examined all the other fixings of the cabin with a new respect; she went upstairs into the loft and sat upon the bed, bouncing a little.

"That's a dandy bed," she said.

"Mother made it for me. It's all genuine white goose."

"God! Imagine! I ain't seen a genuine white goose since I come up here. Your ma must have been a knowing person, Mrs. Martin."

She tried the spinning wheel, saying it ran nice but felt a little light for a woman like herself. "I'll bet, though, that a dancey body like yourself would get a first-rate tone out of it."

But what inevitably attracted her was the peacock's feather. She stopped again before it, holding her hands before her petticoat, tight down against her legs. Her curving nose looked rigid with the wonder of it. Her kindly mouth was hushed. Her gray eyes shone. Beside her Lana looked small and young and frail.

"My," said Mrs. Weaver. "I'll have to tell George about it right away."

As a result, George Weaver came at noon, a bulky, square-faced man, with solid wrists and a deliberate way of talking. He stood before the feather, breathing loudly through his nose, for quite a while, before he turned to Lana and Gil.

"A man could hardly paint a thing like that," he said, pointing to the heart-shape in the eye. He shook his head. "No, sir, not hardly. You've married yourself quite a girl, Gil."

His slow, good-humored eyes fixed themselves on Lana with respect. "Would you mind showing that thing to John and Cobus sometime, ma'am?"

"Why, I'd be glad," said Lana.

"I'll send them over sometime, then," he said.

"You ought to tell Demooth," Mrs. Weaver said. "I'd like to have his Missis look at that. Maybe she won't feel so fine and mighty."

"Now, Emmy," said her husband in his slow fashion. "She ain't so bad. It's just the way she talks."

Mrs. Weaver snorted.

"Anyways," she said, "if you stand there admiring all day you won't get any dinner to eat."

They went outside, Gil and Lana following them to the door.

"You come over any time you're mind to," Mrs. Weaver said to Lana.

"Thank you, Mrs. Weaver. I'm pretty busy right now, but I'd like to later on."

"Everybody's busy settling a new house." Mrs. Weaver nodded.

The two Martins watched their neighbors move off down the cart track: the faded calico hanging limp down the woman's straight, vigorous back; the man's woolen shirt drawn tight over his round shoulders.

"They're nice people, Gil," said Lana.

He agreed.

"They're plain," he said, "but they're good neighbors."

Word of the peacock's feather got round Deerfield in a day. First John and Cobus Weaver came to see it. Gil was finishing his last hoeing of the corn and Lana was boiling clothes in the iron kettle at the outdoor fireplace. They stared at her curiously, rather as if they expected to see the feather sprouting on her.

John, fourteen years old, was spokesman for the pair.

"Are you Mrs. Martin?" he asked.

Lana nodded cheerfully. Their freckled faces were very sober. They examined her from head to toe. Cobus, who gave promise of his father's beamy build, rubbed the calves of his scratched, bitten legs together; but John stood upright on both feet, his hands behind his back, his shirt and trousers parting company to show his belly button, and stared frankly.

"Pa said you had a feather you'd be willing to show us."

"Yes, if you want to see it. Come inside."

She wrung the water from her hands and led them in. They did not say a word, but stood side by side, and stared, but when they left they thanked her with gravity and marched solemnly down the cart track to the woods. Just as they reached the brush she heard them yell, and looking up she saw them running home with all their might.

The Realls came over in a mass: Mrs. Reall, a talkative woman, dressed in a French red short gown, though her face was almost colorless and her hair light faded brown; and Mr. Reall, a sly-looking meaching man, if ever Lana had seen one, carrying the youngest child in his arms. The other seven trailed behind in a gradation of age and size to the three-year-old, who was barely able to keep up. They had a rascally look about them, and they swarmed all over the cabin, chattering back and forth as if the Martins had never been.

The children wished to take the feather down, but Gil was good-humoredly firm about that. "They might break it," he said, "even without meaning to."

"That's the truth," Mrs. Reall said tolerantly to Lana. "There ain't a thing they won't break or destroy some way, if they get a-hold of it. You know the way children act."

The youngest child, on Christian Reall's lap, began to bawl, and she snatched it from him, opened up her blouse, and started nursing it. Throughout the rest of the visit, the child continued nursing, puffing and sucking away, even when Mrs. Reall went upstairs to examine the bed.

"My, my," she said, surreptitiously lifting the coverlet to feel the blankets, "you surely have nice things. I used to myself, before I got to bearing children." She shifted the baby to the other breast and led the way downstairs. "You and Gilly will have to come on over to our place next Sunday," she invited. "Most generally Kitty reads us Bible Sundays. Weavers come, and sometimes Mark Demooth. Missis come once, but the children seemed to bother her. She ain't been in two years." She whispered significantly, "Kitty, he's a great reader. Reads as loud as any parson. You'd be surprised, the meaching kind of a man he looks."

They went away like a tailing swarm of bees, or like a bunch of rabbits, as Gil said. "Reall's religious," he said to Lana. "But they're just like rabbits, all of them, the way they breed, and run around."

"Nobody seems to like Mrs. Demooth," Lana said. "What's she like?"

"She's all right, I guess," said Gil. "But he married her somewhere down near Schenectady. Her folks had money. I guess she don't like it up here much. And Mark being a captain in the militia, she likes to tend her place."

Mrs. Demooth did not arrive for several days. When she did come for her call,—she emphasized the fact that she was calling,— Lana had been helping Gil clear brush.

Mrs. Demooth made her feel conscious of her heat and soiled-ness. The woman carried a parasol against the sun, a faded thing, ridiculous to see in the woods, and she wore a white cap on her hair. She bent her head when Lana invited her in from the heat and perched herself on their one chair, beside the hearth, while Lana sat on a low stool across from her.

"It's real nice of you to come and see me," Lana said, anxious to be polite.

"Don't say so," said Mrs. Demooth. She dabbed her face with a small handkerchief. "I meant to come much sooner. I would surely have come. But you know how it is. I have to watch that hired girl of mine during wash days. I declare sometimes I think it's more work having hired help than doing the work yourself."

Lana, who was tired and hot, and cross with herself, felt like saying, "Oh, indeed, Mrs. Demooth." But she nodded instead.

"That's a real nice teapot, isn't it?" said Mrs. Demooth. "What is it, Wedgwood?"

"I don't know," said Lana. "It's white chinaware, I think."

And it was Mrs. Demooth who said, "Oh, indeed." Her voice made Lana bristle; she flushed all the way to her eyes and bit her lip.

Mrs. Demooth was looking round her.

"You've got one of those feathers, I see," she said, pointing at the peacock's feather with her parasol. "We used to have a bunch of them at home, but it was terrible the way they collected the dust."

Lana only stared at her, and after a moment more Mrs. Demooth rose.

"You're tired," she said kindly. "Do you like it up here, Mrs. Martin?"

"Yes; why?"

"I suppose one's bound to when one's just married. But it was dreary for me, coming here. These cabins. We've lined ours with boards, anyway. That helps. But one gets so tired of the woods; first they're so still you hear yourself breathing; then at night there's all the noise—the frogs, the bugs. It's terrible." Her voice broke for an instant, and her thin and sullen face puckered so childishly that for an instant Lana could feel sorry for her. "And now there's this awful war. My folks were King's people. I don't understand what everything's about. And now Mark's a down-right Whig, on the Committee, captain of the militia. He ought to know, I suppose. But I feel so terrible when he's away. He says there's chance of the army coming down against us from the west. He talks about our moving down to Herkimer. Of course Mr. Butler wouldn't do anything to me, but the Indians—you can't ever tell about what they'll do. Every time Mark goes to a meeting, I'm left alone. . . ."

Her voice trailed off.

"Yes," said Lana, finally. "It must be lonesome. But I guess there's nothing a woman can do about it." She tried to shift the woman's thoughts. "Nobody's got a right to be taxed," she said, "without their say-so."

"Probably not," said Mrs. Demooth. "I don't know, I'm sure. It don't seem right—the price of tea, I mean."

She halted in the door.

"I'm sure," she said over her shoulder, "that some real tea would be a tonic to you. You must come and visit with me and have some. You must really, Mrs. Martin. It's such a pleasure to me to have found one woman up here I can talk to."

"Thank you," said Lana in a muffled voice.

"And, my dear girl," continued Mrs. Demooth. "You shouldn't work so hard in the fields. That's a man's job. They bring us here and shut us up here. And I say they ought to do their own work. You're overtired. Overwrought. Remember. Come and see me."

She went out.

When Gil came in to see why Lana had not returned, he found her hunched upon her knees and sobbing.

"What's the matter?" he asked irresolutely from the door. "Did she turn nasty on you?"

Lana looked up at him with wet eyes.

"She said I hadn't ought to work with you. She said I got too tired."

"Maybe she's right," he said doubtfully. "If you wasn't tired you wouldn't be crying now." He looked defensive. "I said you hadn't ought to come out with me to-day. Brushing's the hardest work there is."

"I don't care," said Lana. "I'm strong. I want to work. I want to be out with you. It's all there is to do." She looked round her contemptuously. "This place," she said scornfully, "why, a little girl could mind it in half a morning." Her eyes traveled over Gil's uneasy face and fell upon the feather. "Oh, Gil. She said it was an awful thing for collecting dust!"

In a vague way, Gil understood. He clumsily put his arm over her shoulders and kissed her.

"Gil!" she said. "I could have *bitten* her. I like it here. I love being here with you. I'm not afraid when I've got work to do."

"Why," he said, "what's there to be afraid of anyway? I'm looking out for you, ain't I?"

"I don't know, Gil. Not Indians. I don't know."

Their eyes met, and they smiled.

"I guess I am just mad, Gil. I thought it was so fine in here till she came in." She wiped her nose. "I can't imagine. I ain't been homesick hardly at all. I been busy trying to be useful."

"You've helped fine. I guess it was that woman. No doubt Mark's told her muster day will be next week."

He stared through the window at the green, shadowed edge of the woods.

"Muster day?" asked Lana.

"Yes. The four of us has to go down and drill with our company at Schuyler. I never thought of it before."

"You have to go?"

"Yes," he said. "The fine's five shilling if you don't turn up. I can't afford to pay that. I guess I'll go down and see the captain to-morrow about it."

2

Captain Demooth

Next morning Gilbert Martin walked down to see Demooth. Though they had no children, the Demooths lived in a double cabin. It was big enough to have the air of a house, perhaps because they had let in so many glass sashes, even in the gable ends of the loft. Inside, also, it was boarded with pine. A kitchen on the ground floor, and a sitting room, where the captain had his desk of mahogany wood; a hall between that joined the two halves of the cabin—it seemed like a manor in the woods.

A small separate cabin housed his farm hand, Clem Coppernol, a cantankerous elderly man, who lived by himself.

"Where's Demooth?" asked Gil, meeting Coppernol in the cornfield.

Coppernol raised up from feeling a squash and pointed his thumb.

"Writing letters in the office," he said.

Gil went to the house.

Mrs. Demooth had not yet appeared, and Nancy, the hired girl, with a long braid down her back and big stupid blue eyes, was clearing the breakfast dishes.

"Morning, Mr. Martin," she said, rolling her eyes towards Gil, and then immediately rolling them away. "You want *him*? He's inside."

Gil thanked her and crossed the big kitchen with its bricked-in hearth, went down the short hall that connected the two halves of the house, where he saw with envy Demooth's rifle and shotgun hung on deerhorns, each with its powder flask and shot pouch, and tapped on the door of the sitting room.

"Come in."

Gil opened the door.

Captain Demooth was a small, slight-built man, in his middle thirties, with dark hair and eyes. He was sitting before the mahogany desk that was one of the marvels of Deerfield. It had taken three men to get it into the cabin.

"Hello, Gil," he said. "What can I do for you?"

Gil prevaricated.

"I came down to make sure when muster day was."

"It's Wednesday. You knew that."

"Yes, I did," said Gil.

"What's on your mind?"

Gil looked down at the floor.

"I never stopped to think of it before, Mr. Demooth. But do you think we ought all of us to go?"

Captain Demooth smiled.

"It makes a difference being married, eh?" He leaned back in his chair and stretched out his legs. He wore lightweight, fitted boots. He had small feet and hands, about which his wife often made satisfied remarks, and in which he himself seemed to find his own satisfaction. Gil looked at him again and thought that he must be going down valley, for he had on a blue coat and a lace stock over his linen shirt.

"Yes," said Gil. "I guess it does."

"Your wife's nervous?"

"She don't say so."

Captain Demooth sighed.

"I hope she's got more nerve than Sara. By the way, Sara

told me she'd called on Mrs. Martin. Says she's a mighty nice-appearing girl. Congratulations."

"Thanks," said Gil, wondering if that was what he ought to say and trying not to flush. Then it occurred to him to wonder if that was what Mrs. Demooth had actually said.

Captain Demooth smiled a little, watching him. "Yes, Gil. I think we ought to go. We've got to do our part. With Wolff in between us and Schuyler, it don't hurt to have him see us going down in arms to muster. And it don't hurt some people between Schuyler and Herkimer to see our muster day."

"Who would that be, sir?"

Captain Demooth glanced at him sharply.

"Who is there, do you suppose?"

"Why, there's Shoemaker's tavern." Gil paused. "But I thought he was on the Committee."

"Yes, he is. There are a lot of people on the Committee. But some of them used to be King's men a couple of years ago. Shoemaker was King's justice. He was a Butler man, too. That's more to the point. When it comes to war, if it does, it won't be King and Congress up here, Gil, as much as us against the Butlers and Johnsons. They don't give a damn about Congress, and I don't know that I do about the King. But they do hate our people as having settled on the best land in the Mohawk Valley. That's what makes them mad." He tapped the table with his finger. "Sit down, Gil."

Gil sat down.

He said, "Yes, sir. I guess that's so. But ain't it all the more reason for leaving somebody to look out after the women?"

"It might be." Captain Demooth thoughtfully stared between the white curtains at the surrounding woods. "But what good could you do if we left you? One man. Look at that."

"Yes, sir." He looked down at his fists. "What right have we got to leave them here?"

"None. If you look at it that way. I know we don't do much at muster day. But we have a good time, that's something."

"Well, I've got to go. I can't afford to pay a fine, Mr. Demooth. But I don't see what right anybody has to make me pay it if I don't want to. Ain't that what we're fighting a war about? About paying up without our say-so?"

"Officially. Up here, Gil, we're going to fight, if we have to fight, to save our necks."

"Then why don't we stay home and look after ourselves?" He felt belligerent; he thought that Captain Demooth was baiting him in some way he could not understand. "I don't care who's running things so long as I'm let alone. I've got to clear my land. I've got a wife to support. And I don't want to leave her where a parcel of Indians can come in and bother her without anybody to stop them."

Captain Demooth looked at him gravely.

"Listen, Gil. Do you think I'd leave my wife here if I thought anything was going to happen?"

"No, sir. I don't suppose so." He met the captain's eye. "But how do you know?"

"It's my business to. I'll tell you. Everybody knows there's queer people going up and down the valley. Running news. In this kind of war there's bound to be some people making money every way they can. Some of those people run news for both sides. They have stations like Shoemaker's. You can believe them if you want to. A lot of them draw pay in Niagara as well as Albany. Well, we have a few people we can believe in. It's my business to collect news from the west and sift out what's likely to be true. Spencer's one of our men."

"The Oneida?"

"Yes. He's somewhere out at Oswego. Another's Jim Dean. He's near Montreal somewhere. I check our other men against what those two say. Right here on this table I've got a better idea of what's happening than they've probably got in Albany this minute. I know that Carleton's building a fleet on Champlain, and anybody can see that he'll drive our side back to Ticonderoga. That means that our frontier isn't going to be Canada any more. It means as sure as shooting that the British will try to take Albany next summer. And it means before they can do that they'll have to get hold of the Mohawk Valley."

Gil said, "Yes, sir."

"I'm telling you this, Gil, to ease your mind. You can keep your mouth shut. Now listen. All along they've been telling us we'd better come around before the Indians come down on us. But the Indians haven't come. There's been a little trouble round Schoharie, but nobody's been damaged much. There hasn't been any up here. The nearer we are to Canada the less there's been. Have you stopped to think why?"

Gil shook his head.

"It's more than a year since Guy Johnson had his Indian council down at Cosby's. That happened just before you got here. They sat around one day and then moved up to Stanwix. They had chiefs from every nation there. But nothing happened, even though it's known Guy Johnson and Daniel Claus and maybe Sir John wanted the Indians turned loose. The hitch was Butler, according to Spencer. He was Sir William Johnson's man. He knows that the Indians are good for just about one big fight. Once he started letting them loose in parties he'd never get them together again. And he's been holding them off until he can get an army to come with them. That's my idea. You can say John Butler don't want to start an Indian war. But I don't think any Butler has that much decent feeling where a German's concerned. He would like to lick the pants off of us. But he's got enough sense to know that in a country like ours he can't accomplish anything by just picking off one farm here and another there. It's the whole hog against the brisket. He'll go for the whole hog any day. That's the Irish of it, too."

Gil drew his breath.

"Then you think there ain't anything going to happen this year, but next year we'll have a bad time."

"Just so," said the captain. "The bigger army they can send down here the more they figure to take away from any army defending Ticonderoga." He smiled wryly. "The one thing they don't figure on, though, is that those people down in Albany aren't going to take any chances, any more than the ones in Philadelphia or New England are, of weakening themselves. Do you know what they call us, Gil? Anything west of Schenectady is called 'bush-German' country."

"Then we've got to look out for ourselves."

"Oh yes. They write us about patriotism. And the great cause. And tell us to look after ourselves and not cry for help. They won't send us troops. The damned Yankees don't want to leave home. They hear that the likker's poor west of Albany. They won't send us powder even. Not even lead. Right now Herkimer's making out an order to take sash weights out of any window that has them between Schenectady and my house. No, boy, we'll have to look out for ourselves. Then if we win the war we'll see if we can get representation in our Congress. It won't be easy, I expect. You see the Yankee merchants started this business because they couldn't make a 12 per cent profit any more. They used the Stamp Tax just to make the country people mad. Who gives a damn for the Stamp Tax, come to think of it? How much money have you paid out to it yourself?"

"That's so," said Gil, wonderingly. "It ain't bothered me." He looked up at the captain. "Why do we have to go and fight the British at all?"

"Because, now the war's started, people like the Butlers and Johnsons will be in power if they win and they'll take it out of our hides, the cost of it."

Gil said, "Yes." As far as he could see, though, they were just about where they had started. Captain Demooth had risen and there seemed to be nothing more to say. He felt the captain take his arm as he went towards the door.

"Don't get scared," the captain said. "And don't let your wife get nervy, either. I've got people of my own, patrolling west and north of here. You know Blue Back, don't you?"

"The old Indian who traps the Canadas in winter?"

"Yes. Mr. Kirkland's guaranteed him. He's got the northern beat, and if there's any trouble this year, I imagine it would come from there."

3

The Farm

When he reached his own place, Gil Martin found that Mrs. Reall had come over to borrow some soft soap. "I don't know how I come to be out of it." She had the baby under one arm. "I don't know what a person can do anyway with a family like mine."

"Make some of your own and quit borrowing everything all your life," was what Gil wanted to say. Instead he stood beside the door frowning down at the frowsy woman and gloomily watched Lana measuring out some soap in a chipped cup.

"Gil's just been down to Mr. Demooth's," Lana said brightly, in an effort to make them all easy. She knew that Gil did not approve of her lending so many things to Mrs. Reall.

Mrs. Reall perked up at once.

"It's a pity," she remarked, "that a nice man like Mark Demooth hasn't got a decent woman to look out for him."

"Did you see Mr. Demooth, Gil?" Lana asked hurriedly.

"Yes," he said. "He's getting ready to go down valley this morning. He said muster day was Wednesday."

Mrs. Reall looked surprised.

"Why didn't you step over to our place? It's shorter, and Kitty would have told you. He keeps all such things wrote down in a book. He's such a methody man."

Gil was nettled.

"I knew when it was. I wanted to see him about something else."

"Well, that wasn't what you said first," said Mrs. Reall with perfect good humor. "Of course you needn't tell me what you did go down for. I don't mind." But she made no move to get up.

Gil knew that she was likely to stay till noon if the humor seized her. With strained facetiousness, he said, "I went down to see if he didn't think we had ought to leave a bodyguard for all you women."

Mrs. Reall laughed heartily.

"My, my," she said, dabbing the baby's nose with the front of her blouse. "Bodyguard! Why, I'm always that relieved when Kitty goes to muster! I figure he's safe enough for one day. If he don't break his legs coming home drunk the way he does. It's one strange thing about a God-fearing man like Kitty, the way he gets drunk muster days. But then, as he says, war is war, and religion is religion, and both is pretty well concerned with hell."

"What did Mr. Demooth say, Gil?" asked Lana.

"He said we ought to go down. He didn't think there was any trouble coming for a while."

Gil wheeled and went out through the door. Mrs. Reall rose and said, "Thank you for the soap, Lana dearie. I'll return you some the next time I get around to making it."

Lana watched her go, then started after Gil. Gil had begun work on clearing a three-acre strip along the creek behind the place. He was felling the trees in windrows widthwise of the land, preparatory to the autumn burning. The sound of his axe in the heavy August air had no ring, but when she found him he was laying savagely into a tree, sinking half the blade at every stroke.

She watched him awhile, her dark eyes anxious.

"Gil," she said.

He stopped, leaving the axe driven, and turned round. His head and neck were covered with sweat and sweat drops ran slowly down his arms. The sun beating down on the newly uncovered ground brought forth a suffocating, tindery smell, as if it might start the firing of itself at any minute.

He stood for a moment looking out on his work. With what he already had cleared, he could see in his mind's eye the first beginnings of a farm taking shape. Next year his present patch of corn would go to wheat. Two years from now, he ought to have eight acres sown to wheat. Once a farm could produce a hundred bushel of wheat the farmer had got past the dangerous years. He could begin to count on a yearly income of around two hundred dollars. He could then consider building him a barn. From where he stood, Gil saw where he would build his barn against the slope. A sidehill barn. It was going to be a great place to pasture stock in. Later they would plan on building a framed house.

But women, he knew, put stock in board walls and a board floor. And Lana deserved a house. When he had married her, he hadn't considered such things, or the fact that she would have to be left here on muster day. There were a lot of things to being married he hadn't considered at all.

She said again, "Gil!" quite sharply.

In her work clothes, with her slim legs bare and her dark hair in a braid down her back, she looked light enough for him to raise her with one hand around her waist, like a daisy stem.

She stamped her foot and the dust powdered her ankle.

"Speak to me! Don't stand there staring like a crazy man gone deaf! What's on your mind?"

"I was just thinking how the place would look, in five years from now."

He looked so sheepish that she laughed. "I'll bet you were thinking about a barn and the cows in it."

"Horses. And I was thinking how long it would seem to you before it would be right for me to build you a decent house."

"What's the matter with the cabin? Don't it look nice?"

"It does. But I thought you'd probably be hankering for a house."

"Well," said Lana, "I probably will be. But that doesn't mean you've got to moon about it so. When I get discontented I'll let you know it fast enough." She sat against the bevel of a stump. "What did Mr. Demooth actually say?"

"Just about what I told her. He said I ought to go down. I told him I wanted to stay. It does seem kind of hard." He repeated everything the captain had said.

"Who's this Blue Back?" she asked.

"He's an old Indian. Once in a while he stops with me."

"It's a funny name."

"Yes, it is. If he ever comes round when I'm out, you treat him nice, Lana."

"Of course," she said. "Why wouldn't I?"

"Well, you know how Indians is."

"You mean drunk."

"No, he don't drink much. For an Indian."

He glanced at her.

"You won't be scared, being left here?"

"No."

"You could pass the time with Mrs. Weaver."

"Maybe I will or go to Reall's. But I'll get back to have your supper."

"You wait for me at Weaver's. No telling when we get back," he said. "If I got time, maybe I'll fetch you something from the store."

She laughed.

"Me. I don't need anything. Lord! You're kind of silly about me still, aren't you?"

"I'm just about crazy," he said, grinning.

"This isn't time to start that kind of business," she said. "What do you want me to do, now?"

"If you mean work, you could drag the lopped branches so the tops lay on the logs."

She set to work. The tree trunks lay where they had fallen almost end to end, sometimes overlapping. She dragged the lopped branches so that they lay over the trunks, the tops all pointing eastward to favor the prevailing west winds of fall, when the burning would take place.

They didn't talk. The dust and the heat choked them both. But as her brain dulled with the labor she kept wondering whether a man would continue to feel like Gil when his girl began to lose her looks. After a while, she even began to forget that. There was just the work.

They stopped at noon, and ate, and came out again into the heat, the flies following them from the cabin and then going in again, but a new swarm met them in the lot. The leaves were already wilting on the cut branches.

It was like that, day after day. At sunset Lana stopped to hunt the cow and milk her. She had dropped off in her milk and only gave a quart at night.

Then Lana started their supper. She gathered a few green ears from the cornfield, stripped the kernels out, crushed them in a bowl, and cooked them in the milk. The milk tasted of cherry and wild onion. All the time, as she worked in the kitchen, she could hear the strokes of Gil's axe.

He came in at dark all soaked with sweat and they went down to the creek together where a pool was, and stripped and washed side by side.

Each night, to Lana, that marked the beginning of life again. She felt tired afterwards, her back ached, but she was clean; and while she ate, the natural uses of her body gradually returned. And the sight of Gil naked, knee-deep in the slow flow of the creek, was still the one exciting thing she had to see. Even when she looked up at the peacock's feather in the dark, his lean white shape came between it and her eyes. One did not see the burned hands and face in the dark, only the whiteness.

They could begin to talk a little. They talked about a certain tree that had been hard in falling, or the way the mare was swelling in her neck from the flies. Gil would then go out with some of their precious salt in a cup and mix it with water and swab the mare's shoulder, while Lana was clearing up. When he came in again, they would be wordless, and would wait only for a term of decency before going up to bed.

All day, her place to him might be taken by anything with hands and arms and the knowledge to cook. When they lay down together, she was Lana Martin, who had been Lana Borst, once, long ago.

4

Muster Day

When he came in from work on Tuesday evening, Gil took his rifle down from the pegs over the door.

"Where's the sweet oil?" he said to Lana.

"Sweet oil? You'd better look on that shelf in the woodshed. Maybe I stuck it up there somewhere. It started to smell bad."

Without a word he went out to the shed, where she could

hear him stirring round with a heavy hand and muttering to himself. But he came back after a moment, carrying the earthenware saucer.

"It does smell kind of bad," he said, and sat down near her, with the saucer on the hearth between his feet and a filthy bit of woolen rag in his hand. "George Weaver's a particular man on muster. You wouldn't think he was, to look at him. You wouldn't think," he went on, glancing at her slyly, "looking at him and me, that he was a sargint over me, would you?"

Lana refused to meet his eye. But she said, "I think George Weaver would make a better sergeant than you, Gil. You get up your mad too easy. The way you was getting ready to because I'd moved out your smelly old oil."

"Mad! Listen, Lana, you just ought to hear him curse and swear on muster day."

"He wouldn't do that to me."

"Who's talking about you anyway?" He had run the scourer down the barrel with the rag wrapped round it, and now he was examining the result with the rag held close to his nose. There wasn't any rust. He let the ramrod fall and patted her head.

"Don't do that," cried Lana, wriggling off from him. "You'll have me smelling just like a gun."

But he had taken to wiping the barrel. "I wouldn't mind it if you did."

"Gil!" she cried. "You wouldn't talk that way to me before we married!"

"You wouldn't have been dragging out my sweet oil on me, before we got married. Ain't it a dandy rifle, though?" He held it in his hands. "I bought the barrel from Wolff. He ordered it from Albany." He turned the gun over and looked at the scroll behind the trigger guard. "It was made in Peekskill. G. Merritt, Peekskill. Come and look at it, Lana."

She felt suddenly jealous of the gun, which she had seen ever since she came to Deerfield, hanging in place over the cabin door. It had been just a thing till now; but when Gil put his hands on it, it seemed to have acquired the power of life. However, a queer little sense of wisdom compelled her to obey, and she looked down over his shoulder at the nicely etched name. She wondered if the man who put it there could have any idea that the barrel would come so far westward and have the power there to make a woman jealous.

But though she looked at the name, she would not praise it. "That's nice wood," she said, tapping the stock.

Gil blushed all over.

"I carved that out myself last winter. It's a piece of black walnut Mark Demooth gave me. I spent pretty near every night all winter working on that stock."

He put the gun back on its pegs, replaced the ramrod in the slot, and again looked round the cabin.

"Do you remember where I kept my hatchet?"

"What do you want with it?"

"I've got to have it to-morrow. You have to have an Indian axe or a bayonet."

"Oh," she said. "Well now, you listen to me, Mr. Martin. You just sit here till you've had your supper. After that I'll hunt up everything you want."

However, he found the axe for himself. Then he greased his boots; and after supper, all there was for Lana to do was to get down his hunting shirt.

"It's filthy dirty," she said.

"That don't matter. So long as your gun's clean and you've got your four flints and your pound of powder, nobody cares."

"I care. As long as you've got to go, you'll go looking decent. What would they say about me if they saw you had the same shirt on and it hadn't been washed since last muster?"

She held it up under her nose, as he had held up the scourer under his, and made a face at him. Then she stuffed it into the iron kettle and put some more sticks on the fire and set about boiling the shirt. It came out finally, looking rather pale.

It was made of heavy linen, dyed butternut brown, with long fringes or thrums round the shoulders and down the sleeves. Ironing it out was a hard job. By the time she had finished, Lana was flushed and heated and the whole cabin smelled steamily of soft soap.

She felt out of sorts until her eye fell on Gil laboriously turning up the brim of his hat, by tacking the edge to the crown in three places.

"What you doing?" she demanded.

"Well," he said, "you're fixing the rest of me so fine I thought I'd ought to make my hat look smart."

"You ought to have a cockade on it then, Gil."

"That would look fine. But aren't you tired?"

"No, I'll make you a cockade. What do you want?"

"Something red," he said. "Red's the color of our party. George Herkimer's company's got a solid red flag. It's handsome."

Lana went upstairs to her trunk with a candle and found a piece of French red calimanco. They sat quite peacefully together while she gathered pleats in it and sewed it on. The light of the candle flashed on her white teeth biting the thread.

"Put it on," she ordered.

He sheepishly did so.

She thought he looked even handsomer the next morning, starting off down the track. She had promised to visit with Mrs. Weaver as soon as she had got the dishes cleared, but halfway down the clearing he wheeled to remind her of it.

"I will," she called.

He waved his hand and went off with long strides. She leaned against the door. The early morning sun was just beginning to reach down under the level of the treetops, making islands of light in the clearing, and showing the glitter of the night's dew. Gil's feet had left a dark track through it.

"But I'll bet he won't think about me once all day," she thought.

He had reached the Kingsroad by now. Christian Reall was waiting for him there on the edge of the underbrush. They saluted each other stiff as two dogs meeting at the corner of the fence. Then they moved off side by side into the woods.

On muster day, Christian Reall was a different man from the meaching Bible reader his wife professed to admire. Gil had never been able to understand why in his family he should pretend to such devoutness if he wished to be such a rip hell once he got loose from them. His very walk was different. He cocked on his toes at each step, instead of flat-footedly shuffling the dust, and as soon as they were safely in the woods he clapped Gil on the shoulder and told him he looked like a God-damned gentleman.

"You don't look so bad yourself," Gil said good-humoredly.

Walking with a swing of his outthrust elbows, Reall preened himself like a jay bird.

"Not too bad," he admitted, "but by Jesus it takes more than clothes to get the girls to look at you. You got to have something. Like a gentleman. Not just lace around your neck or a handkerchief to blow your nose in. *You* know."

"I can't say I do."

"Well, you could. You've got it. Look at the girl you got to marry you! Lana's prettier than the nigh side of a peach. But that ain't what I mean. Who actually wants to marry? Gentry do and gentry don't, but they always have a trot with the girls notwithstanding." He shouldered his rust-pitted Spanish musket and jerked his flopping hat brim over his eyes. "The stories I used to hear when I was down in Caughnawaga was a caution. The way the young gentry went around the country. Just like a bunch of stallions. Why, a girl of fourteen couldn't hardly dast get up a sweat without fearing one of those gentry would be tagging on her heels like a breed bull. Young Sir John, and they say young Walter Butler. And Claus and Guy Johnson. And young Cosby. The whole lot. They rutted the year round. Mostly they hung around the Indian camps or went up into the Sacandaga bush clearings."

"I've heard some of those stories," Gil said. "But I don't believe the half of them."

"You don't? You're a fool then. Everybody knows Sir John had Clare Putnam living in sin in the Fort with him when he got married to Miss Watts. Even Sir William Johnson kind of dabbled in such things. He didn't marry the Weisenberg woman till she was ready to die. He bought her for his bed the way a man would buy new sheeting. Then he had two Indians. One afore Brant's sister. And God knows how many he happened against. All you've got to do is look at all the Jacksons there was in the Lower Castle. It was a joke he had. He let all the papooses born in the house get called Johnson. All outside he called Jackson. Otherwise, he said he'd be feeding half the Mohawk nation. By God, he ought to know, too."

"Well, he was a great man," said Gil. "I'll bet if he was alive he wouldn't have run off to Canada."

"Well, maybe he was. But he surely could rip hell around."

"It's just the fashion with gentry."

"*Fashion*, that's the word I tried to remember." Christian Reall licked his lips. "Wish to God I had some of it myself."

Gil laughed out loud.

They passed Cosby's Manor about when Wolff and his wife must have been having breakfast in the store, for smoke was still trailing out of the chimney. There was no sign of the storekeeper or the woman, but a couple of Indians, like two sleepy cats, sat in the woodshed in a patch of sunlight.

"What's them?" whispered Reall.

"I don't know," Gil answered. "I never seen them."

"They've shaved fresh, look at their heads."

"Yes."

"Do you expect they're painted?"

"I don't know. Not on their faces anyways."

Gil took a good look at them. They didn't seem as stocky as the Mohawks he had seen. But they weren't Oneidas. They were too dark, he was sure, to belong to either tribe. They were thin, almost starved-looking. As they sat under their blankets, they made him think of snakes.

"Morning," he said to them, walking by.

They said good-morning with their mouths. But their heads did not move. Nothing about them moved but their brown eyes, which were small and bright and followed the two militiamen slowly across the front of the woodshed.

A moment later, in the woods once more, Reall said, with a quick backward glance, "Who do you think they was, Gil?"

"I don't know. I think they might be Cayugas. Or more likely Senecas. But I don't know."

Reall drew a shuddering deep breath.

"My God," he said, "the way they stared at me. I've heard the Senecas and the Erie tribes eat human meat."

Reall quickened his pace. "We ought to tell Demooth right off there's a couple of Senecas at Wolff's. God knows what they're up to. They must be from Niagara. Niagara's where John Butler is. Oh, my Jesus, Gil. Maybe he's down here too. Wolff's looked shut up pretty tight."

"It always does," said Gil. "That don't mean anything."

"Wolff's always been a King's man. Always said so." He

looked round again. "We ought to tell them the first thing." He had that fixed in his mind.

The men of Demooth's company of the fourth regiment of Tryon County militia were gathered along the barnside fence in Kast's field, opposite the ford. There were twenty-five of them. They had the half-uneasy look of men who have been caught loafing on the job. When one happened to laugh, two or three would join him explosively. Then they would spit and look away from each other and eye George Weaver, who was standing a little down the fence.

He said, "Captain hain't here to-day. I ain't got a watch. Anybody know what time it is?"

"It ain't time yet."

"Must be past ten," said Weaver. "I'm to fine anybody's late."

"There comes Martin and Reall now. There ain't anybody else missing except them that have a lawful excuse."

At that moment Kast came out of his house in a brown coat. "It's two minutes to ten," he said. "By the clock."

Somebody laughed.

"Time's always by that clock of his, when Kast's around."

Martin and Reall walked up.

Reall cried out immediately, "George."

"Yes," said Weaver.

"There's a couple of Seneca Indians up to Wolff's. They're shaved. Reckon they're going to paint. Maybe Butler or somebody's hanging around there."

"How do you know they're Senecas?" Weaver asked sourly. He didn't want anything to interfere with the muster. With Captain Demooth away, the whole responsibility devolved on him.

"Ain't I telling you, George?"

Just then, tardily, Kast's clock wound itself up and struck seven. The notes came feebly metallic to the waiting men.

"That's ten," cried Kast. "She hurt her inwards somehow coming up here, and the bell's never caught up to the time since."

Weaver took his tobacco from his mouth and cradled it behind him in his hand while with the other he held a paper before his eyes and rattled off the names.

"Adam Hartman."

"Here."

"Jeams MacNod."

"Here."

On down the list. Now and then a man answered, "He can't come. He's gone to the Flats getting flour." . . . "Perry's home. Doc Petry told him his wife might most likely freshen this morning." . . . "He cut his foot grubbing brush in the stump lot."

Obedient to the prescribed ritual, Weaver turned round to face the absent captain.

"All present or accounted for."

It brought the plug in his hand into view. He recovered too late. Restoring it to his mouth, he roared thickly, "Shoulder arms."

The line raggedly shouldered their guns, some to the right, some to the left. They faced Weaver with the gravity of corn-stooks. No two of them were dressed alike. Some had coats, of homespun or black cloth; some, like Gil, wore hunting shirts.

Weaver stared at them as if he were hypnotized. Without the captain he couldn't think what should be done next.

Someone said, "Can't we have the inspection and get it over with? It's damned hot standing here."

"Sure," said Weaver.

He went down the line. Now and then he took a rifle and looked it over closely. Once he made a man lift his shoes.

"You got to get new soles on them. I ought to fine you, Marcy."

"I got paper in their inside," said Marcy.

"Law says shoes equipped for a month's march."

"I couldn't walk that far if I had the shoes."

"It's law." He came to Reall. He looked at him for a long minute.

"Give me your gun."

Reall handed it over.

"It's clean, Sergeant," he said. "I cleaned it yesterday myself."

"Give me your ramrod."

"It's in the gun," said Reall, with a wink.

"No it ain't."

"God, one of the kids had it, I guess."

"Give me yours, Martin."

He took Gil's ramrod and dropped it down the barrel. It sank less than halfway. Weaver took it out, then tipped the gun nose down and whacked the stock with the palm of his hand. An assortment of bean seeds dropped out. Somebody started laughing. Reall stared.

"Them boys been playing bean game," he said. "I couldn't find the seeds. They said they threw them out. Ain't that a place to hide them!"

Weaver handed back the gun.

"Private Reall, dirty gun, one shilling."

The inspection was finished.

"Fall out."

The men drifted apart.

"Say," said someone. "How about eating early? Then we can go home. I got my two-acre patch to finish to-night."

"That's a good idea."

"Maybe it ain't legal," said George.

"We ought to do something."

"Let's eat first."

They had a meal cooked for them by Mrs. Kast. She and her two daughters scurried and finished the cooking of it and brought it out with six jugs of beer. The men lay around on the stubble of the hayfield and drank and ate and got up a company pool on the time of arrival of the expected Perry baby. Sixpence a ticket. Reall took two. That made twelve shilling. Two for the baby and ten for the winner.

After the beer was finished some of the more serious-minded thought they ought to try keeping step once around the field. Everybody thought that was a good idea. They wrestled up and got their guns. They formed threes and did their best. They were all blown when they got back to the barn. It was the best muster they had had in a long while. They felt like celebrating.

Jeams MacNod said seriously, "I bet we could lick the whole British army, marching that good."

Weaver admitted they had done well. He had seen them coming round the corner. They were all in step but Reall, but he was the odd man at the rear and didn't count.

Reall came up now, briskly, his eyes a little bloodshot, saying, "How about them Seneca Indians up to Wolff's? Why don't we march up there and see what they're a-doing?"

Weaver thought they might as well. They could dismiss at Wolff's and he and Reall and Gil wouldn't have to walk home so far. He gave the order.

As they marched past Mrs. Kast they took off their hats to her.

5

Arrest

The company went up the Kingsroad in two ragged files, each taking a rut. There was a good bit of laughing, and some talk. They hadn't much idea of what they were going to do when they got to Wolff's store; it seemed like a kind of joke. Most of them had been there only one or two times in their lives. "Does he keep any likker?" they wanted to know.

"I don't think so," Weaver said. "Cosby didn't like him having too much on hand, with the Indians coming round all the time. Only in spring when they brought in their peltry."

He plodded along, hunched forward, as if he had a plough in front of him. By nature he was an abstemious man and the beer had gone to his head, what with the heat, and the responsibilities of running the muster; and nearly all the way he kept trying to think what he ought to do when they got to Cosby's. As it turned out, it was Jeams MacNod, the school-teacher, who had the great idea.

He said, "If them Indians ain't there, what are we going to do?"

Nobody had thought of that. Jeams said, "Suppose Thompson has some men around, he might get nasty."

"Thompson cleared out a month ago," Reall said.

A kind of deliberate sunrise of intelligence dawned in the school-teacher's narrow, befuddled face. He was a poor man, and he led a hard and thankless life. He wiped the sweat out of his eyes with the cuff of his coat sleeve and said, "Why don't we take a look around the manor then?"

"Ain't that thieving?" asked Gil.

MacNod shook his head. "No, it ain't. Not when there's war. That's what they're a-doing down the valley. They done it in Johnson Hall when Sir John cleared out. There was some of the Flats people in Colonel Dayton's regiment. They went right over the place. They didn't steal nothing. Captain Ross, he said it was confiscated property and he went around with them showing what he wanted retained for himself. Retaining ain't like robbery."

The suggestion gave them the feeling of being on military service. They were doing what regular army troops had done in command of a regular army officer, and they were doing it of their own initiative. By the time they came to Cosby's they were, as Kast said afterwards, looking sober enough to eat hay. They wouldn't have seen the British army, perhaps, if it had been drawn up in squares round the big house, but they saw Mrs. Wolff all right. She was just coming in from the corn patch with a squash in her arms, like a baby.

When her eyes first fell on them, entering the clearing, she started instinctively to run. A woman of forty-five or fifty, her bleached hair half fallen to her shoulders, the bone pins clinging here and there, loosely, like oversized white lice.

Then she caught hold of herself and stood still.

"Mrs. Wolff," said Weaver, when the company had drawn up behind him, "where's your husband?"

"What do you want with John?"

Weaver said heavily, "We're militia on duty. Where's John?"

"We hain't done nothing," she said in her dull voice. "John, he's out in the lot."

"You call him in," said Weaver.

She stared at them for a moment more. When her eyes met his, Gil felt vaguely ashamed. But she didn't say anything as she turned for the log store. She went onto the porch ahead of them and took a small hand bell and swung it slowly.

They all waited for John Wolff.

He came in a moment with a dead pipe in his hand. A little charred corn silk sticking over the bowl showed that he must be out of tobacco. He was a year or so older than his wife, but he had a healthier color, and a set stubborn jaw.

"What do you want?" he demanded. He didn't try being friendly. Everybody knew which way he stood. He thought they were damned fools.

"Where's them two Seneca Indians was around here this morning?"

"There wasn't any Senecas around here."

Reall's voice piped up from the back of the line.

"Yes there was. Me and Gil saw them. Setting in the woodshed."

"Oh, them. They wasn't Senecas. I don't know who they was."

"What were they doing here?"

"They come in last night. Hungry. I let them bed in the barn and give them something to eat. I never saw them before."

"You admit they wasn't Oneidas or Fort Hunter Mohawks."

"I don't admit anything. I gave them something to eat. What the hell business is it of yours, Weaver?"

"John." His wife breathlessly touched his arm. "Don't get angry, John."

"Shut up," he said. "What right have these Dutch punks got coming onto my land?"

"We're on duty. We got to keep track of people without business in these parts."

"Why don't you ask them what their business was, then? I don't know."

"Where are they?"

"Go and find out. They left here at nine o'clock."

Weaver stood uncertainly on the porch. Jeams MacNod went up to him and whispered. Weaver put his finger in his ear.

"Yes," he said. "You stay in the store. Both of you. We've got to investigate the grounds."

Wolff said, "Suit yourself. But you can't do anything to me."

"I'll just go through your place first," said Weaver. He called for Gil and MacNod and Kast to come with him. The rest were to surround the store and wait till he came out.

The inside of the store was a long room with a fireplace at the end and a bed in the corner. There were rough shelves along one wall and storage chests along the other. There were two benches set end to end down the middle of the floor. The benches were made of split basswood logs with hickory legs let into them. Two windows allowed some sunlight to filter through the fly specks.

There wasn't anything an Indian could hide behind. Weaver went into the woodshed. He found about a month's supply of wood stacked sloppily, two pairs of snowshoes, an axe, a wedge, and a maul. "No one out there," he said, and helped the other three lift aside some axe helves, a keg of lamp oil, and a couple of rum kegs. The oil keg had four inches of oil. The other kegs were empty.

They stood looking round. It was so still inside the store that they could hear the men outside talking softly through the buzzing of the flies.

Jeams MacNod tried to lift the lid of a chest.

"It's locked," he said.

Weaver turned on Wolff.

"Give us the keys, John."

"Like hell I will."

"Then we'll have to take an axe to the chests and bust them in."

"All right," Wolff grinned thinly. "You'll find it's a hot job."

"Get the axe, Kast. It's in the woodshed."

Kast returned with the axe.

Wolff said, "You spoil them chests and you'll hear of it. I'll make a complaint to Captain Demooth." He drew his hand over his thin mouth. "I and Demooth had a talk. He said I could stay here as long as I didn't do nothing. I ain't been looking for trouble. He said he'd look out for me. You touch them chests and you look out."

Weaver had begun to get mad.

"Go ahead, Kast. Bust the lock if you can."

Kast swung the axe like a hammer.

"You stop that. There ain't nothing in them," said Mrs. Wolff. "Don't you spoil them."

"Let them do it," said Wolff.

"No, I won't. There ain't anything in them. I'll give them the keys."

"You do that and there won't be any bother," said Weaver.

Wolff stared at his wife, but said nothing. She gave them the keys to open the chests. They found some blankets for the Indian trade. Some cheap knives. Some flour. Some salt beef. There were two bales of skins in the last. When they opened the lid a rank smell came out. "Shut it," said Weaver. Kast started to obey, but MacNod, who was a curious man, pulled up the bales. "Look here," he said.

Two twenty-pound bags of powder lay in the bottom of the chest.

"That's my powder," said Wolff. "I've had it a long while."

"We'll have to take it. I'll give you a paper. It's more powder than we've got for the company."

"You leave me a couple of pounds, anyway."

"What do you need it for?"

"It'll save you wasting it on your damn muster days, anyways."

"All storekeepers been asked to turn their powder in and make a statement of it."

"That's my business."

"You set down," said Kast. He leaned towards Wolff.

"Set down, John. Please." Mrs. Wolff touched him timidly. He threw her hand off his sleeve. After a minute he sat down, though.

Mrs. Wolff turned to Gil.

"You can't take it all. We hain't got fresh meat. We need some." She looked frightened. "Make them leave us a little."

"I'm sorry," said Gil, flushing. "George is in charge. He's sergeant."

A little breath went out of the woman. She sat down beside her husband.

Weaver listened to MacNod. He nodded his head.

"You stay here, Wolff. We've got to look over Thompson's house."

"That's illegal entry," said Wolff.

"You mind your business and we'll mind ours."

Probably Gil and Weaver were the only two among the company who had ever been inside of Thompson's house, and neither of them had been beyond the little office to the right of the door. They had found Mr. Thompson a decent neighbor, but the big house had overawed them with its black slaves who seemed to feel contempt for any white man who didn't own people like themselves, its sounds of voices from the parlor doors, and the tinkle of a spinet coming down from upstairs. To them it had been the expression of all the possessions they vaguely hoped to have come to them in their time. Weaver had been there twice to see about the loan of a yoke of oxen in the early days. Gil had come to sell a large buck he had shot once when some gentlemen had been stopping there.

Standing on the wide verandah that fronted the river, they now felt the same awe in the face of the closed shutters. Most of the men with them caught the feeling. Only Jeams MacNod, who had some education and a fanatical contempt for all success other than his own, was ready to break down the door. He threw his weight against it, but the heavy pine panels had no thought of yielding to a Scottish scholar.

His gesture, however, had been enough to renew their appetite. There had been nothing exciting at Wolff's; they had come a long way, and the wearing off of the effect of beer had left them spoiling for action. When Jeams pointed out a heavy pole lying on the dock by the river shore, half a dozen of them ran down for it. They swung it against the door together. But the bars held solid. The sound of the blow was like the tap on a gigantic drum, sounding hollowly throughout the house.

It stopped them for an instant; then they shouted. They swung the pole again; and again they got no more than the hollow crash, as if the whole house joined in one derisive shout.

To Gil, however, the empty sound was upsetting.

"It'll take too long to break it down," he said. "Why don't we open a window?"

The others let the pole drop.

"That's right," said Weaver. "There ain't no sense in spoiling a good door."

They swarmed against a window together, hacking round the shutter bolts with their hatchets. In a few minutes they had the bolts cut out, the boards pried off, and Reall had thrown his hatchet through a pane. The glass tinkled chillingly into the dark room. They lifted the sash and climbed in, one after the other.

The room was the office, with Mr. Thompson's desk and chairs, and little else beyond the ashes of paper on the hearth where wind in the chimney had stirred them from the grate.

"Hell," said Kast. "There ain't anything in here. Let's look around."

There was a short commotion at the door, before one man at last stepped into the hall. As soon as he had crossed the threshold, the others trooped after him.

The size and darkness of the hall were impressive. The wide boards under their boots creaked a little to their shifting feet, but for the instant it sounded more as if some ghostly person were descending the staircase. While they stood still to listen, chipmunks behind one of the walls took sudden fright.

The sound of panic reassured them. The men broke apart, going from room to room. Gil and Weaver, remaining in the hall, listened to the stamp of boots overhead and back in the kitchen. When men walked overhead a thin dust sifted from the cornices.

"I can't find the cellar stairs," shouted Kast.

"Where are you?"

"In the pantry."

"Try the closet off the dining room," said Reall.

Weaver turned to Gil.

"I don't rightly know what we're doing here, Gil."

"I don't either," Gil said.

"Maybe we'd better go around and see they don't get too rough with things."

"All right, I'll go upstairs."

Gil wanted to get away from the big downstairs rooms. The fine black-cherry dining room table and the delicate chairs worried him; for they were things he would have liked Lana to have. But seeing them against the papered wall, dark though the room was, made him realize that a person could not merely own them.

The holland cupboard in the hall, with its wax figures, half like persons in spite of their small size, the soft feeling of the green carpet under his boots, gave him the same uneasiness. It was not until he stepped onto the bare wood of the stair treads that he felt remotely like himself.

But even on the stairs, the voices of the militia had an alien sound, as if by their entry they had done more than violate a house. They had put an end to a life. The house, shut up, could have fallen to ruin in dignity.

On the second floor, however, seeing the bedrooms opening from the hall, with the big beds unmade, as they had been left by the Thompsons, Gil felt a kind of unreasoning anger. By abandoning it, the people, apparently, had thought no more of the house than the militia had in forcing an entrance. And those that were abovestairs felt no compunctions.

One was holding up a flimsy dressing gown.

"Would a man or woman wear this?" he was asking.

The lace that edged the sleeves hung limply, and his calloused fingertips rasped on the silk.

"You can't tell what they wear," said a muffled voice. Christian Reall came backing from under the bed dragging a piece of crockery. "Look at this, Van Slyck. It's got gilt on it."

Van Slyck glanced down with lukewarm interest. "Yes, it's a nice article," he said politely. He dropped the dressing gown. "I wish I could get me one of these good and warm."

Reall crouched over the chamber pot. "It would be a handy thing. My wife gets chilblains horrible in winter."

They were as conscienceless as men inspecting a line of goods in a store. Gil wandered into the next room. There was less in it to interest one, perhaps, for there was only a narrow bed and a great closet of dark wood standing in the corner. He was curious to see what might be inside the closet.

He found it empty of everything except, lying in a corner, a piece of silk that might have been used as a head wrapping. It was bright green with little white birds printed on it. He picked it up almost mechanically, thinking suddenly how well it would look on Lana's dark hair. Glancing round, he saw that he was alone. It made him feel like a thief, but he comforted himself with thinking that it had no real value. And he had meant to bring Lana something. He had not been so long away from her since they were married. Inevitably it went into his pocket.

Then he looked round him. He felt that he ought to do something, to show his zealous sense of duty.

In the corner of the room behind the door a ladder leaned against the wall. He had not noticed it at first. He would not have noticed it now except that in the pale light creeping through the shutters the dust on the rungs looked disturbed.

At first Gil thought that there might be rats in the house; but he did not see why rats should be climbing to the attic. He decided to have a look.

He had to lift a trapdoor.

The attic seemed no darker than the rest of the house, and he could see quite plainly. The two central chimneys came up side by side out of the floor and continued at a slight outward angle like the trunks of a double tree. Between them was a bed.

There was nothing else in the attic. Gil stared a long time to make sure before he hoisted himself through.

He kept well away from the chimneys until he had circled both of them. On their outside edges the dust lay thick and unmarked, but sometime recently a man had come through the trap and gone to bed. Even if it had not been for the tracks, Gil would have noticed the faint tobacco smell.

He sniffed at the blankets. It hadn't been an Indian. The bed would have had the sickish sweet smell, a little greasy, that Indians had. It had been a white man. Gil sat down on the bed.

Whoever it was, the man must have cooked downstairs, or have got food from Wolff's, for the bed had the appearance of being used often. But the man could not have used the fireplaces except at night or the smoke would have given him away.

Without being quite sure of what he looked for, Gil began poking round. He couldn't find anything except the old dottles of pipes and some small bits of paper. They didn't have writing on them. He got up and began a circuit of the attic. Coming back, he noticed that when the chimneys began to slope towards the roof the bricks were laid in tiers, making small shelves. He went back to the bed and stood on it. On one of the chimneys he found a piece of black cloth. He could just reach it.

For a minute he could not tell what it was. But as he held it in his fingers, his mind went back, for some strange reason, to his wedding day. He remembered how they had left Fox's Mills and how he had hardly been able to take his eyes off Lana, and how pretty and bashful she had seemed when they came to Billy Rose's tavern. They had had the place to themselves except for the one-eyed man who had talked so brashly against the Continental Congress.

Gil caught his breath. It was the patch for a blind eye.

George Weaver's voice came through the trap rather plaintively.

"You up there, Gil?"

"Come up here, George."

George grunted and the ladder shook as he climbed. He took a slow look round him, and listened to what Gil had to tell.

"You're right, Gil."

"The man's name was Caldwell."

"Well, he ain't here now."

Jeams MacNod, the curious man, appeared on the ladder. Immediately he had ideas.

"No doubt he's one of them spies that George Herkimer's rangers keep chasing after all the while. There's a great leakage of news." He took the patch in his hand. "No doubt he ain't blind at all."

"What's he wear this for?"

"So a person will know what he is without having to ask. There's been men with bad eyes, and a man with a lame hand. Herkimer's never been able to catch one of them."

George Weaver said, "I don't know about it. Where's the rest of you?"

"Reall's down in the cellar. They've broke it in. They've got some good gin and they're bringing it up to the dining room. They had to use a chair or two breaking in the door." He lifted the patch. "What are you going to do about this?"

"I don't know. They hadn't ought to be breaking things. I'll get into trouble."

"Listen," said MacNod. "We'll all get into trouble. There ain't a man here hasn't got something out of the house unless it's you and me and Gil." Gil had his own doubts about what MacNod had taken. The man looked too satisfied. "But," continued the schoolmaster, "this here shows that there've been unlawful people using this house."

Weaver said, "I got to get down before the boys do too much damage."

Gil said, "He must have boarded with Wolff," before he meant to. He didn't want to get into trouble.

"How do you mean?" asked MacNod sharply.

"He couldn't use the fireplaces here daytimes."

"No," said the schoolmaster. "He must have gone to Wolff. We can tell easy, looking at the fireplaces. Look here, George. You don't have to worry what the boys do now. You've got proof of unlawful doings. If you find he ain't used the house to cook in, you can arrest Wolff. That'll get you out of trouble."

Weaver said, "I don't want to get John into trouble."

"Man," said MacNod, "ain't he a traitor?"

"I don't know about that."

"Well, you better do it to keep yourself out of trouble."

Downstairs they found that the fireplaces had not been used. In the dining room the men had started building a fire of the broken chairs. They were drinking gin out of blue china cups which they handled carefully.

Weaver broke in on them.

"You boys'll have to step out smart. We're going to arrest John Wolff."

"What for?" they wanted to know.

"Hiding King's people."

"Oh hell, leave him alone."

"Get up!" said Weaver. "You can bring the gin along."

He got them out with arguments and cajolery and finally had them lined up on the porch. From where they stood they could see Wolff's backhouse. Mr. and Mrs. Wolff were coming back quickly from the door.

"My God," said Weaver. "I never thought to look there."

He broke into a run, and the rest streamed after him, Reall at the end, carrying his chamber pot in both hands so as not to spill the gin.

Mrs. Wolff gave a little cry, but her husband only looked sullen and stood his ground.

"Who'd you have hiding there?" demanded Weaver.

"Nobody. My wife felt sick. I went out with her."

"You swear to that?"

"My God," said Wolff, turning away.

"John Wolff," said Weaver, fumbling for the proper words, "I'm going to arrest you."

"Oh, my Jesus, John," said Mrs. Wolff.

Weaver had to go back with the company, but he dismissed Gil and Reall. Reall had a little trouble on the way home, and lost the gin. But he said at parting that it was the best muster he ever attended.

Gil stopped at Weaver's to pick up Lana and to tell Mrs. Weaver that George had had to take Wolff down to Herkimer.

Emma Weaver was not disturbed by the news. "Likely he'll get back after dark," she said. "I'm sorry, though, to hear about John Wolff. What'll they do to him, Gil?"

"I don't know, Mrs. Weaver. Where's Lana?"

"She went home about an hour ago to get your supper ready."

Gil was annoyed. "I told her to stay till I fetched her."

"Now don't get cross with her, Gil. She said you'd be tired and didn't ought to have to wait. She's a real good girl."

"I don't like having her alone."

Mrs. Weaver smiled.

"You men all think a woman can't take care of herself, don't you? Well, we ain't so frail. You think she's so slim, and so pretty, and just about like a stem of grass when you lay hold of her, and you hate the idea of her being in that there cabin where anyone can get at her? Listen, mister, a lot more women get worked to death by their husbands than is killed by other men."

It seemed a long way to his own turn-off. He was almost running when he came in sight of the cabin. He seemed for the first time to see how lonely the place looked. The small cabin, and the stump lot, and the ragged corn, and the swale out beyond.

6

Blue Back

When he opened the door, Lana was in front of the hearth, on which the fire had caught briskly. She started up at his entrance, smiling, her welcome in her eyes.

"Oh, Gil, I'm so glad you're home."

"Miss me?"

"Some."

"Come here."

She still held the spoon, covered with batter.

"You're going to scold me, ain't you?"

"Come here."

She obeyed meekly.

He fished the green silk out of his pocket and put it round her neck.

"I ought to take you out back of the woodshed and shingle you proper."

"Isn't it beautiful? Oh, Gil, where did you get it?"

"The company marched up to Cosby's. We had to break into Thompson's house. Somebody had thrown this down when they was clearing out, as if they didn't want it." He felt shamefaced to tell her. "It's hardly a real present. Only when I saw it I thought how pretty it would look on you."

"Imagine leaving a thing like that. I wouldn't; not if I was being driven out naked to the north pole. Oh, it's lovely, Gil."

She had no compunctions about wearing the thing.

"Look at those birds, those little white ones. Oh, look! Do you know what they are?"

"No."

"They're peacocks."

"No!" exclaimed Gil. It made him feel better about the whole business. He put up his gun over the door and loosened his hatchet.

"You got supper ready?"

"Pretty near. I bet you're hungry. You set down there on the stool and tell me what you did."

He told her the whole business, seeing the Indians on the way down, mustering, the return, finding the place in the attic, and the discarded patch for a blind eye.

Lana turned white at the recital.

"Oh, Gil, supposing he'd been there! He might have killed you."

"He wouldn't dast shoot with all the rest downstairs. And I didn't give him a chance to get hold of me."

"I was afraid of that man in the tavern. He didn't have a nice face. It wasn't just the eye. It was all of him."

Gil became serious.

"Suppose you'd found him here when you came home alone, Lana."

"Him? What do you mean? What would he want here?"

"I don't know, exactly. But this is the house furthest west in the valley except at Fort Stanwix." He said very seriously, "You see, Lana, that's what I meant about you waiting at Weaver's."

"I never thought. I will next time, Gil. It's awful." She returned to her cooking, speaking to him over her shoulder. Gil sat down and watched her. Even though they had been married more than a month now, she seemed like such a young girl. And for the moment he could see that she was afraid. "A man like him might be out in the woods this minute and you and I couldn't tell it. Not till they came right to the door. And then there wouldn't be anything we could do at all."

"Lord," he said. "You mustn't get scared, Lana. Just because we arrested a man."

"What will they do to him?"

"I don't know."

"I feel sorry for his wife. Maybe she felt the same way about you, the way I'd feel about that man."

"I didn't think of that. I guess she did. She looked scared."

"And the Thompson people. They'd be mad if they found out who broke into their house. They'd be mad at us if they saw me now wearing this silk."

"You don't need to wear it, Lana."

"I will, though. I don't care. You thought of me when you saw it and I'd made up my mind you wouldn't think about me all day."

She smiled a little furtive sidelong smile, and rose from her crouch with the quick lithe movement Gil liked to see. "You can put the forks and spoons on the table, mister."

They ate, sitting across from each other, Lana with her back to the door. They were nearly through their supper when Gil rose quietly and went round the table. He stood in the door, with his hand against the jamb, over his head, looking out.

"What is it, Gil?"

"Somebody's coming."

It was the mare, at the far end of the swale, that had caught his eye. She had thrown her head up. She was tossing it now, and snorting, though she was too far off for him to hear her. Then on the edge of the bushes near the river he saw a man. It was impossible to tell who or what he was, for he ducked back out of sight almost immediately. But the mare's nose, swinging like a needle to a magnet, showed the man's course. He was following the edge of the swale towards the house.

Lana crept up behind Gil.

"Who is it?"

"The mare acts like it was an Indian."

"How do you mean?"

"See her stomp her hoof? She don't like their smell."

"Ain't you going to shut the door, Gil?"

"No."

"But you ain't going to stand there in plain sight like that?"

"What's got into you? You didn't mind coming here alone, did you?"

She shook her head.

"I hadn't thought."

"Well, you needn't act like a scared bitch just because a horse has seen a man."

He didn't turn around, and Lana stood stock-still, her hand halfway raised to her mouth, staring at him. After a moment she backed quietly to her place at the table and sat down with her face between her hands. She didn't say anything. But her eyes seemed to have enlarged.

Neither did Gil say anything. He kept his eyes on the swale and the edge of the creek bed, and he kept his hand over his head, within reach of the rifle. The only sound in the cabin was the everlasting low buzz of the flies.

To Lana the wait seemed unending. But she could not force herself to look at him. "He's got no right to say such a thing to me. I wasn't scared only for myself. If I was near home, he wouldn't do it. I could go home if he did. But he knows I can't up here."

She showed no sign of tears. But her jaw set tight, and her eyes narrowed.

As for Gil, he didn't think at all. All his energy was in his eyes, which he kept unwaveringly on the clearing.

He saw the man the instant the battered felt hat came up over the creek bank, only half a shot from the cabin door. As soon as he saw the crown of that hat, he relaxed. He said over his shoulder, "It's Blue Back, Lana," and stepped outdoors. "Hello there, Mr. Blue Back."

The Indian climbed out of the creek bed and walked forward slowly with a grin on his broad face. He was obviously an old man, and he liked to go slow.

"How!" he gave Gil greeting. "You fine? I'm fine." He shook hands with satisfaction.

"I haven't seen you for a long time," said Gil. "I've got married since I saw you last."

"Yes?" said the Indian. "Got good woman?"

"Come and sit down inside and see her."

"That's fine," said the Indian. He followed Gil through the cabin door.

Lana forced herself to get up and face him. She saw a brown

wrinkled face with dark eyes on which the lids seemed shrunk, a broad, rather flat nose, a simple grinning mouth.

Gil was standing at the Indian's shoulder.

"Mr. Blue Back," he said, "meet Mrs. Martin. Lana, this is Blue Back." Just as if he were a white man.

The Indian had a paunch. He seemed to be pushing it out like a turkey cock. His face did not change, but he said, with great sincerity, "Fine."

"How do you do?"

Lana bowed her head slightly. The man's smell had already taken possession of the room. It was sweetish and greasy. If water had ever touched him, she thought, it had only been when wading the creek; and his moccasins showed how the dirt stuck to them afterwards.

He wore leggings, he had a battered skirt arrangement of deerskin with a few beads on the edge, and a weathered hunting shirt, which, if it had ever had a color, was now so greasy that it was impossible to tell. On his head was the felt hat, with a hole in the pointed crown through which the stem of a basswood leaf was sticking. He also carried a brown musket, a knife, and a hatchet.

"Fine," he said again and sat down on the bench Lana had just risen from.

"Is there any milk left?" Gil asked her. "We haven't any rum, but Blue Back likes milk fine. Don't you?"

"Fine," said the Indian, grinning and slapping his hand on his stomach. "Yes, fine."

Lana threw Gil a glance, she didn't care what he thought of it. The Indian's feet were making muddy pools on her clean floor. And her stomach felt queasy. Then without a word she went out to the spring for their jug of milk. She brought it in and set it on the table.

"Get two cups," said Gil. "And pour him some."

Lana said, "You can pour it yourself."

After one look at her scarlet face, Gil silently did so. He said nothing to her as she went up the ladder to the loft. Blue Back, apparently, took no notice, but fixed his brown eyes on the peacock's feather. He obviously admired it, but said nothing. He accepted the cup of milk.

When he had finished drinking it, Gil asked, "What are you doing this way, Blue Back?"

It always amused him that the stout stodgy Indian had been named for the noisy blue jay.

"Looking for deer." In his broken English, interspersed with innumerable "fines," the Indian explained that he had been hunting over the Hazenclever hill. He had shot a doe which he had left in a tree down by the river to take home. He had a haunch there for Gil if Gil wanted it. But it had taken a long time.

He had found the tracks of two Seneca Indians. He thought they must have come from Cosby's Manor. They had had a small fire and lain around on top of the hill all day. Then they had been joined by a man with shoes on. They had taken the trail for Oswego, he thought. He was going to take the doe home and then he was going up north and west for a scout. He wanted to tell Gil that if he saw two fires on the hill at night, he had better look out. Gil could tell Captain Demooth. Blue Back, in explanation, went on to say that he had heard that the Senecas had sent word to the Oneidas that a party might come down to the head of the valley soon and the Oneidas were to mind their business.

"Thanks for letting me know," Gil said.

Blue Back said it was all right. "Like you. Fine friends. Me. you. Fine." He finished his second cup and got up.

"I'll come for that deer meat," said Gil.

He accompanied the Indian down to the river where the doe

had been hung in a willow crotch. The Indian butchered off a hind leg and then turned aside and after some search selected a willow switch. This he peeled and handed to Gil.

"Got fine woman. You young man. You use this on her. Indian don't need it. English man do. I know. I old man. You lick her. She fine woman."

He beamed at this indication of his own sophistication in the matter of white man's culture, shouldered the carcass of the doe and took to the ford.

Feeling very foolish, Gil wiggled the switch and watched him cross the river. It was annoying that Lana had had the poor taste to get up a mad before a guest, even if he was an Indian. Perhaps the greasy old fellow was right, and she needed discipline to take her mind off herself. It made Gil unhappy that he should have noticed.

7

Talk at Night

Gil walked round the outside of his cabin, taking a piece of flannel from the woodshed on his way. He wrapped the haunch of venison in this and hung it from a branch over the spring where it was cool. He thought he heard Lana in the kitchen, but if she was she was working in the dark. At any rate, when he returned, she was not downstairs.

He saw that she had cleaned up the supper things and washed the two cups he and Blue Back had used. She must have gone back up to bed.

He sat down in the dark by the table, wondering what he

ought to say to her. He was half angry, half nettled; and yet he felt sorry for her, too. It was the first time he had wished that they lived close to neighbors, for he would have liked to be able to get the advice of George Weaver, or even of Emma. He did not know what a man ought to do.

Whatever was the matter with her, she had no business talking and acting the way she had before anyone he chose to bring into his house. But on the other hand she had been frightened just before, and a frightened woman could not rightly be held responsible for much, he supposed.

It seemed very serious to Gil. To him it was the kind of thing that shouldn't be let pass. He should not just go up to bed without having it out, and discovering, if he could, what was wrong in her mind. Their whole future life might hinge on what he did. And then it occurred to him what a silly business it was, and he got up angrily from the table.

He didn't light the tallow dip. He took his shoes off in the dark and felt his way upstairs.

The loft was like ink, with the window in the gable showing only a pale gray set of squares. The air smelled faintly of Lana and of spruce wood. Standing beside the trap, Gil stripped to his undershirt.

The boards gave springily as he walked slowly to the bed. His hand touched the foot and then guided him round to his side. He sat down on the edge and said, "Lana."

She did not answer. He held his breath and could not hear her breathing. He put his hand out cautiously and felt her hip under the blanket. She was lying with her back to him, and she must be holding her breath.

They were both holding their breath.

"Lana!" He spoke explosively.

She rolled over on her back and said in a very low, calm, forced voice, "Yes, Gil."

"You going to listen to me?"

"Yes, of course, if you want to stay awake."

Dutiful as damnation.

"You didn't have no right acting the way you did."

"What way?" she asked with such deliberate sweetness that he wished he could see her face.

"The way you did in front of Blue Back."

"I brought you what you asked me, didn't I?"

"You could have poured his glass, couldn't you?"

"I didn't know my marriage contract called for waiting on the heathen."

"He ain't a heathen. He's one of Reverend Kirkland's Indians." Gil swallowed. "I bet he's a better Christian than either one of us, for that matter. And even if he wasn't you or me could go into his house and they'd offer us anything there was in it."

"It's too bad you didn't marry an Indian girl."

"It don't matter what you think, Lana. You've got no right to shame me in front of a visitor."

"You've got no right bringing any muck out of the woods into my house, using my things; and I won't stand for it."

"You won't? What will you do?"

She said furiously, "I'll take them and myself back out of here."

"You won't either. As long as we're talking this way you might just as well understand you couldn't do that if you wanted to. There ain't a thing you own here under the law. Now, you listen to me. You behave decently and I won't talk about it. But you can't act like this and expect me to allow it."

He heard her draw a deep breath.

Then she cried out, "You can't stop me. I don't care what the law is. And I don't care what there is in here, either. You can have it. But you can't talk to me that way." She breathed again. "I'll just walk out of here, that's all. You won't know anything of it."

"Now, Lana." Gil tried to talk calmly. "We didn't marry to act this way."

"I don't care what we married for. I won't stand it. I don't mind living here alone. I didn't as long as you was here. I didn't mind working my share outdoors. I didn't let myself get scared. I done everything I thought you'd like. I tried to be good to you. And then you call me a bitch."

"Bitch?" He didn't understand. "I never called you a bitch."

"Yes, you did. When you told me to shut my mouth and not act like a scared bitch."

"And you got mad because of that?" He reached for her hand in the dark. "I didn't think what I was saying. I didn't mean it. Honest, Lana. I wouldn't call you that. I was scared myself, and I didn't want you scaring me worse."

He had sense enough not to try to hold her hand. He felt her shaking. But he got into the bed and lay on his back.

"I never thought that things could begin to work up here the way they are. I don't know what I ought to do."

He waited in the dark. He felt beside him the trembling lengthen into jerks. Suddenly she rolled over against his side. The way she cried was almost brutal.

"Oh, Gil. I hadn't ought to've done so. Only he smelled so bad. I couldn't think he was nice. Oh, Gil!" She put her face against his undershirt. "You were right to call me so. I did act like a bitch."

He didn't say anything, for he felt as if all nature had upheaved inside his chest. He let her go on crying until she had quieted.

Then, when he was just dropping off to sleep himself, damned if she didn't start poking him.

"Gil!"

"Yes."

"You awake?"

"Yes."

"Gil, I better tell you sometime, and I've been trying to all day."

"Tell me what?"

"You and me are going to have a baby."

8

Trial

The trial of John Wolff for treason was set for the twenty-fifth of August, Sunday, so that witnesses against the prisoner would not be discommoded in traveling down to Herkimer. It would make no difference to the prisoner; he was already there. They had kept him under guard in the new fort; but the trial, though handled by the military, would take place in the office of Dr. William Petry, son-in-law of the accused man, and a member of the Tryon Committee for German Flats.

The office, which adjoined Dr. Petry's framed house, had originally been a small log barn. One end of it was the general store, the other and smaller section, the dispensary. A sort of counter ran across the room with a removable leaf in the middle, so that doctor and patient were continually within view of those who were buying or who were waiting their turn with the doctor. In that way, a very suggestive and double-ended atmosphere was maintained. People waiting would be prompted to buy—groceries or goods; and store customers would be reminded of the fact that their children needed sulphur, or rhubarb and soda, or be encouraged to show the doctor the thumb they had sprained the week before and that had somehow never got just right since.

The doctor was a choleric, tall, and heavy man, invariably dressed in a black coat and a shirt with no cravat. He served both sorts of customers simultaneously, naming prices as he looked down a patient's throat; or, leaving the gut and needle in a cut, he lifted the counter and took down a bolt of calico.

On the day of the trial he was leaning back in a chair under the diploma from the Electoral Palatine Medical Assembly at Mannheim which announced in no uncertain terms that William Petry had successfully answered all questions as to *wounds, in general, contusions, tumors, fractures, luxations,* and *anatomical* and *surgical operations.* The fact that the fort was still noisy with carpenters and joiners had led him to suggest that his store be used as the largest available room in the settlement, the fact of the recent arrival of a shipment of French cloth goods having, naturally, no bearing.

When Lana entered with Gil, the room already seemed unpleasantly crowded. People had lined the counters, until there was hardly passageway up the middle of the floor. They sat wherever they could find a perch, on the grindstones, on the kegs of oil, applejack, and molasses and rum. Even on the road outside people were gathered between the houses: farmers in their best homespun coats, with their wives on their arms, carrying prayer books in their hands, and still with the chilled damp look of churching on their faces.

Someone pointed out herself and Gil as new settlers up under Hazenclever hill; Gil as the man who had uncovered the evidence. As soon as he helped Lana down from her place behind him on the mare, they gave way readily, offering little encouraging half-words of praise that made her realize that Gil had made a mark in the community and become a person of importance. It was even more impressive as they entered the store. At the door a soldier in a brown coat asked Gil who he was, and when Gil gave his name bawled out in a high, untuneful nasal voice: "Witness for the United States."

A little lane opened for them. Lana would have stayed in the background, but Gil still held her hand, and perforce she had to move forward towards the counter or make a scene. There, at what was now the bar of justice, he let her go and she shrank against the wall, holding her small chintz pocket in both hands.

A terrific smell of snuff causing her to look to her left, she met the quizzical eyes, under shaggy black brows, of the doctor himself. He stared at her with such frank curiosity that the blood flowed to her head and she wondered dizzily whether an educated doctor could tell from merely looking at a girl in a bonnet if she was pregnant.

Gil was standing at the edge of the transverse counter beside George Weaver. Beyond them, sitting down, the lean bright face of Captain Demooth was turned a little away from her, as he talked to the lieutenant from the garrison at the fort who was to preside. Then the lieutenant looked at Gil, and nodded, and met Lana's eye. He pulled out his cuffs very slowly. Lana looked away. When she glanced back again, Captain Demooth was talking over his shoulder and the lieutenant was staring her way, and as their eyes met he smiled.

He must be a young man,—about Gil's age, she thought,—but when he was serious he looked older, less impulsive, and rather lonesome. He had a narrow Yankee face with a snubbed nose and an oddly thin wry mouth that was a little sad. He looked like gentry to Lana, for all his homely face.

Gil was reaching up his right hand to scratch the top of his head as Captain Demooth talked to him. Just in the nick of time, he remembered how carefully he had oiled and combed his hair, and his hand hovered, as if he couldn't think how to disguise the gesture; and the back of his neck got bright red.

Lana's heart swelled. That little piece of defeat on his part showed her how much she loved him. She let her eyes close under the shade of the bonnet and locked her fingers round the pocket strings, and prayed.

"Oh, God, let Gil show up well before the gentry."

The Committee of Safety had committed various disaffected people remaining in German Flats before this. But in a case like Wolff's, in which the suspect was believed to have harbored spies, they had preferred to turn the matter over to the regular army. Lieutenant Biddle had been appointed by Colonel Dayton to handle the business. The colonel was busy with arrangements for the repairing of Fort Stanwix before fall and, as he said, "These damn valley Dutch seem to think the army ought to send up a general for their housecleaning."

"Do you know anything about the case, sir?"

"No. I don't want to. All I want is to get Stanwix decently fixed, but I can hardly get a team out of these people. If I had my say we'd fall back on Fort Hunter and let them take their medicine."

"Yes, sir." The lieutenant swallowed. "But what ought I to do? What line should I take, sir?"

"Please yourself, Mr. Biddle. It doesn't matter a hang to us one way or the other. We'll be the butts any way we do it. I'll stand behind you."

Lieutenant John Biddle looked at Gilbert Martin, and he knew that both of them must have the same unhappy feeling on their breakfasts. He wished to God the sergeant would bring in the poor devil and get it over. All about him the German faces kept staring at him. They weren't easy people to get acquainted with. They distrusted soldiers of any rank. The girls were as standoffish as unbroke fillies.

He glanced towards the door again, meeting Lana's eye on the way. He thought, "There's one girl that looks as if she had a heart in her. But Demooth says she's married to the witness, and just as God-saving as the rest of them."

The people outside the door were moving left and right. There sounded the clicking walk of men in step. The sergeant pushed his face through the door, with his hand still wiping his lips, saluted, and announced the prisoner.

"Bring him in," directed the lieutenant. He sighed and took a last look at Lana. The old turkey cock of a doctor was stretching his neck at the girl.

The sergeant drew a paper out of his pocket, and announced: "The prisoner, John Wolff, of Cosby's Manor. Accused of harboring the King's spies and trafficking with treasonable persons."

John Wolff entered. Lana saw his face, stubborn, rather pale, the eyes fixed on the lieutenant. There was another stir at the door and Mrs. Wolff squeezed through. "I got the right," she was saying in a subdued, desperate voice. "I'm his wife. I got the right, ain't I?"

The lieutenant rapped his pistol butt on the counter, and some capsules collapsed in a bottle.

"Order, please."

There was a silence.

"You are John Wolff of Cosby's Manor, as represented?"

"Yes, I am."

"You can stand over against the counter," the lieutenant said.

"Easy on the jug," said the doctor. "It's got acid in it."

Captain Demooth, as a member of the Committee, and the commanding officer of the company of militia which had made the arrest, read the indictment. It caused no titillation. Everyone knew what was in it.

Lana thought, "He'll call on Gil now."

But George Weaver had to give his evidence. . . .

"What were you doing downstairs, Sergeant Weaver?"

"I was kind of keeping my eye on the boys."

"What were they doing?"

"Most of them was looking for Thompson's cellar."

"Did they find it?"

"Yes, they did."

"Did they break in?"

"Yes, sir."

"What were they looking for?"

"I don't know. But they found gin, anyway."

"In other words, they were just looting?"

George hawed a little.

"I guess you could call it that," he admitted.

"Were they all so employed?"

"No. Gil Martin, there. He was looking up in the attic."

"He was sober, I take it."

"You could of fed him hay," said George.

"How did you know he was there?"

"I went to see where he was. I got upstairs and hollered. He said for me to come up. I went up in the attic. We found where there had been people sleeping. We found evidence that there had been a man named Caldwell there. A blind man."

"What is the matter with this man Caldwell?"

"The Committee says he is a spy. George Herkimer's been looking for him."

"Thank you," said Lieutenant Biddle. He wondered where all this was getting him. There was no proof at all about Wolff's harboring spies.

"Gilbert Martin."

Gil was sworn to tell the truth. He spoke in a clear hard voice. It didn't sound quite like his voice, even to himself.

"You are acquainted with the prisoner Wolff?"

"Yes, sir."

"Have you ever to your personal knowledge known him to be associated with treasonable characters?"

"I know he's always stood out for the King's side. Mr. Thompson went after the Johnsons this summer. John's always said the way he stood on things."

"He is known for a Loyalist?"

"Yes, sir."

The lieutenant considered. Then he asked Gil to tell what he had found in the attic, and Gil did so. He further described the man he and Lana had seen at Billy Rose's tavern. He was asked for and gave his deductions. He did so plainly and simply.

"Why hadn't you arrested Wolff when you first caught him in the store?"

"We didn't have nothing on him. Only the powder."

"Were you drunk when you got to the clearing?"

"Some of us was a little lit up, sir."

"That will do," said the lieutenant. Lana felt the doctor touch her leg.

"Your boy's done all right," he whispered. "He was fair enough to John, too."

Gil had stepped back. He stood quite still, perspiring. People murmured and nodded. It was all how you looked at the matter. Nine-tenths of them thought that there was reasonable cause to judge the prisoner guilty. But there wasn't much proof, not the way the lieutenant was asking questions. Only that business about the eye patch.

The lieutenant turned to Captain Demooth. He asked if there were any other witnesses against the prisoner. There were.

Story Grebb was called. He said he lived the west side of Fall Hill, beyond Bellinger's. He testified that three days before the arrest he had been awakened by his negro man, Hans. He had shut the negro out because the negro had been in the habit of sneaking down to the Herkimer place where they had a black wench named Frailty, and Esquire Herkimer was being annoyed. Hans was frightened because he said there was two Indians on the road. They was asking the way to John Wolff's store. He yelled to them to keep on moving, and he let in Hans and tied him up in the pantry and gave him a hiding.

The following witness made the greatest impression. He was a heavy-handed oldish man, with a white moustache stained at the ends and edges. He said his name was Hon Yerry Dorsch. He lived just west of Eldridge Patent. He testified that on the evening of July 14 he came home from settling a paper with Isaac Paris. That he had taken all day to the trip back, and in the evening when he got to James Jones's house there was a man with a lame left hand sitting in it. That he had on a speckled under jacket, a brown surtout coat, blue woolen stockings and strings in his shoes. . . .

Lana caught her breath as Dorsch continued with circumstantial relish.

That the said man was lame in his left hand; that Dorsch asked him, Jones, where the man came from, and that Jones said he did not know; that the man stood him, Dorsch, a drink, and that then the three of them set out along the Kingsroad in company; that as they went he asked the lame-handed man what his name was, but he would not tell him, but told him that he came up from Albany; that Dorsch was sure the lame-handed man was carrying a bundle of letters, because he stumbled against him once and felt them crackle inside the man's shirt; that the lame-handed man said he was meeting a man with a blind eye, and did Dorsch know such a person, which Dorsch said he did not and would take oath to same now before the lieutenant if need be.

Lieutenant Biddle, listening to the tortuous slow testimony, became aware of the excitement in the audience. The stupid Dorsch had brought with him a peculiar nervous tension. The prisoner Wolff stood against the counter, apparently not hearing a word. The woman who had said she was the prisoner's wife had her hand to her mouth. The pretty girl beside the doctor looked a little better now that her husband had testified, though the stuffiness of the store seemed to be getting on her nerves.

Dorsch droned on in his monotone:—

That they had had to spend the night in the woods, but that in the morning they had come to Billy Rose's tavern and he, Rose, had asked them to come in and sign their names to the Committee Register, and that he, Dorsch, had done so, but that Jones and the lame-handed man had gone out and sat under the apple tree in Rose's yard.

Next witness, William Rose, tavern keeper, corroborated the occurrence, as also Martin's testimony about the man Caldwell. Further said, when he went out into the yard with the register, the lame-handed man had gone, but that Jones was sitting there with Jacobus Seeney.

The lieutenant felt sorry for the prisoner, who had to bear all this on his feet.

"Any more, Captain Demooth?"

There was some similar testimony that took fifteen minutes. It began to seem as if the whole United States had been converging on Cosby's Manor, but Captain Demooth made the point that nobody ever knew the business of any of these people; that it stood to reason from what was reported that many of them were hostile to the United States; and that indubitably some of them had stopped with John Wolff.

A little murmur went out of the room and into the group of people outdoors.

"John Wolff, have you heard the testimony of the witnesses?"

Wolff's mouth twisted sarcastically.

"Some of it."

He met the lieutenant's eye. He saw that the lieutenant looked friendly. But he had lost his own temper listening to all these insinuations.

"John Wolff, have you ever assisted King's people?"

"Yes, I have," he replied in a loud voice. His face was a little pale and his jaw was set. His wife stifled an "Oh, John!" The lieutenant did not notice. His voice went on quietly, with a queer sort of encouragement.

"How did you assist them?"

"If they came to my place without grub, I gave them something."

"When they couldn't pay?"

"Sometimes they paid."

"You haven't a permit under the Committee of the County to run a public house."

"Hell, no. But I don't sell likker over the counter."

"Did you sell them any?"

"In jugs if they could pay for it. Store purchase."

His jaw snapped. His voice was beginning to sound ugly.

"Have you done so lately?"

"I haven't any more to sell," said John Wolff.

"Would you if you had?"

"Yes, I would. I got to make a living."

"Did you feed the two Seneca Indians referred to?"

"Yes."

"Did they pay?"

"No."

"You gave them the food?"

"They was hungry."

"Did you do so willingly?"

He was giving the prisoner every chance to crawl out. But John Wolff was raw. He was sick of the business.

"Yes."

"Why?"

"I couldn't turn them out, could I? They behaved decent. Didn't break in nor nothing like those God-damned drunken Dutch!"

The lieutenant hammered his pistol butt on the counter.

"Talk decent, Wolff."

"Nobody else has."

"Would you have assisted these people on their illegal King's business if you had known?"

"I knew they was on King's business. I didn't know what it was. Why, mister? I didn't ask. I minded my own business, see?"

The lieutenant patiently overlooked it. He could see how the man felt.

"Would you willingly assist the King in his oppression of the United States?"

"If he'd promise to exterminate these damned Dutch I would."

"Is that all you have to say for yourself?"

"Do you want more?"

"If you can't justify yourself under the law you'd better not say anything."

"There ain't any law I know of. Except the King's law. I ain't busted that."

"That will be all."

Lieutenant Biddle looked down at his hands on the counter. He hoped he hadn't marred his pistol hammering with it. As far as he could see, the prisoner was only suspected. Suspected persons, however, were not wanted here. It was his business to call him guilty.

He thought, "Guilty of what?"

"John Wolff," he said, "you have been heard before this court, with the witnesses against you. You have produced no witnesses in your own cause. In the opinion of this court sufficient testimony has been given to prove reasonably that you have entertained people whose business is hostile to this country. You have not denied your entertainment of them, and you have not shown that you have not shared in their business. I therefore find you guilty as charged of being a Loyalist. Therefore, according to regulations, you shall be taken back to Fort Dayton and there imprisoned until such time as you shall be taken out by a squad and shot. The court is now adjourned."

A little murmur again flowed out of the room. Outside people said, "They're going to shoot him."

Lana saw Mrs. Wolff standing like a post, a peeled post, white and brittle.

Gil Martin's jaw dropped open. George Weaver went white and red. The man was a neighbor. The lieutenant got up and signaled to the sergeant. The men took the prisoner by the arms and walked him out the length of the store. Then the lieutenant followed them.

9

Fate of Wolff

Clumping along on his old horse, George Weaver overtook the brown mare just outside of Schuyler. The mare was moving at a walk for the comfort of Lana, who sat sidewise behind Gil. She asked, as if George had happened into the midst of an argument, "Are they really going to shoot him, Mr. Weaver?"

"They are, according to law, I guess."

"But why *shoot* him? I can't see that he's done any real harm."

"Why," said George, "I don't know that he has, either."

"Then, *why?*"

Gil spoke from the encirclement of her arms, crossly, so that she thought she felt the words rise through his body.

"That's what she's been asking me till I'm just about ready to get sick."

Lana lifted her chin and stared at George.

"What did you really arrest him for, Mr. Weaver?"

George uncomfortably scratched his head. Lana's dark eyes had a sort of seeking-after-truth look that made him want to get the rights of it in his own dim way.

"I don't know, Lana. It was Jeams MacNod's idea it would keep me out of trouble for letting the lads into Thompson's house. I didn't have no idea John Wolff would get killed for it." He colored. "Honest, Lana."

"Of course," she said. "I know you wouldn't want to hurt anybody, Mr. Weaver."

"What makes it real bad," continued George, "is that it didn't do no good anyhow. I got a regular tongue roasting off the lieutenant. Why, you'd have thought I was a thief, the way he talked. Mark Demooth stood up for us, though. He said it wasn't a cobbler's patch on the way the Yankees have been stripping women and girls down in Albany County."

"I know, I know. But this is terrible. We ain't Yankees."

"Yes," said George. "I expect it really is. I asked the lieutenant. Mister, I says, are you going to shoot poor John *dead?* And he said, well, what do *you* expect? As if I was responsible."

"What's ever going to become of Mrs. Wolff?"

"I don't know. She's a sour kind of person. Doc Petry offered her a place in his house (she's his wife's stepmother), but she said she'd go back to Cosby's and starve afore she'd do that."

"I don't blame her."

"Doc ain't so bad," George replied earnestly. "He's the only doc hereabouts, but he takes care of anybody he can get to, whether they pay or not. He don't press you. It took us a year to pay for Cobus. Eggs and a sucking pig. Me and Emma made our minds up to pay for Cobus afore he got weaned, and we did."

"I thought he looked cruel."

"Oh, I guess he'll get John's life saved. He's got influence. He's gentry."

"I don't believe it."

Gil broke in, "Oh, hush your noise, Lana. It couldn't be helped. The King's people didn't think anything of beating the tar out of unarmed men while they had the strength. Look at the way they licked Jake Sammons when they raised the liberty pole in Caughnawaga, last year."

Lana was silent. She could tell that the business was preying on Gil's mind. She made up her own mind to see if she could do anything about it. She thought, maybe, she could get Mrs. Demooth to interest the captain.

Next day, while Gil was away at Christian Reall's, helping the little man clear logs off a piece, she went down to Demooth's. When she came into the clearing she saw Clem Coppernol leading the captain's horse round to the barn. She went herself to the kitchen.

"Is Mrs. Demooth inside?" she asked the hired girl.

"God!" said Nancy, dropping a platter. "I don't know."

She stared with petrified blue eyes at Lana. But the crash had brought in Mrs. Demooth.

"Nancy!" she said in a hard voice. "If you've broke it I'll have Clem put his belt on you this time."

"It ain't broke, Mrs. Demooth." Nancy began to blubber. "Honest it ain't, only a piece. I'll fix it. I got startled so."

Mrs. Demooth then saw Lana. The swing of her skirts stilled and she became calm all in a gesture.

"How do you do, Mrs. Martin? It's nice you came down. Come into the sitting room with me."

The incongruity of polished dark wood furniture, of fine chairs, and board floors with carpet on them, all within log walls, made Lana feel shy. She sat down straight and silent and did not look at Mrs. Demooth. Overhead she could hear the quick steps of the captain moving back and forth.

"Captain Demooth's just got back," explained Mrs. Demooth. "Will you move out of the sunlight or shall I draw the curtain for you?"

"Please don't trouble. I like the sun," said Lana, not without a momentary malicious pleasure as she looked at Mrs. Demooth's carefully powdered face. "Mrs. Demooth, I came down to see you. To see if you would speak to Captain Demooth. About John Wolff."

"Oh," said Mrs. Demooth, who had sat down beside an embroidery frame. "Oh. You don't mean the man that got arrested in Cosby's Manor?"

"Yes."

"Is he a friend of yours? I understand Mr. Martin was one of the men who arrested him. He found the evidence of that awful blind man's being in Thompson's house. I never had much of an opinion of the Thompsons," she ended with satisfaction.

"Gil was there," said Lana slowly.

"Yes, Mark said some very complimentary things about your husband."

"I know. Gil was trying to do what he ought." Lana had a

momentary thought of the silk piece, but let it go. "But he feels bad about Wolff's being shot."

"Oh, that!" Mrs. Demooth gave a brittle little laugh. "Do you think it matters much?"

Lana said slowly, "Yes, it does. Gil wouldn't say anything. But I don't want him to have an awful thing like that on his conscience."

"My dear," said Mrs. Demooth, "what can women do? It's men's business. Killing each other. I believe personally that the man must be guilty."

"Not to be killed," said Lana.

"I try to keep things peaceful here. It's hard enough to make life pleasant. Mark gets so fretted. I'm sure you'll understand."

Lana's small dark face became almost grim.

"I'm bound and determined to do something. What I can. I can't sleep myself, thinking of Mrs. Wolff." She stopped. She had seen Mrs. Demooth look up. Now an automatic brightness came over her face.

"Oh, there you are, Mark. Have you met Mrs. Martin? She's been so obliging as to call on me."

Captain Demooth stepped into the room.

"Good morning, Mrs. Martin."

Lana rose and curtsied, hardly knowing how to look at him. Nor did she know how to judge a man like Demooth. The doctor may have been gentry, as Weaver maintained, but he had none of the captain's air of self-containment. By his very politeness in bowing to her he put her definitely outside of his life.

"It's so nice to have you back, Demooth," his wife said. "Are you going to favor me for any time?"

"A day or so," he said, looking straight at Lana. But when he spoke it was to his wife. "My dear, I didn't mean to eavesdrop, but I heard you and Mrs. Martin talking about John Wolff." He helped himself to a little snuff, flicked himself, and sniffed. Lana thought he did it like any other man, except more quietly. Then he looked at Lana and his smile was quite pleasant. "What is it you want of me?"

Lana took hold of her courage.

"Are they going to shoot Mr. Wolff?"

"I'm not sure. You don't want it to happen?"

"No," said Lana passionately.

"Neither do I. For the same reason."

Lana discovered that she and Captain Demooth could talk quite frankly. She was afraid to look at his wife. She knew that if she did, she could not go on talking, even though he sounded so impersonal.

"For Gil," she said with a little nod.

"For the whole company. They were just lit. And they tried to find an excuse."

"Gil didn't!"

"No, he was just doing his duty. He took orders. That Jeams MacNod is the whole trouble. School-teachers ought to get more pay. They sometimes have brains. Then they get discontented. I'm afraid Jeams MacNod is going to make trouble."

"I don't know him."

"He's honestly patriotic. To me patriotism doesn't mean a great deal. So are the Butlers, you see. I wish they weren't."

Slapping his boot, he walked over to the window. He saw a hundred yards of worked ground, a split rail fence, then the rising waves of treetops, all the way up the Hazenclever hill to the sky line. No break, but the running water, all the way to Canada. The split rail fence was a frail dam against the wilderness.

He turned so that his face was in shadow against the clean panes. "I tried to get John Wolff off. The best I could do was to get a stay of one week. Dr. Petry went down to see Colonel Herkimer. He was willing to back the petition in confidence, but he could not put his name to it. It's essential that we get him appointed general of our militia because he's the only man that could pull the valley together in war. Otherwise it would be easy to get Wolff off."

Lana said "Yes," but her righteous anger was aroused. Now Wolff would die because a man wished to become a general. She raised hot eyes to the captain, and she was surprised to see him smile.

"Mrs. Martin," he said, "believe me, Herkimer doesn't like this. We advised him to keep out of it. We had to. But Petry will have to get other names and he's blistering mad about it. I was trying to keep him calm enough to write to Schuyler. We'll get John Wolff off, though. I promise." He paused. "And I understand your feeling, and I think you're dead right."

Lana could not think of anything to say.

He turned to Mrs. Demooth.

"Sara, don't you think we might have a glass of sack?"

"Yes, of course. Mrs. Martin ought to have something against the walk home." Mrs. Demooth's voice was smoothly acid. But she left the room. The captain said quietly, "You'll understand, Mrs. Martin, that I think John Wolff has been working against us. That he was a dangerous man to have around?"

"I know," she said. "I guess so. But what's going to happen to him, sir?"

"Well, if he does get off, he'll have to go to jail anyway. A lot of people have already been sent for less offense than his."

"Where will they send him?"

"Simsbury, I suppose. The mines." He let the matter drop. Lana understood that she was supposed to do the same. She took the slender stemmed glass and drank the sack without tasting it.

Dr. William Petry was boiling with rage. He marched through the front door and out on the verandah that faced the river. He stopped there, thinking of some of the things he might have said to Nicholas Herkimer. It would be beneath his dignity to go back and stick his head inside the door like a fishwife; but if he waited a moment or two Nicholas Herkimer might come out to see why. Then he would tell him.

The Herkimer place was the finest farm west of Johnstown. A lot of people thought that the high brick house, painted a bright red, was as impressive to look at as Sir William Johnson's fancy hall. Certainly the wheat and corn were as good as any you could see in the valley; and the herd of mares in the willow pasture along the river bank were the kind that most men only dreamed of.

The mere sight of them served to enrage the doctor more. When Herkimer obliged him by coming out and saying, "Well, Bill," Dr. Petry started swearing, without even turning his head.

"Now, Bill," said Herkimer.

But the doctor had remembered something.

"I forgot you don't speak English decent," he said, and repeated his remarks in German. His translation was free, fluent, and forceful. German was a good language to curse in.

They stood in the sunlight—the doctor at the edge of the steps, red-faced, twitching his black eyebrows, standing very erect in his rusty black coat, and fixing with his eye the astonished little black negro who was holding the old gray saddle horse. Behind him Nicholas Herkimer came barely to his shoulder blades. He had round shoulders and a big head with an unkempt mop of grizzled hair. His eyes were coal black, passionate, and very sharp. But just now, like the long upper lip of his loose mouth, they showed amusement. He looked more like a farmhand than the owner of this opulent farm.

As the doctor caught breath, he said quietly in his heavy accent, "All right, Bill. If you say so. But it don't make any difference. I won't do it. You can get Wolff off all right; but I can't.

If I make a move for Wolff there is a lot of people who will say I'm interested in the other side—with my brother in Canada."

"You don't have to give a damn," exploded the doctor.

"No I don't," Herkimer said. He flushed slowly. "But I've got to listen. There's nobody else could get our own militia out. You know that."

But the doctor, whose passion was still up, refused to see sense.

"All right, General," he said. "Go your own way. Be a general if you like. If you want to hang a man to be one. But if you get hurt with your damn war, don't come to me to get your arm fixed." He snorted. "By God, though, I'd like to do one operation on you."

He stamped down the steps, snatched the old horse's reins from the hand of the negro, and humped himself goutily up into the saddle.

"Bill," called Herkimer, "you write to General Schuyler."

"I'll do what I like," roared the doctor. He kicked the old horse's side and headed him for the river. Herkimer sat down on the steps. He grinned a little. Bill Petry had forgotten that you had to ferry over the river there. He waited until the doctor had turned back from the bank.

"Hello, Bill," he said. "What is it?"

The doctor cursed.

Herkimer turned to the negro.

"Trip," he said, "take the doctor over."

"Yassah, Cunnel," said the negro, and rushed to the scow.

Herkimer got up and went into his house.

"Frailty," he shouted. "Bring some beer in the blue mug."

He went into his office and sat down at his desk. A slim negress, with high shoulder bones showing through her print dress, brought in the beer. Then his wife entered.

"Hon," she said quietly, using his old name, "there's another Indian out there."

"Bring him in."

His wife ushered in a young Indian buck. He was without blanket or shirt. Sweat made beads on his greased, yellowish-brown hide. His kilt twitched over his knees to his deep breathing. He handed Herkimer a letter tied to a stick.

Herkimer opened it.

The Reverend Mr. Kirkland was writing from the Oneida town. He had had word from Spencer that a party had set out from Oswego towards the east. They had not touched Oneida Lake, therefore they must be going through the woods to the north.

The little man's big head nodded. Hazenclever's and the upper part of the West Canada Kill should be watched. Up above Schell's blockhouse. He forgot about Bill and John Wolff.

"Frailty," he shouted. She came in on her broad feet.

"The men are busy," Herkimer said, over his shoulder, as he wrote in his crabbed laborious way: "Tell George to send oud ten men nord of Schell's to find a party of eight peeble. Pass the word to Demuth to look out at Deerfield also."

He said to the negress, "You can run pretty fast?"

"Yassah, pretty good, Cunnel."

"You run like the devil to Mr. Dygert's and give him this."

"Yassah, Cunnel."

He looked at her sharply.

"Frailty, you feeling all right?"

"Yassah, Cunnel. Good enough."

"Has Mrs. Herkimer spoke to you?"

"Yassah. She say I can have de baby in de house again dis time ef'n I pass my promise not to have no more on her."

"Whose is it this time?"

"I guess hit's from dat Hans of Mr. Grebb's, Cunnel. He de pesteringest nigger. I jus' couldn' think of no other way to get rid of him. Dat's de truth, Cunnel."

"You run," he said.

As she went out, his eyes came back to the Indian, who had been standing immovably through this conversation, with his brown eyes seeing everything, but showing nothing.

"Come on," said Herkimer, "I'll get you one drink."

The Indian nodded intelligently.

Dr. Petry had been framing in his mind the letter he was going to write to General Schuyler. But at the turn-off he recollected that Mrs. Small was expecting and that he had promised to attend her. He thought he would look in and see how she was coming on with it.

He stopped off at the blockhouse the settlement was erecting, and found that the stockade had been completed. Jacob Small was not there, but one of the Helmer boys was putting the spy-loft roof on. He called down, "Yes, Doc, Cap'n got word from his house to go down there. He ain't come out since. I know. I can see pretty near everything in the country from up here."

The doctor grunted. He could foretell what he would find. The woman, after going through ten years of married life as barren as a bedpost, had now started labor two weeks ahead of time. She was thirty-one years old and Jake was sixty-five, and he had told the red-haired hussy at the time that she had no business marrying a man that old. He didn't like this way of men of fifty taking girls to bed. Better look around for a widow their own age. It irritated him; and the girl had laughed in his face.

She was a sharp-spoken girl, officious, pushing, pert, and he had a feeling she must have known he might drop in and have planned the labor just to catch him when he had other things to do. It would take a long time. She was built like a trout, with no pelvic bone worth the name, and she was old enough anyway to have a bad time. The business was going to be hell for everybody, and especially for her. Well, it might be a good experience for her to go through. A good lesson.

That thought eased him as he swung himself grumpily off the horse and took the saddlebags off his withers. He knocked on the door and found himself effusively welcomed by Captain Small.

"By God, Doc, the Lord must have brought you. I sent Joe Casler after you two hours ago. How'd you get here so soon?"

Doc explained. "How long's Betsey been at it?"

"Commenced just after breakfast. She let herself go at some griddle cakes and they seemed to settle right down in her."

"Five hours," grunted the doctor. "Where'd you bed her?"

"She's back in the bedroom. We didn't have time to carry the bed in here. Jake, she says, Jake, just let me get right down on a bed. And don't you touch me, Jake. My God, Doc, it's a hell of a thing for a man my age to come up against."

"Pains bad?"

"Terrible. You ought to hear the way she takes on."

"She always made a lot of noise," said the doctor. "She's a fresh girl. You needn't act like a run sheep, Jake. I bet you hurt your ma just as bad. That's the only sensible way to look at it."

"You think so, Doc? Crimus, once or twice I felt like laying down dead myself."

"Have a drink. Got anything in the house?"

"I got some distilled apple juice."

"Get some, but bring it to me first. Who's with her?"

"She wouldn't let me send for anybody. Said she didn't want them mussing up her house."

The doctor glanced round the immaculate kitchen, with its shining brass pans and the copper kettle and the dishes in the dresser. Somehow it made him think of Betsey herself, pert, and spicy. She'd told him off before. Now she'd have to eat pie. People never thought of that when they spoke their piece to the doctor.

"You go and get in a woman."

"There ain't nobody handy but Mrs. Helmer. Betsey can't stand her."

"Good," said the doctor. "She's just the person. Fetch her right off. But bring me that apple juice first."

He walked into the bedroom with a heavy tread. It was a nice bedroom, with a good, solid, four-post bed. The white curtains drawn over the window moved gently with a stir of air and took the curse off the smell of pigs from the yard out back. The floor had a crocheted round rug on it and there was a good chest under the window.

"Well," said the doctor, "you're damn well married at last, ain't you, Betsey?"

He carried along a stool with his foot and sat down beside the bed. The woman lying on the bleached sheet seemed younger than her age. Her waving red hair was a tangled wet mop on the pillow. The pins had fallen out and lay all over the bed. Her face was thin, quite white, especially about the mouth. The eyes staring at him were blue and looked feverish. Her body under the rumpled coverlet was shaped like a sixteen-year-old's.

She didn't answer. She was holding on to the coverlet with clenched, thin, and slightly freckled fists, and the doctor said nothing as he watched the progress of a pain. But he pulled out his watch and laid it on the bed and then put his hands in hers and let her have something to clinch on.

When the pain was over, she raised her eyes to his and drew a tremendous long breath.

"Hello, Doc," she said. "You've been a long time getting here."

"So have you, Betsey."

Her lips drew back over her teeth. They were uneven, but

strong and white. They and her natural smile were, for him, her saving grace.

"Where you been?" she asked.

He told her. "And now you've got to start this when I'm trying to get John Wolff out of trouble. You always were a contrary devil of a girl."

She closed her eyes and said, "God damn," under her breath, and the doctor glanced at his watch. The husband came in carrying a jug and two glasses. He poured one sloppily for the doctor and set it down. "I just can't drink, Doc," he said. "I got to run."

He bolted out of the house after Mrs. Helmer.

"Where's Jake gone?"

"After Mrs. Helmer."

"I don't want her."

"I've got to have a woman. Jake's no good. And you're down now, and you can't do anything. Nobody can help you but the Lord, unless it's me. You'll just have to lay down and take what's coming. See?"

"Damn you, Doc," she said. She grinned. "It's a hell of a business."

"Swearing won't help," the doctor said with gravity.

She laughed in his face, and he felt better.

"I'm going to take your clothes off," he said.

"Why can't you wait for Mrs. Helmer?"

"You'll feel better. And I'll have to take a look at you anyway."

"All right," she said.

She sighed, after he had undressed her and tightened the sheet. He went out into the kitchen, built up the fire, and put on a couple of kettles. When he came back, he sat down beside her.

He said, "When you married Jake you thought he was too old to corner you like this, didn't you?"

She nodded.

"Well," he said, "it serves you right."

She said, "My mother died when I was born."

"Yes, I remember. I did the best I could."

"It's just a curse with us, I expect."

"You ain't built right."

"I know." She turned her eyes to his and said, "There's one thing, Doc. You won't believe it, but I'll tell you anyway. I loved Jake and I still do. We had a lot of fun."

"I'll bet," said the doctor dryly.

"You troubled about John Wolff?"

"He's a mean sort of cuss," said the doctor. "I never liked him. But he's Kate's Pa. I've got to do something."

She nodded.

"It's all a mess," she said brightly, and then caught hold.

When Jake returned with Mrs. Helmer, both breathing hard, the doctor drank his apple juice and let the woman attend Betsey. Mrs. Helmer was a stout German *Frau*. She had had twelve children of her own and she probably knew as much about it as he did. She looked at Mrs. Small's bare body with a critical eye and then went out to see how the water was coming.

Jake Small gulped at his glass and looked away from his naked wife. He felt that the world had turned immodest. He couldn't control it; but it didn't seem right for a human being to be handled that way. It was his doing, too; and to think that he had been quite delighted at first! It was one of those surprises that happen to a man after a long life. It just went to show.

"It's a terrible thing for a man my age, Doc."

"Now, Jake. Don't say that again."

"All right, Doc." He paused and fumbled the glass with his hands. He was looking for a nice outside topic. "You think they're going to shoot Wolff?" he inquired.

"I don't know," said the doctor. "I can't get help from Herkimer.

And Colonel Dayton won't see me. He's all twittered on account of not being able to get teams to haul stuff out to Stanwix. Schuyler wants the fort finished before spring. He's got some crazy notion of the British coming down on sleds or something."

"My God!" said Small. "You don't say?"

"Everybody's got crazy ideas about this country."

A motion on the bed made him look at his watch again and Jake went over to the window and leaned out. Mrs. Helmer came bustling in from the kitchen and bent over the footboard. But Betsey shook her head. "No, thanks, Mrs. Helmer." Her voice held no gratitude for the woman. "Listen, Doc. If Dayton feels that way and you can get him four or five teams, maybe he would get John Wolff off. Jake would send ours, I guess."

"Sure," said Jake, explosively. "Casler owes me work too. You fix her up, Doc, and I'll promise you two teams, maybe three, for a couple of weeks."

Dr. Petry got up and leaned over the bed with admiration on his homely face.

"Betsey, you're quite a girl."

She stuck her tongue out, bit it, and shrieked.

"Get out of here, Jake," said the doctor. He took Betsey's hand. "I'll fix you up all right, Betsey, if it's the last job I ever do."

Her lips drew back. Jake took one look at her and fled.

Dr. Petry arrived at Fort Dayton after dark. He had a job getting in to see Colonel Dayton, but when he did he came right to the point.

"How many teams do you need?"

"Do you know of any, Doctor?"

"How many?"

"How many can you promise?"

"Would four teams be any use?"

"I'd shoot my grandmother for that many."

"You needn't shoot any. You can have those teams if you let John Wolff off."

"What the devil . . ."

"I don't care what you do to him. I mean I don't want him shot. I married his daughter, see? I reckon you can fix it."

"I'll have to send him to jail for the duration of the war; I can't do better than that."

"That's all right with me. I just don't want the poor fool killed."

The colonel got up and shook hands.

The doctor went home and routed his wife out of bed.

"They ain't going to shoot John," he said flatly.

She came out of the bedroom in her nightdress and stared at him with her pale face that so resembled Wolff's.

"Oh, Bill," she said. They stared at each other. Then she asked, "Where've you been all day?"

"Getting John off," he said crossly. "And attending a case."

"You must be tired," she said. "You coming to bed?"

Her voice invited him. She was making up for the way she had acted since her father's arrest, as if that had been his fault. He couldn't really blame her. He supposed you got fond of your father sometimes, even if he was John Wolff. But he shook his head. He went down to the kitchen and stirred up the fire and got some rum from the store. He was thinking about Betsey Small. He wouldn't have believed it was possible to have got a baby out of a body like that, and have both live.

Dayton had said that Herkimer had had word of trouble to be expected on the West Canada or at Hazenclever's. Some of the rangers had gone up the Kill before dark. They had sent word to Demooth.

When he finally changed his mind and went into his

bedroom his wife found him difficult. She couldn't understand why he should act so, but she accepted her lot like a martyr.

Two mornings after the birth of Jacob and Betsey Small's first child, John Wolff was prodded on his blankets by the muzzle of the sergeant's musket. It was close after sunrise and the fort was yet quiet.

"Get up," said the sergeant. "Your wife wants to see you."

He said, "My wife."

"Yes, she wants to say good-bye to you."

John Wolff sat dumbly on the edge of the blankets, with his hands round his knees, his dull eyes staring at the soldier's Yankee face.

"They ain't going to shoot you," the sergeant said with contemptuous kindness. "They're sending you down to Albany." He walked out of the door, holding it open behind him. Through it Wolff heard his wife sobbing. It seemed to him the last unnecessary jab of fate that he should have to put up with his wife's weeping before breakfast. But he knew that he had a duty to perform. "Come in," he said. "And quit that crying."

"Oh, John. They ain't going to kill you."

"No," he said dazedly.

"Where are they taking you to?"

"I don't know," he said.

She had sat down beside him on the blanket. She was sniffling her sobs back into her nose. Her clothes were put on whichway and her hair was still braided.

"How long will you be away, John?"

"I don't know," he said. He began to feel more kindly. "Listen, dear." (He hadn't called her *dear* for a good many years; she was a fool woman, always scared to death of something. She got on his nerves; but he had to admit she was loyal, if she was weakminded.) "Listen," he said, "what are you going to do?"

"I don't know."

He said bitterly, "There's fourteen dollars hid in the store. But that won't last so long. Maybe you could live with Kate."

"She asked me, but I said I'd rather die than stay in his house."

"I don't blame you. But it's the only thing."

"I'll get the money. I'll board with somebody. Maybe I can get work somewheres. Maybe I'd move down to where they're taking you, if we knew where it was.

"People look at me here," she added plaintively. "How long will they keep you away, John?"

"They can't keep me after the army comes down. That won't be long. Maybe next spring. Then I'll get back here."

"Oh, John!"

He put his arm round her shoulder and kissed her.

"You look out for yourself," he said.

He stood uncertainly as the sergeant waited for him. He couldn't understand how you could get fond of a person without ever knowing you were. Then he handed her what silver he had on him.

"It's only just over a pound," he whispered. "I won't need it. If you could get to Canada, you could see Mr. Thompson or Mr. Butler. Walter Butler, he's helped people. He helped Witmore a couple of years ago with his land. But I guess you can't get there." He faced the sergeant. "Where are you taking me to?"

"Albany."

"Well, good-bye, Ally."

"Good-bye, John."

They put him in a wagon with two soldiers and drove out through the settlement towards the Kill ford. There was still morning mist over the creek, and as the team hauled out on the Kingsroad on the far side, they surprised a doe drinking.

The afternoon of the third day, the sergeant delivered John Wolff to the keeper of the Albany jail. He was put in a room with four other men, and the room was so small that they could not all lie down in it.

Two days later they were all five ferried over the river and put into the hands of a teamster named Bush, who was getting five dollars for taking them to Simsbury with two sheriff's officers as guards. They traveled by the way of Canaan and they were two days making the trip—the longest John Wolff had ever made, for he had been born and spent his life in Tryon County.

He did not feel sociable, either, with the other prisoners. He kept thinking of Ally all the time, of the way he had never managed decently to appreciate what a good woman she was, whine or no whine. It preyed upon him. It was the worst part of going to jail. Even when he was informed that two of the other men were Mr. Abraham Cuyler, the former mayor of Albany, and Mr. Stephen DeLancey of the great family that ranked with Schuylers, Johnsons, Van Rensselaers, and Livingstons, it made no difference to him. He answered their request by telling who he was, and what had happened to him; but he listened to their furious indignations like a person outside himself.

When they reached Simsbury, the heel of the moon was over the barracks on the high hill. The horses climbed the road painfully and walked through the gate. An officer in underdrawers and a black coat and hat took them inside. He led them through a door into the face of the hill. They found themselves in a room with no windows. It was the guardroom. The officer kicked one of the soldiers, who got up and started a small forge working in one corner.

The officer said, "You can have new irons for twenty shilling apiece. Or you can take rusty ones." One of the five, a tailor, with an instinct for getting on the right side, purchased new ones.

John Wolff watched the dexterous soldier hammer on the manacles. They were joined together by a chain of long links, which in turn was linked by two chains to the anklets. The whole affair weighed over forty pounds. The heated iron burned his wrists, but he hardly felt it at all. He seemed dazed. Mr. DeLancey gave his name for him when the officer checked the list the sheriff's officers had handed him.

Then the blacksmith opened a trap in the floor.

"That's where you're going," said the officer. "If you don't make trouble, I won't trouble you. You can come up every other day, when your name's called. You'll get your meals lowered down like the rest."

He watched them with apathetic eyes. The two gentlemen went down the ladder first. They did not even look at the officer. The tailor shuddered at the dank smell of stale water. The fourth man, like John Wolff, seemed to be dazed. He was being sent down for beating up a soldier who had molested his wife. John Wolff went last.

They found themselves twelve feet down in the mine, in a small sentry room. There were a couple of soldiers there with a lantern and a pack of cards. As the prisoners descended, one of these opened another trap and said, grinning, that there was another flight.

He held the lantern over the hole for them to see. Far down below they saw men lying on a patch of damp sand. The men yelled when they saw the light. "Company's coming," the soldier roared, and laughed. He dropped the trap over John Wolff's head, barely missing his hands.

John Wolff went slowly down a slimy iron ladder, which had been grouted into the stone. It was hard work; the irons were heavy to handle, and the chains clashed on the rungs. The air grew damper and cooler. He began to shiver. His eyes were lustreless when he reached the bottom at last. A bearded man in the remains of a cravat and broadcloth clothes took him by the hand.

"You'll get used to the cold," he said. "It never gets colder, even in winter. It just stays about the same temperature as that."

He pointed at the water. Now John Wolff saw that it was like an underground pond at one end of which he stood. Directly overhead, the walls rose into obscurity. "It's seventy feet to open air," said one of the men. "They've iron bars over it." John Wolff lowered his eyes to the water again. It filled two passages of the mine; and all around, the trickle and drip of water sounded unceasingly from every wall.

"You can't get out," the man explained. It was obvious.

Mr. DeLancey asked through chattering teeth, "What are those for?" He pointed to three braziers.

"Charcoal. We burn them or we suffocate. If we make trouble they threaten us by keeping back the charcoal. It's all very simple." He smiled. "I've been here over a year now. I got taken by the Committee. I come from Virginia. My name's Francis Henry."

There were thirty men or more, lying on the sand. They didn't get up. They didn't speak. They lay there like half-dead beasts.

Mr. Henry said, "It's the custom for new arrivals to attend to the braziers. You can settle it between yourselves."

John Wolff spoke for the first time that day.

"I'll look after them. I want to get warm."

Mr. Henry showed him the charcoal box.

"Don't fall asleep," he said. He pointed to the dark water. "We've a rule. Anybody who goes to sleep tending fire gets thrown in there. It takes you a week to dry out."

"I won't," said Wolff. Then he looked up. "Mister, do they let you write letters?"

"It's against the rules. But one of the guards can be bought. It costs a pound."

John Wolff sat down. He watched Mr. Henry return to his dirty blanket. Then he watched the braziers, and the smoke from them curling up to the ceiling. It went straight up, but when it reached the ceiling, seventy feet above, it started slowly seeping back down the walls and slowly licked away into the shafts of the mine. It seemed to be floating on the water like canoes.

One pound. He wondered whether Ally had gone back to Cosby's Manor yet. He wondered if she would be as scary by herself as she was when he was round to be complained at.

10

Nancy Brings a Note

About a week later, Lana was alone in the cabin. Gil was working out time against the fall logging and burning he expected to do, when he would want George Weaver and Christian Reall and Clem Coppernol for two or three days. He was paying off Captain Demooth in grass from the swale. The trees were mostly girdled, and already had dried out on the lower branches, the leaves turning brown, with only tufts of green at the tops. From the window Lana could see in a vague way how the new land would lie, straight to the west of the cabin.

She felt listless and dull-headed. There was no doubt in her mind now that there was a baby on the way, and though she could have wished that there might have been a year or so without one, Gil was pleased. A man could clear his land well enough, but when he began to work crops he needed help; and there was only one way to get help in the back country, and that was to lay up children against the time. She wondered whether he would be displeased if the child were a girl. Girls weren't much use around a farm. But the main thing for a successful wife was to prove herself fertile. The sex of her offspring was generally ascribed either to an act of God or to the male parent, according to the reaction of the man himself. She thought, in any case, she wouldn't have to be afraid of Gil.

He had recently bought a fleece from Kast, in Schuyler, and he had told her that in his absence she had better not try to keep on with piling brush. It would be better if she stayed indoors and carded and cleaned the fleece. She forced herself to the task, now, for she had been putting it off all day, on the pretext that the cabin needed a doing over. She had cleaned and sanded the floor and swept out the loft. All the pans had been taken down to the brook, where it was cool, for scouring. But there was no other thing to do after that and she had finally forced herself to come back to the hot kitchen.

The wool had a greasy smell; it put oil on her fingers; it was matted and torn from grazing on the edge of the woods; and the leg fleece had clay dried hard as shot that must be carefully removed. It was too precious to waste a hair of it.

From where she sat, Lana could look up from time to time at the peacock's feather on the dresser. Sight of it made her think of home. By now they would be finishing the wheat harvest; her sisters would be binding sheaves, laughing with the reapers. With the team hitched to the crib wagon, her father would be driving down to them. Her mother, standing in the door, would shade her eyes against the sun and stare after him, westward over the field, westward; perhaps thinking of Lana, trying to see her.

During the past week she had had a feeling of her mother's solicitude, when she herself sat down alone with her thoughts, when she took to dreaming with the peacock's feather.

She resolutely set to work. It made her feel better when she got down to it and could see the time of spinning coming nearer. Spinning was the next best thing to music: the vibration of the wheel entered your body; its humming got into the heart; the thread mounted on the spindle, like dreams come true when you were a girl, or hope fulfilled when you got older, or like the memory of life itself. When a woman spun, she had her destiny in her own hands to make. A man had no place in spinning.

Lately she had noticed a queer thing in herself—that though her mind might wander, and her body lose awareness, senses like sleeping dogs awoke and walked. It was so now. She had heard nothing. Her hands were occupied with the comb and wool. She was not thinking any more of her girlhood home or her home with Gil. If she had been thinking at all, it had been of herself as a being past herself, growing without her own volition, like a lone plant in the woods.

Yet long before she heard a thing, before her mind wakened her senses to the approach of anyone, she knew that some person was coming near the cabin. When she finally did react, it was to start up in a cold sweat with the greasy fleece clutched in both hands like an apron over her knees.

She faced the door, slender and dark, her eyes clouded like damp glass, completely defenseless.

The person stopped before her in the door, hesitantly, awkwardly, half frightened.

"It's me," she was saying. "It's just me. Nancy. I've got a letter for you, Mrs. Marting."

"A letter?" Lana said mechanically.

Nancy looked into her face and swallowed noisily.

"Yes, Mrs. Marting, from Mr. Demooth. Capting, I mean." She thrust a folded piece of paper out at arm's length. "I don't aim to stay. I'll just give it and get along."

Lana came to herself.

"Oh, no, Nancy." The girl's foolish face and wide blue eyes looked pitifully afraid of her. "Come in, Nancy."

"Oh no, Mrs. Marting. I couldn't set in with you. Missis is always after me, reminding me I'm just a hired help. I've got no place inside your house. I know it. Only sometimes I forget it."

"Of course you have. I'm glad to have company. Come in."

Nancy put a tentative foot across the threshold. It was shod in an old blue cloth shoe of Mrs. Demooth's, too small, and slit to let the toes out. As she took the letter, Lana felt like weeping, to think how nearly she had deprived the girl of a great excitement.

Nancy was got up with care. In spite of the heat, she was wearing a blue camlet cloak over her dress, which was a calico, also obviously handed down. She had a string of beads round her neck, of blue and red glass, and a red ribbon in her yellow hair. The hair, too, had been brushed with thought and elaborately braided round her head.

Now she came in and sat down on a stool, denying herself the backed chair. Her china-blue eyes made one rapid revolution of the room.

"My," she said, with an unconscious imitation of Mrs. Demooth's inflection, "you have a nice place, Mrs. Marting."

"Do you like it, Nancy? I'm glad."

"You haven't any picters. But that feather's prettier than a picter, I believe."

"I'm fond of it."

"We hain't got feathers in the big house."

Lana read the letter.

DEAR MRS. MARTIN,

I am writing you this to let you know that John Wolff has been sent to Simsbury Gaol instead of shot. I know you will be glad to hear that, as I am. He will be out of harm's way there and we need have nothing on our consciences. But I wish we all could feel as impartially on both sides as you do.

> Respectfully,
> MARK DEMOOTH

P.S. I understand that Mrs. Wolff has returned to her house at Cosby's. If so, she must be there alone. I shall try and drop in and see her.

Lana's eyes filled with tears.

"What is it, Mrs. Marting?"

"I think Captain Demooth must be a very good man, Nancy."

"Yes, he's a nice man. Sometimes Missis is hard on me. But she says I'm stupid and I guess I am. I think Mr. Demooth likes me. He said so once. He said, 'Nancy, you're a pretty girl.' Then he got on his horse and went to town."

Lana, surprised, looked at Nancy.

"Why, you are," she said.

It was quite true. When any rational emotion showed behind the doll-like eyes, Nancy was pretty. She was a large girl, with strong square shoulders. Under the dress her breasts showed firm and high. She was long-legged and she moved with an unconscious sleepy grace when she was walking. She reminded Lana somehow of a well-bred filly, in her body, now that she tried to see her with a man's eyes.

"What's your name, Nancy?"

"Schuyler. Nancy Schuyler." A trained sort of pride entered her voice. "My mother was Elisabeth Herkimer. She's sister of the colonel. I do hear he has a fine place. I been there once, only I don't remember it very well, only the nice horses and the cherry trees. They was in bloom, not bearing. Do you like cherries, Mrs. Marting?"

"Yes, I do. Have you any brothers or sisters?"

"I've got two brothers, Mrs. Marting. Hon Yost. He gave me these beads. He won them off an Indian down at Canajoharie. Nicholas, he's younger, and black-complected, not like me and Hon."

"Do you have to work?"

"Pa's dead. Ma put me out to work with Captain Demooth and the Missis for four years. She gets three pounds a year in English money for me. I was sixteen then. Unless I want to get married after I'm nineteen. I'll be nineteen next month. Did you want to get married?"

"Yes," said Lana, with a smile.

"I wonder what it's like."

"You've never wanted to?"

"I don't know. Old Clem Coppernol, he's always bothering me to come sleep in his cabin. It's dirty there. I don't think I'd want to. And Missis puts me in my room every night anyway and locks me up. I wouldn't mind sleeping with Captain if he told me to. But that ain't marrying, is it?"

"It isn't quite the same," said Lana, gravely.

"That's what Hon Yost told me. He said, 'you and me ain't got much brains, Nancy, but we've got looks to beat all. You make a feller to marry you if he wants anything. Don't you trust a feller,' he says. I think Hon Yost has got some brains, don't you, Mrs. Marting?"

Nancy leaned forward on her knees. Her back was straight. She had a kind of animal strength that was invigorating to see, in spite of her foolish eyes.

"You'll stay and have some milk with me?" Lana suggested.

"Oh no, I couldn't."

"Yes, please."

The girl beamed.

The milk tasted a little bitter from cherry browse. But it was cool from the spring. And Nancy chattered happily. Her brother had gone off to Canada. He was making money in the army. She supposed she wouldn't see him for a spell, but maybe he might come next year.

"How do you know?" asked Lana with a tightening of her breath.

"He sent word down to Nicholas. He sent word to me he'd try to fetch me an officer, too. I wouldn't mind it if the army was to come down here, would you, Mrs. Marting?"

She finished her milk and rose.

"I'll clean the things," she said. "It's getting late."

"No, I'll do them."

"I wouldn't feel easy, Mrs. Marting. Missis might scold about it. It's nice you letting me set with you this way, but I'd feel better if I could."

She looked so anxious, Lana let her wash the cups. Afterwards she repeated Lana's message of thanks to the captain.

"He'll like that. It's real nice to say it so. I'll tell him after supper when he comes to clean his rifle in the kitchen."

She went away.

11

Blue Back Hunts a Buck

The old Indian, Blue Back, had crossed the Hazenclever hill and gone down the north slopes for the valley of the West Canada Creek. He had kept on the west shore northward towards the big falls, and there, on the edge of the chasm, in a small forest swale he had come on the bed of a deer. He moused around in the grass like an old hound dog until he picked up the track, which he followed through all the deer's morning manœuvres.

They led Blue Back to where the deer had watered, dunged, drunk, and browsed. A little later, a couple of miles to the north-west, they brought him to a pond in which the deer had pulled lilies. By then the Indian knew that he was dealing with a heavy buck. He didn't want a big deer, now that he had come so far from home; he wouldn't be able to carry the half of it back to Oriska. What he was supposed to be after was a nice young doe or a grown fawn. His young wife, Mary, recently baptized by Mr. Kirkland, had asked him to get her a nice doeskin for a kirtle she wished to make for herself.

But Blue Back couldn't let the deer go. He wanted to see the horns. He was what Joe Boleo, the trapper, called meat hungry. Every autumn, when the nights grew frostier and the trees began to get a tinge of color on the ridges, Blue Back began to feel an urge to get hold of big meat. Big horns. Something big in the way of a deer, to start the hunting; something that, when you ate the meat of it, didn't digest so easy as a fawn, but kept the belly tight for a long time.

Last night, sitting in the door of his hut at Oriska, and hear-ing the creek flowing towards the Mohawk River with a misty sound in the dark, it had come into his mind that he ought to take a hunt north just to keep track of things the way he had promised Captain Demooth. When his wife said she wanted a doeskin, he said all right, he would get one. But he knew he wasn't going to look for does.

He had started in the hour before dawn, fording the Mohawk and going down towards the Martin clearing. He thought of stop-ping in on the Martins, but he wanted to get well north early. In the swale he roused out the foolish brown mare and watched her kick her heels through the mist and thought it was a pity, the way she was getting fat, that she belonged to his friend Martin. Otherwise he could slip over any time with a bow and arrow and do some neat night work on her. Horse meat was good meat, and very handy.

But Martin was his good friend, and the squaw was getting pleasanter. He let the horse go. It was well past noon when he came to the big buck's bed.

With the patience and phlegm of a shadow he trailed the buck through the afternoon until he found that the animal was circling. Then he left the tracks and struck out across country for where the deer had bedded the night before. He trotted steadily, his kilt of deerskin flapping up and down on his knees, the fingers of his leggings jumping and shaking. The sweat came out on his hunting shirt, staining it where the grease would let it through. Sweat made a dark ring round the band of the disreputable felt hat. As he went, he gnawed at a small loaf of pressed dried meat and blueberries, got himself a mouthful, sucked till the juices enlivened the meat, and chewed it. It was all the food he had with him; but he was not troubled by that. It was good to get hungry before you killed a big deer. You wanted to bring it home when you were on the point of famishment. Then you would throw it down in the house and lie down on your bed, and watch your young wife cut it up and put it in the kettle. Now and then you would tell her to hurry. It was pleasant to see her hurried and anxious, to smell the steam from the cook kettle, and to lie with your hands on your belly.

The air had a bluish thickness of smoke. It lay all along the horizon. That smoke was another sign of the autumn. It enlarged the trees and made the land look flat when you came out of the woods. You saw a deer on a day like this and it was a deer worth seeing.

Blue Back got back to the swale a little before sunset and made a long examination of the weather. There was no wind, and there would be none till moonrise. Then it would draw from the southeast for an hour or two. But by then the buck would have come to bed, to graze a little before he lay down. At half an hour before dawn, the wind would rise from the southeast again; later it would probably turn to the west.

Blue Back took his post a half-dozen rods from the edge of the swale on a knoll where big hemlocks were standing. He lay down on the needles, with his head on a root and his musket by his hand, pulled the unspeakable hat over his wet face, and went to sleep.

He woke at dusk, looked out into the swale, but saw no sign of the buck. Grunting, he rolled back on the ground. He was a good Indian, so he said a prayer before he went to sleep again.

"Our Father God, I am hungry, I want a good buck, I have been a good man, I will sell the horns to Demooth for a drink of rum, but I will give Kirkland a piece off the shoulder. But if it has twelve points I will give Kirkland a piece off the leg and not take his tobacco for a week. I am a good man. For ever and ever, Amen." A Christian prayer that was. Then just for safety he repeated in his mind, without moving his lips, a prayer he used to say.

He woke once more to hear the buck come through the woods from the northwest, against the wind, just as he had expected, and realized that the Lord was taking an interest. He put his hand under his cheek and slept without snoring.

A squirrel twitched its red tail on a stub of a branch twenty feet up the purple trunk of the hemlock. "Be still, little robber," Blue Back said in his mind, and the squirrel cocked his head. He was still. But he went from tree to tree, forty feet above the forest floor, in the wake of the wet, greasy, crawling old Indian.

A kind of twilight, like a left-over of the day before, hung in the swale. The high gray-green grass was topped by mist. There was yet no sign of the sun, but flying birds were astir in the upper air. Their voices came down in double sweetness through the mist.

Blue Back lay down behind a fallen tree on the edge of the

grass. With great caution he found a rest for his gun and pointed it to where the deer's bed was. He himself was stretched out behind the butt of the musket so that Indian and gun made one brownness on the brown ground.

As soon as the mist began to rise, a slightly tenser quiet over-settled the quiet already in the old man. His eye came into the notch of the rear sight. It was beautiful to fit so well together— gun, sights, man's eye, man's finger on the trigger, God in Heaven and the birds in the mist. All that was lacking was the buck.

The buck rose and lifted its beautiful head. Twelve points anyway, thought Blue Back. By damn God, he was meat hungry now. He let his finger tighten as if the will of God were in it. A flat, belly-filling roar of the musket sent swirls through the mist after the round heavy ball. The birds above broke into a cacophonous twitter. The deer leaped straight up, snapped down its tail, leaped again, keeled over. The black powder smoke, rank as rot, came in a wreath over Blue Back's broad brown face. It filtered off, showing the face wreathed in a wide grin. The old Indian, rather like a bear, was humping through the grass. He bent over the dead buck, cut the throat with his long knife, turned the deer over, slit the belly to the ribs, and plunged his arms, sleeves and all, into the vent. The hot steamy smell of the buck's entrails was all about, seeming to blow his belly full of wind. He hauled the entrails out and then went to look at the deer's head. Fourteen points. God was surely working.

He grinned; he hadn't agreed with God about any fourteen-point buck. But maybe he would give Kirkland a rib or two at that.

With true Indian carelessness he had not bothered to reload the old musket. Now, in the silence that had succeeded the shot, he heard a couple of men coming out of the woods. He looked up in time to see them pointing rifles at him. There was nothing he could do but lift his hand in greeting, blood and knife and all.

The first man blew on a little silver whistle. The note was sharp, carrying, and peremptory. He was answered by a shout behind Blue Back.

"I've got his muskit, Captain."

The man with the whistle then lowered his own gun and advanced through the waist-deep grass.

"Hello, there."

Blue Back went on with the business of cutting up the deer. He waited till the man was standing by his hand. The man was wearing moccasins. He had on Indian leggings, but his shirt was green, and had a kind of strap arrangement over it to hold his powder flask and shot pouch.

Blue Back looked up still further to meet the cool gray eyes above the thick nose and pursy mouth, and gave greeting.

"That's quite a deer," said the man in a friendly enough way.

Blue Back agreed.

"You alone?"

"Yes," said Blue Back.

"Hunting alone?"

Blue Back ran his knife down just before the short ribs. He nodded.

"What are you? Oneida? Onondaga?"

"Oneida. Turtle Clan. My name's Blue Back."

The man with the whistle held out his hand. He said, "My name's Caldwell."

Blue Back gravely shook.

Several other men had come through the grass. Eight white men, he counted; they were dressed in moccasins and leggings like the first. But they weren't trappers. Trappers, white men, couldn't stand each other's company. Then on the edge of the swale a couple of Indians stood out of the mist with the sudden quiet of ghosts.

Blue Back took one look at them with his glistening brown eyes and saw that they were Senecas. They had paint on. Vermilion stripes across the cheeks. One had a blue turtle on his chest. That was all right. He could claim clans even though the Seneca nation had been sending deputations to find out why the Oneidas hadn't joined Guy Johnson and Butler at Niagara.

"Got one good fine buck," he observed. "You want meat?"

"Thanks, Blue Back," said the man named Caldwell. "We'll take what you can't carry."

Blue Back put his arm around the deer, as a man might put his arm around the waist of a girl, just below the cut he had made. He braced his stocky body and heaved suddenly, breaking the backbone. Then he took his axe and cut off the horns.

He pointed to the front half of the carcass.

"Thanks," said Caldwell, again.

"Now I go home," said Blue Back.

"Where do you live?"

"Oriska."

"Listen, Blue Back. Do you know where the Deerfield Settlement is?"

"Yes, at the big bend of the big road."

"Yes. But where is it from here?"

"You going there?" Blue Back asked, raising his brown eyes.

"Yes. But we come by the north, and these Indians," he pointed to the Senecas, "got mixed. Is that the Canada Creek over there?"

"Yes."

"Is there any short cut?"

"Yes."

"Who's living there now?"

"Demooth, Reall, Weaver, and Martin. You want to see them?"

"Thought I'd like to see Mr. Demooth. Is he there now, hey?"

"Yes," said Blue Back.

"Where's this short cut?"

Blue Back got up slowly. He called to the Senecas. They were dark thin men. He talked to them in Indian. He explained the route. They nodded. It was quite clear. They would surely find the way now.

Blue Back smiled. He nodded, too. It was four miles longer than his own route would be.

"You'll come and eat with us?" suggested Caldwell.

Blue Back would. He needed some food. He took up his half of the buck and went to their camp, half a mile back in the woods. On the way one of the Senecas told him that he had been making an early cast round the camp and had found Blue Back's tracks. They had sent out a scout.

The camp was a fire in an opening on a knoll. There were three bark shanties set up. There were also four more Indians. All of them looked as if they had come a long way, for their moccasins were worn thin.

Blue Back listened while he sat with the Senecas and ate boiled stump-ground cornmeal. The party had run out of salt and their tempers were not good. They looked tired and a little feverish, some of them. When he had finished, he shouldered the hind quarters and took his musket in his hand. He thanked them. They were breaking camp when he left.

Blue Back went slowly at first, making a cast to the west. He stopped on the first ridge and waited for five minutes, till he was sure he wasn't being tailed. He wouldn't leave the deer meat yet. But he started a steady plodding trot to the southeast.

When he came to the top of Hazenclever hill, he hung the deer meat in a tree, wrapped in his shirt, the legs through the arms, and set off for Deerfield.

12

Logrolling

To Gilbert Martin, that began as a great day. When he woke up, he got straight out of bed and sprang across to the window. Lana watched him from the pillow. His brown hair needed cutting; it was tangled as a crow's nest.

"What are you looking at, Gil?"

He turned from the window as if her voice had broken a spell. But his eyes still shone.

"Oh, just the land," he said.

"The land?"

"Our place." He came back to the bed and looked down at her. "What's happened to it?"

"My Jesus!" he said. "You ain't forgot, have you? We're rolling logs to-day."

Lana felt immensely shamed.

"I guess I'm not all the way awake yet," she said apologetically.

"I guess you aren't." He laughed, tousled her hair with both hands. "Get up, Lana. You'll be busy cooking for those men."

"I will, I will, Gil. I'm getting up now. Leave go my hair."

He started putting on his clothes, saying half to himself, "We'll roll towards the creek. The boys can begin burning on the far side." He glanced at the window again. "That's right.

Wind's southerly. It'll be a fine day. And the wood's dried out fine."

There were ten acres to log and burn. Two days from now, his farm would look like a farm in fact. He would have to think about getting his own yoke of oxen.

He never considered the heat, and the dirt, and the labor. He would see the fashioning of his own place; the cutting he had worked a year on would be laid bare to the eye. His opinion would be deferred to; every minute of the day would be his own—both those he spent himself, and those of the other men.

"Hurry," he said to Lana, and went down the loft ladder with a clatter.

By the time she got downstairs he was in with the milk. He had milked for her this morning. It made him grin. "I had to do something." He looked down at the pail. "She surely is a fine cow to have bought off a minister."

Everything pleased him.

At six-thirty, about an hour after sunrise, Gil, from the slashing, saw Demooth's fine red oxen turning up from the road. The heavy-shouldered beasts with their great jointed knees, fashioned as if to hold still the earth, came slowly towards him.

"Hey, Clem!"

Clem Coppernol glanced at him with an unfavorable eye.

"Hello, Martin."

His voice was dry, but Gil could take no heed of that.

"It surely is kind of Demooth to send his oxen over."

"Well, maybe. I'd consider it was kind of him to throw me in. But it's easy being kind when another man has got to work it out for you."

He sat himself on a stump while the oxen stood with lowered heads and drowsy eyes.

Five minutes later, George Weaver appeared with his own yoke. They were smaller than Demooth's good Johnson cattle. A black and a red-and-white, rough-coated, narrow-shouldered, they did not have the pulling power, but they were quicker on their feet, as well as twice as hard to handle. But taken together, the two yokes made an ideal combination to log a piece of land.

George Weaver said, "Sorry I'm late, Gil. The boys tried to sneak off and fish the spawn beds up above Reall's. I had to get them back. They'll be right along now, though."

"That's all right."

"You going to wait for Reall?" Clem asked hopefully.

"No," said Gil.

"Hain't no sense in that," agreed Weaver. "That man never got on time to anything except a drink. How do you want to start?"

In a few words, a little self-consciously, Gil outlined his idea. He felt relieved when both men nodded.

"We hadn't ought to start the burning till we get that mass of boys. Emma's coming up with them," said George. "She'll be handy helping Lana, or working out here."

"It'll burn fast," said Clem.

He pricked his nigh ox with the goad and swung the yoke for the heavy beech logs, up against the woods, that Gil had not been able to fell into windrows. The beasts moved off at their lethargic tread, the hoofs spreading with deliberate consideration of their weight and power, the heavy chain, like an iron snake, weaving along the dirt behind them.

By the timber, Clem wheeled them. They moved like smooth,

slow-going, well-greased wheels, presenting their rumps to the end of the log. The sour old Dutchman hooked the chain round a butt and spoke in Dutch, and the chins of the beasts lifted a little, their necks went out, the chain straightened its links, and the thirty-foot stick began to slide like taffy, inch by inch and foot by foot.

Before they had delivered it to Gil at the edge of the creek, Weaver had arrived with his smaller stick, and started back. But Gil had no eye for anything but Demooth's fine yoke. Power like theirs was dignified by slowness.

He helped the Dutchman roll the log in place along the brush that crumpled under its weight. He had no thought of the fine tree that had drawn its life through that stick. He thought of the land the felling of its top had opened. Beech trees killed the soil. It made him glad to know there were so few on his place.

Weaver's boys came sullenly. They stood in their unaccustomed boots, put on against the burning, and looked enviously at the nearly naked Realls. All the children but the sucking baby had accompanied their father, who walked behind them with the downcast look of an unsuccessful Sunday-school teacher.

Gil felt a moment's hesitation at putting them under Reall's command. He thought that with a shiftless man like that the fire might get out of hand. But he himself wanted to attend to the burning of the big logs. It was important to burn them clean as could be.

He had not, however, taken into account the childish streak in Christian Reall. The little man led the chase to the hut to get the first brand. His entry, with the flood of children after him, nearly submerged Lana, who was thrust against one wall and had to watch the spoliation of her fire with mingled amusement and annoyance. Every child wanted some fire.

But Reall, using his Bible voice, squelched them.

"No one sets to burning but me!" he roared. "You get your-selves some branches to beat with."

He marshaled them along the first windrow.

"All right, Gil?" he shouted, but he did not look for Gil's raised hand. He thrust the brand into the dried twigs and watched the first small flames take hold. They seized the points of the twigs, the curled leaves, making innumerable tiny contoured shapes, each in its own entity. The flames ran together. They grew and swelled and merged under the brush. The sputtering subsided in a long deep draught of sound, and the first big flame came up, like a pointed heart.

The children screeched at sight of it. Reall stood with the brand on his hip watching it. Then he sprang down the windrow, crablike, all head and arms, and set another section afire.

In half an hour the whole windrow was burning. The fire, making fast from the inside, filled the early autumn air with the voice of its increase.

Gil, on the creek bank, piling logs and drawing brush across them, felt the smoke in his lungs. White acrid clouds of it drew past him; ashes and swirling sparks, light with the instinct to leap up, came against his sweating skin. It seemed to him that he smelled the burning of the shadow of the forest, the fungus growths, the decay, the gloomy things. The yelling of the chil-dren and Reall was hardly to be heard above the noise of burning.

Punctually to their times, one yoke or other of the oxen would appear with a new log to place, coming through the smoke with heads kept low, Weaver or Coppernol walking beside them.

At first they had a word to say.

"She's burning clean."

"The logs are taking hold real active."

"It's going to make a pretty piece for wheat."

"You've got deep soil here, Gil."

The windrows now were all ablaze. The smoke appeared to run from the tops of them like lines of fleeing rats. Only when it had drawn over the creek, above Gil's head, it lost its first mad impetus and rose on the gentle wind. When he turned, Gil could see it, a great cloud, filtering through the branches and slowly mounting the hillside. Its immensity filled his heart. He hardly heard Clem Coppernol, "I'll have to drag to the next windrow, Martin. Fire's getting too close for the beasts."

They were working fast now, the burning, the heat, the smoke, half smothering them all. Each log stirred up a cloud of ashes as it was dragged.

Lana appeared with a kettle of water. Drinking it, Gil seemed to feel the coolness flooding all his system, rising to the skin, as if after the fire the touch of water could make him new. He grinned when she stared with horror at his singed hair and crusted face. But he waved his arm for her to see the accomplishments of the fire.

They stood for a moment, looking together at the raging holocaust that once had been green trees.

"Oh, Gil!" she cried. "It's beautiful!"

Her lips left a heart-shaped print of freshness on his cheek.

Whether they wanted to or not, they had to leave off at noon. The fire had mastered all the slash. The great logs were being eaten, and they discharged sounds like shots. All sat outdoors, watching what they had started. Grimy, singed, parched—food tasted like ashes in their mouths.

It was Emma, shading her eyes, who said suddenly, "Who's that?"

They saw a shape at the far edge of the burning, running towards them through the smoke. Then one of the trees along the creek caught fire, making a torch that for the moment seemed to take all blue out of the sky and turn it black. The suction of the flame drew off the smoke, and all of them saw the Indian, stripped to the waist, trotting towards them with his old felt hat drawn low over his eyes.

13

Catastrophe

Lana stood dully in the box of the cart, stowing away what things Gil and Blue Back handed up to her. There had been no time to pack properly. Their clothes, the two trunks, the chinaware, the axe and gun and knives and scythe and hoes, the churn, all these things were jumbled up like Lana's thoughts.

One moment they had all been sitting there before the door, watching the emergence to reality of their plans; the next the old greasy Indian had arrived. Ten minutes after not a soul was on the place but themselves. George Weaver had said, "We've got no time to lose. Blue Back says an hour, maybe they'll come quicker."

"Where'll we go?" asked Reall.

"We'll head for Schuyler and the Little Stone Arabia Stockade. Clem, you'd better hit right off for Demooth's."

The sour old Dutchman shook his head.

"*Nein,*" he said. "I will not leave mine oxen."

"Turn them into the woods," said Weaver. "We'll find them when we come back with the militia."

"I will take them with me," said Clem. "They are good beasts. I have a place to hide them there."

"Then get going now, you fool. Blue Back said the Senecas told him they'd be left to themselves. There ain't no Indians worse than Senecas. I went with Johnson against Fort William Henry. I know. But, my Jesus, then they was on our side."

As Coppernol set off, Weaver turned to his fourteen-year-old son. "John, you run to Captain Demooth's. Tell him what we've heard. Remember, eight whites and six Indians. Blue Back says they're Senecas, and they're painted."

"Yes, Pa."

"Run like God Almighty, John."

"Can I leave my shoes off? I can't run in them so good."

"Yes, Cobus will fetch them home. Now git."

Cobus took the shoes from John. He asked, "Can I take mine off too, Pa?"

"Stop asking questions," bellowed Weaver, but Emma Weaver nodded at the little boy. "Reall, you'd better light out right away. Don't try to bring anything heavy. You'll have a little time to hide stuff in the woods. But not over twenty minutes. Meet us at my place, but we won't wait for you."

"We'll be along."

Reall was amazingly unperturbed. He gathered his children as a man might herd his calves, started them off up the path, cut himself a stick, and flogged on the laggers.

Weaver turned to Gil and Lana.

"You got the longest way to travel. You'd better get to work."

Gil was already striding off to catch the brown mare. His face was set. Lana said, "Do you think they'll do harm?"

"God knows," said Weaver, catching Cobus by the hand. "We just don't dast to chance it. They want Demooth."

"Poor dearie," said Emma, glancing back at the burning. That day she had been reminded of her own bare start.

"Emma!" shouted George from down the track.

Lana realized that she was alone with the greasy old Indian. He was still puffing a little, but his brown eyes looked at her kindly.

"You pack your load," he suggested. "I'll help."

Lana felt dizzy. She hardly knew where to begin. The smell of the Indian, when he followed her inside, suffocated thought, but now it roused no animosity. He looked at her a moment, pushed his hat back on his head, and picked up her spinning wheel.

"You go up, get blankets," he suggested.

Lana went.

Gil came with the mare. They piled what had already been gathered into the cart. Then he and Blue Back brought the bed downstairs and took it bodily out into the woods above the spring. After they set it down among the hemlock thicket, they came back for the dresser. To Lana they seemed to act like the confused half-drunken figures one meets in dreams.

Gil shook Blue Back's hand.

"Thanks." His voice was tight and dry. "You're a good friend, Blue Back."

The Indian nodded.

"Oh sure," he said. "Fine friends."

"Maybe we'll be seeing you again."

"Oh sure. But you go way now. Men come pretty fast soon."

"Did you know any of them?"

"One man with a whistle was named Caldwell."

"Caldwell!"

He struck the mare. Lana caught herself against the lurch of the cart. They both looked backward as they rolled down the track. They saw the slash still sending clouds of smoke against the hill; but the flames were lower. On the other side of the cabin the corn stirred its leaves in the slight breeze. The Indian had vanished and the place already looked forlorn.

Gil said roughly, "Don't look at it, Lana."

Obediently she turned her face away. But her eyes filled with slow tears. She had hated the cabin at first. She still hated it on certain days. And yet to leave it was like leaving a part of herself, and a part of Gil.

Through the window glass, Blue Back watched them go. They were fine friends. It was too bad.

When they had turned the corner into the Kingsroad, he stopped looking through the glass and carefully began to take it out of the frame. He had always wanted a glass window. He did not have much time to waste; he had a feeling that the man Caldwell wouldn't be a friendly person to anybody when he found the settlers gone. He took the glass under one arm, and laid hold of his musket with his free hand. He trotted out past the burning and slid down the creek bank. He waded in the creek until he came to the river. There he stood in deeper water, with his eyes just over the level of the bank. He waited perhaps fifteen minutes before he saw the hooped headdress of the Seneca rise over the grass on the far edge of the swale.

The dark, painted face was still as an image. It made no move at all. From the look of it, the man behind it might be using his nose, the way a good dog would.

Then the Indian raised his hand. Another appeared by his shoulder, so like him that together they lost all human aspect. They were like two foxes you might see together, two weasels, two cats.

"Cats!" thought Blue Back, with contempt. The Indians began to move through the swale, but unless you had seen them

first you would not have known they were there. Blue Back followed their progress anxiously. He hoped they would not strike
the creek bank where he had come down.

But they missed the place. They lay against the bank for half
a minute looking at the cabin. Then they rose up. One waved.
A whistle blew on the far side of the burning and the rest of the
party came bursting through the smoke. They thronged together
at the door, they rushed inside, they poured out again and stood
in a group before the door.

Suddenly the six Indians slid away and began working over
the ground like foxes hunting mice. They went to the edge of the
burning, returned, went up the path towards Reall's, reappeared
in the edge of the woods, and knelt at the wagon track.

A little apart from the rest the man Caldwell watched them.
Now they ran up to report to him. Even at that distance Blue
Back saw his face flush up; and unluckily for her, at that moment
Martin's cow came out of the underbrush and looked at all the
visitors. One of the Indians pointed at her, and Caldwell nodded.

It was over in an instant. The cow raised her tail, but before
she could whirl out of reach, the Indian had leaped beside her
and drawn his knife across her throat. Plunging away down the
track after the cart, she seemed to go blind, suddenly, crashing
head on into a tree. As she bounced off, she bellowed once so
that the whole hill made an echo. Then, until she fell, she stood
in silence, head out, pouring blood.

In the meantime one of the white men had seized a stick from
the burning brush. He ran into the cabin with it, and laughed as
he came out at Caldwell's whistle.

All the men ran straight down the wagon track for the Kingsroad. Blue Back straightened himself as the last man turned the
corner. At the first puff of smoke in the doorway of the cabin,
his hand went under his deerskin kilt and emerged holding the
peacock's feather. He put it through two holes of his hat, so that

the eye end dangled in front of his face as he walked, where he could see it all the time. Blue Back had coveted that feather ever since he had first laid eyes on it. But it was too bad about the cow. He had thought to come back and use that cow himself, if Gil Martin left it behind. To go back for it now, though, would be unwise.

Besides, he had to retrieve the hind half of the deer from the top of the Hazenclever hill. His wife would be annoyed with him for shooting a buck, but he would pacify her with the feather.

14

Little Stone Arabia Stockade

Gil lashed the brown mare with the reins and Lana had to hold on hard. The wheels bucketed, the box creaked and strained and banged, and the jumbled load in it clattered deafeningly.

"You didn't do much of a job packing," he said savagely.

Lana did not answer. The jolting made her sick: each bounce was like a fist delivered in her back, her abdomen. She remembered something about not riding in a cart when you were pregnant; she wouldn't have thought it would have made a difference so early. For her body was like a dead weight on the seat. She had to fight herself to keep from being sick, to keep from crying, to keep from falling off. It was a pain to get a breath.

Gil took one look at her and lashed the mare again. He hadn't yet begun to feel. But he drove in a blind resentment against fate.

The road reëchoed to the noise of flight. At Weaver's the cart picked up Reall's wagon. Reall was driving a superannuated black and weedy stallion. He had bought it for next to nothing with the idea of getting rich on stud fees; but nobody had seemed to fancy that particular horse as sire of a colt. He looked like a doubtful proposition anyway.

Mrs. Reall sat on the seat beside him with an anxious face. She felt obliged to carry the baby, but neither did she dare to trust her new possession to the children's care. So she had wedged the baby into Thompson's chamber pot and thus held both together.

The children perched in the body of the wagon wherever they could find room, and stared behind them, hoping to see Indians. They shouted shrilly as the brown mare galloped past.

The Weavers came last. Both George and Emma looked grim. He waved once to Gil; then he handed the reins to Emma and climbed back into the cart and took his rifle from Cobus. He shook the priming out, refreshed the pan, and leaned himself against the rack. It was a comforting feeling, to know he was watching the rear.

At Demooth's they found John waiting for them, a small white-faced figure under the trees. He said that the captain had taken Mrs. Demooth in the light wagon and driven straight off for Schuyler to gather the militia.

Clem Coppernol had hidden the oxen in the woods, and he and Nancy were now somewhere ahead with the odd horse.

The mare was laboring when Gil swung her into Cosby's Manor. Reall's ancient stallion was going weak in the knees. Lana struggled in the respite to regain her senses. She felt half dead, and after the first blessed relief she felt more pain in standing still than in the fury of travel on the jolting road.

Gil handed her the lines. "I've got to tell Mrs. Wolff, if she's here."

He jumped off and ran onto the porch of the store. The building looked as deserted as Thompson's house; but when he knocked, Mrs. Wolff opened the door.

"What do you want?"

Her white face stared at him as if he were someone she had never seen. He said, "We've had warning of a party of British and Indians up above our place. Lana and I can give you room in our cart."

"Thanks."

"You'll have to hurry, though. They can't be far back."

She still stared at him.

"I'd rather trust to Indians than you people," she said.

The Weavers came into the clearing and drove up beside the Martins' cart.

"You'd better come with us," George said.

"I'll stay here." She raised her voice. "I told John I'd stay here and wait for him. I don't want help from you. You put him there. You tried to get him killed, George Weaver." She gave a little unnatural laugh. "I've been praying lately, Weaver. And I guess the Lord, He's heard me."

They all followed her look to the westward. When they saw the fresh smoke, they knew it wasn't from the Martin place. More likely Weaver's.

George Weaver turned back to his wagon, walking heavily. "Get back into the wagon," he roared to John. His boot just missed the terrified boy. He hauled himself up after and said to Emma, "Start the horse. If she wants to be fried by Indians, let her. I won't feel sorry."

The three wagons were halfway to Schuyler when they heard the bell begin to ring. It was a small sound at first, hardly to be heard over the crash of wheels and rattle of harness. But when one of the Reall children called attention to it they all heard the sound quite plainly, even Lana.

As they proceeded she felt the slow harsh clamor growing in

her. It beat with the hammering of her heart; now with the dinning of this bell through all her being, it seemed to her that she
would never clear herself of the sound.

She hardly heard Gil shouting at her. He had to yell into her
ear to make her hear, and she had to fight herself upward into
consciousness, like a drowning person.

"What's the matter with you?"

She wrenched the words free: "I can't stand it any more."

"You've got to."

He grabbed her as she started to slide away; and all the rest of
the way he had to hold her on the seat.

The three horses were all played out when they broke out of the
woods at Schuyler and found the level road at last. Now the bell
was clear in the open air.

They saw the sky, the fields, the fences, houses that looked
secure. The cattle that had gathered in the pastures to listen
to the bell turned curious uneasy eyes to their passage. Women
hovered in their doorways, staring across the river to the fort.
Beyond the ford was Demooth's light wagon, towards which men
were running.

As he saw the scene, the power to think returned to Gil. He
let the brown mare splash through the river and drew her up
beside Demooth's wagon. The captain had already got down and
was examining his rifle.

He said, "All here?"

"All but Nancy and Coppernol."

"They've gone into the fort. You'd better leave your own
things there. We're going right back now."

Emma Weaver said, "You go along, Gil. I'll look after Lana."

The stockade made an irregular square, the twelve-foot posts
following the level of the ground around a well. In the width

of the valley it seemed a puny resource against the chances of Providence. Even the blockhouse, projecting its second story five feet higher than the palisade, made but a tiny show against the autumn sky.

Inside, the place seemed smaller yet. Along the four sides of the stockade, low sheds, whose roofs served for rifle platforms, crowded the enclosure, and the slope of the roofs brought the eaves so low to earth that Lana had to stoop as Mrs. Weaver helped her in.

You would have thought that Emma Weaver had lived there all her life. She showed neither dismay nor impatience. She made the two boys bring her blankets for Lana's bed, and then sent them out to find fresh hay to make a pallet. As Nancy appeared, she ordered her to get her water and build a fire against any need. When Mrs. Demooth demanded Nancy's services, Emma strode out and confronted her.

"You ought to be ashamed," she said, her strident voice filling the entire place. "Nobody's asked you to do a thing, yourself. But Mrs. Martin's bad sick and you'll let Christian-hearted people help her, or you'll get outside."

Mrs. Demooth made a frightened defense: "I'll have to tell the captain."

"Go ahead. Just go ahead," said Emma grimly. "And if he doesn't put a strap to you the way he ought, I will. For my own sake, if not for yours, Mrs. Demooth."

But Lana was neither conscious of this bicker nor aware of the straggling arrival of the women and children of the settlement. Under the guidance of a few old men and younger boys, everyone clustered in the fort. The arrival of the Deerfield people brought the number to over fifty souls. They bestowed their bedding and their more easily fetched belongings where they could. The boys then scrambled onto the shed roof; the old men went to the blockhouse where Clem Coppernol with Grandfather

Kast was watching from the spy loft, in which at last the alarm bell ceased its tolling.

The Schuyler folk were not alarmed particularly. But they were eager to hear the story of the raid. It was the first occurrence of the kind in the western end of the Mohawk Valley, though in Schoharie there had been some trouble.

The women crowded the entrance of the shed where Lana lay like a beast upon her bed of hay. Their thronging faces watched every move of Emma's.

"She going to lose it?" they wanted to know.

They suggested remedies. One said, "You'd ought to lean a board against the wall and lay her with her head down on it."

It was, in Emma's opinion, the first sensible idea.

"Who said that?"

"Me," said an elderly, wrinkled woman. "I've see it work once when I lived in Rensselaer Manor. They did it to a nigger woman. But I don't know will it work here."

"Well, find a board."

There wasn't one to be found in the stockade. One of the boys volunteered to go out and look for one across the river at Kast's, the nearest place. But it was then getting dark and his mother refused to let him go. So four women held Lana in her struggle.

It was like a corner of hell. The darkness that the Betty lamps made yellow firefly glows in, the silhouetted figures of the women under the shed roof, the restless boys on the roofs, trying to see what was going on. The hushed female voices and the guttural tones of the old men in the blockhouse punctuated with silences each articulation of the sufferer.

After the first half hour, Lana was only fitfully conscious of her own part in it. She knew that the bell had stopped, but her own pains had taken its place. At moments she was conscious of unfamiliar hands. . . .

When she awoke in the black of the night, the stockade all dark but for one low mass of coals and the small flame of the lamp quivering in a draft of air, she found herself alone with Emma.

The raw-boned woman was sitting at her feet and staring into the dark.

"What happened, Emma?"

"Poor dearie." Emma turned. "You feeling better now?"

"Only sore. And kind of sick. What happened?"

Emma's eyes filled slowly with tears. The unaccustomed compassion in her face made it ugly.

"Don't you fret." She smoothed the dark damp hair. "Poor pretty thing."

Lana lay still for hours it seemed. Finally thought and words coincided in her tired brain.

"Did I lose it?"

Emma nodded.

The militia bivouacking at Demooth's burnt house and barn slept on the ground like tired dogs. Only Gil and George Weaver, who had asked for the duty of keeping watch, were awake. Faint glows in the sky to west and north told them that all the places were destroyed.

They sat together now, beyond the rim of firelight, not speaking. Demooth's wheat had been fired and trampled. There was nothing left. They knew that nothing would be left of their own crops.

Gil said, "What do you plan to do, George?"

"I hain't had time to think. We haven't any money. You don't get a chance to save money up here."

"I'd saved enough to buy some oxen with," said Gil. "But it won't last long, unless I can find work. Lana's having a baby, too."

George nodded. "Work for money's going to be hard to find."

Gil said, "A man could join the army, maybe."

"I'd thought of that. But now, I don't know. If people all join the army, who's going to look out for this country?"

"I didn't really believe it till now," Gil said. "It don't seem possible for a man to work as hard as I did, just for nothing."

There was nothing left west of Cosby's Manor. Houses, barns, Reall's mill, even, that had no stones, were burned. The militia, at Martin's place, found Gil's cow in the road, untouched, but dead. Somehow that raised their anger more than any other thing, even as they skinned a quarter and cut off steaks for their lunch.

They did find Demooth's oxen and one of Weaver's yoke and drove them back on the slow march home. They ate at Wolff's store.

Of Mrs. Wolff there was no sign. The building, as well as Thompson's house, was deserted. Footprints showed that Caldwell's party had come so far. Whether the woman had gone off to Canada of her own free will, been taken, or been destroyed somewhere in the woods, they could not tell. There was no sense in following the trail with the start the destructives had had, and there was no telling what they might have done. The whole raid seemed such an ugly senseless thing to happen.

For the first time they began to realize that there was no protection for them except in themselves. An unpredictable force had been born in the Mohawk Valley, with potential destructiveness as devastating as the old French rapes. It seemed a pitiful remonstrance when, in spite of Demooth's wishes, Jeams

MacNod led on the company to burn down Thompson's and Wolff's store.

When Gil came back with the company that night to Little Stone Arabia Stockade, he found Lana speechless with pain and shame. She tried to meet his eyes, then burst out crying. Emma unexpectedly kissed him before going out of the shed.

He sat down on the earth beside Lana's bed and held her hand. He could not say, "Never mind." He could not think of what Reall had said in breaking the news: "It's too bad, Martin. But there'll be plenty more." He merely held her hand, because it was all he could think of to do.

15

Winter

The house Gilbert and Lana Martin had rented for the winter— it was no more than a shack, with one room, for all it had plank walls instead of logs, and a small, poorly drawing fireplace— stood opposite the old ford in German Flats, and close to the river bank. From it, the West Canada Creek could be seen across the river, coming straight out of the woods. The house had belonged to Mrs. Schuyler, Nancy's mother, but now that one son was working for himself, that the daughter was in service to the Mark Demooths, and the other son working out, Nicholas Herkimer had good-naturedly offered his sister a room in his house below the high falls.

It was Nancy, who had developed a great admiration for Lana

since the day of the call with the captain's letter, who suggested it. They had been able to rent the place for one dollar a month, and in October they had brought their effects from Little Stone Arabia Stockade and moved in.

Lana had been cooped up there all winter. Every morning Gil went upriver to a farm, which Demooth had repossessed when the Herters went down to Schenectady, and worked with Clem Coppernol. He returned after dark, restless and irritable, for he felt that Captain Demooth had given him work out of charity. Even an old man like Coppernol could have handled the cattle and horses single-handed during the winter.

Lana had tried to persuade Gil to take her back to her father's place. There was plenty of room for them there, and plenty of work for him to do. Her family would have been glad to have them. It was better, as long as he felt the way he did, to depend on one's family than on one's neighbors.

But he would not listen. Her mother, he said, had been doubtful about his taking Lana westward. He would not go back now, within a year, to let them get an unjust satisfaction out of it. When Lana tried other persuasion, he talked so harshly that she dropped the matter for good.

At first she had been afraid, living alone in the little house. Though they were within sight of Fort Herkimer, she felt more lonely than she had even in Deerfield. Nancy Schuyler came once a month, for her afternoon out had become a regular institution when the captain learned where she spent it, but the simple-minded girl, for all her natural cheerfulness, depressed Lana; and it was Nancy who first brought to Lana's notice the disappearance of the peacock's feather.

"You hain't hung up that feather of yourn anywhere," she said on her first call. "I should think you would. It would make the place seem homey to you."

At the moment, Lana was pleased. She said, "I'll get it out

right away." But it could not be found. She and Nancy turned over all the pitifully few belongings in vain.

"I packed it," Lana said. "I remember taking it off the dresser when I went to get the white china pot."

"You must have put it somewheres. Or maybe Mr. Marting did."

That night she asked Gil, but he swore he had not seen it. "You ought to know where it is, Lana. You did the packing."

She left the subject, listlessly, continuing the preparation of his supper. It was nothing but stewed corn mush. They put water on it, having no milk except when Nancy kept a little out of the Demooths' supply and sent it down with Gil, and salt was so dear that they used it only once a week. She put his bowl before him and stayed crouched down on the hearth herself.

"You'd better eat," he said.

"I don't want anything."

"Doc said you ought to eat." He glanced down at her. Her face was pale and thin, it seemed to have lengthened, and there were unnatural shadows under her eyes. She still looked young; but she looked as if she had been hurt. "You know why," he said, roughly.

"I know," she said. "But I don't dare."

"You ought to."

"Who wants a baby now? Living like this. We haven't any chance of getting started again this year. If ever."

"We'll get back in the spring, maybe. That's why I want to stay up here."

"Go back there? To Deerfield?"

"Where did you think I meant?"

"It's so far away, Gil."

"It's no further than it used to be."

She did not answer. She did not even look at him. She heard him finish his supper and drop the spoon back in the bowl. He got up and walked across the cabin, got his rifle down.

"What you want with that?"

He said, "To-morrow's Sunday. I'll go up in the woods and see if there's any deer come down."

He cleaned the rifle in silence.

She said, "Isn't the snow too deep?"

"Adam Helmer's lent me a pair of snowshoes. Maybe he'll come with me."

Adam Helmer was a new friend of Gil's. He was a young man, very tall and heavy, almost a giant. He had blond hair and a thin blond beard, and strangely bright gray eyes. Women admired him, for his strength and his good looks. But he had never married. If he married, he often said, he would have to go to work. As it was, any girl was glad to give him supper. Lana had not been glad. She felt that he was taking Gil away the only days that he might have stayed at home.

Helmer shot a thin doe that Sunday, but Gil missed three. They split the deer and parted in the village below Fort Dayton. When he noticed the light burning in Dr. Petry's office store, instead of heading for the house across the river, Gil went to see him. He found the doctor alone.

"Well," said Dr. Petry, raising his heavy brows, "what do you want?"

Gil handed him a steak he had cut off.

"Here's some deer meat, Doc. I guess you don't remember me. My name's Martin. My wife was taken sick in Little Stone Arabia last September. You came up to see her."

"Yes, I remember her, and you too. It's too bad she had a miscarriage. She's a fine girl. But you paid me for that visit."

"Yes."

"How is she now?"

"That's what I want to ask you about. She don't seem healthy. She don't eat hardly anything. She just moons around the house all day."

"She ought to be getting over it by now. Maybe I ought to see her again. Fetch her up."

"It wouldn't do any good. She's afraid of you, anyway. She's afraid of everything." Gil blushed suddenly and looked at a bottle on the wall marked *Sal. Ammon.* Like a girl's name.

"What's the trouble, Martin?"

"She's scared to death of having another baby, Doc. She's so scared of me, I just have to leave her alone. I don't know what to do."

The doctor grunted and looked at him.

"Do you think I ought, Doc? It gets hard on me. But I can't stand to see her scared."

"Women get notions," observed Dr. Petry. "But she seemed like a sensible girl to me."

"Why, she always used to be. She's a damn good wife. She was."

"Was she scared about the first?"

"Hell, no, Doc. That's what beats me so. She was about all a man could expect to handle. She made jokes about it. Not but what she's modest. She's a decent girl."

"Yes, I understand that."

"But sometimes I wonder, Doc, if she wouldn't be better off if I treated her different."

Dr. Petry drew a long breath and let it out again. He remembered Martin's wife—a pretty girl, he had thought then, sensible, and full of feeling. He didn't know the first damn thing about this young man's problem. No man could. Take Jacob Small's wife. Since she had successfully had a baby she was crazy for another, though he had warned her and Small that it was just about likely to kill her. And this Mrs. Martin, who was equipped to have a dozen or fourteen and had probably started out with every intention of having them, was scared to death.

He wondered if the girls of his mother's and grandmother's times had been so unpredictable. But he couldn't tell. He had trained for an army surgeon, and then he had come over to this country. He had located here in German Flats fourteen years ago, and he had delivered probably a hundred women, or women a hundred times, and yet when this young man asked him a perfectly simple question, he couldn't possibly answer him.

He would like to help him, too. Help them both. Dr. Petry, having married no beauty himself, felt a cranky tenderness for all pretty young women; but he was going to have to admit to Martin that he didn't know the answer, any answer.

Watching the doctor's red, heavy, Bavarian face, Gil began to feel frightened.

"Doc," he said, "you don't think there's anything gone wrong with her? Inside, I mean."

The doctor exploded with a solid German curse.

"No, I don't. She just had the devil shaken out of her at a bad time. Three weeks later, maybe, and she'd have been all right. That girl's able to have all the brats you can get. Baskets of them. Oh, I know she's small; but not when you look at her with my eye, boy."

Gil felt weak.

"Her mother said that to me. She said all Borst women had babies easy. But I got wondering. And now . . ."

"Yes," said the doctor, "and now . . ." His eyes swelled as he looked over at Gil. "I don't know. Do you see? I don't know."

Gil nodded. "I guess it's hard to tell."

"You feel as if I'd let you fall down," growled the doctor. "But I can't help that. I can set bones. I can sew up cuts. I can deliver a baby." Suddenly he fell back on religion. "But God's supposed to look out for the soul. You can't expect me to know everything."

"I shouldn't have asked. Only I didn't want to make a mistake."

The doctor got up with him and shook hands.

"You're a good man, Martin. But there's some things we have to trust to luck about. Or God. Or whatever. I guess this is just one. I wish to God I could answer you. I can't. I'm tired. You better go have a drink and get to supper."

Gil picked the half of the doe up off the floor and started out.

"But listen," the doctor said after him. "It's awful easy to get impatient. See? You've been patient. It won't hurt waiting a while."

Gil went down to the river and crossed on the ice. He wanted to leave a cut of the meat at Demooth's. When he got to the house, there was nobody home but Nancy. She told him, smiling, that Captain and Missis had gone down to Herkimer's place and were spending the night. Coppernol was out. She held the door open for him to enter, the candlelight making ripples on her yellow hair when she moved her head.

"You better set down and get warm," she said, taking the cut from him. "I'll put this away, Mr. Marting, and fetch you some cordial. Captain would want for you to have it."

The kitchen was warm. There was a deep fire on the hearth. Gil couldn't resist the cheerful heat, the wide comfort that the slate-gray walls enclosed. He was tired from the long cold hunt, and the heat seemed to go all through him. He sat drowsily, waiting Nancy's return, listening to her footsteps in the storage pantry and then in a back room. She took quite a while. When she came in she carried a glass for him. As he took it, he saw that she had put a red ribbon round her head.

The ribbon made him look at her.

"Sit down here with me, where it's warm," he said.

She giggled a little and sat down on the settle between him and the fire.

"You're real pretty, Nance," he said.

She flushed up to her ears and turned her slow blue eyes on him.

"Oh, Mr. Marting!"

He sat quite still, watching her struggle in her mind for something to say. The stupidity on her face made no impression on her prettiness. He kept thinking of Lana's listless paleness, and comparing it to Nancy's full smooth pink skin. She seemed so incredibly warm and bursting with health.

"Here," he said, extending the glass. "You've got to have your share."

"Oh, Mr. Marting, Missis said I wasn't ever to drink, with my head."

"Nonsense. It ain't going to hurt you. I don't get much fun any more."

"Mrs. Marting's so poorly," she said.

"Yes. It's not her fault. Go on." His voice hardened.

She sipped from the glass, her eyes wide on his. She choked a little, laughed, and had another sip.

He watched her face. The liquor fixed her flush. But her eyes became almost animated. She sat up for a moment, with a queer animal expectancy. Her voice sounded quite bright. "Oh, Mr. Marting!"

Gil threw his arm round her waist and pulled her to him. He felt her waist swell under his hand. While he kissed her the sheer force in her seemed to lift him. Then she let herself sag into his arm and lie like a dead weight, her head thrown back on his shoulder, the full round of her throat bare to the light, and one hand ineffectually pulling at the laces between her breasts. But her quiescence let her hand slip down again to her lap. Her mouth slowly relaxed, the lips shakily finding their normal shape. Almost the only sign of life in her was the formation of sweat beads on her forehead and her upper lip.

He stared down at her a moment and saw the mouth form itself for words. *Oh, Mr. Marting!* He knew she would say it. And it made him feel sick. He shoved her back into her corner of the settle and got up.

The night was piercing cold, the air clear as ice, the wind like the edge of a knife. Gil, with the deer on his back and his rifle freezing to the palm of his mitten, walked home along the snowy road.

Across the river, the lights of the old Palatine settlement were contracted to points. The fort was a dark square on the snow-buried knoll. Along the road small houses and barns stood like little empty boxes. Further down the valley the earthworks and the low palisade atop them of Fort Herkimer, with the two blockhouses and the old stone church raising their roofs among the stars, were hushed in dormance by the frosty night. The only sound was the steady rapid squeak of his snowshoes.

Gil did not even hear them. He did not see the valley. He walked in a blind rage, Nancy, Lana, himself, and human decency like fumes in his tired brain. He hardly saw the Schuyler shack and the single pitiful light its window made against the river ice.

Lana was waiting with his supper when he flung open the door.

"Here," he said, "Adam shot a doe. Let's throw the mush out and fry a steak."

He sat unmoving on the stool, staring at her slow and listless obedience before the hearth, smelling his own sweat rising through the steam of his clothes, feeling contempt for the tiny room with its leaky walls, rage against himself and her and Petry. Petry didn't really know; he had said as much.

As Lana put the steak on the table, he caught hold of her wrist.

"Sit down and eat some."

"I don't want it, Gil."

"Sit down and eat some, I said."

She said, "I've had my supper."

"I said sit down and eat some."

She sat down.

"Get a plate. You can't eat off the table."

She got a plate, mutely accepted the helping, sat staring at it.

"I can't, Gil." Her eyes filled with tears. He watched them come out beside her nose and follow down her cheeks with ugly slowness.

"You're going to, though. And you're going to quit this business of treating me like this. You're going to start to-night, see?"

He watched her struggle with the meat. He thought she was going to be sick. But she wasn't. She got through it somehow. But when she looked up at him, as a dog might for a kind word of praise, he saw that she understood what was in him. Her face turned deathly white and her eyes showed fear as tangible as tears. She never said a word.

They didn't speak to each other the next morning. They went several weeks without any words but absolutely necessary ones. Gil kept trying to tell himself that he was doing better than having to do with Demooth's hired girl, but when he looked at Lana he had to check himself from fleeing the house. She was completely compliant now. Yet her compliance had the fearful quality of a misused dog's.

On Christmas Day he broke down. He had brought her, from the store, a piece of ribbon, which he could not well afford, and as he watched her mechanically putting it in her hair, with mechanical gestures of pleasure, like a travesty in female flesh and blood, he cried out, "For God's sake throw it away."

Her hands stopped at her hair, and for a long while she stared at him. Then when he sprang up to get out of the house, she stepped before the door.

"Gil."

Her face was so white that he was afraid of her. Then his hand raised and clenched. And suddenly he broke down.

"It was all wrong, Lana. I was all wrong."

After his words the silence between them in the shack was as complete as the silence of winter beyond the door. He could hear his own heart beating, and then, with amazement, he heard her breathing.

"Maybe it wasn't," she said.

"You're like a dead person." He felt the words rush from his heart. "As if I'd killed you."

"I don't know, Gil." Her face for all its pallor became thoughtful. It hadn't the quick responsiveness any more. Looking at it, he felt that that had gone forever. "It wasn't you altogether, Gil. It was me, too."

While they stood there, they heard the bell of the old church, which had been taken out of the belfry to make room for the alarm gun and hung over the barrack door, send its slow notes over the snow.

Gil saw the pathetic question in her eyes.

"Let's," he said.

They went to church across the snow. They had no joy in the service or in the Reverend Mr. Rozencrantz's ponderable sermon on God's nearness in the wilderness or his prayer for the continued fruitfulness of God's earth. The water in the flat pans between the pews, placed there to draw the frost from the stone walls, the white icy light that filtered through the panes, the slow measured encroachment of the damp chill air to their very bones, were all beyond their senses. They sat side by side, untouching, yet close.

III

ORISKANY (1777)

I

Council Fire

To the west of Deerfield, where the Mohawk River made the great bend from north to east, the wooden ramparts of Fort Stanwix, striped with new palisades to patch the old, rose on their embankment above the swampy, snow-filled clearing. Beyond the cleared land the woods looked contracted in the frosty air. Sentries on the walks looked out at them through clouds of their own breathing, lethargically, for there was nothing, as there had been nothing since November, for them to see. Not even the river, which ran under ice; no movement about the two small deserted farms lying under the protection of the fort. Nothing at all but the snowshoe tracks of the five Oneida Indians who that morning had approached the glacis from the west and been admitted through the sally port.

Now they were in the commandant's quarters, a low frame building, of the shape of a cattle shed, set against the north wall. The smoke from the end chimney rose in a blue, thin, transparent tape against the gray sky.

The commandant's office was also the officers' messroom, walled with hand-hewn boards, furnished with tables of milled plank, and heavy chairs, the product of the garrison. There was not one in which a man could be comfortable. At the end of the big table, Colonel Elmore, of the New York line, sat in his shirt sleeves, his back to the roaring fire, with his coat hung over his chair. Down the table before him four of the Indians huddled in their blankets, sweating, putting their odor in the room, staring with eyes that missed nothing while they seemed to be unseeing. The fifth Indian stood at the end of the table opposite the commandant.

This Indian was an old man, but his bearing was like a young brave's. His thin, tan, hawk-featured face was turned steadily toward Colonel Elmore. He spoke in a slow deep voice that rose and fell rhythmically, while one of the officers of the garrison, at another table, scratched down his own translation with a squeaky goose quill.

"We are sent here by the Oneidas in conjunction with the Onondagas. They arrived at our village yesterday. They gave us the melancholy news that the grand council fire at Onondaga has been extinguished. . . ." His voice was raised for a moment. "However, we are determined to use our feeble endeavors to support peace through the confederate nations. But let this be kept in mind, that the council fire is extinguished. *Brother, attend:* It is of importance to our well-being that this be immediately told to General Schuyler. In order to effect this, we deposit this belt with Tekeyanedonhotte, Colonel Elmore, commander at Fort Stanwix, who is sent here by General Schuyler to transact all matters relative to peace. We therefore request him to forward this intelligence in the first place to General Herkimer. . . . *Brother, attend:* let the belt be forwarded to General Schuyler, that he may know that our council fire is extinguished, and can no longer burn. . . ."

• • •

Joe Boleo, the news runner, was a thin man whose joints seemed always on the point of coming loose. He used snowshoes of the Algonquin shape, with spurs at the back, that left prints in the snow like the hind finger of a heron's foot. He went out from the fort while the Indians were still working their jaws on the salt pork Colonel Elmore had served them. He did not take the road along the south bank. He followed the river, where the snow was packed hard on the ice by the wind.

At noon the old Indian, Blue Back, sticking his nose outside the door of his bark shanty at the mouth of the Oriskany, saw the runner and looked long at the bent lank figure, shuffling past beneath the big coonskin cap, at a steady four miles an hour.

"By damn it," he said to his wife. "Joe Boleo's in a hurry."

"Why don't you holler for him to come in?" she said, gathering spit to work into the doeskin.

"It's too cold to holler," Blue Back said, shutting the door. "Besides, he always knows if there's any rum."

"We haven't got any," she said.

Blue Back sat down and put his hand on his stomach.

"No," he admitted, "but when I smelled Joe Boleo I'd want some myself."

He lay back on the bed and looked from the peacock's feather over his head to his young wife. She was growing a belly. The sight of it filled Blue Back with conflicting emotions. It was gratifying at his age to be able to show the tribe a legitimate offspring; but at his age, too, it was going to be hard work hunting for three people.

• • •

Joe Boleo had seen the group of Indian shanties and his squirrel-like, round, small black eyes had noticed the closing chink in Blue Back's door.

"God damn," he thought, "that old timber beast has got some likker and he's afraid I might turn round and visit with it."

He glanced up two hours later to see what was left of Martin's cabin at Deerfield. A corner of the log wall, charred away in sloping angles, thrust broken black teeth through the snow. The sight meant nothing to Joe. If anything it made him feel pleased to think that the settlers for a few years would be held back from the trapping country.

Joe Boleo hadn't many convictions in life, beyond the fact that he was the best shot in the Mohawk Valley; that women couldn't get along without him—not in their right minds, they couldn't; and that if rum wasn't a very good substitute for whiskey, whiskey was a first-rate substitute for rum. He was also annoyed at the British efforts for regulating the Indian trade and price of peltry. If it hadn't been for that he might as well have tailed along to Canada with the Johnsons. But if you couldn't cheat an Indian, who in the name of God could you cheat in this Godforsaken country?

Men were coming in from barns and cattle sheds when he passed Schuyler Settlement, and the setting sun drew Joe's shadow long before him on the crust. It put a spark of red on the lip of the alarm bell in Little Stone Arabia Stockade. The farmers were hurrying so that the milk would not freeze in the pails. Farming, Joe considered, was a hell of a life. You milked and milked at a cow for half a year, and just about as soon as you got her dry, the animal would get herself a fresh supply. But when he saw the warm vapor left in the evening air by the closing doors, it seemed to him there were advantages. A farmer in winter could sit at home and order his womenfolks around, while a scout might have to be running thirty miles to tell General Herkimer that a fire in an Indian lodge had gone out.

Joe wondered whether that had been an accident, or whether the old women watching it had gone to sleep, or whether the God-damn thing had been put out a-purpose. The Indians said the fire had been lit in the early life of mankind, and the Iroquois had kept it alive ever since. Even when they moved they had carried it around with them in a stone pot.

An hour after black dark he slogged his way up to Fort Dayton, handed in the news, and asked for a sleigh to take him down to the falls. The commandant got him the sleigh and a driver and packed him off with a pan of rum in his inside and called in the members of the Committee, Demooth, and Petry, and Peter Tygert, and gave them the news in front of the fire in his own quarters.

Their faces animated, even at the bad news, for having a new thing to talk about. The commandant said, "I'm from Massachusetts, but maybe I'm wooden-headed. What difference does it make?"

Demooth answered him soberly.

"It means that the Six Nations can't act together any more without the fire to confer around. That means that the Senecas and the Mohawks and the Cayugas and anyone else are free agents. While the fire was lit, no single tribe could go to war unless the other five were in agreement."

Herkimer, who had been appointed Brigadier General of the Tryon County militia in September, wrote a letter in his crabbed English to Schuyler and then had Eisenlord the clerk translate it and transcribe it while he and Joe Boleo did a little sober drinking.

Herkimer wanted Joe's opinions.

The scout, sprawling at the table in the white-paneled room whose windows looked out on the river and towards the falls, rinsed the liquor slowly round what teeth he still had claim to.

"If you want to know what I think," he said, "it just ain't safe hanging onto Stanwix. The wall's rotten. They've spiked in enough pickets to keep the others from falling down. If a man's got a cold he dassn't do sentry work there, for fear he'll sneeze and level the whole shebang. Poor old Dayton done a lot of complaining, but that ain't never stopped a leaky roof so far's I know."

Herkimer said he hadn't seen the fort.

"You needn't," said Joe. "Because I'm telling you about it. It would take a regiment four months to fix that place. And it don't do nobody any good way up there. It might have been a pertection for John Roof while he was living there, but he's come down here to your farm, since Deerfield got burnt. If the British was to come that way they could march right round with their pants off."

Herkimer said, "Maybe they won't think of that. Not if they send an army officer. An army officer has got to keep his line of communications open."

"My God!" exclaimed Joe. "What's that?"

"Well, he don't want anybody cutting in on his back trail."

Joe scratched his head.

"Oh, you mean he wants to know which way he's going when he has to run home. I thought it was a bowel complaint. But you could cut off his communications if you had a decent garrison at Dayton and Herkimer. They're a whole lot better forts, and they're handy for us to get to if we have to help them out. Take Stanwix, now: it's way the hell off from nobody's business. It stands to reason that it ain't sense making two armies in a war walk a long ways just to kill each other. Somebody ought to have some comfort."

Herkimer was looking older than his fifty years. It wasn't the liquor. His face was grim; the firelight showed it cut all in angles, the big nose, the heated black eyes, the long lips closed.

"I guess our militia ought to have one good fight in them, anyways. *Verdammt!* If they get in deep enough." He looked at Joe. "Have you heard from Joseph Brant? Any news anywhere?"

"We ain't had any word of him," Joe Boleo said. "What's on your mind, Honnikol?" He gave Herkimer his old name, the one he had had when they went hunting together as boys, before Herkimer got to be a successful man, a landholder, second only in wealth to Johnson. It was queer how the young lads diverged as they grew up, he thought—look at Honnikol, a brigadier general; and look at Joe Boleo, a plain scout. Just the same, Joe bet he could outshoot Honnikol nine times out of ten at a hundred yards.

2

Mrs. McKlennar

"Listen, Gil," said Captain Demooth, "you're a fool even to think of going back to Deerfield. You've seen George Weaver, haven't you? And Reall?"

"Yes."

"They aren't going, are they?"

"No."

"Well, I'm not. I'm going to stay down here until it's over. Even if we all went up we wouldn't have a chance when they turn the Indians loose."

"Do you think they will?"

"Everything goes to show so. Schuyler believes it. Herkimer believes it. You'd be as good as murdering your wife to take her up there. If you've got to go, leave her down here."

"I can't afford that, Mr. Demooth." Gil stood beside the table, touching it with his hands. He wanted to lean on something, but he didn't know whether it would look polite. His face had thinned during the winter. The lines beside his mouth had deepened, and under his eyes. His eyes had a misery in them. "When I think about my land," he said. "All the work I put in it. Burning off the new piece. And letting it just go back to woods."

"I know," said the captain. "I feel like that. But look here, Gil, the militia's bound to be turned out. You'll have to come. You'll have to bring Lana down with you then."

"Oh, damn the militia!"

"That don't do you any good."

"I've got to live. I'd made a good start. We were real happy up there. There's no land for me to work around here, and there's no real work for me on your place, you know that."

"Well, now look here, Gil." The captain crossed his legs and tapped the table with his fingers. "I don't suppose it's any good if that's how you feel, but I'd been thinking about you. I just heard that Mrs. McKlennar's man has left her. No doubt he's run off to Canada. Ever since they started rounding up the disaffected people down the valley, others have been leaving here." Gil knew about that. The Albany Committee had taken charge of four hundred wives and children of departed Tories. The idea was to hold them as a kind of hostage. "Mrs. McKlennar asked me about a man to work her place. I said I'd speak to you."

Gil frowned. "I don't want to work for a woman."

"Think it over. She's a decent woman, and she's able to do well in the world, Gil. She's got a temper, but that's because she's Irish. And listen, things have changed. There's going to be real war. Now Carleton has driven Arnold off the Champlain Lake, the British are bound to make a try for this country. There's already action starting at Oswego. Spencer writes that Butler's moving out of Niagara in May. They'll surely bring an army down this way, and if they do, Deerfield's right in the track of it. Now if you take a job with Mrs. McKlennar for a year or two, you'll know your wife's handy to a decent fort. Eldridge Blockhouse is close by, and she could also get to Herkimer or Dayton, if you were off on militia duty. It's a small farm, but it's good."

"I don't want to work for a woman," Gil repeated.

The captain was exasperated.

"It won't hurt you to go and talk to her, will it?"

He spoke so sharply that Gil looked at him.

"No," he said slowly.

That was what Lana said to him after he had told her about the captain's suggestion. Her face was sweet and comforting. Even though it was subdued, though her mouth had a downward bend, he could rely on her eyes, the honesty in them. The winter had been like a nightmare to Gil; it must have been to her; he thought it was time they moved out of this shack, and there was nowhere else to go, if they did not go back to her family. He didn't want to use that argument even to himself, but she helped him by reminding him.

"We won't have to go back to Fox's Mills," she said. "If we like the place we can stay, and maybe we can save up for what we'll need when we go back to Deerfield."

They walked down to Mrs. McKlennar's farm on a Sunday. The river had opened, spring was in the air. That spring of 1777 had come with a rush. One night when Gil and Lana were going to bed they had seen mist over the river ice. And before moonset in the early morning, they had been awakened by the breaking of the ice. It had cracked first in one long traveling report that carried eastward nearly to the falls.

In the morning the whole valley had changed. The air had been soft and moist; and the rising sun, a red ball on the misty hills, already warm. But the wonder, after the long silence of the snow, had been the sound of water. Water was everywhere. It was flowing in its accustomed channel of the river, dark and soiled against the white banks, but catching a red glitter on the rift below the ford. It came across the low land with a steady seeping sound, overflowing the frozen marshes and putting long lakes in the sleigh ruts. And everywhere on the dark slopes of the hills arched yellow falls burst downward.

Gil and Lana dressed themselves carefully, he in his good black jersey coat, and she in her striped blue and white short gown and striped petticoat. She wore her shawl over her head, but she had a white cap on her black hair, and to Gil she seemed unexpectedly dainty as she walked beside him, for all her muddy feet, and carried her chintz pocket before her, almost with demureness. He kept looking down at her, as if in the soft air he had rediscovered the girl in her body, and she looked to him too fine and gentle for a hired help.

In Lana must have run some inheritance from the old Palatine persecutions. The history of her race was one of oppression and of the struggle to survive against it. It was that which made the Palatines strong—through suffering they had preserved their personal independence.

So now, instead of arguing with Gil, she let him take his own way, contenting herself with the presence of spring, the steady drip of trees, the shimmer of the water, the scent of earth unfettered of the snow, and the clear infinity of the April sky. It was good to be walking so, beside Gil. It was the first time all winter, except when they had gone to church. Through her own contentedness she softened his resentment, and they were walking almost peaceably when they first saw the McKlennar farm.

The land lay prettily for a small farm, bordering both sides of the Kingsroad, its back against the sudden rise of river hills, its front upon the river. At a single glance the eye could comprehend the system of the land. The pasture went along the river on a long low round that carried above flood water. Enough willows grew there to give shade. The great trees spread wider, and their branches to-day lifted their upthrusting twigs like brassy arrows against the violet shadows on the southern hills.

Behind the pasture the fields lay level to the plough, rich black bottom land. In spite of himself, Gil felt his heart swelling when he saw them, with an ache for Deerfield. This land had been worked for many years. And there was a good hay bottom, with bluejoint in the wet and a sod that looked like English grass in the higher portions. He could see that the fences had been well set up.

Gil found himself eagerly searching out the farm buildings. What he saw was even better than he had supposed. The house he let pass; it was a stone-walled house, with a piazza facing the road. Behind it in a slope of ground was a farm barn of hewn logs, laid up with plaster joints and a pine shingle roof. The very look of it was warm.

But Lana was looking past the barn to the small house that stood to the right of the springhouse. It also was built of hewn logs, but she could tell by the way it sat above the ground that it had a board floor laid on actual sills. And in front of the door, in the sunny place, were reddish-orange fowls busily prospecting in the dirt.

"Gil!" she cried. "They keep poultry."

Now she began to be afraid that Gil would shy off from the place, that he wouldn't like the woman of the place, or that the woman of the place would not like them. She closed her lips tight, and she said a small prayer in her heart, and she dared not look ahead.

When she did look up again, it was because a woman's voice had roused her.

"Good morning. Is your name Martin?"

"Yes, ma'am," Gil was saying.

"I'm glad you've come," said Mrs. McKlennar.

From her appearance there, Lana would never have supposed that she was gentry. Her boots were muddy, the tops of them showing plainly underneath her petticoat, which Mrs. McKlennar had pinned up all around, nearly to her knees. Her hair she wore clubbed up at the back of her head in a string net that looked as if some birds had put it together in a hurry. She looked hot and she smelled of her stable.

"Yes," she said, suddenly meeting Lana's gaze. "I'm hot and I smell and I look like the devil and I'm mad as well. Every time I lift a fork of cow manure I am reminded of that damn man of mine. He sneaked out of here without so much as a word. The first I knew of it was the freshened heifer bellowing in the barn. I thought he was drunk and I went down to haul him out of bed. I don't mind a man having his likker, Martin, but if he doesn't do his work he can go somewhere else. The quicker the better, for him."

She snorted like a bell mare and stamped her feet as she went up the steps.

"Come inside."

She led them into the kitchen of her house, a lovely place, to Lana's eyes. The stone walls had been sheathed in wide pine paneling and painted a snuff brown. Overhead the beams were painted black with bright red undersides. Mrs. McKlennar sat on one settle. She pointed to the other, and Gil and Lana sat down side by side.

"Now," said Mrs. McKlennar, "you're here on business. Let's get down to it. I want a man. Demooth says you need a job. Is that so?"

"Yes, ma'am."

"You're a passable farmer?"

"I had my own place."

"I heard about it being burned. Too bad. Well, it's an ill wind. And it's neither here nor there. Mark wouldn't have sent you here if you hadn't known something about it. I don't do much farming. Just keep up the meadows and feed my stock. I'm a widow woman. My husband was Captain Barnabas McKlennar. He was with Abercrombie. I may as well say I've had army life all my life, and I expect to get an order obeyed when I give it. Whether you like it or not. Is that understood?"

Gil flushed. "If I take your pay, I'll do the best I can."

"Well, I don't want you coming around afterwards and complaining. How much do you want?"

"I've never worked for anyone else," Gil said. "What did you expect to pay?"

"Well, I asked Mr. Demooth and he suggested forty-five pounds a year, with the house, with the wood, and with the food. It's not a big wage, but if you work well you'll have a good home here. Besides, if your wife can sew, I'll pay her for sewing for me. Can you sew, what's your name?"

"Lana."

"That's a nickname. Magdelana, I suppose."

Lana nodded, blushing.

"Well," said Mrs. McKlennar tartly, "can you sew, Magdelana?"

"Yes," said Lana.

"Would you do sewing for me?"

"I'd like to," Lana said shyly.

"That's understood. I hate to sew. I hate housework, so I do the barn myself and let Daisy, my nigger, do the cooking. I took care of my husband, but now he's gone I'll do as I like. I've got a long nose, Martin, and I poke it where I like. You may think I'm a nuisance."

"Yes, ma'am," said Gil, at a loss for what to say.

"A nuisance?" she said sharply.

Gil flushed.

"I hadn't meant it." Then, meeting the glitter in her eye, he couldn't help but grin. "But I guess I'll think so if you do."

Lana's heart contracted. She looked quickly towards Mrs. McKlennar and was surprised to find the woman's bold stare fixed upon herself. For a moment the face seemed more horse-like than ever. Then the weathered cheeks twitched a little, Mrs. McKlennar put a large hand to Lana's hair and gave it a pat, as she would have patted a dog's head.

However, her voice was uncompromising.

"Your thoughts are your own property, Martin. But keep them to yourself when they arise. And don't presume on your good looks."

"No, ma'am," said Gil.

Lana sighed. She could tell that Gil was amused, that he had made up his mind.

"Perhaps," said Mrs. McKlennar, "you'd like to see your house?" She glanced at Lana and lifted her voice. "Would you, Magdelana?"

Lana bestirred her senses. "Yes," she said timidly.

Mrs. McKlennar snorted, rose, and led them out the back door. As she did so, she said, "I'll expect you to use the back door when you want to ask me for anything. I don't want muck tracked through my kitchen. I track enough myself."

A stout negress in a bright bandana watched them from the woodshed. But Mrs. McKlennar ignored her, and walked with hard-heeled strides towards the little house.

"It's a mess. McLonis never cleared out. A single man. You'll have a sight of work here, Magdelana. But there's water running through a puncheon, a good spring. Have you got bedding?"

"Most of our things were burned," said Gil.

"Well, I'll help you out with a bed." She opened the door. "It's a good chimney, and it's a dry house."

The inside surfaces of the logs were mellowed. Mrs. McKlennar stalked to the middle of the floor and stood there. "You've got a good-sized bedroom upstairs. It's light and airy. It's the original house. Barney was possessed to build the stone one, but I always fancied this house. I lived here a good many years."

Lana looked round her. It was a good chimney, the kind that would be easy to cook at. It had an oven. It made her think of her mother's oven. She turned to look at Gil.

"It's a nice house," she said softly.

"I'm glad you've sense enough to see it. Well, as for me, you can consider the job yours. It's up to you, now, Martin." She paused. "Maybe you'd like to ask some questions."

Gil said, "Yes. I'm in Mr. Demooth's company. If the militia gets called, and I go out with it, will I get paid my wages?"

"Fortunes of war." Mrs. McKlennar nodded. "I'll expect Mrs. Martin to do the milking."

"I will," Lana said eagerly.

"There's another thing." Gil spoke hesitantly.

"Yes?" Mrs. McKlennar was gruff.

"I'd have to know if you were in the right party."

"A woman hasn't got political opinions. I run my farm. And I'll shoot the daylights out of anybody, British or American, that thinks he can come here monkeying with my business. Does that satisfy you?"

Gil said, "Yes," quite seriously.

"Then maybe you'd like to talk it over."

"That ain't necessary, Mrs. McKlennar. We'll do the best we can for you. I like the farm. And you'll find my wife useful, I guess."

Mrs. McKlennar grinned.

"That's fine." She held her hand out like a man. "When can you move in?"

"To-morrow. I've got a mare."

"You can keep her here."

Lana said, "Would it be all right for me to mind the chickens, ma'am?"

"Chickens?"

"Yes. I used to mind them at home. I missed them up in the woods."

The widow snorted.

3

A Prayer

The people had sat down. Now they bowed themselves forward. The pews stopped creaking. Inside Herkimer Church, there was no sound at all but the sudden cracking of the Reverend Mr. Rozencrantz's knees as he got down from his chair, buttoned his coat, and folded his hands in front of him; and through the open windows the tread of military boots upon the sentry walk of the surrounding fort sounded like the impersonal slow laborious ticking of a clock.

Mr. Rozencrantz was a well-advised man, who knew as well as anyone did that to hold his congregation a preacher must give them something to talk about on their way home. Hell and damnation didn't get far when followed by a Sunday dinner.

In the forefront of the church, high up, in the shadow of the sounding board, he knelt—his white hair hanging to the collar of his shirt, his thin face, his high arched nose, his eyelids stretching tight over his eyeballs as he closed his eyes, the easy mobility of his colorless lips forming themselves for the first word:—

"O Almighty God, *Father of our Lord Jesus Christ, hear us, we beseech Thee, answer our prayers and bring succor and guidance and consolation according to the needs of those we are about to bring to Thy divine notice.*"

The domine's stertorous breathing punctuated the pause. He gathered himself visibly, raised up his voice again, and then let it get to business.

"O Almighty God, *we are thinking right now of Mary Marte Wollaber. She is just fifteen years old, but she is going with one of the soldiers at Fort Dayton. He is a Massachusetts man, O God, and it has come to my attention that he is married in the town of Hingham. I have had her father and mother talk to her, I have talked to her myself, but she won't pay attention. We ask Thy help, God Almighty, in bringing her back to the path of virtue, from which, we believe, she has strayed pretty far.*

"O Almighty God, *You have brought us an early spring, keep off the frosts until the fruit is set. O Lord, the English codlin Nicholas Herkimer has grafted onto his Indian apple tree has bloomed this year. May it bear fruit. It is a wonderful example of Thy ways, and worth our going to see, and Nicholas Herkimer will show it to anybody. Also,* God Almighty, *our* Heavenly Father, *we return thanks for the good lambing we have had this year, particularly Joe Bellinger, who has had eleven couples lambed from his twelve ewes, which is a record in this county.*

"O Almighty God, *we ask Thy compassion and aid for all of us who are in sickness. We ask it for Petey Paris, who got the flux real bad on Saturday. His Uncle Isaac Paris sent the news up to us and asks our prayers and says that he has got in a new supply of calicos, French reds, broadcloths, Russias, fancy hank'chers, some new hats and heavy boots, scythes and grindstones.*

"O Almighty God, *give comfort to the following women, both expecting mighty quick, especially Hilda Fox,*

*who is only sixteen next July and getting close to her time.
It is her first. And also for Josina Casler, who is due the
end of this month."*

The domine halted once more, let go a strong breath, and
resumed:—

*"O Almighty and most merciful God, Lord Jehovah,
who is also God of Battles, come to our aid, we beseech
Thee, hear the prayers of Thy people, gathered here before Thee, bring them aid against the British. It surely
looks like war was coming on us directly. There is activi-
ty, O God, at Crown Point, and they say General Burgoyne is bringing an army of 10,000 men, with Russians
and Indians, against Ticonderoga St. Clair is in charge
there, so help him, God. And we thank Thee, O God,
for sending up the Third New York to Fort Stanwix. We
have faith in them, let it not be displaced. For Spencer
sends us word that Butler and Guy Johnson and Daniel
Claus are meeting at Oswego, and they are hard men,
as we know. They aim to bring the savages. It certainly
looks like war.*

*"O God Almighty, our own Colonel Peter Bell-
inger wants the fourth company to muster at Dayton
to-morrow, June sixteenth. He is marching them to Canajoharie to meet up there with Herkimer, and they are going
to try to see Joseph Brant, the chief of the Mohawk savages,
who has been making trouble down to Unadilla. May all
the militia be punctual to assemble and let them come back
in time to defend this settlement if Butler comes quicker
than we do expect him. O Lord, we ask only to be allowed
to lead our lives here in peace and fruitful cultivation of
our land.*

"The muster will be at eight o'clock sharp on Monday morning.

"For Christ's sake, Amen."

Gilbert Martin, bowing behind the back of Mrs. McKlennar, who sat by herself in her own pew, looking stiffly elegant in her black silk dress and smelling violently of a rose scent, felt Lana's hand come quickly into his. He did not move; he did not look at her; he felt the same surprise that the whole congregation, by their utter stillness, showed. It was the first time that the realization of the imminence of war had been brought home to them.

In the stillness, the cracking of the Reverend Mr. Rozencrantz's knees could be distinctly heard as he got to his feet.

4

Unadilla

The militia had no uniform. Demooth's company came nearest to it, with the red cockades they had adopted. They marched better because of them; nearly half the company were keeping step. The Massachusetts garrison of Fort Dayton, lined up in front of the palisade, gave them a cheer, the derisiveness of which was entirely lost on George Weaver. "Hup," he said, "hup, hup, hup."

Half the women of the valley were there to see them off, and while he watched the shrill adieus, Gil Martin felt glad that Lana had not come to say good-bye to him. He had persuaded her not to, saying that she would see him pass Mrs. McKlennar's anyway. And Mrs. McKlennar had backed him up, with one of her snorts.

"Mush," she had said. "I remember when Barney went off

on Abercrombie's expedition. He kissed me in bed and gave me a wallop behind and he said, 'You stay here, Sally, old girl, and keep it warm against the time I get back.' He couldn't stand anything sentimental, you see."

But when she heard the ragged tapping of the militia drums coming along the Kingsroad, she went stamping down to the fence behind Lana like an old warhorse, to wave at the officers and clap her hands like any girl.

The colonel's mare went past, blasting air in her excitement at the drums behind her tail, while astride her Colonel Bellinger himself tried to look as if he were unconscious of her failing, as well as of Christian Reall's bawling that it was too bad they didn't have a trumpet for the mare to blow on.

The two women stayed by the fence, watching the familiar faces of the men, with the red flag of the regiment flapping at its head against the green river hills, and the slant of their rifles, until they saw Gil walking towards them between George Weaver and the angular Jeams MacNod. Gil looked so dark and tall between them, and his face was so set, that Lana's throat grew tight. She was grateful for the squeeze of Mrs. McKlennar's large hand on her arm.

"He's a handsome man," she said. "God save him."

The German Flats company was five days marching down to Unadilla. At the evening of the first day they encamped at Palatine Church, above Fox's Mills, where on the following morning a detachment of the Palatine company joined them under Colonel Jacob Klock. The two companies together, nearly two hundred men, continued east, and reached the rendezvous at Canajoharie at noon. There they pitched camp again, between the Canajoharie company and a company of regulars from the First New York Line sent up from Albany under Colonel Van

Schaick. The presence of the regular troops in their uniform blue campaign coats was inspiriting, particularly on the following morning when the drums beat them to parade. The regular troops had three-foot-deep drums with a resonance beyond compare, finer than the militia drums. All that day, the militia marched south from the Mohawk behind the drums. Again and again they found themselves keeping step as they went up through the hills.

But at Cherry Valley, Colonel Van Schaick halted his men and announced to General Herkimer that he could go no farther as he had to wait for his provisions. However, he would be ready to back up the general if the Indians got out of hand.

Herkimer, on his old white horse, sat moodily staring away from the colonel towards the palisade that enclosed the Campbell farm and made the only fort for the protection of the settlement. He listened without comment, his black eyes staring on the landscape, the green field set in a saucer of the hills. Since winter a foreboding sense of gloom had come over the little German, and now it seemed to him it was fulfilled.

He touched the cocked brim of his hat to the army colonel and swung the old horse to the road. Waiting for him, Colonel John Harper stood at the head of a small company of rangers, and the sight of him and his men seemed to brighten Herkimer. He asked him whether Brant were still at Oghkwaga, and when Harper nodded asked him if his company, knowing the land, would act as scouts. Harper agreed. Herkimer gave the word.

The militia started forward like the disjointed parts of a snake. Twenty minutes later, the head of the little army of three hundred men was past the settlement on the path to Otsego Lake. In half an hour they had all disappeared into the woods.

On the twentieth they pitched camp on the south shore of the Susquehanna, three miles below its junction with the Unadilla.

A runner was sent out that afternoon to Oghkwaga to announce to Brant that Herkimer was waiting to see him and talk as neighbor to neighbor.

The militia had no tents, except the general's. They peeled hemlocks and laid the bark on poles, facing the north, for the weather was hot. The next morning, under orders, they set up a bark shed, fifty feet long, on a knoll a quarter of a mile below, in an irregular growth of apple trees, some of which were still in bloom.

During the course of the morning the runner returned from Oghkwaga and went at once to Herkimer's tent. The general was sitting alone in his shirt sleeves, a field desk on his knees and a quill pen in his fist. He never felt like writing, and writing this way made it pretty near impossible.

Joe Boleo sat down.

"I seen him."

"Will he come talk with me?"

"Oh, sure, in a few days, he says."

"Did you get a look around, hey?"

"Not much last night. But I looked around pretty good this morning. He ain't got so many Injuns there."

They looked at each other.

"Honnikol," said Joe Boleo earnestly, "you want to tie up this twerp, don't you?"

"Yes. But if I go after him now and don't catch him it's an act of war."

"He ain't got two hundred with him."

"Yes, but Congress still thinks they're going to get the Indians on their side. A bunch of them went down last year and called John Hancock a great tree, or something."

"Is that all they called him?" asked Joe Boleo. "My God, they missed their chance."

"Yes, I'm to get Brant to agree to keep neutral. But, by God, I'd like to shut him up somewhere."

"Why don't you grab him when he comes over?"

The militia lay around for seven steaming days and didn't do a thing. Then, on the morning of the twenty-seventh, the scouts fell in towards camp with the news that Brant was coming up four miles below. At noon an Indian walked into camp and asked for General Herkimer.

He stood like a post under his blanket, his small dark eyes flickering here and there over the camp. General Herkimer emerged from his tent, pulling on his coat as he came.

The Indian asked, "What do you want to talk to Brant about?" in English as good as Herkimer's.

"I want to talk with him as an old neighbor."

"That's fine," said the Indian. "I tell him all these men be his old neighbors too?"

He did not look amused, but Herkimer grinned.

"Yes, tell him that."

The Indian turned. In half an hour he was back suggesting that the already erected shed would do as a meeting place if Herkimer came with fifty unarmed men, which Brant also agreed to do on his part. The shed was out of shot from the surrounding woods, and the bare approach to it was a guarantee against any treachery.

A little after noon, Herkimer walked up the hill and sat down in the shade of the shed roof. He took with him Colonels Cox, Harper, Klock, and Bellinger, and each colonel brought a squad from his own company. Gil was in Bellinger's squad.

They sat around on the benches for ten minutes before Brant appeared at the edge of the woods.

It was the first time Gil had ever seen the man whose name since winter had come to be on everybody's tongue. He was under six feet, but he walked like a taller man. His clothes were made in the Indian fashion, but, except for the deerskin moccasins, they were made of English cloth, and instead of the traditional headdress he wore a cocked black hat bedizened with gold lace. His blanket was a vivid blue, turned back from the shoulders to show the scarlet lining.

Behind him his companions were dressed like shabby replicas. There were five of them, in front of the warriors. A white man in deerskins, whom Brant introduced as Captain Bull, and who smirked a little as he bowed; a half-breed Indian who turned out to be Sir William Johnson's bastard son by Brant's sister, a dark-skinned fellow with an Irish face; a Mohawk chief whose name Gil didn't catch; and a half-breed, negro-Indian, whom Brant didn't bother about.

Brant smiled a little as he looked down at Herkimer and shook him by the hand. His features were straight, well shaped, and full of animation. He kept looking round on the militia as if to see what their reactions were. But their reactions to himself, not to the situation. It took but one look at him to see that he was vain.

Though he was pure-bred Mohawk, Joseph Brant could easily have been mistaken for a white man, and he talked more educated English than old Herkimer could have mastered had he been thrice reborn and three times sent to college. He had a great dignity of behavior, too, that made the militia look like simple men; but it was not the natural dignity of a plain Indian. It had the manners of a white man who has been to a royal court. It was filled with pride, which even so meaching-minded a man as Christian Reall could see was an unnatural thing.

Joe Boleo, watching his back, grunted to George Weaver, "Brant used to be a nice lad, too. But now he wants the world to know he's a nice man."

Joe Boleo had put his finger on Brant's weakness. He wanted to be admired, by both Indians and whites, gentlemen and farmers. He wanted to be a great man, by both standards, with whatever person he was at the moment engaged. It was an attitude that later would account for his irrational kindnesses and friendships, as well as his cruelties and hates. The mistake he always made was his utter inability to understand that forthright people like Boleo or Herkimer or Gil could see straight through him. Vainer people, he enraged.

Brant's complaints had been that the Mohawks who had stayed at the Indian town in friendliness to the colonies were held as virtual prisoners, together with their minister, Mr. Stuart; that Butler's wife and children were kept as hostages; and that forts were being erected on Indian property.

Herkimer had asked if the Indians would remain neutral if these complaints were met, to which Brant replied that the Six Nations had always been allied with the King of England, that they still were. Beyond that he could not go. Herkimer then asked him whether he would talk again to-morrow, and Brant agreed. But as he turned to go, he said quietly, "I've got five hundred men. If you start trouble, they'll be ready."

That night Herkimer talked with Joe Boleo and another man named Wagner, and George and Abraham Herkimer. "It's no use at all," he said. "Brant's made his mind up. And there isn't a damn thing we can do about it. He's got five hundred men, and if he wants he can wipe us out."

"I could draw a bead on him," Joe Boleo suggested.

Herkimer shook his head.

"Shucks," said Joe. "We can lick them Indians. If we get Brant, the rest of them will run like rabbits."

"I can't take the chance. I've got to get these men back to the Mohawk. We're going to need them all."

His nephew George said, "What if he starts trouble to-morrow?"

"That's what I want to see you about. If he does you're to shoot him. You can lay behind the top of the hill. They won't see you if you go before sunrise. Lay in those ferns. But don't you start anything."

Nothing happened on the next day. Brant greeted Herkimer blandly with the announcement that the Indians under no circumstances would break their allegiance to the King. Herkimer shrugged.

"All right, Joseph," he said. "There's no sense in talking any more."

That was all there was to it. Three hundred men had marched southward ninety miles; they would march ninety miles back.

"No sense," Brant agreed. "It was nice to have the visit." The sarcasm was barely veiled. "Seeing you're old neighbors, all of you, we'll let you go home. And we won't bother this country now. As a matter of fact, I've got to go to Oswego to meet Colonel Butler."

Herkimer nodded, stood up, shook hands, and watched Brant calmly walking down the knoll towards the woods with his fifty men behind him. As if he had half a mind to signal to Joe Boleo and Wagner, he kept his hands clenched in his trousers' pockets. He did not move until the last Indian had stepped into the underbrush.

Then he said, "Call up the men."

The militia, held under arms, came quickly up the hill and formed companies. At the same moment, a wild yelling burst from the woods; the brush suddenly disgorged a band of Indians. As they came into the open, they brandished their muskets, tossed up their tomahawks, and yelled again.

"Don't anybody notice them."

Herkimer's voice was calm and contained. He had lit his pipe and now he stood in front of the militia, puffing it and staring up at the sky.

"God damn," he said. "I didn't see that storm coming up. But I guess we'll all get wet anyway. Let's break camp and go home."

The Indians were still yelling and prancing at the woods' edge. But now they too heard the thunder. The clouds suddenly engulfed the sun, a still sultry light came over the rolling valley, and then the rain, in large drops, like a volley from heaven, struck the land. The Indians dove back into the woods and the militia were left alone in the falling rain.

Then they too broke for their own camp. They heard the Indians popping off their rifles through the woods, but the sound was like play in the noise of wind and thunder.

When the last man got into camp, the general's tent was struck and he was hunched on the back of his miserable old white horse. Joe Boleo said, "They've all skedaddled."

Herkimer grinned. "They're touchy as women about their paint when they've just put it on."

"It was war paint," said Cox.

"Yes, I saw it." He was unruffled. "It's time we got back home." He raised his voice above the rain. "This trip ain't altogether a waste. We've learned to march together and get along without scrapping between ourselves." He grinned and rubbed the rain off his mouth. "Boys, it looks like a bad time was coming. But you've seen painted Indians, now, so you'll know what to shoot at."

Plenty of the men had been wondering what the expedition had been for. But as they listened to the little German talking to them through the rain, they realized that they had a man who could take them into the woods, and who wasn't scared of Indians, and they felt that when the time came he could set his teeth in a situation and hang on. "Boys," he said, "go back and get your haying done as early as you can. Peter," he called to Colonel

Bellinger, "I'm going back the way we came by. We have food waiting for us at Cherry Valley if the Continentals ain't ate it all. But I give you enough extra so you can take a short cut. Follow up Butternut Creek. If these Indians ever make a shy at German Flats they'll come that way. You ought to see the country. Joe Boleo'll show you how to go."

So the German Flats company crossed the Susquehanna at the ford above the Unadilla and headed home straight north without more than an Indian trail to follow the course of the Creek.

It was wild land. Gil, floundering through a swamp, found Adam Helmer, whom he had hunted with during the winter, beside him. "It's great hunting country," Helmer said. "I've hunted it for years. I know it like my fist and I'd like to see the Indian who could catch me in it. Or that I couldn't catch."

When they came out at Andrustown Helmer asked permission to leave the ranks. He wanted to visit one of Bower's girls. When he got permission he dropped back to Gil's side. "Why don't you stop off? Polly's got a sister that can give you fun."

Gil grinned and said, "I'm a hired man, Adam. I got to get back to work. You heard what Herkimer said about hurrying the crops."

"You mean you're married." Helmer shook his big blond head. "But you're kind of behind with your sowing, mister." He laughed, stepped out of line, and entered the woods. All girls were does to Adam, and some had to be still-hunted.

The company tramped through the little cluster of eight farms while the women and children ran to the fences. For the Indian trail turned suddenly into a road that ran straight to Fort Herkimer.

That evening, on the second day of their march, the company disbanded. By dark, Gil had got home. There was no light in his house, so he went to the stone one. Looking through the door, he saw Lana and Mrs. McKlennar and Daisy, her negress, sitting together.

They all made much of him, and Mrs. McKlennar went down cellar for some sack, which all three white people drank. She snorted a good deal at his description. "It sounds just like rioters trying to get up their nerve. What we need is regular troops."

"Herkimer has nerve enough," said Gil.

"I don't doubt it, when he gets pinched. But you don't win wars by pinching." She snorted, sipped, and grinned, showing her teeth. "But we're glad to have you back, my lad. Ain't we, Magdelana?"

Lana seemed subdued, and at the question she dropped her eyes to her sewing and flushed.

"Hup, hup," said Mrs. McKlennar. "Leave that and go to bed. That's where he ought to have found you, anyway. Go on."

Gil hardly felt Lana's light touch on his arm. She was looking up with tenderness in her eyes. "I'm glad you're back, Gil." And then, "Gil, are you glad? Because I'm real glad."

"Yes," he said. "But I'm hungry as sin, too."

5

Proclamation

The summer was like any other summer in the upper Mohawk Valley, except for the heat. No one remembered such heat as came in that July. Day after day of it, that even dried the woods so that ranging cattle returned early to their barns. The air was sultry, and there was a dusty smell in it, as if a spark dropped anywhere could set the whole world blazing.

Men swinging their scythes through standing grass could feel the brittle dryness of it through the snathe from blade edge to palm; and the women, at work with the rakes, found the hay cured almost as fast as they could handle it.

In German Flats, people, starting the haying, found it hard to believe that war was going on in other places. The plain farmer, thinking of his hay and wheat, had no real idea of what the war was about. In the evenings, reverting to the subject listlessly, all he recalled was the early days of 1775, when the Butlers and the Johnsons and their sheriff, Alexander White, had ridden the length of the valley to chop down the liberty pole in front of Herkimer Church, as they had done at Caughnawaga. But now they were all skyhooted off to Canada for these two years.

It seemed they couldn't take account of the messengers riding horseback up and down the Kingsroad. Men who went at a gallop and didn't stop to drink. All they thought of it was that you couldn't find day labor any more for love or money. Congress was paying men to work up in the woods around Fort Stanwix, a crazy notion for a crazy place—as crazy as the heat.

Up at Fort Stanwix two men had taken charge. One was an apple-faced young Dutchman with a chin as sullen as a growing boy's and very bright blue eyes. His name was Peter Gansevoort, he wore a colonel's epaulets, and was so gentrified about his linen that one soldier, whose wife (by courtesy) had come along, was doubling the family pay. The other was the second in command, Lieutenant Colonel Marinus Willett, a man who looked like a farmer, with a lantern-like face of rusty red all over, and a nose like a grubbing hoe. When he first appeared the settlers said the very smell of him was Yankee;

but he came from New York, and he was able to laugh and enjoy himself.

The five hundred men in the garrison considered that their commanding officers were slave drivers. Not only did they start rebuilding the entire cheval-de-frise, they burnt John Roof's place to the ground, they cleared the scrub laurel from the clearing, and worse than that they sent two squads out every day to fell trees across Wood Creek. To the local labor, that didn't make sense. What was the use of repairing the fort if, at the same time, you made it impossible for the British to get there?

Then like a thunderclap, on the seventh of July, word came up the valley that Fort Ticonderoga had been taken by Burgoyne. Though half the people did not know where Ticonderoga lay, the very sound of the sentence had the ominous ring of calamity.

All at once, George Herkimer's company of militia was mustered and turned into squads of rangers. They blocked the roads to the four points of the compass—west at Schuyler, east at Frank's tavern beside Little Falls, south at Andrustown, and north at Snydersbush. Rumor said that the Butlers and the Johnsons were returning to the valley, bringing their Indians and the wild Highlanders of whom the Germans were as fearful as they were of the Senecas themselves.

Reports came in of men in the woods at Schoharie, and at Jerseyfield. Overnight the little town of Fairfield was deserted. A man named Suffrenes Casselman had led the Tory villagers westward. The word was brought down by a settler on Black Creek, who described them: twenty men, women and children with them, carrying what they could.

As they finished the haying, the people of German Flats were aware of the rebirth of their old racial fears. The Committee of Safety began enforcing their new laws. A negro was shot for being out after dark without permission. Communities began repairing the old stockades. The hammering at Eldridge Block-house came up the valley on those still days, so that Gil Martin, struggling with Lana to get the last of the hay under the barrack roof, heard it plainly.

That evening Jacob Small rode down from Eldridge. He said, "We've got a cannon set up in the tower," as proudly as though Betsey Small had borne another son. "If you hear it go off, it's Injuns. If she shoots twice, don't try to fetch anything, but run like sixty. If she shoots three times, try to get across the river. It means they've got so close you couldn't get inside the fort."

After supper Gil got down the Merritt rifle. And seeing him clean it, Mrs. McKlennar, who had dropped by in the dark, nodded her head from the door.

"Don't look so scared, though, Magdelana. They haven't got here yet."

A canoe came down the river in the dark, cutting an arrow through the moon. In the bow a big-shouldered man stroked steadily. In the stern, Joe Boleo was paddling with his usual appearance of exhaustion.

They ran the bow aground above the falls and took the path down the hill by Warner Dygert's. They found Nicholas Herkimer sitting on his porch.

"Who's that?"

"It's Spencer, Honnikol."

Herkimer got up. The big man shook hands.

"Where you from, Tom?"

Spencer said, "Onondaga."

"What's up?"

"The Indians are at Oswego. Both the Butlers. Sir John Johnson."

"How many all together?"

"They've got four hundred regular soldiers. The Eighth Regiment and the Thirty-fourth. There's about six hundred Tories. They're wearing green uniforms. All the Senecas are there. Brant and his Mohawks. The Cayugas and some Onondagas. A thousand, maybe."

Herkimer grunted.

"Who's in command?"

"A man named Sillinger." (Spencer gave the local contraction of Colonel Barry St. Leger's name.) "He has a big tent and five servants."

"I never heard of him," said Herkimer. "Is he an army man, Tom?"

The Indian blacksmith said, "I don't know. He wears a red coat with gold strings."

"Thank God for that," said Herkimer. He yelled for a negro.

"Go get Mr. Eisenlord. He's at Frank's. Go quick." He turned to Joe. "I can't write this myself. It's too damned hot to-night."

Eisenlord's neat hand made English of the general's dictation:—

Whereas it appears certain that the enemy, of about 2000 strong, Christians and savages, are arrived at Oswego, with the intention to invade our frontiers, I think it proper and most necessary for the defense of our country, and it shall be ordered by me as soon as the enemy approaches, that every male person, being in health, from 16 to 60 years of age, in this our country, shall, as in duty bound, repair immediately, with arms and accoutrements, to the place to be appointed in my orders; and will then march to oppose the enemy with vigor, as true patriots, for the just defense of their country. And those that are above 60 years, or really unwell, and incapable to march, shall then assemble, also armed, at their respective places, where women and children will be gathered together, in order for defense against the enemy, if attacked, as much as lies in their power. . . .

Spencer had already started back to the woods to watch Wood Creek for the first arrival of St. Leger's advance guard.

Eisenlord had been ferried over the river with copies of his proclamation to be distributed through the county. There was nobody left but Joe Boleo. As he said to himself, he was dry enough to make a hen quack; but old Honnikol sat so grim and still in the darkness that he couldn't bring himself to make any suggestion. He tried to think of a funny story, but the only one he remembered was the one about Lobelia Jackson and the hired man, and Honnikol had never taken much to dirty stories.

So in the kindness of his heart Joe Boleo set himself to thinking about a draft of beer. He thought about it in steins, and in a blue glass, and a pewter mug; and by and by he got so thirsty with his thoughts that he thought of beer in a keg, with the bung open and his mouth the same and the beer establishing a connection.

Herkimer shook himself. "Yah," he said. "You're thirsty, Joe."

"How'd you guess that, Honnikol? I didn't say nothing."

For a moment the little German's voice was deep with amusement.

"Yah," he said. "That's how."

"Well," Joe admitted, "if you come to mention it."

"Maria," called the general.

His wife came out on the stoop. She was a young, plump,

serene woman, who might have been the general's daughter. She came to the steps and he reached out and put his arm round her knees.

"Maria, Joe Boleo's thirsty. And I think I am. Bring us both beer. In the two big mugs."

"All right, Nicholas."

He said apologetically, "I don't want the niggers round just now."

"I know," she said.

It seemed to Joe she was a long time coming back. But she came. Her husband made her sit down beside him and held her in his arm.

"Well, Joe"—holding up his mug.

Joe almost made his usual reply about a catamount's biological necessities; he restrained himself in time.

"Here's to you both, Mister and Missis."

The beer was cool from the cellar. The night was dark. The moon was low upon the falls and the rapids were a living shine. The sound of broken water reached dimly towards the house.

"I'm getting to be old," Herkimer said quietly. "Maria's young." His arm tightened. "When my wife died I never thought I'd marry her niece."

"All in the family." Joe was trying to ease the general's voice.

"Yes," said the general gravely. "That's how it is here—too. Schuyler won't send help. He writes I ought to be ashamed to ask it. He says I had no right to agree to anything with Joseph Brant. And now Cox and Fisscher and some others are blaming me because I did not shoot Brant, because I don't get troops from Albany. They will send some Massachusetts people up to Dayton, that's all. But everything else I do is wrong."

"Hell, Honnikol, all the people are back of you. The dirt farmers and timber beasts like me."

"That's good. We'll have one damn fight anyway. All in the

family, Joe. Our side and Johnson's. There won't be any soldiers at all. You could say it's got nothing to do with a war at all."

6

Muster

FORT STANWIX
July 28, 1777

SIR:

We have received accounts which may be relied on that Sir John Johnson has sent orders to Colonel Butler to send a number of Indians to cut off the communications between this place and German Flats who are to set out from Oswego in five days from this, perhaps sooner, and that Sir John is to follow them with 1000 troops consisting of regular Tories and Vagabone Canadians with all the Indians they can muster. I hope this will not discourage you, but that your people will rise up unanimously to chastize these miscreants and depend upon it we will not fail to do our part.

I am, Sir, etc.,

MARINUS WILLETT

When General Herkimer received this he blew through his lips and put on his best coat. He rode right up to Fort Dayton and walked in to speak to Colonel Weston.

Colonel Weston was a man of sense—the first Massachusetts soldier that had managed to grasp just what the German settlers faced. He didn't like Germans, particularly, but he liked still less anything that smacked of British aristocracy; and he agreed at once to send up provisions from his commissariat and two hundred men under Colonel Mellon, as soon as he could get them ready.

On the twenty-ninth, Tom Spencer sent down a message to Herkimer. It was the first definite assurance of the friendly stand of the Oneida nation in the face of war.

> *At a meeting of the chiefs, they tell me that there is but four days remaining of the time set for the King's troops to come to Fort Stanwix and they think it likely they will be here sooner.*
>
> *The chiefs desire the commanding officers at Fort Stanwix not to make a Ticonderoga of it; but they hope they will be courageous.*
>
> *They desire General Schuyler may have this with speed and send a good army here, there is nothing to do at New York, we think there is men to be spared, we expect the road is stopped to the inhabitants by a party through the woods, we shall be surrounded as soon as they come. This may be our last advice. . . .*

There was one thing left to do. Before night, Herkimer sent men down the valley as far as Johnstown to muster the militia on the third of August at Fort Dayton.

It gave Gil a strange feeling, on that Sunday morning, to hear the church bell ringing across the river at Herkimer; to look out from his doorway and see the farm peaceful in the still hot August air, the blue river, and the wooded hills beyond.

Children, playing outside the ramparts of the fort, were stilled by the ringing bell and began their reluctant straggling into church.

The sight brought back the bitterness he had felt when his own place was burnt; it made him think of the winter and of the happiness he and Lana had had together before that time. It had seemed to him, lately, that she was slowly regaining her old ways. But since Adam Helmer, now become a ranger, had brought the muster word, she had grown quiet again.

She was so quiet now, working in the kitchen, that he wondered what she was doing. When at last he turned back, he found that she was sewing a new cockade on his hat, while the tears dropped slowly down her cheeks. Her bowed shoulders and her silent crying made him tender.

"You mustn't be like that, Lana."

"I know," she said. "I hadn't ought." She did not look up in replying. "But the last two days, Gil, I've been remembering. I've been feeling different. And now I wonder if it isn't going to be too late."

"Too late?" He tried to understand. "Oh. You mean I might get killed. . . . I won't get killed, Lana."

"No, no, no. Not that. I wondered if it was too late for you to love me again."

"I do," he said.

"I know. No girl ever had a better man, Gil. I want you to know that." She got up swiftly, her hand like a head under the hat. She smiled and wiped the tears away with the back of her hand. "Put it on."

He obeyed, standing in front of her the way he had before that first muster down in Schuyler. But it was different now. They both felt it.

"Lana. You'll be all right. You stick to Mrs. McKlennar." He paused. "If anything goes wrong . . ."

"Yes, Gil."

Mrs. McKlennar strode down the path from her house.

"Still here?" she asked. "I'm glad. I wanted Gil to have this."

She held out a small flask fastened to a loop of rawhide.

"It's brandy," she said. "Brandy's the next best thing to powder in a fight."

Lana said politely, "Isn't it a pretty flask?"

"It used to be Barney's." There seemed to be some kind of stoppage in the widow's long nose. "It's no good to me, now," she said briskly. "I thought it might come handy to you."

Gil thanked her.

They stood a moment awkwardly. Then Mrs. McKlennar's head lifted.

"Drums," she said.

The steady rattle of the drums came up the Kingsroad. Gil stepped to the door. His voice lifted a little.

"That's Klock and the Palatine regiment," he said. "I've got to go."

He turned to kiss Lana, but Mrs. McKlennar stepped between.

"I'm going to kiss you, Gilbert Martin. I'd better do it now. You don't want to go off tasting a widow on your mouth."

She took his face and kissed him firmly.

"Good-bye, lad."

She stepped through the door with a snap of skirts.

Bright crimson, Gil stooped down to his wife.

"Good-bye, dear."

Lana lifted her lips. Her eyes closed suddenly. He saw the tears welling at the roots of her dark lashes.

"Good-bye," he said again. "We'll make out all right. The both of us."

He caught the rifle up and tossed the blanket roll across his shoulder. He tramped down to the fence. He turned there, waved his arm, and stepped over into the road, not a hundred yards beyond the oncoming Palatines.

Lana could only stand and watch. He was walking along the

road behind the railings, rifle on his shoulder, the long barrel like a finger pointing back towards home. Then for a moment the ragged rattle of the drums submerged her senses.

She felt an arm round her waist, and Mrs. McKlennar was breathing harshly beside her ear.

"It's hard on a woman," said the widow. "Many a time I've seen Barney go off just the same way. Good-bye. And he's off. Maybe he waves, but he ain't seeing you. He's thinking about the men, you see. All the men together."

The arm tightened.

"It's bad enough when he's your son, or even your father." Her stoppage seemed to trouble her again. "A man can't help it if he's your son—and almost any man can be a father. But there are so damn few good husbands in a woman's life."

Gil was by the turn of the road now; he hadn't looked backward again. In his place the uneven files of Palatine farmers trudged along the road, bent over in their walk, as if they followed a plough. Men and officers were indistinguishable—except the colonel, who sat like a sack of meal on the thumping black mare he used to draw manure with.

7

March

The men made an uneasy, sprawling mass throughout the little settlement. On the edge of the knoll the fort had been built on,

Nicholas Herkimer straddled his old white horse, leaning his hands heavily on the somnolent withers.

He was using his deep voice to good effect, now giving orders in English to an officer, locating the muster ground of each company, now checking the list of supplies that trundled past in carts drawn either by oxen or by horses, now hailing in Low German some neighbor or acquaintance.

When Gil preceded the Palatine company into the village, he saw the general in the same position, in his worn blue campaign coat, warm enough in the stifling heat to keep the sweat steadily rolling down his cheeks. He was listening to the bombastic voice of Colonel Cox.

"All right, Colonel," he said finally. "If you want to push ahead to-night, you can. But don't go beyond Staring's Brook. And don't go until your whole regiment's here, either. Leyp's and Dievendorf's companies haven't showed up yet."

Cox, flushed with heat and drink, said loudly that they were wasting time, he'd undertake to lick the Tories with his own company, and he could look out for his company, too, without being told.

"Those are orders," Herkimer said, tartly, for once. "I make Colonel Weston witness, if you don't like them."

The commandant of the Dayton garrison nodded brusquely, met the embattled colonel's eye with a Yankee gleam in his own, and said, "I've noticed them already."

"Where's Bellinger's regiment?" asked Gil.

"Beyond Doc's house," replied a delighted farmer from Snydersbush. "Cox had to haul his tail down that time." He grinned. "He used to hunt around and raise hell with young Johnson, and now he thinks he's drawn title to being a gentleman."

But Gil noticed what the Snyders man had not, that several

of the other officers were looking after Cox with sympathetic eyes. Like him they rode good horses, with English-made saddles and polished riding boots. In their company, Herkimer's faded outfit, horse and coat, looked like a shabby imitation. No doubt they thought him one.

George Weaver greeted him. "You're only just in time, Gil. How's Lana? We ain't seen her in a month, now."

"She's fine," said Gil. "How's Emma?"

"Just the same. She's been considering going down to visit Lana to get a quilting pattern off her. She said she might go down while I was away."

"That's fine," said Gil.

Finding the company mustered took him back more clearly than ever to the time before his house was burnt. Reall, with his gun clean for once, was there; and Jeams MacNod, looking a little pallid at the thought of war; and Clem Coppernol.

Gil said, "I thought you were over sixty."

The white-haired Dutchman said, "Too old? By Jesus a Dutch man ain't ever too old to take a pot at the British."

Weaver said, "We're to camp along the road to-night, right here. We've got to wait for Fisscher's Mohawk company, and Campbell's Minutemen."

"I thought they'd have to stay, with Brant around there."

"Brant's cut back west again," said Weaver. "He's at Stanwix now."

A man gaped. He said, "That Indian can move through the woods faster than you get the news of him."

"He'd better look out where he shows his head," said Reall in a boisterous voice, raising his gun and aiming at a cabbage in the doctor's garden.

George Weaver smacked the barrel down, roaring:—
"Do you want to kill somebody?"

That evening it looked as if the drought might break. Slate-colored clouds with traveling veils of white lifted their heads over the southern hills. There was a distant rumble of thunder, but no rain came. Fires broke out beside the ox carts. Eatables were unloaded. Pork and bacon frying made an odor through the village. Men sat together, grumbling because they had been kept out of decent beds—men like Fred Kast who couldn't see the sense of walking east seven miles one day to walk back seven miles the next, merely for the sake of sleeping in a blanket on the ground.

"I ain't complaining of your company," he explained. "It's just the idea."

"You ought to have brought your bed along," a man said.

"Yes, with Katy in it," said Christian Reall.

Kast laughed.

"I thought of that, and then I thought I couldn't find no room in it, with all you ground pigs trying too."

George Weaver looked down the slope of ground to the river, where Peter Tygert's house was. Herkimer was staying there. Few noticed the late arrival of the Mohawk regiment until they saw Colonel Frederick Fisscher, dapper and dandy for all his gray hair, go cantering down to Tygert's.

"Well, they got here," Weaver said. "I'm going to bed."

He rolled over in his blanket. Reall said, "You'd better pull your feet out of the road, though."

Demooth came round at breakfast time, wearing the homespun coat he used around the farm. The men were pleased to see him.

They had got sick of the handsomely outfitted officers of the other regiments. It made them feel too much like the plain bush Germans the others claimed they were.

"All present?" he said to Weaver.

"Yes. There's nobody missing."

"That's fine." His dark face, lean, alert, quick-eyed, looked them over.

"Boys," he said, "Herkimer was going to put us in front. But the way feeling is, he had to let Cox go up ahead. Bellinger's regiment and Klock's are going to be the main guard. Fisscher's so tired he'll just naturally have to come behind. You can fall in when you hear them cheering Herkimer off from the fort. When he goes by, you just drop in behind him. I've got to send Cox off now, but I'll join you up the road."

"Yes, Captain," said George.

They both grinned.

It took them all one day to get to Staring's Brook. Ten miles. The companies straggled along the road, taking it easy in the heat. Up ahead, Cox lead the Canajoharie men, festering all the time in his wounded vanity. Then, after a long gap, came Herkimer, musing on the old white horse who picked his footing with such caution. With Herkimer rode half a dozen officers, Colonels Fisscher, Veeder, Klock, and Campbell, and Paymaster Isaac Paris, talking volubly on how a campaign of this sort should be conducted, making a bright patch of blue coats, like out-of-season gentians in the woods; and then the German Flats regiment and the Palatine, perhaps five hundred men. Then another gap, and the long line of ox carts jolting on the road, making their painful crawl, beasts and drivers choking in their own dust, stung by horse and deer flies. And after another gap, the Mohawk regiment, taking its ease along the way.

The total force of the army was eight hundred men. The number weighed heavily on Herkimer's mind that morning. He knew that St. Leger had four hundred regulars, that he had six hundred Tories, men just as good or better than his own straggling militia, and in addition almost a thousand Indians.

At Fort Stanwix, Gansevoort had seven hundred men under arms, but Gansevoort couldn't be expected to send them all out. His duty was to hold the fort. But if it were put up to him in time, he might be willing to spare a couple of hundred of them for a diversion.

The advance guard crossed Staring's Brook early in the afternoon. It took three hours for the train of carts and wagons and the rear guard to arrive. The army pitched camp wherever they could find room along the road, a scattering, unorganized mess of men, nearly two miles long. The fires were like glowworms in the big timber—the men lying beside them, talking softly, hugging close to get in the smoke, cursing the flies, and wondering how things were going at home.

In the morning camp was broken at ten and the troops set out at a good pace. A little before noon, Gil and Weaver, marching side by side along the road, came out in Deerfield, on their own land.

It was incredible how quickly the land had become overgrown, as if the mere fact that men had moved away had emboldened the weeds. The burnt acres on Gil's place already had a scrub of blueberries, and tall clumps of fireweed were flourishing among the charred stumps where corn by now should be beginning to tassel out. The houses were no more. Only the black lines of dead coals marked the squared outlines where the walls had stood.

"It don't do any good to look at it, Gil."

Weaver turned his face towards the alder bottom, through which, deep-rutted by the army carts that had passed that way last fall, the road headed straight to the river.

In the ford, a mile away, Cox's regiment was stirring up the mud.

"Thank God the water's low," said Captain Demooth. "All these wagons going through at once are going to cut the bottom out of the river."

The passage of two hundred men had softened the bottom. By the time Klock's and Bellinger's regiments had waded over, the mud was getting pulpy.

Klock and Bellinger halted their companies on the bank and ordered them to stack arms and take their pants off. But with the way the mosquitoes were taking hold, the men preferred wet leggings and shoes to bites, and raucously refused.

They had to wait an hour before the horns of the first yoke of oxen appeared at the bend of the Kingsroad. The animals came on, snuffing the corduroy and planting each hoof as if they wished the things to grow there. When they reached the riverbank, they came down willingly enough, then stopped and drank.

The teamster swung his bull whip on them, but they refused to stir. Behind the tailboard yoke after yoke was halted, until the train filled all the alder swamp, a dozing mass of beasts, with switching tails. Other teamsters came forward and applied their lashes to the first yoke. The cracking of the whips banged like musketry. There was no room to bring another yoke around the first cart. The whole army was held up by a pair of lousy steers.

Even Colonel Fisscher had time to overtake them. He came storming and swearing along the edge of the road on his bay horse and stared and said loud enough for all the men to hear, "You'd think they were a couple of brigadier generals to look at them."

The men looked up. This militia business, with its high-toned colonels all over the lot, was new to them. They couldn't think what to say. But Bellinger had also heard him. He jumped off his horse and waded into the ford.

"Just what did you say, Fisscher?"

"I said they were like brigadiers, the way they take their time."

"Perhaps they wanted to see whether you'd catch up," said Bellinger.

The Palatine and German Flats outfits guffawed. But the teamster, who was embittered by the whole concern, turned the situation off. "It's got me beat," he said, helplessly. "The buggers don't even want to move their bowels."

Fisscher splashed his horse through the water to find Colonel Cox.

"Can't you do anything?" Bellinger asked the teamster.

"I've licked them. I've twisted their tails. I bit the off one by the ear. It's got me beat."

Old Coppernol crossed the ford. He said, "I've cut me an ox gad. If you bush twerps will make two lines and look like fences, these critters might mind a sensible man."

People laughed. But Demooth called to Bellinger, "Clem knows oxen. Let him try."

Clem said, "You see, these animals have got intelligence. They wasn't born for Baptists and they have to be convinced. Besides, they're kind of bored with all the colonels around."

"Meaning me?"

Clem looked at Bellinger.

"Hell, no. You ain't even a brigadier's nephew. You only married his niece."

In the laughter, Bellinger said good-humoredly, "All right, Clem. Try a hand."

The men waded into the ford and formed two lines, like

fences for a lane, but Clem Coppernol acted as if he didn't see them. He talked to the oxen, patted them behind their horns, and then he walked the length of the ford and back, between the lines of men. He said to the oxen, "If an old man like me can do it, you two God A'mightys ought to."

Then he pricked the off ox with the stick and said, "Hup."

The oxen, miraculously, blew their breaths out, lowered their heads, and lifted their knobbed knees. The cart creaked, sank into the mud, but did not stop. The beasts had got to work again.

Clem bawled, "The others will come now, but don't let one get stuck. If it starts to stop, lay hold of the spokes and pull like God A'mighty."

To the admiring teamster he said tolerantly, "You can fetch my muskit for me. Somebody's got to show these twerps the way."

He went ahead as unconcernedly as the slow brown beasts, talking to them happily, as if for the first time since the muster he had found something he could do.

That night the head of the straggling column got as far as the Oriskany Creek. Colonel Cox picked his camp site on the eastern bank, opposite the little hamlet of Oneida huts. But the huts were empty, and Joe Boleo explained that the Oneidas had cleared out the same day the British Indians left Oswego.

Along the road the rest of the army bivouacked as they had the night before, wherever there was room. It was nearly dark when Demooth's company were finally fed and ready to lie down in their smudges. But as they sat on the ground, quietly in the dark, with the firelight streaking the boles of the trees, and a white mist creeping towards them from the river flats, a man floundered down the line, calling over and over, "Captain Mark Demooth. Captain Mark Demooth."

"This way," Demooth answered for himself. "What is it?"

"Herkimer wants to see you in his tent."

"Who are you?"

"Adam Helmer. Do you know where Joe Boleo is?"

"Right here," said Joe. "Has Herkimer got any likker on him?"

Herkimer's tent was pitched in a natural clearing a little behind the Canajoharie militia. His old white horse, ghostly and gray in the mist, was grazing stodgily beside it. They could hear the steady crunching of his teeth, and the small tearing sound of the parting roots. There was no sentry. Nobody hailed them. Even the horse didn't trouble to prick his ears.

Joe pulled the flap open and asked, "What's bothering you, Honnikol?"

"Come in, Joe."

Seated on his blanket, the little German was thoughtfully smoking his pipe. "Sit down," he said when they had entered. "Spencer's bringing Skenandoa."

The low tent was rank with the tobacco, but none of them noticed that. Even Joe Boleo, when he saw the general's troubled face, forgot the liquor question.

"Those bug-tits been dripping again?" he asked.

"If you mean Cox and Fisscher and Paris," the general said quietly. "Yah." He pushed the tobacco down in the pipe bowl with a calloused thumb. "It ain't them bothers me."

But they could tell by his voice that the officers were getting under his skin.

"It ain't them," he said. "Spencer says Skenandoa thinks that Butler has moved out of camp and that he's waiting for us." He cocked his head towards the west and for a minute all four men were so still that the flowing of Oriskany Creek on its rift in the mist was audible in the tent. And queer mingling sounds come with it: the clink of a halter link on a tied horse; the raised voice of a distant man; the hooting of a small owl back in the hemlocks; the grumble of a frog by the waterside.

"Spencer's bringing Skenandoa." Herkimer stopped again. "That must be them outside."

The two Indians had come quietly. Turning, the four white men saw Spencer's blacksmith hand pull back the flap. Then the old chief of the Oneidas stepped in. He bent his head with dignity. He was wrapped around in his blanket, and he scarcely seemed to crease it as he squatted down in the door, so that they saw his dark-skinned wrinkled face, and the red head covering against the fire on the ground.

Spencer said above him, "Skenandoa's young men have come back."

Herkimer said nothing. After a minute more, Skenandoa nodded his head. "They say Butler and Brant have moved the Indians down the road from the camp. They are doing it now. The white men are coming along soon."

Herkimer thanked him quietly.

"That's all?"

"Yes."

"Have you Oneidas made up your minds?"

The chief seemed to have withdrawn inside his own old thoughts.

When he replied, his voice was low. "The Mohawks and the Senecas have sent threats. Mr. Kirkland is my good friend. Some of us will go."

"Thanks."

The two Indians departed, almost as quietly as they had come.

"You see," said Herkimer. "It's what we would expect. But these military gentlemen, they want to ride right through, banging on drums. Cox says it is disgraceful we ain't got trumpets!"

"What do you want us to do, Honnikol?"

"I've been thinking, all day. I think if we could get Gansevoort to send out men against their camp, eh?"

Demooth nodded.

"You, Joe, and you, Adam, you know these woods. Do you think you could get into the fort? With the Indians coming this way, you could go round and get inside?"

Helmer laughed.

"Sure," he said offhand.

"I can't let Bellinger or Klock go. Mark, will you? You're the only other officer that knows these woods and Indians."

"What'll we tell him?" Demooth asked.

"Send out men if he can, and fire three cannon to let us know." He got up and walked to the door. "It's misty. You'll have good cover." The pipe smoke mingled with the mist. "You better get going now."

In the morning, Herkimer sent out a call for all commanding offi-cers to come to his tent. While the men were cooking breakfast they arrived. They made a knot of uniforms, bright, light-hearted, against the dark hemlock boughs. Cox with his bellicose flushed face and staring eyes; Bellinger, raw-boned, simple, honest, look-ing worried; Klock, stodgy, chewing snuff and still smelling faintly of manure and already sweating; Campbell's gray face freshly shaved; Fisscher, dapper and dandy in his tailor-made coat and new cocked hat; and the black-coated, clerkly, calculating Mr. Paris. Behind them assorted captains and majors waited, watching.

Cox had the first word, as he always did.

"Well, Herkimer. Going to give us marching orders?"

"Pretty soon."

"Why not now? The sooner we get going, the sooner we'll have Sillinger making tracks for home."

"Listen, the Oneidas told me last night that Brant and Butler have got the Indians somewhere up the road. They moved down after dark. Johnson's troops ought to be there by now."

"Fine," Cox said boisterously. "We can lick the Tories and then we can tend to the regulars. Like eggs and bacon for breakfast."

Herkimer looked thoughtfully from face to face, looking for support, perhaps, or perhaps just looking for what was there. Only Bellinger was attentive—and maybe Klock.

"We won't break camp for a while," Herkimer said. "I've sent Demooth and two men up to the fort. They'll send a party out and shoot off three cannon when they do. We'll move when we hear the guns."

For a moment no one said a word. But they all looked at Herkimer in the sunshine, while the morning birds cheeped in the surrounding trees.

"You mean we've got to sit here on our arses?" demanded Cox.

"If you like to wait like that," said Herkimer. "I do not mind."

"Personally," said Fisscher, "I'm getting sick of waiting."

Herkimer said nothing.

"It's a good idea," Bellinger said loyally.

"You getting scared too?" said Paris.

Herkimer held up his hand with the pipe in it.

"There's no sense fighting among ourselves."

"What's the matter? We'll outnumber them. The whites. We can handle the Indians on the side."

"You've never seen an Indian ambush," said Herkimer.

"Oh, my God," cried Cox, "this isn't 1757! Can't you get that through your thick German head?"

Rumor had gone down the road that the gentry were having words. The men abandoned their fires to hear the fun. Many of them left their guns behind. They pushed off the road, surrounding the clearing, till the little German seated before his tent was the focal point of over a hundred pairs of eyes.

Gil Martin, coming with the rest, listened among strangers. For over an hour the silly fatuous remarks went on. Some said you could not hear a cannon that far; some said that the three men would surely get captured; some said that probably they'd never gone to the fort at all. That was Paris's voice.

Herkimer sat in their midst with the voices flinging back and forth above his head; his shirt was still unbuttoned, showing his stained woolen undershirt. Now and then he took his pipe from his lips to answer some remark that had a rudiment of sense behind it; but the rest of the time he kept his head turned to the west, listening. Apparently he was unheeding; but the men close to him could see his cheeks flexing from time to time and the slow even reddening of his skin.

It was Cox who finally touched the match.

"By Jesus Christ," he shouted in his roaring voice, "it's plain enough. Either he's scared, or else he's got interest with the British. I didn't bring my regiment this far to set and knit like girls." He looked round with his staring eyes. "Who's coming along?"

Fisscher cried, "I am."

Suddenly all the officers were shouting; and the men, following their voices, filled the woods with shouts.

It seemed to Gil that nobody was looking at Herkimer but himself. He saw the old man sitting there, his face pained, his eyes worried. He saw him knock the pipe out on his hand, blow out his breath, and lift his head.

"Listen to me, you damned fools." He used German. He was getting on his feet and yanking his coat over his arms. But his voice was enough to stop them. "Listen," he went on in English. "You don't know what you're doing, you Fisscher, Cox, the bunch of you. But if you want to fight so bad, by God Almighty, I'll take you to it."

He climbed aboard the old white horse and sat there, looking down on them for a change.

"God knows what's going to happen. But I'll tell you one thing," he said bitterly. "The ones that have been yelling so much here will be the first to pull foot if we get jumped."

For a moment they gaped up at him.

"*Vorwaerts!*" he shouted, and put the horse toward the creek. Some of them were still standing there when he splashed through and waited on the other side. Then the officers were running to their companies, yelling, "Fall in. Fall in."

The men went scrambling through the brush to find their guns and blankets.

"March! March!" The word was in all the woods where the abandoned breakfast fires still sent up their stems of smoke among the tree trunks. Up ahead at the ford, a drummer gave the double tap or the flam. It was like the first nervous beating of a drummer partridge. It was too early for such a sound, but there it was.

Then the whips began their rapid fire along the wagon train. The cartwheels screeched in starting. The still heat in the woods was overflowed with shouts, stamping hoofs, the rattle and slam of carts along the corduroy, the treading feet. The dust rose over the column. All at once it was jerking, getting started, moving.

At the head of the army, Cox moved his big horse beside Herkimer's. His face was triumphant, almost good-humored once more, because he had planted his will on the column. He felt half sorry for the little German farmer. But he would help the little bugger out.

The rough road went nearly straight along the level ground of the Mohawk Valley's edge, following the course of the low hill. Now and then it dipped down sharply to get over a brook. But the bottom was solidly corduroyed. The wagons didn't get stuck. They had even moved up a little on the marching men.

Blue jays squawked and fluttered off, cool spots of angry blue against the leaves. Squirrels, chattering, raced from limb to limb. A porcupine took hold of a tree and climbed it halfway, and turned his head to see the thronging, jumbled mass that heaved and started, checked, and went again along the narrow road.

The men marched in two lines, one for either rut, their rifles on their shoulders, their hats in their hands. When they came to a brook, the thirsty fell out and drank. Nobody stopped them. When they were through they wiped their mouths and looked up, startled, to see their company replaced by another. They got out of the way of other thirsty men and floundered in the bushes to catch up. There was no room left on the road to pass.

Even George Herkimer's company of rangers, who were supposed to act as scouts, would stop at a spring. And when they went ahead they crashed in the undergrowth like wild cattle. There was nobody to stop them. There were no tracks. The woods were dusty. Branches, whipping on hot faces, stung like salt. The heat grew. Not a breath of air in the branches anywhere, not a cloud in the bits of sky high overhead, nothing but leaves, nothing in all the woods but their own uproarious, bursting, unstemmable progress on the narrow road.

Gil, pushed on from behind, pushing on George Weaver just ahead of him, heard the birds singing in the dark swamp ahead. The ground fell steeply to a quiet flowing brook with a cool moss bottom. He felt his own step quicken with the instinct to drink and cool himself. Looking over George Weaver's thick round shoulders, he had a glimpse of the road turning into a causeway of logs across the stream; of George Herkimer's rangers crowding down on the crossing to make it dry-shod; of the Canajoharie regiment floundering in the swamp and drinking face down by the brook; of Cox turning his red sweaty face to Herkimer and bawling, "Where did you say Butler was?"; of the two banks, precipitous and thickly clothed with a young stand of hemlocks, so soft and cool and damp and dark that it made one wish to lie down there and rest. Now he felt the ground falling under his feet, and the resistless push at his back thrusting him out on the causeway. They had passed half of Cox's regiment and were plug-ging up the other side. The stamp of Klock's regiment came down the bank at their backs. Behind in the woods the jangle and rattle of the carts, the steady cracking of whips, and little futile *rattle-tats* of Fisscher's drummers. All in the moment: "I meant to get a drink of water," Reall's voice was saying at his shoulder. "So did I," said Gil. "My God," said Weaver, "what was that?"

At the top of the hemlocks a little stab of orange was mush-roomed out by a black coil of smoke. They heard the crack. Cox's voice, caught short in another remark, lifted beyond reason. His big body swayed suddenly against his horse's neck. The horse reared, screamed, and, as Cox slid sack-like off his back, crashed completely over.

A shrill silver whistle sounded. Three short blasts. The young hemlocks disgorged a solid mass of fire that made a single impact on the ear. Gil felt George Weaver slam against his chest, knock-ing him sidewise on top of Reall. A horse screamed again and went leaping into the scrub. As he got up, Gil saw the beast fall over on his head. It was Herkimer's old white horse, galvanized into senseless vigor. He felt his arm caught and Bellinger was shouting, "Give me a hand with the old man." The old man was sitting on the causeway, holding on to his knee with both hands. His face was gray and shining and his lips moved in it.

But the voice was lost.

Gil stood before him with his back to the slope and stared down into the ravine. The militia were milling along the brook, flung down along the bank, like sticks thrown up by a freshet, kneeling, lying on their bellies, resting their rifles on the bellies of dead men. They were oddly silent. But the air around them was swept by the dull endless crash of muskets and a weird high swell of yelling from the woods.

Then beyond them he saw the Indians in the trees, adder-like, streaked with vermilion, and black, and white. From the head of the rise the first orderly discharge went over his head with a compelling, even shearing of the air, as if a hand had swung an enormous scythe. He saw the green coats on men firing at him; but he bent down and grasped the general by the knees and heaved him on up the bank while Bellinger lugged him by the armpits.

The colonel was swearing in a strange way. He wiped his mouth on his sleeve and said, "By God, Fisscher has pulled foot!"

East of the causeway, where the rear guard had been, a dwindling tide of yells and firing fled backward into the woods. They dumped the general down behind a log and fell beside him. Gil put his rifle over the log and pulled the trigger on the first green coat that filled the sights. The butt bucked against his cheek. He yanked the rifle back and tilted his powder flask to the muzzle. He saw the man he had fired at lean forward slowly in the bushes, buckle at the hips, and thump face down. He felt his insides retract, and suddenly had a queer realization that they had just returned to their proper places; and he thought with wonder at himself, "That's the first shot I've fired."

"Peter."

"Yes, Honnikol."

"It looks as if the Indians was mostly chasing after Fisscher. You'd better try and fetch the boys up here."

The little German's voice was calm.

8

Battle

There was no sense at first in any of it. The opening volley had been fired at ten o'clock. For the next half hour the militia lay where they had dropped, shooting up against the bank whenever they saw a flash. Their line extended roughly along the road, beginning with the disrupted welter of the wagon train, and ending at the west, just over the rise of ground, where a mixed group of Canajoharie men, and Demooth's company of the German Flats regiment, and what was left of Herkimer's rangers, made a spearhead by hugging the dirt with their bellies and doing nothing to draw attention to themselves. If the Indians had stayed put or if Fisscher had not run away, the entire army would have been destroyed.

But the Indians could not resist the temptation of chasing the terrified Fisscher. More than half of them had followed his men as far as Oriskany Creek before they gave over the attempt. And a large proportion of the rest, seeing easy scalps ready for the taking, started sneaking down out of the timber. When, at last, Bellinger began to rally the men and get them up the slope, the Indians made no attempt to follow them, for they had discovered that killing horses was an intoxicating business.

The ascent of the slope was the first orderly movement of the battle. It also revealed the initial mistake of the British side. Their flanks made no connection with the Indians, and they had to retire from the edge of the ravine to the bigger timber. It gave the Americans a foothold. They pushed to right and left along the ravine and forward with their centre, until their line made a semicircle backed on the ravine.

No single company remained intact. It was impossible to give intelligent orders, or, if that had been possible, to get them carried out. The men took to trees and fired at the flashes in front of them. And this new disposition of the battle, which remained in force till nearly eleven, was the salvation of the militia. They began to see that they could hold their own. Also it was borne in on them that to go backward across the valley would be sheer destruction.

The general, by his own orders, had been carried still farther up the slope until he could sit on the level ground under a beech tree, and see out through the tall timber. His saddle had been brought up for him to sit on, and Dr. Petry sent for. While the doctor was binding up his shattered knee, Herkimer worked with his tinder box to get a light for his pipe. Then, finally established, he looked the battle over and gave his second order of the day.

"Have the boys get two behind each tree. One hold his fire and get the Indian when he comes in."

It was an axiomatic precaution that none of the militia would have thought of for themselves. Gil, moved up behind a fallen tree, heard a crash of feet behind him, turned his head to see a black-bearded, heavy-shouldered man plunge up to him carrying an Indian spear in one hand and a musket in the other.

"You got a good place here," said the man.

He drove the butt of the spear into the ground.

"It may come handy."

"Where'd you get it?"

"Off an Indian." He turned his head. "Back there. They're scalping the dead ones. There's one of the bastards now."

He pushed his gun across the log and fired.

"Christ! I missed him. You'd better do the long shots, Bub. You've got a rifle there. I ain't a hand at this stuff."

Gil had found a loophole in the roots. He poked his gun through and waited for a sign. While he waited he said, "My name's Martin."

"Gardinier," said the bearded man. "Captain in Fisscher's regiment. Don't ask me why. We didn't have the sense to run when he did. There's fifty of us left, but I don't know where they are. Old Herkimer told me to get up in front. He said he wanted to see us run away next time."

Gardinier cursed. Gil saw a shoulder, naked, and glistening with sweat, stick out on the side of a tree. He pressed the trigger, easily. The Indian yelped. They didn't see him, but they saw the underbrush thresh madly.

"Pretty, pretty," said Gardinier. "We ought to make a partnership. You take my musket and I'll load for you. Jesus, you ain't a Mason, are you?"

"No," said Gil.

"You ought to be." He touched Gil's shoulder with the rifle barrel. "Here's your rifle, Bub."

Gil caught a spot of red over a low-lying bough. A headdress. It was a pot shot, but he let it go. The Indian whooped and the next moment he was coming in long buck jumps straight for the log. He was a thin fellow, dark-skinned like a Seneca, and stark naked except for the paint on his face and chest.

Gil felt his inside tighten and rolled over to see what had become of Gardinier. But the heavy Frenchman was grinning, showing white teeth through his beard.

He had set down his musket and taken the spear. The Indian bounded high to clear the log and Gardinier braced the spear under him as he came down. The hatchet spun out of the Indian's hand. A human surprise re-formed his painted face. The spear went in through his lower abdomen and just broke the skin between his shoulders. He screamed once. But the Frenchman lifted him, spear and all, and shoved him back over the log.

"Hell," he said. "No sense in wasting powder."

Gil turned back to face the woods. The Indian, with the spear still sticking out of him, was trying to crawl under some cover. The odd thing was that he wasn't bleeding. But he kept falling down against the spear, as if his wrists had lost their strength.

"For God's sake shoot him."

The Frenchman stuck his head over the log.

"Jesus!" he remarked. He made no motion.

The Indian heaved himself up. He half turned toward the log. Then his mouth opened, and, as if a well had been tapped by the spear, and all this time had been necessary for the blood to find its level, it poured through the open mouth, down the painted chest, turning the front of his body wet and red.

Gil yelled, jumped up, and fired straight down into the pouring face. The Indian jerked back and flopped, raising the needles with his hands.

Gardinier said, "You hadn't ought to have done that. Wasting ball that way."

"For God's sake kill the next one, then."

"All right, all right. You don't need to get mad." But after a moment, he muttered, "I wish to God I'd pulled that spear out first, though. It was a handy tool."

All a man could see was the section of woods in front of him. The woods were dark with a green gloom, made by the high tops of the hemlocks, through which the sun came feebly. The heat was stifling. There was no movement of air. Only the bullets ripped passionate sounds out of the heat.

The ravine behind the militia had long since quieted with the death of the last horse. But now and then a solitary war whoop lifted in the trees to right or left; and the answering shot was like a period marking off the time.

In the American line, out of the disruption, figures began to grow into command that had no bearing on their rank. A man who shot better than his neighbors began to give orders. Jacob Sammons on the left began the first outward movement by taking twenty men in a quick charge against the Indian flank and halting them on a low knoll of beech trees. They started a cross fire against the white troops in front, and the militia in the centre, finding the woods cleared for a space, moved forward. Gil went with them. Gardinier stood up and scouted.

"There's a first-class maple up in front," he said.

They took it in a rush. Then they had a breathing space in which they could look back. They were surprised to find that this new view disclosed men lying on the intervening ground.

Back at the edge of the ravine, old Herkimer was still smoking his pipe. He had taken his hat off and his grizzled head showed plainly from where Gil and Gardinier had taken stand.

Gardinier laughed out loud.

"Look at the old pup," he said. "I wish Fisscher was here."

Both of them realized that they had one man they could depend on, though there was nothing one man could do for them. But it was a feeling all the same.

The lull did not endure.

In the woods ahead they heard a whistle shrilling. The firing had stopped, except for sporadic outbursts way to right and left, where a few Indians still persisted.

Then Herkimer's voice came to them surprisingly loud.

"Get out your hatchets, boys. They're going to try bayonets."

To Gil it seemed as though the fight had begun all over again. Lying behind a tree was one thing. Standing up in the open was something he had not thought of.

But Gardinier suddenly found something he could understand. He heaved his great bulk up and asked, "What you got, Bub?" When Gil merely stared, "Hatchet or bagnet, son?"

Gil reached for the hatchet at his belt with stiff fingers.

"All right. You give them one shot with your rifle. I've got a bagnet." He was fixing it to the muzzle of his army musket. He wheeled back and roared, "Come on."

He seemed surprised when some of his own company came round the trees behind.

Gil saw them coming. They all saw them, in the green gloom under the trees which covered their faces with a pale shine. They were like water coming toward the militia, flowing round the tree trunks, bending down the brush, an uneven line that formed in places and broke with the shape of the ground and formed.

There was a moment of silence on both sides as the militia rose up confronting them. It was almost as if the militia were surprised. Herkimer's warning had suggested to them that regular troops were going to attack. Instead they saw only the green coats they knew belonged to Johnson's company of Tories, and men in hunting shirts and homespun like themselves.

As the line came nearer, they saw that some of these men were the Scotch from Johnstown who had fled with Sir John. They weren't Sillinger's army at all. They were the men who had passed threats of gutting the valley wide open. For a moment the militia could hardly believe what they were seeing.

Then it seemed as if the senseless glut of war would overflow. Men fired and flung their muskets down and went for each other with their hands. The American flanks turned in, leaving the Indians where they were. The woods filled suddenly with men swaying together, clubbing rifle barrels, swinging hatchets, yelling like the Indians themselves. There were no shots. Even the yelling stopped after the first joining of the lines, and men began to go down.

The immediate silence of the woods was broken afresh. Gil, jostled and flung forward, saw a face in front of him met by a musket stock. The face seemed to burst. He swung his hatchet feebly against the arm that clubbed the musket and felt the axe ripped from his fingers. The man he had struck cried out, a small clear sound as if enunciated in a great stillness. Then Gil's ears cleared and he heard a man crying and he stepped on a body and felt it wince under his boot. The wince threw him, and he hit the dirt with his knees, and at the same time a gun exploded in front of him and he thought his whole arm had been torn away.

The boughs of the hemlocks heeled away from him, and the back of his head struck the ground and a man walked over him, three steps, down the length of his body, and he felt sick and then he forgot entirely everything but the fact that he was dying.

He did not feel any more. He was lying on the ground. It seemed to him that every needle leaf and twig on the ground stood up with painful clearness beyond any plausible dimension. A little way off someone kept yelling, "For God's sake, oh, for God's sake." He thought that if he could look he could see what the sound was, but he could not look.

Then the forest darkened. There was a blinding flash. He felt a man's hands taking hold of his shoulders. He felt himself moving backward while his legs trailed behind him. He was jerked up and put on his feet, and he knew that it was raining. He thought, "The drought's broken."

Peal after peal of thunder shook the hemlocks. The rain fell directly down, hissing on the dry ground, and raising mist in the trees. There was no sound left but the pouring rain and the continuous devastating thunder. You couldn't see when you opened your eyes. Only the tree trunks rising close to you, shining black with wet and the falling rain and the distortion of the lightning glares that lit up crooked alleys in the woods and shut them off again.

He felt himself being shaken, and a voice was saying, "Can you walk, Bub?"

He tried to walk, but his feet were overcome with a preposterous weariness.

"Put them down, Bub, put them down. Flat on your feet and stand up. Have a drink; you're all right."

He opened his eyes again and saw the beard of Gardinier matted with rain, and the wild white teeth and staring eyes of the Frenchman.

"Brandy makes the world go round," said the Frenchman. "It makes the girl handy, it makes for boys and girls, Bub. It'll fix you. Hell, you ain't only creased in one arm, and me, I've lost an ear."

The side of his face was streaming blood into his collar.

"They've quit, Bub. They're all to hell and gone. We've licked the pus clean out of them. Come on. Doc will fix you."

He sat Gil down on a mound, and then Dr. Petry's big fleshy face, muttering, looking enraged and tired, bent down. The Doc was splashing alcohol of some sort on his arm. He was being bandaged. The stinging revived him, and he looked up and saw just above him old Herkimer, white in the face now, but still puffing at his pipe, which he held in his mouth inverted against the rain.

"They'll come back," Herkimer was saying. "They're bound to. But we'll rest while it rains."

A little way off a man was eating on a log. The rest were standing, lying on the ground, steaming in the rain. Everyone looked tired, a little sick, and ugly, as if there had been a tremendous drunk a while before.

Nobody was keeping watch. They merely stood there in the rain.

The rain passed as suddenly as it had broken. The men got up and kicked other men to get up, and picked up their rifles. They drew the priming and reprimed, or loaded entirely fresh.

Gil got to his feet shakily, surprised to find his rifle still in his hand. It seemed a long time since the rain. The woods had changed so that he did not know where west lay, or east, or any direction.

Then he saw that Herkimer had moved the position so that the militia were in the centre of the level ground between the first ravine and a smaller, shallower watercourse. Any new attack would have to take them on a narrow flank, or directly up the new slope on top of which their line was formed.

The first shots came scatteringly. The Indians were firing from long range. They seemed to have lost their taste for war. They were being very careful now. Everybody was being careful. The militia stood their ground, but kept to cover.

In a line running north and south through the new position, a broken mass of men lay on the ground, like an uneven wind-row of some preposterous corn. They seemed almost equally made up of militia and the green-coated troops that had come through the hemlocks. They lay in queer positions, on their arms, grasping knife or hatchet or musket, the purpose still on the blank face like an overlying plaster; or else they lay on their backs, their empty hands flung out as if to catch the rain.

The militia stepped over this line impersonally. There was an Indian transfixed to a tree by a bayonet, waist high, with his legs dangling lifelessly against the ground. But he kept his eyes open and the eyes seemed to Gil to turn as he went by.

A little way along a face struck him as familiar. He looked at it again. The possessor of the face had fallen with his chin over a log so that the face was tilted up. Gil looked at it curiously before he recognized it for Christian Reall's face. He had been scalped. The top of his head looked flat and red; and the circumcision of the crown had allowed the muscles to give way so that his cheeks hung down in jowls, tugging his eyes open and showing enormous bloody underlids.

The two armies merely sniped at each other for an hour. Then the second attack by the enemy developed from the southwest along the level ground. At first the militia mistook them for reënforcements from the fort. The direction they came from and the fact that they had pinned up their hat brims to look like the tricorn hats of Continental soldiers were deceptive.

The militia broke cover, cheering, and rushed forward to shake hands, and the enemy let them come. There was no firing. It was only at the last moment that the sun came through the wet trees, dazzling all the ground and showing the bright green of the approaching company.

Gil was not in the direct contact of the two companies. From where he stood he seemed divorced from the whole proceeding.

But another company of green coats was coming round the first in his direction, with the same quiet march, and the same bright glitter on their advanced bayonets.

He became aware of the instinct to run away. It suddenly occurred to him that he was hungry. Not merely hungry as one is at supper or breakfast; but a persisting, all-consuming gnawing in his intestines that moved and hurt. He felt that it was not worth staying for. He was too tired. And the oncoming men looked tired. And it seemed to take forever for them to make a contact. But they came like people who couldn't stop themselves, while he himself could not make his feet move to carry him away.

• • •

They made less noise. The rainstorm which had broken the drought had not had power to take the dryness from their throats. They seemed to strike each other with preposterous slow weary blows, which they were too slow to dodge, and they fell down under them preposterously.

It couldn't last.

Gil found himself standing alone in the militia. There were a few men near him, but there was no one whose face he recognized. They kept looking at each other as if they would have liked to speak.

On the flank, the firing continued where the Indians still skirmished. But that, too, broke off except for stray shots, the last survivors of all the holocaust of firing.

The Indians were calling in the woods. A high barbaric word, over and over. "Oonah, Oonah, Oonah." Suddenly a man shouted, "They've pulled foot!"

At first they thought another thunderstorm had started. Then they realized that what they had heard, with such surprising force, had been three successive cannon shots.

The messengers had reached the fort, and the garrison was making a diversion.

A deliberate understanding gradually dawned on all their faces. They leaned on their rifles and looked round. The woods were empty, but for themselves, for their dead, and for the enemy dead. The living enemy had run away.

Those that could walk began a retrograde movement to the knoll on which Herkimer was sitting under his tree. The old man was looking at them; his black eyes, yet ardent, passing feverishly from face to face, and then turning slowly to the lines of dead.

One of the officers spoke fatuously, "Do we go on to the fort now, Honnikol?" He paused, swallowed, and said, as if to excuse himself, "We know they know we're here."

The little German swung his eyes to the speaker. The eyes filled and he put his hand over them.

Peter Bellinger and Peter Tygert came up to him and touched his shoulder. They said to the officer, "We can't move forward."

They picked Herkimer up by the arms.

"I can't walk, boys." He swallowed his tears noisily. "There's still Sillinger up there. With the British regulars there ain't enough of us. I think we'd better go home."

He asked first that the live men be assembled and counted. It was a slow business, getting them to their feet and lining them up under the trees. The earth was still steaming from the rain. There was a sick smell of blood from the ravine.

The naming of men took too long. The officers went along the wavering lines, cutting notches in sticks for every ten men. They figured that after Fisscher pulled foot with the Mohawk company there had been about six hundred and fifty concerned in the ambush and battle. Out of them about two hundred were judged able to walk. There were forty more who were not dead. How many had been killed and how many taken prisoner no one could say.

Stretchers were made of coats and poles, and the worst wounded were piled onto them. Those who were not acting as bearers dully reprimed or loaded their guns. They started east.

It seemed a long way to the ravine where the battle had started. It seemed a long time, longer than they could remember, since they had seen it last. It was sunset by the time they reached Oriskany Creek.

From there men were sent ahead to order boats rowed up the Mohawk, to meet the wounded at the ford. The whole army lay down when they reached the ford. They lay in the darkness, along the edge of the sluggish river, until the boats came up. They were apathetic.

Only when the boats arrived did they get onto their feet and help put the wounded men in. Several of them afterwards remembered Herkimer's face in the light of the fire. He had stopped smoking, though the pipe was still fast in his teeth. He wasn't saying anything. He sat still, holding on to his knee.

At the time they had just stood around watching him being loaded aboard the boat and laid out in the bottom. Then they had been told to march through the ford, and along the road. They went wearily, too exhausted to talk, even to think. And tired as they were, they were forced to do the same march they had taken three days to make on the way up.

They did not look at the terrified white faces of the people when they came to the settlement. They were too exhausted to see. The word had already gone down the river. People were expecting the appearance of the enemy.

It was a calamity. The army had looked so big going west that nobody had thought they would not get through to the fort. Now they were back; they looked licked, and they acted licked, and they had not even met the regulars. It was pointless to think that the enemy had left the scene of battle before they had.

An officer, some said afterwards that it was Major Clyde, yelled from the foot of the fort stockade that they were dismissed. They were to go home and try to rest while they could. They should expect another summons very soon.

But the men did not stop to listen to him. Ever since they had come out of the woods at Schuyler they had been dropping from the ranks. The instinct to get home was irresistible. They weren't an army any more, and they knew it better than anyone could have told them.

IV

STANWIX (1777)

I

The Women

Mrs. McKlennar simply would not hear of removing to a fort. "What's the use of women being left behind in a war, if they can't stay home and do the man's work?"

"Yes, ma'am."

Captain Jacob Small, who had been placed in command of Eldridge Blockhouse, shifted his feet on the kitchen floor, turned his hat over twice in his hands, and looked anxiously towards the fireplace. "It's orders, though. 'Where women and children shall be gathered together,' it says. And me and other men over sixty and under sixteen is to collect with them and protect them."

"Pshaw, Captain Small, don't you think I can look after myself?"

"Yes, ma'am." Captain Small was uneasy. "But them's the orders. You're rightly in my district. But if you don't want to come to Eldridge, you can go over the river to Herkimer, I guess. Only we've been keeping the corner space in the shed for you."

"Shed!" snorted Mrs. McKlennar. "Do I look like the kind of

woman at my time of life who'd go live in a shed? Herded up like a freshened heifer. With everybody else, eh?"

"Yes, ma'am." Captain Jacob looked appalled. "I mean, no, ma'am."

"Well, look at me, damn it, man. Can't I take care of myself?"

"Yes, ma'am." Captain Small raised his eyes and turned them abruptly away again towards the fireplace.

"If you want to spit," said Mrs. McKlennar, "for God's sake, spit, and get it over with." There was an almost piercing look about her long nose as he availed himself of the ashes. "I suppose it's nice of you to come down here to make a damn-fool woman see some sense. The trouble is my idea of sense just doesn't coincide with yours."

The captain said, "Well, I only tried to be neighborly. But if you change your mind we'll have the corner space ready for you. Phil Helmer has got his cows in it now, but we'll move them right out any time."

"Thank you, Captain."

Captain Small hawked a little, as he reached the door. He looked over his spit at Fort Herkimer beyond the river.

"See there," he said significantly. "Ma'am, there's some women coming to the fort now."

A line of teetering carts, overloaded with goods and women and children, dragged across the flats from the southern hills.

Mrs. McKlennar blew out her breath.

"I've been seeing them for two days. I'm sick of the sight. Scared as rabbits."

Mrs. McKlennar watched him trudge away down the road. Then she stamped over the porch and down the steps and went towards the barn. "Indians!" she said to herself.

She saw Lana coming down from the springhouse with a crock of butter in her arms. "How much did it make?" called Mrs. McKlennar.

"About three pounds," Lana replied. She looked cool and pink, but her eyes seemed to darken. "Was that Captain Small, Mrs. McKlennar?"

"Yes, it was."

"Did he have any news?"

"He was down to try to persuade us to move into his block-house. He's got a stall ready for us. There's some cows in it now, but he was cordial enough to suggest he would prefer us."

Lana smiled slightly. She was getting used to the widow's way of talking.

Mrs. McKlennar said, "And then he pointed out some women going in to Fort Herkimer. And he said a lot more about the way Indians handled women." She paused and looked keenly at Lana. "What do you think about it, Magdelana? Getting scared?"

Lana said, "No," quietly. She wasn't looking at Mrs. McKlennar; with the crock still hugged up in her arms, she was staring westward. "Gil expected I'd stay here, unless we got news things had gone wrong out west. When he comes back, he'll probably expect to find me here."

"Good for you," said Mrs. McKlennar. She tramped away to the barn to curry the horses. It was a job she fancied just then. She didn't have the faintest idea of what might happen, but in any case she had no intention of living like a pig in a sty and having all the farm women constantly peering at her to see what kind of underclothes she wore. . . .

On her way from the stone house to her own kitchen, Lana heard the widow hissing like a whole stableful of grooms. She stopped again in the doorway to look out over the valley.

Two days—and they had had no news. The valley was still and hot; the earth was dry; the river, shallow and slow. Whenever she looked across it, Lana had a feeling of the hills drawing together. She felt the presence of the woods behind her back, as if, on the north bluff, the wilderness crept close and watched her movements through the day with an invisible intelligence.

At the departure of Gil, life as it was known on the farm seemed to have departed too. The three women, in spite of Mrs. McKlennar's noisiness, were imprisoned in a green silence. There was nothing to hear but the crows at evening, or the sounds of their own voices. There were not even any wagons on the Kingsroad, now. No boats on the river. It was as if the valley held its breath; as if the going of the militia drained it of all the things that made for life. One stopped one's talk suddenly for no reason except an unexpected instinct to listen. Listen for what? Lana did not know. But her breast ached.

A thought lived in her with the beating of her heart. He would surely die.

Sometimes it occurred to her that since last fall both of them had been dead. Even in the little Schuyler hut she had had that feeling, though they had felt crowded there, so near that they withdrew from each other, as though to avoid physical encounter. Later, in the early summer, life had seemed easier. Work had been good for Gil. He was the kind of man who needed to be tired. But on Lana's part, living had been merely a slow regulation of the breath. What they did, what they said, had lost all personal significance.

Then had come the first muster and Gil's departure for the Unadilla. And then he had come home, and her first quickening had come and gone like a moth's temptation. She was healthier. But she had not been able to regain her vanished impulse towards happiness.

Gil seemed unaware, detached, and baffled. Often Lana had heard women say of other women that they "got along" with their husbands. She wondered whether that was how she was living with Gil. She submitted to him as she had submitted to the fact of the destruction of their farm, wordlessly, blindly. Blindly

until she had seen him making the turn in the road to Fort Dayton, with the erratic flamadiddles of the Palatine drums passing
after him. When it was too late she had had the choking thought
that he would surely die.

As she looked westward she could see the Schuyler house.
The little shack stood by the river, shuttered and forlorn; but it
seemed to her that she was again lying on the narrow bunk bed,
exhausted, still, cold, pressed down entirely by the bleak terror
and her sense of outrage. She struggled against the memory. Her
mind worked vaguely with the words with which she must try to
tell him they were not themselves then. That she had got past
that time. That it was neither his fault nor hers, but that they
both had been forced by something which was neither of their
making nor of their understanding. Her effort to find words and
reasons was pathetically inadequate. She wrenched herself away
from the sight, turning into her own kitchen, with an awareness
that when two people acted so against each other it was beyond
the power of their minds ever to retract the moment.

It was Mrs. McKlennar who first heard Gil coming home.
The night before, she and Daisy and Lana had been roused by
the noise of Fisscher's fleeing rabble. She had come down to the
farmhouse and knocked on the door.

Lana went down the stairs in her nightdress to open it. Mrs.
McKlennar was standing in the moonlight, her hair stringily
fringing the edge of her white cap.

"Did you hear them, Magdelana?"

"Yes."

"Something's gone wrong with them," said the widow. "I'm
going down to the road and see if I can find out how bad it is.
Give me something dark to throw over this and go up and make
sure Daisy don't scuttle off somewhere."

"I'd like to go with you," said Lana.

"Well, you can't. No telling who they are. They sound

almighty like licked militia to me. But if there's anybody chasing them, a pretty girl has got no business hanging around in a nightgown."

Lana fetched her shawl.

"Will you be all right?"

Mrs. McKlennar grunted.

"Don't be silly!"

But as she went down to the road, Mrs. McKlennar almost wished she didn't feel so safe. She remembered how Barney once said to her, "Now don't you go traipsing round the militia camp at night. You can't tell about militia. And, begod, in the dark you've got a figger would make a lion out of a rabbit."

But that was long ago, when he liked her in a green silk night-gown, to go with her red hair. Now her body had taken after her face, with angles and joints, and no waist that Barney used to try to enclose in his two big hands. All that was left of those days was the fact that the militia were an unpredictable force.

She stood by the rail fence until she saw a man drop beside the road to take off his shoes, and she moved over behind him and prodded him with her forefinger.

He jumped and yelled and swung his gun round.

"I'm only a woman," said Mrs. McKlennar, "and I'm too old to bite."

"Oh, my Jesus," he said. "I thought the Indians were still after us."

"What happened?"

He cast a look down the road after his comrades, a dark disorderly shadow hurrying on the white dust.

"God! I got to get going."

"Is the army licked?"

"I don't know. I guess so. We was in back and then they started shooting out of the woods. You couldn't see. Fisscher came back and yelled the army was licked. That's all I know. We ain't seen anybody since. Only we heard them yelling after us in the woods. And I seen some. All painted. To look like devils."

He was already down the road. Edging off from her, breaking into a weary shuffling run.

Mrs. McKlennar sniffed and turned back towards the house. There was no use waiting for more, the way those men had gone.

She walked into the kitchen, getting an "Oh, my Gawd, Mis'," from Daisy, shut the door and dropped the bar.

"We'd better stay here to-night. You too, Magdelana. And I think we'd better not light a candle." She made her way through the moonlight from the window to the settle and sat down. "Stop your jibbering, you black baboon." When she had sat down she repeated what the militiaman had said.

"Fisscher's run away. And I guess they've surrounded the rest of the army. John Butler always was a clever devil."

Lana's voice surprised herself. She said quite calmly, "They'll be killed."

"Some of them. Magdelana dear, that's the business of war."

"Gil will be killed," Lana said.

Mrs. McKlennar pulled her shawl tighter.

"Go ahead and think so if it does you any good. I used to be just a baby myself when Barney was away. But there's no sense in it." She straightened herself with a slight shake. "I think we'd just better sit quiet here until morning. Then we'll see what's actually happened. I'll even move to a fort if necessary. Hush your noise, Daisy."

"I was only saying de Praise-God-from-whom."

The widow would not even let them light a fire until she had come back from the road. She went down, dressed, soon after sunrise, and held up a horseman with her brandy flask. He turned out to be a dispatch rider from Fort Dayton, starting down to

General Schuyler's camp somewhere below Fort Edward. But you couldn't expect a soldier to disoblige a lady with a flask.

"No, ma'am, we don't know what's happened to the army. We've just got word they had an action up the river. They've sent for boats to fetch down Herkimer. He's bad hurt. But they say the British left the field."

"God bless you," said Mrs. McKlennar. "Take the flask with you."

The rider accepted it, touched his hat with it, and spurred his horse. Mrs. McKlennar watched him go with a small swelling of her heart. A nice-looking lad, a poor soldier—God knew what would happen to this country if a regular army ever came against them. She was humming a dim alto to something or other as she came back to the stone house.

"There's been a fight. They've stood the British off. I don't see why we should move yet. Magdelana, get some sleep. You look a sight. I'm going to wash and eat and lie down myself. Daisy can milk this morning."

Lana was upstairs in her house. She had prayed for Gil. It seemed futile to pray, now that the battle was over, but it was the only thing she could think of to do.

She was still on her knees, her elbows deep in the bedtick, her head in her hands, when Mrs. McKlennar shouted from the yard.

"Magdelana, Magdelana! Here he is!"

For one breath Lana was like ice. Then she got on her feet and went down. She went out into the yard, where, in the hot sunlight, she saw him kneeling at the horse trough, drinking, while Mrs. McKlennar stood at his side and splashed cold water on his head with her hand.

All Lana could think of was how dirty he looked. His face was dirty, almost black with grime; his hair was matted with sweat and hemlock needles. His shirt was torn and his trousers looked as if he had been lost in a briar patch.

He raised his face at her across the trough, and she thought he looked indescribably old. Then, as if he had seen enough of her, he put his lips to the cold surface of the water and drank.

Mrs. McKlennar nodded.

"Come here, he's had plenty. We must get him to bed."

Lana went to his other side. His shirt sleeve had been torn off and there was a dirty rag round the upper part of his arm. The rag was stiff with a brown clot.

"Gil," she said softly.

But Mrs. McKlennar was abrupt.

"Up, lad!"

He got up. The two women bolstered him on either side as he made slowly for the farmhouse.

"We'll get him some brandy," said Mrs. McKlennar. "It'll put him to sleep like a poleaxe, the way he is. We can look after him when he's sleeping."

"Don't you think we ought to fetch the doctor?"

"Doctor?" Mrs. McKlennar stared. "Anything that old fool Petry can do, I can do. And this arm is nothing. He walked home, didn't he? All he needs is a little sleep."

"Yes," said Gil, unsteadily. "I'm tired."

2

Gil

He had gone to sleep, as Mrs. McKlennar had foretold, within ten minutes of swallowing the brandy. Mrs. McKlennar had

taken charge in a way that allowed Lana no protest. As soon as
Gil's eyes had closed, she started cutting free the bandage with
her sewing scissors. She held the dirty rag by the tips of the scissors and took hearty sniffs of it. "It isn't mortified," she said. "But
anyway we'll swab it out." She dipped the chewed birch twig
that was her toothbrush in the brandy and swabbed it through
the bullet furrow. To Lana it looked like a brutal operation.
"Nonsense," said Mrs. McKlennar. "So long as he don't feel it we
might as well be thorough."

"He might wake up."

"Don't be a fool. I don't know whether you've ever seen him
drunk before. But he couldn't be any drunker if he was lying in
a ditch."

She bandaged the arm deftly.

"Now," she announced, "I'll help you bathe him. You get his
clothes off while I fetch some warm water."

While she was gone, Lana worked quickly. Gil lay like a log.
She found that he would not wake no matter how she shoved and
heaved, and for some reason she was glad to have him stripped
and a blanket over him by the time Mrs. McKlennar returned
with towels and a pail.

"Pull back the blanket," ordered the widow.

"Thanks," said Lana. "I can do the rest myself."

Suddenly Mrs. McKlennar laughed.

"Don't you think I ever saw a naked man, Magdelana? And
I old enough to be his mother, or his grandmother, too. Heaven
help me! Oh, come on!"

Her decisive hand laid hold of the blanket and peeled it
back, and she looked down on Gil's straight brown body with
frank curiosity. Then she raised her eyes to Lana's.

"Don't look so shamefaced, girl. He's nothing to be ashamed
of. Why, damn it, you ought to feel proud!"

But Lana could not feel that way. It seemed unrighteous for

her and the widow woman to be working over Gil like that. But she said nothing, only dried the parts of him that Mrs. McKlennar had done washing.

The widow, to do her justice, wasted no time.

"There," she said. "He ought to have one blanket. He's tired. But no more, or he'll wake up with a head like a punkin."

She picked up the pail and the soiled towels and said, "I'm going now."

"Thank you, Mrs. McKlennar."

The widow snorted.

"Thanks, my foot. You're just wondering when the old fool's ever going to take herself off." She stamped deliberately down the stairs.

Gil slept all through the day. He was still asleep when the sun set. But as darkness came he had a spell of restlessness. In the first dusk, while Lana was getting a bite of supper, she heard him muttering overhead, and stole swiftly up to him. He was saying over and over, "I won't run. Oh, God, I won't run." She put her hand on his forehead and he flung round in the bed and shouted, "For God's sake, kill the next one." She shuddered. His face had not changed, but his voice frightened her.

His forehead was slightly feverish, and she went down again to get cool water, with which she bathed his head until his muttering stopped. Then she fetched the Betty lamp, lit it, and sat down where she could watch him on the bed.

Now that he was quiet again, the look of age went gradually out of his face. He had turned on his side with the complete rest of a boy.

As the night crept over the valley, she heard the widow finish milking and turn the cattle into the yard. A little later the light in the window of the stone house went out. There was no further sound except the last sleepy clucks of the hens settling on their roosts. All the farm was dark but for the light in their own room. It brought her a queer feeling of the world withdrawing, leaving them together, just they two. And as she watched his face, hour after hour, she lost all track of time.

A breath of air stirred in the room, flickering the lamp. Looking up from her hands, Lana saw Gil's eyes upon her.

She got up from her chair and went to the bed.

His eyes followed her. His hands lay on the blanket in front of him.

"It seems a long time, Lana."

"It does to me, too."

"You didn't see me."

"I didn't see you wake up."

"I was watching you. You made me think about the way you were when you were burning flax. In Fox's Mills. Do you remember? On the side of the hill?"

Her voice had a small catch. "I was thinking of it too."

"Were you?"

Suddenly she put out her hand to touch his. At the touch he turned his hand over and grasped her wrist.

"Have you been sitting up with me?"

"Yes."

"How long was I asleep?"

"I don't know. I don't know what time it is."

He did not comment. But he began increasing his pressure on her wrist. It frightened her, and she had to force herself to look at his face. She made herself relax until his grip was so strong that her fingers spread apart and stiffened.

He let go.

"I'm sorry. I didn't mean to do that."

"It didn't hurt."

"It must have."

"A little," she admitted.

"I'm sorry."

"Do you want to do it again?" she asked suddenly.

"Do you want me to?"

"I don't know."

She felt that a spell had come upon her. Whether it was the darkness or his hand upon her wrist, or both, the fatigue of her long watch was transmuted. She was no longer afraid of him, and yet she was afraid. In that moment when he had taken hold of her wrist his dark eyes had lost uncertainty.

"Sit down."

His hand guided her so that she sat beside him. She could feel herself trembling; but if he felt it, he did not mention it.

"What are you looking at?"

"There's a light," she said. "Up beyond the fort, on the hill to the west."

A pale tongue of flame was lifting from the hilltop. He hoisted himself, without letting go her wrist, and looked at it. While he watched, it mounted rapidly, and sank again.

"That's Indian fire."

"What does it mean?"

"I don't know. It makes you realize we've got no way of telling if the fort surrenders. They might come down any day."

"Yes."

"Are you afraid?"

The fire dropped, before she could answer. In a moment it was gone. They were just they two again, in the low-ceilinged room, with the wide bed and its swelling feather mattress.

"Tired?"

"I was."

He was watching the small oval of her face, with its dark hair.

As she spoke her lids closed and the curves of her lips softened and filled. She sat beside him as if entranced.

She could not stir for the swelling blood; she felt it in her helpless quiet through all her body, breasts, thighs, and arms. Suddenly he let go her wrist, and she raised both hands to her temples, pushing the hair back. She turned her face to him.

He saw that she was tremulous, half shrinking.

"Lana."

"Yes, Gil."

"When I was up there, I kept thinking about you."

"Did you?"

"About what it would be like coming home."

The pause drew out. Her heart started beating.

He said quietly, "Are you coming?"

"If you want."

"Yes."

She got up slowly from the bed. Her fingers had a feeling of fullness as she took the laces of her short gown. She met his eyes and flushed painfully, and slowly. It was no use to think that he was her husband. He was a strange person who had acquired a right; and she felt completely without power or desire to thwart him. But her instinct made her turn from him towards the far corner of the room.

She did not recognize his voice.

"Don't go away."

She hesitated.

"Turn around."

Again she obeyed. Then her hands went to her hair.

"No," he said. He was smiling now. His eyes were deliberate. "Leave it for last," he said.

She felt the last drop of strength going out of her. It almost made her cry out as she surrendered. She pulled away the laces of the short gown, put it back over her shoulders, and let it drop from her bare arms.

The lamp put a soft shine on her skin as she bent her neck and undid her petticoat. It fell round her ankles. For an instant she stood so, half bent, in its encircling rough folds. Then she stepped from it, timidly, and for a brief moment encountered his eyes, her hands raised tentatively to undo her hair. She had no will of her own under his deliberate and amorous dominance; and she seemed held for an eternity in her submissive pose.

His nod released her. Her fingers flew to the pins, loosening them and letting her hair fall of its own weight down her back. Her breath came out of her breast with a shudder, and the pins dropped from her hair with a little sprinkle of sound on the broad planks. She stood quite still with her hands hanging limply at her sides, the palms turned childishly forward.

For a moment more Gil watched her. Then he smiled slowly, stretched out his hand, and pressed it down over the small flame of the Betty lamp.

3

At Herkimer Fort

The same evening, across the river in Fort Herkimer, Emma Weaver sat on the hearth considering all the things on her mind. What chiefly troubled her was the effect this garrison life was having on her oldest son. John had turned fifteen during the winter and grown fast. Already he was almost as tall as his mother, and since he had been issued an old French musket and appointed to regular sentry go, he considered himself a man.

It wasn't that he was undutiful to her; but she could tell that in the last few days he no longer acknowledged her authority in his personal affairs. She had only to look up from her shed against the stockade wall and see him passing, lanky and rawboned, with stiff strides back and forth upon the walk, to know that John had passed beyond her reach. And when he came in from his duty and sat down to supper she saw the impatience in his face to be through with the meal and get off to the blockhouse on the east, where the squad of soldiers bunked and where he could listen to what he now considered man's talk. The rough laughter, in the evenings, would pass heavily across the enclosure.

Emma didn't mind man's talk. Men together were entitled to their own ways of fun; but John was too young yet. Careless ideas took hold too hard. And with the way the place was crowded, so that there was no privacy, she was afraid that John would get entangled with some girl she herself could not like. There were plenty of them, and there were plenty of times when she had seen John, with the exhibitionism of the first impulse of manhood, stretching himself out in the sun before the blockhouse. He would take off his shirt, like the other men, baring his skinny torso, and drawing deep arching breaths with his chest, while he pretended to doze.

So far, she thought, he had not made a shine at any particular girl. It was just the idea of manhood getting at him now. But there were one or two girls her maternal eye had noticed watching John. Young Mary Reall for one, the Realls' oldest. She had no special urge against the girl, except that the Realls were idle, shiftless, loose-thoughted people, and if John were to marry early he ought to marry a girl with a settled way of seeing things. She wished George would come back so she could put the matter in his hands. George was sure to stamp on any nonsense. For all his easy-going temper, George had an instinct for righteousness that would put a curb on the boy, as it had curbed her own quick temper in their first married days.

The Realls, two partitions down, all reveled in the life. There was no steady work to do. They had no cattle to look after. Mrs. Reall eased about all day, letting the brats run wild. Peebles, the baby, had been weaned, and scurried like a puppy all over the parade ground on his hands and knees. In the evening he had to be hunted up and brought to bed, but Mary had taken on that duty. Mary was doing all their cooking, and it was also Mary who swept out their eight-foot square of space when she could borrow a broom, shook up the hemlock bedding, and saw that one of the boys carried their night's pail of slops to the dumping ground outside the stockade. It was a comfort to have a child at last grow up, and Mrs. Reall let herself luxuriate. She had another baby on the way and it did her good to be idle.

Mary Reall was fourteen now, a colorless girl, with light brown unbraided hair down her back. She had her father's rather pointed and effeminate features, but in her narrow face they were appropriate. On the rare occasions when excitement or heat or worry brought color to her face, it startled one who knew it, seeming beautiful. Not until the gradual cramped settling down of all the people had she noticed the lads being handed out guns. There were thirty boys, and only seven guns, and looking at them while she leaned idly against the wall of the shed, her eyes had singled out John Weaver.

Like the other boys he looked excited and tense. It would be an honor to be given a musket by the army sergeant—a man who knew war and men and guns. He was a grizzled old fellow with a swollen red nose and a lewd mouth and sharp eyes, and he lined the lads up before him and learned their names and looked at them. John Weaver, standing with the others, tried to keep his eyes on the sergeant, but he also felt that people were

watching his back. He sent a sidelong estimating glance round
the stockade, and met Mary Reall's gaze. He did not show that
he recognized her. He let his eye run past, quickly faced front,
and colored to his hair. It had surprised him to see how she had
grown. Her faded cotton short gown was tight over her breast
and her long slender legs looked less slatty.

"You first," said the sergeant, and tapped John with the point
of his forefinger. John turned quite white and weak and unbe-
lievingly stepped forward to accept the musket. Though some
of the boys were older, he had been singled out the first. He felt
the envious stares of the other boys on his back, as surprised as
himself, then, following the sergeant's nod, went forward into
the door of the blockhouse, walking a little stiffly like a young
dog, into the company of men.

Mary Reall did not change her position for several moments,
but leaned where she was, thinking about how often she used to
meet John Weaver up in Deerfield and how he had seemed to
her just any dirty boy. But now she saw how tall he had become,
how his shoulders had begun to fill at the back like a man's; and
it came to her with a sense of awe that she had been brought up
almost next door to him, so that in a sense she shared the honor
of his first promotion.

When she went inside their hut, she was ashamed to see that
supper had not yet been started. Mrs. Reall snickered when the
fact was pointed out. "What difference?" she wished to know.
"What difference?" Mary could not say rightly even to herself.
But there was a dim apprehension that if John could do a man's
part it was time for her to think of a woman's. She set to work at
supper, and then cleaned out all the magpie mess of their inhabit-
ing, picking up the children's shirts where they had been trodden
into the dusty earth of the floor, shaking them and hanging them
up, and borrowing a broom from the next shed to sweep with. "I
declare," said Mrs. Reall. "You've made it look real homey."

Mary felt proud and tired, but also ashamed when she was through and, looking up, beheld John, for the first time, marching back and forth across the opposite sentry walk. His beat took him behind the church, so that she saw him first at one end, then the other. She could have cried because they had not even a tallow dip that she could light, for him to see her work, and herself sitting in the entrance. Instead she had to move over to another door and stand there, trying to be noticed by him while at the same time she kept out of sight of the people whose light she had unobtrusively borrowed.

It was there that Emma first noticed her, and it was there also that John saw her again, for he was paying as much attention to the interesting interior of the stockade as he was to the outside and faceless night.

And on being relieved he went back to the blockhouse the long way, passing the hut, and finding her still there.

"Why, hello," he said carelessly, "ain't that you, Mary Reall?"

"Hello," she said, with an effort at surprise. "I hadn't seen you before, John. How are you?"

"You didn't?" He couldn't help contradicting her. "I thought you was watching when they passed the muskets out."

"Well, I was," she said. "But I didn't notice anyone particular."

He was huffed. But he didn't like to say he was the first selection. So he said, "I hope you're all well."

"Nicely," she said. "And you?"

"We're fine," he said. "It's funny you didn't see us, though. We came in this morning."

"It's so crowded," Mary said. "You know how it is."

"Yes," he said. "We're awful crowded."

He paused a moment, then shouldered his musket awkwardly.

"Well, I got to report to Sergeant," he said, and stalked off. "See you again, maybe."

Mary watched him go. Then she hurried back to her own

space and crept in over the sleeping bodies of her family. She lay down in the corner space reserved for her, glad that there was no candle now. For she was crying, and wondering what in the world had made her talk the way she had.

The fort was a stifling place. The twelve-foot pointed logs of the palisade cut off what air might move. The bark-sheathed roofs of the sheds, only a foot over the people's heads, were their only shelter against the sun, which burned through the heavy air with the intensity of a burning glass. Even in the church, whose stone walls kept it relatively cool, the air grew so stale that people left it for the outdoor heat.

The life was enervating; there was no chance to exercise, except to walk round the fields in sight of the stockade, keeping a safe distance from the woods or fields of standing corn that might give cover to an Indian. They dared go only to the nearest farms, since the garrison could offer them no protection beyond the walls. And after their first few morning chores were performed, the pails emptied in the ditch, the sheds brushed out, and the water drawn, there was nothing left to do but get their meals and talk.

Even the talking petered out. There was not a family who didn't have a father or brother or son in the army that had gone west with Herkimer. Once the first conjectures had been interchanged and the family news caught up with, nothing remained to be talked about except the heat.

They had no news from the army. They had no news from Fort Stanwix. They had no news from the east. All they could do was to listen and wait, and watch with a growing concern for the first possible appearance of the enemy.

Only the squad of Massachusetts soldiers in the blockhouse kept up a kind of conversation in their nasal Yankee voices; but they kept their talk to themselves. They feared and disliked the Palatines as much as the Palatines disliked them. Most of the time their captain, who commanded at the fort, went over the river to pass the time with Colonel Weston, at Fort Dayton, returning after supper in the dusk, giving the countersign outside the gate, marching through in his rust-colored coat and cocked hat, looking neither to left nor to right, as if he held his breath against a troublesome smell, until he reached the blockhouse. He passed through the guardroom with a curt good-night and mounted to his quarters in the upper room. The people could see his shadow there at times, drinking brandy by himself—or sometimes he leaned from the window, smoking a last pipe.

It was queer how quickly all these things became familiar parts of their existence, as if they had spent long lives already in a confined space. It made them apathetic, resigned, and fearful, and the soldiers spoke contemptuously about the German race.

In the midst of it, Mary and John continued their gradual approach in a kind of hushed expectancy. They moved their separate lives through the crowdedness and the dirt and the hostility as if they made a mist in which they apprehended each other's shapes, dimly. Yet the meetings had poignance that only two such beginners could be aware of.

The time when Mary, rising in the middle of the night, heard the sentry steps halt overhead and recognized them for his, and realized that he must have heard her stirring, was mysterious and intimate; and the next morning when she encountered him at the well and they said good-morning to each other with formal politeness, they saw in each other's face that both had shared it.

In spite of Emma Weaver's doubts, that was as far as either of them had got till the night of the sixth, when, long past sunset, a boat was rowed across from Fort Dayton and the news of the retreat delivered.

Then, three hours later, the first bateaux had arrived with

General Herkimer. The fort had been hailed. The gate opened, and the general was carried in past the waiting silent people, holding torches here and there, to the church. After the gates were closed the people moved up to the church windows and talked softly to those who had their beds inside, and learned that the general was wounded in the leg. The men who had brought him lay down in the western blockhouse and would not answer any question. They slept like animals.

In the next few hours other boats arrived. One of the first brought George Weaver home, and John was one of the garrison sent to help him to the fort. As he entered with his father, he saw Mary standing beside the gate, her eyes searching the faces of the new arrivals, and it came to him that alone of all her family she had the interest to look for her father.

He helped put his father down on the hemlock bed and stood back while his mother unwrapped the bandage from his chest.

His father said, "Hello, John."

"Hello," said John.

Emma said, "I'll tend to Pa. You'd better get back where you belong. Cobus can fetch me things."

"I will," said John. He looked down on his father's big body hesitantly.

"Where'd you get the gun, son?"

Emma said, not without pride, "He's one of the watch."

"You'd better get along." His father lay back and groaned as Emma ruthlessly pulled away the cotton. Then he opened his eyes and met John's. "What's on your mind, son?"

"Did Christian Reall . . . ?"

He saw his mother's back stiffen.

"I don't know. I didn't see him. But Jeams MacNod's outside. He'll know." George closed his eyes. Without opening them he said almost apologetically, "I got this at the first beginning, son."

John left them with a sudden realization that they might like to be alone. He returned to the gate where the schoolmaster sat in his tattered black coat, hatless and unshaven, a venomous kind of terror still printed on his face.

He looked up at John's question.

"Kitty Reall?" he said. "You want to know where Kitty Reall is? Well, I can tell you. He's laying with his face over a log. He's scalped. But he ain't half of what there is to see. . . ."

John said savagely, "You know he's dead?"

"I'm telling you. . . . What do you think? They ain't satisfied with just killing. I never saw Indians before. It ain't war. My God!"

Turning away, John saw Mary Reall standing by the corner of the church. She was watching him still, her thin pale face a little lowered, looking out from her brows.

A wave of sick pity went over John and he walked up to her, taking her arm without a word. She didn't protest, but went with him quietly. As he walked her forward he kept searching for a place they could be private in. But there was no unoccupied corner within the stockade, till it occurred to him to look up at the sentry walk.

All the men were round by the gate, looking down over the points of the palisades at the river.

"Come up with me," said John, and climbed the ladder. They could stand in the angle of the walk made by the palisade and the blockhouse wall. No one could see them from below.

John waited for her, with his eyes on the faceless night beyond the stockade. She came up quietly beside him on her bare feet and leaned with him against the pointed upright logs.

It was the nearest to him she had been since he had first become aware of who she really was. Her dress touched his side, and through the dress he could feel the slim round hardness of her body. Her hair had a faint smell of its own, like spice over the body scent.

She waited for him to speak. She had not yet said a word on her own part. But she leaned beside him against the stockade, taking one point between her breasts like a spear, and when he turned his head she did not turn hers.

"Mary," he said.

"Yes." She waited again; but when he could not go on she asked quietly, "Did you hear anything about Father, from that man?"

"Yes."

It seemed an awful thing to say. As if he were killing Christian Reall with his own words.

"He's dead, isn't he?"

She was making it easy for him.

"Yes, Mary."

She did not cry or do anything that he might have expected. But she turned suddenly to him, so that he saw her face oval against the peeled logs of the blockhouse.

"It was kind of you, John, to find out. I wouldn't have known how to ask."

"It's nothing. I wanted to help."

"I'm grateful to you."

He felt himself grow stiff and his voice tightened.

"It's awful. But, Mary, I'll always be willing to help you. Whatever there is you need, you'll let me know. I think you're the finest girl in German Flats."

It wasn't what he had set out to say, but he meant it. And she was standing just as stiff as he. "You've been so good," she was saying. "I'll always remember how good you've been, John."

"I wanted to tell you myself," he said. Then suddenly he leaned forward over his musket. She bent a little towards him and they kissed each other, briefly.

He pulled back quickly, and then, as she looked at him, held out his hand. She put her own in it and they held hands for a moment. Then he said, "I ought to get back to the gate."

"Yes, John."

"You'd better go down here, and I'll go down the walk." They stood silent for a moment and he added, "It would look better."

"Yes, John."

She went down under his eyes, shy and swift, and he turned round the sentry walk, marching openly with his musket on his arm.

It was a wonderful thing to have a girl like Mary Reall. It made him feel protective, as if the musket really meant something. As if Sergeant had picked him out for the very purpose. And it was a wonderful thing to have someone accept your opinions the way Mary did. It was a wonderful thing to be betrothed, he thought.

4

Marinus Willett

As the wounded were brought into the stockades, and the last of the Palatine and Canajoharie companies departed for their own precincts, a pall of terror settled on German Flats. Even the garrisons in the two forts became irascible and bitterly sarcastic about the German race. Everyone thought it was only a matter of days before the Tories and Indians would be among them.

Word got round that among the wounded at Dr. Petry's house was a man who had been scalped, and many people were moved by a morbid curiosity to see him. He turned out to be George Walter, a stout German farmer living below Fall Hill, well known for his good humor. It had not deserted him now. He was entirely willing that people should come and look at him and offer him drinks behind the doctor's back.

"*Ja, ja,*" he would say. "I was lying behind a tree, und the Indian comes und shoots me, und then he comes with his liddle axe und hits me und takes the top off mine head, und he goes away mit it. He thought I was dead." He would pause to grin, and say, "I thought I was dead too," as if that were a peculiarly funny coincidence.

It was that grin that was described around the settlements. They said his face had lost all its fatness and the features seemed on the point of running out of his chin, and that when he grinned all his features seemed to get together there, down below his face. He did it so much that the stitches tore out and the doctor had to work on him all over and lock him up on the top floor. But even so, small boys climbed the maple tree across the road to look at him through the window.

Other sufferers, less picturesque than Walter, had circumstantial stories of Tories recognized in the opposing side. People began to repeat from them how Ritter had been dragged off by two Indians and how the Indians had been driven off by Ritter's former neighbor, Casselman, who had then cut Ritter's throat with his own hand. There were stories of some Scotch Highlanders in Sir John Johnson's regiment scalping the militia just as if they were Indians themselves.

A few people made feeble efforts to the effect of combating these horrors. Domine Rozencrantz read in church from the Ninety-first Psalm:—

"He shall cover thee with his feathers, and under his wings shalt thou trust: his truth shall be thy shield and buckler.

"Thou shalt not be afraid for the terror by night; nor for the arrow that flieth by day."

But the Lord's presence was not an active thing like John Butler's before Fort Stanwix. People in the stockades began to talk about how he used to be Sir William Johnson's right-hand man when the Indians were taken care of, bribed and pampered, so that any man might take up land in safety, and Joseph Brant was just a neighbor. More than one man began to shake his head and think that he had been a fool, and wish for the old safe days back again.

The members of the Committee of Safety in German Flats were well aware of the swing of popular feeling. On the ninth of August, Peter Tygert wrote the Albany Committee as spokesman for his district by virtue of his own survival.

Demooth and Helmer and Joe Boleo had left Fort Stanwix on the night of the sixth, and it had taken them three days of circuitous traveling to elude the Indian scouting parties. They brought news to German Flats of the increasing shortage of provisions and ammunition. Colonel Gansevoort had put the garrison on a single daily ration. The one bright spot was the account of a sortie led by Lieutenant Colonel Willett against the Tory camp on the day of the battle. It was a daring raid and it resulted in the removal to the fort of all the munitions and food the enemy's camp contained, together with Butler's and Johnson's papers and half a dozen flags. They spoke with admiration of Willett's conduct. They said he was a cool, unhurried man. But they also said that the fort could not hold out indefinitely, that the Indians and the regulars were keeping a tight network of lines round the fort. They said that in Butler's papers they had found endorsements for scalps taken, at eight dollars per scalp. When they got through, the sortie seemed a drop of victory that was ironical.

Tygert, writing these things down, continued with the battle itself:—

> Gen. Herkimer is wounded; Col. Cox seemingly killed; and a great many officers are among the slain. We are surrounded by Tories, a party of 100 of whom are now on their march through the woods. . . .

Gentlemen, we pray you will send us succour. By the death of most of our committee members, the field officers, and Gen. Herkimer being wounded, everything is out of order; the people entirely dispirited; our county at Esopus unrepresented, that we cannot hope to stand it any longer without your aid; we will not mention the shocking aspect our fields do show. Faithful to our country we remain,

Your sorrowful bretheren,
THE FEW MEMBERS OF THIS COMMITTEE

But two days after this letter had been dispatched by Helmer, a scout escorted two men into Fort Dayton. One of these was a young lieutenant named Stockwell; the other was Lieutenant Colonel Marinus Willett. As soon as they arrived they were taken to Colonel Weston's quarters, and he in turn immediately sent for Tygert, Demooth, and Dr. Petry.

These three took comfort from the very look of Colonel Willett. He was standing before the fireplace, and at their entrance withdrew his hooked nose from the glass in his hand, a drop hanging from the tip of it, and eyed them with unwavering hard blue eyes. As he was being introduced to the three Committee members, the drop fell to his waistcoat. He said to them bluntly, "Gentlemen, I've had you sent for to know what you've written to Schuyler."

He nodded again when Tygert had repeated the gist of his letter to the Albany Committee.

"You put it to them pretty strong. But they'll send the letter on to General Schuyler. I'm going to see him myself." He smiled at them. "Somebody needs to raise a stink, and Gansevoort seemed to think I could do it."

His big nose seemed to arch.

"Just how bad are things up at Stanwix?" asked Dr. Petry.

"Bad enough. We've got food enough for a while, but we're low on shot. Right now St. Leger's busy writing letters about what he's going to do to us and to you people if we don't surrender. But the troops are taking them right. We made a flag on the new Continental pattern and flew it over the flags we took in the sortie, and that tickled them. And then I thought to read them the passage in the Book of Joel." His blue eyes twinkled close on either side of his high nose as he solemnly quoted:—

"'But I will remove far off from you the northern army, and will drive him into a land barren and desolate, with his face toward the east sea, and his hinder part toward the utmost sea; and his stink shall come up.'"

There was a commotion in the parade yard, and an orderly looked in to announce a dispatch rider. He entered with his papers in his hand.

"Colonel Weston?"

"Yes."

"Papers from General Schuyler."

Weston did not ask to be excused. He immediately opened his letter. Then he looked up.

"Schuyler's sending up General Arnold and Learned. He hopes to add the First New York Line."

There was a silence in the room through which the panting of the dispatch rider's horse came heavily. They all looked at one another. Then Willett wiped his mouth. "Maybe you ought to give this lad a drink," he suggested.

"Yes, yes," said Weston, and filled his own glass. He turned to Willett. "Do you think you'll have to go down to headquarters, now?"

"By God, yes. I want to be damned sure they don't waste any time. Is that decent horse you spoke of ready yet?"

"He's outside."

They all went to the door, then walked to the gate after he mounted. He paused there, gathering up the reins.

"Who do I have to pay if I spoil this horse?"

He grinned and kicked the horse into a canter before he was answered. They watched him down the road towards the creek ford. He sat straight in the saddle, like an electrified ploughman; but as they saw his square shoulders disappearing under the low maple branches they remembered the hardness of the blue eyes, and the big nose in the long face. He wasn't the kind of man who would return without what he was after.

"They'll hear him even if they hold their fingers in their ears," the doctor said. "What was that flag he was talking about, Mark? Did you see it?"

Mark Demooth nodded.

"Yes. It's got thirteen stripes, red and white ones, and a blue box in the upper corner, with thirteen white stars in a ring. They made it out of ammunition shirts, and a blue cloak, and a woman's red petticoat." He grinned thinly. "She's got to be a heroine with the men up there. They say it's the first time she ever took the petticoat off in an honest cause."

Tygert looked solemn.

"I hadn't heard of it before. It sounds like a fancy pattern for a flag, though."

5

Nancy Schuyler

The party of one hundred Tories that Mr. Tygert had mentioned in his letter to the Albany Committee materialized in the form of a party of fifteen who turned up on the thirteenth at Rudolph Shoemaker's house.

Shoemaker was an anomalous person. Before hostilities commenced he had been a Justice of the Peace under the King. In '75 he had signed the Loyalist manifesto against sedition and treason. But he had not chosen to move west with the Butlers and Johnsons later that spring. Instead, relying on his kinship to Nicholas Herkimer, he had joined the German Flats Committee of Safety. Since then his public house had become a sort of neutral ground, and it caused no particular surprise when the news went through the valley that the hostile party had taken up quarters there.

Captain Demooth first heard of it when he asked Nancy at suppertime where Clem Coppernol was. She flushed, as she always did when the captain asked her a direct question.

"He said he was going up to Shoemaker's."

"What's he doing there, do you know, Nancy?"

"He said there was some people from the westward."

Captain Demooth frowned, and Nancy, looking down on his dark head, saw his neat hands hesitate as they put the pudding on his plate. He hurried to finish his supper and then went out again. He said to his wife, "I ought to ask Weston about this, Sara. He may have heard something."

Mrs. Demooth was petulant; but Nancy hardly noticed her. It never occurred to her that this news, more than any other news, could have any importance in her life. She cleared away the dishes, washed them, wiped the table, and fetched Mrs. Demooth's lamp, and then retired to her own corner of the room.

Nancy Schuyler had not been happy in German Flats, though she had expected to be. She had thought the life would be exciting there, with the soldiers in the two forts and the young men on the farms. In such a place she had supposed there would be unmarried men who might be interested in her.

But such men seemed not to exist for Nancy, and, if there had been, Mrs. Demooth kept her so closely under watch that she would have had no opportunity. Her one moment of excitement had been that night in early winter when Gilbert Martin had stopped in with the deer meat and she had felt so sorry for him. Whenever she thought of that night, she felt a shiver take her. She thought that she must have been in love with Gilbert Martin on that night; at the time she had thought that he was in love with her. As she had sat in his arms, she had felt her very being swim into a high kind of happiness. And then abruptly, for no reason she had ever discovered, he had left her and gone home.

Later she had recalled how her brother Hon Yost used to warn her against married men. He had said a girl should never put dependence in a married man. She supposed that must be Gilbert Martin's trouble.

Sometimes she wished that she could talk to Hon, who was the one member of her family who had ever understood her. Perhaps that was because, as he said himself, he was light-headed too.

Nancy's mother had made a visit at the end of the preceding year, coming, as she said, to see what kind of girl Nancy had grown into, and also to collect her daughter's pay for the year, and Nancy had glowed with pride to see her mother in her black shawl facing up so well to the captain's wife.

"I hope Nancy's satisfactory to you, Mrs. Demooth."

"Oh yes, Nancy means very well." Mrs. Demooth used her chilly, lady voice; but it had no effect on Mrs. Schuyler's dark dominant Herkimer eyes.

"She's never been lazy," said her mother. "I'm sure she earns every penny of her wages. Now, if you'll kindly settle the account, Mrs. Demooth, I'll get back to my brother, the general."

"Will you fetch my pocket, Nancy?" Though Mrs. Demooth had not apparently noticed what Mrs. Schuyler said, Nancy was aware that she was impressed. She fetched the pocket and Mrs. Demooth took out three paper bills, saying, "Captain Demooth left the money in case you called."

Mrs. Schuyler looked at the bills.

"Why," she said, "these aren't pound notes."

"Oh, no," said Mrs. Demooth. "They're Continental dollars. They're five-dollar bills."

"They are pretty with those harps drawn on them," Mrs. Schuyler said, "but I'd rather have the money in English if you don't mind."

"I'm sorry, but it's all I have in the house. Of course, if you like, I'll speak to Captain Demooth about it. But he says these are just as good."

"The contract called for three pounds a year," Mrs. Schuyler objected. "I'm not used to these new dollars."

"They'll buy just the same, Mrs. Schuyler. As a matter of fact Captain Demooth said you were getting more than three pounds' worth, but as we did not have the change and Nancy had been a good girl he said you might give her the change as a present if you did not want to take more."

That was what her mother wished to know.

"Thank you," she said. "Maybe I'll buy her something with it. But, you know, I think she's better without money of her own."

The two women bowed to each other, and then Nancy walked out with her mother to the corner of the road.

There they had parted.

"Mrs. Demooth speaks highly of you, Nancy," her mother had said with satisfaction. "I am pleased. Your uncle will be pleased. Be a good girl."

"Yes, Mother."

"You don't get homesick, do you?"

"Oh no," said Nancy.

"Well, good-bye, daughter."

That was the way her mother always said good-bye. Calling Nancy "daughter," as if the word were a gad she pricked her own heart with. But it was a relationship that had no meaning. Her mother did not really belong to her. She was the general's sister. All her talk was about the general, or his big house and the figure he now made in the nation. She never mentioned Nancy's father. That was a mistake the general wished to have forgotten, since the man was dead. Nancy and her brother Hon were the only reminders of their mother's indiscretion, for the other brother, Nicholas, was black-complexioned and quite steady. Mrs. Schuyler never talked about Hon any more than she did of her dead husband.

Sometimes, sitting by herself in the corner of the room, Nancy could feel her heart swell with her own loneliness, and then she would pray that Hon might come down to German Flats as he had promised a year ago. She wished that he could write and she could read, so he might tell her what he was doing. He was such a light-hearted man that Nancy felt that it would do her good just to hear what he was up to.

Now, as she stitched away on her piece of handkerchief linen, she amused herself with remembering all the things she could about Hon Yost. She knew, for instance, that he had joined a regiment of regular troops. She even remembered the name of it—the Eighth King's Regiment. And she remembered his last message. She had once repeated it to Mrs. Martin when they were in Deerfield. The very words came back to her. "He said he'd try to fetch me an officer, too."

Her mouth curved over her sewing, and Mrs. Demooth, looking across the room, thought petulantly how easy it was for a simple-witted woman like Nancy Schuyler to be happy.

It startled both Mrs. Demooth and Nancy when they heard the captain's voice outside hailing Clem.

"Where've you been, Clem?"

"Up to Shoemaker's."

"What did you go up there for?" The captain sounded stern. Clem answered gruffly.

"I heard there was some British there. I thought it wouldn't do no harm to hear what was going on."

"What were they doing?"

"Nothing much."

"Look here, Clem, if you don't tell me what I want to know, I'll have to take you to the guardhouse in the fort."

"Why don't you ride over there yourself?" the Dutchman said sourly.

"Stop your impudence."

"They ain't doing nothing but set around and drink. Ensign Butler has a paper he's reading out of."

"Butler?"

"What I said."

"John Butler! No, he's a colonel."

"No, this is a young man. Nice-spoken, too. He's Ensign Walter Butler of the Eighth King's Regiment, he says. Wears a red coat. They all do, barring the Indians."

"How many are there?"

"Ten or a dozen. I didn't count. They was reading this paper saying how anybody going over to their side will be pertected. And anybody not will be cut up by the Indians. There was only four Indians, so I didn't put stock in that part."

The Eighth King's. That was Hon's regiment. In spite of Mrs. Demooth's "Nancy!" she went out to the two men.

"Clem," she said breathlessly. "Did you see Hon?"

"Hon?" Both men turned. Then Clem guffawed in the midst of his aura of rum. "Yes, by God! I did see him. Why?"

But Nancy had stepped back into the house. Already she had made up her mind to do a desperate thing. She would go up and see Hon herself. It might not be safe for him to come so near the fort, so she would go to him at Shoemaker's, no matter what Mrs. Demooth would surely say. She wouldn't even let them know.

As she sat down on her stool her heart beat so fast that she was unable to thread the needle. She tried again and again, knowing that Mrs. Demooth's unsympathetic eyes were watching her. Finally, in desperation, she merely pretended that she had succeeded. She made the motion of drawing the thread through the eye and with the empty needle began to take fine stitches in the handkerchief seam.

The color glowed in her soft cheeks. She realized that she had fooled Mrs. Demooth. She had never been clever like that before. It seemed like a good omen. Outside of the house the night was uninterrupted. Clem had gone off tipsily to his bed in the barn. The captain had hurried back to the fort. All through the grass crickets were singing. The rhythm of their united notes swung into the beat of Nancy's heart, bringing the darkness close to her.

All she need do was wait until Mrs. Demooth should go to bed, and Mrs. Demooth was already yawning.

6

Tories at Shoemaker's

It was nearly a two-mile walk to Shoemaker's. Nancy followed the road as fast as she could, but though she knew her direction, and had traveled the distance before, the darkness handicapped her. Now and then on a good patch of the road the ruts failed to guide her and she found herself walking in the rough grass at the side.

There was neither moon nor stars. No sign of life showed anywhere except the light of two torches that appeared in the main gate of Fort Dayton. But they were too far behind Nancy to look like more than sparks, and shortly after she had first noticed them, they vanished. With their going the intensity of blackness became deathly. Even the crickets were still, as if they felt the imminence of storm.

In her secretiveness she had pulled a dark shawl over her head, so that with her plain dress she was nearly invisible. A man rising suddenly in the darkness on the other side of the road never saw her at all, and she had time to shrink into the grass with the timid stillness of a deer.

He was coming away from Shoemaker's, and like herself he seemed in a hurry and anxious not to be noticed. She could not tell who he was, but she smelled the rankness of tobacco in his clothes and a strong breath of rum was left behind him after he had gone.

Nancy waited until his footsteps had faded out before resuming her own way. She was not frightened, but she did not wish to be seen by anyone who might know her, lest the word of her adventure might get back to Mrs. Demooth. She was too absorbed in her desire to see Hon to feel afraid.

It took her half an hour to reach Shoemaker's house. As she approached it she encountered more men coming away; and one or two men overtook her, going in her own direction. The queer thing about them was that none of the men spoke. They moved furtively, and they seemed anxious even to avoid each other. Since her first encounter she had traveled more cautiously, listening for every footfall on the road, so that she had time enough to step out of the way, sometimes standing by the side of the road, and sometimes finding one of the old river willows near enough to hide behind.

Shoemaker's house stood back a little from the road. When Nancy reached it, it was merely a darker square against the sky. The shutters were closed over the windows, so that the frames were barely indicated by threads of light. The only sign of life was the recurrent faint mumble of voices.

Nancy stood on the far side of the road, pressing herself against Shoemaker's pasture fence. Now that she had come so far, doubts overcame her and she felt suddenly shy of Hon. It seemed to her that the business the men were conducting must be very important, and her original plan of walking up to the door and asking for Hon, if he were not outside, was quite impossible. She did not want to do anything that might embarrass him in front of so many people. Not that she thought that Hon would be annoyed with her; but all her life she had been made to realize her unimportance before people.

With the opening of the front door, she suddenly discovered herself full in the light. She had one glimpse of the interior of the house. It was full of farmers, standing along the walls. They did not appear to be saying anything. Their faces looked stupid in the tobacco smoke. They were all staring through the door into Shoemaker's taproom.

Nancy could see through the door also, but only enough to have a flashing glimpse of a scarlet coat or two, and, beyond, the face of one man, pale, young, and dark-haired. He was addressing the gathering in a high, decisive voice.

Then the men who had come out on the stoop closed the door, and the darkness was returned. As the men stepped off the stoop. Nancy felt herself seized from both sides. She was taken by the arms and hauled stiffly erect. She started to cry out, but a hand put over her mouth checked the cry. The men who held her did not move until the men leaving the house were well away down the road.

Then a voice said, "You come now."

She was led quickly towards the house, but not to the front door. They turned the corner to the left towards the kitchen porch. Nancy stumbled a little on the steps.

She was not afraid now, only surprised, and bitterly ashamed that she should have been discovered and have been brought to Hon's attention in so humiliating a fashion after she had tried to be so careful. She could not understand how the men had got so close to her. She had not seen them even when the door was open. And now on the porch boards their feet made hardly a sound.

One spoke to the other, and she felt him taking hold of her with both hands, and as the other moved towards the door her nostrils were filled with a strong sweet greasy odor and she knew that the two men must be Indians. As the door opened she looked up at the man who held her.

He was a powerful thickset man. He wore a red cloth head-dress, with a single eagle feather hanging down over his left ear. From the waist up he was naked, his hairless chest beaded through the grease with tiny drops of sweat, so that the light shimmered on his skin with a bronze sheen. He was looking curiously down at her, the eyes a strange parody of intelligence behind the red and yellow painting of his face.

"You be good," he said, and relaxed the pressure of his hands slightly; but he did not let go of her.

The door opened again, showing her the second Indian and a soldier in a scarlet coat.

"You can let her go," the soldier said to the second Indian.

He looked down at her. His coat was unbuttoned. Between the flaps Nancy saw that his shirt was wringing wet. He blew out his breath. "God, it's good to get some fresh air. It smells like a Dutch funeral in there. Well, Missy, what do you want here?"

Nancy flushed within the protection of her shawl. She tried to find words.

"All right, Missy," the soldier said. "Nobody's going to hurt you."

"I know," Nancy replied. At the sound of her fresh young voice the soldier looked at her more closely. "I didn't mean to make a bother," Nancy went on. "I just heard my brother Hon was here and I haven't seen him for two years and I wanted to say something to him."

The soldier said kindly, "You've got a brother with us?"

Nancy nodded.

"What did you say his name was?"

"Hon Yost."

"We ain't got anybody named that with us. What's your name?"

"Nancy Schuyler."

"Nancy is a nice name." He hesitated, still looking at her. Then, as if he couldn't help himself, he took his hands from his belt and put the shawl back from her face. She stood in the light, hesitant and flushed, looking up at him with large eyes. Her full lips trembled a little.

He seemed to miss the simpleness in her eyes. He kept looking at her face, her lovely mouth, her heavy yellow hair, and the long soft curves of her body showing through the thin dress.

"Is your brother Jack Schuyler? He looks a little like you. Not really, you know. Jesus!" He drew his breath. "I haven't seen a pretty girl since I left Montreal, last April." He seemed to recollect himself with an effort. "Jack's got yellow hair like you. Do you think he'd be your brother?"

Nancy was staring in a trance. But her eyes were on the glittering sergeant's stripes, on the red coat, and the white breeches, now stained from his passage through the woods. She did not see at all the eagerness of his face, the almost feverish brilliance of his eyes.

"I don't know," she said timidly. "He had yellow hair. But I always called him Hon."

"That's Dutch for John. The Eighth is supposed to be all

English. I'll fetch him out, anyway. I'd do a lot for you, Missy."
He smiled deliberately at her. "You just stay here." He put his
hand on her shoulder, letting it slide down her arm as he turned
away to the open door.

"Where's that half-wit Schuyler?" she heard him ask another
red-coated man.

"What do you want him for?"

"His sister's outside. She wants to see him."

"His sister?" The man laughed out loud.

He disappeared in the throng and one of the Indians closed
the door, leaving Nancy and themselves in darkness. She heard
their catlike tread moving past her along the porch, and presently she made out their heads, shadowy silhouettes, staring east
together from the steps.

She had to wait quite a while before the door opened again.
But it was not Hon Yost; it was the soldier who had gone to look
for him.

"Jack can't get out right now," he said.

She asked timidly, "Did you tell him I was here, Mister?"

"Yes. He said for you to wait. I told him I'd look after you."
He leaned himself against the wall of the house and stared at her.
He had left the door open a crack, so that the light shone on her,
but when she moved he put his hand out.

"Don't move. Please. You don't know how it is, in the woods.
So long. You get half crazy with the heat, and the flies, and there's
nothing to see but men like yourself. You don't know what it is
for a man just to look at a pretty girl."

Nancy stood still. She couldn't see his face now—only his
brown hair over his ear in the edge of the light; but she could see
where his eyes were.

He said, "I used to live down here. Down beyond Fort Dayton. On the other side of the Canada Creek. I worked for an old
woman named McKlennar. It's funny I never heard of you."

Nancy could not think of anything to say. She was listening and looking for Hon. But the soldier's voice sounded so unhappy that she turned her face a little towards him and smiled her slow smile, with its meaningless warmth.

He said, "My name's Jurry McLonis."

"Yes, Mr. McLonis."

She smiled again and he was silent for a time. Through the door the same decisive voice she had heard before came with the stilted precision of a man reading:—

> ". . . For which reasons, the Indians declare, that if they do not surrender the garrison without further opposition, they will put every soul to death—not only the garrison, but the whole country—without regard to age, sex, or friends; for which reason it is become your indispensable duty, as you must answer the consequences, to send a deputation to your principal people, to oblige them immediately to what, in a very little time, they must be forced—the surrender of the garrison; in which case we will engage on the faith of Christians, to protect you from the violence of the Indians.
>
> "Surrounded as you are by victorious armies, one half (if not the greater part) of the inhabitants friends to government, without any resource, surely you cannot hesitate a moment to accept the terms proposed to you by friends and well-wishers to the country.

"It's signed by John Johnson, D. W. Claus, and my father John Butler. It's plain honest sense, and the last chance you people will have to save your necks. I'm going back day after to-morrow. Every man who goes with me gets a uniform coat, a musket if he needs it, pay in good English money, and a land bounty when this war's over."

Again the silence, and again the low mumbling of voices.

"God, I'm sick of hearing all that, Nancy. The same thing over and over for two days." Jurry McLonis touched her arm. "Jack can't come out a while. Let's go out where it's quiet and dark." Her eyes turned to him, large and questioning and hesitant and foolish. "He told me to look out for you, you know."

"Yes, Mister. I don't mind. While Hon's busy."

The steady sound of Butler's voice had muddled her head. McLonis's arm round her waist was comfortable to lean against. The Indians moved over on the steps and glanced at them, and moved back.

McLonis led her out, his arm tightening round her as she found the footing uncertain in the darkness. He took her behind Shoemaker's barn. There he let her go and leaned against the log wall. But Nancy did not move away. She stood where he had left her, within reach of his arm, quite still, thinking that it was a long time to have to wait for Hon, but glad to be away from the house and the Indians. She could hear his steady breathing just beside her.

Suddenly she was caught again in his arm and swung in front of him. His free hand came behind her back, forcing her against him so hard she thought she could almost feel the logs through his body. She felt his face feeling for hers, his chin scraped across her shoulder in the opening of her dress, moved over her cheek, and his mouth fastened upon hers. For an instant, startled and dizzy, she was inert against his chest. Then under the pressure of his arms her strength came to life. She put her arms around him, pulling herself even closer to him, and lifted her face.

She was silent as an animal. When suddenly he let her go, she stood before him trembling and still; but when he put his hands out again, she moved hard into his embrace. Her hands pressing into the small part of his back became clumsy. Her breath came out with a little moan at the end and her breast arched. She had no recollection of Hon left, only of herself and the man in her arms. He kept saying, "You . . ." without finding any other word to add to it.

Nancy lay in the long grass. The soldier was standing up, like a tower in the darkness rising from her feet. For an instant he was motionless. Then without as much as saying good-bye, he broke into a run away from the barn. Not towards the house, but back up the hill from the river. For an instant her disordered senses followed his crashing progress through the underbrush. Abruptly, the sound ceased, and Nancy, coming to herself at last, knew that something had gone wrong at Shoemaker's.

She heard men shouting, and feet stamping on the other side of the barn as men ran past. She sat up in the grass, fumbling for her shawl. Her hair was snarled and full of grass. Panic swept over her, and without thinking of Hon, only of the instinct to get hidden at home, she found the shawl and started running towards the road.

As she scrambled over the yard fence a man shouted, "There goes one!" A musket roared behind her head, but she was too close to hear the bullet. She ran frantically, sobbing, and yanking at her skirt. For a moment she heard men pursuing, then she was out down the road and going for her life.

She did not stop until she was nearly home, and she stopped then only because she could not run another step. She veered from the road like a hurt deer and fell full length. She kept drawing her breath in great sobbing gasps.

She was still there when she heard the men tramping towards her down the road. Her first instinct was for renewed flight, but immediately afterwards she drew down into the sheltering brush like a hare in its form, to stare with horrified eyes at the approaching group.

Several of the men were carrying torches, and under the smoky light their bodies made a dark throng in the road, with the willow limbs like arms lifted above them.

They came without talking, in open files, their muskets on their shoulders, soldiers from the garrison at Fort Dayton, with the prisoners between them.

With them, at the head of the procession, Nancy's appalled eyes recognized Captain Demooth, and Gilbert Martin, his arm still bandaged, and one of the officers from the fort, a Colonel Brooks, who had sometimes come to supper at the Herter house. But as the files passed her she took her eyes from them and stared into the prisoners' faces. The first was the man who had been reading in Shoemaker's house, the man she had heard addressed as Ensign Butler. It was her first sight of Walter Butler, with his whittled attorney's face, black hair cut short, and black eyes. His mouth reminded her a little of McLonis's, long and thin-lipped, but, unlike McLonis's, tipped with a passion of contempt.

He was dressed in a scarlet coat with an ensign's tabs on the shoulders, and the men who followed him between the tramping files of Massachusetts soldiers were of the same regiment. She kept looking for McLonis, but he was not with them. He must have escaped. Her heart rose, even in her fright, until, as the last of the white prisoners passed, she saw her brother.

Even in the uncertain light Hon Yost looked as she remembered him, his yellow hair reaching to his shoulders, his straight features and red cheeks, and the blue eyes, irresponsible. He walked jauntily, as if he hadn't a fear in the world; but watching the faces of the garrison, Nancy sank down still lower in the brush, and bit her hand to keep from crying aloud. Before she could think what she should do, the tail of the procession was going by with the last torch shining on four captured Mohawk Indians.

The light flashed over their painted cheeks, picked out a wolf's head on the chest of the first, a drooping eagle's feather in his headdress. The light made a dark shine on their oiled skins.

It was not till long after they had gone, until she had seen the torchlights reflected in the water of the ford, that Nancy stumbled to her feet.

The Herter place was dark when she reached it, but, though she was still sobbing softly, she moved as quietly as she could round the corner of the barn. She had crossed halfway to the house when Clem Coppernol rose up in front of her, surrounding them both with his fog of rum.

"Who's that?" he asked unsteadily. As she tried to elude him, he stumbled forward and caught her skirt. He used it to help himself off his knees. "'S a pullet anyways," he mumbled. "'S you Nancy, ain't it?"

"Yes," she whispered.

"Been out. I seen you going. I seen you. You can't lie." He nodded against her shoulder. "Been to Shoemaker's. See Hon?"

She shivered and the tears gathered under her lids.

"No. No. I want to go to bed."

"Saw somebody. You tell me and I'll let you go," he said slyly.

"Yes. I saw a soldier."

He chuckled.

"Nice girl. So awful nice with me, ain't you? Bet a dollar you got laid."

"No," she said frantically.

"Did, though. Or you wouldn't act this way. Where's Hon?"

Her sobs started again.

"They caught him. They've taken him to the fort. What are they going to do, Clem?"

"That's good. Good business." He scratched his head with his free hand. "Probably they'll hang him. Hang the bunch. Yes, sir."

Nancy managed to whisper, "Please let me go."

"Maybe I will, and maybe I won't. You got to be nice to me now, or I'll tell."

"I'll be nice."

"I'm still kind of drunk."

"Yes."

"But I ain't real drunk, neither." He paused to wipe his mouth. "You're a good girl just the same, Nance. I'll stand up for you. If you've got fixed, I'll marry you if you want."

Nancy sprang out of his grasp and fled for the house. He made no move to chase her. He was open-mouthed in the darkness, trying to recollect what he had just said. Long after she had crept inside the house, he remembered.

"By God!" he said aloud. "I am drunk."

7

Death of a Brigadier

The unexpectedness of Butler's capture and the ease with which it had been accomplished did much to hearten the Committee members of German Flats. It had had an immediate effect upon the people, checking all danger of wholesale desertion to St. Leger's camp. Word got out about when the prisoners were permitted to exercise and curious people went to look at them in their regimental coats, walking up and down the small parade space in the middle of the fort.

It seemed a wonder to them. The last time they remembered Walter Butler was on that day in the spring two years before when he had ridden up the valley with Sheriff White to cut down the liberty pole in front of Herkimer Church. Then he had been a man to fear, as all the Johnsons and Butlers were, with the law in his fist. Now they saw that he was a slight man of nervous action, who took his exercise deliberately, making ten circles of the parade,—they counted them, always ten,—looking neither right nor left, his pale face inclined slightly forward. His soldiers might stop and chat with the guard or with the Palatines themselves; Hon Yost sometimes greeted former acquaintances and asked about his family; but Walter Butler seemed unaware of his surroundings. To the spectators he was more like the four Indians who always kept apart by themselves, not even speaking to each other.

Gilbert Martin, like the others, stopped one morning to watch, and afterwards went on to speak to Captain Demooth. He found the captain at the Herter house and asked, "When will those men be tried?"

"They're under military law. They'll have to be court-martialed, Gil. And Weston wants to wait for General Arnold. Technically he's under Arnold now, you see."

Gil said, "I should think it was better to get it over with. Some people there at Shoemaker's will lose their nerve."

The captain smiled a little.

"There are plenty of witnesses who won't. You, for one. That's why I sent for you the other night." His face grew serious. "And personally, Gil, I'm just as glad to have it put into the army's hands. I used to know the Butlers. They've got powerful friends. Some of our Committee would be afraid to convict him if the responsibility was on our shoulders."

"What will they do to him?"

"He'll be tried for a spy," Captain Demooth said dryly.

"How about the others?"

"I don't know about them. They were under orders. Prison, I guess. Except Hon Yost Schuyler. He's a deserter. He's on the rolls of the Third Company of Tryon militia. We can't let him off light."

"Has Nancy seen him? I've heard she was very fond of him."

"Mrs. Demooth's been having trouble with Nancy. She was hysterical when she heard about it. We thought it was better for her not to see her brother. Her mother thought so, too."

"He's just a half-wit," said Gil. "I don't see why he should be shot."

"It's not in our hands, Gil. And as I said before, I'm glad it isn't. How's your arm?"

"It's doing fine. But I can't use it much yet for work. That's one reason I came to see you. Mrs. McKlennar wants to know where she can hire a man. Our wheat's begun dropping."

"So has everybody's. If it isn't reaped inside the next two weeks we'll lose more than half the crop." He shook his head. "I don't know where you can find a man. There are plenty doing nothing in the forts. But they don't want to work. They don't want to do anything until Arnold gets here."

Gil said, "Yes." He hesitated. "Mrs. McKlennar wanted to know if you'd heard how General Herkimer was. She thought she might be able to rent one of his slaves for a week."

"I haven't heard from Herkimer for several days. His leg got mortified. And Petry can't get down to see it, so we don't know much."

"Do you think it would be all right if I went down to see him?"

"Why, yes. He'll probably be glad to have some news. You can tell him from me we've heard the First New York has got as far as Klock's."

Gil went down on the brown mare next morning. It was the

first time he had ever been at Herkimer's house, and the size of it, together with the well-kept fields, impressed him.

A full-breasted negress met him at the door and said, "Gener'l ain' seein' nobody," in an impressive voice. Gil was ready to turn away when the right-hand door opened into the hall and Mrs. Herkimer came out.

"What is it, Frailty?"

"Dish yer man he's askin' fo' de Gener'l," Frailty said contemptuously.

Gil removed his hat.

"I'm from Mrs. McKlennar, ma'am. She wanted me to come down and find out if you could rent her a slave for a few days to get her wheat in. I work for her myself, but my arm's no good, now."

She glanced at the arm.

"Were you at the battle?"

"Yes," said Gil.

The pained look in her eyes increased. But she stepped back through the door.

"Come in. Honnikol's always glad to see anyone who was with him up there."

The general's big bed had been set up in the northwest room with its head to the fireplace so that he could look through the windows towards the river. Herkimer was wearing a flannel nightshirt open at the throat, showing the black hair on his chest, and to Gil, seeing him against the pillows, his shoulders looked heavier than he remembered them.

Herkimer's face was drawn, the mouth set, and it was obvious that he suffered a good deal of pain. But the black eyes stared keenly at Gil as he said, "Good morning."

His wife came over to the bed with a lighted candle for his pipe and he sucked on the stem without turning his eyes from Gil's.

"You want to see me about a nigger, *ja*? I heard you. Haw's Mrs. McKlennar? They keep me cooped up here, and I don't hear anything, not even how my neighbors are. I'm done with—old Herkimer—he lost his army. . . . Look! Aren't you the lad who picked me up mit Peter Bellinger and histed me up the hill?"

Gil turned brick red. It seemed to him a miracle that Herkimer, badly wounded, in the midst of that confusion, should remember a strange face. He nodded.

Herkimer said nothing either. Then he held his hand out. His grip was still strong.

"Sure," he said suddenly in a deep voice, "you can have a nigger." He looked across at his wife, who had sat down again in a corner, looking on with swimming eyes. "Tell Trip he's to go back with—what's your name, young man?"

"Gilbert Martin."

"Tell him with Mr. Martin, Maria. Tell him if he don't work hard I'll lick him myself when I get on my two feet." He made a gesture with his hand, as if he brushed the business aside, and at the same time he lifted his eyes to Gil's.

His eyes were tired and sad and, in a queer way, very shy.

"Will you be honest with an old man?" As Mrs. Herkimer made a cluck of protest, he shook his head. "I know. I'm only fifty-one, Maria, and young women don't like their husbands to say how old they feel." His smile made Gil feel the sadness more. "But it makes me feel old, nobody coming down here, nobody telling me anything. The army gets licked and I am brought down here in a boat and left here, *ja*. Tell me, Martin, what they're saying about me."

Gil did not know what to say, but the general did not help him out. "Tell the truth or don't say anything."

"They're saying nothing."

"And what do they think?"

"I don't know," said Gil miserably. Then he remembered the

knoll before the second charge. "But, by God, there are plenty who were up there who wish you were back and kicking, Mr. Herkimer."

"Kicking." He looked down at his leg. He looked up again and sucked on his pipe. "I let myself get into a mess. I didn't have the insides to stand up to all those downriver gentlemens. This house, it was a mistake to build a big house just because I could. They did not like it." He came back to the point suddenly. "It was a good fight, though, once the fools was killed or run away."

The room was silent. Finally, Herkimer asked from the pillows, "What's the news? What are they going to do with Butler?"

"They're waiting for General Arnold, sir."

"Benedict Arnold. He got up to Quebec, and then he didn't take it. I heard he was coming. Trip heard it in Frank's across the river," he added bitterly.

His wife spoke. "Honnikol, people don't think the way you think they do."

"No? Hardly anybody comes here. Only Warner und Peter und John Roof, because he's staying with me here." He shifted his shoulders. "When's Arnold coming?"

"Captain Demooth said to tell you the First New York was at Klock's last night. They ought to come by here this morning."

Herkimer's eyes brightened.

"That's good," he said. "Ja. Maria, open the window, so I can hear them when they come."

His depression lifted and for a while he talked to Gil about the early days in the valley. He talked about Oriskany and the men and what he had seen during the fight. It was surprising how many men and how many individual acts he had seen, until Gil remembered how he had sat up on his saddle throughout the whole six hours, in plain sight of everything.

He was still talking when they heard the first sound of the troops. At the moment it was like the distant ruffle of a drummer partridge in the still air. Then, suddenly, all three people in the room recognized the beat of drums. They heard the slap of bare feet running round the corner of the house from the slave cabins; a boy's voice shouting down at the dock.

"I can see them." The voice was shrill. Some of the negro children took it up. "*I can see them. I can see them.*"

Inside the room the three people stared at each other. For a moment all the yelling had obscured the sound of the drums. Mrs. Herkimer moved towards the window.

"*Nein,* Maria. Let them make a noise. I feel the same way also." He put his pipe down carefully. "But I can't see them."

Maria Herkimer's eyes filled again. Then she looked at Gil. "Do you think we could drag his bed to the window?"

"No," said Herkimer. "Call in the men. Trip, Joseph. Martin's got a bad arm."

Gil understood her silent pleading. She couldn't bear to have anyone else in the room. "Sure we can drag him." It took all their strength, he with his bad arm, she a slight woman, but they got the bed beside the window, and Herkimer heaved up on his elbow.

The drums, even from across the river, had now mastered the raised voices of the children. "It's the *flam,*" said Herkimer. The staccato double tap brought the shivers to Gil's spine. These drums hadn't the rattletrap sound of the militia. He felt courage as the flam was repeated, three times, a pulse between each beat. And then the drums with a crash banged out the opening bar of "Roslyn Castle."

With the pronouncement of the rhythm a sigh issued from the negroes' throats. Herkimer's fingers started picking at the blanket. "Fifes," he said suddenly. "*Ach Gott!* It is the army."

Through the beating of the drums the squealing of the fifes swept over the river like a cold wind, and close on the heels of the sound, made small by the distance, but clear against the dull green hillside, the troops came marching up the Kingsroad.

They made a compact blue stream above the fence rails,

keeping close ranks, their rifles slanting rays of wood and iron on their shoulders, their cocked hats in rows for the eye to see. They marched like men who were accustomed to covering the ground, with a long stride, their faces stretched forward against the pull of the blanket rolls. They reached along the straight stretch of the road, two hundred and fifty men behind the drums, and slowly covered the great bend westward for the falls.

A break came in the line, and wagons passed to the same pace, the teamsters alert, keeping their horses up to the mark. Another break and two light cannon bounced on their light carriages. Behind them rode a group of officers, their horses' heads on the edge of the white powdery rise of dust. Then the rear guard. Fifty men.

Already the drums had passed from sight behind the river willows. But the fife sound floated behind. Long after it was still and gone, Gil thought he could hear the sound of them. He turned suddenly to Herkimer's voice.

"*Ach Gott*. One gompany. If they had only sent me up one gompany."

His face did not change. He didn't hear the quiet crying of his wife.

Gil helped to move the bed back to its first place so nothing showed that it had been moved but the scrapes of its feet on the wide boards. Then he left. He did not say good-bye to the general, for it was obvious that the general could not talk. But Maria Herkimer followed him into the hall. "Trip will go back with you, Mr. Martin. God bless you." She reached up both her hands and took his face and kissed him.

Outside, Gil looked round him for the negro. He was surprised to see him coming from the ferry with an officer he had just rowed over, a fresh-faced young man in blue regimentals carrying a bag. He asked Gil, "Is this the Herkimer house?"

Gil nodded, and Mrs. Herkimer came out again to the hall.

"I'm Maria Herkimer, sir."

"General Arnold's compliments. I had instructions to stop in at General Herkimer's and see whether I might do anything to help him." He took his hat off, bowing. "Robert Johnson, ma'am. Surgeon, *pro tem*, First Regiment, the New York Line."

Waiting for Trip to reappear with his belongings, Gil overheard their voices.

"Come in, Doctor. *Ja*. You can look at my leg."

A pause.

"Is Arnold far behind?"

"Ought to come by to-night, sir. He's been in a tearing hurry."

"It was kind of him to send you here."

"He was particular. Said something about you being too good to lose. Said it must have been a great piece of fighting."

Herkimer's voice deepened.

"*Ja*. He should have been there."

Another silence. The doctor, saying in his fresh young voice, "I see. I see."

"You think it should come off? Petry said I should keep it. But he iss hurt und can't come down."

"Off? By gad, sir, it ought to have been off a week ago! With all respect. But these back-country surgeons sometimes . . ."

"Petry's a stubborn cuss. Don't get sick, Maria. It's no good to me anyway. I want some rum und my pipe. The one with the big bowl on it. *Ja*."

Gil realized that Trip was standing beside him. The negro's eyes rolled round to his.

"Yassah."

Without a word, Gil went down to the ferry.

● ● ●

It was all over in the northwest room. The surgeon, hat in hand, was saying good-bye. "I have to report to-night at Dayton."

Herkimer looked at him calmly with his black eyes. The room was full of smoke. The negress Frailty was gingerly carrying out the bloody sheet they had used to cover the table. Mrs. Herkimer, pale face swollen, swayed a little as she waited.

"Goot luck, Doctor. Thank General Arnold for me."

"Thank you, sir."

"Tell me something. Did you ever cut off a leg before?"

The surgeon blushed.

"No, sir."

"Don't pe ashamed. A man has to start somewhere. I remember the first deer I shot." His face brightened suddenly. "Maria, have one of the poys find out if Boleo's at Warner's." He set down his pipe in the candlestick. His eye fell on the bundle in the corner.

"Give it to Johnny Roof to bury. It should please a poy to do that."

He sank back and closed his eyes. Nobody had heard him make a sound beyond the grinding of his teeth. Now his breathing was like a blow repeated and repeated against the walls of the room.

While he slept, two boys took the severed leg and walked with it in the orchard. They did not know where a good place would be until one thought of the ox-heart cherry tree the general was so fond of. They dug the hole and filled it.

While he slept, one of the negro lads went up to Warner Dygert's tavern and gave the news of the amputation. Joe Boleo started getting sober then. "My Jesus, what did they do that for?" He picked his rifle from the corner and ambled unsteadily in the negro's wake. Already it was getting dark.

There was no light in the northwest room while Herkimer slept, for Maria, from exhaustion, had fallen asleep herself in the chair by the hearth. She was awakened by Joe Boleo's hand on hers. "It's Joe."

"Oh, Joe," she whispered back.

"They took his leg off?"

"Yes."

"I thought the nigger was lying."

She stirred softly under his hand and left the chair and went into the dim light of the hall. She fetched a candle back. Together she and the gangling trapper leaned over the bed.

"Poor old Honnikol. He never could get round very fast, anyways."

She gasped. She wasn't pointing at the white face in which the nose seemed to have grown overlarge. Her finger pointed at the blanket.

Joe looked at the drench of blood and swore. He went right out himself and woke the entire lot of negroes.

"Get up to Fort Dayton," he ordered. "Get Petry. Doc Petry. Bring him down in a canoe if he can't ride. Tell him a fool army man cut off Honnikol's leg and it's still bleeding."

He returned to the house.

"Hello, Honnikol."

"Joe?"

"Shut up," said Joe. He helped Maria Herkimer twist a tourniquet on above the bloody stump. "We'd better leave the bandage on. It might clot yet."

"I don't think so." Herkimer spoke quietly. "Get me my pipe, Maria, and one for Joe, and beer for both of us. We both need beer. Me, I'm thirsty. How about you, Joe?"

"Oh, my Jesus, Honnikol. I ain't drank in two weeks."

They smoked and drank through long hours, while Herkimer talked fitfully about old hunting trips. They didn't mention war. "Remember the trout above Schell's riff?"

"Sure," said Joe. "Sure, Honnikol."

"I don't know what's become of all the fishing, Joe."

When Herkimer finally went to sleep, Joe left the room, wandering hopelessly to the river side. There was nothing to see. They couldn't bring Petry down before morning. And the bleeding did not stop.

Making a restless circuit of the house, he met Johnny Roof and the other lad standing in the orchard with two spades. "What you doing?" Joe asked sourly. They said they'd heard the general was dying. They were wondering about digging up his leg. "What for?" They said to bury with him. He merely cursed them. He walked around for an hour in the dark, leaving Honnikol to his wife. It was what a woman expected.

In the morning, Herkimer was not talking. Even when Colonel Willett came over the river and reported that General Arnold was passing on the north shore, Herkimer did no more than stare.

About nine, however, he rallied and asked for his pipe. When he had been smoking a little while he asked for his Bible, opened at the Thirty-eighth Psalm. He started to read aloud in a strong voice, but as he went on the voice started to fail. He did not appear to be aware of it, but read on, moving his lips slowly, and only now and then achieving utterance, so that his wife and the lank, uneasy woodsman, who leaned against the sunny window frame, heard only snatches:—

"'O Lord, rebuke me not in thy wrath. . . .'"

8

Arrival of a Major General

The death of Herkimer shook the people. He had been the squire, the man with the money who had built a great house that rivaled Sir William Johnson's Hall. Now they remembered that he had been one of themselves, a quiet man, who came to dinner in his shirt, likely as not. They missed his steadfastness. The men who had been with him at Oriskany battle recalled how he had lit his pipe. Now that he was gone they had no one to depend on.

For three days. On the morning of the twentieth, officers on good mounts, wearing the blue coats of the regular army, rode the length of German Flats reading a proclamation.

> By *the Hon.* BENEDICT ARNOLD, *Esq., Major-General and Commander-in-chief of the army of the United States of America on the Mohawk River.*
>
> WHEREAS a certain Barry St. Leger, a Brigadier-general in the service of George of Great Britain, at the head of a banditti of robbers, murderers, and traitors, composed of savages of America, and more savage Britons (among whom is the noted Sir John Johnson, John Butler, and Daniel Claus), have lately appeared in the frontiers of this state . . .

It was not what the proclamation said that roused the people. There were too few Tories left in German Flats to make the promised amnesty applicable to themselves. It was rather the choice of words. Here was a man who put down what he said as if he meant it, who wasn't afraid of calling scoundrels by their proper names.

Militiamen who hadn't thought of heading west again began to talk of going along with Arnold's army. He was the man who had taken troops overland through Maine and would have conquered Quebec and all Canada but for one unlucky bullet that got him in the knee. In the knee, like Herkimer; the coincidence was striking. They listened to his invitation to all able-bodied men, militia or exempts, to join him in a victorious march against St. Leger's camp. But they waited awhile to see what he would do.

He did a lot. He made an inspection of the forts round German Flats. In each he made another speech about his expedition. He also urged the people out to take care of the wheat.

"This valley's not only got to feed you; it's got to feed General Washington's army. And the army will pay you high. Right now it's buying unmilled wheat at seven shilling." They listened to him, watching him—a black-visaged, hawk-like man, with arrogant round eyes and an opulent mouth. "You've got more than your families to look out for here. You've got the bread of the army in your care. That's what St. Leger's after. And that's what Gansevoort's saving by hanging out in Stanwix, and that's what we're going to save Gansevoort for." His face was flushed high; his voice had a queer habit of sliding up the scale; but they liked the way he walked up and down, light on his feet, like a man who knew the woods.

"Listen to me. Over in Bennington, Vermont, Colonel Stark and a bunch of minutemen captured and licked and manhandled five hundred Hessian cavalry. Do you know why the Hessians went over there? Because Burgoyne's getting pinched for food. General Schuyler has him bottled up. His murdering Indians have gone home, they can't find any more girls to kill, like Jenny McRae. He's just sitting still and praying for St. Leger, and that's what we're here to stop. Lick St. Leger and you lick Burgoyne. You people can do it. You damn near did. I'm here to help you take another whack at it, and both of us together can win this war, right here."

He had Learned's artillery manœuvre in Petry's field, and the men went from all the forts and stockades to look at cannon dragged on wheels. The soldiers lined one up and fired it down the river, and the awed people saw the heavy ball send up a tower of spray three hundred yards downstream. They thought of what that would have done to the Indians at Oriskany, and Arnold had a battery.

"By Jesus," said Joe Boleo, making his first emergence from his gloom, "I calculate I'll go along and see one of them balls let loose after Sillinger myself."

Arnold's next step was to court-martial Walter Butler. He appointed Willett Judge Advocate, which made men shake their heads and say conviction would be pretty near conclusive, with that arrangement. When they found that the trial was open to any and all spectators, they so crowded Dr. Petry's store that a guard had to be thrown round it to keep out late comers.

It gave them a strange thrill to see one of the men who had run the valley standing up before an officer. Butler was self-contained but scornful. He argued in his clear attorney's voice that he had come with a flag to parley with the inhabitants of German Flats. He did not know anything of this new law, he only knew the King's law. He did not consider it necessary to report to Colonel Weston, for he did not know of any Colonel Weston or of any Fort Dayton. The natural pallor of his face was not accentuated when he was brought back into court and sentenced to the pain and penalty of death. The new law he had scorned, as administered by Willett and Arnold, had ground him down. It gave all men pause for thought.

By contrast the succeeding trial of Hon Yost Schuyler as a deserter from the Tryon County militia was an anticlimax. But it showed that General Arnold was not missing any tricks at all; and some of the spectators were reminded how nearly they might have found themselves in Schuyler's shoes, guilty, and sentenced to a hundred lashes.

Arnold had no authority for court-martialing Butler. Both Gates and Schuyler had sent definite orders that the captured

men be removed to Albany. But he and Willett had been putting on a show to divert attention from their unavoidable delay.
The militia were not coming in as they had expected, and the
commissary train as usual was lagging no one knew quite where.

That night while he and Willett sat together in headquarters
tent trying to think up some new game and wondering whether
they dared disobey instructions and execute Butler anyway, the
guard announced two women to see the general. The women
were Mrs. Schuyler and her daughter, Nancy.

Both officers were men to whom directness invariably appealed.
Mrs. Schuyler wasted no time in pleading her own shame, she
only mentioned that she was Herkimer's sister, they could see her
position for themselves. She had brought a proposition from her
son. If Arnold let him off, he guaranteed to go to Sillinger's camp
and, pretending he had escaped from the American army, to put
the fear of death into the Indians. He volunteered the information
that when he left with Ensign Butler, the Indians were already getting restless. He believed that if the Indians left, the Tories, and
maybe Sillinger himself, would lose their nerve.

It was the kind of notion to appeal to men like Arnold and
Willett. They admitted it. But Arnold said, "What guarantee
can you give us of your son's good faith?"

"I've brought my daughter with me," said Mrs. Schuyler.
"You can keep her for a hostage."

Arnold studied Mrs. Schuyler and then glanced at Nancy's
face. Nancy was pale and her eyes were wide with emotion. As
she met the general's eye her lips parted. She had made the suggestion herself to her mother, and she was ready, if anything happened to Hon, to take his punishment.

Arnold smiled grimly.

"Mrs. Schuyler, you're too intelligent to think I could accept
a girl for a hostage. What would people think of me if I ordered
my sergeant to give a girl a hundred lashes on her bare back?"

Mrs. Schuyler sighed.

"I thought so. Very well, my son Nicholas has agreed to put himself in your hands till Hon returns."

Nancy's face flushed darkly, then it went pale again. And she stood there shivering. The two officers smiled sympathetically. It seemed quite natural; they admired her heroism. Her mother said, "Be still."

Nancy did not move or speak.

9

Relief of Stanwix

On the twenty-first of August, militiamen began to appear at Fort Dayton. They came from as far east as Klock's, and with the arrival of the first groups the men of German Flats started to turn out. By nightfall the count had reached three hundred, and Arnold called Willett and all local militia officers into his tent for a council of war.

"Gentlemen, we start to-morrow."

His eyes swept over the circle of faces, and fastened on the hesitant ones. Peter Tygert murmured, "Give us another day and maybe we can get another hundred rifles out for you."

"In another day," said Arnold, "Colonel Gansevoort may have to cut his way out of Fort Stanwix. It's my opinion we could be more useful there than here. You can fetch the other hundred along to-morrow." His eyes protruded at them. "This country's rotten with its hemstitch policies. It's time somebody acted. I'm going to. How about those militia? Are they decently organized?"

Captain Demooth said quietly, "They're pretty disorganized.

A lot of the officers got shot or captured. Most of these men were in the first two companies."

Arnold nodded.

"Very well. I suggest that they be turned over to the surviving officers and made into an irregular brigade. Bring them along in the rear. They ought to shake down as we march. We march to-morrow after sunrise."

It was a still morning, a little cooler than usual. The river lay like glass between the rifts, not stirring the reflection of a leaf.

At dawn, so still was the air that from Little Stone Arabia Fort to Eldridge Blockhouse people heard the muster rolling of the army drums. Gil Martin, reporting, was appointed temporary sergeant of those of the Schuyler company whom he could get together. Of twenty-five he found eleven. Reall was dead, Weaver wounded, Kast wounded; of the other eleven men one was known to be dead, two taken prisoner, three wounded, and the rest disappeared.

Survivors of other companies even more unfortunate, Joe Boleo and Adam Helmer among them, asked to be attached to Demooth's company. They made a compact knot of men when Demooth himself rode up to count them. "Good work, Martin," he said, and wheeled his horse to let General Arnold pass on the narrow road.

But the general reined his horse.

"Is this your company, Captain?"

"Yes, sir."

"They aren't all sound."

"Sound enough, I think," said Captain Demooth.

Arnold smiled suddenly.

"By God, then, let them come. Do they know the woods?

Good. I suggest they act as an advance guard." He turned to Gil. "Keep a quarter mile ahead of us."

The way he said it made Gil feel inordinately proud.

"Yes, sir." Then he asked, "How far will this day's march go, sir?"

"Just as far as we can get." Arnold grinned again. "You do a thorough job of combing the woods and I reckon we'll keep up."

They took the road, with the rolling of the drums recommencing behind them. It prickled their scalps to hear the fifes break out.

The woods covered them with their green silence and they went swiftly westward. In Gil there was a lifting of the heart. He nodded when Helmer said, "This beats the militia. Being our own men and eating nobody's dust." As soon as they had passed Schuyler, Joe Boleo and Helmer took over the direction of the company, but Joe Boleo was tactful about it.

"You ain't timber beasts like me and Helmer, Martin. The two of us can find out a whole lot more of what's going on if we don't have you to keep track of. The rest of you keep on the road and go a little slow. We'll let you know fast enough if we find anything. Wait at the ford until we pick you up though."

The two men broke away and trotted forward into the woods, one on each side of the road. Their moccasined feet made no sound. Gil and the others continued along the road.

They could still see traces of the first march towards Stanwix; deep ruts off the road where an ox cart had bogged down, a rotting blanket, a dropped bayonet. But already the growth of the woods was beginning its work of hiding them. The ferns had straightened round the edges and grass was growing through a hole in the blanket. A deer runway crossing the road had blotted out the wheel tracks.

Well before noon they passed Deerfield and turned toward

the river. There, where the oxen had balked, they sat down on the bank and ate.

They were still eating their food when Gil heard a hail from the woods across the river. Helmer appeared with his hand raised. A moment more and he had splashed over the ford. One look at his big handsome face told that he carried good news.

"Joe's got a squad of Gansevoort's men up the road. They say Sillinger's pulled foot."

"Pulled foot?"

"Yes, pulled foot. Bag and baggage. The Indians lit out yesterday. The whole mess of them, and Sillinger pulling his foot with the rest. They've left everything they've got behind." He burst out laughing.

The other men suddenly joined in.

"By Jesus!" A British brigadier galloping hell for leather down the Indian track towards Oneida. They could see it themselves. Bed, tent, writing desk, and chest of liquor, cooking pots and silver forks, sword, spurs, epaulets, and oaths. They saw the whole shebang. "Pulled foot." It was a joke.

They fell silent after a few minutes and started looking at each other.

"Where'd you find them?" Gil asked.

"About where Honnikol camped, at the crick."

"What are they doing there?"

"Eating," said Adam. "Eating their lunch. When Joe walked in on them they asked him to set down and eat."

Inexplicably they all burst out laughing again.

The rest of the march went swiftly. As soon as Arnold was notified he let his baggage and artillery come on at their own pace and pushed ahead with the troops alone. The army crossed the Mohawk early the next morning. Two hours later they had reached and forded Oriskany Creek.

Gil and his small company marched at the head of the column. As they went on they began to recognize the lay of the land and their talking gradually stopped.

It was Joe Boleo who first began sniffing. He stopped his shambling stride and lifted his face, and the others crowded up behind them.

"What's the matter, Joe?" Gil asked.

"Smell for yourself, lad."

He started forward again. The road was familiar now, running in the gloom of hemlocks above the river bottom. And as they proceeded they began to pick up more strongly the odor of decay that the woodsman had spotted long before.

It became an overpowering stench. It rose up in their faces, like a wall, through which they felt they could hardly pass. They found themselves suddenly on the edge of the ravine, staring down at the causeway. They all stopped again. Then Helmer said, "God! Come on," and they went down the incline and out along the corduroy.

Some of the men looked curiously right and left, but Gil, after one glance, kept his eyes to the track. And even then more than once he had to step carefully round the disintegration of the dead.

They lay, not as they had fallen, but as the foxes and wolves and Indian dogs had left them. The grass or ferns were trodden down around each body, impartially, horse or man, Indian or white; and the half-opened skeletons were like white roots of a miasmal wilderness.

Along the rising bank the corpses thinned out, the air seemed to lighten, and the men could hear each other breathing. Then on the plateau the frequency of dead was resumed, always thicker till they reached the edge of the gulch of the farther side;

and here they lay so close together that the preying animals had not disturbed them all—postured as they had fallen, in the attitudes of fighting, or grasping the earth with swollen hands.

As they saw the end of the battleground ahead, the little knot of living men began to quicken pace. They were running when they finally rose on the far side of the gulch.

Presently, while they waited, they heard the sounds of the marching army far behind across the blanketing silence of those bodies. The tramp of feet coming down on the corduroy, the rattle of harness, and the jolt and clatter of the munition carts. There was a momentary disorder and halt, and Joe Boleo's sardonic voice inquired at large, "I wonder what Mr. Benedict Arnold makes of that?"

It was the first word any one of them had spoken. They looked in each other's faces, seeing them sallow and wet.

But then the first bluecoats were visible along the road. They came in two columns, their white breeches and the white facings on the buttoned-back skirts of their coats swinging steadily, as their solid boots trod heavily on the rough ground. They were marching at attention, eyes to the front, muskets at right shoulder. Above the heads of the first company, the shoulders and flushed face of Benedict Arnold rose to the extended branches of the trees, and his lips moved as if he talked to himself. His eyes looked blazing mad. Demooth's company of militia turned, all twenty-five as one, and took up the march again towards the fort.

At three o'clock the advance companies came out on the vlaie land at the great bend of the Mohawk. Half a mile ahead, the

walls of the fort stood square and brown above the grass, surrounding the low roofs of its four buildings. The sun, westering,
picked out the sticks of the stockade along the south wall facing
the army and shadowed the sally port.

But above this shadow, on the main or northeast flagstaff,
the new flag hung in its bright colors. Even at that distance the
men were able to make out the red and white stripes and the blue
field. The air was too still to move it.

Men were moving across the fields outside the gate; a wagon
was crawling towards the sally port from some abandoned tents on
the high ground to the north; nowhere was there any sign of war.

The gathering resonance of the deep army drums reached
onward past Gil's moving head. He saw a man spring up on the
sentry walk and the men in the field scramble to their feet. The
wagon halted momentarily. The horses turned their heads.
The banging of the drums grew stronger, putting a lift in the
tramping feet. The sun over the fort glanced in two sparks
from the shoulders of an officer. Man after man appeared
behind the points of the stockade. They seemed to stand in a
frozen silence. Then, suddenly, hats were scaled in the air. Four
cannon on the southeast station let loose orange bursts of flame
and the entire side of the fort was engulfed in a black cloud of
smoke. The thudding roars beat down the sound of drums; but
they swelled again triumphantly. At a signal, the fifers licked
their fifes and filled their cheeks. The shrill notes leaped upward,
piercing the valley.

As he walked, Gil watched the black smoke from the cannon rising over the stockade until it obscured even the flagstaff.
Then it began to drift gradually towards the north. When it had
vanished he saw the flag as it had been, limp against the flagpole.
But now it brought him a strange sensation that it was his and
that it hung in victory and peace.

Dr. Petry Sees Two Patients

The mid-October sun was already low over the southwest hills as Dr. Petry rode his old gray horse homeward past Herkimer Church. The fort looked almost deserted. Only George Weaver's family and the Realls were living in it now, besides the small remaining garrison; and George Weaver no longer needed his services. He was just as glad, for Emma Weaver had become so concerned about her son John and one of the Reall girls that she was unpleasant company. The jealousy of an ambitious mother: Emma, for all her homely face, had strong passions for all her menfolks. And then, he was tired.

He was so tired that if it hadn't been for Bell's abominable hen squawking in the sack behind the cantle, Dr. Petry would have been dozing in comfort.

He had long ago caught the trick of sleeping in the saddle. The old gray horse had a steadfast sort of ambling gait; his back was flat and broad enough to lay a table on, and he knew every road, bridge, ford, and footpath in the western half of Tryon County. People said that he knew every patient as well, and what was wrong with him, and what the prescription ought to be.

Now the doctor took off his hat and banged it behind him against the sack, causing an unexpected fluttering commotion. The silence was grateful and complete. He put his hat back on his head, tilting it well forward, and closed his eyes under the brim. Well, when he got home, he'd take his boots off and sit down and have a drink before the fire. A fire would feel good.

The cold was getting more pronounced and he thought they were not far off from frost. He could feel admonitory twinges in his wounded foot. It was a good thing people were getting in the last of the corn. They had got it all in at Andrustown; they were going to have a bee there next week for the husking and had asked the doctor to spread the word of it.

"God damn that God-damn hen." She was making a little moaning in her nose, or bill, or wherever it was. He hadn't wanted her. He was sick of poultry round the house, but George Bell swore she was a layer, and an egg in his rum, now . . . Well, a man oughtn't to complain. It was all Bell had to pay with. It was all the pay he had collected for his thirty-mile ride. He had started at four o'clock that morning, and here it was past five in the afternoon.

But a man ought not to complain. The crops were in and they were good this year. The price of wheat was soaring. Bill Petry ought to collect on a few back accounts this winter. It surely looked as if the war were over, now that St. Leger had skedaddled back to Canada, frightened off by the simple lies of Hon Yost Schuyler. Hon himself, the hero of the day, seemed to have returned to his American allegiance. Fort Stanwix was in first-rate order, with that unswerving, stolid Dutchman, Gansevoort, returned to the command. And best news of all, a battle had been fought with Burgoyne at a place called Freeman's Farm, three weeks ago, and it had been a stand-off. But they said the American army had swelled to twenty thousand men (that ought to make an earful for the King of England) and Burgoyne couldn't even run away. They had him, and they ought to lick him any day. There wasn't any question that Great Britain would have to give in and recognize American Independence. . . .

Let the damn hen squawk. The doctor grinned a little and the old horse pricked his ears and turned for the ford. They were home in half an hour; the horse amiably waiting while Doc uncreaked his weary legs and got them off, and then taking his own way to the barn. The doctor let him go. He entered his kitchen, carrying the bag, and sniffed at the pot on the fire. "What is it?" he asked the negro woman. "Dat's rabbit stew"— with turnips and cider vinegar and flour gravy thickening in the pan to a dark, rich, voluptuous brown.

"Bring me a glass of the Kingston rum," said the doctor, "and here's a hen for you to mind."

The negress, eager for something new, made little soothing sounds as she cautiously opened the sack.

"You ain't been 'busin' her, has you, Doc? She lay so daid. My Lawd, de messin'es' bird. My Lawd! Oh, de poor perty . . . Watch out! You make any of dem desperate messes in mah kitchen and you's gwine to fin' yo'se'f de makin's of de gravy, chickun!" Her black hand had the pullet by the neck.

The doctor chuckled, and went to the store to enter a note in his ledger against the government. He was writing it down in his careful hand:—

> 1777, October 14, George Bell, to one stab wound in thigh, and scalped. Dressed scalp twice a day. Under my steady care six weeks and this day visited and dismissed, cured . . . . £16.0.0.

A knock on the store door startled him. The evening was already growing dark, but he could hear a timid hand fiddling with the latchstring. "Come in," he called.

The door opened and closed quickly at the farther end of the store, and the doctor said heavily, "I don't see people this time of day."

The woman stopped short, timidly. He peered at her. But she wore her shawl all the way over her head.

"Who the devil are you?" he demanded.

"I'm Nancy Schuyler." Her voice was hushed and breathless.

"I know it ain't the time to come and see you; but Captain had to go to the fort after supper and Missis went with him; she wanted the air."

"Well, girl, what's that got to do with it?"

"I didn't want them to know I was here."

"Oh," he said. He began grumbling half aloud, something about the old business, and a man having supper, and he supposed he ought to look. "Well, what's the matter?" he asked aloud.

Nancy was flushing inside her shawl so painfully she thought something in her would burst. But at his question she turned white.

"I don't know," she said. "I've been being sick. Sometimes I can't hardly get to do my work in the mornings. But I don't know."

The doctor groaned and heaved himself out of his chair. He went to the windows one by one, closing the shutters, and then pulled in the latchstring. Then he took a sulphur wick and went out into the kitchen and lit it at the fire, and came back and lit the lamp on the counter. He cleared away some blankets, a jar of bear grease, a pot of bean seeds, and some Indian beads.

"Well," he said roughly, "get up on it."

Nancy was trembling so badly that she hardly had the strength to get up on the counter and lie down. When he touched her she shivered convulsively.

"That's all," said the doctor, going behind the counter to a pail and basin and starting to wash his hands, giving her time to get down and straighten herself out. "When did it happen?"

"In August," said Nancy in a hushed voice.

"*When?* I said."

"I don't know. It was the day they arrested Hon."

"Was it one of them?"

She nodded. He glared down at her through his frowning

long-haired brows. She was so damn good-looking and there were times when she almost looked intelligent. As now, when she was worried; the way she lifted her chin at him, chewing at her lip. "How in God's name did he get at you at Demooth's?"

"I went up to Shoemaker's that night."

"Where were you when we got there?"

"Out back of the barn."

"I bet."

Nancy didn't notice.

"He got away, they never heard him, but they chased me."

"Then you were the fellow they chased down over the fields? They shot at you?" Nancy nodded, and the doctor breathed through his nose. "They said it was a heavy man, about six foot tall, with long black hair! You must have run like blind destruction."

"I was scared."

"What are you going to do about this, Nancy?"

She was silent.

"You want that I should straighten it out, hey? Well, who was the fellow did it?"

"Jurry McLonis," she said in a hushed voice.

The doctor swore.

"That black-complected Mick, eh?"

"He was nice to me," Nancy said.

"He seems to have been. Well, there's no way I can get hold of him that I can see. He's probably in Niagara, Oswego at the nearest. I guess you'll have to button up and make the best kind of a job you can. I'll see Captain Demooth, if you like. You went up to find Hon, of course, and then this fellow took advantage of you." He was sarcastic.

Her eyes filled with tears.

"I did. But he didn't, Doctor. It just was."

"You'd like to marry him if I can get hold of him?"

"Yes, Doctor."

"Well, I'll see what I can do. Now get out. I want some rest. I've ridden thirty miles to-day." He put his hand on her shoulder, marching her to the door.

"But, Doctor?"

"Well . . ."

"You didn't say was I going to have a baby?"

"What do you think I was talking to you about? Yes. Yes. Yes!"

"Thank you, Doctor. When will it?"

"It takes nine months." He counted his fingers savagely just in front of her face. "May."

"It wouldn't be sooner?" she asked eagerly.

"Hell, no. The insides of a girl like you are just like a clock. Say May thirteenth at half-past twelve at night." He pushed her through the door, slammed it after her, and went back to his chair and called to Chloe. "Chloe, bring that rum here and then get me another glass ready. I'll drink the second one in there."

"Yes, *suh!*"

Chloe came sweeping in behind her bosom, the little finger of the hand that carried the glass cocked doggily. "Missis say supper's ready when you is." God help all doctors.

"Yes, Chloe. I want to sit down first. Here. And then by the fire. I want to edge up to eating."

"Yes, *suh!*" Chloe whipped her huge bulk away with her uncanny nimbleness. The doctor sipped his glass. The door was tapped.

"Who's that?" roared the doctor.

A woman answered. He didn't recognize the voice. "Go away," he shouted. Then he was ashamed. If he hadn't been so tired he could have sent her away, but being so tired he couldn't defend himself. He would work himself to death.

"Wait a minute," he shouted, and closed the door into the house. Then he opened the store door.

"I didn't mean to disturb you, Doctor."

He peered into the darkness. "Who is it?"

"Magdelana Martin, Doctor."

His face cleared suddenly. Of course, Martin's pretty wife. A bright girl. It would be fun having her after that half-animal half-wit. "Come in, Mrs. Martin. You mustn't mind my growls. Did you want to see me about yourself?"

"Yes, doctor. But it won't take long."

"Well, come and sit down. Do you like egg and rum? Never tried it? Where were you brought up? Taste some of my glass."

Lana obligingly bent forward towards his hand. It pleased him to hold something to her lips. She took it like a bird. He began to feel sentimental.

"Like it?"

Lana nodded.

"Chloe. Bring that second glass."

"Oh no, thanks, Doctor."

"Do you good."

"I oughtn't to now. That's what I came to see you about." She looked at him frankly. "I'm pregnant, Doctor, and I want to find out if after—after that time, I ought to be especially careful about anything."

"Lord, no. You're all right. If you want it."

"Yes, I do."

"That's fine. I'm eternally glad, I tell you. I was sorry about you. It's the best thing. It's woman's natural function, Mrs. Martin, and you're a fine healthy girl. When do you expect it?"

Lana, remembering, colored slightly; but she smiled at the same time.

"Sometime after the first week in May."

The doctor didn't even swear. He just popped out his eyes and stared.

He looked so funny that Lana started laughing.

"I must be kind of a ghost."

"Oh, no. No, indeed." He cleared his throat. "It just happens another girl is expecting almost the identical time. She was in just before you and I'm beginning to wonder what's been going on with my patients." He glanced at her. "Will you be round this district, then?"

"Yes. Gil said we'd stay till the baby was born. He seems so pleased." Her lips trembled. "Oh, Doctor, I feel as if I'd just begun living again."

"Yes, yes." Chloe knocking, he called her in. "Give that to Mrs. Martin. Drink it, girl. It's a good thing to celebrate with. Here's to Gilly or Magdelana second. Or both!" He laughed.

Lana laughed and drank with him.

"Afterwards, Gil talks about our moving back to Deerfield. He thinks we might get back in time to get our spring corn in. The Weavers will go with us."

"Fine," he said. "Fine. How's your husband, by the way? Arm troubling him any?"

"Not a bit. He came down to meet Captain Demooth at the fort. We thought it might be about their taking Burgoyne, and I walked along hoping I'd see you.

"We ought to be having news."

He showed her out and sat down again. A fine girl. He was feeling better. He was going to have a busy spring, though. Very busy. Well, he might as well get in to supper.

He went in and kissed his wife dutifully and Chloe served them. He was just starting on the rabbit stew when Demooth appeared.

"Doc," he said. "Can you come down to Ellis's at the falls? Right now. I said I'd drive you down."

"What's the matter, Mark?"

"There's been trouble in Jerseyfield. You know that man George Mount who wouldn't move down when St. Leger was at Oriskany?"

Petry nodded and stuffed his mouth full.

"Well, I saw him in Ellis's a few days ago. He'd brought his wife down to buy some things at Paris's. They were gone from home a week, and they'd left the two boys there with his nigger. Well, he went back. He found his place burned and the two lads scalped. One of them was still alive and he brought him out with the nigger. They hadn't touched the nigger. The boy's only seven and they say he can't live, but Mount wondered whether you'd come down."

The doctor dropped a morsel of rabbit.

He stared like a fish.

Then he wiped his mouth, and spoke slowly, "It isn't over, then."

Demooth's face was drawn and bitter.

"It was two Indians that used to stay with Mount. Caderoque and Hess. The nigger recognized them. There were some white men in the same party. They didn't do any scalping. They only shot the first boy."

"Did the nigger recognize any of them?"

"He recognized Suffrenes Casselman. And he said the head man was called Caldwell."

V

JOHN WOLFF'S JOURNEY (1777)

I

The Cavern

John Wolff had been in Newgate Prison for over a year, but he wasn't sure himself how long it was. He seemed to have lost the sense of time. There were days when he couldn't have said offhand whether it was *to-day*, or *yesterday*; they were days beyond track.

Sometimes he would catch himself saying the days of the week, "*Monday, Tuesday, Wednesday* . . ." Or the months of the year. There were many things he used to say. "*Lucy Locket, lost her pocket* . . ." Sometimes he would wake up some of the nearby prisoners and they would throw odd pieces of rock at his bed and yell. It was awful when the men yelled. It started the echoes whirling in the high air shaft, seventy feet high. It was fifty feet across at the bottom, they said, though you couldn't find that out by pacing because the water lapped against the far side. But at the top the shaft was four feet across with an iron grating fixed into the stone; and what with the smoke from the charcoal braziers one could hardly tell where the sun was in the sky, except at noon. A little before and a little after summer solstice, you could see the sun itself upon the grating if you waded out into the water far enough. You could even imagine a faint warmth from it on your head. John Wolff had felt it, and the next man, walking out, felt it also, but he started a convulsion, and they had to haul him out of the water for fear he would drown.

But when the men started yelling and got the echoes going, it used to make John Wolff feel sick. The voices would start picking each other up, catching and passing each other, and coming up and down, until the echoes managed to acquire individual personality of their own, having echoes of their own, and the echoes had echoes, and it went on and on, a bedlam that wouldn't die even when the trapdoor opened above the iron ladder and the guard looked down and yelled back furiously. Then the men would work on the echoes and a queer singsong rise and fall would be worked out that, even after everyone was tired, kept the echoes working endlessly.

It was like the eternal drip of water magnified. The drip of water had the same effect, when everyone was silent. At first you would notice it on the wall right beside you. Drip, and a pause; drip, and a pause. Gradually this soft impingement of a single drop would lead you to listen for drops farther away, and soon your ears would become attuned to drops much farther off. Then you would begin to be aware of the graduation of loudness that distance made, and all at once the drop you had first noticed would have the regular clang of a ringing bell. You couldn't then put it back into its proper equivalent in the sound of sense.

Sometimes a man would get up from his wet straw and work at the bare rock for hours to change the direction of an individual drip, so that its sound would be altered and thus restored to a sane proportion.

But one night when the men were making their singsong, it happened that the guard was drunk. Maybe the guard went a little crazy himself. Anyway, he opened the trap and fired his musket. They could all see him, fifty feet above their heads in the

lighted square of the trap, his furious red face, and the musket
pointing down like the finger of wrathful retribution. The bullet striking made no sound through the yelling voices and they
yelled twice as loud. Even John Wolff yelled that night. And the
guard lost his head entirely. He fired again and again, and finally
a ball ricocheted and killed one of the prisoners. He was the man
who had come in with John Wolff, the man who had beaten a
soldier for molesting his wife. But they did not notice he had
died till it was time for them to go up the next day.

They had to haul him up with a rope and carry him to the
smithy so that his irons could be taken off. Then he had been buried, and the commandant, Captain Viets, in a fury, had had half
a dozen men flogged, choosing the ones the outraged guard who
had committed the murder pointed out, and one man, who owed
the guard three shillings, was hung by his heels for an hour and a
half. Nobody had had any food for two days, but the guard did well
instead, for it was necessary for the prison to consume its full ration
of beef if the commandant were to receive his regular allowance.

It was odd, after that, to think of the dead man. He was buried in the prison yard. And yet he was sixty feet above any of
his fellow prisoners. He was decomposing somewhere underground, but they were still more underground than he. Waiting
for him to come down, one man said: "to come down in drops of
water." He embarked on an intricate calculation of how long it
would take the first drop to come down to their level. John Wolff
started watching the drops on the stone beside his bed.

Now and then long fiery discussions would start up over the
progress of the British army. They all knew one was on the way.
But the guard would give them no news. The guard struck a man
if he asked. They gathered from that that the army was making progress. But one night the commandant himself opened
the trap and they saw his bare legs squatting under his nightshirt as he yelled down, Did they want to hear about General

Burgoyne? They let the drops answer. But Captain Viets wasn't
to be stopped. "He's surrendered his entire army. Seven thousand
men," he bawled. "And the Hessians have been licked at Bennington, Vermont, and Sillinger has been driven off from Fort
Stanwix by Benedict Arnold. How do you like that? Hey?"

Purely from habit they started their singsong and he had to
slam the door shut. They kept the singsong up all night. They
knew now that all hope of their being rescued from the caverns
must be deferred. In fact it was a question now if they ever would
get out. People didn't even know where they were, a lot of them.
They didn't really know themselves. They were conscious only
of the vast formation of rock that was above them. Black tons of
it, they thought. A person wouldn't think of looking for a man
so deep down in the rock.

For a week afterwards they beguiled themselves by saying what
they thought of General Burgoyne. They imagined General Burgoyne if he were put down among them. They wondered if he
would be. But people like General Burgoyne, who made war and
brought Indians and wore epaulets and carried his private whiskey
with him, weren't ever put in places like this. Only a person who
preached in the pulpit for the King, or who said he was a Loyalist,
or who owed a new Yankee judge some money, or who hit a soldier
who was raping his wife—only that man was an atrocious villain.

2

The Drainage Level

Most of them thought John Wolff was going crazy. He was not
aware of it himself. Only he liked to repeat things he knew. And

he also dictated to himself letters to his wife every week, though he hadn't money to smuggle them out if he had been able to write them. He would ask her to write what she was doing and then he would say what had happened in the prison. The letters sounded pretty much alike even to himself. He got tired of them. The day after the captain delivered the news of Burgoyne's surrender, he wrote Ally about it; but then he could think of nothing to add. The Mr. Henry who had first welcomed him to the caverns asked what the trouble was. "I'm writing my wife, Alice," explained John Wolff, "but I can't think of anything new to tell her."

"Have you described this lovely home of ours?" said Mr. Henry.

"No, I haven't."

"Why don't you? Take a look around and see what there is to see."

Several men laughed, but John Wolff did not mind. It was an idea. He began looking round and made up his letter, about the air shaft and the beds and the queer beach of sand and the water. "The water is queer," he said, "the water keeps dropping down off the walls all the while and the water don't never get higher nor lower." He realized that he was saying something nobody had noticed.

Suddenly John Wolff came out of his daze and he had a long fit of the shakes. But they were not the damp shakes that everybody had. He was shaking with excitement. He went and looked at the water.

He said, "Has anybody ever tried to wade out there?"

"It's too deep," one of the men said.

"Has anybody tried to swim?" asked John Wolff.

A roar of laughter went up. One of the men reached out and rattled the chains connecting his ankle and wrist fetters. "Try and swim with forty pounds," he suggested. John Wolff stood in their midst looking at their faces, gaunt and filthy with rock dust and charcoal smoke and unwashed beards. It came to him that he must look like that himself. His hand went to his beard. He had never had a beard before. He had always shaved.

Then his eyes grew cunning. He felt them growing so and closed the lids lest the other men should see it, and he went and lay down. They were still making jokes about him when the guard opened the door and shouted at them to "Heave up!" for their exercise.

From his bed, John Wolff watched them clambering toilsomely up the ladder, their chains clashing against the iron rungs, as they fought upward with one hand and carried the night buckets with the other. The smoke from the braziers drew into the guardroom and the guard stepped away from the door. John Wolff lay there till they had all gone up.

"Hey, you!" the guard yelled. "What's your name, Wolff!"

John Wolff didn't answer.

"Come up."

John Wolff remembered all the filth he had ever heard and sent it up to the guard. The guard laughed. "All right," he said. "Stay down. Stay down for a week." Wolff was a harmless man, not worth coming down for and lugging up and flogging. He slammed the trap shut.

John Wolff got up. He clanked slowly down to the beach, looking at the water. Then he started rummaging in the straw beds. Some of the prisoners had bought pieces of plank from the guard, to put under the straw. He hadn't any himself because they cost a shilling a foot. Moving with the slow, half-hopping motion the irons forced him to use, he took down planks and put them in the water. They floated soggily. He got more. He laid them on top of each other, side by side. Then he waded out and straddled them and tentatively pulled up his feet. The planks sank under him and he rummaged for more. He finally had enough to float him and he tied them together with strips torn from his blanket.

He straddled the raft and pushed it out with his feet. He paddled with his hands. The weight of the irons made his hands splash no matter how careful he was. But he had only a little way to go to get out of the brazier lights.

John Wolff had thought a long time about which shaft to choose. But as he could not make up his mind he chose the farthest. When he entered it, the noise of his splashing diminished. The light behind him was circumscribed by the low ceiling of the shaft and the flat level of the water. Looking back, it seemed to him that he had come a great distance. He could not see far ahead, because the shaft made a turn. He paddled slowly round that, and then in the darkness that instantly became complete he felt the front of his raft strike the rock. The blow was very slight, but it almost knocked him forward off balance. He barely saved himself by lifting his hands and bracing himself against the rock wall. He realized that the drift was filled to the ceiling, and that there was no way out. He felt all round the water level to make sure and then tried to turn his raft.

There was not room to turn it in the darkness, and he had to back out. It was a laborious and painful process. His arms dragged and his legs had gone cold and numb, except for the ache the cold made in his ankle scars.

When he came back into view of the sand beach and the smouldering braziers and the mussed straw of the beds he had despoiled of planks, he was sobbing with exhaustion. He lay forward along the boards, eyes shut. From a vague sense of habit he started dictating a letter to Ally.

"The right drift is full of water so I can't get out that way. I shall have to try the other one. It is so hard to paddle."

Then it occurred to him that he could not wait another day. It would take almost as long to get fifty feet back to shore as to paddle into the next drift. In either case he would not have time to put the planks back under the straw. They ducked men who monkeyed with the beds of others. It took two weeks to get dry.

John decided to paddle into the next drift.

Again the splashing he made seemed to crash against the upward walls of the air shaft. But again the noise was shut off when he finally entered the second drift.

He had been working for an hour to cover his hundred feet or so of progress and the men should be coming down soon. He forced himself to keep at it until the last reflected light of the water was left behind. Then he came to a slight curve and continued round that, and then he stopped.

He had a sudden new sensation. The sweat was pouring out of his skin. It was the first time he had sweated for months. It made him feel weak, as if the whole energy of his body had been put to work at the process of creating sweat in him; but at the same time he felt an access of courage because he was able to sweat.

It gave his hands power to paddle on. Behind, and far away, shut off by the rock wall, he heard the muffled clanking as the men started coming down the ladder. He kept on.

It was dark now, and he was scraping the side of the drift. But he kept paddling. When he heard his name called behind him, the sound was dim and the echoes that entered the drift were mere whispers of his name,—*John Wolff, John Wolff,*—like voices for a person departing this world.

His arms lifted and fell and lifted. He had gone a long way. He was not completely conscious any more of what he was doing. He was quite unprepared when the raft struck a projection of the wall, dumping him sideways off the board into the water. His last flurry broke the wrappings of the raft and the boards came apart. He thought he would drown. Then he struck bottom. He stood up and his head came out of water. Against his wet face, in the dark, he felt an icy draft of air.

He started wading. The bottom was quite smooth, but the water deepened. It reached his chin. He knew that he was going in the right direction, because the air still drew against his forehead.

The boards were now out of his reach and it was too dark to see anything, anyway. John Wolff stood still in the water, thinking aloud: "Dear Ally, the water is up to my mouth. It is getting deeper. But there is surely air coming along this drift and I can't get back and I figure to go ahead. It is better to drown than to stand still in water. It is not very cold water, but it makes me shake some. Otherwise I am well and hoping you are the same. . . ." He drew a deep breath and took a full stride forward.

The water fell away from his chin, from his throat. He felt the cold air against his wishbone. He drew another breath and took still another step and the water dropped halfway to his waist. He shouted.

It was thin sound and it was drowned by his sudden threshing in the water. All at once he was reaching down, holding tight the chains to his ankles and floundering knee-deep along a narrow stream. The air was cold all over him. He went on for half a dozen yards and shouted again. There was light on the righthand wall. Faint, but actual light. Daylight. He turned the corner to the left and saw the dazzle on the water which now ran downhill quite fast through a small tunnel that seemed to narrow to the dimension of a large culvert. He had to bend and get on his knees. He took another turn as he dragged himself in the water, and he saw ahead of him the gray of woods in October.

But between him and the woods was a wooden grille.

It shocked and amazed him to find that grille after so long and baffling a distance. It seemed to him a malicious manifestation of the godlessness in man. In its way it seemed to him infinitely more wicked than the trial which had sent him to prison in the first place.

He dragged himself up to it and put his hands against the lower bar and rested his head on his hands. The shakes were getting hold of him again. He closed his eyes, and let go of his body.

He felt the grille shaking as he shook and opened his eyes. It came to him that the wood was old and the joints the crossbars made with the frame were very rotten. He braced his feet against a stone and threw his weight against the grille.

The whole business gave way, tumbling out under him down the steep hillside. He fell with it, with a last clank of his irons, rolled over down the slope, and came to rest with his face upward, seeing the breast of the hill against the sky. He lay still, weeping.

A cold rain was falling steadily.

3

The Hammer

In two hours, he had covered a mile and a half through the woods. He had got beyond caring about the noise he made. Just after sunset he struck a path that led him into a pasture.

The pasture sloped toward a valley through which a road ran. On the road were a small house, with a barn attached to it by a woodshed, and a building that had a chimney and looked like a forge. The wet bricks shone faintly in the light from the house window.

He stopped with the rain beating down on him, and stared at the lighted fire visible through the kitchen window. The whole world smelled wet and cold.

Presently a man came out of the house and went to the barn.

John Wolff could hardly credit his good luck as he saw the man lead out a horse and take it to the front door. The man waited there while a woman came out, shawling herself against the rain, and let the man help her onto the pillion. He then mounted in front of her and yelled to someone in the house to bar the door till they came back.

John Wolff could hear the answer in a negro voice. It sounded like a woman's. The man said they would return in two hours. He kicked the horse to a trot down the road in the rain.

As soon as he was gone, John Wolff started down the hill. He went first to the building he thought might be a smithy and opened the door. There was enough light in the banked fire to show him the anvil and the hammers and files.

He was like a man obsessed. He made no effort to be quiet, but picked up one of the hammers and started striking on the seams of his wrist bands. It was hard to get a good swing. His aim was clumsy from the cold and the hammer head kept rolling off the iron onto his arm. But the seam cracked finally and he pulled the iron loose. For a minute he stood looking at the rusty imprint on his wrist. Then he slowly flexed his arm and raised it over his head. He felt as if his fist could strike high heaven.

He broke the other fetter handily enough and began to work on the anklets. These were harder to break, for it was almost impossible to keep his leg on the anvil within striking distance of his arm and yet get a free swing with the hammer. Finally he thought of tipping the anvil over.

It took all his strength to do it, and the anvil teetered a long time before he could overbalance it. It fell with a terrific crash, but John Wolff did not seem to notice the noise until the screaming of the negro woman in the house broke in on his hearing. He lifted his chin and automatically started to join her—as if it were the singsong starting back in the cavern.

Then he remembered what he was doing and held his ankle against the anvil and swung the hammer with both hands. The seam smashed all to pieces. He broke the second at the first blow.

The negress was still shrieking over in the house, and John Wolff listened to her, cocking his head a little, while a queer look of cunning came into his eyes. The hand which held the hammer began to swing with little jerks. Suddenly he became aware of the motion of his hand and stopped it. He stood quite still with a growing excitement on his face and his breath coming and going sharply.

At his first step he nearly toppled over on his face. He recovered himself, went out through the door, and closed it behind him with great care. He stopped for a moment more, turning his head towards the house as if he tasted the fear in the black woman's shrieks. The hand holding the hammer twitched again. He started for the house.

Habit forced his legs into the queer hobbling gait the shackles had trained them to; but the release from the weight deprived them of all sense of balance. He kept lurching forward; and on the second hop he measured his length in the mud of the yard. He scrambled up and forced himself to move more slowly until he had got onto the porch. He knocked on the door. At the first blow the woman stopped screaming.

He forced his hand to knock gently again: this started the woman off on her shrieks and he listened with his ear to the panel. When she stopped, the house was quiet as death, with only the sound of the rain dripping from the eaves.

The drip distracted him until he heard the woman moan inside the house, and then the sound of her feet sneaking towards the back.

It infuriated him. He raised the hammer with both hands and smashed it against the door. It was an eight-pound hammer and he broke in a panel in half a dozen blows. He became intoxicated with the destruction he was making of the door and forgot all about the woman. He knocked in the panels one by one and hammered at the bar behind them until the bar fell away, brackets and all. Then he opened the door and walked into the warm lighted room.

A fire was burning on the hearth and a kettle was steaming. He had not seen a kettle with a spout for more than a year. The hammer dropped out of his hand, clanked on the hearthstones, but he let it lie.

He thought he was standing steady, but he was weaving on his feet. He had forgotten all about the woman; even when she stole down the stairs to see what had become of him he did not hear her. She stood there watching him with her round eyes rolling the whites in her black face and her lips hanging flabbily open.

She saw a man so thin he hardly seemed like a man at all, with a mess of light brown hair showing white streaks and hanging down on his shoulders, and a matted beard and a torn shirt, and rotten wet trousers and bare feet. The feet were bleeding. She saw the blood on the hearthstones. And then she saw the fetter scars on his ankles and wrists.

"Lan' sakes," she breathed. "You ain' no booger, is you?"

His chin lifted, but his glazed eyes did not shift from the kettle.

"If I could have a cup of tea . . ." He sat down weakly.

The negress was a young wench. Her curiosity and sympathy were powerfully aroused. "You one of de prison people," she announced. She nodded as he did not contradict her. "Soon as I lay my eyes on you, I say, 'Leeza, dat am one of de prison people. He got put in jes' like ol' Massa. Dat's what he did.'" She came forward. "Co'se you can have some tea. And I'll jes' bring along some eatables wid it." She flurried about her job, chattering, "Dey takes away de hones' people. Dey takes me away f'um 'em. Mistah Phelps he join de Committee of Safety and he get to be a powerful big man and he get me when dey lock up my ol' fambly.

He's gone to de Committee to-night. He used to go by hisse'f, but since he tuk to fallin' off de horse, Missis she jest obliged to go wid um. Lot of de wimmen folks has to now. Dey have their party and de man they have theirs."

John Wolff shivered with the tea. It scalded him, but the taste was so penetrating that he could not stop drinking. Warmth flooded him. The negress stood beside him, offering a collop of cold pork and a slice of heavy bread. She watched him with a kind of pride.

"Whar you gwine?" she asked softly. "You cain' stay here."

"No," said John Wolff. "No, I'm going to Canada."

"You cain' go dat way." Her courage made her swell herself. "Here," she said. "I'll fix you fo' de trip. I use' to shave old Massa."

John Wolff was content just to sit still. He let the black wench work on him. She shaved him with her master's razor and she hacked his hair short. Then she went upstairs and rummaged an old pair of shoes, and a coat and a pair of trousers.

"Dey're kind of monst'us-lookin' on you," she said, "but you got to cover up dem iron marks."

Her face was proud over her handiwork. She was a clean-looking wench, quite young.

"Thanks," said John Wolff. "Maybe I better be going."

"You take me wid you?" she suggested, making eyes at him.

He said, "I've got to find Ally."

"I he'p you."

"No," he said. "It's too far. I'm going out to Niagara."

He felt strength coming back to him. He hadn't thought of going there, before. But it occurred to him now that he might be able to find someone who had heard of Ally at that place.

The negress sighed.

"I guess you wouldn't take me along nohow. I guess I'll have to stay here."

She watched him sidelong.

"I'll jes' have to chase myself out into de rain," she went on, as he made no sign of having heard her. "Less'n you bash me wid de hammer a couple of times."

He shivered.

"No."

"Den I got to say you bus' in here and took dese things. Oh, Mr. Phelps, he'll lay into me. But he ain' so smart. Ain' none of dese folks is so smart."

John Wolff took his eyes from the hammer. He turned and went out into the rain. The negress called after him shrilly:—

"You take de lef' branch, Massa. Dat bring you into Canaan bimeby."

He went along without a word.

4

Niagara

It was late in November. A light snow had begun early in the afternoon. It drifted down without noticeable wind. But a heavy gathering of clouds in the northwest promised a storm to come.

The walls of the fort looked brown and close to the earth. Even the stone mess house and its two flanking towers seemed to huddle between the parallel expanses of lake and sky. The river and the flat of the land were gray with cold. The smoke from the barracks and the officers' mess rose thinly against the falling flakes and mingled with the smoke from the small Indian camp and the huts of trappers, traders, and independent rangers that made a straggling kind of village beyond the gate.

The people moving down desultorily to the shore seemed

pinched. They talked a little and they stared with a kind of deferred eagerness at the small sloop that was approaching the dock. The freeze was due on the lake any day; and the sloop was the last boat expected till next April.

In their scarlet coats a squad of soldiers from the fort marched down among the Indians and whites and took their station at the head of the makeshift dock, grounding their muskets and standing at a chilled attention. The dock could not bear the weight of many people. At the last boat's arrival it had been swamped and the outer end broken off. But nobody was expecting much of this boat. . . .

John Wolff, staring from the foredeck, watched the low land creeping towards the boat. His eyes wandered slowly over the crowd. He had been six weeks reaching Niagara. He was gaunt and footsore. But his pallor was disappearing.

He had crossed the Hudson at the mouth of the Hoosic and made his way to Ballston village, and there, by chance, he had picked up two men named Kennedy and Miller who had come down from Saint John's to visit their families. They had used their leaves to cross Champlain and tramp sixty miles of enemy country, and the day John Wolff arrived they were planning to return. They took him with them. At Saint John's he learned that Major John Butler was in garrison at Niagara. There was talk that Butler was recruiting a regiment of his own. Nobody knew very much about it, but John Butler was a good man to serve under. If you liked frontier service.

As the boat drew in, people began calling out to the sloop from the shore, and the deck hands yelled back. Nobody said anything in particular. There was nothing to say.

The boat warped alongside the dock and the business of unloading began at once without ceremony, for the master wanted to get back across the lake before the freeze.

He moved up beside John Wolff now, smoking his short pipe, the tail of his red knitted cap hanging down beside his cheek.

He said, "Here's where you get off." His voice was sarcastic in spite of his joke.

John Wolff said, "Maybe I can get to see Mr. Butler and he'll lend me the money."

The master spat over the side.

"I'll collect it next spring. Ain't no hurry." He sucked his pipestem free and stared westward across the river. "That's where you'll live, I reckon."

"Over there? I thought that was the fort."

"'Tis. But that's where they're building the barracks. They ain't got any nails. I just as soon not see Major Butler till I got some nails to bring him. Maybe I'll have them next spring."

John Wolff looked west. Well back from the river shore a low line of log buildings raised bark roofs against the sky. They looked even more bleak, even more huddled under the snow, than the fort.

"God," said the master. "I don't see how folks can stand to live here. They must be crazy. Ain't more than eighty women in the whole place, barring the Indians. And what I've seen of most of them, they wouldn't raise the hackles of a six weeks' rabbit." He looked companionably at John Wolff. "You said you'd lost your wife, didn't you?"

"Yes."

"That's how it is," nodded the master. "You lose them, or something." He gestured with the pipe. "But out here you can't even find them. I don't see why you came out here."

He cocked his head.

"By God," he said, "hear the falls. When they sound that way I begin to expect ice. Well, you might as well get off. I ain't spoiling my time here much longer."

The dock was now loaded with boxes and barrels—shoes, flour, rum, powder kegs, pork, salt beef, blankets.

"I wish there was some nails, though," said the master. He shook hands. "There's a couple of the new rangers coming down. Maybe it's Butler. Guess I'll get below."

Wolff saw three men in green coats coming down to the opposite shore. They got into a skiff and rowed over the river. In the stern sat a short gray-haired man with a red face and black eyes and a long Irish lip to his mouth.

"Grange!" he shouted. "Mr. Grange. Did you bring me any nails?"

"No, I didn't."

The master stuck his knitted cap out of the cabin.

"Why didn't you?"

"I couldn't get them. That's why!"

"Did you hand over my requisition?"

"Yes, I did!"

Major Butler's face was black with suppressed rage.

"Didn't they say anything?"

"They said nails was scarce."

"That's a lie."

"I ain't saying it ain't, am I?"

"What did they say?"

"They said, 'Jesus Christ, you'd think the old bastard was going to win the war with a kag of nails.'"

The major drew in his breath. Then he seemed to collapse back into himself and his eyes became helpless. But he started to grin.

"Why couldn't you tell me that in the first place?"

The master grinned back.

"Well, I didn't just want to crucify you, Major." In his relief, he prodded John Wolff to the side. "Here's a man wants to jine on with you, Major. Come all the way from Simsbury Prison in Connecticut. I thought he might kind of take the place of a kag of nails. He's kind of built like a nail, ain't he?"

John Wolff flinched at the major's direct stare. Then he drew in his breath and stared back.

Butler lowered his voice.

"What's your name?"

"John Wolff."

"Wolff? Wolff? I seem to remember the name."

"I kept store at Cosby's Manor."

"Oh, I remember you now. You want to join Butler's Rangers?" His voice had a kind of pride at the name. As if the organization were something tangible, like hand work.

"Yes, sir."

"And you've been in jail?"

"Yes, sir. I was arrested a year ago last August."

"That's a long time." The red face quieted. "Get into the boat, man, and come back with us. This is Sergeant McLonis. He came from your part of the valley. You may know him?"

John Wolff shook hands with the young man as he got into the boat. He felt shy. He thought he might feel better when he had a good warm uniform coat like McLonis's. He studied the uniform. Green coat, with crossed buff breast straps. The lining of the coat was scarlet. The hat was a skullcap of black leather, with a leather cockade over the left ear and a brass plate over the forehead. The waistcoat was of heavy green woolen, and the full-length leggings of Indian tanned deerskin. It was a good uniform, Wolff thought, fixed for use in the woods.

"Sit down," said Major Butler. "We'll row back, lads. I don't want to see Bolton to-day." He turned to Wolff. "I hear that Thompson's house and your store were burnt by the rebels, Wolff. It's too bad. It's going to be a long while before you can get back, I guess. With the mess St. Leger and Burgoyne made of it. We can't get any government support for a full-sized campaign. By God, we can't even get nails from them."

The skiff smacked over the slight ripple. The drip from the oars had an icy sound. The air was raw and piercing.

"We'll have to do the best we can ourselves," said Butler. "How old are you, Wolff?"

"Fifty-odd."

He was holding his breath to ask. He couldn't seem to get the question out, he wished so desperately to ask.

"That's not too old if you're in sound health. But it's hard work, campaigning through the woods. If you don't feel up to it, I can give you work round here."

"Thank you, sir. I ain't so strong now. But I'll be all right. I used to have good health."

The other men kept watching him. Then he saw that Major Butler was looking too. He saw that his sleeves had drawn back showing the iron scars.

"You've had a hard time," said Butler. "Maybe you can't forget it, but it's better to try to, Wolff." He raised himself stiffly as the boat landed on the shore. "They've kept my wife and children down there. I can't get them exchanged."

"Yes, sir." Wolff's face started to work. He blurted out, "Do any women come here from the valley, sir?"

"Some got through." He was brief. "Why?"

"You haven't seen my wife—Alice Wolff? Ally, she's called. Kind of a pale woman? A little younger than me?"

Butler shook his head and glanced away. The men shook their heads too. McLonis said, "It would be known if she was here. It would be bound to." His voice was gentle with sympathy.

"Can you send letters down there, ever?"

Butler said, "I can send one under a flag, when a flag goes.

But a letter's not likely to reach her unless you know where she is."

John Wolff, walking behind him towards the low log barracks, said, "Yes. I'd forgot. The store got burned, didn't it?"

The snow began to drive a little before the first breath of the wind.

BOOK II

THE DESTRUCTIVES

VI

GERMAN FLATS (1777-1778)

I

Paid Off

Though there had been several light falls at German Flats early in November, the snow had not lasted. But now, as Lana looked out from the kitchen window of Mrs. McKlennar's house, it seemed to her that snow must surely come soon. She had prayed for snow, as all the valley had prayed for it since the murder of the Mount boys in Jerseyfield. Deep snow alone, in the woods between themselves and Canada, could ensure their safety. Until it came, no family living beyond easy reach of the forts could feel secure; and many of them had once more moved into German Flats. At Mrs. McKlennar's, Gil and Lana had moved into the stone house, while their own log house had been turned over to Joe Boleo and Adam Helmer. Both were homeless men, but Gil said that in the event of a raid, he and they together could hold a stone house like McKlennar's safe as a castle.

For two days long lines of steely clouds had been moving out of the northwest. People in the valley could feel no wind; there was no visible sign of it except the clouds, or the sudden bending of the trees on one of the higher hills.

As Lana looked through the window she saw Joe Boleo emerge from the farmhouse, drawing on his foul pipe and studying the sky. She herself was impelled to join him in the yard.

"Do you think it's going to snow?" she asked.

He held his position, eyes aloft, the sparse hair on his half-bald head shivering as if with cold. "Women are the devil," he replied at large.

"Why, Mr. Boleo! I only asked a question."

He turned a sober face on her.

"That's so," he said in obvious surprise.

Lana flushed, then laughed. Her cheeks were bright, against the gray background of the winter trees; her eyes shone. She enjoyed this shambling, indolent, gangling man for all his musky smell that reminded her of pelts. Now she made her voice sound humble: "Well, is it going to snow, do you think, please, Mr. Boleo?"

Joe kept grinning to himself. He wasn't like Adam Helmer, who hated the sight of a pretty girl carrying a baby in her inside because it seemed to take the point out of her good looks. Joe liked any pretty face, and he had grown especially fond of Lana's.

"Sure," he replied. "It's going to snow hard. There's a real storm coming. Feel the cold. No, you can't feel it on your skin. You've got to feel it in your nose. You can smell a big snow before it comes. And look there!" He pointed his long finger at a gap in the tumbling rollers of the clouds. "Just watch there a minute."

As Lana came close to sight along his finger, Joe's eyes slid sidewise. He thought she looked happy to-day. She was a real nice girl, he thought, the way she brought him and Adam things to eat and cleaned their house out for them. "You keep watching." He moved his shoulder so that it touched hers and he could feel the round soft solid curve through her dress. He even felt her draw her breath.

"Oh, the geese?"

"Geese." He nodded. "They've been going by all day. Higher than hell and straight south."

She saw them come and go, leaving the clouds in their wake, a rippling line.

"And there's another thing," said Joe. "Keep still. Don't even breathe."

He liked to see her when she held her breath.

"You mean that singing sound? What is it?"

"That's high wind. You can hear it that way in the westward country where the land lies flat. Down here we get it when the wind blows high."

Her lips were parted, quick and red to breathe the cold.

"Now you'd better get inside," he said. "A girl in your shape has got responsibilities. And anyways, Gil will be hungry for his dinner. He'll want to get started right after."

"Oh yes," she exclaimed. "The paymaster's coming to-day."

"Yes," said Joe. "We're going to draw militia pay. By God, we ought to be rich. Rich enough so I can buy you a present maybe." He eyed her with sly eyes.

"Oh, thank you, Mr. Boleo. But you ought to save your money."

"I ain't a hand at saving. Why, sometimes I've made thirty pounds and spent it all in a couple of throws in Albany."

"Throws?"

"Well, maybe I got tossed around by the girls a little." He spoke with a kind of boastfulness. "Down there the girls get at a man like me. He can't hardly help it." His wrinkled face expanded. "God," he said, "the things that have happened to me, though!"

"Why, Mr. Boleo!" Lana was bubbling with delight.

"Well, I hadn't ought to talk this way to you."

"I'm sure a girl wouldn't rob you. Not up here."

His eyes became lugubrious.

"That's the trouble. Women are the devil."

Gil and Adam came in at noon. Gil with the cart piled high with firewood to add to the corded tiers already in the woodshed, and Adam carrying the hog-dressed carcass of a buck on his broad shoulders. The three men hung up the deer in the woodshed, and all came up to the stone house for dinner, sitting down at the table with Mrs. McKlennar, who derived a monstrous satisfaction from all Joe's stories. She was delighted also with Adam Helmer. Any big man could put a flutter under her ribs, and Adam, with his coarse, good-featured face and long yellow hair, pricked her mettle.

The kitchen reeked of their tobacco-tainted clothes, and there was a wet bloodstain on the shoulders of Adam's deerskin shirt. Beside the two, Lana always noticed Gil's cleanliness with pride. But to-day he was as excited and noisy as they. All three men were bursting with the prospect of ready money coming in. They hadn't decided what to do with it, but Gil had earlier said to Lana that they would need the money. What little cash he had had dwindled away to nothing, and he would not receive his year's salary of a hundred and twelve dollars until April. Militia money would be handy to buy some necessary stuff for clothes, shoes, and store flannel, out of which Lana could work things for the baby during the winter. Besides, their powder was getting short (and the price was high).

Lana and the negress, Daisy, served them with samp and pork, and slices of dried squash fried in lard and flour, and apples baked in maple sugar. In the midst of dessert, Mrs. McKlennar got up suddenly and fetched a bottle of sack from the cellar, pouring them each a glass.

"My husband always celebrated on pay day," she explained. "I ought to start you boys off right."

Joe Boleo rolled the liquor on his tongue.

"I'd like to have met your husband, ma'am. He must have had some right good notions," he said politely. But as they went out of the door, he whispered to Adam, "I'll bet that horny Irishman got him a good stiff drink of rum to wash it out with."

Mrs. McKlennar watched them go. "Look," she said to Lana, "it's started snowing."

Fine white flakes were driving down upon the valley. Already they had made a thin dusting over the earth and the three men tramping abreast towards Fort Dayton left muddy footprints in it.

"Lord," said the widow, "they're three fine boys." Then she flung her arm round Lana's shoulders and her horselike face softened. "Come upstairs," she said. "I was in the attic before dinner and I found some things I thought you might use for the baby."

Lana wondered what Mrs. McKlennar could possibly have that would be useful to a baby.

The house grew warmer as they went up the stairs. Then when they passed through the trap into the attic, the air was cold again. It was darker too, with the snow falling outside the one small gable window. The loose boards clattered under the widow's tread. She bent down suddenly.

"I got these out," she said.

Lana looked down. She saw a cradle and blankets, a miniature plate, and a silver spoon.

The widow breathed harshly through her nose. Two bright spots had flushed her gaunt cheeks.

"One of Barney's soldiers made the cradle, and Barney got the other things and showed them to me on our wedding night for a joke. I remember how we both laughed. But we never used them. I don't know why. We tried the best we knew, too."

Lana said softly, "I think it's awful nice of you to let me have them."

"Nonsense," snorted Mrs. McKlennar. "Don't get sentimental."

She rubbed her nose.

"Take them down to your room. No, I'll carry them; you better not lift such heavy stuff."

The snow was driving hard against their faces when the three men forded West Canada Creek and came in sight of the fort. The number of footprints on the road made Adam laugh.

"I bet the militia never turned out as good before."

Joe Boleo grinned.

"How much do you think the pay amounts to?" Gil asked.

"Plenty," Adam replied. "I don't know how they figure it, but we commenced in June, going down to Unadilla, and we was pretty busy right along till Arnold went home. It's pretty near three months, up here. Down east the campaign was longer. Maybe they'll pay us for the whole campaign."

They encountered George Weaver going through the gate. He was looking so solemn and embarrassed that they asked him what was bothering him.

"Why," he said, "Mrs. Reall wanted to come along to collect what was due on Kitty's pay. She asked if she could come with me. And Emma didn't like it much on account of John and Mary Reall. But I said it wouldn't be neighborly not to take her. She's just ahead."

Mrs. Reall, looking surprisingly cheerful, turned back to greet them. She had her daughter Mary with her. Mary, Gil thought, was growing into a nice girl. There was a still, brown earnestness in her eyes he didn't expect to see in any Reall. And she looked a little appalled by all the men round her and her mother, a little ashamed that her mother should have come, perhaps. Gil held his hand out, introducing his two companions to the Realls.

Adam smiled at the girl and said to the mother, "You come with us, ma'am. We'll all go in together."

The soldiers' mess had been turned into the paymaster's office for the afternoon, and a couple of the garrison were assigned to guard duty at the door. When Adam worked a lane for his companions through the crowd, the soldiers barred the entrance.

"When does this paying start?" Adam demanded.

"When he gives us the say-so." One of the soldiers jerked his head back toward the door.

They stopped and chatted with the men round them. Some people eyed Mrs. Reall and Mary curiously, but nobody took notice of them more than to say "How do you do."

Then a pompous voice cried sharply from the messroom, "All right, lads." One of the soldiers turned and bawled, "Do I let in the whole shebang, mister?"

"No! Let in twenty or so, that's all the room will hold comfortably; and then close the door until they're paid off. Then let in another lot. We can't freeze, you know."

With Adam's broad shoulders clearing a path, Gil and Weaver and Joe and the Reall women were among the first to enter.

The room seemed dark after the swirling whiteness of the snow outside. And the snow itself, when one looked out at it, seemed to lend to the darkness. A log on the hearth was disintegrating into a mountain range of coals. With his back to it, in a black coat, red waistcoat, and soiled white tie, sat the paymaster, come up from Poughkeepsie at Colonel Bellinger's request. He had the roll of the regiment before him and the colonel's muster sheets, and these he was comparing and checking against each other. He finished as the men crowded in and barked a little in his throat. "Line up," he said. "Line up down the table. I can't handle you all at a time."

As he stepped up to the table, Gil noticed that Colonel Bellinger was in the room. The colonel looked grim. Gil could not understand why.

"Hey, there," said the paymaster. "What's that woman doing in here?"

Mrs. Reall, who was third in the line of men, stepped out of it and drew herself up before the paymaster.

"I came to collect my husband's pay."

"*Hak, hak, hak,*" went the little man. "No women allowed in here, ma'am."

"But I said why I came."

"What's his name? Why isn't he here himself?"

"His name is Christian Reall," said Mrs. Reall. "He's dead."

The little man examined his list.

"He ain't marked so. Now, ma'am, will you kindly get out?"

"Just a minute." Colonel Bellinger came forward. "I don't know why Christian Reall isn't marked on the list as dead. But he was killed and scalped. I saw him myself. I think his widow is entitled to his pay."

The little man looked angrily at the colonel.

"I'm sorry," he said. He seemed to swell with the importance of his position. "I'm appointed to pay militia wages. I don't pay dead men." He gave his little barking cough.

"But where do I get his pay? I'm entitled to it. I'm his lawful wedded widow," said Mrs. Reall.

"Claim against the state. Swear it to a justice. File the claim. *Hak, hak.*"

"But I ain't got any money. I need it. I've got children, mister."

"They're no business of mine."

"Look here," said the colonel. "Surely he earned his money as well as any man could. I'll swear to the time of his death and to Mrs. Reall's being his wife. Can't you pay her for his time up to then?"

"My dear sir," said the paymaster. "We don't do things that way. I've explained the procedure. The claim will be filed before the auditor-general and passed by an act of Congress."

"Jesus Christ, listen to the bug-tit."

Adam Helmer's voice was heavy with admiration.

"Sir?"

No one answered.

Colonel Bellinger took Mrs. Reall's arm. "I'll see you get it, and I'll see you have something on account." He led her to the door.

The men turned back to the paymaster, who was clearing his throat. "Give your names," he said. "I've got the money sorted for you."

A man named Hess and a man named Stoofnagle drew pay. Then it was Gil's turn.

"Gilbert Martin."

"Company?"

"Mark Demooth's."

"Oh yes, Captain Demooth's. Here you are. The account's different from the other companies. You get no pay for the five days' service with General Arnold. You were requested to act as scouts for Continental troops. Therefore your expenses will be due you from the United States Congress. You will receive it in due course. That makes your pay $4.27 instead of $5.52, which is the regular private's pay for last summer's militia service in this regiment."

A stunned silence fell upon the room. The two men who had already received pay began counting it. Gil looked down at the money in his hands. Four dollars and twenty-seven cents. Suddenly his throat swelled. He thought of Oriskany. He didn't feel like waiting for the others to be paid. He went towards the door.

Perhaps the little man felt uneasy, for he started coughing again as Joe Boleo gave his name. The gangling woodsman slouched over him.

"Thanks," he said. "It sure is fun to lick the British."

The little man coughed.

"It's the regular pay according to the regulations of the New

York Congress. Militia serving in its own precincts draws pay only for actual duty. In your case, expedition to Unadilla—fourteen days. You were then discharged. Expedition to relieve Fort Stanwix, unsuccessful—five days. You were again discharged. Expedition under General Arnold, successful—five days. Twenty-four days at twenty-three cents a day is five dollars and fifty-two cents. It seems plain to me."

"You said the word, bug-tit."

Joe followed Gil out into the snow. The roofs of the buildings were whitened. The stockade looked black against it. The air was getting colder; soldiers blowing into their hands on sentry walks made clouds of steam that whipped rapidly away among the swirling flakes.

Adam Helmer overtook them. He was laughing loudly. "I ought to have brought my purse along."

Gil had nothing to say. He went out through the fort gate and turned left for home. The snow was making fast.

The other two men walked in his footprints, Joe at the tail end, muttering to himself.

"What you talking about?" Adam demanded.

"I was wondering how in hell those buggers got to be that way."

"How in hell what buggers got to be what way, Joe?"

"Those Congresses."

2

The Snow

The snow lay two feet deep when the storm cleared. The weather remained cold. Winter, thought Emma, had come to stay; and she walked along on her husband's bear-paw shoes with a feeling of complete security.

She hadn't told any of her menfolk where she was headed for. She had merely announced at dinner that she was feeling house-bound and that a romp in the snow would do her good. The cabin seemed awfully small for four large people: herself; and George, a solid man; and John, nearly a man; and now Cobus was catching up to John. All three had looked at her from over their plates; all three had said, "All right, Ma," grinning their boys' grins. She was proud of her menfolk, and as she left the house she had a comforting assurance that they were proud of her. Even John was, preoccupied though he had been these past months with the Reall girl. She felt sure that he had no idea that she was going to Fort Herkimer, with the deliberate intention of talking to Mary Reall.

She had not seen the girl since they left Fort Herkimer to live in the cabin on Peter Weaver's place, where George had agreed to give his time and the boys' for a third share in the farm produce. She had had no intention of ever seeing the girl; when George announced that he was going to take Mrs. Reall to the pay-off, Emma had been hurt, as if by doing this George were taking John's and Mary's side against herself. But as soon as he told her how the paymaster had treated Mrs. Reall, all Emma's natural wrath had risen blazing.

"I wish I'd been along," she said; and "I wish you had, Emma," said George. "The girl seemed to take it hard, ashamed to see her Ma put down, and all."

"It's a wonder you men didn't stand up for them."

"There wasn't nothing we could do. Bellinger was there. He couldn't and he's the colonel, too."

She let it drop. But the idea came to her, now that she felt the Realls had been put upon, that maybe Mary could be talked into a state of sense. It was just as important for the girl, after all, as for Emma's John, not to hasten to a wedding.

As the blood started flowing through her body, she pulled the shawl back from her gray hair, drawn uncompromisingly to its honest knot. The cold whipped up the color in her cheeks. Her stride was masculine; the weight of the snowshoes made her swing her feet. She ought to have been wearing trousers. She kept kicking the loose snow from the webs. It was powdery and it glittered when she flung it off. She trod down hard to hear the squeak, putting her weight forward over her knees.

God hadn't granted it to Emma to have a pretty face; but she had a fine, well-working body. Walking by herself made her conscious of its strength and vigor, feeling herself in every part; yet to tramp this way, for the sheer muscular delight, was an expression of her underlying femininity. Where pretty women who had looking-glasses might have examined their naked selves, Emma, instead, renewed acquaintance with herself by means of what she called her romps.

To Mary Reall, who saw her swing through the gate, Emma's hearty good health was an expression of ruthlessness. The girl was afraid of her. She knew instinctively, even as Emma asked to see Mrs. Reall, that John's mother had come down to talk to her.

They had a corner of the northwest blockhouse, which they shared with two of the Andrustown families. Mary's mother was lying on one of the bunks originally built for a garrison. A fire in the centre of the floor gave all their heat to the three families. The smoke had blackened the rafters and the ceiling boards. It found its way upwards through the trap and out of the spy loft when the wind allowed. It was a miserable place.

"It's surely nice of you to call, Emma!" said Mrs. Reall.

"I was just out for a walk." Emma looked round her. No chance in here to talk to Mary. "How are you making out?"

Mrs. Reall explained that Colonel Bellinger had lent her money out of his private purse. He was such a nice man. So gentrified.

"Yes," said Emma, forcing herself to be agreeable. "But you can't live like that forever. What will you do next year?"

Mrs. Reall was not disturbed.

"I've sent in the claim for damages that Kit made out before he got killed. I guess I ought to hear of it pretty soon. I showed it to Mr. Rebus White, and he said it ought to be honored by the state." She used the words with importance.

"Who's this Mr. White?" demanded Emma.

"He's the corporal here. He comes from Massachusetts. He's a real nice man, Emma, and thinks maybe he'll settle here. He's talked about my keeping house for him."

Emma gave a neutral grunt. "George talks about making a claim. How much did yours mount up to?"

Mrs. Reall began to shuffle among her bedding. "I've got it somewhere. The copy, I mean. Oh yes, here it is. It comes to two hundred seventy-one pounds and fifteen shilling."

"Two hundred pounds! How on earth did you figure it out that way?"

"Jeams MacNod wrote it out for Kitty. One dwelling house, a hundred pounds. One grist mill, twenty-five; one bedstet, four-teen pounds; one hollan' cupboard, seven pounds." She rattled off the items, having them by heart.

Emma's jaw fell open.

"But that ain't so. They never was worth that much in hard money. That bed. And that hollan' cupboard—you never had one."

Mrs. Reall was not disturbed.

"I've always wanted one. Mr. MacNod said it was best to put down everything, because sometimes they cut down on the list."

Emma stared.

"Well," she said suddenly, "it's not my business." Her eyes swung round to Mary. The girl was watching her. Her thin face was dark red. "My Lord!" thought Emma. "She's ashamed."

"You see," continued Mrs. Reall, "we got our government

now, we ought to use it for ourselves. That's what Mr. White says, too."

"It's how you look at it, I guess." Privately Emma considered it stealing; she never had trusted the Realls. But she must not show her thoughts too plainly. "How are you fixed for the winter?"

Mrs. Reall laughed.

"I guess we'll make out all right. They're sending food to us, and we all share in here. It's hard on the little ones, not having shoes. They've started chilblains early this year. But there's always Providence."

There always was for people like the Realls. Out of her sense of shame, Emma said, "There's some shoes Cobus has outgrown. I'll send them down." She got up and said good-bye. She was glad she had two miles to walk home, to get some fresh air into her.

"Good-bye," called Mrs. Reall.

Emma halted outside the door to put on her snowshoes.

"Can I help you, Mrs. Weaver?"

Mary had come out with her.

Emma said, "I guess I'm still young enough to put them on myself."

The girl drew back as if she had been slapped. Her thin face was quite white. It made her eyes seem larger.

"Mrs. Weaver," she said quietly. But her voice had the tenseness of a child's. She looked like a child in her ragged, poorly sewn petticoat. Even in her rough home-knitted stockings her legs were thin. Emma felt like pitying her as she would pity any miserable object, man or beast.

She got up on her snowshoes and stamped her feet to settle them in the laces.

"What is it, Mary?"

She looked at the child's face. She wasn't getting enough to eat. She didn't look half strong enough for her age; why, at her age Emma had had a breast and shoulders, whatever her face looked like. The girl drew a shuddering breath.

"You mustn't think too bad about Ma. She doesn't think that's stealing. It's just the way she thinks."

Emma said heartily, "I know. She can't help it."

Then she was caught by the girl's level gaze. Whatever else you could say about her, the girl was brave. She was scared to death, but she was standing up to it. Emma liked that.

"What you mean is we're all the same, don't you? You think so because John and I are in love with each other."

"In love." The words bounced from Emma's lips. "What do you two children know about love?"

"What did you, Mrs. Weaver, when you were fifteen?"

"Nothing," said Emma, staunchly.

"But you got married, didn't you?"

The girl had spunk. Her forehead looked too big for her face, thin the way it was. And her underlip was shaky. But she looked straight at Emma, and Emma, instead of getting angry, found herself liking it, to her surprise.

"Have you ever been sorry?"

"Not more than most women, Mary."

"Has Mr. Weaver?"

Emma suddenly smiled. "He hasn't said so." She drew a deep breath. "Will you walk to the gate with me?"

The girl came. The snow seemed to pinch the calves of her legs as she stood beside Emma outside the palisade. She held her hands in front of her and waited for Emma to speak.

Emma thought for several moments before she did speak.

"Do you and John see each other often?"

"He comes down when he can." Mary's narrow face was wistful. "It's not often, though."

"John's a good boy." Lord knows how they make love here in this place, Emma thought.

"Mary, I don't mean to be hard on you. Or on John. But you don't know anything about getting married."

Again the small half-smile.

"I know," said Emma hastily. "A girl has to begin. I'm thinking of you, too. How do you know you love John? How do you know John loves you? I'd hate for either of you to be unhappy."

"We ain't scared to try, Mrs. Weaver."

"I know. I know. You're never scared at your age. Or at least not much. Do you think you could make a good wife? Look at it that way."

Mary's eyes were downcast.

"I don't know. I'd try. I never had much chance to learn things."

"I should think you hadn't!" Emma's contempt got the best of her. "Not but what your ma means well, though—in her own way."

She saw the girl taking another deep breath. Again the eyes met hers in the same level regard.

"I wanted to tell you, Mrs. Weaver, that John and I are in love and we aim to get married. If he wants to keep on we'll do it anyway." Her color rose. "You couldn't stop me without killing me, Mrs. Weaver."

"Look here," Emma said. "I'm not going to stand in your way, Mary. But I want you both to be sure. Will you promise me not to get married for a year?" And meeting the eyes again, "Or not to get married without talking to me first?" Her mouth twisted. "After all, it wouldn't be easy to do that up here, without banns, you know."

The girl gulped.

"We won't."

Emma believed her. "Don't start crying," she said abruptly.

She swung away for home, making her best pace. She didn't look round; but kept at her work. She felt her blood restored to its racing beat that she enjoyed so much. She was flushed and breathless when she got back to the cabin, barely in time to start the evening meal.

She looked at John's face. "You can't guess where I've been," she said, laughing at him. "No you can't. I've been to Fort Herkimer seeing the Realls."

John blushed.

"I thought it would be nice for John to go down for me with some shoes of Cobus's I promised. I thought while he was there, he might ask Mary to come up here for Christmas dinner."

John had turned brick red to his eyes. George merely looked at Emma. He was used to her, but there were times when he felt quite confounded. Her and her romps in the snow!

3

March Thaw

The winter in German Flats passed uneventfully enough. The cold continued and the snow lay deep. Unmilled wheat was fetching seven shilling a bushel at Little Falls, where Ellis's Mills were grinding for the army. Almost every week the mills shipped flour to Albany. When men heard stories of how the Continental army was starving at a town called Valley Forge, they found it hard to believe. They wondered where the flour was going to.

Occasional sleds that passed along the Kingsroad, Lilliputian in the still white world of snow, reminded the inhabitants that men were yet in garrison westward at Fort Stanwix. The sleds stopped the night at Fort Dayton and in the morning put out for the upper fort. They followed the river—hauling on the ice, a natural road. They went without a guard. The army, evidently, had no apprehensions. It made the people feel secure. Some even came to regard the murder of the Mount boys as the trick of drunken Indians; nobody could tell what to expect from a drunken Indian, least of all the Indian himself. It made them discount the story of the presence of white men. That depended entirely on a nigger boy's say-so.

Up at McKlennar's, the further the winter drew along, the more Joe Boleo expressed misgivings. When he and Adam and Gil were off hunting in the woods, Joe would keep tracking along the ridges spying across country, and he never came to a creek bottom without following it for half a mile or so. "Indians always hang to water," he said. Gil and Adam Helmer often laughed between themselves at the figure he made, bent over on his snowshoes, his long neck outstretched, among the snow-loaded balsams. "You can laugh, you twerps," he would say. "But wait till the snow starts going down." Then he would strike off and bring them to a deer yard, and he and Adam would begin killing deer.

Adam was inclined to be jealous of Joe's shooting. In his own overflowing strength, Adam liked to strike cross-country, running on his shoes for miles on end. But it was generally Joe, mousing along quietly, who found the deer. Then he would squat with his narrow tail just over the snow and wait for the other two to come back to him. He would sit there, looking at the deer, who always herded to the far side of the yard and stared back at him with their queerly lambent, soft eyes. Joe would be saying, "Poor pretty, poor pretty," in a sorry sort of way, like an old woman sort of woodpecker, according to Adam, and then when Adam came he would begin shooting. Sometimes the two of them would shoot three or four deer, picking out the marks, calling the shots, pacing off the distance from the wall of the yard, before Gil stopped their senseless killing.

"Hell," said Joe, "we got to keep our eye in."

"Shoot at a tree," suggested Gil.

Adam would be scornful.

"You can't waste powder and ball on a tree."

Then they would select a doe that looked fairly plump and kill her and leave the rest lying in the yard. They kept not only McKlennar's well supplied with meat, but carried deer after deer to the forts and the settlement, sometimes selling the meat, sometimes giving it away. It depended on how they felt.

In the evenings they would light a great fire in the farmhouse fireplace and lie in front of it, drinking rum and molasses; and Gil generally went down to sit with them. Up at the stone house the women took to sewing things, making things for the baby, spinning. Mrs. McKlennar liked to spin with her big wheel, working the treadle with her vigorous foot, and making a hum come out of the whirling wheel like a voice against the cold. They talked about things, the three women together. Daisy, the negress, sitting in a corner, made a rug for the baby with a wooden crochet hook and strips of rags. Daisy couldn't sew and she was unhappy till the widow suggested that she make the rug. She embarked upon a five-foot project, though what good a five-foot rug could do a baby nobody ever figured out, unless it was Daisy herself. Sometimes she had a run on a color, like red; sometimes she spent two nights with brown, as if that were the color of her thoughts. It was no place for a man.

In the farmhouse atmosphere, with the two woodsmen sprawled on the floor before the fire, telling each other tales or passing off the gleanings of the valley news, a man could be at ease.

Joe liked to have the news from Herkimer's house. There was talk of raising a monument that had been voted down in Albany, on the other side of the house from the well. Five hundred dollars had been mentioned. Joe went down one day to see how it would look. He returned still wondering.

In February there was some talk that the Massachusetts garrisons of Dayton and Herkimer were returning to their homes, having completed their service. It was said that they would leave in March. No provision was made for their replacement. Demooth and Bellinger had been down to Colonel Klock in Palatine to organize a protest. All three men were trying to have Fort Stanwix abandoned and the German Flats forts strengthened. But Congress would not listen to their arguments. Congress held that Stanwix was the strategic defense of the valley. It was intimated that they might send some troops to Cherry Valley, but that was all.

Joe shook his head about it.

"They might just as well have nobody at all. You wait till the snow leaves. You'll see."

"See what?" asked Gil.

Joe grunted. "Indians."

Adam Helmer said skeptically:—

"They got their medicine up there at Oriskany."

"That's the trouble. If they hadn't been whipped so bad, they might wait to come along with the next army. But the way it is they won't wait. They'll want to get their face back. They'll be after scalps. They won't care whose. They'll feel they've got to. Hell, boy, I've lived with the Senecas, and I know."

"You lived with them, Joe?" asked Gil.

The gangling trapper stretched himself on the hearth to kick over a log with his heel. The fire blazed upward, pouring a ruddy light across his sweating body. The room reeked of the men's smell, tobacco, and rum. It was stifling hot, making them all drowsy, and Joe's voice was pitched low.

"Oh yes, when I was young, like you lads. I used to trap up the Chinisee. I got along real good with the Senecas. I had a wife out there. She was a real nice girl, too." He stirred himself lazily. "They ain't as light as the Mohawk girls, but they're thinner."

He drank a little rum and turned his eyes thoughtfully on Gil and Adam. Outside the wind had died down with the coming of darkness, and the burning of the fire was even and fierce.

"I never knew you was married, Joe."

"Sure," said Joe. "I stayed there with her four years, without ever coming out." His reminiscent grin made his face unbelievably homely. "My God, that girl was set on me!"

Adam was crouched in front of Joe. The firelight made his big face scarlet and threw lights in his long yellow hair. He held his glass in both hands, his hands passed over his knees. The shadow of his broad shoulders filled all the opposite wall. Now he turned a facetious eye on Gil. Gil grinned.

But Joe knew what was going on in their minds. He said seriously, "You ought to have been along with me, Adam. You'd have liked it. Gil, now, he's a settled kind of man." He drew his breath, slowly, and belched. "Along in those days, a white man was just about the finest thing that could happen to an Indian girl. It made her important in her town. When I first went out there, the Indians treated any white man like he was one of their sachems. Like a big bug, see, come visiting. They gave him a house in the town and then they sent in all the best-looking girls so he could take his pick and feel comfortable while he was staying. It was a good idea. Only it wasn't so easy making your pick. Some of them girls was pretty nice." He poured himself another drink and stirred the molasses in with his finger. "Some trappers got the idea of staying and then going off for a day and coming back and beginning over. There wasn't any harm in that. It don't matter what a girl did till she got married, see? But it didn't happen that way to me. I got to the Chinisee Castle, the one they call Little Beard's town now, and they sent in eighteen handpicked ones. But right away I knew the one I wanted. I knew she'd suit me fine. I was young-and-coming, see, and I suited her too. Don't laugh, you timber beast. It's truth. She stood with the rest of them looking on the ground, the way they all done, but as soon as she made out all the rest was looking down, she just took one look at me and it fixed me. Boy, she could throw her eyes at you!"

"I believe you," Adam said.

"Go to hell. I reached out at her and I said, 'You, you me fine!' I hadn't learned the language then. But she understood all right. The others went out, leaving just her. And as soon as they'd gone she just looked up at me, kind of scared and shy. I was pretty young, I guess, but it made me feel big.

"She didn't come only to my shoulder and she had braids reaching down to the middle of her thighs. She wasn't only medium dark, too, and she was pretty in her best clothes. She had on a kind of red overdress, what they call Ah-de-a-da-we-sa, and a blue skirt with beadwork on it. She was a great hand with beadwork. It was what made her come high in marriage. And her pant things was doeskin with more beading on the foot."

"She come high?"

"I didn't know how I could pay her ma," Joe said seriously. "I didn't have only a bare stake. No beads for trading. I needed everything I had, see? The girl's ma was something big. One of the chief's lines. They keep their family on the female side. The way the girls act up they've got to if they're going to keep the children anywhere near straight. . . . But I've got away from me and the girl. Soon as we was alone she signed for me to set down by the fire and take off my shirt. She took a bone comb out of her belt and started combing my hair. She greased it and picked out the ticks and took pains where it was curled. She liked them curls. I had fine curly hair, you know."

Even though Joe looked so serious, they had to laugh. They stared at the shiny expanses of bare scalp between the remnants of his past beauty. Joe rolled over and turned his back and lifted his shirt to let the heat strike against the rum in his belly.

"Lord," he said over his shoulder. "When I went to bed with

her it was pretty dark. But I didn't have to see her to know she was good-looking. I told her in the morning I'd like to marry her."

"I thought you said you couldn't speak the language."

Joe looked hurt. "You don't have to when you've done that to a girl. I just said so, and she caught on all right. She colored some. Most Indians don't show color, but that was one of the things about her. That and teaching her to kiss. The way she caught on. You can fool around with all the heifers between here and Albany if you want to, but you won't know just what teaching a wild Indian to kiss is like. Well, she said she'd like to fine, so I said fine, and she said what did I have to buy her with? Well, I opened my pack, and she went through it like a dog after a rabbit. She shook her head. She made it plain there wasn't anything good enough. I felt bad, and she looked sorry. Then she clapped her hands."

"Yes," said Adam, "she clapped her hands."

"God damn you, Adam. She did." Joe began to look embarrassed. "I'd been getting dressed and she come up to me and put her hands on my waist and made the motions I was to take my drawers off. I had red flannel drawers."

The two young men guffawed.

"Honest to God," said Joe. "I told the chief how I felt, and I got him to take them round to the old lady and she went near crazy over them. Later I heard she'd gone right in and tried them on. They was some tight, but they stretched enough. Though she had to rig a kind of tassel in front when she wore them in the turtle dance. She made a little bark box for them and hung them over her bed. They were still in good shape four years later when the old lady led the Okewa for Lou."

"What's that, Joe?"

"It's the woman's all-night Dead Song."

"Your girl died?"

"Yes," said Joe. He blew smoke against the logs and watched the flame snatch it up the chimney. "After we got married, I and

Lou went up the Chinisee. I built us a hunting cabin up there. It was good beaver country and a wonderful range for fisher. And she was a first-rate woman for a man. Knew how to take care of me. She was the only woman I ever had around that didn't get on a man's nerves. When I felt like laughing, she was ready to bust with it herself. Never saw anybody so always happy. She wouldn't call me Joe. Just Boleo, only she couldn't ever say the B. She called it Do-le-o." Joe's face was deeply concentrated. "And when the trap lines weren't bearing so good, she didn't make a lot of talk—what a white woman would call distracting you. She minded her business. I knew she was around, that's all. She was good to have around. And she never got lonesome. Seemed as if I was good enough for her. Of course we'd go down to the Castle every once or twice a year. I had to trade my fur pack, see? . . . It was a good life. And healthy. The way she kept me healthy. Used to make me hemlock tea to keep my skin open. Her cooking was Indian cooking, but she learned a few things, to please me. I told you she learned kissing. But it was a funny thing, she never got to be like a white woman. She was always shy about the way she acted with me. She wouldn't wash with me in the crick. Sometimes it got me mad. I never saw her naked in plain light. A bear kilt her while she was berrying." Joe drank and drew a breath. "The queer thing was we never had no children."

"What's queer about that?" Gil asked.

"Why, those girls could have children easy as letting go a crock of lard. John O'Beal now. He come out there and traded; he bought my furs. He married a girl too, and had a mess of children. One of them's got to be a chief. His name's Cornplanter."

"You said John O'Beal?" Adam asked.

"Sure, he was quite a lad, too. But he soured on it. He came back here and lives down the valley somewhere."

"Near Fort Plain?" suggested Adam.

"Sure, that's the man. I ain't seen him in some time."

Joe Boleo lay full length on his back, draining his glass.

Gil asked, "What did you say her name was, Joe?"

"Well, her Indian name was Gahano. Means something like Hanging Flower. But I told you I called her Lou. You ought to have been out there in those days, Adam. You'd have got along good. But now they ain't so friendly about white men. You can marry all right. But they don't trot the girls out for you any more. I quit myself when Lou died. . . .

"But that was the way for a trapper to live. All you had to do was run your lines, and you had a nice cabin to come back to, and your dinner cooked, and a woman to mend your clothes. You just lay around, and got up warm in the morning. It didn't cost you a cent." He looked at them again. "Most trappers came home in summer. They cleared out with the furs and spent their money, and the woman took care of herself while they was gone. Some kept two families going. But those buffaloes never spent the summer the way I did. We'd take trips, her and me, and lay around fishing. We'd go off where there wasn't anybody, not even the tracks of anybody but ourselves, for three months. We'd build a summer shanty and she'd plant corn. Yes, sir. You'd just lay around listening to a big fish jump and wondering if it was worth the bother putting the worm in the water. Lou worked all the time we was on our vacation, readying hides and putting up quitcheraw against the winter. I whittled her a little press for making the cakes in, which tickled her a lot. And then she'd go berrying to make pemmican. That was when the bear got at her. An old she-one with a couple of cubs. I spent a while tracking them and I killed the lot—" Joe paused and spat. "But, hell," he went on, "that's not what I set out to tell you. Indians ain't no good. This country would be a whole lot better off without any Indians. We'd be better off right now, I tell you. And I wouldn't be setting here listening to that drip off the roof."

Adam Helmer stirred himself. Adam had been wishing he had been born in a good time of civilization so he could have gone out to the Indian country. His full lips were compressed and wet just thinking of it. A little lithe hard girl like Joe's Lou, right now, would suit him fine. "Drip?" he asked.

"Yes," said Joe with scorn. "Drip. The thaw's commencing."

Gil got to his feet. He went to the door of the cabin, opened it, and stood there, leaning out.

The wind had turned to the south. He felt it damp against his face; he could feel it even with the outrush of overheated air from the kitchen.

"You're right, Joe," he said over his shoulder. "It's the thaw beginning. Sugaring ought to start early this year."

"Shut that door!" yelled Joe. "Do you want to freeze us?"

4

Fairfield

Towards the end of the month, when the sugaring was in full progress and the smoke from the sugar bushes made pale blue wavering ribbons against the hillsides, a horseman left the Snydersbush stockade and rode full gallop the eight miles south to the falls, turned west along the Kingsroad, and flogged his way through the slushy ruts as fast as his blowing horse could lay foot to the ground.

The spattery thudding of his hoofs was audible in Mrs. McKlennar's sugar bush, high though it was above the road. They were boiling for the fourth day and some of the Eldridge people, the Smalls and the Caslers and the Helmers,—Adam's cousins, Phil, his wife Catherine, and son George,—were attending. The women were knitting by the fire, minding the kettle. Adam, on his own initiative, was bringing the wood for the fire and hanging round the women as much as possible. He was wearing a new hunting shirt, colored after the pattern Morgan's Riflemen were supposed to wear. It was of heavy white linen with long green thumbs along the sleeves, the double capes, and the bottom hem. He looked inordinately handsome in it; his yellow hair was carefully combed, and he had shaved.

Gil and Captain Jacob Small and George Helmer were hauling in the sap on hand sledges from the trees where the boys gathered it from the small pails. It was a sunny, windless day, warm enough to make sitting in the open pleasant. The steady drip in the pails was like the ticking of a clock, as if the trees together combined to mark the passage of the time. The distance one could hear a drop fall in a bucket was surprising; it was audible even above the women's voices.

Of all the men, only Captain Small, and Adam and Joe Boleo, had brought their guns. Adam and Small had left theirs in the little bark shanty before the kettle. But Joe was prowling the woods. They did not know that he was making a cast three or four miles to the north and west. They would have laughed if they had known. The snow still lay more than five feet deep in the woods. Even with snowshoes it made heavy going.

When they heard the horseman coming up the road, Gil and Captain Small left their sledges and walked to the edge of the bluff. From there they could look down on him. The horse was floundering, but the man's arm rose and fell with pitiless fatigue. Jacob Small took one look.

"That's Cobus Mabee. He looks scared." He took his hat off and rubbed his grizzled head and stared incredulously at Gil.

Adam, seeing them move to the edge of the bush, left the women and joined them.

"What's going on?" he asked.

Small said, "Cobus Mabee just went up to Dayton."

Adam laughed.

"Maybe he's after Doc."

"He didn't look to me like that. Did he to you, Gil?"

"He was spoiling his horse," said Gil.

Adam's face sobered.

"That's serious."

They looked at each other.

"Do you think we ought to move down out of the woods?"

Adam said, "No. Joe's back there in the woods."

Small said, "One of us ought to find out what's happened. Gil, there's George Helmer on the edge. You send him down and let him ride your mare up. No sense scaring the womenfolks. It's the first party of the year."

Adam went back to the shanty. He got his gun. "I'm going to see if I can get a partridge," he explained. "You ladies have got wood enough?"

"Oh yes, Adam." They smiled at him. They went on with their talk. All except Lana. Suddenly Gil found her staring at him. He forced himself to smile. But she wasn't deceived. And he shook his head and put his finger to his lips.

His heart was like something shrunk inside himself as he watched her face. He thought, "What's it going to do to her?" Her face went deathly white. Then suddenly her chin went up and she said something in a quick high voice to Mrs. Small that made the latter laugh and pat her red hair. Mrs. McKlennar nodded, looked at Gil and smiled. Mrs. McKlennar had the instinct for such things. He guessed that she had caught on even before Lana.

He made himself go back to his sledge and haul it to the kettle. Nobody had missed George Helmer. The sugaring continued. But he and Captain Small managed to bring the children to trees closer to the fire without anyone's noticing, and themselves kept a watch on the woods. They would hear Adam shoot if anything went wrong, and he would hear Joe. Now the drip of the sap seemed startlingly loud.

Two hours passed before George Helmer returned. He came quietly without fuss, and without fuss Small and Gil joined him at his trees. He told them at once.

"The destructives have been in Fairfield. Indians and Tories. The whites was all the Fairfield people who went off before last August. Suffrenes Casselman, and Countryman, and the Empies. They killed little John Mabee and they took everybody else prisoner but Polly. She got away from the Indians. But she seen the rest. They've burnt every house and barn in the town. There ain't a thing left."

George Helmer was an earnest young man, and he was scared.

Captain Small said, "Did anybody see which way they went?"

"They went out on the Jerseyfield road," said George. "Cobus Mabee had it all planned to move down to his uncle's place in Indian Castle. He's moved his wife and the baby down and he was going back to get Polly and John and the cow. He stopped for dinner in Snyder's. When he got up to Fairfield the houses was still burning. Hadn't nobody known a thing about it, anywheres else." He caught his breath sharply and looked over at the shanty. "Do you plan to stay here, Jake?"

Jacob Small said, "Yes. Ain't no sense in moving till Joe or Adam comes in. Don't you go acting scared, George. We got to make sugar. We got to make enough for next winter, same as we'll have to do our planting."

"My God, Jake!" The young man's face was pale. "How can a man go out and plough and plant with *them* in the woods?"

"I don't know," Small replied. "But either you got to die hungry or you got to raise food."

George said unsteadily, "That's right." But his eyes kept rolling towards the woods. It was he who spied Joe and Adam coming in abreast. Joe was wringing wet with sweat and snow. He came over to Gil and Small and rested the rifle butt on the toe of one of his snowshoes.

"Where's George been to?" he asked, and pointed to the horse lather on the inside of George's pant legs.

They told him.

"That's good," said Joe.

"Good?" cried George Helmer.

"That's what I said. If they hadn't gone there, they'd've come right down here. They had an open camp six miles back. I guess they wanted to make sure of Fairfield before they hit so near a fort." His eyes were owlish. "There was about twenty of them, nine Indians. They struck out some time yesterday for the northeast."

The five men stood together a moment.

Joe asked, "How much more boiling have you got to do?"

"We could finish in a couple of hours."

"I guess you might as well finish," said Joe.

"You don't think they'll come back?"

Joe pursed his thin lips.

"Not that particular bunch, maybe. Maybe nobody right off, either. I've took quite a circle and there weren't no signs. This time of year, jays holler easy."

5

At Demooth's

Nancy was inside the house when the news of Fairfield was brought to the captain by a soldier from the fort. She had just finished clearing up after dinner, and in the silence she heard the captain go out into the warm sunshine and she heard every word the man told him. When the captain came in she saw that he was worried. He looked almost frightened to her.

"Where are you going?" he asked sharply.

"I'm going to give this to the pigs, sir."

She held a plate of food scraps, and she stared at him with wondering blue eyes.

"Pretty good food for pigs," he said irritably, but Nancy forgave him that. With the doctor, the captain had stood up for her against Mrs. Demooth. She couldn't have borne it otherwise. All day long Mrs. Demooth was after her with stinging, small remarks. Mostly low, unladylike things about her shape, how big her belly was, and how bastard children always showed more—things Nancy would never have believed Mrs. Demooth capable of saying.

"Men are fools," Mrs. Demooth said. "If I had my way you'd be turned out. Girls like you ought to be whipped before the town. But your own mother wouldn't have you round—I don't blame her—and the men say you couldn't starve. Men all take a sneaking pleasure in it. They always do if the girl's young. Get out of here. Get out of my room, anyway, if you won't get out of my house."

Nancy knew she was big, but it had seemed natural at first. The soldier had been a big man, and she was a big girl, and sometimes she thought the child would be big even if he was lawful. But as time went on and the captain seemed to notice her more, the sight seemed to make him irritable with her, and she began to think that what Missis said must be true.

Hon Yost laughed about it. Hon Yost would pat her belly as if he were patting the child itself.

"I'll bet it's going to be a dinger of a boy. Just like you and me, Nancy. But we get fun out of life."

Hon Yost had had a wonderful time the first half of the winter.

He had never done less work in his life. For a long time every-body seemed glad to talk to Hon. Men slapped him on the back wherever he went and stood him drinks. He had been a regular public hero and generally drunk. But he was a harmless drunkard and came home every night to the barn, where he shared the stall with Mr. Demooth's horse. Nancy took him out what scraps of food she could steal. That was the plate's destination now.

But lately nobody paid much attention to Hon. At first he had been unhappy about it; disbelievingly, he would stick his face into Shoemaker's tavern, or the place across the river, and say hello. Once he even started the story of how he licked Sill-inger with his wonderful account of Arnold's army. He got to where he said to the Indians, "Can you count the leaves on the trees?" Meaning, of course, that Arnold's army was as big as crea-tion. But they kicked him out of the tap. He hardly ever got a drink. He once thought that if he enrolled in the militia he would get popular again, and saw Captain Demooth about it. But the militia were disorganized. Captain Demooth said Colo-nel Bellinger was trying to have new companies organized. New officers were needed. Over half the old ones had been killed.

Captain Demooth was sorry. He said that he appreciated Hon's patriotic sense and that as soon as the new organization was complete he would be proud to have Hon on his own com-pany's roster.

At first Nancy was happy about it. While Hon had been a public figure she hardly ever saw him, but now that nobody else would talk to him, he hung around the Herter place. He seemed to like to talk to her. He was pleased when she asked shy ques-tions about McLonis. McLonis was quite a man. The Butlers thought high of McLonis. Some people thought it likely McLo-nis would get to be a commissioned officer some day.

"Yes, Hon. But what is he like?" asked Nancy.

Hon poked her.

"Gee, *you* ought to know!" He burst out laughing, flinging himself back in the straw so that his long hair gathered chaff. Hon had a nice voice, for all he was dim-witted like herself. She loved to hear him laugh, and she smiled a little herself. Sitting in the cool light of the barn window that day, Nancy looked like a goddess of fecundity. With her yellow hair down her back and the lids of her eyes full and her lips half parted in the remnant of the smile, she might have been the original mother. Hon always made her feel that her accident was a distinction.

But now that he was on the subject of McLonis he liked showing his familiarity.

"Jurry," he said, "he's a fine, ruthless man. That's quite a word. I heard Major Butler call him that. I was right close to Major. It was the night we camped at the Royal Blockhouse coming down here."

"Do you think we'll ever see him?"

"I will," said Hon.

"But I've got to see him, you know."

"Well, maybe you will."

"Do you think he'd like me now?"

"Say," said Hon. "If you ever got to Niagara you'd be just about the queen of the company there, Nance."

"What do you mean?" She was breathless.

"Why, there's not a white woman there looks half of you."

"Oh. Then he might marry me out there."

Hon suddenly was silent.

"Mightn't he, Hon?"

"Well," Hon shook his head wisely. "If he gets to be an officer, maybe he wouldn't."

"But you said he would."

"That's when he was a corporal."

"Yes, but I'm me, aren't I?"

"Yes," said Hon. Hon did have a few ideas. He had seen

enough to know that an ambitious man would not marry a girl like his sister. The trouble with Nancy was that she had been happened on by an ambitious man. He liked Jurry and he wanted to keep friends with him. And it didn't seem important.

"But I've got to get married," Nancy said urgently. "Mrs. Demooth says I am the living sin."

"Old Clem said he'd marry you."

Nancy shuddered. "I couldn't marry Clem. He always smells so sour every morning."

"Listen, Nancy. I used to say for you to marry. But now I don't know. Out there at Niagara lots of the women ain't married. They're nice women too. Some of them in the officer barracks. Maybe you could get in the officer barracks."

"Couldn't you take me out there, Hon?" she pleaded.

Again he slapped her belly.

"With a load like that, Nance?"

"I can walk all right."

"If you had it on your back, maybe." Hon laughed at his own joke. But Nancy looked as if she were going to cry.

"Sometimes I get scared you'll leave me here."

"Why shouldn't I?"

"I get so scared, Hon. *She* keeps talking at me some days. She says it makes girls awful sick. She says sometimes they die—bad girls do. It ain't like having honest children."

For the moment Hon was troubled. He was fond of Nance, in a way. After a minute or two he said, "I don't believe you'll die."

She was called to the house by the tinkle of the captain's bell, to Hon's immense relief. She was the devil to reason with. He took himself away from the barn before she could return.

Nancy had thought of late that Hon was getting restless. As the snow softened towards the end of March, and mists rose in the valley, he had been acting more and more uneasy. He kept making excursions into the woods. At last he spent a night away.

Nance was terrified. But he had come back the evening after; he was in the barn at supper time when she carried out his plate of left-overs. He was sitting on some straw he had raked out of the mare's stall, whetting his hunting knife on his boot sole. She thought he looked excited.

"I found tracks where a party had been across West Canada Crick," he said. "Three or four days ago."

"A party?"

"About twenty. I guess they was some of ours."

"Ours, Hon?"

He was impatient with her. "Sure. What do you think? From Niagara, maybe?"

"Oh, Hon! You don't want to go with them?"

Immediately he was sly.

"How could I go with them? They're way the hell off by now. I wish I knew where they went to, though."

In her relief she wanted to please him, and she repeated everything the soldier had told Demooth. But as soon as she was done, she saw that she must have been dim-witted. Hon didn't say anything at all. He reared up like a dog and looked through the open door towards the woods.

"Please don't go, Hon. Not till I'm through."

When he didn't answer, she sneaked back to the house. She thought if Hon went she would surely die.

He was gone in the morning. Clem told her. Clem was feeling pretty grand; he had thought for some months that things were bound to come his way. With that damn fool out of reach, maybe he could work on Nancy.

The way she drooped in the soft morning sunlight, there in front of him at the barn door, he felt lustful. He didn't want to be a lustful man, particularly, but he thought what a damn fool he had been to be drunk that night when Hon was captured. Any sober man could have horned in on the game.

"Don't cry, Nance. You've always got me to look out for you." She just looked wilted.

"Do you know he's gone, Clem?"

"Yes, he told me to tell you good-bye." Seeing her frantic glance at the woods, he laughed. "He didn't go north. He went by Unadilla. He'll need to get food in the Indian villages. Him and Indians get on good. He'll be all right."

"That's why he didn't ask me for any." Nancy gave a small miserable nod.

Clem said harshly, "You needn't figure on catching up with him. He'll be going like a wild hog. You couldn't ever keep up with him, girl."

"Why?" she said like a child.

"He don't want anybody catching up with him." Clem thought it might be just as well to give her a little plain sense. "Hon may be a half-wit, but he knows what'll happen to him if they catch him another time."

6

Mrs. Demooth

Only a little over a week later a second attack was made on Snydersbush. Word came to German Flats on the fifth of April. This time the information was complete. The enemy were over fifty strong, half white, half Indian. They had left the stockade alone. The people inside the stockade possessed a swivel they had let loose when the enemy first appeared in the road. The roar of it had kept them from the fort. They sashayed up the road instead.

They took Garter at his mill and burned the mill in plain sight of the fort. At Windecker's they cut off a threshing party, four men and two boys, and took them prisoner. They sent Indian scouts ahead to pick up the four settlers on the edge of the town and took them all: Cypher, Helmer, Uher, and Attle. They moved with great swiftness and discipline. They burned the farms, houses, barns, barracks, even Attle's brand-new backhouse. They killed all the horses and cows in their way. They headed for Salisbury; and swept that settlement at dusk. There they captured only three men, for the other inhabitants had moved into the Mohawk Valley down around Klock's and Fox's Mills and hadn't yet returned. But the destructives razed the town. Then they headed out along the old Jerseyfield road, northwest, past Mount's, the scene of their first irruption.

The leader of the party had attracted a good deal of attention in Snydersbush because of his uniform. It was a strange one; nobody had seen anything like it. A green coat, it was said, and deerskin breeches, and a black leather hat like a skullcap with a brass badge on the front of it. He roused a great deal of morbid speculation. Some of the old settlers said it reminded them of the uniform worn by the French commander, Beletre, back in '58. It was over a month before a report from James Dean, outside Niagara, informed them of Butler's Rangers. With his usual precision in detail he included a description of the new uniform.

The conviction gradually took root that John Butler was making an attempt to cut off German Flats. They knew that he had always hated Germans; and he had always been jealous of their rich soil. . . . They pointed to the fact that the number of each party had been just adapted to the strength of the place struck. Each party had burst out of the woods unheralded, had burned and killed and taken prisoner, and then hightailed it back for Canada. There was no point in even calling out the militia, let alone chasing them. They had the whole northwestern wilderness to make cover in.

Mrs. Demooth was terrified. Mark would not take her away, he would not even send her. She stayed in the house all day, but she was always listening. She had nothing to distract her, no one to help her in the house but that miserable wench, whose mere presence was an insult to a decent woman—first with her constant sickness, now with her swollen belly and her great blue stupid staring eyes. Whenever Mrs. Demooth saw Nancy she had something to say to her; whenever she sent Nancy out of her sight, she began to think of sayings that would give her pain.

Mrs. Demooth was not consciously torturing a half-wit. Far from it. Having, like a dutiful wife, been forced to violate the nicer feelings, in her own household, she told herself that she was merely trying to make Nancy understand the enormity of her fornication. At first she had started her tongue lashings in the captain's presence, but he had not liked it, and now she never spoke to the girl until he had left the house.

He was away nearly all day now. He was down at Palatine, seeing Colonel Jacob Klock. Mrs. Demooth could always tell when he had been to Klock's because he smelled of manure. It made her think that the Klocks must keep the cows in their kitchen.

The men were trying to reorganize the militia and above all to get regular troops sent up from Albany. Demooth even went to Albany to confer with General Stark in person. But all the great hero of Bennington would say was that he needed every man he had to defend the Hampshire grants, and the Hudson Valley north and south. He refused to consider the opinion that these raids were parts of a larger plan. He called them mere riotous excursions. He cursed about the useless militia and said that if German Flats and the Mohawk Valley could not take care of themselves like other frontiers they might as well lie down and die. Even Philip Schuyler spoke in the same vein. The security of Albany made all of them sound patriotic. Schuyler showed Demooth General Washington's reply to his reports of Klock's demands for troops. Washington said the same thing exactly. Let them take care of themselves like the other frontiers: the New York militia had been the least effective of any state's. The logic seemed thin to Demooth. He pointed out that troops were being sent to the Virginia frontier.

He returned, worn-out and hopeless. By the end of the month, the sum total of encouragement was the announcement that Alden's company of Massachusetts troops would be sent to Cherry Valley as a base from which they could operate against any important incursions of the enemy. It made one want to laugh.

At the end of the month the hamlet at Ephratah, to the north of Stone Arabia, was struck. This time the invaders were a small party, entirely of Indians, according to first reports. They burned the Hart house, killed Conrad Hart, took his son prisoner, and murdered a four-year-old boy. But a day later, the word reached German Flats that the man who had killed the boy had been seen by Mrs. Rechtor to have blue eyes, and when he raised his sleeves to rinse his hands, his wrists showed white skin.

Colonel Bellinger, sitting with Demooth and Petry in the Herter kitchen, nodded.

"It was bound to start some day. That's not a regular raid. But there'll be plenty more like them now they've seen how easy it is."

Dr. Petry also nodded. "They'll start picking off all the little places. They'll start hanging round the field fences. And it's time planting began. Already they're ploughing at Weaver's."

Demooth said bitterly, "Schuyler told me the Indians had never been effective in battle. He said we'd demonstrated that ourselves at Oriskany. Couldn't we act like men?"

"If we had wings," said the doctor in his heavy voice. "But my feet weigh too much."

Nobody even grinned, it was too true. No one could be

expected to rush off after raiders leaving his own place unde-
fended. They couldn't make anybody realize that the valley was
ninety miles long, that the Tories had the whole of the wilderness to hide in, but that everything the militia might do would
be plain to see. It was as if the leaves of the trees had eyes.

"There's one thing we can do," said the doctor. "Everybody
out of reach of the forts should be told to move in. If they want
to work their farms from the forts, they do it by themselves."

They all agreed.

Demooth made another suggestion.

"We ought to have a company of rangers of our own. Somebody to watch the trails. Mostly to the south. Any big force will
have to come at us from Unadilla or Tioga."

"What can they do?" demanded the doctor.

"Give us warning. If we can get inside the forts we can hold
them off, barring cannon, no matter how many of them come.
It's a long way to bring cannon. And men like Adam Helmer
or Joe Boleo could make it risky for their scouts." He paused.
"They might be able to pick up a few of these murdering parties, too."

"How'll you pay them?"

"Militia money. We'll list them in different companies and
work out 'service' for them."

"It's not regular. They're good at making smells in Congress."

"I'm responsible," said Bellinger. "I can stand some smells."

The doctor got up. "While I'm here I might talk to that
Nancy. How is she?"

"All right. You'll probably find her out in back."

Dr. Petry stamped heavily into the small back room. He
found Nancy sitting white-faced, very upright, on a chair. Her
hands were on her knees.

As he saw her, the doctor's brows gathered.

"What's the matter?" he asked in his harsh voice.

Nancy's lip quivered.

"Doctor, what does the fornication look like?"

"What!" he exclaimed.

"She said the fornication would be my death."

Dr. Petry started a German curse.

"She? That woman. She's crazy." He was exasperated and confused. They were all crazy. He turned on Nancy. "Don't talk blasted nonsense at me."

Nancy began to blubber.

"I don't want to die."

"You won't die," shouted the doctor. "I tell you. Listen to me. You won't die."

Nancy was appalled at the way the doctor looked down at her with the breath-making noises in his nose.

"Did Mrs. Demooth say that?"

Nancy nodded.

Without another word he turned and stamped out. He had his own war to wage and he laid down the law to Demooth. Nancy heard it all. Her terror increased. She was afraid that Mrs. Demooth would want to kill her. In her heart she had the unavoidable conviction that Mrs. Demooth knew better than the shouting doctor. She wanted to find somebody, Hon, McLonis, any friendly person, before she died. . . .

The doctor had reduced Mrs. Demooth to tears. He not only dressed her down, he told the captain what he thought of him for letting his wife behave so to a poor, defenseless girl. His whole big face was flushed and his eyes stared at them as if they would burst out of their sockets. Nothing could stop him until Mrs. Demooth began to laugh. She went off into peals of screaming laughter, one after the other, drowning all other sound.

The doctor took one look at her, stepped to the pantry, where he found the water bucket, and doused the woman with the entire bucketful. He slammed the bucket on the floor, swore once, and told her to go and dry her face. Then he stormed out of the house to his horse.

After the doctor had left, Nancy listened to Captain Demooth leading his wife to her room. She sat where she was, not getting supper, not even moving, but listening to the continued sobbing in the bedroom. Over and over, Mrs. Demooth kept saying, "I'm so frightened, Mark. I've been so frightened. I can't sleep. I don't see how you can sleep. I dream about them. I dream about Indians. They won't let me even sleep. . . ." The sun set. Twilight came into the small room, cool, with a wet smell from the sopping land. The snow was nearly gone. Only here and there stretches of it left in the folds of the land made shimmers in the dusk.

The house gradually quieted. A long time after, the captain came into the kitchen. Nancy could hear him moving there. She saw the light come on in the crack under the door. She tried to stir herself, and she got as far as the door.

Her own face was swollen from crying. Her eyes felt as though they were filled with blood. When she opened the door the captain was standing by the table.

He turned his face.

"Yes, Nancy."

"Do you want me to get some supper?"

He looked at her gravely.

"No, thanks."

Nancy forced herself to speak.

"How about *her*?"

"I don't think she needs anything. I think you'd better not go to see her. I think she's sleeping."

Nancy swallowed. Her contracted throat gulped with the effort.

"I'm sorry, sir."

The captain's face was not kind. It was not unkind either. It frightened her. She would rather have had him swear at her the way the doctor had.

"You'd better stay in your own room, Nancy. I may have to move you somewhere else for a while. But I'll take care of you till your child's born."

"Yes, sir."

"I've got to go over to the fort for half an hour. I think she'll be all right. She's sleeping."

Nancy's eyes widened as she saw him go through the door. She knew better. She knew that *she* wasn't asleep. It was just a pretense to get him to go. To get him to leave Nancy alone. As the door closed after him, Nancy gave a little moan. She couldn't cry to him to come back. Her voice wouldn't work. She wrestled with her brain to make her voice work, but it would not. The bedroom door had opened.

"Don't you dare to make a sound."

Mrs. Demooth was standing in the door. Her hair was bunched about her head in wild damp masses, but her eyes, which stared at Nancy, were dry and brilliant inside the red lids. Crying had made her voice hoarse and nasal.

Totally unable to stir, Nancy watched her in horror; but Mrs. Demooth stayed in the door. Both listened to the diminishing sound of the captain's footsteps along the muddy road. It was a full minute after they had died away before either woman spoke.

"He said I wasn't to leave the room."

She did not raise her voice; but for a moment her eyes wavered, as if even yet she feared that the captain might hear her. For a moment she was silent. There was no sound at all but the rapid beating of Nancy's heart. Then Mrs. Demooth lifted her chin.

"I never hired you. He hired you and then he told me. I didn't want you to begin with."

Suddenly Nancy started shuddering. The shudders brought

little repercussions of sound out of her throat, a hushed animal whimpering. Her mouth began to open. "Stop it." Mrs. Demooth's voice was raised a note; it was still hoarse. Nancy closed her mouth and swallowed, and wiped her mouth with her hand and wiped her hand on her apron.

"You're nasty," said Mrs. Demooth, watching her. "You're not only a whore, you're nasty." She nodded. "Don't you move. He said I mustn't leave my room. I was younger than you when he married me. I used to live in a fine house in Schenectady. Our servants weren't idiots. There weren't any Indians. There was a wall round the town. I came with him. I went into those awful woods and lived in a log cabin. I never said 'No' to anything he wanted. And he hired you. Do you know I've always hated you? Do you know how I've wanted to kill you? Answer me. Answer me, will you?"

Nancy could barely nod. The motion opened her lips.

"You're nasty. Nasty. But you can't move. Neither of us can move. Do you understand? It's what he wanted. It's his orders. It's the will of God. You can't move. I have to stay here. He made me promise. I never said 'No' to him. But I'm going to kill you, Nancy. I'm going to kill you, do you understand? I know *I'll* be killed soon. The Indians are coming to kill me. But I'll kill you first. The Lord will let me live long enough for that. To kill you and that abomination inside your body. Don't move. You can't move." She laughed deep in her throat. No one had ever heard her make a sound like that. She laughed again, listening, herself fascinated. "God has made me an instrument in His hand. He removes all unclean things from His earth. He comes and walks the earth to do it Himself, or else He makes instruments like me. He walks the earth. Do you hear me, you?"

Nancy's eyes were dull. Suddenly she put her hands to her abdomen, taking hold of herself.

Mrs. Demooth began to laugh.

"It knows. It is dying. I told you I would kill it."

Nancy screamed.

"You know I hated you, but you didn't go. You couldn't. He wouldn't let you, because he wanted me to kill you. Now He comes walking. To see you die. You and what's dying in you now."

Nancy's knees buckled. She seemed to collapse over herself onto her face.

Mrs. Demooth watched her. There was no tremor to the open flame of the lamp. There was no tremor in Nancy's body. Mrs. Demooth smiled. She looked right and left, listening. Her smile deepened. Her face seemed even paler. Little bunches of flesh swelled beside her nostrils. Slowly she took a step over the threshold of her room and stopped. She looked right and left again and listened. Then she walked over to where the girl lay and bent down and lifted her shoulder. Nancy rolled partly on her side, and lay limp, bent slightly at the hips, preserving the position. Mrs. Demooth let go the shoulder and straightened up. Then deliberately she kicked Nancy.

She returned to her room and paused for a moment to look back at the prone figure with exalted eyes. She raised her eyes slightly, closed the door, and went to bed.

The evening mist drifting into the shadows drew across Nancy's face. Her lids fluttered. Gradually she opened her eyes. There was no sound. Her eyes rolled slowly towards the bedroom door and found it closed. Tears came into her eyes and rolled down over her face.

Suddenly she blenched. She put her hand to her belly and pressed against herself. Her face was contorted with the effort to rise soundlessly. Her long legs moved with infinite care. She took off her shoes and tiptoed to her room. There the horror overwhelmed her completely. No longer trying to be quiet, she gathered her belongings in a panic,—her dress, her comb, her nightgown, and her cloth shoes,—and twisted them into her shawl. She came back through the kitchen, bent slightly forward, keeping her eyes from the door, and went out into the darkness. She ran heavily.

On Captain Demooth's return he found his wife rigid on her bed, with a slight froth drying at the corners of her mouth. He could not waken her and called for Nancy. When she did not answer, he went into the kitchen and rang the bell. Then he went to her room and found that she had gone.

He took the lamp into the yard, shouting for Clem, and with the old Dutchman searched the yard. By the fence they found Nancy's fresh tracks. She had climbed the rails and crossed the meadow towards the south. They managed to follow her tracks as far as the woods. But there they had to stop.

"There's no use in looking any more."

Clem shook his head: "Only an Indian could foller her through that brush."

"Didn't you hear anything at all?"

"I was sleeping pretty hard. I was tired."

"I'll have to get back to my wife."

"Anything wrong with her?"

"She's had a fit, I think. Her mother told me she used to have them when she was little. Will you go fetch Doc, Clem?"

Clem said, "*Tschk, tschk,*" in his best manner.

"Hurry up, Clem. I feel as if I was going crazy myself. We just had an express from Albany. Walter Butler's escaped."

"God help us," exclaimed Clem; but he was thinking about fording the river. The water was high, now.

7

The Indian

When, a few hours later, Nancy broke free of the woods, she found herself on one of the bare, hillside pastures. Looking back, she saw the mist lying below her in the valley. She had come a long way.

Her shawl was a sodden bundle hanging from her clinched fingers. Her short gown was torn over one shoulder. Her petticoat clung wetly to her legs. She felt like a flogged person; she was reeking with sweat and wet from the whipping branches. Her hair hung round her face. A little stream of blood trickled from a cut cheek.

She fought hard to gain her breath, turning her back on the valley and fixing her eyes on the stars. Gradually against their distant patterns she made out the dark shoulder of the hill. When she saw it, she started once more at her heavy walk. Her body was like a dead weight precariously balanced on the arch that joined her legs.

Somewhere under the mist behind her, a dog rushed out of an invisible house. She could hear his furious barks traveling back and forth. All at once the dog's voice deepened, fixed, and she realized that it had picked up her scent.

But at the same moment a long whistle pierced the mist. It was followed by a man's incensed shouting. "Prince! Come back here, Prince!" Nancy heard the name quite plainly. The dog stopped barking and then, a moment later, yelped; and the night became still. A long shuddering breath went out of Nancy. She set herself with a desperate deliberation against the hill.

A half hour later she stopped on top of the hill in a scattered grove of maples to draw deep breaths. Though she knew that she was out of reach of pursuit, she did not dare stop for long. She was convinced that what Mrs. Demooth had told her would surely take place. The pain she had carried out of the house had died, but she was sure that it would come to life again. Even now she could feel its premonitory stirrings.

She tramped nearly all night. The general slope of the ground was downward, but at times she was brought up against sharp rises that took interminable climbing. A little before dawn she lost her sense of direction. She could no longer see the stars; the sky had turned to a dull gray with neither light nor shadow. The ravine in which she floundered was gray, like the sky, and the wet touch of branches on her cheeks or breast was cold.

She stumbled into a small stream without seeing it and came at last to a halt in water that pushed icily against her knees. She put her hand down and lifted a little water to her mouth. Her lips felt swollen to her hand's touch. She could not drink.

After a minute she gave up and wearily forced her way out of the water. Her knees would not lift her feet the height necessary to climb out on the bank, and she struggled futilely, feeling the cold earth against her thighs. She splashed heavily, though she did not hear it, and fell face down on the thick dead sodden grass, and lay there.

It was then that the pains returned. Nancy lifted her swollen, pale, and tear-streaked face and cried out. Her voice was not loud, it was utterly forlorn. It made the Indian think of a rabbit in a faulty snare.

The Indian had been scouting down towards the flats when the dog scented him and barked. His first intention had been to sneak up beside the corner of the barn to see whether he could pick up an easy scalp. He wanted to save up for a new gun; his old French trade musket that he had inherited from his father shot very badly. For hunting he even had to carry his bow. He had picked up two scalps that month, one down at Ephratah, and one of a lone trapper between Edmeston and the little lakes. The one he had got at Ephratah had not come off well and he was not sure whether he would be able to get the eight-dollar bounty for it at Niagara. He ought to take another to be sure.

But the dog had so obviously spotted him that the Indian decided to give up that chance, and he legged it up the hill with the dog chasing him. The man had called in the dog; and the Indian had nothing to show. But then he had heard somebody floundering in the wet way above him. When he reached the pasture, whoever it was had disappeared, but the Indian found plain tracks and a tatter of cloth together beside a juniper. He could not understand it; it was too dark to see the tracks, but just on the chance he had started following. In the dark, that was slow and painful work. As soon as it got lighter, however, he made the surprising discovery that the footprints had been left by a woman. He fingered the pouch under his belt in which he carried his *Oki*, the skin of a red-headed woodpecker, and realized that at last it was bringing him a little luck. You got eight dollars for any scalp regardless of sex. This ought to be an easy eight dollars. The woman was alone.

He went at a trot, for the trail was easy to follow, and a little past dawn he broke out on the edge of a steep ravine and looked down on her. She had fallen forward on the bank of a small stream.

The Indian ran down the bank, jumped the stream in a single leap, and stood beside her, fingering his hatchet. He had several ideas. He might shoot her—he hadn't shot anything with his musket this trip—or he could bang her on the head and save the powder. He was still considering when Nancy looked up at him and screamed again, and he realized that she had not seen him at all or heard him either until that instant. Then he saw that she no longer saw him. She was unconscious. He caught her by the arm and hauled her out of the water and looked at her. He found out that she was in the act of giving birth.

He was very much puzzled. To find a woman like her there alone in such a case was extraordinary. It made him uneasy. He decided that he had better think things over before he killed her, so he dragged her over the ground to a clump of hemlock and built a fire. He left her on a slight incline, with her legs downward, and sat down himself with his back to her.

The light increased gradually while he sat before the fire. Birds moved in the branches. He heard their voices all through the woods and the smooth musical sliding of the water over a sunk log. While he watched the birds he took out of a pouch a piece of pemmican and began sucking and gnawing at it. He considered that his wife had died that winter and that he had no children and that he might get eight dollars for the torn scalp anyway. But he was not sure.

He seemed oblivious of the event taking place behind him. But suddenly his dark eyes were attracted by the flashing passage of a woodpecker. Black and white, and the red head like a traveling spark. A great twittering and fluttering broke out in a tree, and a moment later the woodpecker returned in hot pursuit of a female. The Indian grunted, relaxed, and went ahead with his chewing. He decided that she was a strong girl, or she would not have journeyed so far. And her light long hair and her blue eyes interested him; he was different from most Indians in his own town. He liked to live solitary and had a small log house on the outskirts of Deodesote village. He had never been markedly successful on a warpath. Two scalps and this woman prisoner might make him some reputation. If, now, he decided to marry her, it wouldn't be necessary to give presents, either.

He waited complacently for the woman to finish the business.

When some poor order emerged from the flux of Nancy's consciousness and she opened her eyes to the world before her, she saw the Indian sitting in sunlight before his fire with his blanket drawn over his shoulders. The musket was leaning against the stub of a dead hemlock branch and the bow and quiver were hung beside it.

The sides of the Indian's poll were shaved and the scalp lock was braided like some queer kind of handle to his head. One battered feather hung from it. He looked comical to her light-headed fancy, and she felt sorry for him, he was so dark and ugly. When she tried to speak, and he turned, she almost laughed at the way his face looked with smeared paint, white and vermilion, in stripes. She even remembered how it had terrified her when she saw it on the bank of the stream; then it had appeared like the arrival of the abomination itself. But now Nancy knew that she was alive.

To her awakening senses came the sound of the water in the stream, the birds' voices, and the smell of smoke from the Indian's fire. Her body felt torn and sore and exhausted, but it was alive. She met the Indian's expressionless eyes with a slight smile; then struggled to sit up.

As she did so he rose to his feet and moved away from her. He went down the ravine to a piece of dry raised ground and started peeling sheaths of bark from a big hemlock. He used his hatchet and scalping knife together.

For a while Nancy watched him erecting a tiny bark shanty. Then she made her eyes look down at herself and at the small, soiled, male shape to which she had given birth. For a moment she was chilled by the old fear; but her movement upset the child so that it rolled over and bumped against her knee; and suddenly it opened its infinitely small mouth and gave a flat bawling wail.

It was alive. Nancy laughed. Then she picked up the baby and moved it into the sun and went down to the stream with unsteady steps and washed herself as well as she was able. While she was there she found her bundle, and, bringing it back, unwrapped it and took out the nightgown, which was of worn flannel. In the dryest piece of this she could tear out, she wrapped the baby, after first wiping its body with the other portions.

When she was done, the Indian came back to her and said something she could not understand. He was a squat, slightly bow-legged man who did not quite come to her shoulder. He pointed to the shed he had made.

"Oh yes. Thank you very much."

Nancy smiled wanly and managed to follow him. He did not offer to help her with the child or her belongings, but he put down his blanket for her.

He tapped himself on the chest.

"Gahota," he said. "Gahota."

Then he poked Nancy's breast with his forefinger and stared at her. She giggled slightly. He poked again. Finally she understood.

"Oh, my name's Nancy."

He repeated it. Then he said, "Gahota."

"Gahota," said Nancy. The Indian smiled. Some of the paint cracked on his cheek. He watched her sit down on his blanket, put some more wood on the fire, took his bow, quiver, and musket, and disappeared into the woods.

Nancy sat still for a long time, holding the baby in her lap. Finally she lay down with it and slept.

It was nearly dusk when she smelled cookery and woke again. The Indian was squatting before the fire. He had fashioned a bark dish in which he was boiling some meat. Every now and then with a small ladle of birch bark he would skim off a wet mass of feathers. But as soon as he saw that Nancy was awake, he moved over and gave her the ladle, signing to her that it was time she assumed the woman's job.

The two partridges boiling away in the soup smelled strong, for they had been immersed, feathers, entrails, and all; but Nancy was hungry. She skimmed with good will. When the two carcasses fell apart she took the bark dish off the stones it rested on and set it between herself and Gahota. As she started to dip her ladle, the Indian took it from her hand.

He ate slowly and steadily until the soup was half gone. Then he shoved the vessel towards her and tossed the ladle in. Nancy was ravenous. While she was eating the baby began to cry. But she did not heed it until she had finished the soup. Twice she saw the Indian stare at the child, and the third time she reached for it and set it on her lap.

A little later in the evening she felt the milk filling her breasts. Clumsily she lifted the child. She caught Gahota's eye. He looked contented now, indifferent. He had removed his shirt and was slowly rubbing his belly.

Nancy felt a great friendliness for this kind man.

"Will you help me find my brother?" she asked.

He did not turn his head, nor answer.

"My brother, Hon? Hon Yost Schuyler."

He did not answer.

"I must find him," said Nancy, with a slight panic. But the Indian continued to ignore her. She dropped the subject, for she thought obviously the poor heathen did not understand the English language. Besides she felt warm and soothed and preoccupied with the tugging at her breast. Almost as an afterthought she said companionably, "He lives at Niagara, you know."

Gahota, whose name meant Log-in-the-Water, had been politely ignoring her bad manners in addressing him. But now he grunted.

"Deodesote," he said flatly.

He did not look at Nancy. But Nancy nodded behind his funny back. She was contented for the first time in many months. Quite happy.

"Deodesote," she repeated in a dutiful voice.

They started just at daybreak.

8

Smoke

As the days of May went by, the settlers in German Flats became increasingly aware of the gradual closing in of the destructives. Captain Demooth was asking for volunteers to add to the Ranger service. He had been able to find only ten men willing to spend all their time in the woods. There had been thirty at first, but as the sun grew daily warmer, and the earth dried, many of them returned to work in their fields.

Gil was one of these. He knew that Mrs. McKlennar would have willingly found another man and taken care of Lana into the bargain; but the farm was on his mind. He had to see to the planting of the corn himself. When he was out with Joe and Adam, he found himself uneasy, after the first two days, to see how the wheat was growing.

"He ain't nothing but a farming man," Joe would say, disgustedly. They had set up a tiny lodge a few miles north of Edmeston, which was still inhabited by several Tory families. From the hillside, as he lay on his belly in the leaves, Gil could look down on the clearings and watch the small ploughings; the women putting in the hills of corn and squash and beans; the children fetching the cattle at dusk and dawn.

The children were the only people they had to be careful of. Sometimes the cattle strayed near the shanty and had to be driven off, though once or twice, before he did so, Gil took their kettle and filled it with fresh milk.

The other two would never allow Gil to make one of the

weekly solitary scouts to the southward. They said he had no
sense in the woods; he would get killed surely. An Indian squaw
could hear him coming half a mile. They made him stay at the
lodge, and when they thought they had any news, he had to run
up the back trail fifteen miles to the next station. There a man
was always waiting to relay the word.

Gil was not as bad in the woods as they made him out to be.
He became quieter as time went on, and they admitted that he
was turning into a good runner—not in Adam's class, of course,
but better than middling. But he had no eye for things. He
couldn't tell what a crow or jay or kingfisher was chattering of.
They said tolerantly that he would never learn.

There were odd times when he felt the lazy contentment
creeping into him. When for days they just lay round on a hilltop, when the sun was hot and the sky dry, watching the tops of
the trees to the south and particularly the east.

Once old Blue Back came into the camp. He had taken his
wife on a spring tour to Unadilla to visit a Tuscarora family as
soon as she had her planting done. He had left her there and
struck north to give them the news.

They saw him sauntering up the hill, shifting his eyes left and
right, looking everywhere but in their direction. Joe muttered,
"The old twerp seen us a hundred yards back. He looked me right
in the eye. Now he's going to act surprised."

He did.

He beamed all over and said "How" to all of them, shaking hands and holding his hat up to each in turn. He had not
shaved his head. He looked greasy and brown and dirty and he
smelled of fish. He said they had been curing bullheads for three
days in his friend's cabin. They had all the windows and doors
closed to keep the smoke in the cabin. He said it got pretty hot,
sometimes, so he came up to see how Joe Boleo was, and his
friend, Gil Martin. He said an Indian couldn't get any drink in

Unadilla or Oghkwaga either. The white men laid hold of all of it. He thought somebody up north might have a drink. He had a twitching in his right leg when he went without it too long himself. Did Joe ever have that?

Joe resignedly handed him a small swallow of rum and Blue Back sat down. He said he needed a new hat.

"Go to hell," said Joe. "You can't have mine."

"Too big," agreed Blue Back. "Yours too big." He pointed at Helmer.

"What you going to do about that, Gil?"

Gil grinned and said he needed his own hat himself.

"Me make trade," suggested Blue Back.

"No, thanks," said Gil.

"What's on your mind?" asked Joe.

The old Oneida sighed and said that Joseph Brant was in Unadilla. He was gathering the Indians. There were already about fifty whites under Captain Caldwell there, and quite a lot of runaway negroes. He hadn't talked to Captain Caldwell himself, because he thought they might not be friends. But Captain Caldwell drank a great deal. All the white men drank a great deal. Sometimes it seemed to Blue Back that they were sick or afraid of the woods.

"Brant still there?"

Brant, said Blue Back, had gathered together about two hundred and taken the party eastward. But he was due to return soon. He had to meet with John Butler at Unadilla in the end of June.

Boleo whistled under his breath.

"Adam," he said, "you better take a cut through Springfield and pass out a warning. They won't pay no attention, though."

"No," said the Indian. He had been that way himself. People just kicked him out. He hadn't even had a drink. He had only managed to steal a couple of young pigs.

"What did you do with them?" asked Adam hopefully.

It appeared that they were eaten.

Joe said, "When did Brant move out of Unadilla?"

A week ago, said Blue Back.

Joe swore. "Why didn't you come here right away, you old timber beast?"

"No good."

He's right, thought Gil. The people wouldn't move, now that crops were in the earth, and there were no troops to send to them. He looked at Joe. Joe was standing up and staring eastward.

"By God," he said, "Brant's on the loose already!"

Gil could not see the smoke for a long time. It was such a pale, frail, insubstantial thing, a mere mist in the sky.

"You better pull foot for home, Gil. Tell 'em Brant's burning Springfield way. Me and Adam will make a scout, and Adam will come back here and I'll report at Herkimer."

They had their own path marked out. They did not use the old Iroquois trail. Their route lay along the ridges, above it, following deer runs.

Gil hit a steady pace. He was going all the way through to the forts. On such long running—even on this one, when he knew that the destructives were loose—he had a singular feeling of freedom. Often he thought that if he were making such a run with Adam, he would quite easily break off with the easy-going giant to a party with the Bowers girls. Adam had pestered him about it more than once when they were lying before their fire at night.

The sunset was fading when Gil came out on the top of Shoemaker hill. He paused for a moment to get his breath for the last miles down to the river.

The sky was like a great silken sheet over all the world, misty in the north, but edged with sunset to the west. Under it, on a level with Gil's eyes, the wilderness rolled northward—mile upon mile, ridge upon ridge, until the mountains lifted against the sky. The color of it in the late spring was like water, gray-green, with darker shades where the evergreens marked out the long pine ridges or the balsam swamps, and with occasional frothy streaks of white of the wild cherries in bloom. As the light waned, the whole panorama conveyed a sense of motion; the ridges rolling higher and higher, as the hollows of the balsam swamps were deepened.

The valley itself was like a crystal under his feet through which he could look down on a picture painted in miniature. The bright line of the river was still tinged with the sunset; the two forts—from this elevation they looked close together—were geometrical shapes in the irregular varicolored fields; the fences between the fields were like small stitches painstakingly made to patch the surface of the flats. But the houses and barns alone in the farther clearings were infinitesimal blocks in the crooked fingers of the wilderness.

As he started down the bald slope of the hill, Gil's eyes searched across the river, picking up the line of the Kingsroad and following it towards McKlennar's. He could see house and barn, and the stone house behind the blooming apple tree. The sunset made the windows blind burning eyes in the stone face. But the rest of the place was clear, even to young John Weaver turning the cows into the yard. Lana, of course, would not be milking. She was two weeks overdue. Gil trotted downward.

Then he saw a familiar figure moving along the road. He knew at once who it was. It moved into a lighted stretch, showing the gray horse and the heavy, upright, black-clad rider. He was going out from German Flats. He was approaching McKlennar's. Now he turned in, and John Weaver's small dog rushed out barking to meet him.

It was Dr. Petry. For some reason, Gil remembered what Mrs.

McKlennar had once called the doctor, when she saw him riding his gray horse along the road. "Like death on a pale horse," she had said.

9

Night on the Farm

Young John Weaver tingled with excitement, curiosity, and dread. He could tell by Daisy's voice that things had started in the stone house. He had just finished the milking; it had taken longer with the spotted cow freshened, as she had that morning; one hind quarter of her bag had shown a sign of caking and he had to work on her. The negress stuck her calico-wrapped head in the barn door and called, "You, boy!" He knew it then, but he didn't like being called "You, boy," by a nigger, even though he was hired help; and he didn't answer. Daisy peered in and said, "Oh, white boy!"

"What is it?" John asked gruffly.

Immediately Daisy put on her importance.

"You got to fotch me mo' wood."

"I took it in before I went after the cows."

"Dat trash! I want birch. I want a lot of it. Fust thing dey'll holler fo' hot water, and whar Daisy den? W'en ol' Miss wants something she wants it first off, immeedjut, and now. I got to have birch split fine to fotch de bilin' wid de fust bref. Here, give me dat milk and get on de mare and go tell Doc Petry. And don' you spare de hickory stick on'r."

John wrenched the halter off the mare, bridled her, and mounted bareback. He rode hard, hunching himself over the withers, and wondering, "Will I be in time?" He drew up at the doctor's and called in through the window.

"They just told me to fetch you."

With agonized eyes he watched the doctor pop in a tart of preserved currants and wipe his mouth. "I thought it might start to-night," said Doc. "Well, well. You might unhitch my horse— he's all saddled—and bring him round here."

John flung off the reeking mare and got the doctor's horse, lugging him by main force. He waited till the doctor came out and mounted. "Hup," said Dr. Petry. It was like winding a piece of clockwork: the spring seemed jammed for a minute; then the insides of the gray animal whirred and rumbled and his legs started to gesticulate, and all of a sudden you realized that he was actually walking away. John clambered onto the mare and caught up. The mare was hot and full of fettle.

"Excuse me, sir," he said to Doc. "I think I'd better get on back. They want me to split some more wood."

The doctor, who had got the hiccoughs from starting out on a new-filled stomach, put his hand to his mouth, and then turned his staring eyes on John.

"Oh, yes," he said. "Split wood. Just what we need. Half a cord."

But the mare was already helling away up the road like the backsides of forty rabbits. John rushed her into her stall and yanked his axe out of the shed and got to work on the wood. As soon as he had three or four armfuls he delivered them to the kitchen. He could hear Mrs. McKlennar moving round the front room and talking. Daisy bustled in. "Dat's enough in here," she said. But John still stood there. He wasn't sure. Yes, it was—her voice! Mrs. Martin was talking! Thank God she was still alive!

He went back to the woodpile and chopped and split enough wood to boil water for all the babies this side of China. But he was thinking, wouldn't this be an awful time to have the destructives strike the flats? Of course the scouts were out. Of course there would be some warning. But to move her! Move her now! It was too late. Why hadn't she moved into a house close to the fort? When the doctor came there would be two of them, though. John left off chopping and got down his musket and reprimed it. He wished that Gil was back. He felt a tremendous responsibility. But he wished now that the doctor would hurry up. Then he remembered that he hadn't turned the cows out, so he did that. And then the doctor arrived.

"Chopped the wood?" he inquired gravely as John took his horse.

"Yes, sir," said John.

The doctor went into the house. When John came back to the porch and sat down with the musket on his knees, he could hear the doctor's heavy voice rumbling away to Mrs. McKlennar, a pause, laughter, and then Lana's voice joining in.

Young John felt the blood rush all through him. He positively burned with the thought, "By God, women were brave!"

He thought what it would be like when he and Mary got married. What it would be like, being in there, watching her, seeing her go through it. It seemed awful. Mary was even slimmer than Mrs. Martin was. But it had to be. A man couldn't get away from facing it. It was right, too. It was what you expected.

He heard silence fall heavily in the room. Then he heard Mrs. Martin give a gasp and the doctor say with unction, "They're picking up, aren't they?"

"Well, for God's sake, John Weaver!"

He turned to see the widow looking at him. Her horse face was flushed high with excitement. But she appeared to struggle with something in her own inside.

"What on earth are you doing, John?"

He tried to explain. But Mrs. McKlennar seemed to understand. "Very good idea," she said. "Yes indeed. But I think you ought to patrol the place. You better keep marching round the buildings. Suppose an Indian should be coming up from the back?"

John wasn't a fool. He blushed. He knew that she meant he wasn't to sit there right outside the window. He couldn't imagine how he had come to do it.

"Yes, ma'am."

Now he was marching round the yard. Now he was down on the road, looking to see if anybody were coming. He leaned against the fence rails, and thought, "Even if we get able to marry this summer, that couldn't happen for quite a while."

For he and Mary had it all settled. They had realized last winter that John's mother still didn't want them to get married, and that she had asked Mary up just for John to see how little Mary knew. But Mary had been apt at picking things up, and Mrs. Weaver hadn't liked that. She had stopped asking the girl in March.

George Weaver had taken it pretty much to heart. He had said to his son, "That's how your ma is. You've got to take her the way she is, John. I've done it, and she's been an almighty good wife. She's been a good mother, too. If times were different I could give you something to get married on. As it is, you'll have to work for yourselves. When you get enough, you'll have my agreement, and I'm not going to take your pay, as I might otherwise. You go ahead, and you work it out when you can, and you get married. Mary's a fine girl, and your ma's just notional now. Once you've gone and done it, she'll come round."

It was the longest talk he had ever had with his father. He had gone down to see Mary about it the next week. That was the day when Mrs. Reall had announced that she was going to go back to Massachusetts with Corporal Rebus White. Mrs.

Reall was taking her family, but Mary had refused to go. She was ashamed. She broke down with John and explained that Mrs. Reall would not marry Mr. White until the state had paid her widow's claim. It was shameful.

Mary had stayed. She had, through March and April, eked out enough, by working for the garrisons, to feed herself. But it had seemed pretty desperate to them both. At first John could not get work. Then when the spring came there was plenty of work to do for widow women, but there was no cash money involved. There was almost no money left that people were willing to lay out in hired help.

But at the end of April they had had a great stroke of luck. Captain Demooth's hired girl had run away and the captain had been willing to let Mary go there and try the job. And then Gilbert Martin had joined the Rangers, which took him away part of the time, and while he was gone he paid John half a shilling a day to look after the McKlennar place. They realized they were getting along. For a while they even talked of getting married right away, until it occurred to Mary that it might interfere with her job; so they decided to wait a few months longer and save maybe twelve or fifteen dollars.

John had wanted to join the Rangers, but they said he was too young. They did promise to enroll him in the militia, though, when the companies were reorganized. He told Mary about it.

His mother never spoke about Mary. Every time John returned to see his family, she cooked some dish she knew he would like, but she froze all over if he mentioned the girl. She seemed bitter and unhappy. And now John, thinking of what one day Mary would surely have to go through, never considered that his mother had been through the same process to bring him into the world.

All he thought of was Mary. Since she got her job, she had taken to winding her braids round her head. Her neck showed slim and pliant. There were moments when she greeted him with a dignity and fondness through which her slim ardency emerged as a thing so surprising that it took the breath of them both. It gave John a queer feeling that her visible maturing, instead of giving her defenses against himself, was putting her in his power. She was so anxious to improve herself, she was so conscious of the fact that she had come between him and his mother, that she wanted to do everything to please him.

Even John did not think she was pretty, except in the way any girl that wasn't too fat was pretty. He didn't know why it was he had fallen in love with her. She was long-legged and she had an abrupt way of moving; but every now and then, when she looked at him, she seemed struck in a moment with grace.

He tried to figure it all out. She was never malicious, and she was always honest; and yet she was shy. He realized vaguely that she was fine, but it was hard to understand that, with her parents and her upbringing. That was what he called her to himself. She was fine.

It was quite a beautiful discovery for a boy so young as John to have made.

He tried to imagine how it would be when they were married, what kind of room they would have, and what Mary would have on. He wondered whether he would be shaving by then. Mary had once said she hoped he would never let his beard grow. He thought of her lying slim and snug under the blankets, and himself shaving over the slop basin.

Young John shouldered his musket and marched back to the road with his little brown dog trotting before him like a fox. He wondered how long the dog had been with him; he had not noticed; he had not even noticed that he had strayed away from the road. With surprise he saw that it had become dark. A still, black night, in which sounds carried long distances. He could hear a whippoorwill in the cornfield as plain as though it were in the road beside him. The peepers down by the river began to whimper into their night singing. John shivered, and looked back up the slope towards the stone house.

The windows of the bedroom were lighted. Against the curtains he saw the silhouettes of the doctor, bent over like a grubbing bear, and the dragoon-like figure of the widow.

"God," thought John. "It's happening now."

The sweat came pouring out of him. Then there was one uncontrollable welling of sound that he would never have taken for Mrs. Martin's voice. The doctor ducked down. Mrs. McKlennar bent forward. They were like people smitten out of the power of life.

And then the doctor straightened up, and John suddenly relaxed weakly against the fence. He had forgotten all about destructives, Indians, war, Mary, his mother, himself. It was over. But John stayed still and struggled with himself, to make himself go up, to find out what had happened.

Then the little brown dog started growling.

"Shut your mouth," said John savagely. He aimed a cuff at the beast, but the dog eluded him and spun off down the road barking high and shrill. Then John heard a man running towards him.

"Hello, hello. That you, John?"

"Is it Mr. Martin?"

"Yes. I saw Dr. Petry coming up when I was on the hill. What's happened?"

John said with a strangely controlled voice:—

"The baby's just got born."

"Is everything all right?"

"I was just going up to see," said John, "when I heard you coming."

They turned towards the house. They saw the door open and a path of light shoot towards them down the slope. Mrs. McKlennar was standing there with a bundle.

"John! John Weaver!"

"Yes, ma'am."

"It's all right. I thought you'd like to know."

John's throat filled.

"Yes, ma'am. Here's Mr. Martin. He just got back."

He felt Gil take hold of his arm. They ran that way, full tilt up to the porch. Mrs. McKlennar stood waiting for them, grinning wide, but with tears sliding bumpily down beside her nose. She was snorting and sniffing like a dog with a breathful of smoke.

Gil shoved right past her and went into the room; and John couldn't help peering through behind him. Dr. Petry was in the act of covering up Mrs. Martin. But the thing that surprised John was that Mrs. Martin had her eyes open. She gave Gil a small smile.

The doctor grunted.

"Everything went off first rate, young man."

There it was. There in Mrs. McKlennar's arms. She pulled back the wrapping and showed John the red small face with its intimations of humanity quite plainly to be seen already.

John breathed hard.

"It's a perfectly beautiful boy," said Mrs. McKlennar.

10

Andrustown

Whatever she might be doing, Mrs. McKlennar beamed like the rising sun. She would not hear of Lana's working more than to wash the baby and change its diaper cloths. One day when Lana was bathing herself and the baby started to yell, Lana asked Mrs.

McKlennar whether she would change the cloths for her. Mrs. McKlennar did. "Nasty, nasty," she said. "He's just like a man already, the way he don't care how he musses." That afternoon, when John showed up to say good-bye, she gave him the brightest shilling she had in the house. "Don't you put it away," she said to him. "You go down to Petry's and buy your girl a hair ribbon with it." John was amazed. He looked at the shilling in his soiled palm and he looked at Mrs. McKlennar. Her horselike face was still beaming because she had been asked to change the baby's dirty cloths.

John went down to the hay piece to see Mr. Martin. He had already been paid; he had nearly three dollars in his pocket, but he thought he ought to say good-bye again. And he hated to leave the farm. Somehow it had become associated in his mind with the life he and Mary were going to start as soon as they were able. He had lately imagined themselves in such a place.

Gil was mowing some of the corners along the bottom land and he rested his scythe on the point of the snathe when he saw John coming and began to whet the blade. The stone against the steel gave ringing notes in the still heat.

"Well, John. You're going?"

"Yes, Mr. Martin."

"I hate to let you go."

"I kind of hate to go myself, Mr. Martin."

"I'd keep you here if I could afford to. The hay's standing heavy and I'm going to have a lot of work with it, now my wife can't help on the cart."

They accepted this gravely. But Gil was obviously proud and pleased that he was going to have to do extra work.

"Yes, sir," said John.

"You've got another job, John?"

"I promised Mr. Leppard I'd make a trip over to Andrustown with him and help him get in some of his hay."

Gil was thoughtful. "I hope it's all right."

"They only figure on staying a couple of nights. There's been no news in, has there?"

"Not that I know of," said Gil. "But it's pretty far off."

"I guess we'll be all right."

"Joe Boleo's down towards Edmeston, right now. Who's going?"

John said, "Mr. Leppard said him and both the Bells, and Hawyer and Staring, and then young Bell's wife and Mrs. Hawyer and Mrs. Staring. They're coming to rake and to cook for us."

"They oughtn't to take the women."

"I guess it'll be all right," John said again.

"Well, good luck, John."

John raised his hand. "You've treated me real well," he said. "When I come back I'll come around here. Maybe I can give you a couple of days if I haven't got other work."

Leaning on his scythe, Gil watched the lad go. John was a good worker and it would have been fine to keep him round the farm. If it hadn't been for having to pay Dr. Petry's fee, Gil would have hired John out of his own pocket, just for the sake of the place. Another hoeing wouldn't hurt the corn, with all the wet there had been; there would be a big hay crop; and the wheat looked absolutely clean. It looked pretty close to a record harvest all along the line.

But Gil couldn't lay half a dozen sweeps of hay without having to look up towards the house. And then he would naturally swing his eyes across the valley, taking in the sky line from Eldridge Blockhouse to Fort Dayton. Then he would look back to the house again.

The house was always the same. He could see Mrs. McKlennar and Daisy doing their jobs, and nowadays he could see Lana doing fine work on the verandah—Mrs. McKlennar wouldn't hear of their moving back into the farmhouse, any more than she would consider moving down to one of the forts herself. "What's the sense of your staying in that hot cabin?" she would demand. "You ought to keep the baby cool nights like these." And she was right about the forts, too. They were overcrowded. Since the word had come, at the end of last week, of Butler's attack on Wyoming, the people in Schuyler had moved down. Little Stone Arabia Stockade could not contain all of the local families. Now, with the people from up the Creek Valley and from south, by Andrustown, the forts were jammed. "Me live in a fort!" Mrs. McKlennar's voice was raucous. "Have you *smelled* them? Have you seen the flies? I'd rather be scalped!" But the people wouldn't live outside—even some people with near-by houses came into the fort at night, since they had heard of Wyoming. There had been Wyoming Tories in Butler's brigade. They had been the ones who had searched out fugitives. They hadn't hurt the women and children to speak of; they had just driven them into a swamp without food, to make their own way to safety as well as they were able. There weren't any berries ripe at that season for them to live on; many of those who were lost starved to death. Of those who managed to reach the settlement of Wilkes-Barre, more than half were naked and so stung with flies and infected with ague that it wasn't expected they would survive. Blue Back, who had got the story from his Tuscarora friend in Unadilla, said the swamp was named by the Indians "The Shades of Death." It didn't seem possible that civilized man could allow such things even in war.

A dog was barking over the river to the eastward. Gil's scythe stopped. Now all he could hear was the high screech of the locusts in the woods and he cursed them silently because they obliterated any distant sound. Looking over the river, he saw that men at work in their fields had also stopped. A few were moving slowly to the places where they had left their rifles. The whole valley seemed to have become still. It had happened that way again and again, all the men Gil could see, stopping, and looking in the same direction. He glanced back at the house. That was all right. Up there the baby was squalling about something or other and they had not even noticed.

Then the dog's barking picked up and made a fluent ascent of the hillside woods and everybody knew that he must be running a rabbit; yip-yapping for hell and gone as if the one object of creation were a rabbit and a dog to chase him. Mechanically Gil's scythe sheared again through the standing stems of grass.

Up at the house, Lana opened her dress for the baby's second feeding of the day. She had never felt so much contentment since her first wedded days. In her heart she felt that it was even better than that time. She no longer worried about herself and Gil. The baby was a tangible expression of their success together in the world, while at the same time he was a defense against the world and Gil. She took no thought for the future, except vaguely, thinking of the boy as a man; she was too full of love and the sense of her own easement in feeding her son to feel beyond the moment. It made her proud to know that she could feed him; small as she was, she had a splendid flow of milk; and he was a big demanding child, moreover, who had weighed ten pounds on the doctor's estimate, a child many a larger woman would have envied having.

Mrs. McKlennar often noticed Lana's passionate preoccupation at feeding time. She did not, like many women, take it as a chore; her whole day seemed governed by the expectation that led up to the appointed time. She was a natural mother, Mrs. McKlennar thought, and knew that she herself, supposing she had had a child, would never have felt like that. From now on, Gil would have to walk behind the family cart. He would no longer be the girl's husband, but the father of her family. It was the patriarchal instinct from her Palatine blood. Some of those girls were wonderful things to see before they married; then they became great mothers. "She'll shut him out of both their lives until she wants him." It seemed queer to an Irishwoman.

And yet it was not altogether so. Lana always greeted Gil with happiness and anxiety for his comfort. He was to be pleased, to have just what he wanted. But there it was again; he was the father. Mrs. McKlennar wondered how Gil would stand up under this attitude.

Three mornings later, Joe Boleo appeared at the house for breakfast. He had reached the valley late the night before, sleeping in Demooth's barn. Now he said he wanted a good meal, a wash and shave, and a bed with feathers in it. Nothing was up in the south that he had seen. There was no news. He must admit that he preferred Daisy's cornbread to Adam Helmer's idea of nocake.

After feeding he dropped down to the hay meadow to pass a few minutes with Gil.

"The boy's a dinger," Joe said gravely. "He's growed since I was here before."

Gil grinned.

"He gets lots of nourishment."

"By God," said Joe heartily.

"Who's down in the lodge?" Gil asked.

"Hain't nobody," said Joe. "I got sick of being by myself, but Adam's due back there to-morrow."

"Where's Adam?"

"He's picking up John Butler's trail back to Niagara. There weren't no point in staying down. They've all gone from Unadilla."

"Listen, Joe. Did you see any of the Andrustown people?"

"No, I didn't. I didn't come through Andrustown. I took a swing west of there. Why?"

"There's a party gone there to cut hay."

Joe swore. "Why didn't they tell me?"

"They supposed you were down south."

"Well, I can't stay there all the time. I hain't been out of the woods for two weeks. Everybody's so busy cutting hay they don't think of a poor timber beast like me. Dingman wasn't at the second lodge, either." He leaned against the fence. "Hell, nothing's going to happen."

"Dingman's haying for Mrs. Ritter. They spent last night there."

"No," said Joe.

"They've took their women with them."

Joe gawped. "What do they think they're doing?" he demanded.

"Cutting hay. Like me. Like anybody else. They thought the Rangers were out."

"Now listen," said Joe. "Everybody's cutting hay and nobody spells me and Adam. We got to get some time off, ain't we? Look here."

Gil said, "We better see Demooth. I think you and me had better go after them." He hooked his arm through his scythe snathe and picked up his rifle.

Joe stared.

"By God, you are an earnest man, Gil."

Gil did not answer.

They reported to Demooth and set out before seven o'clock. They kept to the road. The tracks of the two wagons were plain in the road. Joe pointed to them scornfully. "What do they think it is, a frolic?"

"What do you mean?"

"All of them riding in the wagons. Probably singing songs. I hope they took along some cider for the girls."

Gil thought grimly that they probably weren't singing,

anyway. But it was true that they hadn't sent a man ahead. There wasn't a sign of a human foot anywhere. But there wasn't a hostile sign along the road, either. The woods were still and close with the July heat. Only the locusts made a sound. Nothing moved but the two men trotting along the road.

It was eight miles south to Andrustown by the road. They had left the Mohawk Valley and were cutting through the hills when Joe pulled up sharp. "Listen." Gil stopped beside him. He himself had thought it sounded like a shot. Now, after a short interval, they knew. Half a dozen shots were made in quick succession.

"God," said Joe. "I wonder if they got him."

"Got him?" Gil's brain was dazed.

"Yes." Joe was irascible. "That was firing after somebody running. Probably trying to reach the woods. They must have been lined up." He started running. "Run," he said.

It was surprising how his shambling stride covered the ground. He ran like a dog, with his head up, as if he took scent out of the wind. Now that he was started he seemed perfectly calm. He even jerked some talk over his shoulder to Gil.

"So long as they're shooting they'll all be watching the houses," he said. "Must have got them inside the houses."

Twenty minutes later, Joe slowed down. There had been two more shots, but since then there had been not a sound. He and Gil had covered a little over three miles.

"No sense in running right into their laps," he said. "Your wind is licked anyway. You couldn't hit a standing barn." He himself was breathing deep but easily. The only sign of his running was the sweat on his forehead, which stood out in big drops. "We'll kind of edge up and see what they're doing."

He circled to the west in order to get up on the slope of the hill. If you were going to be spotted and chased, it was good to begin running halfway up a hill. That meant that the man chasing you would put on his first spurt, nine times out of ten, the full length of the hill, so you had him licked before he could ever get in shooting distance.

He and Gil circled round till they could look through a slash in the trees down onto the little settlement. It was a small place—just the seven cabins and five small log barns, and the barracks under which the crops were stored. It was familiar enough to them both, except that about four acres of hay had been mowed and half of it cocked. But the two men were not looking at the hay.

What they were looking at was the group of people on the road. There were about sixty Indians, painted for the most part. The hot sunlight glistened on their greased hides and the feathered tufts of hair on their heads. They were standing around a cabin which they had just set on fire. The flames ran along the bark on the logs. The flames were dull red and yellow and tipped with thick smoke. The smoke went up against the trees and rolled into the sky. The bark roof caught with a gush of sound, and suddenly the whole cabin seemed to be enfolded with fire. It was unbelievable that a house could burn so fast.

Joe said suddenly under his breath, "There's somebody in that house."

"How do you know?"

"They wouldn't be bothered to watch it otherwise. Look, they've got everything they could out of the other houses."

It was an effort for Gil to take his eyes from the burning cabin. Now he looked carefully at the crowd of Indians. He saw the three women standing among them. They were not making any demonstration. They stood perfectly still, watching the cabin with a dull kind of fascination. The way sheep will look at something dreadful. They stood like that until the roof fell in. If there were a man inside he made no sound. "Killed himself if he had sense," Joe said. "Look, they got somebody there."

Gil saw for the first time the body hanging on the fence. It was old Bell. He was caught with one leg through the rails up to the crotch and both arms hanging over the top rail; his head tilted to one side, against his shoulder. He had been scalped. The top of his head was like a red gape against the sunlight, with a little halo of flies.

Joe started moving from tree to tree, to get a fresh view, while Gil followed him. When they had moved far enough to look past the other side of the burning cabin, they saw two men lying on their faces in the road. One was young Bell, in front of his own door; the other they thought must be Staring's son, but they could not be sure from that distance. Joe began to swear.

Gil had a crazy impulse to take a shot at one of the Indians, any one, to put a shot into the midst of the whole bunch; but Joe, who seemed aware of it, whispered, "Don't shoot. We can't do anything. I don't see Leppard or Hawyer or young Weaver anywhere. Maybe they got away." His rifle muzzle twitched up in his hands. "They ain't all Indians either, Gil. Look there."

A man in a green coat with a black skullcap on his head had come out of the Leppard cabin. He seemed unconcerned. He went over to the Indians and watched the burning cabin with them. Then he said something that started them picking up burning sticks.

"That's one of Butler's Rangers," said Joe. "Do you suppose Leppard or Weaver would have the sense to get back to the fort?"

Gil did not know. He was too fascinated by what was happening to think of anything except that this was how his own place must have looked with the Indians burning it.

Butler's man turned round to the women and his face was towards Gil.

"Joe!"

"Don't talk so loud," said Joe.

"That's Caldwell!"

He remembered him as plain as if his wedding night had

happened only a week ago. Even without the patch over the eye the man's face looked the same.

He acted perfectly quiet, as if he knew just what he was doing. He motioned the women to walk north along the road. He kept saying something to them. The women looked back at him almost stupidly, and he jabbed the air with his hand. The women turned and started walking along the road. Every now and then they turned their heads to see the Indians setting fire to another cabin or barn. The Indians were swarming all round the settlement now. A couple of them were even going through the hayfield touching off the cocks.

One of the women began to run and the other two brokenly took their pace from hers. As if the Indians had heard their quickened footfalls, half a dozen of them broke away from the burning and yelled. The women started to run hard. They looked ineffectual scurrying up the road. They ran with their heads back, stiff above the hips, their legs working furiously and twice too hard under the heavy petticoats. The rest of the Indians, hearing the yell, threw down their sticks and yelled themselves and poured out on the road.

Gil was trembling like a dog. He felt sick and cold. Even his hands seemed to feel nausea. He started shouting at Joe. "We got to do something."

Joe whirled on him and struck his face with his open hand.

"Shut up. God damn you, shut up." He turned back to watch. His eyes had a glittering kind of interest in the proceeding. The women did not bother him. There were plenty of women. He wanted to see. But he kept saying over and over to quiet Gil, "We can't stop them. Not even if we shot."

Gil saw that he was right. The Indians were overtaking the women easily. They weren't even hurried about it, but the women were too terrified to realize that. They still ran along the road, erect and desperate, with the funny skittering motion that a woman has when she tries to run. The Indians let them get almost to the beginning of the woods, then they yelled again with the piercing high note that an Indian can make and surrounded the three women.

Six or seven bucks caught the women by the shoulders and threw them down on the road and fell on top of them. The rest of the Indians crowded round. They were still yelling, but some of them were laughing.

Joe said suddenly, "I guess they ain't going to kill them."

Gil saw that the white officer was standing in the road looking after the Indians. He was making no motion to stop the proceedings. Even from that distance he looked almost amused by it. Then he turned his back and started systematically to feed the fires where they were not doing their job.

Gil looked back at the women and Indians. The crowd had given back a little. Now there was a shrill whoop and one of the Indians bent down and straightened up waving a petticoat. All the Indians whooped. Then another bent down and came up with a short gown. In a moment a couple of dozen of them were waving pieces of the women's clothing. Then they all backed away so that the two men on the hill were able to see the three naked bodies of the women lying in the road.

The Indians looked down at them for a while, shaking their clothes at them, until the man in the green coat put a whistle to his mouth and blew a shrill blast. The Indians answered it stragglingly. They left the women.

The women lay where they were, beaten and stupefied, until the Indians were quite a way off, when one by one they got up slowly. They stood naked looking back at their burning homes, at the Indians, and the three dead men. Then they stampeded for the woods. The Indians sent a few whoops after them, and at each yell the women seemed to buck up in the air and come down running harder. They weren't like women any more without their clothes. They were like some kind of animal, and they went a great deal faster than they had before.

Joe whispered to Gil, "Come on, we got to head them off."

He led Gil at a rapid rate back through the woods until they got to the road. The women heard them coming and ran like fury, but Gil and Joe did not dare call to them. The women were too scared to look back. They had to run them down. It was only when two of them fell that the white men were able to overtake them.

The women were Mrs. Leppard and Mrs. Hawyer and young Bell's wife. The oldest woman, Mrs. Leppard, was the first one to recover her wits. She said the Indians had come up just before the men went out to hay it. They had got Bell and had shot old Bell when he was going to get a horse. Young Crim, who had decided to join their party at the last minute, got into his house and would not come out, so the Indians burned his house with him in it. The three men in the hayfield had made the woods. John Weaver had been down by the spring and had got away too.

Joe helped up Mrs. Staring, who was a pretty girl, quite young, and urged all three off the road. While they were still talking, young Weaver, unarmed, came down the hill to them. His face was white and he looked terribly scared. But he had stuck around. He said he thought something might turn up for him to do.

Joe grinned at him.

"Did you see Leppard and the others?"

"They went for the fort."

"You take the women back and tell them I and Gil are going to camp on their trail for a while."

The men gave the women their hunting shirts and started them off for Fort Herkimer with John. Then Joe and Gil returned to the edge of the clearing and watched the Indians burning the rest of the settlement. It took them about an hour more before the white officer was satisfied. Then they picked up their loot and made packs of it. They had a queer collection of odds and ends, which Indians were apt to value, like small mirrors and a china bowl; but the men with the women's clothes were the ones that seemed the most envied. Some of them tied the clothes round their heads. They rounded up the two horses that had brought in the carts, which had already been burnt, and took off south down the road, a compact mass of men, moving, now that they had finally got started, quite fast. They made Gil think of wild dogs which had been running sheep. They kept no order in their march, but stuck together with the instinct for killing.

I I

Adam Helmer's Run

The destruction of Andrustown was something that Adam Helmer had missed: he had made a long swing to the west with old Blue Back, following John Butler and his thousand men on their trip back from Wyoming. He had gone all the way to Chemung behind the army. Butler had left off some of the men at Tioga, but he himself was indubitably headed for Niagara. Helmer and the Oneida had struck back cross-country with the news that Brant had met Butler at Chemung and had gone back to Tioga to pick up the Rangers left there, and his own Indians at Unadilla. There was some talk of attacking Cherry Valley, apparently; but Helmer believed, and so did Blue Back, that Brant would strike at German Flats.

At the news of Andrustown the first impulse had been to chase the raiders down to Unadilla. Conrad Franck had immediately set out with twenty volunteers on the understanding that Colonel Klock, whom Congress had appointed chief of the militia battalions, should bring up the Palatine companies to join Bellinger and back them up. But Jacob Klock got no farther than the sight of Andrustown; while he was still apprehensively eyeing that smoking ruin, a runner came from Little Stone Arabia Stockade to report a new irruption by the enemy. They had burned houses in Schuyler and taken two men prisoners, one of them George Weaver, and killed four. That was enough for Jacob Klock. He would not listen to Bellinger's protests. He gave orders for Bellinger to return to Fort Herkimer while he himself took his companies overland to the falls, and as soon as he was home he sat right down and wrote a letter to Governor Clinton.

The puffy old colonel was so disturbed that he got his sequence of events completely muddled; he even dated his letter June 22, instead of July 22. He wrote:—

Sir, Tryon County has once more experienced the Cruelty of a restless Enemy. Springfield, Andrewtown, and the Settlements on Lacke Osego were at once attacked and destroyed last Saturday. House, Barns, and even Waggons, ploughs and the Hay Cocks in the Meadows were laid in Ashes. . . . As soon as the news came, I ordered immediately the Militia to March to stop the progress of the Enemy. The same Instant I received a Letter from Coll. Peter Bellinger of the German Flats, that the Enemy was burning Houses within four Miles of the Flats praying for Assistance. I did order up five Companies of the Palatine and Cona Johary Battallion; The rest I marched straight to Andrewtown; ordering Coll. Bellinger to join me in order to intercept if possible the Enemy. But on my March thiter I learnt that he the Enemy was gone; and nothing was left, as to scour the woods, as I got information, that still a strong part of the Enemy was left to do mischief. As soon as the Flats Militia was on their March in the woods, the Enemy fell out at the Flats and toock two prisoners. . . . We are informed that Brandt boasted openly that he will be joined at Unatelly by Butler, and that within eight days he will return and lay the whole County waste. . . . Harvest time is at Hand & no prospect of a speedy Assistence. . . . Last Sunday Morning I dispatched an Express to general Ten Broeck, and desired the recommendation of the Situation of our County to your Excellency & to gen Starcks, but did not receive an Answer. Your Excellency, the common father of the good People of this State, upon whose fatherly Exertions the People of this County relieth, and which keepeth the many poor, the numerous widows and the fatherless still in hopes, will, we fervently pray, grant us such speedy relief, as your Ex'llcy in your wisdom shall see meet; & In case it chould be an impossibility; to afford us any Assistance with Batteaus, to bring off wifes and Children, that they might not be prey to a Cruel Enemy. Having tacken the Liberty to macke your Excellency aquainted with the Situation and Sentiments of the people I remain as in duty Bound Sir Your most obedient and most humble Servant

JACOB KLOCK

While Jacob Klock was busying himself with this effort and Colonel Peter Bellinger was crossing the hills north again as fast as his men could set down their feet, Conrad Franck and his thirty volunteers were sitting on their tails round Joe Boleo's lodge on the hill above the Edmeston settlement. They were waiting there for Bellinger and Klock. Gil and Joe had intercepted them on the road barely in time to keep them from being run over by Brant's main gang, which was returning from the little lakes. Brant and Caldwell had joined just above Edmeston, making an army of three hundred men, and the thirty farmers from German Flats lay up in the witch hobble and sumac, a quarter of a mile off, and looked down on the fringe of the army. It was apparent to them that Caldwell was but an offshoot of Brant's main army, and it might well have been that the whole three hundred would have turned that afternoon. Instead, however, they bore off south into the woods, passing Edmeston. They made a motley army: Indians for the most part, Cayugas, Senecas, and Mohawks in their paint and feathers, Eries with strange headdresses made of the dried heads of animals, greencoat soldiers, with their black caps and leather gaiters, a few scattered remains of the old Highland guard of Fort Johnson, dark limber men, wearing tartan kilts and knee-length leggings of deerskin and carrying long-barreled, smooth-bore rifles and Indian war clubs. They came down the trail with the long loose stride of woodsmen, their tread light on the ground, but their voices were upraised in talk as if there were no other living thing in all the woods. They shouted back and forth, calling each other's names, lifting the fresh scalps from their belts,—those that had them,—roaring to know whether the bounty still held at eight dollars in Niagara.

Gil and Joe Boleo and Conrad Franck, lying well beyond the line of their men, plainly saw Caldwell and Brant meet and report to each other. The dour unemotional white man was nearly a head taller than the Indian. Watching the latter's temperamental face, Gil could not help but remember how Brant had towered over Herkimer that day at Unadilla thirteen months ago. Herkimer was dead; Herkimer must have known what would happen with Brant loose in the woods with armed men to manage. Even to Gil, who knew little of the general strategy of war, it seemed that Brant was the leading actor in the gradual encircling of the flats. He wondered for an instant whether it would be worth while to shoot Brant where he stood. A fair mark, with his red blanket over his shoulder and cocked hat with yellow lace and the silver gorget on his chest that a man could hold his sights just under. But even as the thought occurred to him, Joe Boleo touched his hand and shook his head. "There ain't no Indian worth getting killed for," he whispered. Before Gil could think it out in his own mind, the army was on the move.

They disappeared as quickly down the road as they had come. A few of the Senecas deployed in front; a few of the Mohawks spread out in the rear, loitering along until the main body was well ahead. One man came within a hundred yards of where Gil lay. He was close enough for Gil to see the lines of his face under the paint, the broad nose, slightly hooked, with the deep nostrils; the little silver socket that held the eagle's feather over his right ear; the notches on the handle of his tomahawk.

The thirty men stayed where they were for over an hour, but when no one else came from the east or north, they withdrew to Boleo's lodge to take council. They waited for Bellinger and Klock until sundown. Gil found that several, like himself, had felt the itch to draw a bead on Brant. But having seen Brant's army, they felt less anxious to open battle on them.

There was nothing thirty men could do. It was obvious that they ought to go home. But the men were spoiling for something now they were out, and it was Joe who calmly mentioned Young's settlement two miles east of Edmeston, on a branch of Butternut Creek. The inhabitants were all outspoken King's men.

Nobody had any arguments. As soon as it was dark, they moved across the trail. Within an hour they came out on the creek shore and found the wagon ruts that led to Young's; an hour more and their work was done. Behind them the small clearings were alight with the burning farms; three of them, belonging to

Young, Bollyer, and a man named Betty. The men from the flats had found only women and children, but that fact—that Tories felt it safe to leave their families unprotected in the woods— served only to infuriate them. They hauled the women out of bed and drove them and the children down the trail. Then they burned every standing wall, killing cattle and horses and even shooting the pigs that ran squealing round the firelight. They stripped one of the women, who returned to save three pounds in hard money, and laughed at her, dividing the money among themselves, and telling her to talk to Captain Caldwell.

Adam Helmer had missed all these events while he was travers-ing a hundred and fifty miles of wilderness, and he felt bitter at having missed the fun. For a month and a half nothing hap-pened. Every time he returned to the flats, Demooth or Bellinger sent him out again at once. He had hardly had time for more than a couple of visits with Polly Bowers; he hadn't been back to McKlennar's for a good meal at all. He hadn't seen Gil; Gil was too busy getting in his wheat. But the wheat would all be in now; and the next trip down they might be able to get up a decent crowd. Joe Boleo was covering the west since the raid on Schuy-ler in which George Weaver had been taken prisoner. Helmer alone was responsible for the Unadilla trail, unless he included the three men who were supposed to be watching the trail with him. Most likely they were sitting together throwing dice.

Adam combed his hair as he lay in the green filtered sun-light. The woods were dim with the September haze. The August heat was continuing; but it was better to be hot than to lie out in the rain.

His first sight of the Indians came so abruptly that he knew it would be impossible to warn the men beyond him. There were forty Indians, he judged, Mohawks too, coming up the trail at a dogtrot. That many meant surely that there were flankers out. He heard them now. Whatever force it might be, it was coming fast.

At last what everyone had feared had come to pass, and Adam had allowed himself to get caught like a fifteen-year-old boy on his first scout. He knew that there was only one chance of those three fools getting away; and he knew also that some-one would have to get away if German Flats were to be warned in time. Adam did not hesitate. He rolled over on his knee and took the leading Indian a clean shot right under the wishbone. Then, while they milled, he charged straight down the slope and over the trail and up the opposite bank. He made it so fast that the first shots the Indians had at him he was dodging through the scrub.

The musket fire crackled like dry sticks, and the stink of black powder reached out in the still air so that he smelled it as he ran. But he paid no attention to the shooting and yelling on the trail. He dodged into some heavier timber, and wheeled down the bank again. He had judged his course exactly. He hit the trail three hundred yards ahead of his first crossing, just beyond a bend.

He ran lightly, listening to the surge of voices behind him. Up at the lodge a sudden feeble burst of three shots sounded, then more yells. The damned fools hadn't had the sense to cut and run when he gave them the diversion. He knew as sure as he knew which end of himself he ate with that the three men were dead. It left him alone to carry the warning into German Flats.

German Flats lay twenty-four miles to north and he knew he had probably the pick of Brant's Indians on his trail, men who could run eighty miles through the woods between sunrise and noon. But Adam knew that he could run himself, and he knew that he would have to run on an open trail and that once the Indians discovered that, they would know he would stick to it. They wouldn't have to be bothered with tracking.

He eased up slightly, listening behind him. The first surge of yelling had overshot the eastern ridge; now it returned. It would be only a minute before they brought his tracks down to the trail. He began to put on a little pressure to make the next bend; but just before he rounded it he heard the war whoop slide up to its unhuman pitch and a wild shot cut the air high over his head.

His wind had come back from that first foolish burst up and down the ridge. He lengthened his stride. His yellow hair, fresh-combed and beautiful, whipped up and down on his shoulders like a short flapping blanket. His mouth opened as he reached his full pace and he took the slight grade with the bursting rush of a running buck deer.

The Indians had stopped yelling. At the end of the next straight stretch Adam flung a look over his shoulder and saw the first brave running bent over, going smooth and quick and soundless. The Indian knew that Helmer had seen him, but he didn't lift his gun. He wasn't carrying a gun. He had only his tomahawk, which was a great deal more deadly if he could pull up within forty feet.

The Indian must have been gaining, Adam thought, or else he was the leader of a group, following the old Mohawk dodge of sprinting to make the fugitive travel at top speed. The others would take a steadier pace; but as soon as the leader tired another man would sprint up. By keeping pressure on the fugitive in this way they could run down any man in four or five hours plain going. Adam would not only have to keep ahead of the press, he would have to run the heart completely out of them.

He sprinted himself now; not blindly, but picking his next easing point beforehand; he knew the trail, every stone and root of it, from Edmeston to German Flats, as well as he knew Polly Bowers. His easing point would be the ford over Licking Brook. A half mile.

At any time it was worth while to see Adam run. He was the biggest man in the flats, six feet five in his moccasins. With his mass of yellow hair he seemed yet taller. He weighed close to two hundred pounds, without an ounce of fat on him.

He began to draw away from the Indian as soon as he started to sprint. Glancing back again, he saw that the Indian had straightened up a little. He got the feeling that the Indian's face was surprised. Probably the Indian fancied himself as quite a runner. Maybe he was champion of some lousy set of lodges somewhere. Adam could have laughed if he had not needed his wind, but the laughter went on in his inside, sending the blood into his hands. His head felt fine and clear. He figured he had gained thirty yards on the Indian when he hit the brook.

He jumped the ford. It was too early to risk wetting his feet and going sore. But as he cleared the water, he threw his rifle from him. It splashed into the pool below the ford and sank. Now that his hands were free, Adam began unlacing his hunting shirt. He got it off. By the time he came to the big butternut tree, he had wrapped his powder flask and bullet pouch in it, and he threw it over a small clump of witch hobble. Then he tightened his belt and stuck his hatchet into the back of his belt where the handle would not keep smacking against his legs.

He was now naked from the waist up. The wind of his running felt good on his chest, cooling the sweat as it trickled down through the short golden mane. He was a wonderful man to see; his skin white as a woman's except for his hands and face, which were deeply tanned. He was feeling fine and going well. He felt so fine he thought he might almost let the leading Indian pull up and maybe chance a throw at him with his tomahawk. He eased a little, enough to see the Indian. When the buck appeared behind him, Adam saw that he was a new man. He was taller, and his face was painted black and white instead of red and

yellow as the other's had been. He did not come quite so fast, but
Adam's trained eye saw that he had better staying power. Adam
decided then and there that he would put all ideas of a quick
fight out of his mind. The Indians meant real business.

For the next four miles the chase continued with only a
slight variation of the pace, Adam adapting himself to the man
behind. He was beginning to feel the pressure, but he was running with greater canniness. He kept his eyes glued to the trail
now. He did not dare risk a blind step. His ankles wouldn't hold
up as well if he lit on a rolling stone or a slippery root. He had
the feeling very definitely that the race was reaching a climax,
and though he ran strongly, strong enough to lick any man in the
flats at a hundred yards straightaway this minute, he knew that
these Indians were good.

His breathing was still excellent. He had no fear of giving
out; he could run till sundown, he thought; and then it came
upon him that it would be a fact, if he managed to clear the
Indians, that he would hit the flats just about sundown. Even
while he ran, he reasoned it out that Brant must have figured on
reaching the valley at dark and striking in the morning. Adam
wondered what would happen when Brant knew that the word
had gone ahead of him. He doubted whether Brant could get up
his main body anyway much before sunset. But it didn't matter
much. The only thing in the world Adam could do was to reach
the flats. If he got there first some people could get into the forts.

His eyes kept checking in his landmarks and he realized that
Andrustown was only a mile, or a little more, ahead. He must
have outdistanced most of even the first pursuit. He expected
there would not be more than half a dozen who could have held
on as long as this, and if that were so they would have to be
sending up another man pretty soon. And they would all begin
bearing down at the same time.

Adam figured that if he could get through Andrustown clearing he might better take to the woods, for he would have gained as much time as anyone could on the main body.

As he chanced a backward glance, he saw that the Indians were going to try to run him down now. The new man was there and it was evident that he was their best man. He was not tall. He was thickset and had thick short legs. He was entirely naked except for ankle moccasins and breech clout and he was oiled and painted and rather light-colored. He looked like a Mohawk. He wore three feathers. It seemed impossible that he could have kept up with the rest, just to see him at first, for he had a belly that showed out in front. But his belly did not bounce at all. After a minute Adam thought it must be an enlarged place where he kept his wind.

The Indian's legs moved with incredible rapidity. He had already taken his tomahawk from his belt as if he were confident of being able to haul up on the white man. That gesture gave Adam the incentive he needed. He was enraged, and he took his rage out in his running. When the Indian entered the clearing, Adam was already down past the black ruins of the houses and going away with every stride. It was the greatest running the Indian had ever looked at. He knew he was licked, and he started slowing up very gradually. By the time Adam hit the woods, the Indian had stopped and sat down by the roadside.

When Adam looked back from the woods the Indian wasn't even looking at him. He was all alone in the clearing and he was futilely banging the ground between his legs with his tomahawk. Adam knew he had made it. He did not stop, nor even let down quickly on his pace. All he had to race now was time. He would have laughed if he could have got the breath for it. Time? Time, hell!

• • •

They saw the runner coming down the long hill, his body glistening with sweat and reflecting red from the low-lying ball of the sun. He was coming hard. The sentry in the spy loft of Fort Herkimer saw men come out of houses as the runner passed. Then the men ran back into the houses. Before the runner was out halfway over the flat land, the family of the first house he had passed had their horse hitched to the family cart in front of the door and were piling their belongings and children into it.

The sentry let out a yell.

"It's Helmer!"

In the yard an officer stopped on his way out.

"Helmer?"

"Yes, Adam Helmer. He's running hard. He ain't got his gun. He ain't got his shirt on." He paused, looked out again, and then bawled down once more. "He looks pretty near played out." His voice flattened. "I reckon it's Brant."

"What makes you think so?"

"The people are coming in after him."

Without another word the officer went round the corner of the blockhouse on the run for the church. It was Colonel Bellinger. The sentry heard the whang of his feet on the rungs of the belfry ladder.

Bellinger was now in the steeple. He was yanking the canvas off the swivel. The brass barrel glinted in the sunset. Bellinger stood back, waving the match.

The gun roared. One shot.

All over the valley it brought people outdoors to stare at the church steeple. Before dark they were thronging towards the forts by road and river. Those who had already reached Fort Herkimer stood in front of the church and stared at Helmer's naked chest. It was whipped with branches, the white skin welted and bloody. But Helmer was breathing easily again. He had never, he thought, felt finer in his life.

12

A Night—and a Morning

Mrs. McKlennar's barn was a comfortable place to milk in. It was cool and dusky. There were no windows—only the walls of logs and the log ceiling overhead. The four cows stood in a row on rough plank. The whole place was filled with dust and the dry earthy smell, mingled with dung, from the walk behind the cows. It was quiet with the soft breathing of the cows, and the hiss of milk striking its own froth in the pails. Mrs. McKlennar, gray bare head butting one cow's flank, and Gil, face turned to look through the open door, were milking together. They were not making any conversation. They were tired from lashing down the wooden barrack roofs over the wheat stacks. And they were both conscious of the finish of the harvest, a good harvest, one they were both proud of—Mrs. McKlennar because the farm belonged to her, and Gil because she had dropped the remark that it was the best yield they had ever had from the land. He knew that it was he himself who had made that best yield a fact. They were thus contented, balanced on the one-legged stools, when the flat impact of the swivel's roar fell on their ears.

In the first breath, they could hardly believe what they had heard. Then Daisy's voice lifted in a falsetto screech from the house. "Oh, Mis' McKlennar! Hit's de cannon gun over de foht. I seen it going off! Oh, Mis'!"

The widow rose with Gil. Her long face was set. She saw how white he was.

"It's the alarm gun," he said. "It's a raid."

"One gun." Her lips compressed; she nodded.

"We've got to move to the fort."

She nodded again. They were out of the barn now, striding towards the stone house. "Don't run," said Mrs. McKlennar. "We won't get there by running. And *she's* all right."

But Gil had to see Lana. Lana would have been feeding young Gil—christened Gilbert McKlennar Martin, with the widow as sponsor.

Lana was sitting in the kitchen, with Gilly at her breast. Her eyes met Gil's, questioning, terror-stricken, but full of enforced quiet. Thank God, he thought, she hasn't lost her nerve, yet.

"Now, Gil, where do you think we'd better go?"

"We can get to Dayton by the road. But I'd rather cross the river to Herkimer. It's quicker. We can take the cart down to the river."

Mrs. McKlennar nodded.

"We won't try to take much. I'll get my money and some brandy. Daisy, you take the pail from Gil and fill a stone jug. Milk is handy sometimes. And that fresh baking of bread and the two hams. And don't scream. They don't pay for nigger scalps."

"Yas'm."

Gil was surprised to find that he was still carrying the pail. He got the rifle down from the pegs between the beams, and then started through the house, closing and barring the shutters. Mrs. McKlennar collected her money and the brandy and her own clothes and Lana's. She made bundles of the clothes on the kitchen floor and wrapped the brandy and money in them. Daisy brought the food in a basket. "I fetched de new currant preserve and de side of fresh pohk," she said proudly. "That preserve and pohk tas' good together."

Gil was already out of the house. He chased the pigs into the woods, drove out the cows after taking off their bells, and then hitched the mare to the cart. As soon as he brought it to the door, Mrs. McKlennar tossed their belongings in. Lana buttoned her short gown. She met Gil's eyes with a pale face, saying, "I thought I'd let Gilly finish his feed. I thought he'd be quieter."

"Good girl," said Mrs. McKlennar.

He helped Lana into the cart. Daisy and Mrs. McKlennar scrambled over the tailboard. Gil closed the door and poked the latchstring in. They had done all they could. He took the mare by the head and led her down to the road. As they turned into it, they heard the express rider coming along from Dayton. He passed them at full gallop, leaning forward in his saddle. He did not appear to notice them.

The alarm gun at Eldridge Blockhouse made a single dull thud.

"They haven't reached the valley yet," Gil thought. He opened the bars on the far side of the highway and led the mare into the wheatfield. They went at a walk over the stubble towards the river.

Though the darkness was already a shadow in the east, and a mist had begun to hover on the water where brooks entered the river, a hazy after-sunset light reached from beneath a dark bank of clouds rising in the west. Through this dim haze the four adults in the cart could see people moving across the flat land on the far side of the river. The creak of the cart, even the tread of the horses on the opposite road, reached them with startling clearness, but the absence of all talk gave to the approaching night a singular effect of silence.

They themselves got out of the cart without a word when Gil stopped the mare on the riverbank. He drew the bow of the boat on shore and helped the widow into the stern. Then, standing in the water, he passed the baby from Lana's arms to Mrs. McKlennar's lap. The child lay still as a mouse. It seemed to them that it must be aware of what was going on, it lay so still, looking straight up at the unaccustomed sky with wakeful eyes. Lana got in next and helped to stow away the basket and bundles. Daisy nearly upset the boat in her anxiety. Her fat hams filled the bow, her striped petticoat swelling over the gunwales. She sat motionless, holding her treasure, a framed small picture of Christ, close to her bosom. Her face was gray under her bright calico kerchief.

Gil climbed up the bank again and unharnessed the mare. After a moment's hesitation he backed the cart down the bank into the river and threw the harness into it. It would be hard to burn a cart in the river. Then he slapped the mare's rump, slid down to the water side, and shoved the boat out.

It was overloaded. He had to row slowly. He pulled out into the middle of the quiet river and paused for a last look at the mare. She had stopped a little way from the bank to look after them. She kept pricking her ears nervously.

"Hadn't we better start?" Mrs. McKlennar suggested quietly.

Gil pulled upstream. The reflections of the willow trees were fading into the general darkness of the water. The valley was yet quiet. There was no sound anywhere, except the passage of carts along the road, until the Casler family, also rowing up the river, overtook them.

Jacob Casler said softly over the water, "You folks all right?"

"Yes. You?"

"We brought all we could. I ain't got any gunpowder, though."

"They have some in the fort."

Mrs. Casler said with a slight shrillness in her voice, "We got plenty of bullets. Jake made a lot this spring."

They then rowed steadily ahead without further conversation.

The clouds, without rain, gradually filled the sky, and pitch-dark night had fallen by the time the two boats reached Fort Herkimer. Though the gates were still open, there was little noise from inside. Gil got his family on shore and hauled the boat out of the water. Lana carried the baby, and Mrs. McKlennar, Daisy, and he carried everything else. They passed through the gates into the crowded square.

Every inch of space was taken by people standing together in groups, by carts yet unloaded, horses nervous but still. Gil asked for the news and for the first time learned of Helmer's race and the fact that Brant at last was on the way.

He found a place for his family on the north wall in a corner shed which they had to share with Mrs. Weaver and Cobus. Directly across the square from them they saw Captain Demooth arranging his wife's bed with Mary Reall's help.

Mrs. Weaver said "Hello" to them in a dull voice. She had grown gaunt. She kept watching Mary Reall's quiet attendance on the captain's wife. There was great unhappiness in her face. She made no move as John went over to see Mary before coming across the yard to find his mother. Gil drew young Cobus aside and asked in a whisper whether anyone had heard of George Weaver. Cobus shook his head.

"We don't reckon he was killed."

Emma Weaver lifted her voice.

"We don't know. They pay the same for scalps they pay for prisoners." She turned away from John. "We're all right. Cobus looked out for me."

Gil saw that Lana was settled in the corner with Mrs. McKlennar beside her. He bent down and kissed her cheek. "I've got to talk to Bellinger or Demooth," he said.

The yard was now alive with the hushed murmur of people straightening themselves out. Suddenly Colonel Bellinger lifted his voice.

"We've got to get the horses out of here." He caught sight of Gil. "You, Martin. You get them out. All of them, and the carts. Right away."

"I want to keep my horse," a man protested. "The Indians stole my cow."

"All of them, I said. We can't have the yard cluttered up. We haven't room for horses. If they get scared and get kicking they'll damage somebody. Get them out. All the women"—he raised his voice so that it carried throughout the fort—"I want all the women to stay in the sheds or the church until we get the yard clear. If any shooting starts, all the women and children must get into the church. Keep the north pews for a hospital. All men with guns, who haven't been assigned posts on the stockade, report to Captain Demooth on the east blockhouse." As the subdued movement of disentanglement commenced, Bellinger moved over to the central fire, watching them. There was disorder, but it was quiet disorder, as if the people were accustoming themselves to a dark room; and Bellinger was patient. The horses and carts were being quickly taken out into the blackness beyond the gates, unharnessed, and the horses loosed. The banging of dropped shafts was a loud sound. In fifteen minutes Gil returned to report all horses outside the stockade. Bellinger raised his voice again. "One more thing." He waited till everyone's attention was fixed on him as he stood in the firelight. "We don't know where the Indians are. It's a black night and a fog is rising off the river. We can only listen for them. So as soon as you're settled you'll have to be quiet. No talking anywhere. If a baby cries, and you can't hush him, take him into the church and cover him up."

He turned to meet Demooth. He seemed quite calm. His long dark face and broad shoulders made a comforting bulk in the firelight. Gil remembered him at Oriskany, lugging Herkimer up the slope.

He said to Demooth: "Martin here has cleared out all the horses. Have you got all your men up, Mark?"

Demooth's voice was tightly strained, though the strain did not show in his face.

"Yes, I have."

"How much longer do you think we ought to let the fire burn?"

"It ought to be put out now. Nobody's come in for the past ten minutes. We can't check everybody. Some of the people may go to Fort Dayton. We don't expect anybody from Eldridge."

Bellinger said, "I'll put out all lights in ten minutes. I'll have to give the people warning."

He was shouting the warning as Gil climbed up on the west sentry walk. Gil passed young John Weaver, looking white and set in the face. "Hello, John," he said.

"Hello, Mr. Martin," said John.

Down in the yard, Bellinger and Demooth had moved to the gates. They were closing them now, with two men helping. The gates squealed and ground on their straps. The three bars fell heavily into place. The shutting off of light from inside the enclosure also shut off the eyes of the horses outside. The animals had gathered in a small herd to look in at the gate. Now they whinnied in the darkness. The familiar sound, for some reason, was fearful.

Gil found that his position was next to Adam Helmer. They shook hands. Helmer laughed softly. "Did you hear about me running away from those Mohawks?" he wanted to know.

He was bursting with pride. He was wearing a shirt too small for him—there wasn't a shirt in German Flats that would have made a decent fit for him. He leaned easily against the picket points, with a borrowed rifle propped handy to his hand. He talked softly about the run, becoming dramatic as he told about outdistancing each Indian. He made quite a story about the heavy-set fellow who had just sat down and banged the ground with his tomahawk. "He looked like he was crying," said Helmer. "I don't blame him. I've got quite a scalp, by God." He shook his head, tossing his yellow hair, and laughed.

"When the fire's put out, nobody's to talk," shouted Bellinger.

"I mean that. Anybody that can't keep their mouth shut had better plan to get outside."

A couple of men had lugged a great kettle to the fire. They emptied it over the flames. The light seemed to burst and spread with the steam. At the hissing, and the steam smell, and the added darkness, the horses whinnied again. Then they stampeded.

In the fort the darkness was black and voiceless. Lana felt as if the people she had been watching were all dead. She felt alone in the world with Gilly, until Mrs. McKlennar put her hand out. The two women held hands.

Cobus whispered to his mother, "I don't see why they won't let me have a musket up there."

"Hush. Hush your mouth." His mother's voice was savage. Then almost inaudibly she began to pray for George. George had taken a trip up to Schuyler on that fatal day to see about some work he had heard of. He had wanted to get the job as a surprise for John.

Mrs. Demooth was quite docile. She lay on her back on the blankets with her hands folded on her breast. She had a queer notion that her husband had tied her hands after she had kicked Nancy. She thought they were still tied. She would not even dress, or feed herself. Mary had to take complete care of her; but she was nice to Mary. She wasn't afraid any more. She lay there singing under her breath. She sang snatches of a hymn, of which only now and then, by leaning close, could Mary hear a phrase. "A mighty fortress is our God . . ." Mary remembered how her father liked to sing it; he sang it always in German, rolling it out with his surprising deep voice. Her tears came close to her eyes as the woman's colorless voice went on with the hymn. And then, after a silence, the voice sang thinly—it was like the voice of an insect, it was so small—a little light sad tune.

> *"Twixt the water and the willow tree,*
> *There stood I,*
> *When I spied my gallant gentleman*
> *Riding by . . ."*

It went on, so plaintively that Mary hugged her knees tight and tried to see John up on the sentry walk. But since the fire had gone out, she could see nothing. Her heart was sad, thinking of him and herself. It was impossible for him to find work anywhere that paid money. He had worked through most of the harvest for nothing but food and keep. He always seemed to be cheerful when he came to see her, and he was happy that she should be doing so well. It made her feel very humble that she should be earning money while he wasn't.

> *"Oh, my Lord, why did you pass me*
> *In the time gone by,*
> *That only now you speak of love*
> *When death rides nigh?*
> *For I'll never love another*
> *Though the stream run dry,*
> *Though the willow leaf be withered*
> *And my heart doth die."*

Listening to the thin voice, Mary felt her love for John well up in her. She said a prayer for him, addressing God as a literal person who could, if He would, take care of John.

She put out her thin hand to the woman's forehead, in the

dark, and began to stroke her face, very gently. The singing stopped after a while, and a little later Mary's hand felt wet.

In the darkness by the eastern blockhouse Bellinger and Demooth talked in low voices. They tried to feel confident that the fort could hold off Brant and the Indians. They had eighty-seven armed men. Fort Dayton should have sixty-odd. The most dangerous place was Little Stone Arabia Stockade with only twenty, but they believed that the raid would be confined to the flats. Altogether there were one hundred and forty families in the flats—that figure included the Eldridge Settlement, which contained eight families and fourteen men. Men were any male persons over fifteen. They did not know how big Brant's force was. They had no way of telling. All their scouts but Joe Boleo were inside the fort; and the scouts were the nucleus of any real defense. They could not afford to send one out. Boleo, they decided, must have been cut off and have gone over to Dayton.

They had a fair supply of powder, enough for a week, though the often demanded supply had not been sent up from Albany. There was plenty of shot. They knew that an express had been sent down to Cherry Valley, where the Massachusetts Regiment of Colonel Alden had gone into garrison; but they did not expect any succor from him for two days—if indeed any ever came at all. They had to rely on themselves. Their greatest hope lay in the fact that Indians never cared to face fire from behind a stockade.

When they stopped speaking, the fort was still and black about them. Not a light showed anywhere. There were not even any stars to give an outline to the palisade. Nothing moved but the mist eddying damply against their faces in a vagrant draft.

Demooth climbed the nearest ladder to make a round of the sentry walk. All the men were wakeful. Each one whispered as

Demooth passed that he had heard no hostile sound. Demooth paused from time to time to listen for himself.

The only sound he heard was the slow tread of a grazing horse. It seemed to be quite near, but the horse was totally invisible.

The faceless night dragged on interminably. As near as Gil could figure, it was getting on to dawn when his ears were first attracted by the soft blowing of a horse's breath. He nudged Helmer. But Helmer had already heard it.

He whispered, "If that was an Indian the horse would have run."

They waited for several minutes. Then they heard a man whistle.

Adam stiffened. He whistled back on the same note. The answer returned.

"It's Joe," he murmured. "He's edging up to the sally port."

Helmer dropped off the sentry walk, lighting on his feet as gently as a cat. He went quickly towards the gate where he found Bellinger and told him that Joe Boleo was coming in. Together they opened the sally port, and Joe Boleo stepped through like an embodiment of the darkness itself.

"What have you been up to?" Adam asked.

"That you, Adam? I been sleeping with your grandma's aunt. Where's Bellinger?"

"He's right alongside of me." Adam grinned in the darkness. "Did you hear about me running off from the Mohawks?"

"No," said Joe. He turned to Bellinger as the latter demanded what news he had.

"Brant's up at Shoemaker's. He's got a big army. Mostly whites, too, that's the funny part. I couldn't figure out how many—about five hundred all together. They camped there the first part of the night, but two hours ago they commenced moving out over the valley. I thought maybe I'd better come back and get some sleep."

Bellinger asked, "Are they moving all in one bunch?"

"Naw. They've broke up in parties."

"Then I guess they won't attack the fort."

"I ain't guessing," said Joe.

"Well, Helmer. You get back on the walk."

"Come with me, Joe," said Helmer. "I want to tell you . . ."

"Go to hell," said Joe. "Where can I get a drink of water?"

Joe's news was passed from man to man. The whisper traveled the circumference of the stockade like the flitting of an owl through the dark. The women and children could hear the shuffle of feet passing over their heads, as each man moved to his neighbor, whispered, and moved back. But no one bothered to tell the women. They had to stay in their dark and airless sheds, listening and waiting and unwarned.

Lana felt Gilly wake up in her lap. First the slight stiffening of his hard little back, then the bump as he slung his head down against her thigh. He would begin to cry for his feed. He was an early feeder—voracious and demanding, a regular rooster. She whispered to Mrs. McKlennar, as she dandled Gilly, and Mrs. McKlennar leaned away from Lana's shoulder. When Gilly opened his mouth for his first bawl, he found the breast popped in. The smack of his mouth as it closed in surprise was almost like the clap of two hands. He gave a little grunt and, applying himself directly, sucked with noisy gusto. Mrs. McKlennar gave a positive snort of delight.

"The little warrior!"

Lana eased her back, which ached from the long hours of sitting in the darkness, and let him feed. She was glad of the distraction. It was the first thing that had happened all night, and her brain was worn out with her unceasing effort to listen.

A cock crowed.

The bird's voice was so familiar in its accents that more than one person imagined it at his own farm. But as the bird crowed again, the voice became isolated and infinitely distant in the mist. Presently another bird answered, and then a third took it up.

Listening to the birds crowing here and there throughout the valley, Demooth felt that something was out of place. He drew out his watch and read the face by the light of the gunner's match kept going in the church. The watch told him that it was 4.25, almost an hour and a half before dawn.

He climbed up into the belfry to get a higher view. As he went up the ladder into inky darkness, he heard a dog start barking far up the valley.

Standing beside the swivel, under the beam that used to carry the bell, Demooth looked out. He could not hear a human sound. Only the frantic furious barking of the dog persisted. But suddenly the dog yelped and went away yelping through the fog.

At that instant, Demooth lost his illusion. Red glows of light swelled in the fog to the west, and, refracted in the moist air, they took spherical shape. Even as he located their position, new globes of light swelled behind them; then with the unexpectedness of a blow they started springing up on the right and left, north and south of the fort, and finally to the east, so that the fort was surrounded as if by a phantasmal manifestation.

He was so absorbed in the sight that for the moment he was not aware of the stirring on the sentry walks below him. But as the voices of men reached upwards, he was brought sharply to his senses.

"That's Ritter's barn, see."

"Which one?"

"That one, the little one, just to the right of the other and a little back of it."

The globes were dispelled and became bonfires. They seemed to have aroused a wind, for suddenly it began drawing from the west, slowly driving the mist past the fort and appearing to build a wall with it over Little Falls. Looking down again, Demooth found that he could see the sentry walk quite plainly, picked out by the firelight, and encircling the darker well of the yard. But even this darker place had come to life. Hearing the men's voices, the women had stolen out of the sheds. They were standing now with their faces lifted skyward. To Demooth they looked pale and swimming with a queer pained realization of disaster, though as yet they had not been. Then they started moving for the ladders and began to climb up on the sentry walks. They kept shifting, as if they sorted themselves out, to stand with their menfolk, and all together, men and women, they stared out at the burning valley.

The whole valley was alight. Trees stood out against the darkness, distinct and black and two-dimensional. Houses and barns assumed their accustomed shapes with suddenness in a bed of rising fire, then seemed to sink and vanish as the flames went up. The watchers in the fort had ceased talking. Their voices, however, continued; a guttural sort of punctuation of helplessness that swelled inarticulately as they got their first sight of the destructives.

The Indians were plainly silhouetted, darting into the zones of firelight, with their crested heads and their naked shoulders shining. The white men were darker shapes, more governed in their motions. They ran before the fires, or stopped momentarily to watch, before running on. There was as yet no sound of shooting.

Now and then a band of destructives could be traced through the darkness by the burning sticks they carried. They followed the roads as though they were illuminating a map.

On the sentry walk a man shouted, "My God, they've set fire to my wheat!"—he strained out over the picket points, his eyes were incredulous. Beside him a woman stood stiff as a spear, with her face turned outward and her eyes closed, as if she could see the roaring burst of flame against the back of her eyelids. The man stopped muttering to himself, and gradually the entire fort became so still that the noise of the nearer fires became distinctly audible. The Indians were too preoccupied to pay attention to the fort, but the first attempt at a sally, the first shooting, would have drawn the entire mob of them. There was nothing that men could do but stand and watch the swift destruction of their homes.

Gil had been keeping watch on the opposite side of the river. Fires already had broken out as far east as Eldridge Settlement, and the small squat tower of the blockhouse was sharply etched against them. But not until an hour had passed did he see the first small fire start at Mrs. McKlennar's place.

He watched for a moment, identified the barn, then the log house, then the two wheat stacks. They burned so fiercely that after a minute or two they seemed to merge in one tremendous conflagration. In ten minutes half a dozen men had managed to destroy the entire results of his year's work—the best yield the farm had ever had. He felt that if he watched longer he might burst out crying like a baby.

A volley of musket shots distracted him. The shots came from Fort Dayton, where already there had been considerable burning done in the cluster of the village. It was impossible to tell what had happened, whether the Indians had attacked the fort, or whether the garrison had made a sortie. Joe Boleo lifted his thin face like a fox into the wind and listened to the shots. "Look," he said after three or four minutes. "That's a runner. There's some more coming after him. I reckon they chased some of them away from Dayton."

The men on the sentry walk saw the band coming through the ford. They made a dark blot on the water. The water was an almost pearly gray. "By Jesus Christ, it's daylight!" said Helmer.

None of them had noticed the rising sun. It poured a rosy light through the valley, tinting the stray remnants of the mist that hung on the brooks or the edges of the river. The last line of the bank of rainless clouds that all night long had passed from west to east caught fire along its lower edge, burned crimson for a while, and slowly sank away. A flight of plover, riding high against the sunrise, came down West Canada Creek with their soft intermittent calling back and forth.

The runner was passing due south in the direction of the Herter place. As the men followed him with their eyes, they saw that a large group of the destructives stood in the yard. One man kept slightly aloof, in his Indian blanket, with the sunrise catching a faint shine in the gold lace covering his cocked hat. A whisper went the rounds again. "That's Brant."

The runner spoke to him, and the following group of men came up to merge with those that waited. Brant called out several men, who raised their rifles and fired a volley skyward. They loaded, fired again. Once more they repeated it. Then, round the smouldering coals of the Herter barn, they sat down, cooked, and ate their breakfast.

The people in Fort Herkimer did not move. All of them watched the destructives eating breakfast. None of them thought of cooking breakfast for themselves. They were unable, even for a minute, to tear their eyes away. Indians were herding the cattle from the woods. The Indians ran like active dogs, uttering yapping cries; and the cows, confused by the smoke and fire, went in a blind panic-stricken flight before them. Such bands came from all over the valley, apparently erratic, but always converging on the spot where the men were eating. As they approached, the men got to their feet and made ready to mill them.

Other men, white men, were rounding up horses, riding them in singly, or leading a string of them, or driving them hitched in their carts. The process seemed endless.

In reality it took only three hours. The rounding up of the cattle had been thoroughly organized. By ten o'clock the entire herd, inextricably mixed together but moving steadily in their ordained direction to the south, began to stretch out over the flats. They followed the road towards Andrustown. Long after they had disappeared, the bellowing of the cows came back to Fort Herkimer from the hills.

In the fort the people leaned against the pickets in exhaustion, staring with bloodshot eyes at the place they had been accustomed to live in. The wind had died and the fires burned low, but the smoke rose steadily as far as the eye could see in bars against the limitless blue sky.

Gradually the people stirred. Their movements were halting, their voices fumbled at words and gave over the attempt to speak. They looked into each other's blank faces and looked away. Someone had started a fire in the yard and women gathered round it to cook. They did it mechanically, apathetically, silently, as if they sought comfort in the routine of regular existence.

When he came down, Gil found Lana among the other women. She was bending in front of the fire with the same burdened apathy, but when he touched her she lifted her face. Neither of them spoke for several seconds.

Then he said, "The stone house didn't burn."

Lana nodded.

"We were lucky," he said.

She was looking at him.

"The corn's standing," he said.

"And there's the potatoes," she said gravely.

13

Brief Activities of the Military

The express rider who had taken the news to Cherry Valley returned late in the afternoon with a message that Colonel

Alden could spare one hundred and eighty men and was sending them under Major Whiting across country north of the Little Lakes, in the hope of cutting off the enemy. Half an hour later, Bellinger, with two hundred men, recruited during the day from the two forts, Eldridge's and the Palatine companies, set out on Brant's trail.

They knew that they could not expect to give battle to Brant's army; they went with a sense of futility. It was more for something to take their minds off the destruction of the valley. They did not hope to consummate a rendezvous with Alden's troops—if that had been Alden's intention, it was a delusion that any man, they supposed, was entitled to. They had not even bothered to ask for soldiers from Fort Stanwix, where Major Cochran commanded two hundred and fifty line troops in garrison. They knew that his orders from headquarters were definite to hold that fort and let the valley go hang.

They spent two days on Brant's trail without getting anywhere near him. They would have liked to find and kill some stragglers from the army; but the only men they found were the three dead scouts on the hill over Edmeston. They buried the scouts. The people of Edmeston had fled behind Brant, taking their livestock with them.

The militia half-heartedly set fire to their dwellings and turned back towards home with twenty or thirty cows and horses which had eluded the Indian herders. They brought the animals to the forts and tethered them.

It took the people more than a week to figure out the extent of the damage. A few men returning to the ashes of their barns and houses found a cow or a horse waiting uncertainly near by. A few flocks of sheep still remained, but these were being harried by the dogs, which, homeless now, had taken to the woods like wolves, and at night could be heard howling over the hills.

Colonel Bellinger's tabulation, which he sent to General Stark in Albany, offered the following figures:—

To buildings burned:

Houses	63
Barns	57
Grist-mills	3
Barracks of wheat	62
Hay stacks	87

To stock taken and carried away:

Horses	235
Horned-cattle	229
Sheep	269
Oxen	93

Those figures made an impression on even the dogged wits of the hero of Bennington. He began casting round for something he could do, something to balance the German Flats accounts when he sent in his report to headquarters. In this foggy process of thought he remembered that in August Governor Clinton had persuaded him to send in a regiment of Pennsylvania riflemen to the Schoharie Valley. Stark, in a pique, had ordered the commanding officer, Colonel William Butler, to act only defensively, in the only district of Tryon County that was not seriously threatened. Now that he remembered where they were, he dispatched an express ordering Colonel Butler to destroy the Tory base at Unadilla.

For three weeks the regiment had been expecting a shipment of shoes. They continued to wait for three weeks more. Finally they marched without them; but by that time all the hostile Indians and Tories had fled south to Cookoze on the Delaware, where they did some unmolested depredating. The riflemen, however, performed a brilliant march, half barefoot as they were. When at last they reached the Unadilla towns, they found only four or five Oneida and Tuscarora families, who had remained because they were friendly to the American cause.

But Colonel William Butler had come to make war. His orders were to wipe out the Indian towns, so he wiped out the friendly Indians in them, men and women. His riflemen were hard-bitten Morgan men and they had been bored in the Schoharie Valley: they made a spree of the process. Consequently Colonel Butler did not mention the Indians killed in his report. He wrote instead:—

> I am well convinced that it has sufficiently secured these Frontiers from any further disturbances from the savages, at least this winter.

General Stark, feeling that at last he had done something, piously echoed the conviction. He considered James Dean's reports that Walter Butler had left Niagara with a hundred and fifty Rangers and fifty regulars, ostensibly to defend Tioga and possibly to make an attack on the Mohawk Valley, were sheer delusions. Anyway they were not headed for the Hampshire Grants. And shortly thereafter he resigned his portfolio to Brigadier General Hand.

Edward Hand found that there were several reports from spies in the west, all predicting the same raid, and there seemed to be a general trend of agreement that the raid would strike Cherry Valley. Being an earnest man, General Hand decided he would visit Cherry Valley himself in November. He found the fort short of bread and powder and returned to rectify the mistake. He also sent copies of his reports to Colonel Klock and ordered him to collect militia and hold them ready to march to Cherry Valley should occasion arise. He directed Colonel Butler at Schoharie to keep a watch in the same direction. He stopped in to see Colonel Van Schaick, commanding line troops at Johnstown, and said the same thing to him. Then, apparently, General Hand settled himself in for the winter at Albany.

14

Prospects

By the end of October two clusters of log cabins had been erected round the two forts in German Flats. Even to the men who had rolled up the walls, they looked small and pathetic. They had had to work too fast to hew the logs. They were the same as the cabin a man would erect for himself when he first went into the wilderness. To some of the old ones in the community, they restored memories of German Flats when it was known as Burnetsfield—just after the French raid of '57. Though the fields were, perhaps, ten times as wide as the cleared land of those days, they lay as desolate under the thin sifting of the snow. The black jagged lumps that once were barns and houses looked just the same to the old men, except that there were more of them now. The river ran dark and swift and cold in its white banks; and at night the northwest wind howled down West Canada Creek. The expectation of winter confronted everyone.

In the noon sunlight, under the slow downward drift of flakes, children laboriously puddled clay that was stiff with frost, and women were sealing the cracks between the logs. Men worked with adzes on planks for the doors. The few horses and oxen remaining to the community were all at work drawing in firewood and the cornstalks from the outlying farms. Boys were guarding the stooks set up among the cabins. Browse was already scarce in the woods and the cows anxiously tailed the carts in from the fields and had to be driven away.

Men had not felt like building again out of reach of the forts, though it meant that they must travel back and forth to work, next spring. Since the September raid several families who had gone back had been taken up by marauding parties; and as the autumn waned the Indians took fewer prisoners and more scalps. It was difficult to feed prisoners on a two-hundred-mile march through a snowy wilderness.

The surprising thing was that so many people stayed at all. A dozen or so of men who had relatives to the east had left the flats with their wives and children and what remained of their possessions; and a few had gone in the dubious hope of finding work. But most of them felt that they could not afford to leave. With the destruction of their wheat, their only source of income had been obliterated. Besides, many of them did not want to move. They had brought the land from wilderness to farm. In the past two years they had been tasting their first prosperity. To abandon their homes would be, it seemed to them, to give up the human right to hope.

On November first, a train of seven wagons hauled slowly up the Kingsroad. As it passed McKlennar's, Gil came out of the stone house and hailed the driver of the leading wagon. The driver pulled in his steaming team and yelled back.

"We're hauling to Fort Stanwix."

"What have you got?"

"Mostly flour and salt beef."

"You've got a lot of wagons."

"Yes," said the driver. "We're the last train for this year. I ain't sorry, either."

"Haven't you got an escort?"

"We will have. They're sending down a company from the fort. We've got to wait this side of Dayton till they get to us."

"Why this side?" asked Gil. "We haven't heard of any Indians."

The driver laughed. He was a red-faced, lantern-jawed man, a Continental teamster, in a battered campaign coat.

"They ain't afraid of Indians," he said. "They're afraid some of you people will get together and steal one of our wagons."

He spat between the rumps of his wheelers and swung his arms to warm his hands. He added, with a drawled tolerance, "I guess they need wheat up there, too."

"I guess they do," Gil said grimly.

"Ain't you pretty far off, living here?"

"There's always two men, here," Gil said. "There won't be any big parties down now, I guess, with the snow coming."

"I guess not," said the driver jovially. "I guess you've got a pretty comfortable place there. Didn't the destructives burn it?"

"They tried to. They burned the barn and the log house."

"I thought it looked different somehow." His red face shifted and admiration came into his eyes. Behind his wagon the other teamsters had begun to yell. He motioned with his arm for them to haul past. "I'm having a talk with my friend," he bawled. "You go ahead."

Lana had come out beside Gil. She looked small and bright-cheeked in the cold, but there was a queer kind of speculation in her eyes as she stared at the wheat wagon. Now she raised them to look at the driver and smiled.

"Good morning," she said. "Did you come up the valley?"

He said with a sort of gallantry, "From Ellis's Mills, ma'am."

"Oh," she said. "I thought you might have come from Schenectady."

"No. Why?"

"I was wondering how things looked like in Fox's Mills."

"I was through there last month. Hauled down to Johnstown with wheat for Van Schaick's regiment."

"How was it in Fox's Mills?"

"It looked just the same as any place. Why? Do you know folks down there?"

"My family lives there," said Lana. "I haven't heard from them in two years now."

"Well, they ain't been much troubled with destructives. Only at the outside farms, some."

Lana's sigh made a little cloud before her face.

"I ought to be starting, I guess," said the driver. His voice was vaguely suggestive. He looked down at the lines in his mittens.

"Say, mister."

"Yes."

"Ellis will sell you wheat all right, or flour. He's asking nine shilling English money, or old York, if it's silver."

"Nine shilling?" It was incredible.

"It's a good bargain."

"He knows we can't get flour. Our mills are burned."

"I guess so."

Gil said bitterly, "The damned Scotchman."

"I don't like the Scotch so good myself," said the driver. "Look here. I'm a neighborly man. Would you like a sack out of this wagon? I'll sell it for five shillings hard cash."

"No!" said Gil, suddenly.

"It's the best price you'll get this winter. But it's got to be hard money. I don't deal with Continental money, generally," he went on as Gil turned, "but I'll let you have the sack for $6.25 in notes if you like. Seeing it's you, mister."

Gil turned back and stared.

"That's five to one," he said incredulously. "Money'd dropped to four to one the last I heard."

"Oh, no," said the driver. "I was in Schenectady last month. It's down to eight to one now. You'll get a real good bargain, see."

"Go to hell!" said Gil.

"You needn't act like that to a favor."

"Get out of here."

"It's a highway."

"Get out of here before I drag you off your wagon, by God."

The driver stared a moment and then spoke to his horses. "My Jesus," he said. "I never seen such a crazy fool."

Adam Helmer came round the house with his rifle. He had been listening, apparently, for he said to Gil, "Shall I shoot the bug-tit? We could drag his wagon down the road and make it look like destructives. We'd burn the wagon." He lifted his rifle suggestively. "I could scalp him. I ain't very good at it, but I could get it off all right. Then we could give an alarm."

The driver took one look at Adam's great bulk and started to flog his horses.

Going back to the house, Gil said bitterly over his shoulder:—

"Save your powder for something we can eat."

But Adam could not resist putting a ball through the canvas top. The rifle made a roar in the snowy sunshine and as the powder smoke drifted gently away from Adam's big red face he gave a whole-souled grin. The wagon was careening round the bend of the road; the four horses bucking up their rear ends like unanimous rabbits while the driver screeched and flogged them with all his might.

Gil had turned back at the shot.

"You damn fool. Now he'll probably report on you and come back with a squad."

"No!" said Adam. "I hadn't thought of that." And he beamed all over.

Gil had worked hard. He and Adam had rigged up a small log shelter for the horse and the sole remaining cow. It was a great streak of luck that had let the Indians find the other three and leave the freshened cow; but she was already feeling the pinch of light rations and was falling off in her bag. She gave only about a quart at each milking, and Gil figured gloomily that by January she would be giving less than a quart a day. The quality of the milk, too, had changed. It had turned whiter and thinner and it had a peculiar pungent, barky taste that the baby still gagged over.

That did not trouble Lana, who said that she could take care of the baby, whatever happened. She was sure of it, too. It was a kind of inward confidence that made her seem to bloom, even on the day they came back to the farm and saw the familiar sights obliterated—the barn, the log house, even the fence rails leading from the barn, had been burned up. But Gil was not sure in his own mind of Lana's ability to nurse the baby. He felt that they would have meat enough with Adam around most of the time. Joe Boleo was expected to come back also. But Gil doubted whether Lana's milk would hold up on a meat diet.

He cursed himself now for persuading Mrs. McKlennar to let him put practically all the ploughed land into wheat. They had been banking on the rising market of course. But he wished to God he had put more in corn.

The corn was all gathered, the husks braided, and the ears hung by them along the red and black rafters of the kitchen in long rows of gold and maroon. But considered in terms of six adult people, it looked like a small supply.

Occasionally he found Mrs. McKlennar watching him when she thought he wasn't noticing her. She herself was quite happy now that she had got back to her own house. She continually breathed defiance and war at the thought of ever leaving it again, vowing she would rather lose her scalp a dozen times than go away. But she was worried about Gil and spoke to Lana about him.

"He lies around too much," she said. "You ought to get him out. Working. Doing something."

Lana lifted her dark eyes.

"What can I get him to do?"

"It doesn't matter," said Mrs. McKlennar. "Anything."

"But he's done all he can. Now the little stable's finished and he's got the wood cut. Adam doesn't do anything, and he's all right. I guess Gil is."

The widow snorted.

"Adam's not the same. He's just a bear, a big brainless yellow-haired bear. Bears naturally lie up in winter. They lie around and scratch their bellies." She smiled to herself. "I like Adam."

"Gil will be all right," Lana said confidently.

"Well, you're his wife. You think I'm a stuff-budget. All young people think old people are, girls worse than boys. Nobody pays any attention to an old woman like me."

Lana smiled and held up the baby to Mrs. McKlennar.

"Here's two do, anyway. After all you've done for us."

"Go on!" But Mrs. McKlennar smiled and took the baby in her arms, and the baby confidently began to bounce. "The warrior," she muttered. "Lord!" Then she looked across him at Lana. "You're so pretty. And you've got your baby. And Gil loves you. And you aren't afraid. I hope you never will be."

Later she said to Gil, "Why wouldn't it be a good idea to start work on the new barn? We'll need it next year."

"I can't build a barn till the frost's out of the ground."

Mrs. McKlennar controlled her impatience.

"You could cut the logs, couldn't you?"

"Yes," said Gil, doubtfully. "But what's the use? It'll soon be too deep in snow to skid them out." He turned away from her and added, "It would probably get burned next year, anyway."

Mrs. McKlennar allowed herself to be tart.

"Nothing will ever get built again if you think that way."

As he lay before the fire, watching Daisy's broad shape bending down to place a pone on the coals, he wondered where Adam was. Adam had returned to McKlennar's for a purpose. With the Bowers girls at Fort Dayton, he couldn't carry on his commerce if he lived in the community of cabins. It was not private enough. He knew that if he were so handy to Polly he would soon give himself away. Besides that, he had a new distraction in Jake Small's wife over at Eldridge. He hadn't made much progress, he admitted to Gil, but give him a little time. He knew her well enough by now to know that she was crazy for another baby, and that she was beginning to lose faith in poor old Jake.

"I don't say nothing against Jake's powers," Adam maintained honorably, "but I just hang around so she can look at us both at once. She's quite a girl." He combed his hair. "No doubt she'll get the idea."

Gil thought of that and thought of Betsey Small, red-haired, quick-tongued, and thin and tight-looking. For a moment he didn't catch on to what Daisy was saying about Mrs. McKlennar. Then he cursed and told her to keep a civil tongue. He wrenched himself off the floor, got his axe, and presently all the people in the house could hear its clear hard cracks as it bit into a spruce.

At supper time he felt better than he had in weeks. He was tired; but he had felled and cut to lengths twenty logs. He said to Mrs. McKlennar, "I think I'll make the new barn sixteen wide."

Immediately she got up an argument for a narrow barn, delighted to see him get his teeth into conversation. But finally she succumbed. "You probably know better, Gil."

He replied good-naturedly, "Well, you see I've done farming all my life."

He left her in the kitchen and went to find Lana. It was cold in the bedroom, so cold that they saw their breaths between them and the baby. Lana tucked it in, while Gil got undressed, and covered the whole cradle with a thick quilt, making an airless tent.

He watched her slight start when she discovered that he was already in bed. She glanced at the cradle sidewise, looked at him from under her lashes, and, smiling slightly, took her comb from the top of the chest.

He lay still and straight in the deep trough of the feather bed, watching her. He loved to watch her comb her hair when she was in this quiet and contented mood: the way she undid the braids; the way she flung the hair forward over her shoulder and combed it in front of her, head down, looking out at him over it, quiet, refreshed, as if the touch of the comb on a single strand of her hair might soothe them both; the way she lifted it behind her head and combed it from beneath, in long arm-length strokes that were slow, almost languid, with sensation. Her strokes were so deliberate that it seemed as if the thick mantle of black hair to her waist must keep her warm. The comb crackled very faintly as it passed through her hair; and the sound of it made Gil conscious of his own tired ease and the increasing warmth beneath the covers.

"Hurry up, Lana."

She smiled at him in the bed, deliberately going on with the combing. Her voice was soft, and she watched him through the motions of her hands with sleepy, humorous eyes.

"Mrs. McKlennar was worrying about you," she said. "But I wasn't worried about you."

"What about?" His voice was sharp at her irrelevance.

"About you lying around and not doing anything."

"I've started getting logs for the new barn." He stopped himself and said sternly, "What's that got to do with things?"

"Nothing, only I said I wasn't worried."

He grinned.

"You weren't worried a bit?"

"Not a bit," she said. . . .

Captain Demooth walked with Dr. Petry to the latter's store. The doctor had been over to the cabin to see Mrs. Demooth. But the men had not been able to talk; there was no place in the cabin where one might talk without everyone hearing you.

"Come inside, Mark," said the doctor. "I'll get you a drink."

"I don't want a drink."

"Well, I want one. And you better join me."

The doctor went to his office and faced the shelves. He stood for a minute looking at the rows of bottles; then he said: "It was a dispensation of Providence they didn't burn this office. This town could a whole sight better spare a church than those bottles." He reached for one marked *Tarta Emetic* and took two glasses, and poured out a yellow liquid with affection. "Don't get nervy, Mark. It's good Kingston. The last I have. I put it there to make sure it don't get misapplied. Now if it was Tartar Emetic in a rum bottle, that would be something."

He drank and watched Demooth drink.

"How long have you been married?"

Demooth started. He met the doctor's eyes.

"Why . . ." Then suddenly he caught on—the drink, the question. Demooth swallowed and said in the same tone, "Twelve years, Doc."

Dr. Petry grunted, held out the bottle, and poured two more glasses. He closed his eyes as he drank; then he said, "Twelve years is a long time, for some people, and short for others. I've been married only ten, myself. Well, Mark, I might as well tell you . . ." He drew a deep breath.

"You needn't, Doc. I've thought so for some time myself."

"Yes, it went to her head."

"It wasn't the raid, you know," said Demooth. "I was waiting for it to happen. She was scared."

"Weak head, weak head. She was one of the prettiest women, when I first saw her, I ever saw," said Dr. Petry.

"How long do you think she'll live?"

"A week, a month, maybe till next spring. She's strong in some ways. But she doesn't want to hang on."

Demooth turned to the window.

"I think the thing for me to do is to take her to Schenectady. She never got used to living up here. When I see her in that hut, I remember the way she used to look at me when we first settled in Deerfield, before the house was finished. I used to laugh at her then."

"Some people never get over being scared, Mark. There's nothing you can do about it. Yes, I'd move the poor lady down. It might make her happy. It might give her a new lease. But if she dies, don't take it too much to heart, Mark. Try not to. It doesn't pay to get brooding. Not up here. Not now."

Demooth ignored what he said.

"I can take her down to Little Falls in one of those wheat wagons that went up to Fort Stanwix yesterday. They ought to be back by the end of the week. Ellis will lend me his sleigh."

"The sooner the better," nodded the doctor. "Before it gets too cold. She won't stand much cold. Will you stay down there?"

Demooth hesitated.

"Yes."

"Will you come back next spring?"

Again he hesitated.

Finally he said again, "Yes."

"Good thing," said the doctor. "You'll probably be needed. While you're down, try and get me some stuff. I've got a list. I haven't been able to get anything sent up from the army hospital. Good luck, Mark."

They shook hands.

. . . "What will we do, John?"

She wasn't crying, but her eyes were helpless and tragic.

"Won't he take you?"

"He says he can't. He says he'll have to take Ellis's sleigh and there'd be no room for me. He told me, too, that I'd done Mrs. Demooth as much good as anyone could have done. He was very nice, and he gave me a month's wages, too. I didn't want to take them, but he made me. Do you think that was all right?"

"I guess so," said John. "As long as he said so."

They were walking out along the Kingsroad, because they had no other place to be alone. It was snowing a little; there was no sunlight; the sky was gray, and even the snow looked lifeless, as if it died in falling.

Walking through it, both Mary and John looked thin and small and cold. Mary was cold. She was wearing moccasins she had made herself, stretched over rough knitted stockings. Whenever she had to answer him, she drew a deep breath so that her teeth would not chatter. She was afraid he would see how cold she was and make her turn back. But he was too preoccupied to notice her. He walked bent over, watching his own feet in the snow, a frown on his face. The frown made him seem older; she liked him when he frowned, knowing he did so on account of her. Ordinarily it gave her confidence in him. But now she thought, what could even John do in such a situation?

He suddenly blurted out, "If I could get work anywhere . . ."

It was to her a confession of his hopelessness. There was no work—she knew that as well as he—and she knew also how he felt about his mother. Now that his father had been taken by the enemy he felt a natural responsibility for her welfare and for Cobus's. Cobus wasn't yet old enough to be solely responsible. He was a stout strong lad, but he was too young to hunt. Moreover, the Weavers had less corn than almost any other family; and almost no money at all.

"John," she said, "how much money have you got?"

She knew already, but he answered again, glad of something to say, that he had given the money to his mother.

She said, "With what Mr. Demooth has given me, I've got ten dollars, now."

She had not told him before how much. Ten dollars. Ten dollars. He looked at her. The sum automatically reminded him how six months ago they had thought they could get married when they had that much saved up.

"What is it in?" John asked.

"Mr. Demooth always paid me in hard money. He said that was what he had made the offer in and he would stick to it."

John said, "Then you've got—let's see—you've got eighty dollars in American money."

Suddenly they were awed by the miracles of Congressional finance. Just by the word of it, apparently, Congress had made them incredibly wealthy. Eighty dollars—why, some people who were respectable had lived and died with less than that. They started smiling at each other.

Seeing him so pleased, Mary relaxed, and immediately the shivers got the best of her, and because John was looking at her he noticed them at last.

"You're cold."

She only nodded.

"You ought to have told me."

She kept her teeth clinched, but she pleaded to him with

her eyes. And he could not scold her. He knew how she looked forward to going out with him.

The wind had begun to blow also, and it seemed to him that he could see it cutting through her threadbare jacket and shawl. Her face was pinched now with cold, and her brown eyes very large. The freckles stood out startlingly on her face.

John was frightened. He cast a wild look around and spotted Mrs. McKlennar's stone house.

"We can get warm in there," he said. "Come on, Mary."

He grabbed her arm and began lugging her towards the house.

It was midafternoon and they found only the women at home.

"For Lord's sake!" said Mrs. McKlennar. "What have you two children been up to?"

"It's my fault. I brought her walking. She got cold. I didn't notice how cold it was. Do you think she'll get sick?"

John was breathless and white. He couldn't get his eyes off Mary, and now that the shakes had taken hold of her she could not have stopped them with the whole world looking on. They both started as Mrs. McKlennar cried, "Sick! Pshaw! I'll give her some sack. Daisy! Fetch the sack. Now sit down by the fire. John hasn't introduced you, but I know all about you, Mary Reall. John's a good boy and his mother thinks you're lucky, but you're not half as lucky as he is. I can see that." Mrs. McKlennar meant what she said. The girl was already cocking her chin, and Mrs. McKlennar liked any girl who could cock her chin. She gave her some sherry and had some herself and motioned the two young people to sit down on one settle.

She sat down opposite them.

"What on earth brought you two so far—just talking?"

To John, troubled as he was, Mrs. McKlennar's long and horsy face, seen against the ears of corn, and the strings of dried apple and squash, in her large and comfortable kitchen, wore a kind and powerful beneficence. His young mind had been troubled too long with his and Mary's burdens. Before he remembered that Mrs. Martin and the negress were still in the room he had started to tell Mrs. McKlennar everything.

"You see," he concluded, "now Pa's gone, I've kind of got to look out for Ma. And she won't let Mary in the house. It ain't as if we hadn't waited quite a while, and we aren't so terrible young. And then I don't know where Mary's going to live. She can't live alone."

"Can't she stay in Demooth's cabin?"

John flushed.

"He said Clem Coppernol was going to stay there."

"Then of course she can't," said Mrs. McKlennar. "Do you know what I'd do, John?"

She was sitting very straight on the settle and looking down her nose at the two of them. As John replied, "No, ma'am," the end of her nose quivered visibly.

"I'd marry the girl before some man with more brains than yourself snatched her from under your nose." Her deferred snort was quite deafening.

John's eyes shone. Then they sobered again. He had thought of it so many times. "It ain't possible, Mrs. McKlennar. It wouldn't be right to Ma. Taking Mary into her house. And I can't build us another now. I couldn't keep the two in wood. Cobus ain't much yet. Somebody's got to look out for Ma."

Mrs. McKlennar said, "No, I don't think you ought to abandon your mother, and I'm not telling you to. Now listen, John Weaver. What house are you living in?"

"In the cabin at the end of the row near the fort," he said wonderingly.

Mrs. McKlennar snorted once more. "You *are* a stupid boy, John—maybe you shouldn't get married after all. Now I've got to tell you all the things Mary could tell you but has been too sensible to tell you. What I meant was, who built the cabin?"

"I did," said John.

"Item one. You did. How much money of your father's has your mother got? How much of yours?"

"She's got five dollars of Pa's and seven dollars I earned."

"Item two, you are mostly supporting her and your brother. Item three, how much money has Mary got saved?"

"Ten dollars," Mary said softly, but with pride. She couldn't help it. Her voice made Mrs. McKlennar swing her eye round, and a sly little smile pulled the corner of her mouth.

"Then," said Mrs. McKlennar, "marry the girl, take her to the cabin, and tell your mother that you've brought your wife home to your own house, and that Mary has said that she will be very glad and proud to have your mother stay with her." Mrs. McKlennar's grin had infinite relish. "She hasn't another place to live in so she'll have to put up."

"We haven't much corn. Pa was trying to get his money back in wheat. We haven't much to live on."

Mrs. McKlennar tossed her head.

"Mary's money will take care of her as well when she's married as when she's single, and she won't eat more. To look at her I'd say she'd gladly go without food every other day for the sake of being married to you. Shame on you, John Weaver. You're trying to be too respectable. Respectability never made a saint. Saints most always start their careers with some good honest sinning. If you're going to starve, you might as well all starve together. And that reminds me. There's no stores where I can buy Mary a wedding present. So you'll have to use your ingenuity to find yourself something. I shall give you a pound, Mary."

John and Mary both stared at her. Then John looked at Mary and flushed painfully. But she did not flush at all. She merely looked at him. The voice of Mrs. McKlennar went on almost like the voice of a higher power. Lana had told her the whole story; and long ago the widow had thought something ought to be done about it.

"John," said Mrs. McKlennar, "I'll tell you something you don't probably know. Reverend Sam Kirkland's over in Fort Herkimer, and he sent word by an Indian he'd be down this afternoon to spend the night here. He always stops on his way out from the Oneida towns each fall. He won't mind marrying you without banns when I tell him about you. Now—would you like to wait and get it over with here and now? You, John Weaver, would you?"

John glanced at Mary. He looked positively shamefaced. Then he faced Mrs. McKlennar again and gulped.

"Yes, ma'am," he said.

"And you, Mary, would you?"

"Yes," said Mary. Her voice was very low, but very steady.

"Oh, Lord," thought Mrs. McKlennar. "See what I've done now! They're nothing but children. The girl's just a child." But Lana was smiling at her, and black fat Daisy was muttering, "'Clare to gracious, ain' dey sweet?"; and she went on thinking, "God, what nasty sentimental things women are, and God knows why either. Likely as not he'll beat her or something, and she'll be miserable with her mother-in-law, and the two of them will hate me all their lives." But suddenly she began chuckling, and when they all looked at her, she said, "Anyway, Mary's lost her chill."

Now that it was done, it seemed hardly possible. It had taken so short a time. First Reverend Mr. Kirkland had come, and both John and Mary had been impressed with his kindness, and a little awed to think that he was the man who had kept the Oneidas on the American side of the war. He was a tall lean man, dressed like any other man, except for his black hat. He had straight thin features and a gentle mouth, and his eyes seemed completely detached from all the world. But the solemn, nasal tones of his voice as he repeated the service yet rang in Mary's ears.

She felt humble and uplifted together. It was odd, too, walking home, though the daylight had waned, that she did not feel cold. She took John's arm just as they reached the outskirts of the settlement. The feeble lights of tallow dips coming through the paper windowpanes of the cabins were like solemn light brown eyes. Her thin hands were strong on his arm, helping him to walk to the cabin where they would now live together with his mother.

"John," she said. "Are you unhappy?"

He said, "No." But she knew that he was worried.

"I'll always be anything you want me to be, John. I'll always love you, no matter what."

He squeezed her hand against his side without speaking. But he looked into her face as they went under the first window and saw it brave, and patient, and adoring, and so young that he felt frightened to think that she was now his own.

Frightened, and excited, and glad that they would not have to sit through supper. Mrs. McKlennar had given them a supper before leaving. It was a marvelous meal—the bone end of the last ham, some heated chocolate in china cups, a pone with jelly, and apple sauce. It now occurred to him that he and Mary would have to find themselves a place to sleep together. He would take Cobus's bed for themselves, as it was in the corner—though farthest from the fire, it would be more private. They had nothing but two deerskins to make curtains of—he hoped it would not turn so cold these would be needed for bed covers. He felt himself prickling all over; and then with a rush of elated confidence he knew that Mary had felt his elation, and that suddenly she had lost all her courage, and was afraid of him. When he opened the door, the light shone softly on her face, her eyes on his, and the color rushing into her cheeks.

He turned to the room, "Hello, Ma."

Emma Weaver said, "We saved you some supper."

"I've had it," said John. He closed the door behind him and swallowed hard.

"Ma, I've brought Mary home."

Emma turned her head. Her homely face, grown more gaunt, became animate. Anger, doubt, conviction, and fear passed over it.

"John," she said softly, "you mean?"

John managed to nod.

"Mary's staying. We got married this afternoon. Reverend Kirkland married us at Mrs. McKlennar's."

Cobus, who was whittling an ash stick for snowshoes, became all eyes. He turned from Mary to stare apprehensively at his mother. Emma said, "Do you want me and your brother to move out?"

"No, Ma. You know that we wouldn't want that."

Emma said, "I heard Captain Demooth would not take Mary to Schenectady. I didn't know you'd do this." All at once tears, big helpless ones, poured out of her eyes, and trickled unevenly down her lined face.

Mary's breath caught.

"Don't, Mrs. Weaver. Please don't cry. I want to help you, John and me both do. And we can, please, if you'll let us."

She had stepped forward and bent slightly down towards Emma. Now, to her astonishment, and to the two boys', Mrs. Weaver lifted her wet face.

"I'm so tired," she said. "You don't know how tired I have got since George got took." The sobs rose in her breast. She hid her face, and, as Mary touched her, leaned against the girl's knees. John thought that he was going to cry himself. He had never seen his mother licked before; she seemed physically beaten, as if he himself had laid a stick across her shoulders.

They got her to bed on the floor before the fire, where she lay sobbing quietly. John ordered Cobus to bed and then he and Mary moved the chest as he had planned and hung the deerskin up. They blew the tallow dip out and crept under the blankets, dressed as they were, for warmth. They could see the soft glow of the fire-light pulsing over the bark on the log walls. The fire burned without sound.

Over in the other corner, in John's old bed, fat Cobus lay like a hare, unmoving, holding breath, soundless, and all ears. Emma's sobbing continued softly. The deerskin, not completely cured, had a faint tangy rankness that seemed to grow as the fire sank to coals. . . .

In one of the cellar cells, in the very wall of the old fortress at Chamblée, George Weaver was wondering whether German Flats had managed to get through the summer and autumn without suffering the raid everyone had been afraid was coming. He did not know. There were nine other men distributed around the walls of the small cell. They had no window to see each other by. Their faces must be remembered from the brief flashes that the jailer's torch made when he came to bring them their food. Since they had entered the cell they had not been allowed out of their irons; and their irons were fastened to heavy rings in the stone walls.

It had taken George two months to get there. First three weeks of following his Indian captor through the wilderness to a Seneca town, where they had made him run the gantlet. It was his plodding patient strength that had brought him through that, though George would have said it was the fact that they could not beat him off his feet. His captor had become a celebrity on the strength of George's performance and told George in broken English that he had never seen a man take so slow a pace and survive.

George had stayed two weeks in the Indian town before being led on to Niagara, where he was traded for the customary eight dollars to a beefy British major. They had kept him at the fort for eight days before shipping him with some other prisoners on a small sloop to Montreal. All the prisoners hoped they would be kept in Montreal, and most of them were. But George, with two other men who had been captured near Cobleskill, was shipped on to Chamblée.

When he saw the immense square walls of the old fortress, he had thought that it would be a hard place to get out of; but he had had no idea that men treated prisoners the way he was treated. A man could stand up, and he could sit down, and he could lie down if he got in a particular position parallel to the wall. That was bad, but worse was the fact that since the ten men had entered the cell they had not been allowed loose for even long enough to clean the filth out. The place had an unbelievable stench. Some of the men had periods of raving, and others never said anything. George was managing to get used to the stench. It was becoming part of him, like an integral function of his own skin. The only thing that bothered him was his belief that the man in the corner behind the door had been dead for four days. He had not touched food for that period nor said anything nor rattled his chains, and the jailer's light never reached into that corner, except to touch the unused food, which was left lying there. There was quite a heap of it now on the board the man used to use as a plate. But no one else could reach it.

To keep himself from thinking about it, George used to try to think about his family. It came easier to-night because the jailer had said it was snowing outside. George thought what a nice thing it would be for his family if he could write them a letter saying that he was not dead.

15

By Cherry Valley

The same snow that the jailer at Chamblée told George Weaver was falling over the valley of the Richelieu River, in the woods south and west of Cherry Valley took the form of sleet. The scout of twelve men and a sergeant ten miles out on the Beaver Dam road decided that there was no sense in running a scout at all on such a night. The sergeant was sure that he was getting up the beginnings of a chill. He had never been able to stand being in the woods anyhow; and when darkness began to filter through the sleet, he gave orders to halt on the next dry spot, or drier spot, or spot less wet was what he meant, and light one hell of a big fire.

Only one man asked if it was wise to light a fire near the road; the rest laughed or cursed, according to how wet they felt, and began breaking off dead spruce limbs. But the sergeant thought that he ought to take cognizance of such a remark. He set about explaining to the private that they had had rumors all fall of a raid on Cherry Valley, and it hadn't come, had it? What if Colonel Ichabod Alden had sent them out; he had to do something, hadn't he? But he wasn't worried, was he? He was sleeping in the Wells house, four hundred yards from the fort, wasn't he? Him and Colonel Stacia and Major Whiting—and if the private thought that that looked as if the officers expected a raid, he was entitled to think so or to drain himself in the creek, or to kiss the sergeant's great-aunt if he liked. The private responded that to him it didn't matter a damn if the whole General Continental Staff slept in the Wells house so long as Mr. Wells raised no objections; the officers always slept in the houses where there were pretty girls, didn't they? Well, said the sergeant, he wasn't himself going to stand under an eternal and universal piddle while Colonel Ike lay in a feather bed, and not build a fire anyway, and to hell. He sneezed.

In ten minutes they had a great fire going, shooting the sparks up through the drizzle-soaked boughs, and they stood around it, dripping and steaming and feeling sorry for themselves, with the light red on their faces, and their guns stacked under a near-by hemlock tree.

All the Indians under the advance scout of Ranger Captain Adam Crysler had to do was to give a couple of yelps and step in and pick the guns up. The Continental scout of Massachusetts men never offered to leave the fire. They stared and gawped. These were the first Indians many of them had ever seen, painted Senecas with their heads bare to the wet and their blankets sopping dismally about their sides. They looked bulky and stuffed out under their deerskin shirts, but for all that they looked damned ugly, too. The ugliest thing they did was to herd the prisoners away from their own fire and take their places.

The first the Continental scout knew of a hostile British army was when a distant whooping answered the Indians who had captured them. Then for a long time there was not a sound except the crackle of spruce on the fire, the muttering of the Indians, and the everlasting drip and piddle from the branches. Then more Indians came through the woods, more Indians than these Massachusetts men believed existed. They seemed like a thousand. There were five hundred of them. They gathered round and started building new fires. Soon the little valley glowed with light, like a hillside in a dripping sort of hell. Into this infernal glow penetrated the steady beat of shod men marching.

The marching soldiers followed a slender man, swarthy as an Indian, without paint, whose lank hair clung to the back of his neck in wisps. He looked drawn and cold and tired. Behind him came one hundred and fifty men in green campaign coats and black leather skullcaps. Behind them marched fifty British regulars in red. Some of the regulars were even keeping step. All at once the woods had overflowed with living men. It seemed a miracle that they were there.

It was almost a miracle. On the Chemung River the Rangers had been watching the movements of the Eleventh Pennsylvania Regiment. The Continentals had penetrated nearly to Tioga before turning back to garrison Wyoming. Then Walter Butler, young, headstrong, and consumed with his ambition, decided to make a late fall march on Cherry Valley. All year the Canadian command had been making useless plans for taking Cherry Valley, one of the military depots for the Continental army, a frontier fort, and a menace to their own base at Unadilla. It was late in the year to make a start. He had insufficient supplies for his troops, and he had only two hundred men. But he put it up to them and they answered by offering to start next day.

They started late in October, through the cold rainy days, following down the Chemung, then turning up the Susquehanna, on which they met Brant returning towards Canada.

John Wolff would never forget that meeting on the banks of the river, filled with floating sodden leaves and driftwood: Brant at the head of his five hundred Indians, Butler with his two hundred men, showing an order from Haldimand that gave him sole command of any expedition undertaken against Cherry Valley and requested aid from all and any British officers. Brant demanded the command as senior captain. Butler curtly refused. There was a long argument before Brant, bitter and silent, turned his Indians to the northeast ahead of the white troops, and the long march was continued.

A hundred and fifty miles through swamps and along riv-
erbanks and over hills, up the Susquehanna to Otsego Lake,
thence overland to strike this road. There was little talking in
the company of Rangers. They marched with a dogged, damp,
and dreary sullenness. But they never stopped, for always they
had the indomitable nervous figure of Butler ahead of them.

The Indians were unfriendly as Brant himself. They did
not know why they had to come. They hated the rain. They
wanted to go home. Many of the Senecas had been out all summer. The Indian scouts all said it was impossible to take Cherry
Valley. There were two hundred and fifty men in garrison; there
were three hundred more at Schoharie and nearly five hundred
at Johnstown. Better to make a raid in the upper, unprotected
valley.

But Butler was stubbornly setting his heart on Cherry Valley;
his winter in prison seemed to have given him a bitter power. He
drove the Indians on; even Brant, wrapped in his blanket, his
gold-lace hat a sodden scarecrow mockery of himself, no longer
argued.

John Wolff, marching in the last squad of the Ranger company, had fits of nervous fear when he saw the Indians all around
them. He and some of his company thought it likely that the
Indians might turn on them. Once a scalp was taken off a head,
you couldn't tell whose head it had come off of. The white men
were so much easy money for the Indians, if they chose; and
stories went round that that had happened in a small way with
St. Leger's retreating army, and that Bolton in Niagara had paid
eight dollars for more than one member of the Eighth King's
Regiment.

It was a nightmare march, with insufficient food. War had
driven the deer far off the trails, and the wolves had begun running. They heard them at night in the hills above Unadilla as
they came by.

November eighth and ninth and tenth they came through the Tryon country. It was on the tenth that they rounded up the twelve scouts with the sergeant and learned that the officers were at the Wells house. The scouts were willing to talk. Any man would have been willing with all those predatory Senecas squatting round him in the rain. They crowded close to Butler and answered questions.

Wolff heard the order to march as if it were part of a dream. Darkness no longer had any bearing on his thoughts. He shouldered his gun and took his place, and presently his feet began to take him forward through the rain. They had gone a mile when the rain gave up for a breath. The night seemed suddenly to clear and the marching feet left a dark track in the dark, and the mud felt cold and brittle. "It's freezing," said the man next to Wolff. "I hope to God my shoes hold out." Then from the north a flake drifted down, and another flake. The ground whitened under the trees. A luminous imitation of light was counterfeited in the woods.

At twelve o'clock they halted, filed off the road, and entered a swamp. Through the trees on the edge of the swamp they saw white hills dimly rising against the sky, one a steep cone, like a sugarloaf. The word came down the line, "No fires to-night." The men stood crowded close together for what warmth their clothes could give off. The sleeve of Wolff's coat stiffened with frost.

"We'll be lucky if half this army gets back to Niagara."

The man beside Wolff was talking. Wolff did not hear him. He was so cold that even his brain was numb. He did not even think.

At daylight the snow unexpectedly turned to warm rain from the south. A mist that was more like steam rose over the snow and hid the valley. Low orders were given: Eighty men with Captain Crysler to cut off the Wells house and take the officers; the rest to charge the fort, Butler leading the main group;

the Indians to circle the fort and rake the palisade from the far side. Brant appeared and disappeared. A whistle sounded and the army moved.

At seven o'clock they heard a challenge on the road, and the sudden frantic galloping of a horse. The army moved behind it at the double. Wolff's squad followed the main force for the gate of the fort. They passed houses. People were stupidly looking out of their doors. The file of eighty men swung off towards the Wells house. Then in the fog ahead of Wolff the palisade loomed like a dark mass, and he saw the closing gate. Musket shots made little orange blobs. A lieutenant cried, "Lie down." Wolff fell in the slush and felt its cold soak through his coat. He started firing. At the same instant the cannon of the fort discharged over their heads. Behind where the town lay, he heard the wild shrill screeching of the Seneca war cry.

Just ahead of him Captain Butler raised up on one arm to look back. His face was bitter and hopeless. He said distinctly, "Oh, my God. Brant's taken all the Indians into the town." There was no firing from the other side of the fort. Every man there knew—both inside and outside the palisade—that the fort was safe. But they fired at each other for three hours, until the burning houses began to show up the Rangers' position. Whistles shrilled along the line of prostrate, slush-sodden men, and a slow crawling retreat was effected. The men rose up behind the first houses they came to and stayed there in the heat of the burning walls. It was the first warmth they had experienced in forty-eight hours. They began fishing in their wallets for scraps of smoked meat and chewed hungrily. It took them several minutes to realize that the houses burning in front of them must contain better food. And at the same time their numbed consciousness made them aware that the Indians were running amok.

The weary Rangers were mustered and sent to protect the burning houses, but it was then too late. The whooping and

firing had receded into the edges of the woods. Only a few inhabitants were discovered unharmed. All through the settlement
were signs of the Indian work, women lying beyond their doors
indecently soaked even in their deadness, a child, an old man.

Butler was traversing the road like a madman. He gathered
up an old man and his daughter and sent them to the fort with
a flag and passed them in. Brant saw them enter too late to stop
them. He confronted Butler with the warning that the Senecas
demanded that the other prisoners be reserved. He said he could
do nothing. He pointed out that if the Senecas were roused,
they could and likely would annihilate the little army of whites.
His face was expressionless, his voice as casual as if he talked of
driving rabbits.

Butler withdrew his Rangers to the woods behind the Wells
house, where they found Captain Crysler and his men surrounding forty shivering men and women and children. One of these,
a man in a nightshirt, turned out to be Colonel Stacia, second in
command of the fort. He reported that Colonel Alden had been
killed, and surrendered himself to Butler.

The women huddled together like sheep. They did not move
except to turn their heads when Indians whooped in the woods.
When the mist began to clear and a colorless November sunlight
fell upon them, they still looked cold. The ragged, soaking Rangers regarded them without interest.

After a while the army withdrew to a hillside and made a
camp and lit fires. They rounded up some cattle and killed a
dozen cows and skinned them and threw the meat in pots as fast
as it could be dissected.

The Indians, suddenly returning, took the remainder of the
cattle and killed them for themselves. They lay around all day
watching the burning settlement and the palisade of the fort
with all the firing platforms alertly manned. Butler kept by himself. A little way off Brant camped with a few Mohawks and

watched Butler. John Wolff lay on his back with his comrades and digested food. He was too weary to do more.

They stayed all day, and at night they made windbreaks of bark, and brush, keeping the prisoners in the middle of the white encampment. The mist came up again from the snow, smelling of wet earth and charred wood and rotting leaves.

Early in the morning they skirmished the fort for an hour or two; but the business was half-hearted. They withdrew to their camp, and then orders were passed for the long retreat to Canada. Nothing had happened except the destruction of the houses and the murder of twenty-five noncombatants.

The weather was turning colder and a little after noon the snow began again. Butler unexpectedly sent back thirty-eight of the prisoners under guard and waited till the escort had returned. By then it was too late for the Indians to object. Three hundred miles confronted them, cold days, colder nights, and the steady and inexorable increase of snow, and, yet more bitter, the loneliness of the woods and the consciousness of failure. Only the Indians who had scalps at their belts took any comfort. The rest, Indians and white troops, marched on with the touch of snowflakes on their faces, in dogged silence.

VII

ONONDAGA (1779)

I

March 1779

In the opinion of some people, the winter had been providentially mild; but in another way it had been hard, for after the beginning of February the snow had so far decreased in the woods that the deer no longer yarded. With the steady hunting round German Flats, they had also become wild; and by March most of them seemed to have moved south to the grass flies on the Unadilla tributaries. It often meant a two days' hunt for even good woodsmen like Joe Boleo and Adam Helmer to pick up one deer.

But to Gil Martin, the problem was more than one of food. He had worked hard and had his logs all cut and ready to roll for the new barn. Now, as the snow went down in the valley, bringing up to the eye the lay of the soil again, he wondered where he would find seed for his fields. There had been no wheat to plant last fall. He would have to find oats and barley. He had none left. During the first months Mrs. McKlennar had bought oats, and wheat and barley flour, not only for herself, but to help the neighborhood. There was no question of her paying Gil's wages.

Such things as wages and money belonged to a former time. But her supply of cash was nearly spent.

It was in Gil's mind this Monday, the fifteenth of March, to go down to Fort Dayton. He wished that Captain Demooth were back from Schenectady; but failing him, Gil thought he had better talk to Colonel Bellinger.

He stood outside the shed, looking up at the sky. The blue was softer than it had been all winter, and a white cottony tier of cloud hung over the southern hills. Some of the brooks already had opened, loosening a smell of earth.

He said through the open door, "I'm going down to Dayton. I don't know when I'll be back. You'll be here, Adam?"

"Till five o'clock," said Adam. "I've got an errand over to Eldridge's."

Lana smiled over his head and Mrs. McKlennar tossed hers. They all knew that Adam was making his play at Mrs. Small. "Her and her red hair," Adam would say. "And just wasting her time with Jake." So far he had made no progress.

"I'll be back," said Gil.

Whenever he went to Fort Dayton, Gil realized how lucky they were at McKlennar's. The stamp of hunger was bitten deep into all the people's faces. You could see it at McKlennar's, and you could feel it too, in the sharp answers they gave one another. But many of these people looked apathetic, or their eyes were like the eyes of ghosts.

Even Bellinger's eyes were unnatural. He opened the door of his cabin to confront Gil. He was a big man, and rangy, with a great coarse-cut head on his stooped shoulders. He looked tired.

"Oh, it's you, Martin. Come in. I've company." His voice was dry. "But he's about through here. Come in, will you?"

Gil entered.

A man in a brown coat was sitting at Bellinger's plank table. He had a rather studious face and mild eyes. He didn't look like a farmer or a soldier; but by the way he folded the papers before him, it seemed to Gil that the man's soul was filled with a love of writing. For the papers were covered with neat, pointed script, precisely ruled.

Bellinger said tiredly, "Mr. Martin, let me acquaint you with Mr. Francis Collyer. Mr. Collyer has been sent up by the governor at the request of General Clinton."

Mr. Collyer made a slight bow. He took no interest in Gil, but addressed himself to Bellinger.

"Thank you, Colonel. You've given me everything. I'm sorry that I shall be compelled to report as I have told you."

"That's all right, sir. It's your business."

"Of course, Colonel, I have no idea what action Congress will take in the matter. I merely report. I am leaving you a copy of my summation. You know the figures anyway, as you've obligingly supplied them yourself."

"I don't give a damn what Congress does," Bellinger said suddenly. "You can tell the Governor so. Put it in your report, sir."

Mr. Collyer wisely said no more. He took his leave politely and walked to the fort, where his horse waited for him. Bellinger closed the door on his back. He leaned against it for a moment, staring at Gil. Then he began slowly and wearily to swear.

"I've had that gentleman on my hands for a day and a half, Martin. He's made me feel sick to my stomach. It's queer how sick to your stomach you can feel when you're half empty. Oh, he was very polite. A nice quiet gentleman. Mr. Collyer. Sent by Congress! Think of it!" He wiped his mouth and stepped to a stool and sat down. "Listen, you know I took things into my own hands in January and started signing requisitions for food from the army depot at the falls. But, by God, somebody had to do something! I signed the requisitions as on Congress. People had to have flour. I had to keep them. If I hadn't done it they would have been forced to leave. It was the only wheat in this part of the country. Thank God I got a double requisition yesterday! Just in time."

He stopped.

Gil asked, "What's Mr. Collyer?"

"That's it. What is he? He's a damned accountant sent up from Albany to look into all my requisitions of wheat. We were very patient together. We visited people. He heard their stories. Then he made a report. There's the summation. Read it! Read it, will you!"

What Gil read in the precise writing was this:—

Copy of the summation of my report to Governor George Clinton, March 15, at German Flats, Tryon County, State of New York, U. S. A.

(Re requisitions on Army depot at Ellis's Mills by Col. Peter Bellinger, 4th Company Militia, for wheat for the inhabitants.)

Having thus collected all evidence and made due personal investigations thereof, with the aid of said Col. Bellinger, who was in every way obliging and whom I may say I believe to have acted in the best faith, it is my finding that undue employment of his power has been made by said Col. Bellinger and that from my investigation it is plain that most of the inhabitants drawing said rations were not sufficiently destitute to warrant the use of *Continental Army* supplies. Respectfully submitted.

FRANCIS COLLYER

Bellinger was regarding Gil with deep-set angry eyes. "I suppose we ought to have been dead to warrant using army food. My

God! Can't they realize that if we don't stay here, the frontier will automatically drop back to Caughnawaga? Can't they realize anything?"

Gil had nothing to say.

"I don't care what they do to me. I've pilfered, stolen, robbed the damned Continental army of enough to see us through till April. They can't hurt me, now. I'll resign my blasted commission. It won't make any difference if I do."

He stared hard at Gil.

"What did you want to see me for?" he asked belligerently. "You aren't out of food, are you? You haven't been on rations yet." Suddenly Bellinger smiled. "Come on. I won't kill you. Though I'd like to, too."

Gil felt better.

"Maybe this will kill you, sir. I came down to see where I could get twenty bushels of oats or barley for seed."

"Oh, my God!" Bellinger burst out laughing. The little cabin rang with his deep voice. "That's good." He slapped Gil's shoulder. "And I'd clean forgot about seed! Christ, what a man!"

"What can we do now?" asked Gil.

Bellinger got up.

"We'll take some wagons down to the mills. We'll beat the conscientious Mr. Collyer, who's going to leave an order with Ellis not to issue any grain except for Continental use. And we'll take along enough men to make the Continental guard surrender it, too, by God."

It took them two hours to round up men and wagons, and then the half-starved horses went so slowly through the pawsh of snow that they did not reach the mills until late afternoon. Mr. Collyer had already been there. The sergeant in charge of the mills forbade the entrance of the German Flats men. But the sergeant wasn't armed, and neither were the guard. They were sitting in the miller's loft playing a chilly game of cards and drinking beer. Bellinger simply locked them in.

The sergeant watched them with grim eyes.

"What do you dumb-blocks think you're doing?"

"We're going to help ourselves to a little oats and barley," said Colonel Bellinger, returning from the loft. "If we can find any."

"You'll catch it plenty if you do," threatened the sergeant. "I'll name the bunch of you by name in my report."

"You'd better explain how you came to be caught like this. Garrison! As your superior officer I ought to have the lot of you court-martialed."

"Superior bug-buttocks," said the sergeant.

Bellinger's shoulders suddenly hunched towards the man.

"What kind of buttocks did you say?"

The sergeant was furious with himself as well as the world for having been caught without a single guard on duty.

"I didn't name no bug."

"No? Why not?"

"I wouldn't insult no bug," said the sergeant.

The men had forgotten all about the grain and were now crowding the space between the bins to watch. It was too close quarters for them really to see. But even over the roar of the falls and the empty clack of the wheel ratchets, the impact of Bellinger's fist against the sergeant's middle was a solemn sound. The man's wind shot out all beery in the floury atmosphere. His hands went to his middle and his jaw came forward and his eyes swelled directly at Bellinger's fist. The fist traveled beautifully to meet the jaw. The sergeant straightened, went over backwards flat on his back, bursting a sack of flour in the process, so that a white cloud engulfed him. He lay there, dead to the world. The men yelled suddenly as Bellinger breathed on his knuckles. He turned on them. "Get to work," he bawled. "And don't waste any." He waited till they started to the bins. Then he sat down beside the prostrate sergeant and studied the gradual discoloration of his face until the wagons were loaded.

Gil found him still sitting there when he came to report that they had barreled and sacked almost a hundred and fifty bushels of oats, and thirty bushels of barley, and about ninety of wheat they could store for next fall's planting.

"Good," said Bellinger. "We'd better start." He took from his pocket a written requisition he had prepared before leaving the flats, and with a sharpened bullet filled in "150" and "30" in two blank spaces of his badly formed writing. At the foot of the paper he added: "P.S. 90 Bushels wheat too. PB, Col." He bent over to slip the sheet into the front of the sergeant's coat and dusted his hands as he rose. "You know, Martin, I kind of like that fellow now," he said. "Well, we better get going."

As they emerged from the door into the late afternoon air, all misty with the spray from the falls and vibrant with the thundering water, they found Mr. Ellis, the miller, anxiously regarding the five wagons.

"The boys tell me you've taken oats and barley and some wheat for seed, Peter," he yelled.

"We took only ninety bushels of wheat," Bellinger yelled back over the noise of water.

"Where's the guard?"

"They're locked up in the loft. I don't know whether they finished their card game. The sergeant's busted a bag of flour. But he's got my receipt."

"How'd he do that?"

"With his head, Alec."

The men burst out laughing, but the roar of the falls swallowed their laughter. Ellis's jaw dropped.

"You did that, Peter?"

"Sure we did. By the way, where did all those oats come from?"

"It was shipped in last week from Stone Arabia, Klock's, and Fox's Mills," bawled the miller. "I was going to mill the wheat to-morrow." He shook his head as though to clear it of the roar of water. "You'd better take it back, Peter. Honest you'd better. I can fix the sergeant so he won't say anything."

"Like hell I'll take it back."

"Listen. Don't be a fool, Peter. Don't you know they're collecting supplies all over the valley? They say Clinton will muster the line regiments up here inside of six weeks." He watched Bellinger swing onto his starved horse, which had been nudging up to the tail of the nearest wagon and snuffing with exalted shivers of its slatty sides. "Listen, Peter. That grain's for them."

Bellinger leaned out of his saddle, and stared at Ellis, then wiped spray from his eyes. "Where's the army heading for?" he shouted.

"I don't know for sure. Some say they're going to wipe out the Indians."

"What Indians?" yelled Bellinger, as the men crowded up to listen.

"The Iroquois."

"By God," shouted Bellinger. "How?"

"I don't know. But you take that wheat back, anyway. There's going to be five regiments. Maybe a thousand men. You'll get into bad trouble, Pete."

A lull in the wind made his words startlingly loud as the roar of the falls was swept north. Bellinger was leaning on the withers of his horse. He seemed to be thinking with his whole body. He looked tired again. All his men, including Gil, watched him. Bellinger lifted his reins. His voice was as resonant as it had been at Oriskany. They all heard it.

"Like hell I'll take anything back. They can do what they like, Alec. It's worth it to get seed into the ground." He moved his horse to the front, regardless of his yelling men.

The men went at the horses with their whips. The wagons lurched and groaned inaudibly and gathered a semblance of speed against the foot of the hill. The miller, watching them leave, thought they looked like animated scarecrows. Not very animated, either. He lifted his hand.

2

Drums

Scattered bits of news that filtered in to German Flats during the next two weeks seemed to confirm the miller's words. The First New York had gone into garrison at Fort Stanwix and Colonel Van Schaick himself had ridden through to take command. And on Captain Demooth's return from Schenectady in the first days of April, they learned that a great many bateaux were being built in that town for army use. Demooth said it was no secret that Congress intended an expedition, though where and when it would start, nobody knew.

The people listened to the rumors without much heart. Nothing had ever happened before to lend credulity to such reports. More pressing things occupied them—the spring ploughing and the sowing of the stolen seed. Bellinger was anxious to have it in the ground before a company was sent to reclaim it. He himself waited for court-martial papers to be served on him with a kind of grim fatality, and in the meantime thought of ways to hide the seed until it could be sown. He never was court-martialed. He never found out why not. Probably no one knew.

On the sixth of April, Gil went down with the mare and cart to secure his allotment of seed. He had already had a talk with

Bellinger and Demooth, and both officers agreed that he should stay on the McKlennar place. It was the one farm that had a stone house standing that could be defended, and the soil was of the best. The other people had marked off temporary land around the forts, each man with his field to cultivate, to raise communal food. "You'll understand we'll expect you to bring your grain into common stock next winter if it's necessary," said Bellinger.

On the seventh and eighth of April, Gil sowed the oats. The earth had dried fast and worked easily. All day he marched back and forth over the soft loam while the mare on the other side of the fence watched him wistfully. Poor beast, she had been worked to death on insufficient pasturage, hauling the plough and then the drag, until she could hardly stand. Gil had got Adam down to help, and one or the other had hauled with the mare. At that they were better off than some people who hauled their drags without beasts. Now Adam Helmer was resting on the sunny porch, and the women were down by the river gathering the early marigold leaves for their first green food in months. The baby lay on a shawl in the grass at a corner of the field where Gil could keep his eye on him. The boy looked thin, lately, and seemed dull, for they had been feeding him on meat broth since Lana's milk had given out, and the cow would not freshen until June. They borrowed a little milk from time to time—enough, Gil thought, to keep the baby from getting too sick. But he was worried that it cried so seldom.

Lana did not seem worried. She was carrying another child; they thought it would be born in August. But she looked older. She had a queer look of frailness above the waist, while her hips and thighs had grown inordinately heavy. She took no interest in anything but food. But Gil hoped that, when they were getting plenty to eat again, she would brighten up.

He was glad that Demooth was back, for that meant that John Weaver could get work. Though his wife had died, Demooth was fixing up the Herter house, of which the stone walls yet stood, and he needed a younger man than Clem Coppernol now to work what farm he had left. The old Dutchman had not wintered well. He had always been a heavy eater and the thin winter had left him sour and difficult and given to unpredictable and dangerous flights of passion. He had nearly killed a horse that had lain down with him from exhaustion. They said he would have beaten it to death if he himself had not collapsed from the exertion of swinging the fence rail.

All these things had bothered Gil like a buzzing in his head, like the sound of bees outside a window on a hot afternoon. A good many others complained of the same buzzing of the head. They thought it might be weakness that made it, or the unaccustomed warmth.

Gil himself did not put much stock in the rumors of a Continental offensive against the Indians and Tories to the west. Not even when he saw an unusually large munition train hauling west to Fort Stanwix on the sixth.

But on the seventh he had forgotten about them. He had started sowing at dawn. At first he had cast badly and unsteadily. Later the old accustomed rhythm had returned to his tired arm. This morning at last he had felt like himself and the seed fell in even sweeps, and by afternoon, with only four bushels of barley left to sow, he had felt his confidence rise.

The women came back with baskets of green leaves, Lana, Mrs. McKlennar, and the negress, walking through the still evening air. He thought Lana looked better. She picked up the baby, slinging it on her hip, and stopped before him.

"Come back," she said. "You've sowed enough to-day."

"Don't walk on the seeding," he said. "I've only a little left to do."

She obediently stepped off the seeding and let him pass. Her eyes brightened to watch the even swing of his arm, hand from the bag, over and round and back, making a sort of figure eight that the grain traced wide in the air and spread, in touching earth, to make an even sheet. To watch it soothed her. It was a familiar gesture, elemental in faith and hope.

She said, "I wonder how they're fixed for seed at Fox's Mills."

"I guess all right," he said, turning and coming back towards her. "How's Gilly?"

"I think the sun's doing him good. I wish he had more flesh on his legs."

"Where's Joe, to-day?"

"He was back of the house in the sumacs. He had a spade. I don't know what he was doing."

They let Joe Boleo's activities drop. Then Lana went on to the house. She said over her shoulder, "Daisy's going to bake a spinach pie with the greens."

Gil was finishing the last row of the field, at the river-side fence. He thought the buzzing was coming back to his head, but he was tired. He stopped to let his ears clear, letting the last grain trickle through his fingers. After a moment, he turned the bag inside out and shook it. He could not waste a single seed. The field lay square before him, traversed in parallels by his own footprints.

A still clear light lay all across the sky, and a flock of crows traversing the valley from north to south caught rusty flashes from it on their wings. Gil watched them turn their heads to look at the field and wondered whether they felt hungry enough to steal his oats.

Joe Boleo came down the field and said, "Gil. Your wife wants you to come home and rest."

"I'm resting right here."

"I figured so. But a woman don't think a man can rest unless he's where she can talk at him."

Winter had not upset Joe. He looked the same—gaunt, stooped, wrinkled, lackadaisical.

"I can't get the buzzing out of my head, Joe."

"What buzzing?" Joe was never bothered by buzzings.

"It's so loud I'd think you could hear it," said Gil.

Joe pretended to listen.

Suddenly his face tilted.

"By Jesus," he said soberly, "I do." He waited a moment. Then he climbed onto the fence and turned his face southeast, across the river. "It ain't buzzing, Gil," he said excitedly. "It's drums. They're coming up from the falls across the river. Hear them now."

Gil's head cleared. He too heard them. He climbed up beside Joe and stared with him through the infinite clearness of the evening air.

"There they come," said Joe. A file of blue was marching up the road. They saw them, but it was hard to believe.

"They're going to camp," said Joe. "They're falling out in that five-acre lot of Freddy Getman's."

Gil could see the drummers with their deep drums drumming beside the single black stud that was all that remained of Getman's house. Behind them lay the lot. Into it were wheeling a company in blue campaign coats, their muskets all on shoulder. They began to stack arms.

"What are they doing?"

"Taking the fences apart for firewood, I guess."

Another company with white showing through the blue, white gaiters and white vests, followed the first. Then came a swinging company of men in grayish hunting shirts.

The drums were now a stirring resonance throughout the valley. Adam came loping down the field. He asked excitedly what Joe had made out. "Let's go over," he said.

"Sure," said Joe. "You coming, Gil?"

Gil said he would go home. He didn't want to leave the place alone. He was tired, too.

The two woodsmen were like two boys. "We'll come right back and tell you," they shouted, and piled down to where the boat was fastened. Adam rowed, forcing shiny swirls with the oars, and Joe jerked his fur cap in the stern.

Supper was nearly over when the two men returned, but Daisy had kept a plate hot for each of them. They talked together like boys, both at once, both contradicting.

"There's a hundred and fifty soldiers," said Adam. "Two companies. The Fourth New York."

"No, it's the Fourth Pennsylvania. The New York Regiment's the fifth."

"You're crazy."

"Who gives a dang? You ought to've gone over, Gil. Their wagons come in right behind them. Remember how we had to wait for our wagons going up to Oriskany? These bezabors were sore as boils because they had to wait for fifteen minutes for the wagons."

"That ain't nothing. Do you know what they had for supper?" Joe Boleo's small eyes blinked.

"No," said Mrs. McKlennar. "How could we know, you crazy fool?"

"He's just like a bedbug," said Adam. "He gets ideas from humins, but they go to his belly. They had fresh pork. Yessir, Mrs. McKlennar. Fresh pork. I et some. And they had white bread. Soft bread. God, this country's getting luxuries now the army has soft bread."

"You big blond-headed bug-tit," said Joe Boleo. "Anybody could have guessed that. What they had, Mrs. McKlennar, ma'am, was white sugar in their tea!" He pursed his lips. "They offered me some tea, and I said yes. And they said how much sugar in it? And I said, well, about two and a half inches of it, with a spoonful of tea. And the son of a gun gave it to me! I brought it home in my shirt." Chuckling, he drew the cup from inside his shirt and handed it to Mrs. McKlennar.

Mrs. McKlennar began to sniff. She tried twice to speak, and then she said, "Thank you, Joe. I wish we had tea to go with it. But we'll have it in water. Daisy, boil some water."

"Yas'm, sholy does. It's ready bilin'."

Daisy in her ragged dress fluttered round the table laying the cups. She poured the water from the kettle. With great care Mrs. McKlennar put two teaspoonfuls in each cup. Nobody spoke as they stirred. They all watched her till she lifted her cup. Then they sipped together.

"It surely is a treat," said Mrs. McKlennar.

Lana suddenly got to her feet.

"I'm going to see if Gilly likes it," she said. She brought him to the table and sat him on her lap while he stupidly nodded his big head and rubbed his sleepy eyes. They all held their breaths when she put the spoon to his mouth, carefully cooled by her own blowing. He made a face, feebly, then stiffened and was very still. Then he started to cry. Their disappointment was intense.

Lana said defensively, "He's never tasted any sugar."

"Don't be silly," cried Mrs. McKlennar. "All he wants is more."

When Lana lifted the spoon again the child opened his mouth eagerly. "See!" cried Mrs. McKlennar. "I told you."

Everybody felt jubilantly happy.

"Did you find out where they were going?"

"Stanwix," said Joe and Adam together.

"Just there? There's two hundred men there already."

"That's what they said," said Adam.

"It's my idea they're going to make some kind of pass against Oswego," said Joe.

"What would they send Rangers for against a fort?" Adam was scornful.

Gil said, "Do you suppose they're going to go against the Onondagas?"

"By God!" said Joe.

They all remembered what Ellis had said. The Iroquois.

"They'll need scouts, I'll bet," said Adam. Joe met his eye.

"It would be fun going with an army like that and wiping out some Indians," said Joe quietly. "I always wanted to do some destruction against them."

He turned to Gil. "If they do, will you come along with us?"

Gil shook his head. Adam said, "You got your planting done, ain't you? Come on."

"The womenfolks will be safe enough with an army that size flogging around the woods. You ought to see them. They ain't like those Massachusetts boys."

"We ain't been asked," said Gil.

"Shucks," said Joe, blushing, because he had thought of something else to say and barely saved it before women. "You come along. I fixed something for the women in case they should get cut off. It's a hide-hole. I been working on it for three days."

"Really?" Mrs. McKlennar was interested. "What is it?"

"Come out," said Joe. "No, damn it, it's dark. I'll show you to-morrow."

"What's that, Gil?" Lana had risen.

Adam said soothingly, "That's just the tattoo, Lana."

They all went out on the porch with the tattoo of the drums thudding faintly across the valley towards them. It was pitch-dark, but the regularly spaced fires seemed very near.

They stood a long time watching them, in the damp coolness of the night. They saw the sentry figures small and silhouetted. They could even see the stacked rifles.

"They been a long time coming," said Joe.

Back in the house there was a scraping of silver against china as black Daisy scraped the cups for her own taste of sugar. She was humming softly.

3

At Fort Stanwix

Half an hour after sunrise, young John Weaver galloped into the McKlennar yard, waving a letter for Gil. It was a hasty scrawl from Colonel Bellinger asking Gil, Adam, and Joe to report to him immediately at Fort Dayton. While Gil was reading it, the calling of the robins was hushed by a long roll from the drums across the river. Gil ran round the house. He found Adam and Joe watching the camp. They could see the men breaking away from the fires and rolling their blankets.

"It's the general," said Joe. "I've heard it before." He answered Adam's question scornfully. "Not General Washington, you dumbhead. It just means the army's going to march."

Gil gave them Demooth's orders and the men went into the house together to get their rifles.

Lana confronted them in the doorway.

"Gil!"

"Don't get worried," he said.

"Where are you going?"

"Bellinger wants to see us. That's all."

"You're going with the army," she said accusingly.

Adam interposed awkwardly, "Aw, now, Lana. Nothing can happen to Gil with me and Joe along."

She looked white and stiff and her arms hung straight at her sides. Gil said to Mrs. McKlennar, "If we do have to go I'll send John Weaver back. He'll let you know if you ought to move to the fort."

Mrs. McKlennar nodded her gray head.

Joe slapped himself. "Lord, ma'am, I'd forgotten clean about it."

"What, Joe?"

"That hide-hole I made. It'll only take a minute to show it to you. Come along."

He led them quickly out into the sunlight and up through the sumac scrub. "You want to come this way, so you won't leave tracks."

He stopped a hundred yards up the slope.

"There it is," he said modestly.

He pointed to a fallen tree whose roots had lifted a great slab of earth.

"I don't see anything," said the widow.

Joe beamed. "That's it. You don't see nothing. Come here."

He led the two women to the roots of the tree, round to the trunk, and pointed. There was a small hole in the ground. "Don't walk out there," he cautioned them. "That's just poles laid over with dirt. There's room inside for the bunch of you. You can drop right down. I made it soft."

Mrs. McKlennar said, "Thank you, Joe."

Joe said, "You want to remember the way up here. Go over it in your heads so you could do it at night. I don't reckon you'll have to use it, though."

"I don't think so."

"It's a good thing to have handy, though."

He went back down the hillside and found Adam and Gil ready and John Weaver mounted. Lana came, still as death, behind Mrs. McKlennar. The men went down to the road and turned and waved. The widow waved back. Then Lana lifted her hand. Her arm looked frail and white in the morning sunlight.

She began to cry.

"He might have said good-bye to the baby," she sobbed.

Mrs. McKlennar put her arm over Lana's shoulders.

"Don't say that. He didn't want to go any more than you wanted him to. That's why he acted like that."

Over the river the drums beat out the assembly and the troops began to mass along the fence. A moment later the "march" sounded, and the two women saw the lines gather themselves like a single organism and start moving out on the road. They saw what they had not seen last night, that there was a flag in the middle of the line. They had never seen the flag before. The sight of it, clean and bright, with its stripes and circle of stars, for some reason made them feel like crying.

It appeared that Colonel Van Schaick had requested three guides from Bellinger.

"I don't know why he won't take Indians with the Oneidas so close and willing to go. He wanted three white men, he said. I thought of you. He says it will be only three weeks at most."

"Where does he want us to take him?" Joe asked.

"I don't know," said Bellinger. "You'd better start right away. Martin, did you plan for your women to come down here?"

"I think it would be better."

"It may not be necessary. I'll have young Weaver stay out there. But I'll keep an eye on them." He paused. "Van Schaick's got the woods covered to the west and I'll cover the south. And the Oneidas are out. I don't think there's any danger with the size army that's coming." He shook hands with the three in turn. "You'd better go."

The three men reached Fort Stanwix the same day, coming out on the bend of the river just before sunset. While they were yet approaching the fort, a small swivel was discharged and the flag fluttered down from the pole over the gate. It was a beautiful flag, silky and shining against the setting sun; but Gil felt that no matter how often he saw this American flag, he would only see the one that had flown from that same pole two years ago, with its botched stripes of uneven thickness, and its peculiarly shaped stars. Then it had stood for something besides the Continental army.

They trotted up to the sally port and announced themselves to the guard as three scouts from Colonel Bellinger. They were at once admitted and taken directly to the officers' mess. There they found Colonel Goose Van Schaick and his second in command, Major Cochran. The major was well, almost meticulously uniformed; but the colonel was a heavy man with coarse hair turning gray and small calculating eyes, and his collar rode high on his thick neck. He accepted Bellinger's letter and eyed the three Rangers.

"I don't want to be asked questions," he said belligerently. "You'll stay here, you'll live with the noncommissioned officers. Now, does any one of you know the woods west of Oneida Lake?" His eyes had unerringly picked Joe, who was leaning his tail against the table and gazing into the fireplace as if it were a wonder of the world. Now he nodded his head.

"Sure," he said. "I do."

"How about you two?"

Joe answered: "Gil ain't a timber beast, but the young lad's not going to get lost as long as I tell him where to go."

Adam opened his mouth to roar, but he met the colonel's eye in time. There was something about the colonel's eye which quelled him.

The colonel said, "You big ox, if you start fighting around here I'll have you flogged before the fort. I don't want to be bothered with yelling louts like you. And just so you'll know what it

would be like, you can go out on the parade to-morrow morning
and see what happens when a man gets flogged."

He turned back to Joe. "Listen you, what's your name? Boleo.
You're to stay ready to march. You're to report to me an hour
before the first troops start. I'll tell you where we're going. Then
you'll pick the route, though I imagine there's just one way to
get there."

"Sure." Joe was looking out of the window. "Down Wood
Crick and across the lake. You land on the southwest shore,
march over to Onondaga Lake, cross the arm—you can wade
it. It's not over four feet deep. Then hit Onondaga Crick and go
up. That will bring you to the first town. Jesus, Colonel, I used
to play around there as a young lad. You ought to have been out
there then."

The major's Irish face was a study, but the colonel wasn't taking the same pleasure in Joe.

"How did you figure that out?" he asked in a steady hard
voice.

"Why," said Joe, innocently, "I ain't a complete fool or I
wouldn't have been sent here, mister."

"Did you get that from somebody else?"

"No, we figured it out coming up."

The colonel grunted. "Keep your mouths shut. You're sure
you can wade over the arm of the lake?"

"If you don't mind getting wet."

The colonel stared very hard at Joe. Then he said in cold,
level tones, "That's all. If you want to eat you'd better hurry."

As they came out onto the parade, the garrison were fil-
ing into the mess, and the three men followed them dubiously.
These soldiers didn't look quite natural somehow. They seemed
to keep step with a kind of instinct. A corporal came out of the
shadow of the officers' mess and touched Gil's arm. "You the
three scouts?"

They said they were.

"My name's Zach Harris. You're to eat with us." He led them into the mess to a table at which sergeants and corporals ate together. They were greeted friendlily enough and sat down to heaped wooden bowls of beef stew cooked with turnips, tea and sugar, a slab of white bread, and a piece of cheese. The way they ate made the soldiers regard them with curiosity.

"What's the matter, ain't you fed all day?"

Adam replied, "We ain't had a feed like this since last September, Bubby. Does the old man always feed you like this?"

"He's a dinger to get provisions. But he bears down pretty hard on the discipline. Ever since that Dutchman Steuben came around last year, old Goose has been cock-eyed over discipline. But he can act real nice sometimes."

"He looks to me as if he could act just about as nice as a wolverine with the bilious complaint," remarked Adam.

The table roared and the word, going clean round the mess hall, set all the men to laughing. But Corporal Harris's was a dry grin. "I guess I see why the old man wanted you to watch a flogging, mister."

The flogging took place an hour after sunrise and just before breakfast. It was one of the colonel's theories that it made more impression on an empty stomach.

The three Rangers were routed out of bed by Corporal Harris and told to appear on the parade in five minutes. Before they were dressed they heard the drums beating a muster, and as they stepped out into the soft April morning the tap of a single drum came from the guardhouse.

Corporal Harris led them to a position in front of his own company. The entire garrison had been lined up in a hollow square. Set up on the bare beaten earth in the middle of the square was a single post about a foot thick. It made a long shadow towards the guardhouse, and now the tapping of the single drum marked the approach of the culprit along this shadow. He came between two sergeants. He was naked to the waist. He looked neither right nor left, but kept his eyes on the post.

Joe Boleo looked on with an abstracted kind of interest. Adam stood straight. The faces of the soldiers were expressionless as the culprit was taken by the arms, his hands lifted, and two nooses of fine rope passed over the wrists. The rope was then hauled up over a groove in the top of the post until the arms were stretched over the man's head, and his shoulder blades stood out sharp and his toes barely touched the ground.

The two sergeants then stepped back. The sergeant major of the garrison stepped out from the ranks and the drums beat a short roll. The sergeant general read from a paper:—

> *"Private Hugh Deyo, Captain Varick's Company, tried before court-martial and found guilty of stealing a shirt. Sentenced to fifty lashes with the hide whip. April 9th, 1779. To be administered before the entire garrison on parade, by order of Colonel Goose Van Schaick."*

He shifted the paper to read the back. "Captain Wandle's company."

"All present or accounted for."

"Captain Gregg's company."

In turn each company was called and answered.

The sergeant major of Varick's company then stepped forward to the left of the post. He unwrapped the six-foot hide whip from his arm, on which it had been coiled like an inanimate snake, and tossed out the folds in the dust so that they lay flat behind him.

The drums rolled.

"Sergeant, do your duty."

Adam looked up to see the colonel standing grimly with the officers in the opening through which the prisoner had come.

The whip sang forward and snapped with a preliminary report to one side of the culprit. It snapped a second time and cracked solidly across his back. It made a small puff of dust as it snapped. The man's body seemed to leap inside itself. A diagonal welt was marked on the skin, with a break between the shoulder blades, but the man made no sound.

The whip cracked again, and the sergeant said aloud, "Two."

It was beautiful whipping, the second welt appearing a half inch below the first. The welts went down the man's back in parallels. The man still made no sound. At the count of ten the stripes began to climb again and the first overlay occurred. A little spurt of blood was drawn and trickled slowly into the hollow of his back, which looked tight and cupped, to receive it. It went down inside his pants.

Gil could not take his eyes off the man. He saw him duck his head against his arm and bite it. He still made no sound. But at the fifteenth stripe he gave way and yelled for the first time. Then with a pathetic stiffening of the back he kept silent for three more strokes, and then he broke down, and at last Gil managed to tear his eyes away.

He could hear only the whip stroke, the yell, and the stolid counting of the sergeant's voice. When finally it was over the man hung against the post, quite still, but with a palpable throbbing all along his back, which now had puffed and dripped slowly all along the line of his belt.

The flies, which had been buzzing round and round the post throughout the punishment, darted in several times, and then lit delicately. The drums beat. It was over. The companies filed in to breakfast.

As they went the sentry hailed from the gate, and it was

opened to admit four Indians. But Gil did not look at them. If he had, he would have recognized two—the sachem, Skenandoa, the old man who had been Herkimer's friend and who had come to the American camp before Oriskany, and Blue Back.

Blue Back was feeling pretty big these days, for he had succeeded to a sachemship with the title Kahnyadaghshayen, which, in English, meant "Easy Throat." But he still continued his enlightened habits of thought, for he did not wear a blanket like the other three Indians. Instead, he wore a British campaign coat. If the gold braid was somewhat tarnished, the scarlet was redeemingly bright. It was much too tight across the back, which made it uncomfortable to wear, because it bound under the arms and made the lice go down into his leggings. But it did look well with the peacock's feather, which he wore over his right eye. His wife had made a tricorn of his old hat, and as far as Blue Back could see, he was just as handsome as a major general. As he entered the fort, he was convinced that Colonel Van Schaick would hire him to guide the expedition, wherever it might be going, for forty cents a day, though he had made up his mind to accept twenty, so long as he was offered a full rum ration.

It gave him a genuine shock to see Gil Martin. For one frenzied instant he planned to run back through the gate; but as soon as he observed that Gil had not seen him, he took the feather surreptitiously out of his hat and hid it inside his coat. He didn't feel quite so important, but he felt a lot safer. With the other three Indians, he stopped for a moment to stare at the flogged soldier, wondering inwardly why they had not burned him also.

A sergeant came up to lead them into the colonel's office, where they all sat down on benches and accepted tobacco, while Skenandoa announced their names; and none of them looked at the colonel. None of them knew what to make of the colonel; he wasn't like Gansevoort or Willett, and they were a little afraid of him. He had a patience like their own; but it was cold patience in which they felt no courtesy.

Finally Skenandoa remarked that his young men had seen a big army coming west through Dayton. Was it so? Or had their eyes been deceived?

It was so, said Colonel Van Schaick.

So many men must be going on an expedition.

As to that, the colonel did not know. There were no orders. It would probably mean no more than a change of garrison.

Skenandoa looked crafty. That was too bad, because his young men had all come to the fort to offer themselves as guides and scouts. He had sixty young men and three sachems to keep them in order.

The colonel allowed that it was too bad. There was nothing for them to do unless they made an expedition of their own. He wished he had someone to send to Oswegatchie. He would pay five kegs of rum for the destruction of that place. But he had no men of his own to send.

Skenandoa still looked crafty. His men were very young. Maybe the colonel could send two officers to show them how to act.

Colonel Van Schaick thought for a moment. Very well, he had two. When would the Oneidas want to start?

In a week.

Very well, it would be seen to. The great Lieutenant McClellan and the Ensign Hardenberg would go. He called in the two young officers and introduced them and ordered them to report to Skenandoa in the Oneida camp on the seventeenth, equipped for a three weeks' march. The Indians grunted and ceremoniously departed.

"Sorry," said the colonel to the two young officers. "We've got to get them out of here before they get the wind up about the expedition. I'm telling you in confidence, we're to wipe out the Onondagas. If they knew it, the Oneidas might give it away."

Blue Back, passing through the parade, saw his three white acquaintances emerge from the mess. "How?" he said to Martin, and "How?" to each of the others.

Joe said, "You're looking fine, Blue Back."

"I fine," said Blue Back, grinning. "How?" He beamed.

"We're fine."

"Fine," said Blue Back.

"Come and have a drink."

Blue Back hesitated. His fat face was sorrowful.

"Neah," he said. "No drink. Go home. Go make expedition." That was a new word. Sadly he went out through the gate after his companions.

4

Blue Back's Troubled Mind

When Blue Back got home to his new house in Oneida Castle, he lay down on his skins on the floor. His wife found him there when she came in bearing a heavy faggot of firewood. His wife was still pretty and young-looking, though she was big with an expected addition to the family, which now, to old Blue Back's continuing amazement, already amounted to two children. The eldest he had driven out to play with the other neighboring children. The youngest, still on her board, he had hung on the peg beside the door. So when his wife returned, she knew at once that Blue Back was engrossed either in sorrow or in deep thought.

She immediately brought up the fire and put on a dish of stew. And then she did what he always adored—stripped him and began picking him over for bugs.

Old Blue Back liked to feel her hard cool fingers going over his stout body. He liked the way her braids fell over her shoulders and tickled along the temple of his upstanding belly. She was infinitely proud of him and proud too of the way he was proving fertile. She even boasted about him to the women. Where was another man of her husband's age that could get two children like that? And now another coming ten months after the second! She knew young warriors from their first successful warpath that didn't produce as masterfully as that. It must be his belly, they said. Other old men lost their bellies, or they became round and hard like a walnut with shriveled meat, and rattled continually; but Blue Back had a stomach like Ganadadele, the steep hill. Truly, thought his wife, it was a wonderful thing, and her pride and duty to keep it so. She left him for the moment to fetch the meat, wishing that it might be autumn so that she could fill him with new beans.

When the two officers appeared in the Indian town, they brought a keg of rum, which restored some of Blue Back's confidence and made the other sachems feel quite sure that what the officers said was true. Apparently, the new troops under Colonel Willett were to take over the fort, but for the time being both armies were remaining in garrison. The weather had turned cold, said the officers, and there was no point in marching back down the valley in cold weather. One could even see snowflakes falling beyond the door of the house. It was so.

However, being active men, they themselves were eager to join their Oneida brothers on a warpath. And the next morning, since the sun shone again, the sachems called up the young men. There were sixty of them, painted for war. Dressed in their best beadings, they made an imposing array among the small houses and lodges, and they set up a great yelling as they marched off into the woods, with the Indian wives following at the proper distance.

Inside the first woods, the men all took off their best clothes, leaving them in bundles for the women to take back. They painted a couple of trees, and set out. Blue Back left his red coat and put on his greasy old hunting shirt. He did not feel much like marching through the dripping April countryside; he felt vaguely uneasy. As he sobered, it occurred to him that Colonel Van Schaick was an artful man. Suddenly he did not believe anything of all the things that had been said. He decided that he would drop off by himself and see whether the troops were actually remaining in garrison.

He came out on the vale in which Fort Stanwix stood on the evening of the eighteenth, and beheld a sight that confirmed his suspicions.

Large squashy flakes of snow, falling steadily, made it hard for him to see what the soldiers were hauling west from the fort into the woods. Blue Back scouted round through the tamaracks and lay down beside the road St. Leger had constructed two years ago. One of the wagons came groaning by close enough for him to see that it carried two bateaux. After it had passed, he followed it all the way to the shore of Wood Creek.

There he found thirty soldiers encamped as guards for a great number of boats tied up to trees. He listened to the men's conversation, but they made so much noise that he could understand little of it. Mostly it seemed to have to do with women and the new rum, which they did not think highly of.

After a while, Blue Back withdrew into the woods and built himself a bark shed and lit a small fire. He stayed there all that night. In the morning he went back to the fort and saw the troops marshaling outside the glacis, and a couple of wagons hauling food towards Wood Creek.

Blue Back's round face grew rounder with thought. If the army were really going to travel, they would normally have been glad of Indian guides. If they had elaborately sent off the Indians towards Oswegatchie and paid rum in advance, it meant that they did not wish Indians. If they did not wish Indians, it was because they did not wish Indians to know what they were going to do. Even Blue Back knew enough to realize that there was just one objective against which such an army would move—the Onondaga towns.

Though the Onondagas had claimed to be neutrals, Blue Back was aware that the Americans thought the Onondagas had done some raiding of their own. He knew himself that they had taken Caldwell down against Little Stone Arabia. Skenandoa had remonstrated with them about it. They had refused to take warning. They were having all the fun of raiding with little risk of retaliation. Now they were going to be raided by the Continentals.

Blue Back didn't care about that; but what he did care about was the indubitable fact that the Onondagas would claim that the Oneidas had told on them, and would therefore still more indubitably bring the hostile western nations down on the Oneidas. He decided that there was just one thing for him to do, and without wasting another minute he started jogging west towards Wood Creek.

His belly bounced a little at first, but gradually he got the wind out of himself and by the time he reached the shore of the creek he was making good time.

He circled the landing, taking note that no bateaux had yet started, and set off along the bank. He was relieved to see how full of drift the creek was. Bateaux drew so much water that the men would take a full day getting them down to the lake. By that time he himself should have found a canoe and got far across the lake.

He found a small canoe well hidden in a growth of young balsam, turned it over, and found two paddles in it. He picked it up easily and carried it to the water. He sighed with satisfaction when he got in and picked up a paddle and shot off with the roily current.

He looked enormous in the canoe, like some kind of brown frog, corpulent with May flies. But his arms were strong and the canoe handled like a leaf under his earnest paddling. The sweat came out on his brown face, and he took his hat off, showing his braided lock held in shape with a red, lady's shoelace. Before midafternoon he came out into Oneida Lake to meet a rising west wind, and he skirted the southern shore. He paddled all afternoon and evening, making heavy weather of it, and having to land every hour or so to drain the canoe.

Along towards midnight, however, having been compelled to go ashore for the second time in an hour, he decided that he had enough of a lead on the army, and he lay down under his canoe and slept. The snow formed a white backbone on his canoe and dripped off on either side of him as he lay, but neither the cold nor the wet disturbed him.

He was awakened at dawn by the screaming of gulls. The wind was still in the west, but lighter; and the waves had a brittle slap along the sand. It was a clear day with a mild sun that only intermittently could be felt through the wind. The lake was a

cool dark blue, and the sky, still shadowed in the west, had a rim
of brightness all round the horizon. It looked to Blue Back like
a regular rain-making day. He turned his attention to the gulls,
which were streaming past him in groups of two and three, great
white birds, with the sunlight golden on their underwings. Off
to the east a flock of them had collected and were wheeling and
rising and swooping like enormous snowflakes.

For some time Blue Back studied them. He stood on the
beach, the wind flapping the edges of his hunting shirt, his hat
tilted back on his head and his belly feeling as empty as the
windy sky. Slowly an expression of the purest surprise came over
his brown face. He put his hand to his mouth, then took it away
and plodded back up the shore for his canoe. It was sodden and
heavy with snow, but he swung it over his head in his haste as if
it were a brand-new one. His bowlegs trotted under it; he gave
a grunt and heaved it off his shoulders and tossed it into the
water, sprang in, and made two strokes standing—still looking
back towards the east. Then he sat down and paddled, striking
out across the bay called Prosser's, and heading straight into the
wind for the Onondaga landing.

He could scarcely believe what he had seen, though he knew
his eyes were good. They were unmistakably bateaux, about
thirty of them, he thought. They would be carrying about five
hundred men. Even at that distance he had been able to make
out the blue coats in some of them. And the boats were all close
together, though they must have rowed all night to have come
so far. Who had ever heard of an army of that size traveling so
quickly?

Blue Back felt a little quiver far under his fat at the root of
his backbone. Those soldiers weren't going to do anything to the
Oneidas, but it made him uneasy to think that they could move
about the country with that speed. He kept the bow of his canoe
straight in the wind and paddled hard, hoping that he had not

been seen. He knew that he could paddle away from them. But he had figured on having a day or two to break the news.

A couple of gulls started following him and squalling, but luckily the main flock were too interested in the flotilla to be attracted to him, and little by little the canoe drew ahead until it was safely out of sight.

Blue Back did not land at the landing, but a half mile to the east of it. He hid his canoe a good hundred yards up the shore, before starting his stout trot for the Onondaga Castle.

He reached it, fairly tired out, before dark, and helped himself to a good meal before he delivered his news. The largest part of the Onondaga fighting force was in the west, supposedly to meet Colonel John Butler somewhere beyond the Genesee. There were only a few men left in any of the villages, he was informed, and they were mostly older men, or boys. When he told the men that there were five hundred soldiers coming against them, they decided that they must move at once, and started sending out runners to the surrounding villages. They planned to move in the morning. They appeared to feel perfectly friendly towards Blue Back and offered him a bed in one of the best houses.

He was glad to accept, and slept heavily all night; but next day his uneasiness recurred to him. The approaching invasion had nothing directly to do with him; it was rather the sight of all these people starting out into the west that troubled his mind. They were very quiet. Even the multitudinous dogs did not bark. The main town, in which he was, boasted fourteen horses, and these were all loaded to the limit of their capacity until their half-starved, beaten bodies were almost lost to view. The women carried their babies, their seeds, and bundles of their finery, as much as they could manage. Even the little girls were given each a bundle or basket. And nobody said good-bye to Blue Back. They moved off in single file into the southwest to strike the Iroquois trail, a hundred souls of them, without a house to go to.

When he started looking into the empty houses, it made him sad to see how much they had been forced to leave. Green pelts, the larger household dishes—unexpectedly his probing finger found a pouch of wampum beads. His face looked singularly thoughtful as he transferred the pouch from its hiding place to his belt. But there were so many things left. In the council houses were a lot of oldish muskets which Blue Back carefully went over to see whether there was one better than his.

It was well on in the morning before he gave up his investigation of the deserted town and wandered off into the woods. He stopped for an instant to look back on the empty silent houses, most of them with bark roofs, some beautifully rounded in the old Iroquois fashion that the fathers used to know, all scattered any which way in the woods, with the long council house standing alone.

In that council house had burned once the council fire that made the Six Nations a great and undivided race. "Onenh waka-lighwakayonne. Now it has become old; now there is nothing but wilderness. You are in your graves; you who established it." The words entered Blue Back's mind, the beginning of the great hymn. He had not thought of them for a long time. They went through his brain like a lost bird crossing the sky. He lifted his eyes and beheld rain clouds driving down from the northwest.

The old Indian, in his dirty shirt and his dirty moccasins and his limp, leaf-stained hat, shuffled indolently into the underbrush. A patch of bloodroot bloomed like the whitest snow, and among them his feet made no sound.

So, suddenly, he heard to the southeast the report of several rifles, irregular, distinct, but tiny thuds of sound.

5

The Expedition

It had been Blue Back's plan to return to his home before the troops arrived; but now he realized that they must have marched overland from Oneida Lake with far greater rapidity than he had counted on. They were already cutting into the outlying villages, between him and the home trail.

He drifted uneasily up on a low hill from which he could see out over the forest tops. The drizzle had already begun, driving through the stems of the trees and striking him in waves of wet. Four miles south and east a vast cloud of dark smoke was tumbling skyward. Blue Back wondered whether the people had moved away in time. A great curiosity laid hold of him to find out how the army would act. There had been shooting.

He hesitated for only a few minutes; then, like a fat brown shadow in the gray spring woods, he began to move towards the smoke. And in half an hour he had picked up the bluecoat company, led by a detachment of Rangers, coming towards him among the trees.

It was Blue Back's first sight of the Morgan Rangers. He did not like their looks. He could tell by their faces that they would pot an Indian as quick as a rabbit. They would not be troubled to find out what nation he belonged to. He sank down into the scrub, watching them pass with beady eyes. . . .

• • •

For two days, Blue Back dogged the army in the rain, watching everything they did. He saw them burn the old towns, loot the houses, taking very little. He saw them casting muskets into the hottest fire. He saw the store of Indian gunpowder exploded in the main town and the council house curl apart, hissing under the raindrops, and fall in a mass of sparks. He saw a lone return-ing dog, a white dog, looking for food, shot in the head and swung into the fire by its tail. He saw squads of men sticking pigs with their bayonets and roasting them in the ashes of the burning houses.

The troops did everything systematically and quietly. It was not like an Indian raid. It was done with a cold-blooded calcula-tion that overlooked no ear of corn.

On the morning of the second day, Blue Back picked up a small detachment that had surprised the one village in which Indians yet remained. They had rounded up fifteen women and brought them as prisoners, a silent, sullen, hopeless group, wet, shivering, mishandled. Later he found the remains of the village; and here he came upon signs that the discipline had not been observed. There were a few men lying about the open ground, unscalped for the most part. And there were women, some of them half naked. He was not much interested in the dead women until he happened to notice one in the bushes beyond the town. She was lying under a low-growing hemlock, on the soft needles, where it was yet quite dry. She had been hit on the head and was dying. She was quite naked. She was a young woman. Her tangled hair was long and black. She made no sound at all and did not move except for the very slow and painful heaving of her breast.

The old Indian did not let her see him; but he waited near by, dog-like, until she was dead. Then he beat around the town look-ing at the other dead women. Almost all of them were young.

• • •

The army camped that night on the site of the old town with great roaring fires. The officers had a long lean-to set up on a rise of ground. Blue Back, who hung on the outside of the pickets, could see everything they did. He recognized Colonel Van Schaick entering notes in a small book with the feather of a bird and receiving reports from the other officers. He also recognized Colonel Marinus Willett by his huge nose and slab-sided ruddy cheeks. He saw Joe Boleo and Adam Helmer come into the light of the officers' fire to be questioned. He understood enough of what they said to realize that all the towns had been burned and that the army would start its return march on the next morning.

One by one, captains and lieutenants made their reports. When the last one had spoken, Colonel Van Schaick turned to Colonel Willett.

"We've not lost a man," he said with satisfaction. "How's that for a record? Ninety-odd miles into the Indian country, a nation destroyed, no casualties. By the Lord, I'm proud of you all!"

Everyone seemed pleased. Only Willett spoke through his great nose.

"I'd like to know where all the Indians went to, Goose. I'd like to know who warned them. Somebody did, you know."

"I'm just as glad," said Van Schaick. "We've given them a lesson and we've committed no atrocities. I'm proud of you all. It ought to have the effect we hoped for."

"What effect, Goose?"

"Why, it practically guarantees safety to the western settlements."

Next morning Blue Back stayed only long enough to make sure that the army had started back towards their bateaux on Oneida

Lake before cutting off on his own path to find his canoe. He was well ahead of the army when he reached the lake, and he launched his canoe without being noticed by the boat guard.

Two days later he was back in his own house, talking to Skenandoa and eating a hot meal. The ancient sachem was as upset as Blue Back himself. He said he would have liked to protest to Van Schaick at once over the expedition, but to do that would be to acknowledge that the Onondagas had been warned by one of the Oneidas. When they considered everything that Blue Back had seen, they decided it would be dangerous to let the colonel know. They felt singularly helpless. They decided to wait until the news became general and then to demand army protection against the western nations and the British.

After Skenandoa had left, Blue Back's wife combed out his hair and pampered him in his favorite ways. She was immensely proud of him; but at the same time she was disturbed by his persistent staring at her. She did not know that he was wondering whether a white man would consider her young enough, or pretty enough. He felt that he no longer comprehended white men.

6

Destruction of the Long House

Colonel Van Schaick was doing the talking. He stood up before the three men, now that he had shaken their hands in turn—Joe Boleo, Adam Helmer, and Gil. On one side Major Cochran looked on with obvious pleasure. On the other Colonel Willett was preternaturally solemn. But when Adam's restless eye met his, the yellow-haired giant felt like laughing out loud. Willett's right eyelid was perceptibly fluttering.

"I am obliged to you three men," said Colonel Van Schaick. "You have done a splendid job for me. For the whole army. I flatter myself the whole army has done a splendid job, but it would have been impossible without such sure guides. You will now return to your homes, and you will kindly convey to Colonel Bellinger my gratitude for having sent me three such excellent men. Tell him I shall write him personally as soon as pressure of duty permits. Here's your pay. I thank you."

To each man he handed a slip of white paper neatly inscribed, except where his own pigeon-track writing wandered through the letters of his name. The two woodsmen, neither of whom could read, were too dumbfounded to speak. They held the papers in their big hands gingerly and merely stared. Gil tugged them by the sleeves. They followed him out, heads bare.

Joe muttered, "It's like church."

"Shut up," said Gil. Adam burst out laughing. Then they heard a chuckle behind them and found that Marinus Willett had come after them. "You did a good job, boys," he said. "I want to remember you." He shook hands, the way Van Schaick had, but he seemed like somebody a man could talk back to. His big erect shoulders had none of this new drill-masterish stiffness. "I don't know how much good the expedition did, but we did all there was to do."

Joe looked sober. "Those Onondagas will holler like cats with their tails in traps."

Willett nodded.

"I hope they'll only howl."

He nodded his head to them and went away to his own quarters. The three men walked out through the gate. As soon as they were out of hearing, Adam demanded, "What's this paper anyway? It ain't money."

"I'll read you mine," said Gil. "They're all the same."

By Goose Van Schaick, Esquire, Colonel,
the First Regiment, the New York Line.

TO GILBERT MARTIN & GREETING —

You are hereby authorized to impress for your own use as a return for your services in this regiment in the service of the United States, 3 bushels of wheat from any Person whom Col. Peter Bellinger, Esquire, shall deem can conveniently spare the same & whose name shall by him be endorsed on this warrant.

Given under my hand at Fort Stanwix
this twenty-fifth day of April 1779
GOOSE VAN SCHAICK, COL.

"Well, for God's sake!" said Adam. "Who's got three bushel of wheat in German Flats anyway?"

"Shut up, can't you? Always yelling. Look, Gil, does mine say, 'Joe Boleo and Greeting' on it?"

"Yes, it does."

"Show me where."

Gil showed him.

"Well, I'll be God damned. Boleo and Greeting."

"Yes, but what good's this thing to me?" demanded Adam. "It ain't money, it ain't likker, and there isn't any wheat."

"Oh, give it to your girl for dinner," growled Joe, lengthening his stride to pull ahead of them.

"Listen, Gil. Maybe you'd like to buy my paper, hey?"

"I haven't any money," Gil said, with a laugh.

"Well, how am I going to get paid, then?"

"I don't know. You can ask Bellinger."

The road wound out of the grass into the woods. Joe Boleo shambled along in the lead. He didn't act anxious for company. He was bent way over, his lean shoulders hanging and his wrinkled face absorbed. When the other two got in hearing of him, he was muttering, "Joe Boleo and Greeting. By God! Joe Boleo and Greeting. . . ."

The three reported to Bellinger at Fort Dayton and were given supper there. Men crowded round Bellinger's cabin to hear the news of the expedition, and to many of them it seemed—now that Congress had decided to act—that the end of the war could not be far away. They started discussing the feasibility of rebuilding on the sites of their old farms. Some regretted that they had sown their spring seed in borrowed land.

Bellinger told Gil that the women had remained at McKlennar's, for there had not been a single alarm throughout the valley. It was now generally admitted that a powerful campaign was going to be carried on against the Iroquois that summer. Quartermasters were scouring the valley for supplies. In Schenectady they were constructing numberless bateaux. It was believed that one wing of the army would muster at Canajoharie within six weeks. James Clinton was the brigadier appointed to command it—fifteen hundred men. But that was only the wing. The main army would muster in Pennsylvania and come up the Susquehanna. The expedition Gil had just returned from was no more than a preliminary demonstration.

As he walked down the road from the fort after dark, Gil felt a strange sense of peace. The air had turned warm on a southerly wind. It was damp, and it felt like more rain; but a rain from the south would be a growing rain. He was walking alone, for Joe had accepted an invitation to drink, and Adam, having caught sight of Polly Bowers at the corner of the fort, had been overwhelmed with the desire to describe the Indian country to her. Gil was glad to be alone, just then.

The house was quite dark. Either they had gone to bed or they had closed the blinds. He thought that perhaps in a few months it would be safe for people to burn candles in their houses once more, without darkening the windows.

He was startled when a dog rushed barking down the slope. Then he realized that John Weaver must be staying at the farm and he whistled to the dog. The dog recognized him and jumped about his legs, and the next moment the door opened and Lana was pushing her way past John. "It's Gil. I know it's Gil. Let me out," she was saying.

He jumped up the porch steps and put his arms round her. She was whispering, "I was sure you were coming home to-night. I knew it, Gil, but they wouldn't believe me."

He pulled her through the door and they walked together into the kitchen, where Daisy was holding a splinter to the coals and blowing through her thick lips at it. It took only a moment to get the light. It was good to be home, to see women's faces, people he loved. He shook John's hand. John said, "We heard you'd gone against the Indians."

"Yes," said Gil, "we burned the towns. We took some prisoners, but the men were mostly away. It wasn't much but marching."

John's face colored.

"Now you're back," he said, "maybe it would be all right for me to get on home."

"Yes, yes, go ahead, John. And thank you for all you've done." Mrs. McKlennar grinned at his retreating back. "I keep forgetting John's a married man."

They sat down together while John whistled to his dog and set out for Fort Dayton.

"You look healthy," observed Mrs. McKlennar.

"I'm fine," said Gil. He felt Lana pressing his hand under cover of her petticoat. "How have you all been? How's Gilly?"

"Everything's been fine."

"How's the cow?"

"She freshened day before yesterday. She's in good shape," said Mrs. McKlennar.

"What was it?"

Lana smiled.

"A heifer. A nice one. Brown and white."

"That's fine." It was better than fine. It would have been tragic if the cow had dropped a bull calf. With the few remaining cows in German Flats one bull was enough for service for the entire district.

The next evening at sundown the army came from the west, a long line of bateaux rowing steadily down the river. They camped on Getman's farm, and in the morning they continued for the east. Two days later their munition wagons hauled through with a company for escort. The commanding officer brought an order to Colonel Bellinger demanding levies to fill out one squad, and the militia was mustered and lots drawn.

Gil was miserable with the dread of having to leave the farm again; but he did not draw a long straw; and he was able then to feel sorry that young John Weaver was one of the unlucky ones. He could see Mary's face, thin and tragic; and he thought of how Lana would have looked if John's bad luck had happened to him. He tried to cheer John, telling him that he would draw pay for the three months and get a campaign coat, but John only nodded. He had almost an hour to see if he could buy himself off, but having no money to trade with, he was unable to interest anyone else.

He went to see Demooth about it. The captain said he would get Mary for his housekeeper, so that at least she should be taken care of. John marched at sunrise.

In May, having planted his corn and squash and pumpkins, Gil finished the barn roof. It was a great day on the farm. Mrs. McKlennar got out a bottle of Madeira, the last she had, and they drank it together.

Then in June the news came that the army was mustering at Canajoharie. They would have been slow to believe it had not Mary Weaver had a letter from John. She brought it up to McKlennar's to have it read, and Mrs. McKlennar read it aloud to them all. John wrote badly, but his letter was confirmation of the report.

> Dear wife Mary I am now at CONJHARY I am in Col Willets regiment Cap bleeckers comp. Hav a new blew cote am well Nothing remarkabel has happened we have 1500 men, & Pars rifle comp, They say we will merch for Springfeld nex Satday the 19 i think I think of you Mary & wonder if you have found out you are to have a baby yet I send my love with this and also beg you will give love to ma and Cobus
>
> > Your husband, recpectfully,
> >
> > JOHN WEAVER

There was a silence in the kitchen after Mrs. McKlennar finished. They could hear outside a man far away whetting his scythe, and across the river Casler shouting to his team as he brought in logs for his cabin. Casler was rebuilding.

"It's a good, manly letter, Mary," said Mrs. McKlennar.

"Yes," the girl gave a sort of gasp. She reached out for the letter and folded it over and over and stuck it inside her dress. She seemed to be ready to cry. Gil went outdoors. It was no place for a man. He drove down to the hayfield with the mare and cart.

When the bumping and creaking had died away, Mary looked up at Mrs. McKlennar and blushed painfully.

"Colonel Bellinger said he had to send an express down to-morrow and I could send a letter, but I can't write."

"Would you like me to write for you?"

"Yes. Please. John's mother can't write either, and I couldn't ask anyone else."

Mrs. McKlennar snorted softly as she fetched her desk and ink. She sat down again opposite Mary with the desk on her knees, and dipped the quill.

"Now what would you like to tell him? You just say it and I'll write it down."

"Dear husband John—" and then, appalled, she listened to the scratching of the quill and saw Mrs. McKlennar's capable wrist arching along the paper, and she burst into a flood of tears.

"Now, now, child. You mustn't act like that. Remember that he's probably homesick and wants this letter more than anything in the world."

"I can't do it. I can't. I don't know how," wailed Mary.

"Well, what do you want to tell him? He's anxious, you know."

"Yes, he was worried about it. About me having a baby. He didn't know how we could buy flannel for it. His mother doesn't think I could ever be a good breast feeder and we've got no cow."

"Well, dear, are you going to have a baby?"

Mary shook her head. Her face crimsoned, and suddenly she covered it with her hands.

"Then tell him." Mrs. McKlennar drew herself up, without being aware of it, and looked formidable. "Just imagine I'm John and say it to me."

With an effort Mary governed herself. "I'll try."

And Mrs. McKlennar wrote:—

DEAR HUSBAND JOHN,

I am well and I hope you are really well. I am not going to have the baby now but will surely some day. I am sure I could feed a baby even though your mother thinks not. She is well and so is Cobus. I am keeping house for Capt Demooth and he is nice to me but it is not nice to cook for him like cooking for you. I think of you every night and do you think of me? It is my hope to see you home safe soon. I pray for you, and that is my prayer.

Your loving wife . . .

"Would you say 'Mary Weaver,' or just 'Mary'?"

Her breast was rising and falling as if she had run.

"I would say just 'Mary,' I think, myself, though the other is dignified."

"I think John would like 'Mary Weaver' best."

Mrs. McKlennar wrote "Mary Weaver."

They did not hear from John again, except through general news of the movement of the army. On the twenty-third the word came by an express to Colonel Van Schaick at Fort Stanwix that the army was not to march west through the Mohawk Valley, as many people hoped, but to join Major General Sullivan's huge corps at Tioga. Clinton had already started his first troops south from Canajoharie and was hauling bateaux overland to the head of Otsego Lake.

The same express coming east again the following day reported to Colonel Bellinger that Oneida Indians had brought news to Fort Stanwix that John Butler was taking an army up the Genesee, planning to cross above the Indian Lakes and mobilize the Indians at Tioga. That John Butler not only knew of the

American rendezvous but knew the names of all regiments and the numbers of men contained in them. As proof, the Indian named what he could remember, and his figures were correct. That was how Peter Bellinger was first informed of the numbers and personnel of the southern army, and that was how the people of German Flats first heard of it—information supplied by their own spies from observations of the British.

Five thousand men would move against the Iroquois, with cannon and Morgan's rifle regiment, and four states supplying the infantry. It was an impressive thing to think of. To people like Demooth, and Gil Martin, and Bellinger, came the first realization that there was a power in their own country, the country that had been made theirs. A power beyond the unlimited muddleheadedness of Yankee politicians.

They felt that now they would be safe from the Indians as long as that army was campaigning in the wilderness. The whole settlement breathed easier. The women went out on the haying parties, and the last of the hay was brought in with a rush. Gil Martin abandoned his first plan of stacking his hay in small lots hidden in the near-by woodland and stacked it all against the barn. The sight of the new barn, and the high mound of hay which Lana had thatched, working in the cool of the late afternoon, was an emblem of their new security.

Towards the middle of July, Joe Boleo and Adam Helmer returned from a scout to the southeast and reported having been all the way to Otsego Lake to see the army.

"We got down beyond Butternuts and there was a lot of Indian signs heading east, and we figured they was watching the army, so we thought we might as well get a look at it ourselves."

Adam bubbled over with descriptions of the tents, the boats. "They've dammed up the entire lake," he said. "And when they start they'll bust the dam and have four foot of water to float their boats downriver." They had seen the execution of two Tory spies and listened to a sermon by the Reverend Mr. Kirkland and had a drink with Marinus Willett, who wanted them to serve with him as scouts. "Joe figured the rum wouldn't hold out as far as Chinisee," Adam explained, "so we didn't go."

"I wanted to see what fifteen hundred men looked like, all together," Joe said. "I didn't want to make it bigger than it was, though. Somebody would have had to go without his rations."

Bellinger was thankful that they hadn't gone. He gave them each a present of liquor and a little cash, and after Adam had spent one more fruitless day with Betsey Small, he and Joe went into the woods again.

Then people heard that the army had set off. They heard it in the prayer of Reverend Rozencrantz, who gave credit to Rimer Van Sickler, who had returned from Otsego. He was one of the levies taken at the same time as John Weaver. He turned up in church and listened to himself being quoted by the domine, and explained to his friends that he had come back to finish his barn. He figured that the army under Clinton could do just about as well with one less man, but that he himself couldn't get along without a barn next winter. And all it needed was the roofing of one bent, if a log barn could be said to have a bent. It would take him only three days. He said the army had made him lame in the left foot. On Monday he got cheerfully to work. On Tuesday he had finished the roof. He told Bellinger that even if he was a deserter and got taken for it, it was worth more than the regular thirty-dollar fine to roof his barn.

On the night of the twenty-fourth, Lana was restless. She was suffering continually from pains in her legs, and therefore she heard the gallop along the road in time to wake Gil. They sat up side by side in the dark, hearing the furious thudding swell towards them through the night, pass, and die rapidly away.

They got up and went out onto the porch, searching the night instinctively for fires. Mrs. McKlennar woke and came out to join them with an old red coat drawn over her nightdress. They held their breath to listen, but heard nothing except the whimper of the whippoorwills in the wheatfield.

For a while they thought it must have been an ordinary express, though expresses seldom went by at night. But before they had decided to get back to bed, the sound of galloping again was born in the west and swept towards them.

As the horse came round the bend in the road, the rider began shouting, "McKlennar's! McKlennar's!"

"Hello!" shouted Gil.

"That you, Mr. Martin?"

"Yes, who's that?"

They could see him now, the hoofbeats stilling as the horse pulled up, a shadow on the vague pale ribbon of the road.

"Fred Kast. Bellinger says for you to come to the fort. The Onondagas are out! They killed some soldiers up to Stanwix this afternoon."

Lana gave a choked cry, but Mrs. McKlennar said, "Get the baby. I'll close and bolt the shutters."

The horse was stamping. "I've got to get to Eldridge's," yelled Kast. He was off again.

As he hitched the mare to the cart, Gil had a dull feeling that nothing was any use. The destructives would be there. They would burn his new barn. He couldn't turn the cow out either, because of the calf. Better to leave them in the barn than chance a bear's getting the calf. He set down a pail of water for the cow and dragged in some forkfuls of hay.

It was just like the start for Fort Herkimer almost a year ago, except that this time they would go all the way in a cart. Thank God the wheat wasn't yet quite ripe enough to burn!

They were two-thirds of the way to the fort when Kast over-took them. Eldridge's was warned. "They've only got powder for about twelve rounds," he said. "Jake Small ain't been able to get any anywhere."

At Dayton the squad of regular soldiers with whom Van Schaick had garrisoned the fort assigned them to a space along the barrack wall and told them to keep out of the way. The night continued clear, warm, and uneventful, except for an outraged screech owl, and the myriad mosquitoes.

But late the next afternoon they were informed that reën-forcements would be with them in twenty-four hours. The army had not yet left Otsego. About three hundred men were march-ing under Gansevoort.

Everyone breathed easier, except Van Sickler.

Towards sunset of the following day the drums were heard approaching, and within the hour the little army was encamped outside the fort. Gansevoort rode in with his pink Dutch face delighted at having made the swiftest march the valley had ever seen—two days from the foot of Otsego Lake to German Flats. He promised to wait until the Rangers came in, and in the mean-time he arrested and court-martialed Van Sickler for desertion.

But Gansevoort was so pleased with himself that he let Van Sickler off with a fine of thirty-one dollars, and, since the man could not possibly pay it, announced that he would have to be on fatigue for the rest of the campaign.

Van Sickler himself was dubious about it all. At first he fig-ured he had lost sixty-one dollars; but later he decided that he had got his barn roofed for a dollar, and that was a bargain.

As soon as the information was brought in that the Ononda-gas had passed to the south of Springfield, Gansevoort departed. His troops moved fast, their three light wagons keeping close up, their drums banging a quickstep.

The people watched them go and, long after they had dis-appeared, listened for the last faint mutter of the drums. That sound, hauntingly faint, was the last sound of war in the valley until the same detachment appeared, surprisingly, from the west in September.

In the meantime, it seemed as if the great army had disappeared from the face of the earth. They heard no news at all of it, but what it might be doing, whether it had met the army under John Butler,—Rangers, Greens, British, Tories, Senecas, and Mohawks,—whether it would reach Niagara, or even the Seneca towns, was the one thing men talked about in the settlement.

Gil thought little of it. During the last week in August Lana's labor started, and they lived for three days with Dr. Petry in the house. Mrs. McKlennar, and Daisy, and Betsey Small, who had come down to help from Eldridge's, were all worn-out and haggard.

To Gil it seemed as if the thing would never finish. Now and then, even in the wheatfield, he thought he heard her crying. Dr. Petry seemed helpless. He blamed it on the lack of food, on the drain that nursing the first baby had put on her. "Last winter took about everything out of her. And this is a big baby. I don't see how she got to have such a big one."

"Can't you help her some way?" demanded Mrs. McKlennar.

"How can I help her? It's part of a woman's job—that's all. We can't do anything but wait."

"But it's unnatural!" Mrs. McKlennar's voice grew harsh. "It's terrible."

Betsey Small remembered her own painful childbed, but that had been full of violence, and quickly over. Once when Petry was alone with her, he said, "Do you still want another one?" He tilted his head towards the room in which Lana lay.

Though Betsey's eyes were shadowed, her mouth shaped itself impudently. "It's part of a woman's job—that's all. I wonder whether a man or a woman said that first."

"Don't talk to me like that," he growled. "I hear tales about you and the fool Adam Helmer."

"Well, you needn't believe them! I'm fond of Jakey." Her eyes brightened. "But I would like some more, if you want to know. Plenty of them. Poor Jake." She turned her eyes away.

The doctor grunted.

"Will she die?" asked Betsey.

"I don't think so. But you might."

"Not with you looking after me, Bill."

"Oh hell," he said.

Mrs. McKlennar was beckoning him to the door.

The baby was born at noon on the fourth day, a huge and handsome boy. It looked so big to Gil that Lana's body seemed to him completely caved in after the birth. She did not speak to him, but lay inert, eyes closed.

"She's all right," said Dr. Petry. "You needn't whisper. She wouldn't hear the trump right now. She won't be good for much for quite a spell, though. No, don't thank me. I didn't do anything. I just sat here to earn some money."

He growled, and wearily mounted his old horse, and rode away.

"Bill's aging lately," Mrs. McKlennar said.

Betsey Small was dandling the child and calling it her lusty man.

"I'm just as glad Adam's not around," thought Mrs. McKlennar, watching her.

7

The Hard Winter

Throughout the summer and fall their feeling of security was strengthened. After each scout Joe and Adam reported the same emptiness of the woods. Maybe a lone Indian: if they followed his tracks up, they found he was an Oneida or Tuscarora going fishing. Or sometimes they saw the tracks of several Indians; but these parties always included squaws. They weren't war parties. They were Indians looking for the blueberries. "They say it's going to be a hard winter. They're doing a lot of berrying."

It got so that the two men hated to go out. Especially Joe; for Adam generally dropped off a scout and came back to spend a while with Betsey Small, and, when he got sick of getting nothing from that red-haired woman, to make a night excursion somewhere with Polly Bowers. But with the latter he went out just enough to keep his own inside track with her. Betsey Small had infatuated him. It got so that he would pick her a bunch of flowers, maybe, besides bringing her in a good fish or two, or some venison, or a couple of prime partridge. Once he asked her whether she would think any more of him if he brought her a couple of scalps.

"Senecas?" she asked.

"Sure," he said. "Senecas, or a couple of them Tories. If you ever want anybody's scalp, you let me know."

She smiled, veiling her eyes and looking insolent and badgering, studying all his magnificent body as he sprawled on the bench with his back against the table and his chest bare to the fire.

"You like me an awful lot, don't you, Adam?"

He tossed his yellow hair back and grinned.

"Don't you ever get tired waiting around here?"

He kept on grinning.

"If it wasn't for Jake, I'd have had you a long while ago. But I like Jake."

He looked puzzled, as she repeated, "Yes, if it wasn't for Jake."

Jake Small came in. He was getting bald and looked fatter.

"Hello, Adam," he said. "You back for a while?"

"Yes, I'm back. I just stopped by on my way home. How are you, Jake?"

"Fine, boy, fine."

He reached for an apple off the shelf.

"Have one, Adam?"

"No, thanks," said Adam.

"Well, I will," Jake said, biting into it. "I've always had the awfulest hankering for apples, Adam."

He put his arm round Betsey when she came up to kiss him. It was the damnedest thing Adam ever had to look at—the happy way she looked when she kissed him back. He got himself lazily onto his feet and picked up his rifle and went out of the house.

Though Lana was getting about again, she had not much strength. She worked because there was a great deal to be done. Gil was threshing in between days of picking the ripened corn, and he needed help in sifting the chaff. He wanted to get his oats all threshed and safely stored before the fall was over. The steady thump of the flail on the barn boards was like the drumming of a partridge, hour after hour.

The air was cold and very clear, as if frost were in the offing. Lana sniffed it in the yard and looked up the valley. The sky to the west had a greenish glassy tinge. One could almost think that the sky was reflecting the shine from the river. The tips of balsams seemed more sharply pointed, needlelike, and made of iron. The low sun looked like a thin coin. In its light, Lana seemed pale and full of stillness; her black hair was heavy and without lustre. As she stood beside the shed door, the evening found in her the same hushed intentness it found in the darkening woods. Only the front of her short gown moved with her light breathing, showing her full and heavy breasts.

Joe Boleo, stepping quietly in the shed for an extra log of wood, watched her for a moment. He thought she had not heard him, any more than she seemed to have heard the thudding of Gil's flail. But she said suddenly, "Joe, what's that bird?"

"Which bird?"

"There on the bottom branch of the maple. I never saw one like it."

She seemed to have a sixth sense for spotting anything alive. The bird had neither moved nor made a sound.

He said, "That's a Canada Jack. It's early to see one of them—and so close to a house, too. Most generally it means a hard winter."

They both stayed still, and the bird on its limb was still, staring back at them. Then the calf bawled flatly in the barn, and they heard the blatant answer of the cow homing through the woods.

In the kitchen, Daisy rattled her pans.

At sunset the two companies of soldiers swung down the road from Fort Stanwix. They were lean and tired. Their ragged uniforms gave them at first sight a kind of ghostliness. Their long strides brought them swiftly and with an odd effect of silence, for half of them wore moccasins, to replace the shoes they had used up. And the drums of the two drummers were headless.

John Weaver returned with them. He did not look at all like the boy who had started out. He was like a stranger to Mary. She felt even younger than on her bridal night; and when they went to bed in the Herter house, she was shy and half frightened. He seemed so much stronger—even in his happiness with her she was aware that he had been with men and become a man. Though she had never thought of him otherwise, she knew that the John she had married was a boy; and proud as she was of him, now, his touch conveyed to her a strange sense of warning that she would never be as close to him again in all their lives.

Gansevoort had given him his discharge, and paid him in a wheat warrant, so that he felt quite comfortable about feeding his mother and Cobus during the winter. For themselves, he and Mary would stay on with Demooth.

He was glad to get home. The next morning, when the conch horns sent their dim invading wail over the valley, they lay under the blankets close together and heard the cannon fired from the fort as a salute to the departing soldiers. The rising sun, entering the low window, touched the shoulders of his campaign coat, stained, frayed, and faded. . . .

"John, was it awful out there?"

"It was the finest farming country I ever saw. But we got so we were sick of it. Every time we saw a cornfield we were sick. They made us cut it down—all of it. We cut down the apple trees. They had peaches, even. We cut them down. We did at first; but there was so many we just girdled the last orchards. We burned every house. Some of them had nice houses, framed ones, with glass windows. Nicer than this house, Mary."

"It must have been hard work."

"I don't know how much we burned. Captain Bleecker figured it out that the army had destroyed one hundred and sixty thousand bushel of corn. The Indians all went west to Niagara."

"Was there any battles?"

"Only one. It was short. There was five thousand of us and only fifteen hundred of them, more than half Indians. Afterwards they cornered a scouting party. Twenty men. They caught two of them and burned them in Little Beard's town. Chinisee Castle."

He stopped suddenly.

"Poor John," she whispered.

"It was mostly just walking," he said. "Walking every day and sometimes at night. Or burning. Or cutting corn with your bayonet. We got short of food and had to eat our horses. We wished we hadn't burned everything, coming home."

"The Indians will never come again," she said.

"No. They've gone to Niagara. I don't know."

"Were the burned men anyone we knew?"

"No, a Lieutenant Boyd. And a sergeant. His name was Parker. I didn't know either of them. I don't want to talk about them. I been dreaming of the way they looked. It makes me afraid sometimes. I don't want to go to war again, Mary."

She tried to hush him.

"You won't need to."

"I never was scared of the Indians before. But they did things to those men."

"Don't talk." She lifted up her lips. But he didn't kiss her. He lay close beside her, with his face hidden in the hollow of her shoulder. He didn't move.

Gil and Joe Boleo and Adam made a trip up to Fort Dayton to talk to Rimer Van Sickler. The squat, overmuscled Dutchman sat in his cabin among his fourteen children, with his second wife cooking him an apple pie. Her thin face, prematurely aged from bearing children and too much heavy work, was exalted with the social eminence her returned hero had brought the family. Why, only yesterday, Colonel Bellinger and Captain Demooth had spent the whole afternoon listening to her Rimer tell about his western expedition. Here in her own cabin. She had had to send the children over to Mrs. Wormwood's out of politeness, seeing they were gentry, but she herself had stayed. And now here was Mr. Martin and Joe Boleo and that worthless Helmer, who had thought he was a hero himself when he outran the Indians.

Rimer yelled a "Come in" to the men. He was obviously tickled to have them come to see him. Timber beasts.

"Get out some rum for my vriendts," he yelled. "You voman: Py Godt, I think I haf to put my belt across you und learn you again who is boss, hey!" He turned to the three. "I had to do it pefore, I can do it again, *ja!*" He had her almost in tears. The light went out of her face as in obedience she fetched the jug and set it down before him.

He was sitting in front of the fire on a deerskin, whittling calluses on the balls of his feet. "Efry time I cut a piece off I say to mineself, 'Rimer, you old timber beast, dot is t'ree miles from Kandesago to Kanandaque.'"

Joe said dryly, "I always figured that fifteen miles, myself."

"Ach, *ja.* You peen out dere. I haf forget it. You're right, Joe. But, py Godt, dot big hunk over there, dot is twenty-seven und a half we marched Candaya to Appletown. In te afternoon. Py Godt! Efry shtep I feel dot punion grow, like a horn. Dot vas de day mine boots broke through, too."

"Did you kill many Indians, Pa?"

"Don't talk. No, de Indians vas alvays de trees behind, or de hill behind, or de shwamp across. Only once we haf a battle, dunder, shmoke de cannons, und de Indians run right off. Old Pa Rimer couldn't run so fast as Indians. *Ja.*"

They had to listen to the full details of the campaign as witnessed, memorized, and amplified by the aggrandized imagination of Van Sickler; but finally he came to Boyd's capture, telling how the army found the ambush and marched the next day to the Genesee, forded it, and entered the great town.

How, in the open space before the council house they saw the two stakes. Even Van Sickler forgot himself as he described it. Those Senecas, what they could think of! The two corpses half consumed from the waist down before the fires burned out, eviscerated; the nails removed from the toes and fingers, the fingers disjointed or cut off at various lengths. "Ve found two thumbs, so ve knew de nails vas pulled. Dere vas clam shells dey had cut de fingers off mit." The eyes had been pushed out and the nostrils slit, the cheeks pierced, the lips skinned off, the tongues pulled out, and all over the chest slabs of hide removed.

The children listened with popping eyes and a dull apathetic horror came over the woman's face as she stared at her husband, though whether at the torture or at the man, describing each detail with bestial accuracy, she hardly knew herself. "Dey cut de heads off. But de last thing vas de heart." His small eyes glittered as he told it. "Cut out between de ribs, und stuck de mouth into. Only dere vasn't any lips, joost de teeth. *Ja!* It vas a sunny day."

The winter came early, and it turned piercing cold. By the first of October the hills were white in the north, and the leaves fell with the snow. The snow never went down. By November, before the blizzard, it was more than a foot deep on the ground. But after the sixth day of the snowstorm it was four feet deep. It mounted up against the sides of house and cabin and barn until the paths to the door were like inclined chutes, holes in the earth. No one had ever felt such cold or known such snow.

Few people went visiting. Lana, who had thought of trying to see her parents during the slack season in December, gave up the notion. Provisions coming up to Stanwix took two days even on the river ice. More than once horses broke down and froze where they had fallen.

At McKlennar's, Gil was thankful that he had stacked his hay beside the barn. He could never have found it in the woods, once the big snow came.

All day he and Lana and Mrs. McKlennar and the babies hugged the fireside. The negress suffered a strange change in her complexion. It was as if her skin had turned gray with dark brown blotches underneath. She could hardly walk for her chilblains. Joe Boleo never left the place. The idea of raiding parties coming in that cold was simply preposterous. But he took great satisfaction in his idleness. "I can't get them Senecas out of my mind," he said. "They ain't got any food. I bet they're dying every which way." It was a comforting thought to them all.

The only thing that troubled him was having to help Gil get wood. They cut great logs and skidded them in the front door and set the butt ends in the fire. Every hour or so they would pry the log forward into the coals. They kept it going all night, taking turns at watching.

Even so it was so cold in the kitchen that Lana's fingers were too numb to spin, except occasionally when the sun shone at noon. They became silent for long periods. And Mrs. McKlennar seemed to age during the winter, and sat more and more, close to the fire. Finally she succumbed to Lana's suggestion of having her bed moved into the kitchen.

Only Adam went about at all, visiting occasionally at Eldridge's or paying a dutiful visit to Dayton. The cold did not affect him as it did the others. He did all the hunting alone. But hunting was poor, and the deer, when he got one, were terribly thin. The meat was tasteless as old leather.

The wind seemed never to stop blowing. It had a high note on the crust. At night, when it came from the north, they could hear the howling and threshing of the pines on the high ridges half a mile away. But on the few quiet nights, the cracking of frosted trees in the icy darkness was worse to listen to.

In the barn Gil had built a kind of wall around the cow and heifer and mare, banking it every day with the manure that was dropped overnight, but that was always frozen. The three animals kept close together. Their coats were shaggy as sheep's wool. To milk the cow was an ordeal; his bare hands received no warmth from the teats; and the milk froze before he could get it to the house.

But the knowledge of their security was one comforting thing; and when the weather finally broke towards the end of February, they waited uneasily for a week, hoping for more snow. It came at last, heavy, without wind, a deep, protecting blanket between them and Niagara.

Though it came in time to save them, it did not come in time to save the Oneida Indians. On the last day of February, the entire fighting strength of the Onondaga nation, with a few white men and a party of Cayugas and Senecas, fell upon Oneida Castle. In German Flats they never learned the rights of it; all they knew was that a mass of half-frozen Indians,—men, women, and children,—and a few starved dogs, appeared at Fort Dayton and asked for food and shelter. They crowded the fort for two days, making dangerous inroads on the supplies, before Bellinger was able to get them started for Schenectady. The town had been utterly destroyed, but the raiders, they said, had gone back to Canada.

When Adam went down to see them, he found old Blue Back, his fat cheeks mottled with the cold, squatting in his blankets and watching his wife make a sort of hot mash of whole oats. The two larger children huddled against him, and the baby on the squaw's back was wrinkled like a nut, with two enormous eyes. The old Indian accepted tobacco wordlessly.

"They'll take care of you all in Schenectady," Adam said in an attempt to cheer him up.

"Sure. Fine." But the old man obviously did not think so. He smoked, looking past Adam along the soiled snow of the parade. "You watch'm woods close," he said. "They come some more. They mad."

"I wish you was going to be around, Blue Back. It'd be handy having you scouting with us."

"Maybe." He went on puffing. Then he said, "You going back to Martin?"

"Yes."

Blue Back reached a dirty hand inside his shirt, and felt of something.

"You fetch'm this. No luck," he was going to say; but as he touched the peacock's feather it occurred to him that in a white man's town it might be lucky after all.

His eyes grew blank. He shook his head.

"You watch'm woods," he muttered dully.

Adam told Bellinger what Blue Back had said that afternoon, and Bellinger wrote letters to the governor, and to General Clinton, and to Schuyler. Three weeks passed before he got a reply. All three sounded upset and indignant. The army last fall had been organized to wipe out the Indian towns. It had done so. The Indians were bound to be crippled for years to come. The menace had been removed at a vast expense; no other single campaign of the war could compare to it in cost. Over a million of dollars had been expended, purely for the benefit of the frontier. There was some mention of common gratitude. And let him be reminded that such continual fears and apprehensions and baseless alarms would have deleterious effects upon the inhabitants. It was felt in Albany that the time had come for the frontier settlements to stand on their own defense.

In German Flats, the settlers began to look for spring.

VIII

I

Jacob Casler's Tax Problem

Gil was getting some hay into the barn. There wasn't much left. He had been feeding the three animals one good forkful between them. They showed it. The mare was gaunt, and, as Joe said, the hip bones of the cow and heifer stood out sharp enough to hang the milk pails on them.

He heard a man's boots squash through the wet snow in the yard, and then the door opened to let Casler come in. "You in there, Martin?"

"Yes. I'm just feeding the stock. Walk in."

Casler closed the door behind him and walked up to Gil. The light in the barn was a dim, dusty twilight gray, in which the animals looked even more meagre than they were.

"How are you all?" asked Gil.

"We're in pretty good health. How're you, Martin?"

"All right." Gil leaned on his fork and looked at his neighbor. Casler was a good neighbor to have, even though Gil did not see a great deal of him. He was a thin, earnest-looking man, with a slow way of speech, and a hard worker. He had rebuilt on the site of his old house across the river—a tiny cabin, in which he had wintered his wife, his two young daughters, and his three-year-old son.

"It's getting bad footing," he remarked, picking up a straw to chew. "It looks to me as if the snow was going pretty quick now."

"I've been thinking so myself."

They considered that fact in silence for a few minutes, before Casler asked, "You folks going back to the fort soon?"

"I hadn't planned. Mrs. McKlennar is against it till we have to."

Casler nodded slowly.

"She's a stout-hearted woman, ain't she?"

"Yes. I hate to move her, too. She's been poorly, off and on."

"Yes. I hate to move, myself. I was figuring on getting pretty near all my ground working again this season. Now I don't know."

Gil had the feeling that Casler had only got round to part of what was in his mind.

"Listen," he said, "if anything happens, why don't you folks plan to come over to this place? We could hold that house against quite a lot of them. It's as good as Klock's fort."

"That's right," said Casler. "How about her? Would she mind?"

"Mrs. McKlennar, you mean? No."

"I don't allow that anything's going to happen somehow. I ain't really bothering about that, Martin. How about her? Has she got one of these tax papers?"

"Tax papers?" repeated Gil. "I hadn't heard of any tax papers."

"Then they ain't got down this side of the river yet. They've been around Herkimer and they got down to my place this noon. They served them on me. It's that tax law they passed in Albany. It's got to collect eighty thousand dollars out of Tryon County.

They said what German Flats had to pay, but I forgot. I know what I got to pay," he finished grimly.

"How much do you?"

"A hundred and seventy-seven dollars and forty-eight cents!" Casler's mouth closed suddenly and he stared at Gil.

"Did you say a hundred and seventy-seven dollars, Casler?"

"And forty-eight cents. What in God's name is that forty-eight cents for?"

"But you can't pay that!"

"You don't need to tell me, Martin. I ain't got the forty-eight cents, even."

"They can't make you pay it."

"The paper says if I don't pay it in cash and half down in two months' time, it will be collected from me. They'll take my stock—I ain't got only the cow and she's dry now. And they'll forfeit my land for taxes."

Gil said again, "They can't do that, Casler!"

Casler nodded slowly.

"The man told me it's on account of all the cost of that army last year. He said we got the benefits of it, but he said our rates wasn't as high as other parts of the state. But I can't pay it. I want to do what's right, but I can't pay that." His voice began to rise. "I'll do my share; I ain't never missed muster; but if they take my land I can't feed my folks. I thought the reason them Boston people started this war was so we wouldn't have to pay taxes."

Gil tried to comfort him. He tried to show that nobody else could pay more than a small share of such a tax in German Flats. Most of them couldn't pay a cent, any more than Casler could. Even Congress couldn't wipe out a whole community. There was something wrong about it.

"There ain't nothing wrong in what I told you, Martin. It's all wrote out. I'll bet you'll get one yourself for the land you had in Deerfield. You wait. There ain't any money in my house. I got to buy some seed potatoes, as it is, this spring. I got twenty-five cents."

"I'll let you have some seed potatoes and welcome, too. I got more'n enough, Casler. Did yours get froze?"

Casler explained that he hadn't had time to dig himself a cellar last fall. They had sacked the seed potatoes against the chimney, but they had frozen even there.

As Casler turned to the barn door, Gil added, "You remember what I said about coming over here."

"Thanks," said Casler. "That's kind. But I ain't really figuring the Indians will come this spring."

Gil stood in the door and watched him trudge down through the wet snow to the river. The tracks he had made coming showed on the river and up the far bank and across the flats. In the damp air they collected violet shadows for every footprint, over the fields, all the way to the tiny cabin from whose stick chimney a thread of smoke trailed uncertainly.

Gil had Casler and his tax on his mind all the rest of the day. Before supper he told Mrs. McKlennar about it. Adam was out, probably hunting up a girl of his,—the spring unease had hit him a month ahead of time,—but Joe Boleo was there, squatting down in the corner and watching Lana suckle the baby. At first he had been a good deal embarrassed, when the cold forced Lana into the kitchen to feed her child; and he had offered to leave. But Mrs. McKlennar said that was ridiculous, Joe must have played the same game himself, once.

The process, as Lana and the young boy carried it out, took hold of Joe's imagination; and he made up all sorts of reasons why he ought to get back to the house about feeding time. There was something in the full white springiness of the breast and the way the child mishandled it that softened Joe's ideas, so that he seemed to get drowsy with the baby; and he would sit there on the floor, nodding his bare cranium and trying to figure what it must have been like when he used to be doing a similar business.

Sitting on the settle, with her feet wrapped in an old blanket, Mrs. McKlennar held Gilly on her lap. Somebody had to hold Gilly to keep him from getting one of his jealous fits of screaming. He hated cow's milk so, and, though he was only two years old, Mrs. McKlennar maintained that he had all the passions of a grown-up man.

The negress stumped from fire to table, preparing the adult food—the last of the hominy, part of a dark loaf, and some salt pork. Now and then, if she moved unexpectedly, she would give a kind of singsong moan that was an echo of her winter's chilblains.

The sound of Gil stamping his feet in the shed was the signal for all of them to hurry. Lana looked down at her breast and saw the baby's mouth languorous round the nipple and pushed it away.

"He's had plenty," said Mrs. McKlennar. "He's greedy as all get out. He'd wear you to the bone if you let him."

Gil watched from the doorway, his dark face sharp and quiet, while Lana took the baby away to its cradle. Gilly slid down from the widow's lap and started crawling after his mother and had to be fetched back by Daisy, who dandled him and whispered "Honey boy" in his ear. Joe looked up sheepishly and said, "Evening, Gil. What's the news?"

"I was talking to Casler."

Briefly he told them about Casler's tax papers. He turned to Mrs. McKlennar. "If they tax Casler that much they'll try to get three hundred dollars for this place."

Mrs. McKlennar let out a snort that sounded like old times.

"I wouldn't pay it, Gil. I can't, for one thing. And for another, I'll be damned if I do."

Joe let out a shrill "Hurraw!" causing the widow to look down her nose at him.

"What do you mean by that?"

Joe grinned like an old half-rabid wolf.

"I was thinking it would be fun to be around here if they tried to put you off this place."

Mrs. McKlennar snorted again.

"I don't know what I'd do if they did that. I've used up almost all the money Barney left to me. I used to think it was enough to put me in my coffin, till Congress started printing this new-fashioned currency."

Joe said quickly, "I guess you won't have to move."

"I suppose they'd send soldiers. I couldn't do anything if they did that."

"That's why I said it would be fun to be around. I was thinking of me and Adam. I guess it would be quite a lot of fun."

"You're a fool, Joe Boleo," and her long face softened. "Just a gawking lazy fool."

"Yes, ma'am." Joe grinned.

She hitched her shawl up on her shoulders and got up to move to the table. It was a little pathetic to see her walk, when one remembered her former vigor, but there was plenty of snap left in her eyes.

She sat down in front of her bowl of samp and bent her head. "For all we are about to receive, O Lord, make us thankful, in Christ's name." She giggled. "You know, Joe, I think it might be quite a party, you and Adam and a squad of Continentals."

"Amen," said Joe, who enjoyed the formalities. "It sure would."

"I feel sorry for that poor man, though. He's probably just miserable."

Joe pulled his spoon out of his mouth.

"Casler always was an honest kind of a fool," he observed. He dipped his spoon, heaped it, and blew on it daintily, while Gilly watched him with disturbed eyes.

In the course of the ensuing week, a man served Mrs. McKlennar with her tax assessment. The paper was a thoroughly impressive document. It listed one stone house; one log house, floored, in excellent repair; one springhouse; one log barn; three cows; two horses; forty acres tillable land, prime soil; sixty acres wood land; one stand of King's spar spruce, twenty acres. Mrs. McKlennar read it in front of the man, whom she kept standing before her in a state of extreme embarrassment. "Melchior Foltz," she said. "Have you really got the nerve to come down here and serve this paper on me? Asking me to pay you four hundred dollars tax?"

"Yes, ma'am," Foltz said dubiously.

"Then," said Mrs. McKlennar, "I think you are a bigger fool than Absalom's ass. Tell me, where's my barn? Where's my log house in good repair? Eh?"

"That ain't any business of mine," mumbled Foltz. "I'm just hired to serve the papers. I ain't collecting it now."

"You better not," said Mrs. McKlennar, "or you'll get kicked where Absalom's ass ought to have been." A faint color touched her leathery cheek. She peered hard at Foltz and then, in the silence, snorted.

"Yes, ma'am. I guess I'd better leave now. I got to go to Eldridge's."

He was wiping his forehead as he came out.

"That woman just about had me worried," he confessed to Gil. "I ain't doing this because I want to. I get off some of my taxes for doing it."

"Oh, you do?"

"Well, I got to do something, ain't I?"

"There's one thing you better hadn't. That's come around

here again. If Adam Helmer was here, he'd probably take a branch of thorn apple at you."

"I don't want no trouble with Adam Helmer. I ain't collecting the bachelor tax."

"Is there a tax on orphans and lost pigs?" inquired Joe Boleo.

Foltz took a look at Joe and started down the yard to his horse. The two men watched him ride slowly down to the Kingsroad. They went into the house.

"You know what I bet they're doing," said Mrs. McKlennar. "I bet they got hold of the old King's tax list." She threw the paper into the fire.

"For God's sake!" said Joe, sincerely.

Casler came over the river one morning and heard that Mrs. McKlennar had thrown her tax paper into the fire. It heartened him a little; but then he shook his head. "She's gentry," he said. "She knows how to hire law." Gil couldn't think of any way of reassuring him. He tried to talk to him about sugaring. But Casler was not interested beyond admitting that the sap was on the rise and that he planned to sugar next week.

"You'd better sugar over in our bush," said Gil.

"It's too far," said Casler.

He went away a little before noon. He walked like a defeated and embittered man.

That afternoon the weather turned warm and clear. The snow seemed to be falling in on itself. The boles of the river willows stood out thick and dark against it, and their upper twigs gleamed in the sun like brassy spears. The warmth and the sunlight and the lack of wind made Joe so lazy that he refused to try to get a trout through the ice.

Instead, he was plaiting cords of elm bark with which Gil patched the mare's harness. Behind them the house sounded as drowsy as they themselves felt. One of the babies was making a whining to itself, and Lana and Daisy were washing.

"Right now," Joe remarked, passing over a completed cord of bark, "I bet that Adam he's just laying on his back in Betsey Small's kitchen doing nothing at all. That's a shot, Gil!"

Gil looked up.

"Did you make out where?"

"I wasn't paying attention."

Neither of them moved. "I think it was across the river," said Joe. He carefully laid down the elm bark; Gil held the harness on his knees. The valley was hushed; the ice on the river beyond the willows looked sodden and rotten, near to breaking. The only thing they saw was the smoke on the hillside beyond Fort Herkimer, where a party, with most of the garrison to guard them, were sugaring.

Slowly their eyes came down the valley and turned eastward. Nothing there to see but the roof of Casler's new cabin. The walls of the building were mostly hidden by a grove of trees and a growth of brush; but one corner of it showed up in the sunlight. A path went round that corner through the snow to the well.

Now, along that path, they saw someone moving. It was Casler's oldest girl. They could tell who she was because of her two tow-colored braids. She was carrying a bucket, and she was running. She was floundering slightly in the soft snow, and she was not looking back, and the bucket kept slopping little glittering waves of water. Something in the child's attitude brought the two men to their feet. As they rose, they heard, very faintly, almost like a whisper, somebody shouting.

The little girl suddenly turned her head, dropped the bucket, and tucked up her elbows. Her legs looked thin and long under her short petticoat and the two braids lifted behind her back.

At the instant of her leap, another shot cracked with complete finality.

The child's body fell away from it, struck the corner of the cabin, bounced, and dropped in a huddle against the snowbank. For an instant it lay there; then slowly rolled over on its back and slid down into the path.

Powder smoke puffed out all through the bushes, rose, and merged into a thin level line, and a volley of reports succeeded it. Then, distantly, men yelled.

"Indians," said Joe. "Get inside. Close the shutters, Gil, and get the guns down. I'll stay here and see how many there are."

In the kitchen, the washing had stopped and the women rested over the tub, black arms and white, their faces turned together. The baby had stopped whining. Mrs. McKlennar rose from the settle, and, as Gil went to the blinds, reached down the guns.

"Where is it, Gil?"

"Casler's. Fetch the children in here, Lana, and keep them on the floor, near the fireplace. They ain't near us, yet. Joe's outside, watching."

In the house the firing was the faintest tapping of the air. A woodpecker would have made more noise.

Joe came in silent and quick.

"There's about twenty-five or six of them. Indians. Three whites."

"Aren't you going to help the Caslers?"

"There's too many of them. It wouldn't do any good my going to the fort, either. Put the fire out. Maybe they ain't noticed our smoke. Maybe they'll forget about this house. No, don't use water. Get some manure out of the barn, and bury it. Don't look like that, Lana. They aren't any of them over here, I'm pretty sure. By the time I went to the fort for help, them destructives will have done all the killing possible down there. The thing we want is not to be noticed by them. I'm calculating they'll hear the racket over to Eldridge's. Mrs. McKlennar."

"Yes, Joe."

"Can you load guns?"

"Yes, Joe."

"I know Lana can. You two will have to load. Ain't I seen two pistols somewheres round here?"

"My husband's. I'll fetch them. If they get close enough I can shoot them better than either of you. I used to practise." Her face colored and her lips set.

"I bet," said Joe. "Gil! You cover that fire with the manure and then bank the edges with the ashes. That way you won't get smoke. Pack it right down. How much water have we got in here?"

"There's the washtubs."

"By God, what luck! Having a raid on wash day!" He chuckled. "I'll just take another look outside and see what's doing and fetch in a couple pails of water to drink. I don't think they'll come over this way, but we're pretty well fixed if they do."

He slipped out of the front door. Gil finished banking the fire. For a minute all the people in the room were quite still. In their silence, like a faint far patting of the air, another burst of shooting sounded. Lana's face seemed to draw in on itself and her eyes grew dark and still. She sat down suddenly on the floor and caught the two children onto her lap and looked up at her husband. It came to Gil that it was all a dream, a nightmare, and pretty soon he would wake up and find the three years' dreaming was only the space between cockcrow and milking. He went out on the porch to cover Joe's return from the well.

Joe was standing in the open, a bucket in each hand. He heard Gil come out and said, without turning his head, "Take in these buckets." As Gil relieved him he picked up his rifle. But he kept watching all the time across the river. When Gil returned, Joe's speech followed the crack of a rifle.

"I know that feller. He shoots left-handed. The skinny one, see. He sticks his head out forward after he shoots and drops his left shoulder."

"Who is he, Joe?"

"Suffrenes Casselman. I've heard him swear before he quit Fairfield that he'd get his uppings back out of German Flats."

It was no dream.

The Fairfield Scotch had always bitterly resented the fact that the Palatines held all the rich river flat land.

It was easy to follow all that was taking place across the river. There were at least two dozen Indians surrounding Casler's, and though they kept under cover from the house some of them were in open view of anyone at McKlennar's. They kept firing at the window. The paper panes were already torn away by bullets. But now and then from a chink in the logs a dull yellow-red stab pricked out and the valiant roar of Casler's old musket sounded over the other guns. As soon as it had fired, the Indians crept up nearer to the house. They were quite close already. Their bodies left long winding uneven trenches in the wet snow.

Under the firing the body of the little girl retained its motionless, crumpled posture.

Suddenly a couple of Indians sprang up to the corner of the cabin with two bundles of dry brush and laid them against the logs. They leaped back at once, but one of them stumbled, and the roar of the old musket showed that Casler had managed to find one bull's-eye. They saw the Indian behind the brush hopping around and around holding onto his arm. All the Indians yelled, and three of them rushed up to the brush, carrying lighted splinters. They ducked down immediately and ran back to the cover.

Gil turned his eyes towards Eldridge Blockhouse. It seemed incredible to him that no one had yet heard the firing. Joe said, "The air's drawing straight from the south." When Gil looked back to the cabin, the brush was smoking. A small flame ran up several twigs, zigzag, and leaped out into the air. Then all the brush caught and blazed. It was like a picture of fire. The Indians whooped again; their shrill voices, that seemed hardly human to a white man's ear, were like birds' voices.

"The cabin's caught. I didn't think it would be so dry." Joe was leaning on his rifle, resting his chin on his left wrist. "I won-der will they stick it out. Or make a break for it."

The rising force of the fire tossed large loose flames up against the eaves, and suddenly they laid hold of the bark roof. The sheaths curled up, revealing the rafter poles, and the fire swept up to the rooftree and strained into space. The encircling group of Indians drew in on the cabin.

At the same instant the dull thud of the swivel in Eldridge Blockhouse struck the valley, and a heavy somnambulant cloud of black smoke hung in the window of the spy loft. A moment later the thud was repeated from Herkimer Fort; and then, almost at once, but louder, from one of the three-pounders on Fort Dayton.

The Indians in view of the two men at McKlennar's wheeled to stare towards the forts. Then they lifted their muskets and yelled.

"Herkimer can't send any men till the sugaring party gets back," said Joe. "If they send any out from Dayton, they'll come down this side."

Gil found himself shaking. He remembered how he had felt watching the Indians chase the three women at Andrustown, but this time his conviction of horror could not escape fulfillment.

The end happened abruptly. For some moments there had been no shooting from the house. Now, suddenly, he and Joe saw Casler jumping out round the corner of the house. He had his musket held in front of him and he fired as soon as he stopped. It was impossible to tell whether he had hit anyone. Things happened too fast. As soon as he had fired he ran straight at the concealed Indians, who knelt with leveled guns. They let him get just to the bushes before shooting him. Immediately they swarmed all over him. It was impossible to see him under the pile of Indians. Then the Indians drew apart and one of them gave a loud yell and raised his hand.

At the same time, in the snowy field behind the trees, Mrs. Casler appeared, running clumsily with the baby in her arms, while her younger daughter clung to the back of her petticoat. About a hundred yards behind the child five or six Indians, dark lean shapes, ran easily in the path beaten down by the woman and the child. They overtook them without haste. The first one caught the little girl by the back of the neck and raised his hatchet. The woman kept running. The Indian who was now leading leaped clear of the snow and landed hard on her back. They went down together almost buried by the snow. The Indian was like a dog worrying a sheep. He rose up on all fours and got to his feet and held up his hand. The sunlight caught his hand, reflecting on the inside of the scalp. The woman's long hair surrounded his arm.

In the sunset the militia marched down both sides of the river. The Dayton men stopped at the McKlennar house, but Joe and Gil had already crossed to join those from Herkimer.

They had seen the destructives band beyond the house and take a straight path to the hills, striking for Springfield. Joe led forty men on their beaten trail, but there was no chance of catching them with the half hour's start they had. The Indians could outrun militia any day.

Gil stayed long enough to help gather the bodies. They buried them near the house, where the earth was thawed—Mrs. Casler and the two little girls and Casler, all scalped, all with the same lost faces that scalped people had. Only the baby had not been scalped; he had no hair at all.

2

Deodesote

Like all the other Seneca towns east of the Genesee River, Deodesote had been razed by the American army in September of the preceding year. Only one house remained, and that because it was not near the town, but down the Hemlock Lake Outlet, at the northwest corner of the wide-water pond. The pond was all shored with high hemlock timber hiding Gahota's cabin, which was on the low ridge. Behind the cabin, where the evergreens gave way to leaf trees, the small field that his wife worked was open to the sun, a hidden place, warm and well-drained.

The squaw had finished planting the corn. The hills stood in rows of patted mounds. She gathered up her basket and her wooden hoe and stared happily at the work she had done. Her own field: her own corn would soon pierce the brown earth; her own squash and pumpkin vines invade the soil between, lacing the whole together; her own beans climb the growing cornstalks. Beans, corn, and squash—the three sisters, Gahota called them.

Though the time of terror and famine had gone by, no other Indians had returned to Deodesote. Gahota said they would not return. The heavy passage of the army had rolled them irretrievably into the west. But Gahota and Nancy, and the baby, Jerry Log-in-the-Water, and the baby to be born, could all live where they were.

Nancy straightened her back proudly: Gahota would hunt them meat and fish them fish; but it was she who would earn them their indispensable provender of grain. The field was a large one and well hoed. Gahota had grunted and stopped to look at it when he passed it yesterday, and Nancy had been able to tell from his brown lined face that he was satisfied with her.

Her back had rounded slightly, and there was a pad of fleshy muscle across her shoulders. In her doeskin clothes she looked larger than she used to. But her face was as pink and white, her eyes as blue, and her yellow hair fell in two thick braids to the joints of her hips. She left her field like a goddess of earth, placidly secure in her awareness of fruition.

When she reached the cabin, Gahota was sitting beside the door coiling his fish line, with four trout on a pile of ferns before him.

"What big ones!" Nancy said.

Gahota grunted. She passed into the cabin. It had no chimney, only the circular fireplace of stones on the earth floor, and the small opening in the roof above it. All the ceiling was blackened, shiny, and offering a faint bitter smell of soot. In the corner, where she and Gahota slept, the baby was poking his fingers through the eyeholes of the bearskin, laughing the while with long, soft, rich gurgles. He shouted when he saw his mother, rose up on his unsteady legs, and followed his stomach towards her.

She took him by the hand to lead him out and, gathering up the four trout, went down to the lake to clean them for dinner. Gahota found himself a sunny spot against a tree bole and stretched out.

Squatting at the water's edge, Nancy opened the fish with deft slices of her knife, while her son, imitating her, sat suddenly in the shallow water. The splash and the chill made him raise furious wails to the four winds; but Nancy laughed, and let him yell.

A hail across the lake caused her to lift her eyes. She saw at first only the surrounding hemlock trees, with their breathless reflections an inverted forest, and the clear sheet where the Onehda entered the wide water in the south. Beside this stream early azaleas coming into bloom gave a first hint of their clear pink, so ineffably soft that even the untouched crystal of the lake had failed to capture it.

Waist-deep in the azaleas, some men were standing.

"Gahota. Come." Nancy's voice was quiet, untroubled.

She heard her husband's feet pad down behind her. He stood over her, his shadow falling across her bent back, shading his eyes.

"Nundawaono," he said. He lifted his arm and called.

"Who is that?"

"Gahota. You come."

The men disappeared back into the woods. Nancy finished cleaning the four trout and followed Gahota back to the cabin, the baby tumbling along behind like a hungry puppy.

"Nine come," Gahota said to her. He got his pipe and tobacco and sat down at the threshold, leaving her to gather wood and start the pot cooking. Luckily there were three rabbits and the quarter of the fawn.

Outside the door she heard the men arrive and squat and talk in the Indian language. But they did not say much for a while, and what they did say failed to interest her.

When she had finished the stew she carried the pot outdoors and set it down before the men. There were nine of them, as Gahota had said, six Senecas, three white men. One of the white men wore a brown coat and battered pants. He had a lean jutting throat from which his small head pointed like a turkey cock's. Nancy hardly noticed him. She glanced at the other two.

One of them wore Indian clothes. His face was painted with remnants of vermilion and black, and his hair had been awkwardly stained. As she looked at him, he lifted his eyes from the steaming pot, and stared.

"Nancy!"

It was Hon.

Nancy could not speak for several moments. Neither she nor Hon could find words. But the struck silence of their attitudes made the others look at them. Gahota grunted impatiently. A woman's place was not here. Obediently Nancy turned to go.

"It's my sister, Nancy," Hon said. "Don't you remember me telling you about her?"

"Her, who?" The third man licked his fingers.

"The girl you had at Shoemaker's."

"By God." Jurry McLonis looked up. "I never noticed her."

Gahota was watching them with small inexpressive eyes. Nancy had just passed into the shadowed interior of the cabin, but there she turned and her white skin and blonde braids made a ghost of her, as if glimpsed in a twilight.

McLonis rose.

"It's true," he said. "What's she doing here?"

"Set down, you fool," growled the third white man. "Can't you see the Indian's took her for a squaw?"

"That ain't right, Casselman," exclaimed McLonis. "It's bad business—Indians taking white women. Butler's afraid of it at Niagara."

"Butler!" Suffrenes Casselman's lean face became contemptuous. "Who talks about Butler now? The Indians won't go with him any more since Sullivan licked them. Johnson don't have anything to do with him. Let the Indians alone. It's hard enough to get them to go with us."

"Maybe," said McLonis. "But this girl's Hon's sister."

"Yes," said Hon. "She's my sister—Nancy."

Casselman snarled at them both. "Sit down." He leaned forward and said in a lower voice: "Listen, you dumbheads. These buggers we got with us ain't feeling any too good about us. They didn't get no loot out of that house we burned, and the four scalps wasn't enough to go round. You'd better not give them the chance to get mad at us."

The ever-present mistrust of Indians that most of the Tories felt, the knowledge that their scalps, delivered at Niagara, would look the same and fetch as much as any rebel's, made even McLonis pull in his horns. He sat down in his faded green Ranger coat and stared back at the Indians. Their host was still watching him. Now he said something in Seneca over his shoulder and Nancy obediently closed the door. McLonis dropped his eyes and resumed his eating. It was not that he cared where she was, or who she was: it was just that the sight of her, her handsome pink-cheeked face and yellow hair and vacuous blue eyes, had reminded him of that hour behind Shoemaker's barn; and he had been away in the woods now for eight weeks.

Suffrenes Casselman explained to their host that Hon was his squaw's brother, and had not seen her for two years. The Indian nodded understandingly. Such encounters were surprising to a man; he looked more closely at Hon. He realized that Hon was like Nancy, slightly touched.

"You see your sister," he suggested. "Yes?"

Hon nodded.

McLonis whispered to him, "Fetch her out. I'll drop back in the woods. We can take her with us, whatever Casselman thinks. If he don't like it he can go by himself."

Before Hon moved, McLonis rose and wandered off into the woods. He went with studied aimlessness and the Indians paid no attention to him. Some men always went into the woods after a hearty meal.

McLonis found a fallen tree and sat down on the trunk. The

more he thought about her, the more fun he thought it would be to take her to Niagara. A lieutenant up from the ranks had to content himself with Indian girls. If anything better than Nancy came his way he could always hand her over to the privates. There'd be plenty of men anxious for a girl, with her looks, whatever her brain was like. He thought that they could kill a few days on the march back to Niagara. There was no hurry. They had to collect ammunition and round up another gang since the one they had taken east in March had fallen apart. Suffrenes wanted fifty men. He meant to wipe out Eldridge's and the other outlying small forts, and if one of the promised expeditions materialized, he would plan to join it. A little fun before a campaign like that would hurt no man.

McLonis sat on the fallen tree and cleaned his nails and thought he would buy her a dollar's worth of dress goods. It would seem like a fortune to her after a year in that cabin. He had smelled it through the open door. It had the Indian reek. But she looked clean and healthy. She had a kind of perfection, he remembered, a kind of ripe apple roundness to her. It made him realize how eternally tired he was, how lonesome he was, month after month in the woods, with the inevitable return to the barracks and the Indian town and the long uncompromising level of the lake with its level shores, with the everlasting dinning of the falls. Leg-weary and heart-weary.

Hon's arrival startled McLonis.

"Where's Nancy?" he asked.

Hon scuffed the hemlock needles with a moccasined toe.

"She's talking to Gahota," he said. He looked ashamed.

"What did you say to her?"

"I told her you wanted her to come with us. I said you would take her back to Niagara."

McLonis nodded. "Sure. Where is she?"

"I said she was talking to Gahota."

"You mean he won't let her come?"

"I don't know," Hon mumbled.

McLonis got to his feet.

"I'm going to talk to her myself. You've made a mess of it."

"I wouldn't," Hon said. He began following McLonis, then thought better of it and branched off to join Casselman.

McLonis walked straight towards the cabin. Before he reached it he saw Nancy emerging from it behind Gahota. They turned towards him. McLonis halted.

Nancy came straight up to him, stopping before him, with her hands clasped in front of her. She stared into his face now with a curious insistence.

"Gahota says you want to talk to me. He says I better talk to you."

The Indian beamed at her shoulders.

"Yes talk. Yes talk." He turned away and left them.

McLonis found himself swallowing as he looked at her. She looked so indescribably appealing, big though she was, in her soft doeskin costume, with her clear eyes and her clear skin with the whiteness of winter still on it. She looked cool as snow, the kind of snow that sometimes fell at the end of April, a few flakes suddenly, in a day of heat. And she stood there waiting for him to speak.

"Don't you remember Shoemaker's, Nancy?"

"Yes."

"Don't you want to come with me? I'll take you to Niagara."

"No, I don't want to come."

Her eyes had dropped and she spoke hesitantly.

He said, "But you don't want to stay in a place like this. It's not right. It's not decent, Nancy."

"I don't want to go," she said, after a moment.

"You needn't be scared of him. I'll look out for you. Hon will be along."

As she did not answer, his speech went on, more quickly, almost desperately. "But I'll take you to Niagara. Don't you remember how it was? You said you'd—you said you loved me. I loved you. I never forgot you, Nancy. Honest. I said I'd marry you, don't you remember? You can't stay here. I'll marry you when we get to Niagara."

She raised her eyes then to his.

"I am married," she said. "I don't want to go. Thank you," she added softly, and turned back to the cabin.

He stood where he was for a long minute, half minded to overtake her; then he noticed Gahota a little way off, leaning against a tree and idly swinging his casse-tête by its thong. From the waterside Casselman and Hon were yelling to him to hurry up.

3

In the Valley

Days were to come in which Lana would find herself wondering if she were herself, or some fear-deadened creature existing in human flesh. The mounting tide of dread gained impetus with each express that came through German Flats from the east. In April and May they heard successively of smaller settlements cut off, their few inhabitants killed and scalped. The Sacandaga bush, Harperfield, Fox's Creek, in Schoharie, Getman's, Stamford, Cherry Valley for the second time, and isolated homesteads, one by one, to which families had returned in their eagerness once more to work their farms. The Indian parties did their work and vanished before rescuers could so much as start from the nearest fort. A puff of smoke against the warm May sky;

the faint sounds of firing; another name crossed off the militia list; and who knew who was with him at the place. His wife? His children? Sometimes later it was learned that he was there alone.

The Indians were not taking many prisoners, for they were not returning all the way to Niagara after every raid. They burrowed off into the woods like dogs, circling, lying hidden till all threat of a pursuit was by, and then entering a new district. Five times that month of May the man at McKlennar's had been called for the militia. Five times they had marched into the woods. And five times they had found only the burning ruins of the homestead cabin and stayed only long enough to bury such dead as they found.

The militia were positive that white men led the raids. Twice, following up the tracks of the destructives, Adam and Joe had found women at the site of their first camp. In each case it was obvious how they had been treated before being scalped.

Whenever the militia were called, Lana and Mrs. McKlennar had moved down to one of the forts. Once Adam had been sent to fetch them in when Joe and Gil were both on duty. He had taken them to Eldridge Blockhouse, where thirty people were crowded inside a stockade fifty feet by forty. They had spent seven days there, with no news of what was happening.

Jacob Small or Dingman or Robhold Ough was always on watch in the spy loft and from time to time he called down what he saw. Once it was an express riding along the Kingsroad, full gallop into the west. Another time it was a wagon train, presumably for Fort Stanwix, since it was escorted by sixty soldiers. Again, in the middle of one night, the watcher saw fire to the south and west, far up the valley, beyond Shoemaker hill.

It was so still in the darkness that even at that distance a brief session of firing could be heard. Lana and Mrs. McKlennar, sharing a shed with Betsey Small and her four-year-old boy, talked together in low voices, trying to imagine what was happening to keep the militia out so long. As soon as he had brought them safe inside, Adam Helmer had departed to run a single-handed scout, he said, to the northward. But he had been gone six days.

Betsey spoke tenderly of him as she lay on her back and stared at the square roof of the blockhouse against the stars. There in the spy loft Jacob was keeping the second watch.

"I'd miss Adam," she said. "I'd hate to have anything happen to him. He's such a crazy fool."

"He's crazy about you," said Mrs. McKlennar.

"I know he is." She added, after a minute, "I'm fond of Jake."

One of the children turned on his straw bed with the noise a mouse might make in a barn. In the pitch-dark across the stockade another child began to cry. Instantly Jake's voice came down from the spy loft. "Stop that noise." The mother's fierce whispering could be heard. Then again the silence.

The small stockade cut a segment out of the sky through which stars traced the passage of the night.

"The last express said they expected Sir John Johnson would be down; do you think that's it?"

"It might be."

One of the four cows kept in the stockade began to moo; and Jake's instinctive call for silence brought a smothered laugh from a boy. You couldn't tell a cow to hush its mouth. Then, as the cow continued its bawling, the ridiculousness changed to terror. They could see Jake leaning over the sill of the spy-loft window. His voice was thick with passion.

"Take a club to her! My God, are you all idiots down there?"

Betsey whispered, "Jake feels mad. We'd better quit talking."

There were only five grown men in the stockade, to protect the twenty-odd women and children. Both the Snells who had survived Oriskany—seven of that family had been killed there— and the Forbush men and the two younger Borsts had been called up to Dayton. A solider man than Jacob Small would have been frightened by the responsibility. Eldridge's was too far away from any other fort to expect any reënforcement if they should be attacked.

Their only hope lay in keeping a strict silence during the night, and hoping during the day that any marauding party coming their way would be small enough for five men to handle. He thought he could frighten off any bunch of Indians with the swivel. But supposing the Indians were brought by some Tory renegade—like Casselman, for instance; he would know that a swivel mounted that high was next to useless.

The alarm guns at Herkimer and Dayton both sounded three times. That meant that there was a large party of Indians. Jacob wished he knew how large. They must have burned the Moyer place during the night—that would be the fire he had seen. The Moyers, three families of them, had set out to build that spring, he had heard.

The worst time of watching was in the hour before dawn, when light was just beginning and there were no stars. The valley, then, became like a gray blanket, without shape or distance. It was harder for a man to see than during the darker hours, and no sound was reliable.

It was at this hour that Adam Helmer returned. He was crossing the highland on a dead run. Jacob heard him come over the edge and down the slope to the lesser incline on which the stockade was situated.

"Eldridge," he was calling. "Helmer."

"That you, Adam?"

"Let me in, Jake."

Small bawled down the word to open the gate and Helmer came in, his wide shoulders filling the narrow gap. He stood in the yard, breathing deep, while Small leaned out of the spy-loft window to hear his news.

"The Indians are out again, Jake."

"Where?"

"I almost ran into them. They were coming from West Canada Crick. They'd crossed below Schell's and they're headed this way."

"How many?"

"About sixty, I guess. I ran around them, after they'd gone by. I had to climb a tree and they went right under me. Mostly Senecas, and about ten white men. Casselman. Empie. McDonald. I heard their names."

"How far back of you?"

"They'll be here in about two hours."

Small swore.

"That's after sunrise. They'll see us plain."

"They've got the militia after them. But they figured the militia would chase up the crick, I guess. They'll find out pretty quick what happened if Joe's with them."

"We only got five men here, Adam. Six, with you."

There was a silence. All the women and the older children had come out of their sheds. Now they looked up at the spy loft, making a pond of white, strained, frightened faces. They were all depending on him, and he had no more idea than any of them what to do.

In the midst of that silence Mrs. McKlennar's snort was a challenging blast.

"There's fifteen grown women here," she said. "We'll rig up to look like men. If we show up along the rifle platforms, they can't see we're women. They'll go by."

They found a few extra hats and some old shirts. The five men passed their hats out. Betsey put on her husband's; Lana borrowed Adam's. They stuffed their hair inside. Three of the women, having no hats, hacked off each other's hair with a razor. They put on shirts and coats and armed themselves with broomsticks and pitchfork handles. For a moment they stared at each other in the yard, then, hiking their skirts up, they climbed the ladders to the rifle platform.

"Don't hold those sticks so plain," admonished Small from the spy loft. "Just hold onto them as if they was guns, but don't try to show them. If they come while it's still misty you'll look all right. And if any shooting commences, duck."

He pulled his head out of sight, then stuck it forth again for a last word.

"And don't talk. A woman's got no idea how far a woman's voice will carry."

It was so still now, in the misty pre-dawn, that they heard the splashing of Small's brook under the alders a hundred yards away. It was cooler than it had been during the night. Even Jacob Small, twenty feet above them, saw nothing; and he did not hear the padding feet as soon as they did.

The footfalls came along the way that Adam had taken, over the crest of the highland and down the slope, at a run. But before they reached the wheatfield they slowed down and faded out of hearing. For a long time Lana tried to hear them again. She kept staring toward where they had last been audible, away on her left.

She never knew what sound had caused her to turn her eyes straight out from the stockade, but when she did she nearly screamed. An Indian was standing there, vaguely defined in the pale light. She knew it was an Indian. She could see the feather over his ear and the scarlet on his face and chest and the blanket hanging from his shoulder. Her courage seemed to drain out at her feet. She could only stare as a bird would at a snake. She felt her heart beating so hard that she could scarcely fetch her breath; the blood pounded in her ears, stopped suddenly, and the painted figure of the Indian began to sway in her eyes. She thought she was going to faint.

Then Mrs. McKlennar caught sight of her and reached out and poked Adam. He glanced at Lana, slipped over to her, and followed the direction of her gaze. His rifle crept out noiselessly between the points of the sticks.

The smell of his sweat beside her brought Lana to her senses. "Don't move," he muttered. She did not dare move. Out of the tail of her eye, she saw his thick finger bending on the trigger. She could not help herself from looking back to the Indian. As she did so the rifle roared in her ears and the smoke flushed up in her face, choking her. But before it did, she saw the Indian spin on his heels and fall, head towards her, on his back.

"Hell," said Adam. "I must have got him to one side."

The tear of his teeth on the cartridge paper, the cold slither of the ramrod whanging home the bullet, and he was gone back to his post. She found that she was panting.

"Get him?" Jacob called down.

"Got him," Adam answered.

The shot brought on the main body of the destructives. They could be heard on the highland, then coming down the hill. Then their progress faded out. But the mist was thinning, and here and there the vague shapes of them were visible.

A musket flashed from the spot at which the Indian had been killed. The ball whipped over the women's heads with a sharp tearing sound. "Down, you," shouted Jacob.

For a minute there was no other shot. Then a yelling broke out. They loosed a volley at the palisade and the bullets broke splinters off along the points. And then a shrill whistle called out of the mist.

Jacob called down, "They're pulling off. It did the trick. They seen you." He waited a moment. "I think the militia's coming. I heard a conk-shell horn."

Lana turned her back to the palisade and sat down. She also had heard the deep dismal wailing of the conch shell.

"Hey," bawled Jacob. "They're a-going! They're going down the road."

They were trotting down the road in Indian file. Lana, getting to her feet, watched them with the others. About sixty of them, Adam counted, perhaps a dozen white men. They plodded along at a steady pace, not looking back. They carried blankets on their shoulders, and rifles and muskets trailing from their hands. They all looked brown in the thinning mist, dark and dirty and implacable. There were enough of them to have stormed the stockade in five minutes if they had not mistaken the women for men. . . .

An hour later the militia came over the edge of the highland behind Joe Boleo. They came at a trot, also, but the gait was not like the smooth Indian tread. The militia plodded like farmers, stubbornly setting down their feet, forty weary men.

Joe Boleo drew a little ahead of them.

"You all right?" he yelled.

"Yes."

"How long ago did they go by here?"

"An hour."

Joe gave a groan. "All night long I been kicking these twerps to make them run and all we do is get farther behind."

"You're lucky at that. There was sixty."

"They burnt out the Moyers. We got Dolly Moyer, scelpt but not kilt. They'd started to carry her off, but we come up too quick. We was right on them there."

The militiamen fell out of rank any which way and lay down on the grass bank before the stockade. Joe eyed them disgustedly. "Say, is Adam in there?"

Adam was already pushing the gate open.

"Hello, you bug-tit," he said to Joe. "Want to go after them?"

"Yeah. I want to see them out of the valley. Come on."

Lana issued from the fort with the other women, looking for Gil. He was sitting on the bank with his back against the stockade. He looked back at her without smiling.

"Have you got any food?" he asked. "I'm hungry. Young John here's just about played out."

"I'll cook up some wheat right away. There's no flour."

In one corner of the fort was an old burned-out stump, an Indian mill, they called it, in which they crushed their wheat grains to a kind of rough meal. Lana threw some of this in water and borrowed a pinch of salt.

While she was tending it, Gil brought John Weaver in with him and sat down in the shed.

"Are we going home with you?" Lana asked with a nod towards the children.

"Yes. It's over, I guess. Sir John has headed north."

"Sir John? North?"

"I forgot you wouldn't know," he muttered. "Sir John brought five hundred men across the Sacandaga flows. He's struck the valley by Johnstown. They say he's burned down every house in Caughnawaga. He's killed fifty or sixty people. Old Fonda that used to be his neighbor, eighty years old, scalped on his front door. They crucified a man at Tribes hill, they say. There was three hundred Indians. Everything burnt. They say a hundred or more men went off with Sir John. They took their families with them. And the families of Tories that got left behind four years ago." His voice became uncertain. "Bellinger got orders to muster us in case they came this way. But yesterday afternoon we heard they'd headed north. The soldiers hadn't even started after him from Schenectady when the express left there. They'd been called back there until they knew that town and Albany was safe. We were just coming home when we got the word that there was burning up at Moyer's. We started out after them. . . ."

"Don't talk," said Lana. "Stop. Eat something. It's all ready."

Outside the upright sticks at their backs a woman cried, "Tom! Tom! You come back here! You mind your Ma."

A surly voice answered back, "We was just playing Indian, Ma. We was trying to scalp him."

In the sunlit field two little boys with wooden knives were squatting beside the dead Indian.

4

Terror by Night

No man, all summer long, had gone to his field alone. The haying had been done by armed parties, of thirty or more, sent out from the forts. The people in Fort Herkimer attended to the south side of the river, those in Dayton to the north. At the end of July twenty men were sent to help out with the Eldridge haying. The hay was all stored in small stacks within sight of the stockades, but out of shooting range, so that they could offer no cover to the enemy. At the same time, they could be watched and sallies made to protect them against any small force.

The destructives had hung in the woods through June and July. The scouts sent out left and entered the forts under cover of darkness. In July a mob of sixty Indians almost surprised three hay wagons, chasing them right under the Dayton stockade.

Lana had heard the warning gun go off on the southeast rampart of the fort and gathered her children and run them through the gate. She did not know whether Gil was on that particular hay party, but she was not allowed on the rifle platform to see. She had to remain under it, out of the way, with the other women, listening—first to the shooting out across the valley; then to the rumble of the wheels and the squeaks of the racks as the heavy loads swayed in and out of ruts at their mad gallop. Then the thudding of the horses' hoofs and the racket of harness; the screech of the gates swinging open; the yelling of the Indians close behind; and at last the thunder of the wagons rolling into the parade. As the gates screeched shut again a volley from the rifle platforms seemed to split the fort apart, and four swivels went off with sullen booms, and the yelling outside stopped.

Holding the two children to her, she crowded out with the other women, to see the men sliding down off the loads and running to join the sortie forming at the gate. She saw Gil looking over his shoulder at the line of women's faces. His eyes met hers. He did not raise his hand or smile, no more than she. In the next moment he had passed with the others through the opening gates to drive the Indians away from the cabins and haystacks outside the wall.

That was the nearest any party of savages came to the forts that summer. Most of the time they lay in the woods, trying to pick up berrying parties, and burning all the new outlying cabins one by one. The valley now was as desolate as it had been after Brant's raid. Most of the remaining cattle had been killed and eaten by the destructives. The scouts reported that the pigs, left to run loose in the woods, were getting to be as cute as the deer.

Though the women still cooked in the cabins, most families slept inside the forts; for, towards the end of July, Brant had appeared below Stanwix with eight hundred Indians. They had actually seen his army from Fort Herkimer, crossing the valley to the south. He made no demonstration against the forts, however. Instead, two weeks later he turned up at Canajoharie at the site of his old place, and desolated six miles of the Mohawk. Men, women, and children were killed and taken prisoner, one hundred houses were burned, mills and churches. Wagons were destroyed, ploughs and harrows broken. They said that opposite Frey's you could see human bodies in the water.

• • •

After the second burning of the Herter house, Captain Demooth
had moved into Fort Dayton. John Weaver, however, was sent
across the river to Herkimer. Since he had served with the Continentals under Sullivan, he was now classed as an experienced
soldier and was appointed by Bellinger a sergeant of the garrison.

The promotion made Mary proud, and thankful, also, that his
duties kept him entirely in the fort. They lived on the second
story of the northwest blockhouse, sharing space with Sergeants
Stale and Smith and their wives and Stale's two children. They
had no room for privacy between themselves, but they all felt that
it was better, airier, and quieter than living in one of the sheds.

It had been dry and very hot. The green had been slow in
returning to the mown hayfields. The river ran very shallow. But
since August there had been few alarms.

On the north side of the river Mary and John could see
through the loophole next to their bunk the stone McKlennar
house with its shuttered windows. The survival of that house,
the last left standing but Shoemaker's, was one of the mysteries
they often talked about, together, for they liked to look at it and
plan on having a house of their own some day resembling it.

The other women, hearing them, would sometimes smile,
half bitterly, that people could still be so young. But Mary ignored
them. She understood how these two women felt, having lost
everything that belonged to them. She did not try to answer
when Mrs. Smith told her to wait until she had had a child and
seen it sicken from lack of food and die from cold. Mrs. Smith
had taken her child to bed with her during the past winter, but it
had caught a malignant quinsy of the throat. "Doc Petry couldn't
do nothing. He said it needed milk." Her toneless voice went on:
"My own milk gave out. I ain't like some people. I got to have
food myself to breast feed a child. I'm the hearty-eating kind of

woman. I've got another in me now. What's going to become of it?" She glanced at Mary's figure. "You're lucky. You ain't never had one. You talk about stone houses. Well, all I want to think about is a log house of my own again, and dried punkin and corn ears and hams on the rafters. Just to set down and look at them and know they're all mine."

Mary knew how lucky she was without being told. She was growing up. She would be eighteen before long, and John told her that she was getting prettier every day. Her breasts were filling out, and she had more flesh on her shoulders, and her cheeks were rounder. Her legs were still the slim hard legs of a girl; but John liked them, even though he used to tease her about how long they were. "When the war's over," he said one day, "I'm going to buy you a print dress. I'm going to get it made. With a long skirt. Right to your toes. Your legs won't show, and you'll be beautiful."

"I'll powder my hair," she said. "There'll be flour then."

Imagine it, flour enough to use it on your hair.

"I'll ride you over on a pillion saddle. You'll look like a lady, Mary. With your bonnet tied with bows."

These thoughts seemed so possible and real when they looked at the McKlennar house. As if the house might be their own, waiting for them to ride across the river and enter it.

The time would surely come. She did not tell John how she hoped he would look in a new blue coat and snuff-colored pants and polished boots, perhaps, and certainly a cocked hat. She felt too shy; his talking about her like that always made her remember with humility the way he had first noticed her in this same fort, the way he had talked to her and they had got engaged to one another. She was a little skinny brat then, with one braid down her back and one plain petticoat to her name; and he had stood out before his mother for her, and kept on loving her, and finally they had got married. Now he was getting to be a great man. He had been noticed and had started upwards. She had no doubt that the war would be won with people such as John in power. They would make it a fine free country afterwards, and maybe it was not too much to think of owning a black house servant.

Down in the yard there would be a shout for the changing of the sentries and John would have to get up and pull his boots on and go down and stand his watch. The square black room would become blacker after his going down. Mary would huddle herself against the wall and listen to the sounds of changing watch: the sound of men clambering onto the rifle platforms; the thump of Smith's or Stale's feet on the blockhouse ladder; his boots dropped on the floor; his little grunt as he stooped to take his pants off; one of the women, whichever wife it was, murmuring querulously in the hot darkness as she made room on the straw bed. Mary would lie straight and narrow, trying to shut out the sounds from her ears. The grossness of these men compared to John was sickening to her.

The militia reaped the wheat systematically along the valley from west to east and the McKlennar fields were, consequently, the last to be visited. As the farm was so far from Fort Dayton, both Bellinger and Demooth agreed with Gil that it would be simpler to move down ten or fifteen men to the house and let them camp there while the grain was harvested. But Mrs. McKlennar would not hear of a herd of men let loose in her home unless she went along.

"It's my house," she said, looking the colonel in the eye.

Bellinger sighed.

"Besides," pursued the widow, "with a couple of women looking after their food they'll do the work a whole lot quicker."

Lana was delighted that they were allowed to go. It seemed quite safe with all those men close by. The last scout had reported the Indians moving west towards Tioga. The frequency and magnitude of the earlier raids led people to suppose that nothing much more could be expected to happen that fall.

As the first wagon turned off the road and drew up to the porch, the mystery of the immunity of Mrs. McKlennar's house was explained. Just above the front steps a horse's skull lay on the porch floor.

The men noticed it at once, and one asked suspiciously, "How'd that get there?"

"I put it there myself," said Mrs. McKlennar proudly.

"It's a Tory sign," the man said.

"Of course it is; that's why I put it there."

"It's a Tory sign," he repeated, eyeing her.

"Where'd you get that skull?" another asked her.

Mrs. McKlennar snorted.

"It's the skull of my own mare. I found it this spring when I was strawberrying. She was killed two years ago."

The fact that the skull could be identified seemed to make them feel better about it. One man laughed; it was a joke on the destructives; and they all began to lug in their bedding and spread it on the porch.

But when Mrs. McKlennar went into the house she found that someone had been making free with it. Men apparently had cooked at the fireplace, for the hearthstones were greasy. They found a bit of bloody bandage on the floor. Some of the destructives must have used the place, keeping it securely shuttered and lighting a fire with no fear of detection. Mrs. McKlennar grinned wryly. "I guess I didn't have my whole joke to myself, Lana, and I'll bet these men have left their bugs in here." The women opened all the windows to let in the sun and clear away the mustiness, and then, while Lana mopped the floor, Mrs. McKlennar attacked the sooty cobwebs.

She was in a fine temper by the time they had the kitchen habitable. "I'll not leave this house alone again," she said. "I'd rather lose my scalp than go through this again."

Gil had brought wood and Daisy was cooking before her fireplace once more, muttering to herself, as she had to clean one pot after another, "Dear, dear, dear, dear," with a clucking noise like an offended hen. But she had the men's food ready by sundown and they came up from the wheatfield to eat it on the porch, where they sat admiring the swathe they had cut through the grain and eyeing the full moon that rose through a shelf of mist upon the hills by Little Falls.

They spent a week at bringing the wheat up to the barn, and the second week they started threshing. Some of the men had returned to their cabins, a new lot succeeding them, and as fast as the grain was threshed it was barreled and carted to Fort Dayton.

The women worked longer hours than the men. The cooking and washing were far more than Daisy, the negress, could handle alone, and before the wheat had been threshed Gil began pulling ears from the corn and expected Lana to help him. Mrs. McKlennar therefore had to assist the negress.

But they all enjoyed it, even the cow, which had been led down from the fort when it was decided to thresh at the farm. The feeling that they were in a house, that they had a place to themselves, made up for all their labor.

Gil decided to talk to Bellinger about their staying. His first argument was that if the destructives had actually been using the house for a hideout, it was better either to burn it to the ground or else to have a guard upon it. His second argument had more effect. The McKlennar wheatfields were among the best in the valley. It would be of advantage to the whole community if Gil were allowed to plough them in the fall. He thought if he could have six men on hand continually that he could safely keep on at the house. In case of any large raid, naturally, the family would withdraw again to one of the forts. If Bellinger realized that Gil's principal idea was to keep his fields in order, it only agreed with his own passionate conviction that the one hope for the settlers was to hold their land and feed themselves. He agreed. And though the tiny garrison changed personnel every day or so, there were always six men working with Gil at the ploughing or helping Lana to gather the apples which were just beginning to fall.

The leaves were turning and the nights growing colder. Though there had been no frost as yet in the valley, it had touched the hills, and the maples were already scarlet and crimson and flaming orange. The afternoons were hazy and full of silence and without wind.

The two children began to put on flesh, eating the new wheat in mushes and samp from the new corn. It was a quiet time. Though Daisy fell ill of a queer fever and was sent to Dr. Petry to be treated for several days, and Lana had to do all the work, she felt a sense of peace take root in her own being, and now and then she caught herself looking forward. It was something she had not done with happiness for several years.

Mrs. McKlennar spoke of it to her one day. "I can see you're planning things. About you and Gil and the two boys, ain't it?"

Lana nodded.

"There's one thing I want you to know. You needn't tell Gil now. But when I die I want you two to have this place."

The widow's face reminded Lana of that March morning when she and Gil had come to interview her, perhaps in the way Mrs. McKlennar drew her breath. There was a sharpness in her eye as if she dared Lana to answer her back.

"In some ways," she continued, "I've been happier than I've been since my husband died. That's because you two have been like children to me. I've appreciated it."

Lana said softly, "It's nothing to what you've been to us."

"Nonsense. I've just told you. Let's forget it." Then she said sharply, "Maybe, though, you'll want to go back to Deerfield if this mess ever gets done with."

Lana shook her head. "I can't tell. I don't know what Gil thinks—he's never spoken of it."

"Well," said Mrs. McKlennar, "it's up to you. The place is yours to leave or take."

As she went out of the kitchen Lana thought, as she had more than once of late, that Mrs. McKlennar seemed a little frail.

Gustin Schimmel was a little man who could only be described as burly. He walked as if he weighed two hundred pounds, with a hunch to his shoulders, and his solemn face belligerently outthrust. He was a very serious person and he took his duty at McKlennar's very hard.

Two days ago a lone Tuscarora Indian had come in to report to Bellinger a huge army of men moving east of Unadilla. He was so emphatic about the numbers of this army, whose trail he had happened on, that Bellinger wanted a scout sent out. He had summoned Gil to join Helmer and Boleo, and had sent word to Gustin Schimmel that on no account was any man to leave McKlennar's until specific orders were received or others arrived to relieve them. It put Gustin in a very serious position, for it was his first command.

He came into the kitchen that evening to assure himself that all the shutters were bolted and the back door barred. With the colder nights, the men were sleeping in the front rooms of the house and the women and children occupied the kitchen.

"I tended to them myself, Gustin," said Mrs. McKlennar.

"Yes, ma'am. But I got to see *myself*. I'm responsible."

His eyes did not allow him to see Lana hastily veiling herself in a blanket, or to observe the widow pushing the chamber pot hastily under the bed. He wondered how such embarrassments could conceivably be avoided.

Having finished his inspection, he addressed the floor.

"I hope you sleep good, ma'am."

"Good night," said Mrs. McKlennar without hope.

"Good night, ma'am." He backed himself out, closing the door. "You ain't to bolt this door," he said from the other side.

"There isn't any bolt," said Mrs. McKlennar.

"Thank you, ma'am."

They had a good night as he had wished them, except for one interruption: the sound of a horse coming from the falls. The clear chop of his hoofs on the hard road past the farm—increase, diminishment, and silence. Before they went to sleep again, a light rain started to fall. In the men's room the snoring continued on its heavy course; then they heard one man stirring in the hall and the half-stifled breathing of Gustin Schimmel deep in his perplexities beyond their door. He breathed there for some time before he finally once more retired.

The morning showed them the last of the rain. A west wind had begun to blow, to clear after the rain, so powerful in its deep gusts that it was like moving silver on the hills.

The wind blew all day.

Gustin Schimmel stood on the porch from time to time, facing it. He wanted to know what that express had carried. He wished mightily that Gilbert Martin would return and relieve him of this new habit of thought he was acquiring. The unaccustomed involutions of his brain had affected his appetite. Laboriously that afternoon he wrote on the piece of paper on which he had decided to keep a journal of his command.

Thirsdey, Oct. 19. It raind some. it clerd this morning.
Express went by last nit Today nothing remarkabel.

He stared awhile at the paper. For the seventeenth he had
inscribed in his burly hand, "Warm to-day noboddy on the road.
Skvash py for super." Squash pie as an entry disturbed him somewhat, for it did not seem very military. He had put it down to fill
out the line, since he could think of nothing else. Ultimately
he decided to let it stand, folded the paper, and breathed in the
widow's direction.

"If you'll excuse me, ma'am," he apologized, "I think I'll just
go down to the road and see if I can see anybody."

Mrs. McKlennar fixed him with a marble eye.

"I shall miss you, Gustin Schimmel."

"I could send in one of the boys to keep you company," said
Gustin.

"No, thanks, since you can't stay with us, I think we'd rather
be alone."

"That's what I thought, ma'am. I want to see if I can find out
about that express."

Mrs. McKlennar looked at Lana.

"Do I seem like somebody who's going crazy?"

"No," said Lana smilingly.

"I am, though. Raving crazy. He's making me." She smiled
in turn and went on, "Why don't you take the children out? It
would do all three of you good."

"Won't you come with us?"

"No, I'd like to just lie here and rest. You stay out till the cow
comes in for milking. There's no cooking to do with those four
pans of beans all baked."

Lana saw that she wanted to be alone, so she put Gilly's deerskin jacket on him, which made him think he looked like his
father, and wrapped a blanket round the baby. The baby had

thriven for all the moving they had done that summer. He lay like a great fat lump on her arms, as much as she could carry. He hadn't been christened till the spring when, one day, Domine Rozencrantz had come by McKlennar's; and they had named him Joseph Phillip, with Joe Boleo for a sponsor. Young Gilbert, however, had never seemed to make such flesh, and Lana thought it was due to a combination of the hard winter after Brant's raid and her own milk's giving out when he was still so young. The last was due no doubt to the prompt occupancy of herself by Joey; and at the time it had seemed to her a strange and unjust manifestation of Providence that she should lose her milk. But now that Gilly was becoming so hardy she found it easier to accept the ways of God.

For Gilly was a tough little nugget, active as a young squirrel, and for all that he was only two and a half he was able to walk for quite a little way. And he seemed to take great satisfaction in going into the woods, which, of course, meant the sumacs behind the barn.

Lana took the two children a little way up the slope, perhaps a hundred yards, to an open patch she had found one day, where the earth was smooth enough for the baby to tumble about unwatched. The patch was on the brow of the upland, and, there being no trees round about, the sumac leaves, all gold with bloody crimson tips, and the dark red tassels, seemed to touch the blue of the windy heavens overhead.

The earth was fairly dry, even after the night's rain. The sweep of the wind hushed everything. Sitting there, Lana found herself growing drowsy, and after a while she glanced round to make sure that the children were close by and then stretched out upon her back. The house was so near that she could hear any sound that might rise from below, and yet, for all that could be seen of it, it might be under the moon.

Lana wondered briefly whether Mrs. McKlennar were having

a decent rest. Then her eyelids slowly closed. The voice of the booming wind lulled her. Her face was almost girlish as she lay there, the pink whipped up in her cheeks by the wind, and her hair pulled forward under her cheek so that her mouth seemed in a nest.

A few minutes later, Gilly lifted his sharp little face. He acted as if he had heard a sound—a hail from the Kingsroad, perhaps. His mother had stirred in her sleep and the little boy walked up to her and stared down gravely. He glanced at his brother, but his brother wasn't much good at covering the ground, so Gilly, after another moment, walked unsteadily down the slope and into the forest of sumacs. . . .

The hail he had heard had been young Fesser Cox riding his first dispatch from Fort Dayton. Colonel Klock had sent up word from Schenectady that Sir John Johnson had struck the Schoharie Valley with fifteen hundred men. The seventeenth he had laid waste eight miles of the Schoharie. On the eighteenth he had entered the Mohawk and turned west, burning both sides of the river. All people were warned to enter the forts. The militia at Stone Arabia were to stand before the ravaging army. General Robert Van Rensselaer was bringing the Albany militia up the valley to take him in the rear.

Bellinger sent orders to the detail at McKlennar's. It was at once to proceed to Ellis's Mills at the falls and reënforce the garrison there. Fifty militia were about to march from Dayton and Herkimer to back up Colonel Brown at Stone Arabia or join Colonel Klock. A detail would be sent out in an hour to pick up the women at McKlennar's and carry them to Eldridge's, where the men would amplify the garrison of the blockhouse.

Gustin Schimmel did not like it. But he believed in orders. He woke Mrs. McKlennar out of a sound nap and explained that the second detail was on the way and that they would be taken to Eldridge. He himself hated to leave Mrs. McKlennar like that, but it would not be for long. He would prefer to wait until the others arrived or take them himself to Eldridge's, but there it was, plain orders.

"Godsake, man!" cried the widow. "Get along." ("And thank God it's the last of you," she thought, realizing that her cap was caught in the pins over one ear.)

She had been having her first good nap in a long time, but when she awakened she realized suddenly how old she had become. She did not feel like getting up at all, and she thought she would stay where she was until Lana came in. Lana would be down in a moment and could help her with her things. It was hard to have to move again, when a woman began to feel old and tired. Hard to leave the house she had been happy in, so wildly happy sometimes.

She thought of Barney. Barney in his dragoon coat. Barney coming home from the Masonic meeting where he and his friends had been pooling the scandal and news of the valley, Barney coming home slightly tipsy, though he might have ridden fifteen miles, and singing his favorite song—they said he sang it whenever the rum began to seep around a little in his enormous barrel. The words came back to Mrs. McKlennar with her memory of his flushed, handsome face.

> *Oh, I love spice,*
> *I love things nice,*
> *And I love sugar-candy.*
> *I like my life*
> *With my dear wife,*
> *Unless the girls are handy.*

The rascal! He would tumble her hair all out of its cap, her red hair it was, and look as full of sin as the devil himself, and all the time he was as chaste and simple as the brooks he was forever fishing. She remembered the way they dined on warm summer evenings when Sir William once came, with his son,—plain John then,—or John Butler, or Varick, or one of the Schuylers. The gentlemen took off their boots and put their pumps on in her bedroom, and they ate on the porch, with the white table napkin and the candles slobbering with moths, and the hill, the valley, the stars in the sky and in the river, like the finest French paper in the world. The gentlemen seldom brought their ladies, and for that Sally was just as glad, for she had the gift of making men treat her as equals and could crack as hard a joke as anyone if occasion required, and she liked her half bottle of port in the old days, and, *tsk, tsk, tsk*—what a waggery of scandal that would have started if a woman had the telling of it back in Albany. . . . They had planted the orchard together and they had planted a flower garden, but somehow neither of them had had the patience for gardening, or felt the need of being fashionable. It was better to straddle the mare for a gallop to Klock's than to fork the roots of a bleeding heart. It was a pity he should die so long before her, and yet she was glad, for she could not imagine what Barney would have done in these days. He never was much of a man to think things out, poor dear, with his handsome useless head—Lord knew how he could have managed to hold court as Justice of the Peace if the courtroom hadn't been the pub; he could always give both sides a drink and tell them one of his stories if the judgment was beyond him, and then sell them a cock or a foal at the end of it. And come home at night and tell her about it with great rib-swelling roars that tossed her beside him in the bed like being in a storm at sea. And the nice way he liked things, and on the minute—the linen spotless, his shaving water with the crystal salt in it, and the small lace stitched to his good shirts before they were put back in the drawer. Once when she hadn't done it and he had looked in the wrong drawer for a pocket handkerchief, she had really believed he would lift the skin of her back for a minute. But instead he had sat down and explained it to her, the way a grandfather would to his youngest daughter's little daughter, great stupid hand that he was, good only for handling guns or cursing men into level files. Oh, Barney, Barney. . . .

She was not conscious of the minutes passing, or of the time it was, for the whole house had bloomed before her tired eyes and become beautiful and sweet once more. She did not hear the men marching down to the road, and half an hour later she did not hear the detail going by—the detail that should have stopped and taken them. She did not think of Lana, nor why the girl was not yet back with her two children, though it was getting shadowy in the sky across the east window. She had just remembered something that she had not thought of for years, showing how familiarity and custom makes one forget.

This bed she was now lying in so contentedly was the bed that she had been a bride in. (At the tavern in Albany. The best in the house, the landlord had taken his oath, and it was a decent-looking bed for a tavern, though no great piece of furniture in a private house. Just honest maple wood; but in the morning Barney had waked up and looked at her and sat up with the bedclothes over his knees,—and a cold draft pouring down inside her nightgown,—and he had sworn that he would never sleep in another bed unless he had to. He had rung the landlord up then and there. "Good morning," said the landlord. "Your Honor had a good night?" Impertinent, sly-tongued devil: Sarah had sat up beside Barney and flushed furiously in his face; but she hadn't made him change expression. Barney laughed, till he coughed, and swore. "I want to buy your bed, landlord. How much is your asking price?" The man was so confounded that he named three guineas. "I'll give you four and not a penny less," shouted Barney, "and bring me a bottle of the lobo pale for my

breakfast. Oh, and I forgot, what will you have, Sarah, my dear?"
She said she would have a glass of his bottle. "You will not. If
there's one thing I can't stand it's a wife always cornering in on
her husband's drink. Two bottles, landlord, and in twenty-three
minutes to the second. Get out and good morning.")

What a thing it was, this delicious revival in her mind of all
those early days. Sleighing down the frozen river to the barracks
by Hudson Village. Or driving out to the flats at sundown. . . .
No, no, it was better to remember coming to this place and building the house together, and Barney being dumbfounded because
a chimney could not be laid up in a day. . . .

She did not hear the muffled tramp of the German Flats militia going along the Kingsroad—sixty frightened men with orders
to proceed as far as the falls for the night and wait there with a
scout out to the north in case Sir John's Indian forces broke loose
from his army.

She was thinking of Indians though, and the way Barney
would not let them in the house, because they smelled so beasty
it spoiled his taste for claret for three days. . . . He could even
taste it in the cottage cheese the evening one had slept beside
the kitchen fire. . . .

That reminded Mrs. McKlennar that the past was not hers
to recapture. She realized that she was sleeping in the kitchen
and that the house was bare of people and that she was alone,
and it was dark.

No, not alone. Somebody was walking in the next room.
Somebody being very cautious. Somebody carrying a firebrand.
Two people, she could tell it now, carrying torches. The pine
smoke scent came in to her, aromatic, bitter, clearing her head.
The light was coming down the hall. Suddenly it occurred to her
that the detail Gustin Schimmel had apologized about had never
turned up. These could not be they. The detail must long since
have got to Eldridge's. Sir John was in the valley.

The door opened slowly and an Indian wobbled into the room. He was slightly tipsy, having just found and emptied a brandy flask, but not so tipsy as his companion. He held the torch over his head with one hand, and clutched a mass of clothing and blankets and a green glass bottle in the other, and the light flared down on his shaven head with its startled scalplock dangling a broken feather. His face was painted black with liverish yellow spots and a white stripe that went down his nose and over his mouth and chin, as though his face had been put together by an inexperienced cabinetmaker. He was very hot, and he smelled not only of himself, but of the bear grease all over him that had turned rancid in the heat and wet. And he stared at the old lady in her bed as if she were the great snake demon of Niagara Falls.

"What do you mean by coming into my house?" demanded Mrs. McKlennar.

She had sat up very straight in the bed with her wool jacket over her shoulders and her cap awry. Her long nose was sniffing. She was thinking of the cottage cheese. Barney.

The Indian's jaw dropped. He was not used to being talked at so. And though he did not understand English, his companion said he did.

"Owigo," he said softly. "Come quick."

Owigo was a squattish individual with white circles painted round his eyes. He hit the doorjamb with his shoulder and dropped both muskets and spun round till he was facing the bed.

"Speak English," grunted the first Indian.

"Bellyache bad," were the first words Owigo thought of, and he said them.

"Something worse than that will happen to you, my lad," Mrs. McKlennar said grimly. "You talk English. Well, what have you got to say for yourself? Coming into my house like this!"

Owigo teetered into what he thought was dignified politeness.

"How," he said after a pause.

"What are you doing in my house?" repeated Mrs. McKlennar, drawing herself a little more rigidly erect.

Enlightenment traced a devious course through the Indian's fuddled brain.

"Ho. Set house on fire. Burn quick. All burning there." He waved his hand, a wide gesture that embraced the universe.

For a moment Mrs. McKlennar stared at the two. It was true. She could hear the fire now, she could see the faint light on the floor beyond the open door. These drunken, beastly, good-for-nothing, stinking fools! All the Irish in her blazed.

Her lips parted to a stream of invective that might have silenced even Barney. It certainly silenced the Indians. They were appalled. They recognized virtuous outrage when they saw it, and they did not know what to do.

"Burning my own house with me in it!" cried Mrs. McKlennar. "You ought to be whipped. If my husband were here he'd have the hides off your backs clean down to your heels."

"Yes, yes," apologized Owigo anxiously. "You get out quick, you catch on fire."

It was true enough. The very door smelled hot. Already little fingers of flame pointed round the edge and were withdrawn.

But Mrs. McKlennar would not move.

"I'll not," she said. "I'm not a well woman. I can't sleep outdoors on a cold night like this."

The slowly seeping intelligence in Owigo's eyes was transmuted into words. He explained to his puzzled companion what the white lady had said. The companion looked worried. He replied in Seneca.

"Friend Sonojowauga say," explained Owigo, "you get'm out quick. Burn bad. Burn very bad."

Mrs. McKlennar said then, "If I'm to get out of this house, you'll have to move my bed out for me." She tapped the bed and pointed to the door. Sonojowauga understood the gesture while Owigo was still trying to get the sentence translated in his mind.

He grunted. Then Owigo said, "Yes. Fetch it out. Sure, fine."

"Don't look at me while I get up," said Mrs. McKlennar, mastering a slight shiver. She rose and donned a coat.

"Now," she said severely, "you hurry up."

Willingly they caught up the bed and ran it to the door.

"On its side," said Mrs. McKlennar, "like this. And don't scratch it, you careless lazy beast."

"Make quick," panted Owigo.

They blundered through the door and set the bed up in the yard beside the barn, and hurried back for the bedclothes; by then the kitchen was ablaze. Mrs. McKlennar shrieked at them.

"Don't touch my sheets with your filthy hands; I'll carry them myself."

They escorted her, nonetheless, and watched her with mystified faces while she made the bed. Then she got into it.

"Go away, now," she said. "And don't ever come near me again."

Owigo smiled ingratiatingly. "Burn fine."

"Get away," said Mrs. McKlennar. "Quick. I don't like you two. You are very bad."

Owigo looked dismayed. He had done everything. His face was sorrowful. Seeing his friend so, Sonojowauga made his face look sorrowful too.

"We go," said Owigo. They gathered up their muskets and trooped off into the woods, one behind the other, feeling very bad, and still a little drunk.

Mrs. McKlennar looked after them, then she returned her gaze to the house, and watched it burn. The red light covered her in the maple bed, showing her long face very quiet. Her eyelids blinked against the light as she sat there, backed against the pillows, and after a few minutes, slow, heavy, silent tears began to drop over her lined cheeks. She lay down in the bed, with her back to the house, but she could not keep the light away. She did not then think of Lana. Her heart was breaking with the destruction of her house. For three years it had escaped the destructives. Now at last two drunken Indians had set it off.

An hour after she had lain down, Lana had wakened, and after a single glance around her had sprung up in terror. The baby lay sound asleep, but Gilly was gone. She called, but as she started down through the sumacs she had a view across the valley.

In the late afternoon sunlight, for one instant, between two groves of trees, she saw a party of men, proceeding at a trot that was unmistakable. Indians were in the valley.

She stopped with Gilly's name frozen on her lips, overwhelmed with the bitter knowledge of her own criminal foolishness. It was well that she did. Following the fences along the Kingsroad she saw two Indians, painted on chest and face, one red, one black, and Lana realized that they could not have missed the house. They were turning up to it. Utterly helpless, she watched them pad softly onto the porch and nose their way inside like two inquisitive dogs. It was too late to see what had happened in the house. No shooting had greeted the Indians. The six men must have gone.

Not only must they have deserted her for some incredible reason; they must have taken Mrs. McKlennar with them. There was just one thing Lana could think of to do. To hide the baby first in Joe Boleo's hide-hole, then to search out Gilly without calling.

It took her several moments to find the hide-hole from this new direction; but as soon as she did, she lowered the baby into it and wrapped him in her coat. He slept like an angel. Lana pulled herself out of the hole, leaving the baby in darkness on the hemlock twigs, praying that he would continue to sleep. Her heart fluttered as she stole out on hands and knees, listening for any tread that might be heard among the sumacs. There was none. The valley was quiet save for the western wind that drew across the hill with its inevitable booming force.

Carefully and furtively Lana began creeping down towards the house. She kept her head low to the ground, seeking through the stems of the sumacs for a sign of Gilly. She understood now how much like forest trees those stems must look to a baby. She went all along the lower edge of the sumac growth, hoping to intercept him if there were yet time, stopping every little way to listen for a hostile sound, forcing her terror to be calm, her eyes to search through every opening in the brush.

The Indians in the house, if they still were there, were being remarkably quiet. She had now covered all the lower part of the slope and begun to crawl upward once more. She wondered if she could risk a call. She was torn with the desire to stand up and shout to Gilly and anxiety for what was happening to the baby in the hide-hole. If he woke up now and screamed he would be heard, even over the wind, far beyond the house.

The sticky branches of the sumac catching in her hair dragged it loose from the pins. It fell forward over her face, impeding her sight. It was hard enough to see anyway, for the sun was well down. The sky, when she glanced up at it, looked as if it promised cold. She began to fear the night now, almost as much as the Indians. If she did not find Gilly before darkness came, she felt that she would never find him.

The desire to weep was one more thing to struggle against; she felt that if she could lie down on her face and sob and make a noise she would find help. But she did not dare to. Even as the tears streamed helplessly from her eyes, she put her hands and knees out to feel for dry sticks, moving them out of her path with the instinct that hunted creatures have of destruction beyond every leaf. . . .

Her heart was bitter, even bitter against Gil for having left her so. If he loved her truly, he would surely know that she was in trouble. He would come to find her. But she knew that Gil would not come, and that the trouble she was in was entirely of her own making. She started to pray as she went on and on with her nearly insensate patience, forcing her eyes to search ahead through the increasing darkness. And then she heard it. The thin voice. For one dreadful moment she listened—afraid that it was Joey.

But it came more clearly.

"Ma, Ma." He had learned to say "Ma" that summer. He said it so distinctly.

She governed her tired senses, compelling them to a sane judgment of the direction of the voice. Yes, up the slope. Near the little cleared space where they had sat down. He had found his way back to it.

She risked a cry, soft and urgent and clear, "Ma's coming. Hush." It was so dark now that it didn't matter. She stood up and ran, blundering through the bushes, scratched and whipped, to see his little dark shape standing up all alone in the exact centre of the open space.

She caught him in her arms.

"Ma's boy," she whispered. "Hush, hush."

He whimpered a little and settled himself snugly against her breast, and she began to feel her way in the direction of the hidehole and was surprised at the ease with which she located it. She perched the boy on the edge of the hole and lowered herself cautiously in case the baby had moved. Then she stretched up her hands and took the boy down. She sat down with a child in either arm. She did not cry. She kept dry-eyed, alert, in the dark little hole, straining for any sound that might mean danger.

The glow against the sumac leaves visible through the hole first told her that the McKlennar house was burning. She risked one glance above the hole, standing up and peering over the tree trunk. The wind was tearing flames in banners from the roof. She had a glimpse of the two Indians carrying the bed and then Mrs. McKlennar following with the bedding. She could not understand it.

She lingered till the bed had been set down and the old lady ensconced. She saw the Indians depart. And she wondered if she could go down and tell Mrs. McKlennar to come back to the hide-hole. But the babies kept her. Joey was beginning to whine. He would wake up and want his food. Gilly was hungry too. Lana's head swam. What on earth had happened?

Mrs. McKlennar had lain down in the bed. Was she sick? Too sick to move? But she had followed the bed out there.

Suddenly her eyes were caught by the shape of a man, stooping down among the sumacs, well away to her right. She dropped inside the hide-hole. At the same moment Joey let out his first bawl. He had a voice like a calf when he was hungry. She fumbled frantically in the dark for his mouth and pressed her hand on it. She felt his instantaneous convulsion of protest, arms flying, legs kicking, as he tried to get his breath. Gilly started to whimper. "Hush," she whispered. With her free hand she tore at her short gown, ripping it in two, baring her breasts. "Oh God. If my milk doesn't come now!" She huddled Joey up to her and withdrew her hand and pressed his little face towards her. She felt him start to yell, then his surprised jaws clamped on her breast so hard she almost cried out. And then the reassuring pressure beginning.

Gilly was starting softly to cry now. Cold and hungry as he was, the smell of milk was too much for him. He would not hush. She pulled him towards her too and let his face rest against the free breast and left it to him whether he would accept it. They had worked so hard to wean him. But when, fumblingly, he touched the breast, her heart welled over.

The man in the sumacs was Joe Boleo. He and Adam and Gil had returned from their scout reporting that an Oneida Indian had seen the army of hostiles strike the Schoharie. When they had reached Fort Dayton, Bellinger had ordered them to take a detachment of men with Mark Demooth to the south. An express had said that Van Rensselaer's army was fighting Sir John above Klock's, and that the Tories were breaking over the river. If possible Demooth was to capture Johnson or John Butler or some of the leaders.

Gil had asked at once for his family and Bellinger had explained what he had done. "You've got to go, you three. You're the only scouts to find them after dark in those hills. I can't spare one of you." He looked gaunt and haggard and determined. "Your women are all right," he said.

Gil hurried off to report himself to Demooth. Joe Boleo, however, didn't give a damn for Bellinger or General Washington himself, if it had come to that, or army discipline or cause or justice. He remembered that he had a godson in McKlennar's and he was going to make damn sure he was all right. If he felt like it afterwards, he could circle and still catch up with Demooth.

He reached McKlennar's in time to see the roof fall in and the widow lying on her bed. The old woodsman took one look, then bolted down to her. He was sure he had heard stray shots at Eldridge's. More of the destructives were on the way; running the woods like driven wolves, they would snap at anything that crossed their path.

He snatched up the bedclothes and pulled Mrs. McKlennar to her feet. He didn't ask her why she had not used his hide-hole. He ran her up the slope and shoved her in. As he did so he felt the presence of terror in the pit and called, "Lana, is that you in there?" Then he added, "It's Joe."

"Yes." He could hardly hear the word through her release of breath.

"Here's Mrs. McKlennar. You keep quiet and you'll be all right. I ain't coming in. But I'll stay close."

He was right about more Indians. Three of them came to the burning house and started nosing round. They picked up footprints at the edge of the sumacs and began to work up the slope. The women heard their footfalls gradually approaching the hidehole. Then they stopped. Suddenly a man whooped, a terrible ear-piercing sound. Then he was still, waiting for the frightened stir that should point out his victim.

There was a clean, sharp crack. The two others yelled, and at the same time the women heard Joe Boleo shout. The sumacs crashed overhead with the sounds of pursuit and flight, and in only a minute the wind again was audible.

Mrs. McKlennar leaned against Lana and wept.

The clear October dawn woke them—unbelievable as it seemed to wake, to have fallen asleep at all. The babies began to cry.

"It's all right," Joe's voice reassured them from above. When Lana looked out she found him on the fallen tree, cleaning his long rifle. His hatchet and knife were polished at his side. "Three of them." He nodded at her. He helped haul out the babies. "I did a perty on the one that yelled. Twenty rod, right through the head. He's down there."

Lana would not look, but Mrs. McKlennar stared curiously at the dead painted body. "Jurry," she said suddenly. "Jurry McLonis!"

"Deader'n fish." Joe nodded. "Come on. I'll lead you back to the fort." He picked up the baby. "I'll lug Joey," he said.

The threads of news were slowly gathered during the day. The Tory army had disappeared to the west. But they had burned the whole of Schoharie and both sides of the Mohawk from Canajoharie and Caughnawaga to the fording place above Klock's. They had not been caught as they might have been. They had killed forty men at Stone Arabia who had tried to stop their march; and the Indians and destructives as usual had dropped away from the main army in their uncontrollable desire to hurry.

Then the detail that had gone to Eldridge reported that Jacob Small had been caught by the first appearance of the Indians before Fesser Cox had given the alarm. He had gone out to gather apples. He had always liked apples and there was a tree a few rods from the blockhouse, behind some woods, whose apples he particularly fancied. He had been shot and scalped and left where he was in the branches. They found an apple in his hand, with one bite out of it.

Towards dark, Adam and Gil returned with two-thirds of their force. They had been surprised. Demooth and eight men had been captured by Johnson's Greens and Butler's Rangers.

As darkness came that night, the still-booming great west wind brought clouds and the first early fall of snow.

IX

I

The May Flood

The rain as it started on the fifth of May looked like an ordinary spring shower, clouding over a little after noon, and the first cold drops slanting out of the northwest. The river was already high between Dayton and Herkimer. In the falling rain it flowed with a smooth force, which covered the fording place without a riffle.

Lana and Mrs. McKlennar kept the fire going and listened to the steady patter on the bark sheaths of the roof. It was damp in the small cabin that Gil, with Joe and Adam to help him, had laid up after the McKlennar house had burned, though it stood on the high ground north of the fort. Mary Weaver said that her place, which was the next below Petry's store, had a stream running through one corner. Cobus had been trying unsuccessfully to dam it out with clay all afternoon.

After Mary left them, Mrs. McKlennar turned on the negress, who as usual hugged the hearth.

"Can't you stop that chattering?"

"Fo' God I can't, Mis'. Hit's de way dey is, dat's all."

Daisy felt the damp since her fever of last fall. She claimed she felt it on all the bones in her "skelington." "If you could des' leave me have a little drap of rum, Mis'."

"Rum!" snorted the widow. "If I had it I'd drink it myself. Even Dr. Petry hasn't any."

Lana began to prepare supper. They had a small cut of deer meat and a little milk for the children; there was no flour in the place.

Her face had a new quality of transparentness. She was very thin; even her hips that had grown so heavy a year ago were now fined down like a young girl's. She was dressed, as were Mrs. McKlennar and the negress, in a strange collection of odds and ends; her petticoats, raveled out almost to her knees, seemed ready to fall apart with the rottenness of age. She wore clumsy homemade moccasins on her feet and a deerskin jacket poorly tanned over a shrunken woolen shirt of Gil's.

As she set the iron kettle on the logs to boil, she tried not to think of her family; but for months her mind had been conjecturing about their fate. Expresses coming up the valley in November had said that Fox's Mills was one of the settlements entirely wiped out by Sir John's Tory army. Most of the people were believed to have been killed. But there was no way in which Lana, in German Flats, could find out. All that she had been able to discover was that her second sister had been married the year before to a man from Johnstown. Her informant could not say who the man was; it was something he had heard in Klock's. Lana thought that her sister would now be twenty years old. Lana herself was twenty-three; but she felt that she must look much older than that.

Her thoughts went round and round, making no connected sense. When she heard Gil's footsteps hastily squelching through the mud outside, she had to force her face into a smile. She wanted to smile; the instinct lifted her out of the day's listlessness whenever she heard him coming home. But to make her lips respond was an effort of translation which she was always conscious of.

As the door opened to let him in, she turned her head and saw the rain sheeting down in the dusk beyond him, and Joe Boleo standing at his side, dripping in damp deerskins.

"I brought home Joe to see his godson," Gil cried.

"I'm glad," said Lana. The children were always glad when Joe or Adam came to visit. She thought, "I'll have plenty. I'm not hungry myself."

"Come in and sit close," Mrs. McKlennar said. "You poor boys certainly look wet."

"It's quinsy weather all right," said Joe, grinning at them all and hanging his rifle, muzzle down, on a peg through the trigger guard. The two boys came up to him.

"Did you bring us anything, Uncle Joe?" they asked.

"I got a piece of soft pine in my pocket," he said. "What'll I make you?"

They disputed for a moment between a buck deer and a tomahawk. But the vote finally settled on the buck. A buck with twelve points, Gilly specified. Joe looked a little blank. He could whittle pretty well, but a buck deer was a large order for a man with a hunting knife. Then a thought crossed his mind and made him smile, and he set to work manfully on the rear quarters.

"It's quite a rain," said the widow. "Where've you been, Joe?"

"I was over the river to Herkimer seeing Adam."

"We haven't seen Adam much, lately."

"No; he's sitting on Betsey Small's tail, just about. She won't have him less'n he marries her, and seeing she's the first woman ever stood him off it seems like he just can't stand to come away from her."

"I thought Adam had another girl," said Lana.

"Polly Bowers? Sure, but now she's having a baby, Adam ain't interested in her."

"Sinner," exclaimed Mrs. McKlennar, but she did not say it with the proper moral indignation at all. She was too fond of the hulking, handsome, yellow-haired brute.

"Has anyone talked to the girl?"

"Oh, I did, some. I kind of got the idea she was willing to peddle it out to any father, though she had the belief it was one of them Continentals was in garrison here last year for a spell."

"Well, my land," cried Mrs. McKlennar, "doesn't she know?"

"She said she hoped it was the corporal," Joe replied; "but she's trying to lay it onto Adam and I guess that's why he's hanging on after the Small woman. You know how it is with a man like Adam when he finds a woman has acted inconsiderate like that."

"Uncle Joe," cried Gilly, "it ain't got no head on it yet."

"I know. I'm coming to it when I get to it," said Joe. "Even the Lord had to begin somewhere on a buck. I just ain't so quick. This here's quite a rain. Last Wednesday I was up to Stanwix and the water was getting up close to the sally port. Yes, ma'am, I figure it's going to rain real hard. How long? Three or four days. It'll be a flood."

"How can you tell?"

"Wind's passing through the north. You can hear it on the north side of the roof now."

His Adam's apple bobbled a little as he lifted his lean face.

"When the wind passes through the north to southeast you get a real storm."

"Ain't it de troof," Daisy said dismally.

Lana lifted the steaming kettle from the fire and the rich soup smell was a momentary beneficence in the cabin. They hitched up to the plank that served for a table, Joe last.

"There's your buck," he said to Gilly.

"That ain't a buck," cried the boy.

"Yes it is. It's a good twelve-pointer."

"It ain't. It ain't got no horns at all, Uncle Joe."

Gilly's underlip began to twitch.

"'Tis so a buck," said Joe Boleo. "Ain't you got any sense? Who ever seen a buck with horns this time of year?"

Gilly set the crudely carved animal in front of his plate. He still sniffled to himself, thinking it looked almightily like a sheep; but he ate his soup down. And pretty soon he piped up, "It is a buck, Uncle Joe. I can see now."

Joe looked embarrassed. But Lana smiled and caught Mrs. McKlennar's eye. The two women had small helpings; now they watched the men eat. Four men, Lana thought, sentimentally. Four boys, thought Mrs. McKlennar.

The spatter against the north side of the house swelled to a driving gust, reducing everyone to silence. Then it stopped abruptly, and for an instant everyone listened to the eaves drip outside. But in a moment the wind began again, stronger and steadier, and the rain seemed to come all the way across the valley and strike the cabin like the flat of an enormous hand against the south and east.

"She's beginning now," said Joe. "This valley's going to be a wet place to-morrow, when the river gets hold of it."

Listening to the fall of rain all night, like a voice in the dark that would not hush, Gil wondered whether there would be any seed left in the riverside meadows, supposing the river got as high as Joe thought it would. His ears stretched for a sound of the river; but there was no sound beyond the rain.

Lana, with that strange awareness of things beyond her senses that sometimes came to her, thought of all the places down the valley, tracing the brown swelling course of the river, and thinking how desolate Fox's Mills must look, with its close-gathered houses, now burned. It would be hard on older people like her parents to camp out this way. As hard as it was on Mrs. McKlennar.

Sarah McKlennar managed to keep up her spirits during the day. She was the kind of woman that always reacted well to an audience, and instinctively played her part. But when night came and the babies dropped off and the light faded down on the hearth, she began to think of her house. She hadn't many years left to live, she knew, so it did not matter to her as it did to Lana and Gil, who should have inherited the house along with the place. And it didn't even matter to them as much as it did to the house itself. She imagined it now, the scorched stone walls, blackened and split, under the cold rain, streaking the soot marks—no matter if it was rebuilt the house would always wear scars.

Joe Boleo didn't think at all. He knew enough to sleep, when he had food in his inwards and a warm bed. His snores went up and down as evenly as a pendulum.

The rain fell in a continuous grayness over the valley. In the morning the stockade of the fort, only a couple of hundred yards away, was a brown shadow, indistinct, and without visible life. Lana threw a piece of horse blanket over her head and shoulders and went out with Gil and Joe to look at the valley. As soon as they stepped through the door their ears were greeted by the roar of the West Canada Creek away on their left. The sound was nothing like the usual roar of the rapids that came down through the hills. It was more a deep-toned humming, as though gigantic harpstrings had been stretched from bank to bank. Joe said, "The rocks are covered." He thanked them for his supper and went away to the fort. Gil and Lana proceeded until they could see out across the flat land towards the river.

The Mohawk was as smooth as glass, but the color was changed from gray to a roily brown, and the shape of it was unfamiliar reaching back in spots well south across the fields.

There was nothing on earth a man might do now, except gather firewood and wonder how far the water had risen.

No one had ever seen such a rain. When, on the third day, the wind changed to the southwest and the sky opened towards noon, and the first small space of blue appeared like a vision on the top of Shoemaker hill, they saw the flats half covered by a brown and fluid waste. The hillside streams arched out from the hills and stood like carved dark yellow columns clear in the air. Where the West Canada Creek met the Mohawk was a boiling pot of waters, in which a spruce tree, entire, from tip to roots, revolved with a kind of gigantic dismay.

People felt queerly disturbed to see the sunset reflected where they had planted wheat. Men stood in futile groups along the edge of the flood, tossing out sticks and trying to estimate the force of the current and the effect it would have on the topsoil.

Towards dusk a bateau with five soldiers shot down the main current from the west. The four men at the oars swung it into the quieter water and rowed steadily towards Fort Dayton. They were men from Fort Stanwix, carrying dispatches. The woods, they said, were impassable, but coming by river they had covered the whole distance during the afternoon.

The east and north and south walls of Fort Stanwix had been practically leveled by the flood. The parade was under two feet of water, and there were really no defenses left except the pickets on the outer glacis. If an army could have crossed the woods against them now, the garrison would have had to defend itself in the open. It was obvious that the garrison could not repair the damage.

While the men ate, Bellinger read the letter from Cochran, which confirmed the men's story and added that the officers unanimously recommended the transfer of the Stanwix garrison to Forts Herkimer and Dayton. He did not, however, feel sure that the Albany command would receive this recommendation with any more favor than in the past, and suggested that Bellinger write a letter to the Governor endorsing the transfer.

The bare possibility of a suitable garrison of regular troops in German Flats roused a hope in Bellinger that he had not felt since the beginning of the war. He wrote a long letter to the Governor promising local labor for the erection of suitable barracks and for any other work the army officers might require.

But when the boatload of soldiers departed on the following morning Bellinger felt less confident. He had become painfully aware of Albany's fixed habits of thought about the western settlements.

That afternoon, however, any other possibility was put out of the question by the complete destruction of the remaining fortifications at Stanwix by fire. How it had started no one ever told; why, in the saturated condition of the fort, it had not been got under control, no one ever explained.

2

Return of Marinus Willett

The hope and confidence inspired at German Flats by the arrival of the garrison from Fort Stanwix were short-lived. The Albany command had conceded the necessity of their removal in May; before the first week of June they had withdrawn two companies for the defense of the Hudson Valley. At Fort Dayton were left only a few squads and at Fort Herkimer a Captain Moody with his artillery company of twenty men, and two light field pieces which were mounted on the walls.

Bellinger grimly supervised the spring planting with armed guards of militia. The small group of Rangers were no longer permitted to make long scouts, but were stationed close along the hills. It was not necessary any more to have long warning of a raid. The women and children were kept huddled to the forts, and the farming parties were instantly convertible to armed companies that might either cut their way back to the forts without assistance or, if the raid proved numerically small, attack the destructives in the open.

There was nothing left to destroy; and the parties that turned up early in June were only looking for stray scalps. More than half of the planting of wheat had been buried or washed out by the spring flood, and the spring planting of grain came up in serried patches of buckwheat, barley, and oats, put in as seed had been procured.

Gil Martin had made no attempt this spring to work the McKlennar farm. Most of his wheat had been washed out. The gutted walls of the stone house, the sashless windows, like lipless mouths, were good only to house stray hedgehogs. The empty barn, which had survived the burning of the house, was burned towards the middle of the month. The fire was seen from the two forts during the night, burning sullenly, with a small party of men surrounding it, but no one suggested going out against them.

Then, towards the end of June, as he came back to Fort Dayton from scout duty with Adam Helmer and John Weaver, Gil saw ten mounted Continentals riding east along the Kingsroad. Adam and John remained outside the fort to watch them, but Gil went in to make his report to Colonel Bellinger. While he was yet talking to Bellinger he heard the horses enter the stockade, and a moment later a sentry stuck his head in the door to announce the arrival of Lieutenant Colonel Willett.

It was a still hot evening, and the smoke from the cooking fires drew in through the windows, filling the small room. But Gil saw Bellinger's dark eyes brighten as he got up from the table, and he himself felt a quickening of his heart. Both of them remembered Willett's first arrival at the fort while St. Leger was investing Stanwix four years ago. Willett had come through the Indian lines; and Willett had ridden straight on to Albany to hurry up Benedict Arnold. They had forgotten Arnold in German Flats until the news had come last winter of his attempted betrayal of West Point. But for some reason no one had forgotten Marinus Willett.

"That's all, Martin," Bellinger said. "You can go now."

"There's no need of that, is there?" said the nasal voice from the door. "It's his business as much as yours and mine, Bellinger."

Marinus Willett looked just as they remembered him. The hard small twinkling blue eyes, close above the huge hooked nose, the red face, the square uncompromising shoulders, filled the doorway. As he came up to Bellinger he looked even taller, for Bellinger had the regular farmer's stoop. His large nose sniffed while he shook hands, and he said, "I hope you've got enough extra to feed us, Bellinger."

"I guess we can scrape up something."

"I'm glad to know it. There's lots of places down the valley that can't do that. Even at my headquarters in Fort Plain we haven't anything to drink."

"We've had no likker up here since last October, Colonel." Bellinger stopped himself short. "Your headquarters?" he asked. "What do you mean?"

The blue eyes twinkled.

"They've merged the five New York Continental companies into two, and George Clinton came around and pestered me to come up here and command the Mohawk levies. He said I was going to be my own man and would have a regiment to work with and a couple of companies of regulars now in garrison. With that and the militia—me and you—we're supposed to make this frontier safe." Willett sat down and stared humorously along his nose. "I thought, with that, by God, I could do a lot more than anyone has done so far and I said I'd come. I've been up the valley for two weeks. I've reckoned up the men." He didn't look humorous now, his flat cheeks hardened. "I found Stark had drawn off the two companies: now the British won't buy Vermont, he's scared they'll come and take it for nothing. God damn him."

"God damn all Yankees," Bellinger said fervently.

"God damn the whole shebang. I've got a sore tail. Man, I've been to every stockade and fort between Schenectady and this place like a God-damned census taker, checking the militia list Clinton gave me before I set out. That was the '77 list, Bellinger. There were twenty-five hundred enrolled men. Do you know how many of you there's left?"

"I know that we've lost nearly half of our men in this district," Bellinger said grimly.

Willett nodded his big head.

"There were twenty-five hundred in 1777. Now the total, including yours, is less than eight hundred." He stared at Bellinger and Gil. "That's why I said it was this man's business as much as ours. God, it's a mess. Besides the militia I've got one hundred and thirty levies, in good shape. But I'm responsible for Catskill and Ballston as well as this valley. And I'm sending most of them to those two places and the middle fort in Schoharie. I'll leave Moody and his twenty men in Herkimer. For the rest of the valley I'd rather depend on the militia." Suddenly he grinned widely, showing his large yellow teeth. "Clinton's landed me on you, and, by the Lord, I'm not going to run off now. There's nobody outside the forts, and I can get hold of men fast. We'll do the job, one way or the other. Have you got a pipe around anywhere?"

Bellinger produced a clay, which Willett filled from his own pouch. "I've got a few exempts and a few levies not listed and I'll keep them as my own garrison in Fort Plain and as the centre of any army I get together. This section, though, I'm going to leave to you. I'm not going to call you out, either, to go down the val-ley, but I want you to keep your men handy to join me if I ever come this way."

Bellinger nodded with his usual sombreness. But for the first time in a long while there was a gleam in his eye. "We'll be around. Can you get us a little powder?"

"I've got the Governor's ear. By God, I ought to, after tak-ing on this job! I'll guarantee powder. Food's hard to come by. There's plenty of it in Albany, but the Congress has impounded it for the regular army. Even Heath can't get it for his garrison at West Point. Lord knows what's up. But there's one satisfaction in it—the destructives won't find much to eat when they come this way."

3

The First Rumor

One of Willett's first acts was to impound the best horses at the various forts along the valley for use by his expresses. It had an immensely heartening effect on German Flats to realize that there was someone in the valley who was keeping close touch with them; and the first express to arrive brought news of an irruption in Currietown and Willett's gathering of the militia, his quick pursuit, and total rout of the destructives at Dorlach. For the first time a band of the destructives had actually been caught and licked.

The harvest of their mixed crops in August, after that, was comparatively undisturbed, though there were occasional brushes in the woods when stray Indians attacked the berry pickers.

Another effect of the expresses was the bringing of news from the rest of the country. Willett always included in his dispatches to Bellinger whatever word had come to him. Men began to talk about the war in the south as if it were in some way allied to their own difficulties.

It was strange how that simple illusion had restored their courage. They were not aware of it themselves. They did not know that Willett was raising heaven and earth that fall to get even one company of well-equipped regulars sent up to him. To Governor Clinton he wrote how "the prospect of this suffering country hurts me." He even went over Govenor Clinton's head to General Washington, describing the valley as he had first seen it, and as it stood now. But Washington was meditating his march into the south to join Greene and Lafayette against Cornwallis, and he would not spare a man.

In the Mohawk Valley the fall was early, arriving with a long stretch of northwest weather, small cold showers that pebbled the surface of the river, and day after day of rolling clouds. The roads became heavy, and the expresses, when they traveled, were coated with mud to their thighs.

The corn was stacked about the stockades and the threshing went on in the barns close to the forts, and the winnowed grain was carried into the magazines and stored. Joe Boleo predicted a cold winter that would break early. He did not know why he thought so, when John Weaver tried to cross-examine him; but he had no doubt of it.

They were standing guard on top of the Shoemaker hill, bare to the wind, with the clouds passing over their heads, and occasional showers, which they could see entire from their height, leaving wet trails across the tossing wilderness. The trees were mostly bare, and the forests filled the air with the wintry smell of mouldering leaves. Now and then they saw small flights of duck scudding before the rain.

"Winter's coming," said Joe. "It's getting cold. They hain't ever bothered us none after October, only when Butler went to Cherry Valley."

John was glad to believe him. All day he had been keeping scarcely half a watch. He had hardly felt the cold as he crouched down behind the windbreak Joe had constructed. It seemed to him that his whole being was filled with what Mary had told him that morning about being sure that she was going to have a baby.

He thought he would never forget her; she acted so proud.

"Do you think I should tell your mother, John?"

But he said, "Wait till I come home." He wanted to have time to think. His mother hadn't been herself for two years now. She kept very quiet. Sometimes it seemed to him as though a half of her mind had deserted her when George got taken; for while she did her share of work, she had fits of talking vaguely. She never wept any more as she had at first. Though she was convinced that since they had never heard a word of George he must be dead, it was plain that she could not reconcile herself. Sometimes John used to have the feeling that she was only keeping herself alive until she was sure. Now, he wondered what effect this news would have on her. Rarely, she would have flagrant bursts of temper, when she would try to take a strap to him or Cobus as if they were still children. He didn't want to have her start a thing like that with Mary.

But when John reached the top of the hill and the wind surrounded him, he forgot about his mother and thought only of his wife. He had felt a month before that Mary had something on her mind—apparently she had known then, but she had wanted to be sure. She was sure now. Her face shone with her tidings. She had stood with him outside the door in the cold October sunlight, proud and straight, tilting her thin face to speak over the wind, her eyes beaming on him—he could not tell that at last Mary felt that she had raised herself to his level, nor could he ever know the love and gratitude and pride she had in him.

Instead, with the silent Joe on the hilltop, he had been wondering all day, remembering that time when Mrs. Martin's boy was born: how he had been frightened, how slow the hours had gone by, how dark the night had been. He knew that Mary would laugh at him if she ever suspected how he dreaded it. Her face had been gallant and taut like a flag in the wind when she told him.

It made him think of the first time he had noticed her, in Fort Herkimer: the same thin eagerness in her face, the same anxiety to know what he was thinking. It used to make him feel foolish to think how often he had played with her in Deerfield without being aware. He might so easily never have discovered her at all.

Her face stayed before his eyes so vividly all day; she still seemed so young to him. He thought of her now at different times transformed by the same eagerness: that first time in the fort; and again in the fort when he had taken her up on the sentry walk to break the news of her father's death at Oriskany; and again the cold day when they had walked towards McKlennar's and been married, when Mrs. McKlennar put it up to them both; and again when he had gone away to join the expedition against the Iroquois, and when he had come home; and the day that Bellinger had made him corporal in the Herkimer garrison; and once there in the blockhouse when they were planning their own stone house like the McKlennar house.

Sometimes she had been anxious, sometimes sorrowful, and sometimes overflowing with joy; but always in every part of her he felt her love, her eagerness for their life together, and her pride in him. It made him wonder whether Gilbert Martin, for instance, felt the same way about Mrs. Martin, or whether, like most men, he took his wife for granted. At times John thought there must be something unmanly in feeling the way he did about Mary. He would try to be short with her and resolve not to answer her questions, but on those occasions Mary invariably was quiet. She was a quiet girl anyway. He had no chance to act like other men; and he always found out that he had no wish to once he was with her.

He knew that the coming winter would probably bring more months of short rations, and he did not think that Mary was the sort of woman who could nurse a child. A child needed a lot of food in cold weather. Suppose that it was born in March. But Joe Boleo had just told him that the winter would break early. Suddenly he decided to believe Joe. It would have to be a short winter.

John felt that divine Providence had taken a hand in all his life. His eyes were so rapt that the old woodsman hesitated momentarily before touching his elbow.

"Express coming in from the falls," he said.

John saw the rider driving his horse to a sluggish trot through the sticky going. It was growing dark.

"Come on," said Joe. "We might as well go down."

Mary met him at the door.

"Come in, John. I've got supper ready for you."

She kissed him, putting her thin arms hard about his

shoulders, but her eyes were tender and calm. He supposed that women acted that way.

"I've told Mother," she said softly. "I thought it was best. There may not be much time."

She had closed the door behind them and was leaning against it with her hands clasping the latch. He now saw that she was pale and was watching him with that level regard that invariably stirred him so, as if she were hoarding him up like a treasure.

"Time, Mary?"

He heard his mother rise from the hearth. Emma's gaunt face showed that she had been crying.

"I'm glad she did, John. It's made me happy. I ain't been so happy since when . . . I can't think, hardly. I wish your pa knew of it. Maybe he does."

The door swung open, putting Mary aside, and Cobus entered with some wood.

"I wish they'd let me go too. Can't you make 'em, John? You're a corporal."

"What are you talking about?"

"Gil Martin was here just a short spell ago. He said for you to come up to the fort. Butler's this side of Johnstown heading this way."

It was hard to take it in. Even Joe Boleo had thought that the raiding must be over for the year. John stood for a moment staring from one to the other.

"I guess I'd better go up there," he said.

"Can I go with you, John?"

John turned to his brother.

"You stay here, Cobus. I want to know somebody's looking after Ma and Mary."

Cobus looked down at his feet.

"All right, John."

Emma came up to John and put her arms round him. "We'll look after her while you're away, John. Don't you worry. But come back here before you leave, if they'll let you."

"I will," John promised.

He looked at Mary as he picked up his musket, and she went to the door ahead of him. It had begun to snow. He could see the flakes snared in her hair against the light from the small window.

For a moment neither of them spoke.

Then Mary said, "I told her we'd call the baby after your pa, John. Do you mind? It made her happy."

"I don't mind." He answered without thinking, mechanically. He was thinking of the long marches through the woods with Sullivan's army, in the Indian country. He suddenly shook himself out of it. They wouldn't be going into Indian country. "I think it's fine," he said. "Did she ask you?"

"Oh, no. I just thought of it, when I started telling her."

Mary was silent again.

When she lifted her face her eyes were clear.

"You'd better go up now, John."

She hated for him to go. But she didn't want men thinking John behindhand, now he was corporal.

"Yes," he said. "Good-bye, Mary. I'll try to come back before we leave. But take care of yourself."

"Don't worry about me." She made herself smile, not thinking how dark it was. "I'm tougher than I look. You ought to know that, John."

He leaned over her quickly, kissing her, and turned away towards the dark wall of the fort.

The wind was going down. Already, under the falling snow, a heaped bonfire in the centre of the parade was putting light on the inner walls of the blockhouses. The points of the stockade stood out needlelike and black. John saw men moving in through the snow, carrying their guns under their arms, the muzzles pointed down. The dark tracks they left on the whitening ground were like the gathering of a web towards the open gate.

There was no noise inside the fort, except the crackling of the fire and the mutter of men's voices. When John entered, he found them lining up in companies along the four sides of the parade. They went to their own companies; Demooth's (Demooth was gone, but young Lieutenant Tygert was in command of it) had only twelve men left. John, the corporal, Gil Martin, Boleo and Helmer, the Rangers. Clem Coppernol was not fit for a march. And a few men who used to live in Schuyler; Spankrable and the two Kasts. John moved over to join them, asking Martin in a low voice whether he had heard the news.

"The express came in just a little while before you did. The British have burned Warrensbush and crossed the river to Johnstown. They had six hundred men. Willett chased them. He licked them outside of Johnstown. But they got away. They headed west, north of Stone Arabia. Willett was at Stone Arabia when he sent the express up. He's waiting to find out which way they're headed and he wants us ready to cut them off."

"Willett licked them?"

"Yes, with four hundred."

Gil's thin face looked set and red against the leaping firelight.

Before the fire Bellinger was checking in the militia as they entered the fort. The sentries on the rifle platform stood up over him, half lighted against the snowing night, watching the parade inside as much as the surrounding darkness.

Every now and then a man came forward to the fire with an armful of logs and threw them on the flames. Ten minutes later, after another freshening of the fire, Bellinger closed his book.

The men fell silent. He stood, with his rounded shoulders,

staring back at them. He did not seem to speak loudly, but everyone heard him plainly.

"I guess you know what's happened. Butler's in the valley. Butler and Ross with six hundred men. They ain't just Indians. They're Tories and regulars, trained soldiers. But Willett's licked them with four hundred militia."

The silence continued. But Bellinger did not look as if he expected a cheer or anything like that. He was thinking about things, the way all of them were thinking.

"We've had our farms wiped out. It's been four years. We've had the Butlers down here and we had John Johnson last year, and we've never had a real crack at them since Oriskany. We had Nicholas Herkimer then, and we've got Willett now. And we licked them then."

He was looking at the ground, watching the snow melt back from the fire.

"Willett wants the whole bunch of you ready when he gives the word. I don't know when that's going to be. But last June I promised him we'd have ninety men when he asked for them. I want you all to make sure you got powder and ball. If you ain't filled up, get it to the magazines. I guess we all feel just about the same. Go back to bed when you get done. If I want you to-night I'll let off the gun." He raised his face towards the swivel on the southeast corner. "Bring a blanket with you and the warmest shirt you've got. Herkimer men better stay here in the fort."

He turned his back on them and trudged into his room.

So they weren't to go yet. John drew a deep breath. He had powder enough and ball; he had filled his flask that morning. He heard Gil ask Joe Boleo if he wouldn't come back to the Martin cabin, so he himself asked Adam Helmer to the Weavers'. Adam thanked him, but declined.

Adam had figured that he could perfectly well get over to Herkimer and tell Betsey Small what was going to happen. If the gun went off he could run back long before any body of men could leave the fort.

As he slipped out of the gate he saw Doc Petry stumping back to his office in which he now lived, ate, dispensed, and slept.

Adam trotted down to the river crossing and hopped into a boat and rowed himself over. In thirty minutes he was inside the Herkimer stockade. Five minutes later he had got Betsey out and told her.

They stood in the lee of the church wall.

"Listen, Betsey," he said, "Butler's coming up the valley."

"Yes, Adam," she said quietly. "But what are you doing over here?"

"Oh hell," he said, "can't I do anything to suit you?"

Her voice was slow with the same quiet amusement she always showed towards him.

"A lot of things you do suit me fine. But what do you expect me to do? Cry? Laugh? Kiss you, I expect."

"Kissing's better than nothing."

You could have cut his head off with a feather when she said quietly:—

"All right. Where are you?"

She put her arms around his neck, and Adam locked her in his arms. He gave it to her, but he couldn't even make her gasp. And he had been saving up two years just to give it to her. Beside her, Polly Bowers was like putty. It made him mad, and he started casting his eyes round for a place they could get away to, under cover. You couldn't take a girl out in the snow, somehow; but while he was thinking about it, she had slipped out of his arms.

"There. That ought to suit you."

Adam felt suddenly hurt.

"Betsey!"

"What is it?" She sounded so kind, God damn her, she was probably laughing at him.

"I thought we was just beginning," he muttered. "I was just thinking where we could go."

"I'm not one of your girls, Adam." She laughed softly. "Can't you tell the difference?"

"I can," he said glumly. "What do you want me to do, marry you?"

"You've never asked me."

Adam knew he was a fool to say it.

"All right. Will you marry me?"

"You sound as if you was swearing, Adam. But I will. When you leave me to go horning round the country, I want the law."

As she laughed again, he caught hold of her.

"Come on, where can we go?"

"I'll tell you after we're wedded."

"But we can't get married now."

"Well, then, we can't go anywhere. I'm not taking chances, Adam."

He swore at her, cajoled, pleaded with her; but nothing could shake her amused silence.

"By God. I'll wake the domine."

That jolted her. "You can't do that. You'll make a scandal."

"For God's sake, what do you want me to do?"

He stood like a muddled bear, confronting the snow and darkness. She laid her long hand on his arm. "Poor Adam," she said. Her voice grew sober. "You've promised me, ain't you?"

"Yes."

"You'll marry me when you come back? You'll swear it?"

"I'll swear it. Cross my heart. Honest to God, Betsey."

"I want banns read. I want the whole business. So everybody will know I've got you." She gave a low, delicious laugh.

He didn't answer her with words. He knew now that she was acting like a skittish mare, all along. But he knew that she would hold him to his word. He didn't care. As he reached out for her she put aside his hands. "Come with me."

She led him to the door of the northwest blockhouse. Captain Moody's men were quartered in the other. There was no one here but Moody himself, and he slept on the bottom floor.

She put her hand on Adam's lips. Her fingers felt cold as rifle iron, so cold that he had a sense of heat beneath the icy skin.

"He's deaf," she whispered. "But be quiet."

They stole past the captain's bunk and up the stairs to the loft. The paneless window frames were faintly marked by snow upon the sills. The place was empty and bare and smelled of cold; but when Adam followed her up through the loft she met him quietly. There was a sureness in the way she came to him in the dark. He might have known. And then when he had her she went all soft, shaking as if her soul had gone away from her.

4

The Last Muster

The dawn of October 28 was windless and cold. When Gil got out of bed to start the fire up, the valley was white with snow and all the trees metallic from the frozen mist. The sky was so clear, just before sunrise, that it looked colorless.

There had been no sound from the fort. Lana dressed and moved furtively about the cabin as the first sticks caught.

"Do you think you'll have to go to-day, dear?"

"I don't know," he whispered. "We're waiting to hear from Willett."

After that they were silent. The children, Joe Boleo, Mrs. McKlennar, and the negress lay like logs of wood under their blankets, heads covered for warmth. The paleness of the light dimly entering the paper panes increased the sense of cold and made them look as if they would sleep forever. Crouching down before the tiny fire, side by side, Lana and Gil had this waking moment to themselves, and though they could not talk, they were conscious of each other's nearness. In their unspoken thoughts affection served as well as speech. When, without looking from the fire, Gil put out his hand, Lana's was ready to meet it. They stayed so, watching the fire grow, watching the vapor of their breaths diminish, for several minutes, until the first thin warmth made itself felt beyond the confines of the hearth.

Gil stepped outside for more wood, and then took the bucket and his axe down to the nearest spring. When he had gone, Lana's tears welled up. For an instant she let them come in the sheer luxury of her love; then she wiped them away to smile and take the icy bucket from Gil's red cold fist, and fill the kettle for their morning mush. Again they stayed together till the first faint tinkles of the heating water roused the negress, as any sound of warmth invariably did. Probably she had been awake all along, but fire sounds meant nothing to Daisy unless they were hot enough to cook with. Gil and Lana relinquished each other for the day.

The men left the cabin after breakfast. They found the Herkimer militia already cooking at the fort and Bellinger sorting provisions in the magazine. No word had come in from the east. None came all morning.

But in the afternoon a man who stood watch beyond the Canada Creek ford let off his musket. The men mounted the rifle platforms to look out. During the day the frost had melted from the trees and the limbs were black and wet against the sky and the soft gray indistinctness of the hills. The wind, which had returned more gently towards noon, was carrying a high scud of cloud, shadowing the valley. The universe looked cold and smelled of coming snow.

Underneath, along the straight road, they saw the line of men in double files marching towards them. They walked like tired men. They hunched themselves against the wind which picked at their nondescript clothes, and kept the locks of their muskets under their arms, the barrels pointing forward and down. But their pace kept them moving with a dogged steadiness that had the teams on the three provision wagons reeking to keep up in the half-frozen muddy ruts.

Bellinger let off no cannon salute. There was no powder to spare for salutes, and he knew that Willett wasn't the kind of man that wanted one. The arrival of the weary downriver militia and the entrance to the fort were accomplished in a silence as grim as the gray passing of the day.

Willett went straight to Bellinger's room and called him in. He had discarded his long campaign coat for a woolen hunting shirt and high fur cap; except for his square shoulders he looked like any farmer of militia. But under his fatigue was the inevitable twinkle of the small blue eyes. He wiped the drop from his nose and shook hands.

"I hear you licked them," Bellinger said.

Willett grinned.

"We didn't actually whip them. They ran away. It was too dark for me to chase them." He glanced away from Bellinger. "*We* ran away once. But Rowley took their flank, and, by God, we came back again."

He let himself down on his chair.

"I followed them to Stone Arabia, but they'd struck north of there. I sent a scout after them to see if they were heading for Oneida Lake or straight for Buck's Island through the woods. The scout's to send an express as soon as they find out. So I marched up here. It was hard going. Have you got your ninety men?"

"They're waiting."

"Fine. Got any boys who really know the woods north of here?"

"Yes. Boleo and Helmer do."

"Good. I've got about fifty Oneida Indians under a fat old fool called Blue Back. They turned up after the fighting was over. But I don't want to trust them for scouts."

"Blue Back knows every leaf on the West Canada that's fallen in the last forty years. It's his private hunting ground."

"I'm glad to know it. I'll use him with your two men."

"Do you want me to keep the men belonging to this fort inside? The Herkimer men are staying here."

"Let your men go home. We won't start now before to-morrow. Can you help me out with five days' rations for four hundred men? I've brought along about three hundred, including the Indians."

"I think so."

"One thing more. You're to stay here."

"That's not fair," said Bellinger.

Willett grinned wearily in his face.

"I'm not going to argue. They're orders. Look here, Bellinger. You've got to. If anything goes wrong we've got to leave one man here who knows how to hold on to this land. You've had more practice than me."

Bellinger glowered. "It's a dirty trick, Willett."

"If you think you're going to lose credit, you needn't worry.

Nobody's going to get credit going with me. I'm supposed to be turning up at Ballston to protect Albany from Ross and Butler."

"I don't give a damn about the credit, Willett. I just want to get at them once and see some of them knowing they're licked."

"I know," said Willett quietly. "I wish I had a drink."

"Verdammt! You'll have it then, for not stealing my medical supply."

Both men turned round to confront Dr. Petry, who held a small keg in both arms as a man might hold a baby on his chest. He peered at them for a moment through his bushy eyebrows, then advanced to set the keg on the table in front of Willett.

"'For wounds and surgical needs,'" he read the label. "Well, I'm prescribing now. A little glass apiece—and one for the doctor, Peter. I'd get a hemorrhage watching you drink if I didn't have some too."

John had gone home again—the second time after he had said good-bye—and he felt foolish about it. He was beginning to think that maybe after all the army would not march. But the way Mary's face lit up when he came through the door dispelled all his uneasiness.

He told them at supper the extraordinary news that Willett had brought with him, that General Washington had taken his army south to confront Cornwallis in Virginia. They had no idea, any of them, what it could mean; but Gil Martin had heard Willett telling Bellinger in a very excited way, as if it were a tremendous thing for Washington to have done.

Cobus's eyes glistened.

"Next year I'm going to 'list with the army," he said.

John laughed.

"Enlist for what? A drummer boy?"

Cobus's face was still a round one, and now the sullenness of it on top of his skinny body made even Emma smile.

She said to him, "Don't you mind John. I'll let you go, next year, if you want to. But come along with me now."

"Where?"

"I want to visit with Mrs. Volmer."

"I don't want to go. What do I have to for, anyway?"

Mrs. Weaver took him firmly by the hand. "You come along." She said from the door, "We'll be down there for a couple of hours."

As she closed the door, John smiled at Mary. Both of them realized that Emma had never been a special friend of Widow Volmer.

"Ma's making up," John said. "She'll go on making up to you now all her life. You'll see."

Mary said loyally, "She's been good to me ever since we got married, John."

It made him deeply happy.

The wind was not strong enough to make the cabin cold when the fire drew so well. They were like an old married couple sitting side by side upon the hearth, John thought, and he said, "You ought to have some fleece to spin."

Mary smiled. She had been thinking the same thing. She would not need much wool.

"You with a pipe and reading out of a book to me."

"I never read very good," John said.

"You would if you practised at it. My pa used to read real fine. I think he read better than Mr. Rozencrantz. . . ."

Her face stilled with her voice. But even memory of Christian Reall's death at Oriskany could not deprive them of their contentment at having the cabin to themselves. All that was long ago; and John had a queer sense of the three of them sitting there.

"Suppose it's a girl, how can we name it after Pa?"

Mary said, "I knew a woman named Georgina once."

"Why, yes," said John.

The fire popped and sparked and they watched the exploded coal gradually glimmer out on the damp dirt floor.

"Do you suppose that battle down in Johnstown means this war is getting over, John?"

"I don't know. It's only a little battle the way they think of things, I guess. Not like Burgoyne's army. Nor not like General Washington's in Virginia. I guess down there they don't think it's much."

"I mean, would it end the war up here, John?"

"I don't know. I guess not."

She said, "It would be nice, wouldn't it? We could live in our own cabin. Have you figured where it would be, John?"

"Why, I guess we'd go back to Deerfield on Pa's place."

"I'd like that. It used to be nice there."

"Yes," he said.

She lifted her face and looked across at him. She smiled with her eyes. She felt so still, watching his intent face studying the fire. It didn't matter in a moment like this what you said, so long as you talked softly. . . .

The express from Stone Arabia arrived in the darkness before dawn; the horse dead lame and the man's hands so cold he could hardly let loose the bridle reins.

He brought the scout's dispatch. Butler and Ross had taken a circle straight north. The scout thought they must have got lost. Now they were heading west so far above the valley he thought they surely must be striking towards Buck's Island.

Willett and Bellinger, shivering in their drawers, read it in the light of the coals.

"Where would they hit the Creek?" Willett asked.

"I guess about twenty miles north. Blue Back could probably tell you, or Joe Boleo, but Joe's sleeping out."

"Let's get Blue Back."

A sentry routed out the Indian, bringing him in, blinking his sleepy eyes and hugging himself with his blanket. "How," he said to Bellinger, and then to Willett, "How? I fine."

Immediately he squatted in front of the fire where the heat drew an unholy smell from him, and lighted the greasy rounds of his brown cheeks with shiny moons.

Bellinger explained while Blue Back slowly rubbed his belly underneath his shirt and fetched up silent belches one by one.

"Where do you think they'd cross, Blue Back?"

"Indians lost," said Blue Back. "Senecas, Mohawks, no damn good. Get lost. White men go for Fairfield. Make find Jerseyfield road."

"I think he's right," Bellinger said.

"Sure," said Blue Back. "Ask Joe Boleo."

"How far north is that?" Willett asked.

"One day."

"How many miles?"

"One day," Blue Back repeated with firm politeness.

Willett gave up.

"Do you think we can find the army up there?"

"Sure yes," said Blue Back. "Like rum. Like drink."

"I haven't any likker."

"Sorry," said Blue Back. "Walking bad. More snow."

"What time is it?"

Bellinger replied.

"About five."

"We'll have daylight enough in about an hour. You'd better get your men."

As Bellinger went towards the door, Blue Back asked anxiously, "Shoot cannon?"

Bellinger grinned stiffly, nodded, and went out. He felt the cold against his empty belly.

Willett said, "You better get back to your boys and cook breakfast."

"Stay here," said Blue Back quietly. He drew his blanket over head and hat and crouched beneath it, motionless as a dormant toad beneath a basswood leaf.

When the swivel thudded, he gave one convulsive flop, but he did not emerge until he heard Bellinger shouting in the parade. Then he poked out his head and eyed Willett dubiously.

"You take cannon?"

Willett shook his head impatiently.

"Fine," said Blue Back, standing up. "I go too."

The muster was as silent a business as the arrival on the afternoon before. The men entering the fort from the surrounding cabins were told to return for their breakfasts and report in half an hour. The men cooking over the open fires in the parade had little to say. The feeling of winter hung in the air. The sky was lustreless. The wind drew steadily from the north, and though they did not feel it in the shelter of Fort Dayton, they could hear its voice in the woods.

Gil and Joe Boleo ate together with Lana and Daisy waiting on them, and the two little boys, staring like owls, pressed close together across the hearth where they had been told to stay. Their fascinated eyes had watched their father and Uncle Joe oiling their rifles; they had seen the yet more wonderful operation of Joe whetting his knife and Indian hatchet on a stone, sinking the edges into the board table when he was satisfied. He ate between these implements, knife to right and tomahawk to left. The hinges of his jaw worked visibly and audibly in the thin leather above his cheeks. Only occasionally his eye slid round towards the children's solemn faces.

There was a hush in the cabin; partly from the belly-shrinking cold, partly from the thinness of the dawn light, which made one wish to yawn; partly from the anxiety in Lana's eyes that seemed to have affected Mrs. McKlennar as well as Daisy. The widow lay on her low hemlock bed with her coat still thrown over her blankets. Her long pale face was tilted forward awkwardly by her hands behind her head. She had not even a snort this morning, nor a single caustic word to relieve her feelings. But when Gil and Joe got up she said, "Come kiss me, Gil."

Gil got down on his knees on the floor to kiss her and she took one hand from behind her head. Her fingers seemed fleshed with ivory.

"Good-bye, lad," she said. Then, "Good-bye, Joe."

Joe took off the hat he had just put on and said, "Good-bye, ma'am." He turned to Daisy. "When I get back I want one of them hot pones."

Then the two men at last came to the two boys, and Gil kissed them and Joe tossed them once in the air.

They went out through the door with Lana following them, huddling her clothes about her against the cold. The door closed for a moment, then Gilly yelled, "Uncle Joe!" He had been watching that knife and tomahawk all along. When Joe put in his head and saw them, he said, "How'd I come to do that?" He closed the door behind him and put them in his sheath and belt and said to Gilly, "I ought to have you along with me to look after me."

He hesitated with his hand on the doorlatch and met Mrs. McKlennar's eye.

"You've got a good heart, Joe."

Joe blushed brick red and bolted.

The men marched off over the thin snow side by side. Lana, her face all pinched against the cold, watched their bodies merge among the tree trunks, and then pass round the corner of the fort. She put her hand to her mouth. It felt frosty where Gil had kissed her. A few snowflakes, hard as shot, drove scatteringly after them.

The muster in the parade was performed quietly. Willett and Bellinger stood side by side. Once Willett shouted, "I want no dead pans. Keep your priming covered." The men formed lines, holding their rifles under their arms. They kept shifting from foot to foot with the cold. The dim light and the snow ran the assorted faded colors of their clothes into one indistinguishable muddy brown.

Bellinger said, "Every man carries his own rations."

The rations were passed out and folded inside the blankets and the blankets strapped to the backs.

"We're going to march fast," Willett said quietly. "No straggling. Any man we leave behind will have to look out for himself."

For one cold moment more he spoke to Bellinger. Then he called for Demooth's company.

Young Lieutenant Tygert stepped forward, followed by the twelve men. Willett looked them over.

"You boys are to be our advance. I want Helmer, Boleo, and Martin to step forward." They did so. For an instant Willett eyed Helmer's huge bulk; what he thought of him was impossible to tell. "Better have one more. Name one," he said to Martin.

Gil never knew why he called for John. He had not seen him; perhaps it was because John and Mary had been on his mind. As John stepped forward, Willett said, "You look pretty young."

John saluted, and Bellinger said over Willett's shoulder, "Corporal Weaver served with General Sullivan."

"You'll do," Willett said without changing expression. "I want you four men to scout ahead. I'm telling you before the army that Ross and Butler are running away. We're going to try and head them. They've still got more men than we are, but they're running. Blue Back, the Indian, says they'll head for Fairfield."

Joe, characteristically holding his rifle by the muzzle and resting his chin on his hands, nodded. "They'll head for the Jerseyfield road and pass Mount's mill. That takes them on the upper trail across the West Canada, to strike the Black River. Where do you want to hit them, General?"

Willett did not bat an eye.

"I leave it to you where. I want to hit them, that's all."

"We'd better cross the Crick this side of Schell's Bush, by the shallow ford, and then we'll hit for Jerseyfield. Better pick up their trail than take a chance they'll get lost again."

"It's up to you," said Willett. "Strike your own pace, but make it a fast one. We'll keep up. Good-bye, Bellinger."

He shook hands, picked up his rifle, and followed Demooth's company through the gates. Outside they were joined by the fifty Oneidas. These, it was arranged, should screen the flanks, but Blue Back, beaming and saying, "How!" joined the four men at the head. He trotted along with a paunchy jounce, covering the ground as fast as Adam and going as quietly as Joe. Gil and John found themselves pressed to keep up.

They rapidly drew away from the main force, along the Schell's Bush road, and for fifteen minutes held the pace. Then Joe lifted his hand. They jogged more comfortably. The first burst had warmed them, and they thought that the men behind would be a long time getting warm. There was not enough snow to keep the frost from getting at your feet.

"We won't spread out till after we've got over the ford," said Joe.

They jogged along in single file. First Joe, making pace, then Blue Back padding in his tracks, then Gil, then John. Adam, hitching up his blanket, came easily in the rear, swinging his big shoulders and humming to himself.

5

The Two Camps in Jerseyfield

The West Canada Creek rolled down through the hills, opaque and brown and swift, a thigh-deep flood even on the shallow ford. It thrust against them icily as they worked their way across holding each other with their left hands, their right hands keeping their rifles over their heads. Adam stemmed the current for them, surefooted, solid as a rock.

The five men jogged into the woods to make a short circle. Finding all clear, Joe brought them back to the ford. A few moments after their return they saw Lieutenant Tygert lead the advance down to the water's edge. "Tell him they better cut poles and march across in squads," Joe said to Adam. Adam lifted his stentorian voice just as Willett's long red face appeared. In a moment, unheard across the rushing water, they saw the men take hatchets to the nearest maple saplings.

The snow was thickening, falling with a steady slant into the current of the stream as if it urged it onward. On the pointed hills, the pines were swaying their boughs against the sky.

Joe sniffed the air.

"It's making up," he said. "We'd better not get too far ahead." He turned to the Indian. "How about it, Blue Back?"

Blue Back, the only one of them who had not started shivering, grunted. He said his Indians would keep track of them, and pointed. Already two groups of Indians were trotting down from the flanks and taking to the water one behind the other.

"All right," said Joe.

He trotted off, keeping along the eastern shore of the creek, following a trail that was little more than a deer run. He kept Gil and John with him and sent Adam and Blue Back out to right and left.

All morning they trotted into the blinding snow, winding back and forth to find the easier going, but always going north.

At noon they halted briefly to build a fire and soften some salt beef in Joe's small kettle, fishing out the meat with sticks, swallowing the hot lumps whole and feeling them in their bellies, and taking turns at the resulting broth. The Indian and Adam drifted in through the snow while the three were finishing, and Adam cooked his own food. The Indian huddled in his blanket and gnawed a piece of quitcheraw, but accepted a drink or two from the kettle afterwards. While they were still at it, Joe sent John up a tree to see out over the woods, and he reported smoke visible in the south.

"They're keeping close just like Willett promised. That man has got the makings of a regular timber beast." Joe tilted his face and yelled, "Look north!"

They watched John edge around the tree trunk, but after a minute he shouted down that he could not see anything against the snow.

"They wouldn't be this far south," Joe said. "Come down, John."

They left their little fire to be put out by the snow, which was now beginning to drift. The going became heavier, and they dropped to a much slower pace. By four o'clock they were coming out on the black moss country that stretched from above Fairfield to the Mount's Creek Valley.

The wind swept over these uplands unhindered except by small stands of poplar. As the men stood with their shoulders to the storm, the snow appeared to drive horizontally past their eyes. They had to shout when they wanted to make themselves heard.

"We can't find them to-night," Adam shouted.

Blue Back shook his head, and Joe said, "This snow would cover their tracks in twenty minutes the way it's drifting."

The wind was hitting the flats so hard that it lifted the fallen snow in clouds that disappeared in the air like blown dust. The shirts of the men were already stiff and white with it.

Gil and John, less hardened to woods running than the other three, stood side by side, fighting for their breath. Gil thought the boy looked cold. "All right?" he said close to his ear.

John turned his head. The snow had whitened his eyebrows and lashes. His thin pale cheeks suddenly shot up spots of color.

"Yes," he yelled, and once more turned his face into the wind. Gil looked north. It was getting dark—not dark exactly. He had not been conscious of the fading of light. Instead the whiteness of the storm appeared to increase, draw closer, causing an illusion of emptiness in the land beyond it.

But now as he looked with John he had a glimpse of the conical tops of hills, revealed for a moment between the snowstorm and the sky. Blue Back also saw them.

"Mount's Creek up there," he said.

Then the hills were shut off from view.

Joe yelled, "I think we'd better go back. We'll catch Willett in that stand of spruce. It's the only good place to camp."

As they turned, Gil thought he heard voices. They came from the northwest, very faintly. For an instant they sounded to him like lost men calling for help. Then the wind raised itself against his hearing, and there was only that and the hiss of drifting snow, which was a part of it.

But the old Indian was standing still with his flat nose to the north.

"What's up, you dumb fool?" Joe asked.

"Wolves."

"You heard wolves?"

"Hear 'em plenty."

Joe said, "Come on. We can tell Willett we've found Butler."

As he went over the edge of the flats, and the wind leaped off into space above their heads, he said, "Wolves like that must be tagging the army."

He plunged down the slope, knee-deep in the loose snow. John followed him, walking very erect, and the rest kept to their tracks.

They discovered the militia, a brown attenuated streak against the whiteness, slowly pressing towards them. The Indians had fallen in close on either flank.

Joe found Willett marching near the rear guard.

"You better camp, General."

"Why?"

"Can't camp on the flats. No shelter. There's a good spruce stand off on your left. It's out of the wind. We've found Butler up ahead."

"Found him? How far?"

"We don't know exactly where. But we'll let you know before morning." He paused. "You can't tackle an army in a storm like this, mister. Hell, you'd be shooting yourselves half the time."

"All right," said Willett. "Go ahead."

Joe led the way to the spruce woods, where the militia set to breaking off dead limbs. The fires burnt hot under the dark trees, first dull spots of red against the white sheen of snow; then, as they reached upward, creating their own light, and forcing back the storm. The men cut saplings, and piled on lengths of wood while others started sticking up spruce-limb shanties. A little brook served them for water. They lay around on the snow under their shanties, watching the snow melt away round the fires, listening to the hiss, and the crackle of burning. Beyond the confines of the woods they could yet see in the last daylight the driving passage of the snow; but in the woods the flakes descended easily, making a watchful pattern against the darkness, or occasionally a burst came down directly, swishing over the fir branches, leaving in its wake released boughs waving, oddly black.

As soon as he had eaten, Joe Boleo rounded up Blue Back and a couple of Oneidas. The four went over to the shanty under which Willett sat wrapped in his blanket—only his fur cap showing. Joe prodded him.

"General."

Willett's long red face emerged.

"We're starting now," said Joe. "We'll find out where they be and what they look like. We ought to be back before midnight."

"Good luck."

The four figures disappeared beyond the firelight with complete suddenness, as if they had walked through a blank wall. As soon as they were out of sight, Blue Back took the lead. Even Joe admitted that the old fellow knew this country better than any other man alive. Having heard those wolves, he would be able to walk straight to where they had been.

They climbed out of the spruce hollow and got the wind in their faces on the barren flats. It was too dark to see whether the storm were slacking, but the loose-blown snow stung them, and they took a slow hunching pace.

They went perfectly straight for more than two miles through the darkness, seeing nothing, hearing nothing, not even each other, not even themselves. The wind was piercing cold.

Joe had a general idea of where they would come out, and as soon as they entered the woods he realized that Blue Back had struck the Black Creek Valley. They dropped down a long slope of rough going with the snow in places well over their knees, crossed the creek on a huge fallen ash. It was uncanny the way Blue Back had come out within a hundred yards of that ash bridge.

The woods were heavier on the far side, and the wind was a

lofty sound in a higher sky. Under it they heard the wolves following the hills to the north. Blue Back stood still for a long time
listening to them. Then he turned his direction a little westward
and went on.

Joe knew exactly where he was when they broke into the
next shallow valley. The creek ran out of the woods on his right,
broken over rapids, a quick-running black rough water. They
crossed it on the remains of a dam. On the far side they caught
their feet on square timbers under the snow.

"Mount's mill," grunted the Indian.

A little way beyond was where the barn had stood in which
Mount's two youngsters had been scalped so soon after Oriskany.

Blue Back trotted into the woods above the place and then
swung down the valley, due west. The howling of the wolves was
now closer and above them.

Suddenly Blue Back halted. He stood still as a post. Behind
him the woodsman and the two Indians were motionless. Barely
discernible, two shapes broke clear of the darkness, themselves
embodiments of it, and slipped away.

"Jesus, they're getting bold," thought Joe.

Ten minutes more of cautious feeling forward showed them
the first campfires.

No one was standing sentry in the storm. The fires made a long
line through the woods, and the men lay close to them, sprawled
out; many of them had lain still so long that their blankets were
whitened by the snow. In the largest part of the camp, three or
four horses huddled together, lifting their heads and snorting at
the scent of wolves. But the men paid no attention to them.

The whole place, but for the horses, seemed to sleep. It was a
sleep like death, as if the snow that fell on them were a drug they
had had too much of.

But while the three Indians and Joe watched, they saw a man stir in one of the shelters, shake off the snow from his blanket, and rise. His face was haggard. His green and black, stained uniform and his leather skullcap on his unclubbed black hair identified him to Joe. He could have picked him off then, and got safe away without trouble, but Willett wanted to hit the army, not Butler.

The man's eyes passed over where the four scouts stood, swept the camp. They saw his lips move. He walked to the edge of the firelight and bent down and prodded a snow-covered shape with his sword. The man lurched over, rose, and lifted his hand, and Butler struck him with the flat of the sword and drove him out to his sentry post.

The man was a Highlander. The knees under the kilt were black as chilled beef. He looked pathetic and wild, shivering, with the icy musket in his hand, confronting the woods, the wind, and the wild voices of the wolves.

He was within a hundred yards of Joe, but he saw neither Joe nor the Indians. What he saw, no one could tell. His eyes were opened inward on his own thoughts.

For a few moments more the four watched Butler go down the camp, beating out the delinquent sentries, indomitably, patiently, wearily, forcing them to posts. Then the scout backed slowly off. The two younger Indians followed reluctantly. There was easy scalping material around that camp. They knew it—as the wolves knew it.

Blue Back took a straight overland course directly to Willett's camp, where Joe roused the colonel.

"Come in here," said Willett. "It's warmer."

Joe sat down beside the colonel and made his report. "They're only three miles north and they look played out. I couldn't see that they carried much food, General."

"Eating their horses as they go along," commented Willett. "We'll go for them before sunrise to-morrow. You've done fine, Major."

Joe grinned.

"I seen Butler," he said. "He was the only man with gimp to put the sentries out."

Willett nodded.

"I told him once he was going to be hung," he said. "After Oriskany. We've been far apart since then."

"I could of killed him easy."

6

John Weaver

The militia camp began to come to life at the dusk hour before dawn. The low fires were replenished. The men moved stiffly, semi-animate, with the cold in their bones. It was still dark in the spruce woods. They ate briefly of boiled beef thickened with cornmeal. Then Willett called them together.

"The enemy's three miles in the northwest. We'll follow our same formation till we hit them. The levies will follow me to the centre. The rear guard break along their south flank. They'll probably try for the West Canada. We want to turn them into the woods."

Helmer, Boleo, Blue Back, Gil, and John Weaver found themselves again in the advance. When they came outside the spruces, they found that the snow for the time being had stopped falling. But the heavy leaden clouds were still in labor over the shadowless land. The cold felt damper with the snow withheld. The breaths of the advancing brown militia crossing the white upland clung to their faces white as cotton. Behind them the beaten path of their feet stretched to the edge of the valley from which they had risen.

It took them an hour to reach the camp site of the enemy; but the enemy had moved as early as themselves. The trail they had broken was like a wide road through the woods. Ahead along the hills the wolves still howled, marking their place.

Willett jogged up to the front.

He formed parties. The Indians split again and went ahead wide on either flank, two horns to the main body of the militia. Like eyes before the head, the same scouts were advanced for contact.

"We've got a beaten path," said Willett. "I want you boys to take their rear guard as quick as you can. We'll be right after you."

The march was now a steady run in the beaten track of the army. Even so it was an hour before the scouts first came up with the enemy's rear.

John Weaver found himself on the right, with old Blue Back half a dozen yards beyond him. In spite of the hard going and the fast pace, he did not feel quite warm. He could not get his mind on the business properly. The white woods seemed to blur before his eyes, trees swimming together, and his mind kept turning to home.

His first awareness of the enemy was a loud yell from Blue Back. He lifted his head dully to see the Indian flop on his belly in the snow, and, looking over him, he saw half a dozen men in red plaid kilts trot out of a clump of trees. He could not realize what it meant for a moment. His head was full of wonder. He had just thought how it would be if George Weaver were not dead after all, if he were to come home and find a grandson named after him. It was the last thought John ever had. One of the Highlanders had heard the old Indian's warning yell. He turned, sighted the standing boy, lifted his rifle, and fired. The ball struck John square in the chest. He jumped straight up, like a deer, clear of the ground.

As he heard the rifle shot, Gil whirled towards it and broke out of the underbrush to see John pitch upon his face. Blue Back fired at the same instant. The belly-filling roar of the brown musket brought a snow load down from the nearest tree. Two clouds of black smoke wavered a little way apart. But the Highlander was not dead. He lay on a doubled leg. His comrades were like a pack boring into the woods.

As Gil stopped beside John, Blue Back humped forward through the snow. The scalp yell broke from his old throat with an unaccustomed quaver. Gil knelt down beside John. But John was dead as he lay, full pitch in the snow, covering his own blood. At the same instant the cry of the Highlander was drowned by a deep roar behind them all. The militia came through the woods in a brown wave. They passed on the dead run, without much order. And after that first yell they were silent. The battle had begun. Gil was picked up by the mass of men and carried forward, leaving John where he was. He had a glimpse of Blue Back beside the dead Highlander, sticking the wet scalp in his belt and lurching into his fat waddle. Then they were in the woods and taking running shots at the army ahead.

The hostile army never stopped. When a man fell he was pushed aside. Feet trod him into the snow. The rear guard of Highlanders was picked up by the militia and surrounded and disarmed, but the main force continued as if they had heard nothing.

They trotted in two files, making for the creek. A little before the valley was reached, the snow began again. And on the near side of the West Canada, Walter Butler rallied the Rangers. They made a stand. It held long enough to let the army get across. The Rangers plunged in, swimming and being carried down where the two units of Oneidas waited hanging over both banks with their hatchets ready.

But the militia were not to be stopped. They surged down the bank and into the water just as Butler lifted his exhausted horse on the far bank. In a volley of shots he was seen to pitch. The horse flung out on the shore, shook him off, and went galloping after the army, raising wet clots of snow. A couple of Indians coming up the bank found Butler, scalped him where he lay, and passed after the horse.

The snow came thicker. The militia, who had crossed, broke into the woods. All morning they followed the fleeing army, picking them off like driven hares. None of them stopped except to fling their blankets off, then their guns. Finally it seemed as if half the British were running unarmed, west and north, on their blind trail towards the Black River Valley.

It was a little after noon that Willett finally worked to the head of the militia and stopped them fifteen miles beyond the Canada Creek. They stopped from exhaustion as much as from obedience, leaning on their guns in the falling snow and staring westward past the colonel over the wintry wilderness where the disrupted path of the beaten army still bore witness to their panic. Slowly a grin passed from Willett to the men.

The job was done at last. They had not captured the army, but everyone seemed to know that Butler was killed; and everyone knew what would happen to a foodless army in full rout, half armed, in eighty miles of pathless woods.

They turned slowly back, not talking, not keeping ranks, trudging for home. Along the way they saw the Oneidas reaping a harvest of scalps that was beyond the dreams and legends of all Indian history. They left them to their bloody work.

The militia reached West Canada Creek again a little before dark and pushed forward for four miles more on the back track. During the evening, Gil tried to find John Weaver's body. But it was not until Blue Back joined him that they found it. It had not been touched, for the wolves had passed on ahead at the first shooting and were now waiting the completion of the Oneidas' work. Gil found stones and brush to build around the body before it became dark.

The march home went quickly. They came over the ford at Schell's a little before sunset and reached Fort Dayton just at dark. Willett let them fire a full round of shots; and then for the first time they cheered. They saw the women rushing out. They saw the torches waving. And then, with unexampled extravagance, Bellinger let off a salute of four cannon. It nearly graveled poor old Blue Back, until he remembered that he had taken scalps himself. He twisted the hair round the muzzle of the ancient musket and started a crazy screeching which his Indians imitated. But they were hardly heard.

They streamed together into the fort, past the women and children, who began sobbing and crying with them, and rushing into the marching men to join their husbands.

Bellinger stood beside the gates. He kept yelling something. Yelling and yelling. Nobody heard for a while. Then Willett entered and met him. They talked for an instant. Willett's face blazed and went white. He jumped up on the blockhouse ladder and set off a swivel over their heads.

For an instant silence settled with the smoke. Through it his nasal voice came down.

"General Washington's taken Cornwallis in Virginia!"

It came to them all slowly. So slowly that Gil, with Lana under his arm, for an instant forgot. Then he saw Mary Weaver passing from group to group, her eyes searching every face with a stilled panic. He said something to Lana, and both of them moved after Mary.

She lay on her bed without crying. It was Emma who cried. The night was still at last. And the snow fell over the Mohawk without wind. Gil, Lana, and Joe Boleo stayed with them, helpless and wordless.

At his table in Bellinger's room in the fort, Willett was wearily writing his dispatch. He had got through with it. The invasion of Warrensbush, the fight at Johnstown, the loss of the enemy's trail, the sally north from German Flats, the chase through the woods, the bloody crossing of the Creek, Butler's death, only one American killed. He ought to say something to show why he did not capture the army.

He rested his long face on his left hand and finally wrote:—

In this situation, to the compassion of a starving wilderness, we left them. . . .

X

LANA (1784)

Lana brought the stool to the kitchen door for ten minutes' rest. With Gil away she had so much work to do in caring for the farm that these few minutes before the boys brought the cows in for milking were like a gift from God. The baby was asleep in the cradle with a rag over her to keep the flies off. It was a bad season for flies. So much wet, and then the midsummer heat that had brought the wheat on very fast. Too fast, Gil believed; he was afraid of rust. But the corn had thriven as they had never seen corn thrive before.

When they had returned to Deerfield a year ago, their hearts sank at the way berry vines and scrub brush had encroached on their cleared acres. Yet they had ploughed easily. In one season, Gil had restored all the land they had originally worked, and this summer it was under crops, with the corn in a brand-new lot.

The new cabin stood on the site of the old. It looked like the old cabin from the road, but the end that pointed towards the spring had an extra section in which Gil and Lana and the baby slept, while the two boys occupied the loft over the kitchen. The barn also was larger, for they had two cows and two calves; and instead of the old brown mare, which they had had to kill for food the year after the West Canada Creek battle, they now had a yoke of oxen. The oxen had seemed to them the first material evidence of their future prosperity—even to Lana, who longed for a boughten bed with cords and a feather mattress. She no longer slept as easily as she used to. Her back was apt to pain her after a full day's work from four to nine, as when she had to help get in the hay before a rain and leave her household work till after dark. But the boys helped now, raking, and fetching down the baby at her feeding hours, and saving their mother the walk back to the cabin. The oxen had cost Gil seventy dollars and the big cart thirty dollars more. He had had to borrow from Mark Demooth to make up half the price, so that they had a mortgage on the place; but that would be taken care of partially by back militia pay and the indemnity for the first burning of their farm when Congress started meeting claims. It was hard for them to have to wait so long when down in Ulster and New York claims were already being settled; but Mr. Yates had explained to Gil that it was a question of votes and that when the new western county became politically important they would be paid surely. It was a matter of being patient.

It was hard for Gil to be patient. If he had had that pay, he could have bought the black girl Klock offered to sell him the week he went after the oxen. Klock's asking price was only a hundred and fifty dollars. To-day, Lana was inclined to share Gil's bitterness. With a girl to do the cooking and help with the cheese, she would have felt quite fresh for to-night's milking.

She did not resent Gil's absence. She had urged him to it. It was the fulfillment of a long-standing promise to take Mary Weaver into the woods and find John's grave. Lana loved Gil for being willing to take time off. They had left four days ago with old Blue Back, who swore he could go straight to the spot. . . .

The Weavers had returned to Deerfield at the same time as Mark Demooth. George and Demooth had been released from prison a year ago, and though George's ankles had been so burned from fetter sores that he was not able to do heavy field work, the Weavers, due to young Cobus's labors, had done as well as the Martins had. Of course, neither family could afford hired help like Demooth. He employed a young man and his wife, in Clem Coppernol's place, and the woman's sister, a pretty girl, whom Emma Weaver thought Demooth might marry even though she was not in his class.

"A durn sight better wife than the first, she'd make," said Emma.

Emma worked like a man. Though her bodily vigor seemed to have increased since George's return, she had become a fussy woman. Fussy over George, and yet more fussy over Mary and John's daughter, Georgina. At times it got on Mary's nerves, the way Emma interfered to spoil the child. But Mary was grateful for the kindness. She had grown into a fine, full-bosomed woman, whom Lana wished John might once see again—it was so unexpected. And it seemed tragic to her that those two should have had each other and been parted before the arrival of Mary's late beauty.

Just before she set out with Gil and the smelly old Indian, who was again pestering their farms as he had in the old days, with four black-eyed little brats trailing him into idle mischief, Mary had heard from her mother that she and her new husband, Rebus White (they had been married as soon as Mrs. Reall drew her indemnity from Congress), were planning to come west to the old Reall place and rebuild the mill. Deerfield would seem then as if it had never been destroyed.

It had not been hard for Gil and Lana to make up their minds to this return to Deerfield; there had been no other place for them to go to. Both Lana's parents had been killed in the wiping out of Fox's Mills. Only her married sister was left alive of her whole family.

As to the McKlennar farm, they had discovered, when Mrs. McKlennar died in the spring of '82, that her will must have burned in the house. So they had no legal title to the place. When they filed a claim, they were informed that the farm was forfeited for unpaid taxes and that their claim would be considered along with others. The man who succeeded in acquiring McKlennar's was a man from Springfield, Massachusetts, a Mr. Jonathan Allen, a decent man, they were told, though they had never seen him. For when Gil was informed that his claim had been refused in favor of an army veteran for unpaid service to his country, he had packed up his family and come straight to Deerfield. As it was, it had been a hard struggle to meet the taxes. Lana had shared Gil's bitterness then; but soon she had got over it. Here there were no pushing Yankees to remind you that the organized army and the New England states had seized the reins of government. Here she could be reminded of her first arrival as a bride, how she had been afraid of its dreariness and emptiness. Now it seemed sweet to her in the rare moments when she found leisure to look out at it.

She lifted her head to listen for the two cowbells up Hazenclever hill. But there was no sound yet, and she realized how cows hid themselves away in swampy places on these hot days. She rested her head against the doorsill, without fear of Gilly's getting lost. He was uncanny in his knowledge of the place. She felt quite safe about him and Joey.

The late afternoon sun poured over her. She was not disturbed by its heat. She loved it, when she could be still in it. It seemed as though her body never could get enough warmth after those last cold winters. How the children had survived those damp cabins she never knew.

As she rested her head, her hair, brushed back above her ears to the big low knot behind her head, showed silver wings. But her face was still young, in spite of the lines that marked her cheeks, and her mouth retained its tenderness. Only the lids of her closed eyes were thinner, and faintly brushed with a brown shadow like a stain. . . .

In the complete stillness of the afternoon a hammering to the south broke out like the sound of a woodpecker on a tree. But Lana did not lift her head. She let the comforting sound drift into her. She knew what it was. People were building over the Mohawk River beyond the fording place. Several people. She had not met them yet, though Gil had gone over one Sunday with Demooth and reported that they were Connecticut men. But he liked one of them, a sensible, law-abiding man named Hugh White. There would be a town there pretty soon, Gil thought, and they would have neighbors.

Now she heard the cowbells coming down through the woods, and after a while she saw the cows, one behind the other, plod into Reall's brook to dip their muzzles. The two little boys splashed in after them and whacked the water with their maple wands. Lana rose.

In a few minutes she was milking in the stuffy darkness of the barn while Gilly explained how long it had taken to find the cows and complained about how he had had to wait for Joey.

"Joey's not so old as you," Lana said quietly. "He gets tired quicker."

"I didn't get tired," Joey mumbled.

"Go fetch the bucket from the spring then," Gilly said.

"I can't," said Joey. "I want to set here."

"If you ain't tired," said Gilly, "you had ought to get it to help Ma."

"You go and get it, Gilly."

She milked on. The cows were holding up well in spite of the heat.

"Didn't we have a horse?" Gilly asked when he came back from the spring.

"Yes," said Lana.

"I said so. Joey wouldn't believe me."

"I didn't say we didn't."

"What happened to the horse?" Gilly asked.

"We ate it," Lana said.

"Why did we eat it, Ma?"

"Because there wasn't any food left in the fort."

"Did I eat some too?"

"Yes."

"I don't remember it."

Lana tried to forget the time. It was the summer after West Canada Creek. When everyone believed the war was over, when it *was* over everywhere else in the country, Brant had suddenly appeared with five hundred Indians and a few Tories to harry German Flats. It was only the mercy of God that Adam Helmer and old Gustin Schimmel had happened on them. Adam had brought the warning in time; but the Indians had caught Gustin.

Brant had surrounded Fort Dayton for four days, and the food had got so low that every living thing inside was killed that would serve for meat. On the last day, in an effort to draw the men out of the fort, Brant had had Gustin Schimmel burned to death on the open land towards the river.

The Indians had burned him slowly with small fires, so that he would live for a long time, but they had planted the stake out of shot. Not so far away, however, that the poor old German's screams could not be heard in every cranny of the fort. He had started giving out at sunset, but even after that the sixty defenders on the rifle platforms could see the fire, and the slowly charring shape, and hear the cries continuing with a faint insistence.

Then Brant had vanished into the night and the next day

Colonel Willett had arrived from Fort Plain. It was the last time they had been visited by the destructives.

"Come up to supper, boys," she said. As they walked before her, she thought of how she had tried to keep the pleading disembodied voice away from them. She shivered violently at the recollection. She had stretched a blanket over their heads and lain down under it with them. To keep them under it she had pretended they were all three Indians. . . .

After supper was over and they had gone to bed, Lana heated water enough to wash out some of the baby's things, worked for an hour in the steamy kitchen, and then picked up her daughter, who had begun to whimper for her evening feed.

Though night had fallen, Lana blew out her candle and nursed the baby in the dark. It rested her to do so. She needed no candle to see the child's soft hair, which was so light. It seemed perfect to Lana that her daughter should be fair—she remembered how jealous she had been of her sister's yellow hair, like her mother's. She wanted the girl to be a beauty, "tall and fair," like the old song.

The child nursed more gently than the boys had done. Lana smiled at her own conceit. It was like having a woman in the house. Elizabeth Borst. Gil had agreed to the name. He said, when the child was born, that she looked like any little German girl. But he was pleased with her, though he tried not to show it.

Lana still smiled. The cowbells clinked away beyond the brook. The baby's head dropped from the nipple and Lana rose to put her to bed. She had her in her cradle when she heard the man rap on the door.

For an instant all the panics of years past rushed on her heart.

"Hello," the man was calling softly. "Hey! Is there anybody in there?"

Lana forced herself to go to the door.

"Who is it?" she called.

"It's John Wolff. Does Martins live here?"

"I am Lana Martin; what do you want?"

"Please let me in, Mrs. Martin."

Lana knew that he could get in if he wanted to. So she lit her candle at the fire and got down the musket Gil had bought for her when she was alone. She lifted the latch and stepped quickly behind the table.

But the man entered diffidently. He had no gun, and when he saw her he said, "I ain't going to do you harm."

As soon as she saw him Lana lost her fear. He was an old man, with thin white hair and a sad hopeless sort of face.

He said, "Don't you remember me? I used to keep the store at Cosby's Manor."

"Oh yes," she said. "Yes."

"I got sent to prison," he went on, "but I got away. I always wanted to come back. I left my wife here, see? She never turned up anywhere in Canada. Did you see her after that?"

"No," said Lana, quietly setting down the musket.

"Her name was Ally," said Wolff. "I never knew what a good woman she was till I had to leave her. I wanted to come back and find her if she was here. But they chased me out down there. They took my gun away. A big feller named Helmer swore he'd kill me, but some other folks helped me get away. They told me he'd killed three Indians that had come around since. I didn't want to harm nobody. I was looking for Ally."

"No," said Lana, "we never heard from her. They thought she went away."

"I've got a little place near Niagara now. I run the store on Squire Butler's place. I wanted to take Ally to it."

"I'm sorry." Lana could not feel hatred for him now that she was no longer afraid. "Won't you have something to eat?"

"No, thanks. I'll just be getting back."

"Back?"

"Home. To Niagara." He tried to smile. "It's quite a ways."

"You haven't any gun."

"I've got a little food. There's berries now."

"You take this musket," Lana said impulsively. "I don't need it. There's not much powder and ball for it."

"I couldn't do that."

"Oh yes. I expect my husband will be home to-night. Please."

He stared at her with his weak eyes.

"You're kind," he said. "You're the first kind person I've see. And you know about me, too. But I never did nothing to get sent to jail for."

"I know; I believe you."

"She never turned up, you know. She was good to me that last day when I was into the fort, Mrs. Martin. They wouldn't let me write to her, except I paid them money. I didn't have enough."

She thought he was going to cry. But he did not. He left in a little while, and she closed the door once more. Overhead she heard the boys steal back to their bed, but she did not scold them. She was glad Wolff had gone before Helmer found him. Helmer would kill any Tory or hostile that came into the valley if he could. They said he had killed Suffrenes Casselman. But no one knew that really, unless maybe his wife. Betsey was a strange woman in some ways. Gossip had it that she made Helmer swear an oath to bring her scalps before he got in bed with her, and that he brought her the scalps.

Lana did not go to bed. She had the feeling that what she had told Wolff was so and that Gil would return to-night. When he was away she felt only half alive. Everything she had in her, everything she had done or would do, every thought and every hope, was part of him. And yet sometimes he seemed less close to her. She did not know. As long as he stayed with her, came back to her, it did not matter how little time of his life he gave to her, so long as she could see him, feel him, hear him. She thought of that poor hopeless man, John Wolff, returning to his store in the new settled land, somewhere in the west.

When she heard Gil, he was walking with the Indian. She opened the door and called them to come in. But Blue Back was saying, "No, fine. Fine," and backing into the darkness.

Gil chuckled as he closed the door.

"Blue Back won't come in. He wants me to give you this. He says he'll come round some day after you've had a chance to get your mad off."

"What on earth?"

Gil held out to her a peacock's feather, broken, stripped of half its herl, but still showing enough color in the eye to identify it.

For some reason, to touch it took all the strength from Lana's legs. She plumped down on the stool and leaned against the table. The hand that held the feather started to shake. It was silly of her. She did not understand it herself. And to keep Gil from noticing, she asked him whether they had found the place.

"Oh yes. Blue Back found it. The stones were still there. Nothing had got at him."

He was taking off his wet and dirty shoes.

"How was Mary?"

"She cried some," he said. "But after a while I think she felt better. She borrowed old Blue Back's knife and dug up some posies and stuck them around the place. She didn't take long."

"I'm glad you took her," Lana said. "She wanted to go so much."

"Well, I'm glad too. I'd promised long enough."

He was watching her now, over his shoulder. "What's the matter with you, Lana? Did anything happen?"

"Gil, do you remember that John Wolff? He got arrested on that muster day?"

"John Wolff, by God. The man that kept the store. I testified against him."

"He was here before you came back. They'd driven him out of German Flats and he came up here to see you."

"What did he want?" Gil's face hardened. "If he wants to come back to settle, he better not try."

"Oh no, he was looking for some news of his wife. She never turned up in Canada."

"I remember. After they took him to Albany she went back to the store. But she'd gone from there when the militia went up— you remember, after we went to Little Stone Arabia Stockade."

It seemed they couldn't get away from it. Again and again, day after day, the years came back to them. Lana wasn't thinking of the Wolff woman then—she was thinking of the winter night in the Schuyler hut when Gil brought home the half of a thin doe. All at once she realized that it wasn't herself who had been responsible for that long dread between them, nor Gil. She wasn't like that. She wished he had kissed her when he came in. She lifted her face and looked at him. He wasn't looking at her.

Lana's eyes filled suddenly with tears. Those years, they had entered not only herself, and Gil, and through them the children, they had become part of the land, even on this place, remote as it had been throughout the war—the birds of the air, she thought, the beasts of the field. "Man's days are as grass." Herself, Gil.

"Is Dad come back, Ma?"

Gilly's narrow dark little face peering through the trap from the loft. . . . Joey still snoring on like a half-stifled little hedgepig.

"Yes, son. It's Dad. Get back to bed. Me and your ma are going now."

He laid his arm round Lana in the dark, leading her to the room they slept in. The baby was snuffling her breath in and out. As Lana started to unlace her short gown, she discovered the peacock's feather still in her hand. She fumbled for the shelf beside the window and laid the feather on it.

She heard Gil getting down on the bed; the rustle of straw beneath the blankets. Beyond the window the faintly clinking cowbells moved along the brook.

"We've got this place," she thought. "We've got the children. We've got each other. Nobody can take those things away. Not any more."

Printed in the United States
by Baker & Taylor Publisher Services